GENTLEMAN TAKES A CHANCE

"A tour de force." —Jerry Pournelle, on the prequel

THE GEORGE

FRESH FRIES
never frozen

Sarah A. Hoyt

$7.99 U.S.
$9.99 CAN.

ISBN 978-1-4391-3325-5

9 781439 133255

50799

EAN

Tom answere

"Tom?"

"Dad?"

"Oh, good. I've been delayed at the airport again. Look, I really need you to go wait in the loft for the cable guy."

"Dad!" Tom turned around to look at the frozen river. He had a feeling he'd heard something move or slither down there.

"I wouldn't ask if it were just because I want to watch TV, but I'm going to be working from home and I need the cable connection for the internet."

"Dad, I can't get to Denver," Tom said, drily.

"Why not? How long would it take you to fly there? It's only a three-hour drive away. Flying couldn't be more than twenty minutes."

"Flying in the current blizzard would probably take me about three hours," Tom said. He suddenly felt very tired. "And besides . . . look, I just can't."

"You know, I don't ask you to do this stuff every day," Edward Ormson said, in an aggrieved tone, from the other end of the connection. "It's just that this is really important to me, and I thought . . . Well, I thought our relationship was better these days."

Their relationship *was* better these days. And he owed his father for the diner, The George. "If I could at all, I would, Dad. It's just that I'm in the middle of a big mess right now."

"A mess? What type of a mess? Anything legal?" His father was a corporate lawyer and clearly, just now, a hammer in search of a nail.

"No," Tom said. "Look, it's just . . . not something I feel comfortable discussing on the phone."

"Did you eat someone?"

Baen Books
by
Sarah A. Hoyt

Draw One in the Dark
Gentleman Takes a Chance

Darkship Thieves (forthcoming)

GENTLEMAN TAKES A CHANCE

Sarah A. Hoyt

GENTLEMAN TAKES A CHANCE

This is a work of fiction. All the characters and events portrayed in this book are fictional, and any resemblance to real people or incidents is purely coincidental.

Copyright © 2008 by Sarah A. Hoyt

A Baen Books Original

Baen Publishing Enterprises
P.O. Box 1403
Riverdale, NY 10471
www.baen.com

ISBN 13: 978-1-4391-3325-5

Cover art by Tom Kidd

First Baen paperback printing, December 2009

Distributed by Simon & Schuster
1230 Avenue of the Americas
New York, NY 10020

Library of Congress Cataloging-in-Publication Data:
2008020728

Printed in the United States of America

10 9 8 7 6 5 4 3 2 1

GENTLEMAN TAKES A CHANCE

From near and far the creatures gather—winged and hoofed, clawed and fanged, and armed with quick rending maws. Great hulking beasts appear that the world has not seen in uncounted ages: reptiles that crawled in great primeval swamps long before human foot trod the Earth; saber-toothed tigers and winged pterodactyls. And others: bears and apes; foxes and antelopes, all converge on a small hotel on the outskirts of Denver, as a snowstorm gathers over the Rocky Mountains.

Outside the hotel, some change shapes—a quick twist, a wrench of bone and flesh, and where the animals once were, there now stand men and women. Others fly into the room, through the open balcony door, before changing their shapes.

In there—in human form—they crowd together, massing, restive. Old and young, hirsute and elegant, they gather.

Outside the day dims as a roiling darkness of clouds obscure the sun. Inside the men and women who were—such a short time ago—beasts wait.

Then of a sudden *he* is there, though no one saw him shift shapes; no one saw him arrive.

He is not huge. At least not in his human form. A well-formed man, of Mediterranean appearance, with well-cut if somewhat long, lanky dark hair, sensuous lips and a body that would not have looked out of place in a

1

Roman temple. He appears to be in his middle years and wears his nakedness with the confidence of someone who feels protected in or out of clothes.

But it is his eyes that hold the assembly in check—dark eyes, intense and intent—that look at each of them in turn as though he knew not only any of their possible sins and crimes, but also their nameless, most intimate thoughts.

"Here," he says. "It is here. It is nearby."

"Here," another voice says.

"Nearby."

"So many dead. Shapeshifters. Dead."

"We can't let this stand," someone says.

"It won't stand," the leader of the group says. "We'll find those who killed the young ones of our kind. And we will kill them. The blood of our children calls to me for revenge. I've executed the murderers of our kin before and I will do so again."

"The deaths happened in Goldport, Colorado," a voice says from the crowd and a finger points. "That way."

"I will be there tomorrow," the leader of the meeting says. A tenseness about him indicates certainty and something else—an eagerness to kill again.

Kyrie Smith looked up at the ceiling as a sort of scraping bump came from the roof of the tiny workingman Victorian that she shared with her boyfriend, Tom Ormson. The sound reminded her of ships at high sea— of the shifting and knocking of wood under stress. How much snow was up there by now? And how much could the roof withstand?

From the radio—high up on the shelf over the card table and two folding chairs that served as dining nook— came a high-pitched whistle, followed by a voice, "We interrupt this program to issue a severe winter storm alert. All city facilities are closed and everyone who is not emergency and essential personnel is requested to stay indoors. Goldport Police Department is on cold reporting. Should your home become unsafe or should you believe that it will become unsafe, these are the public shelters available."

There followed a long list of public buildings and churches. Kyrie thought briefly that with the weather the police couldn't be on anything but cold reporting—icy in fact—though she knew very well they meant that any accidents should be reported later. Cold seemed such an apt adjective for what was happening outside.

Not that she anticipated needing shelter. The little Victorian cottage had been here for over a hundred years and presumably had survived massive snowstorms. But though it was only three p.m., with the scant light outside, the swirling darkness looked more like stormy midnight than the middle of the afternoon.

It was her first blizzard in Goldport, Colorado. She'd lived here for just over a year, but the last winter had been mild, sparing her one of the legendary Rocky Mountain blizzards. Which she wouldn't have minded so much, except for the fact that those blizzards grew ever larger in the tall tales of all her neighbors, acquaintances, and the regular diners at The George.

For the last week—while the weathermen screamed *incoming*—the clientele at The George had been evenly divided between those who'd say not a flake would fall and those who insisted they would all be buried in snow and ice and future generations would find them like so many Siberian mammoths buried in permafrost, the remains of their last souvlaki meal still in their stomachs.

Kyrie suppressed a shudder, gave a forceful stir to the bowl of cookie dough she held against her jean-clad hip, and told herself she was being very silly. It wasn't like her to have this sort of fanciful, almost superstitious fear. She'd like to think she had imagination enough, but she'd never had time to let it run riot.

She had been abandoned as a newborn at the door of a church in Charlotte, North Carolina, on Christmas Eve, and had lived in a succession of foster homes, having to fend for herself more often than not. She'd grown up slim and graceful, with the muscular body of a runner.

At almost twenty-two, she'd been an adult and on her own for about four years. She rarely stayed at a job for very long. What she had thought for many years were dreams of turning into a panther—and now knew was true shape-shifting—usually scared her away from any given place, job or relationship and had kept her moving before anyone became too close. She'd been afraid of being made to see a psychiatrist. She'd been afraid of being given antipsychotic drugs. Sane or not, she wanted to know her thoughts came from her own mind, not from some chemical. And her madness—as she thought it—hurt no one. It was just dreams.

For years she told herself she didn't miss people, or relationships, or those other things that seemed to be a given right of all other humans. She kept her own house and her own mind. And, until three months ago, when Tom had become her boyfriend and started subletting the enclosed porch at the back of the house, she'd been lonely. Very lonely.

Then suddenly she'd had to believe she was a shifter. That the panther she dreamed of being was her other self. And that there were others like her. This had tossed her headfirst into a sea of new relationships, new ties.

This house and Tom were the closest thing she'd ever had to a family. Probably the closest thing he'd ever had to a family, too. Oh, he'd grown up with wealthy parents, she knew. He'd been raised in New York City by professional, well-to-do mom and dad. But that hadn't made them a family. It wasn't just that Tom's parents had divorced when he was very young. People might divorce and yet raise their children well and as a family. It was more that his mother had never cared again if Tom lived or died. And his father had left Tom to be raised by hired help, and only took notice of him when Tom got in some scrape and had to be bailed out—which he did regularly—possibly because it was the only time he got attention. And then, when Tom was sixteen, his father had walked in on him changing from a dragon to a human, and—horrified or scared—had thrown Tom out onto the streets of New York City in nothing but a robe.

After that Tom, too, had drifted aimlessly, living as he could, without anyone to rely on, without anywhere to call home. And now . . .

And now they lived together. And they were dating, presumably with a view to marriage, not that it had ever been mentioned. Of course, since Tom's father had bought the diner for them jointly, they were already part of a partnership.

And a touch of Tom's calloused hand could still set her heart aflutter, just like a sudden tender look from him, across the diner on a busy day, could make her feel as though she were melting from the inside out.

Still all their kisses and their caresses had an end. Tom always pulled back, before things went too far. Everyone in the diner—everyone who knew them—assumed that, since they dated and lived together, they were sleeping together as well. And Kyrie didn't know what to think. Tom said that he wanted to take it slow, to give them both time to establish a normal relationship before they became more intimate. And yet . . .

And yet sometimes, when he pulled back, she caught a hint of something in his eyes—distance and fear. Was he afraid he'd shift during lovemaking? It wasn't that unusual to shift under strong emotions, so that might be all it was. Or perhaps he'd realized he'd made a mistake and she was not whom he wanted?

A wave of protectiveness and of almost shocking possessiveness arose in her—the need to protect this, the one haven she'd found. Something—someone—must belong to her. And Tom was hers. Oh, not against his will. But hers to protect and hers to love.

Setting the bowl down, she pulled back her waistlong hair with a flour-covered hand, marring her carefully dyed-in Earth-tone pattern—that gave the impression of a tapestry whose lines shifted whenever she moved—with a broad streak of white. She frowned at the little door that led to the back porch where Tom was still asleep.

Would Tom be upset that she had turned off his alarm clock? They both worked the night shift at The George— a long night shift, often seven p.m. to seven a.m.—and he always set his alarm for two p.m. But she had turned it off because she thought there was no point going into the diner today and Tom might as well rest. The chances of their having enough customers to justify the money used in lighting and heating The George were very low. And even though it was only a few blocks away, Kyrie didn't want to drive in the storm howling outside. And she certainly didn't want to walk in it.

Whether Tom agreed with her was something else again. She looked down at the bowl of dough. A succession of never-ending foster homes had taught her that the easiest way of managing men was by setting something sweet down in front them. It tended to distract them long enough that they didn't remember to be angry.

Still, as she knelt down to rummage under the cabinet for her two baking sheets, she tensed at a sort of half-gasped cry from Tom's sleeping porch. Rising, she held the trays as a shield, and looked at the door into the enclosed back porch. Tom didn't cry out in his sleep. The house was barely large enough to swing a cat. If he sleep-screamed, she'd know by now.

He didn't yell again, but there was a deep sigh, and then the slap of his feet—swung over the side of the daybed—hitting the wooden floor of the sleeping porch. The sound was followed by others she knew well, from normal days. A confused mutter that, had she been close enough, would reveal itself as "What time is it?" followed by a cartoonlike sound of surprise, which was followed, in short order, by the sound of the back blind being pulled aside to allow him to look outside, and then by words she couldn't hear well enough to understand but which—from the tone—were definitely swearing.

Then Tom's bare feet padded towards the door between sleeping porch and kitchen. Kyrie, who in her short time of sharing the house with a male, had learned that if you appeared to be totally in command and quite sure you'd done the right thing, men—or at least Tom—were likely to go along with it, so she set the tray down on the card table at which they normally ate and started studiously setting little balls of cookie dough down on the tray, two inches apart.

Tom cleared his throat, and she looked up, to see him in the doorway. Her first thought—as always—was that, despite being all of five-six, he looked amazing, with pale skin, the color of antique ivory; glossy, curly black hair just long enough to brush his shoulders contrasted with intensely blue eyes like the sky on a perfect summer day, and generously drawn lips that just begged to be kissed.

Her second thought was that the most sculpted chest in creation deserved better than to be encased in a baggy green T-shirt that read *Meddle you not in the affairs of dragons, for thou art crunchy and good with ketchup.* Even if she'd bought him the T-shirt. And the best ass in the tri-state area should not be hidden by flannel checker-pattern pajama pants in such virulent green and yellow they could give seizures to used car salesmen.

"I take it The George is closed?" Tom said, and raised his hand to rub at his forehead between his eyebrows.

He squinted as if he had a headache and there were heavy dark circles under his eyes. Granted, skin as pale as Tom's bruised if you sneezed on it, but he didn't normally look like death warmed over. She wondered why he did now. "It's either closed now or it will be very soon. I called Anthony and he said it was pretty slow. He wanted to shut down the stoves and all, close and go home. So I told him fine. I know we could probably walk to The George but—"

"I looked out," he said. "We might very well not find The George in this. Blinding blizzard." He blinked as if realizing for the first time what she was doing. "Cookies?"

"Well . . . the radio said that there will be emergency shelters and I could only figure two reasons for it. Either the snow is going to be so heavy that the roof will collapse, or they're afraid we'll lose power. Can't do anything about roof collapsing. Not that tall. But I can preemptively bake cookies. Make the house warm."

He came closer, to stand on the other side of the little table. Though he was still squinting, as if the light hurt his eyes, his lips trembled on the edge of a smile. "And we get to eat the cookies too. Bonus."

"Make no assumptions, Mr. Ormson." She waggled an admonitory finger. "This is the first time I've baked cookies. They might very well taste like builder's cement."

His hand darted forward to the bowl and stole a lump of dough. Popping it in his mouth, he chewed appreciatively. "Not builder's cement. Raisin *and* chocolate chip?"

She shook her head and answered dolefully, "Rat droppings. The flour was so old, you see."

He nodded, equally serious. "Right. Well, I'll take a shower, and then we can see how rat droppings bake."

Down the hallway that led to the bathroom, she heard him open the door to the linen closet. Using a clean towel every day was one of those things she didn't seem able to break him of. But part of living together, she was learning, was picking your battles. This was one not worth fighting.

She heard him open the door to the bathroom as she put the cookie trays in the oven. She was setting the timer when she heard the shower start.

And then . . .

And then the sounds that came out of the bathroom became distinctly unfamiliar. They echoed of metal bending under high pressure and tile and masonry cracking, wrenching, subjected to forces the materials weren't designed for.

Her first thought was that the roof *had* caved in over the bathroom. But the sounds weren't quite right. There was this . . . scraping and shifting that seemed to be shoving against the walls. The cabinet over the fridge trembled, and the dishware inside it tinkled merrily.

Kyrie ran to the hallway and to the door of the bathroom.

"Tom?" she said and tried the handle. The handle rotated freely—well, not freely but loosely enough that the door clearly was not locked. And yet it wouldn't budge when she pushed at it. "Tom, are you in there?"

A growl and a hiss answered her.

The lion leapt across the entrance of the Goldport Undersea Adventure. He bounded across the next room, amid two rows of large tanks. The private company that had bought out the municipal aquarium had outfitted this room to look like a submarine's control room, with gauges and the sort of wheels that turn to activate pressure locks, and buttons and things. When the aquarium was open and functioning, the screens above the controls showed movies of underwater scenes in various bodies of water around the world.

Now dead and silent, with the aquarium closed due to inclement weather, they were just large, dark television screens. The whole building was empty except for a woman in the back office and the lion, who sniffed his way down the pretend mountain path that wound among tanks stocked with fish from the world over.

As he padded past the tank with piranhas, the lion growled softly, startling the exhibit of sea birds on an elevated area and causing them to fly up till they met with the net that kept them within their space.

The lion didn't care. He had picked up the scent he had been looking for. A sweetish, almost metallic scent.

The smell of shapeshifters. He put nose to the ground and followed it, growling softly to himself, past the little suspension bridge with the artificial river underneath— momentarily disoriented where water had sprayed and diluted the scent. But the scent picked up on the other side of the bridge.

The lion couldn't think why the scent was important. There was a part of his mind—as if it were someone else, another mind, locked deep inside his brain—telling him the smell related to death and killing.

The lion didn't know why death or killing would be important, and he couldn't smell death in the air anyway. There was no decay, no blood. Just a smell of fish and water and chemicals, and the smell of people, many people, some of which had probably passed by days ago but left behind the olfactory trail of their passage.

Then there was the clear bright scent of a shapeshifter. Not that the lion knew what a shapeshifter was, or not really. Just that this was the scent he was seeking, the scent he must follow, deep into the broad chamber decorated with a cement chest and a hoard of plaster coins that his other mind remembered as unconvincingly painted to resemble gold.

The chamber was vast, with a tall ceiling lost in darkness. The lion crouched close to the ground, and followed two trails of smell—or rather, one trail that wound itself around, in front of two vast tanks. Inside the tanks swam creatures the lion's inner mind told him were sharks. Large, with sharp, serrated teeth, they swam towards him, while he sniffed at the glass.

The lion paid them no more attention than he did the

yellow tape that blocked one of the tanks and the service stairs, discreetly hidden behind some plastic fronds, leading back to the top of the tank. There was no smell there at all, and the lion didn't look at it. Instead, he turned to follow the interesting scent out of the chamber, towards the front of the aquarium.

And stopped when he heard a voice, coming from the opposite direction of where he had come. "Officer Trall?"

The words made the lion turn, giving something like a half-grunt under his breath, as he loped very fast back the way he had come. Very, very fast, his paws devouring the distance he had traversed so cautiously.

Steps followed him. Human steps. Steps in high heels—the inner voice told the lion. A woman.

The lion gave a soft, distracted roar as—the inner voice yelled to hide, to change, to do something—he leapt into a corner of the entrance chamber, around the side of the ticket booth, and into the narrow hallway that led to the bathrooms. He hit the door of the men's bathroom at a lope, and rolled into the room.

As he rolled he . . . shifted, his body twisting and writhing even as he tumbled, till a tall, muscular blond man landed, from a somersault, in the middle of the bathroom, by one of the closed stalls.

From outside the door, the voice called, "Officer Trall?"

"In here," the man who had been a lion answered, his voice shaking slightly. "Just a moment."

And it was just a moment, as he reached for his clothes—khaki pants and a loose-cut shirt that, with his mane of long, blond hair gave him the look of a surfer about to hit the waves—and slipped into them and his shoes with the practice of someone who changed clothes several times a day.

In fact, Officer Rafiel Trall of the Serious Crimes Unit of the Goldport Police Department, had clothes hidden all over town and in some of the neighboring towns as well. One thing shifting shape did—it ruined your wardrobe. Though he controlled himself—well enough during the day, with more difficulty at night—he still destroyed clothes so often that he'd developed a reputation as a ladies man throughout the department.

Every time he came back wearing yet another set of clothes, all his subordinates, from his secretary to the newest recruit, elbowed each other and giggled. Rafiel only wished his sex life were half as exciting as they thought it was. Not that he could complain, or not really. He dated his fair share of women. He just couldn't allow any of them to get close enough to see his . . . changes. So he had a lot of first and second dates and rarely a third.

He looked at himself in the mirror, frowning, as he combed his fingers through his hair. Receptionists, women officers, even the medical examiners and legal experts who had sporadic contact with the Goldport Police Department, all warned each other about him in whispers. He'd heard the words "fear of commitment" so often he felt like they were tattooed on his forehead. And it wasn't true. He'd commit in a minute. To any woman he knew would accept him and not freak out. In less than a minute to a woman like him, a shifter. Of his kind.

The thought of Kyrie came and went in his mind, a mix of longing and regret. No point thinking about it. That wasn't going to happen.

Instead, he opened the door—his relaxed smile in place as he met the aquarium employee who waited outside, a slightly worried look in her eyes. She was small and golden skinned, with straight black hair and the kind of curves that fit all in the right places. Her name was Lei Lani—which made him think of her as one of the Bond girls—and she was a marine biologist on some sort of inter-program loan from an aquarium in Hawaii.

Looking at her smile, it was easy to imagine her welcoming tourists in nothing but a grass skirt. Of course, thinking about that was as bad as thinking too much about her first name. Neither encouraged his good behavior.

"I'm sorry," Rafiel said. "One of those sudden stomach things."

"Ah. I was just checking, because I really should lock up and go home. I mean, everyone else has, and I only stayed because I live so close by here."

"Yeah. How bad is it out?"

"Blinding. As I said, if I didn't live within walking distance, I'd have left long ago. I mean, I'm not even sure you should drive in this. Perhaps you should stay at my place till the weather improves."

Was that a seductive sparkle in her eye? Did Rafiel read it correctly? It wasn't that he wasn't tempted, but right now he had other things on his mind.

He shouldn't have been so reckless as to shift shapes while there was someone else in the building, but the hint of shifter scent he'd been able to pick up even with his human nose had forced him to check it out. After all, a shapeshifter at a crime scene could mean many things.

The last time he'd picked it up, it had, in fact, meant that the shifters were the victims. But there was always the chance it meant the shifter he smelled was the killer. And a murder committed by shapeshifters, properly investigated, would out them as non-mythological. Which meant—if Rafiel knew how such things worked—that at best they'd all be studied within an inch of their lives. At worst . . . well . . . Rafiel was a policeman from a long line of policemen. He understood people would be scared of shifters. Not that he blamed them. There were some shifters that he was scared of himself. But the thing was, when people were terrified, they only ran away half the time. The other half . . . they attacked and killed the cause of their fear.

"I'll be okay. I have a four-wheel drive, and I've lived here all my life. This is not the first blizzard I've driven in," he said. He was still trying to process the input of the lion's nose. There had been a clear shifter scent trail throughout the aquarium. It had circled the shark area.

The shark area where, yesterday, a human arm had been found—still clutching a cell phone—inside a shark. The aquarium had been shut down—though the weather provided a good excuse for that. And the relevant area was isolated behind the yellow crime-scene tape. The dead man had been identified as a business traveler from California, staying in town for less than a week.

The question was—had he fallen in the tank or been pushed? And if he'd been pushed, was it a shifter who'd done the pushing?

The sound of the roar-hiss from the bathroom made Kyrie stop cold. Tom didn't—normally—roar or hiss. But the dragon that Tom shape-shifted into did.

She frowned at the door, trying to figure out how Tom could have become a dragon in the bathroom. And why. While Tom was a short human, as a dragon he was . . . well, he had to be at least . . . She tried to visualize Tom in his dragon form and groaned.

With wings extended, Tom had to be at least twenty feet from wing tip to wing tip and she was probably underestimating it. And he was at least twelve feet long and his main body was more than five feet wide, with big, powerful paws and a long, fleshy tail.

Now, your average bathroom might—for all she knew—be able to contain a dragon. But the bathroom in this house was not what anyone could call a normal bathroom. In fact in most other houses it would be a closet and not even a walk-in closet. It was maybe all of five feet by four feet—the kind of bathroom where you had to close the door before you could stand in front of the sink and brush your teeth. There was no way, no way at all, a dragon could fit in there.

"Tom," she yelled again, pounding on the door. "Tom! Please tell me you didn't turn into a dragon in the bathroom."

The sound that answered her was not Tom's voice—in fact, it resembled nothing so much as a distressed foghorn—but it carried with it a definite tone of apology and confusion.

"Right," Kyrie said, as she tried to push the door open. The problem, of course, was that the door opened inward. That meant to get in—or get Tom out—she must swing the door into the bathroom which was, in fact, already filled to capacity with dragon. The resistance she felt was some part of Tom's flesh refusing to give way.

She stopped pushing. She had no idea what had caused Tom to shift. Normally he only shifted involuntarily with the light of the moon on him and some additional source of distress working against his self-control. But what could make him shift, in the middle of a blizzard, in the bathroom?

She needed to get him to shift back. Now. Knowing why he shifted would help, but if she couldn't find out—and he wouldn't be able to answer questions very intelligibly—then she must get him to shift back by persuasion.

The door dated from the same time as the house—somewhere around the nineteenth century, when Goldport had been built from the wealth flowing from the gold and silver mines around the area. The wealth hadn't reached into this neighborhood of tiny houses—originally filled with workers brought from out East to build the mansions for the gold rush millionaires. Oh, the house was still far more solid than houses built today. The walls were lath and plaster or brick, instead of drywall. It was framed in heavy beams. But the doors—as she'd discovered when repairing hinges or locks before—were the cheapest, knottiest pine to be found in any time or place. One grade up from kindling. Further, to make their construction cheaper, they were not a solid panel, but a thicker cross-frame filled out with four veneer-thin panels.

Kyrie silently apologized for any injury she might do Tom, but she had to bring him out of this somehow. She went to the linen closet and wrapped her hand in a towel. Then she aimed at the thin pine panel and punched with all her strength.

The panel splintered down the middle and cracked at the sides. It remained in place, but only because it was held together by countless layers of paint. The dragon inside the bathroom made a noise like a foghorn, again.

Kyrie ignored the noise and, instead, started tearing at the door panel, pulling it out piece by piece. When she had all the pieces out, she leaned in to look into the bathroom. Which was not as easy as she'd anticipated. First because it was dark in there. Whatever else the dragon had done in the shifting, he'd definitely broken the ceiling light fixture. Judging by a sound that evoked a romantic brook running through unspoiled mountains, he had also torn the plumbing apart.

Worse than that, what she was looking at resembled a nightmare by Escher, where nothing made any sense whatsoever. There were green scales, and she expected green scales, shading to blue in spots. But part of what she saw was the bluish-green underbelly of the dragon Tom shifted into. And right next to the missing panel, a claw protruded—huge and silvery, glinting like metal in the moonlight. Next to it was crammed what looked suspiciously like a bit of wing.

"Tom," she said, trying to sound reasonable, while speaking to a mass of scales that, she realized, was *pulsing* rapidly with the sort of panting rhythm a frightened person might breathe in. "Tom, shift back. You can't get out like this. Shift back."

The scales and wing and all slid around, scraping the door. The dragon moaned in distress. For a moment, the huge claw protruded through the opening, causing Kyrie to jump back, startled. When everything was done moving around, a dragon eye looked back at her through the opening. The tile balanced just above its brow ridge only made it look more pitiful.

The eye itself—huge and double-lidded and blue— except for size and the weird additional inner lids, was Tom's eye.

Kyrie spoke to Tom's eye. "Tom, please, you must shift. I understand there had to have been something to make you shift. But if you don't shift back now I can't get you out of there. And that bathroom is going to freeze."

She didn't need to be a building expert to know the tiny window into the bathroom had to be broken. The sudden moisture at her feet made her cringe. First, they were going to flood the house. And then they were going to freeze it. And it wasn't even her house. She rented it. Good thing she'd long ago resigned herself to the idea she'd never see the security deposit again. And good thing she didn't expect to ever be rich. After paying for these repairs, she'd be flat broke.

"Tom," she spoke as calmly as she could, though she felt her heart racing and was holding back on a strong impulse to shape-shift herself. She could feel it as her nails tried to lengthen into claws, as her muscles and bones attempted to change shape. She gritted her teeth and forced herself to remain human. To remain sane. Becoming a panther now would only add to the confusion. "Tom, you must shift back. I don't know why you shifted, but there is nothing that we can't face together. We've done it before, remember?"

The eye blinked at her, panic still shining at the back of it.

"Look, breathe with me—slow, slow, slow." She forced her own breathing to a slow, steady rhythm. "Slow. Everything is safe. And if it isn't, you can't fight it while crammed in that bathroom. You must be human and come out of there first. Then we'll talk."

She spoke on so long that she almost lost track of what she was saying. It was all variations on a theme. The theme of being calm. Very, very calm. And shifting back.

Water was running under the door, covering the pine floor of the hallway in a thin, shimmering film, but she didn't dare move or stop talking. Was she having any effect? Tom's eye continued to glare at her, unblinking. She only knew he was alive because she could hear the dragon's breathing huffing in and out of huge lungs.

And then there was a sound like a sigh. Or at least a short intake of breath followed by a long, deep exhalation. The dragon flesh filling the broken part of the door trembled and wobbled. The distressed foghorn sounded again.

Other sounds followed—sounds Kyrie knew well enough and which she felt a great relief at. Not that she'd show her relief. She didn't want to startle Tom and stop the process. That was the last thing she wanted. Instead, she took deep, deep breaths, feeling Tom breathe with her, while muscles slid around with moist noises, and bones made sounds like cracking of knuckles writ large.

Tom sat there, on the soaked floor of the bathroom, on what remained of his ripped pajama pants and T-shirt. Plaster dusted his hair. His naked, muscular body showed a landscape of scratches and bruises.

He looked at her, mouth half open. Then he keened. It was neither crying, nor screaming—just a sound of long-held, pent-up frustration. He raised his knees and wrapped his arms around them, lowering his head and taking deep deliberate breaths.

She'd seen this before. She knew what it meant. He was fighting the urge to shift back. But he had it under control now. And he would be mortally embarrassed as soon as he had the time to be.

Kyrie did what any girlfriend—what any friend—could do under the circumstances. "Right," she said. "Don't go anywhere. I'm going to go turn off the water valve to the house."

Tom was mortally embarrassed. Once past the panic of the dragon and the heightened senses of the beast and the pain of being forced into what seemed to the dragon like a very tiny box—once he was himself—he didn't need to examine his surroundings to know the damage he had done.

The toilet was broken, the pieces shattered everywhere. The plumbing was torn apart. Faucets bent beyond recognition. Walls with their inner layer scraped off, in a way that was probably not structurally sound. The window was smashed—leaving jagged pieces of glass glinting in the frame. The shower enclosure destroyed. What had, less than half an hour ago, been a bathroom was now a disaster zone.

And Tom was sitting in the middle of it, looking up at Kyrie, who stared back in shock. She was very pale. No doubt toting up the expenses he had caused her. The lease was in her name. They'd be lucky not to get kicked out, even after they repaired the damages. And all because he couldn't control his shifting and had gotten scared by—

In that moment, staring openmouthed at Kyrie—who looked, as she always did, like a Greek goddess who had consented to come down from her pedestal and wear jeans and a T-shirt and a single, red-feather earring—he remembered what had made him shift.

There had been a *voice* in his head. There had been a *voice*—echoing in his mind as clearly as though it were coming through his ears, which it wasn't. The voice had been of an entity known to Asian cultures as the Great Sky Dragon.

Whether he was really the father of all dragons as legend maintained, or not, Tom could not know. What he did know was that he was the leader of Asian triads in the west—that he ruthlessly murdered and stole and sold drugs and did what he had to do to keep his people safe and prosperous. And his people were only those who could shift into dragons. A specific kind of dragon. A kind Tom wasn't.

Their last meeting had brought Tom closer to his death

than he ever cared to go. As close as he could go and still come back. And now he had pushed his way into Tom's head.

Tom shuddered as panic tried to establish itself and force him to shift again.

No, and no, and *no*! Nothing would be served by becoming a dragon. There were threats that the human brain was best suited to handling, no matter how much the puny human body might not be a match to claws and fangs and wings.

He heard himself make a sound—a half scream of frustration at the body he couldn't control—as he lowered his head and concentrated on breathing. Just breathing.

In this state he only half heard Kyrie say something about the water valve. He heard her walk away as he controlled himself. And then he smelled burning. The cookies.

It was, strangely, a welcome relief from other thoughts. He got up. Everything hurt. He felt as though every fiber of his body had been bruised and as if all his bones had cracked, crazed, like plates exposed to high pressure. Groaning, holding on to walls and furniture, telling himself he didn't have time to be in pain, he didn't have time to heal; he padded through the soaked hallway to the kitchen where just the barest bit of water was making it over the little metal lip dividing the kitchen linoleum from the hallway wood flooring. His feet slipped as he hit the linoleum, but he balanced, and rushed to the oven—as much as he could rush without screaming. He remembered one of his nannies reading him the original story of "The Little Mermaid" and how, after the mermaid had traded her tail for legs, every step she took would be like walking on knives. This felt like that, except the knives were also throughout his torso and down his arms, and small daggers seemed to stab through each of his fingers as he flexed them.

Oven mitts on, he pulled the tray of cookies out and set it atop the stove, then carefully turned the oven off. The cookies were less burnt than he'd expected—just looked like they'd gotten a suntan.

Right. He'd best make himself decent quickly. They had bigger trouble than the cookies, and there was absolutely no way he could take a shower now. But if he remembered correctly, when you turned off the water valve to a house, whatever water was in the pipes or in the heater remained. That might just be enough to, at the very least, get the grit of masonry off his skin and hair.

He limped to the hallway closet, full of purpose—because any purpose, and any thought was better than to think again of what had made him change or to acknowledge his pain—and grabbed a handful of washcloths and a towel. And he tried not to think of the pain. It would pass. He would be fine. Shifters healed very quickly. Particularly well-fed shifters.

He wet the washcloths at the faucet in the kitchen, and put soap in about half of them—then retreated with them and the towel back to his room.

Fortunately he was familiar with this sort of ad hoc washing. He'd had to do it often enough when he was living on the streets and only working occasional day jobs, between the ages of sixteen and twenty or so. Contrary to public perception, given a supply of paper towels and soap, it was possible to wash up—at least enough to not stink—at a stall in a public bathroom. It didn't, by any means, beat a long soak in a tub, or even a hurried shower, but it would do if it must. And clearly it must.

He was going through the motions of wiping down with soap, then wiping the soap off, noting that the soap stung in a high number of abraded places, and that just touching his skin brought on a pain on the edge of unbearable, when he heard the back door close and Kyrie call tentatively, "Tom?"

"In here," he said. "I'll be out in a moment."

She didn't come in. Their rules for when they were allowed to see each other naked wouldn't make sense to anyone else. They didn't even make any *rational* sense to Tom himself. But they made *emotional* sense.

Because of the shifting, they had seen each other naked long before they had a relationship, and often saw each other naked in all sorts of situations. But while human and not coming off from a shift, they respected each other's privacy as much as possible. Kyrie would no more walk into his room while she knew he was naked than he would walk in on her in the shower. Oh, yes, they were dating. They were in love, or at least—Tom smiled to himself, as he extracted as much masonry as possible from his long dark hair—he thought so. His opinion might be insufficient, since he'd never had any experience with the emotion before. Still, he would give his left hand, or wing, or claw for Kyrie and she'd proven often enough she'd do the equivalent for him.

But they were both intensely private people. And neither of them had experience of relationships before. So they were taking it slow and trying to establish the feelings and the boundaries before becoming more physical. Not the least because neither of them was sure how the beasts they shifted into would react to *more physical*. The prospect of becoming dragon· and panther during sex could be regarded as either hilarious or terrifying, depending on how macabre one's sense of humor.

Having finished his Spartan wash, he dried with the towel, tied his hair back—after rummaging for the elastic in the bedclothes—and slipped on a pair of jeans and a loose white T-shirt. Remembering the water in the hallway, he put on socks and his leather boots and came out of his room to find Kyrie coming in too, from the other side, duct tape in hand.

"I wiped the water from the floor in the hallway and sealed the bathroom," she said, matter of fact. "So the cold doesn't come into the rest of the house." Then looking at him, she smiled. "You cleaned up."

He felt himself blush that she was surprised he'd take the trouble to clean up. "I didn't think masonry was the in look this winter."

She nodded solemnly, stowing the duct tape in the drawer under the coffee maker. "There's coffee," she said, while pouring herself a cup. "I'd started it when—" She stopped. "Thank you for saving the cookies."

He bit back the obvious answer: "You don't need to put on the politeness. No need to thank me, since I was the one who made you forget them." Most of his life, long before he'd found out he was a shifter, at sixteen, he'd been giving the answer guaranteed to infuriate people and rejoicing in getting a reaction. Any reaction. He didn't know why. That was just the way he was.

It was tempting to say that he'd become a hostile bundle of aggression because both his parents were busy professionals, too busy in fact to notice their son existed. Tempting and, no doubt, some psychologist would say it in all seriousness.

But Tom didn't believe in psychology any more than he believed in any other organized religion. And at some point a grown-up had to stop blaming his parents for his quirks. Perhaps that was what had set him off . . . perhaps not. Perhaps some accidental genetic combination had caused him to be born hostile and contrary. But three months ago, when he'd moved in with Kyrie, he'd decided that habit stopped and quickly too. So now he bit his tongue and sighed. "They are a little too tanned."

She smiled back, as if she knew of the averted response and appreciated his effort. "No matter. Still edible." Picking up a cookie, she sat down.

He got himself coffee. Her whole attitude said *we have to talk,* and he supposed they did. He used the time of filling the cup and sugaring his coffee to think of what he could say that would mitigate what he had just done.

I'll pay for it was obvious, though he had exactly zero clue how. All the money he had—just like all the money Kyrie had—was part shares in The George. And, unlike what he would have imagined before getting into it, profits and debts weren't as clear-cut as they seemed. His father—in an impulse for atonement that could not be gainsaid—had bought them the building and equipment for The George. That much they had. But it wasn't money. You couldn't walk into the mall with five bricks and buy a T-shirt. And there was no way he could swap one of the industrial freezers for the repair bill on the bathroom. For one, because they needed the freezers.

Which was the issue with the money. The George was doing well. Money came in every night and day. The few upgrades he and Kyrie had been able to afford here and there—a coat of paint, new Formica on the tables, re-covering the vinyl booths, a new stove—were drawing in a better clientele, too. In addition to the manual laborers and students who had always drifted to The George, they now got young professionals from the gentrified area a few blocks away, amused at the dragon theme of the restaurant and intrigued by Tom's culinary experimentation.

They were—from what Tom understood of the raised eyebrows of his accountant, who was a man of few words—doing very well indeed, having unwittingly become the spearheads of the push for gentrification in *that* area of Fairfax. But the money that came in went out again very quickly, and the improvements fueled other improvements. There were waiters to pay and Anthony's salary had been raised since he'd become manager. To keep the better clientele, Tom had bought new silverware and dishes and improved the quality of everything from the paper goods to the coffee mugs. His own self-respect as a cook had forced him to buy better quality meat.

His father—when they talked—assured him all this would eventually pay off and while the cycle seemed fruitless and inane right now, eventually the money coming in would outstrip the need for improvements and Tom and Kyrie would find themselves wealthy or close to it. Today was not the eve of that day, though. Their separate bank accounts, if pooled, would net them maybe two thousand dollars. On which they had to live for the month. Not enough for this type of repair.

He could, of course, ask his father for help, but just the idea of it was enough to give him heartburn. He'd solved—he thought—his life-long struggle with his father. While his father was not the best of parents, neither was Tom the best of sons. But still . . . Edward Ormson had forced his sixteen-year-old son out of the house at gun-point onto the streets of New York City on the day he found that Tom shifted shape into a dragon.

Tom could forgive, but he could not forget. He'd accepted the diner, but even that had smarted, and he'd only accepted it because he could tell how much Kyrie wanted it. And he'd talk to his father and be civil when he called because the man was trying his best to establish a relationship. And Tom was not so flush with friends that he could turn down anyone willing to befriend him. Even if it was his own father.

But he'd be damned if he was going to go cadging his father for money. He'd be damned if he'd go back to his father every time he found himself in a scrape. He'd be damned if he gave his father reason to think of him—ever again—as his fucked-up son.

He'd rather live on the streets, he thought decisively, as he made his way back to the table and sat down, cup in hand. He'd done it before.

He looked up, frowning slightly, to meet Kyrie's attentive gaze on him. She was examining his face—probably for signs of the madness that had caused him to shift in the bathroom.

When she saw him looking, she smiled. "Have a cookie."

What Kyrie wanted to know was why he'd shifted. But she was terrified that if she asked him, he'd feel the need the shift again. After all, whatever it was had to be powerful enough to cause a visceral panic reaction. Thinking about it might bring on another shift.

His eyebrows lowered a little and as he took a bite of the cookie, he did it as if it required a large amount of concentration. When he looked back at her, his gaze remained worried and more than a little bit confused.

"I figured," he said, his tone slow and calculating. "I might be able to get a loan. But I don't know how because I don't want to mortgage The George because that's yours too and, you know—"

"What?" She hadn't meant to interrupt, but the last thing she'd expected was for him to start talking money.

"The bathroom," he said, gesturing airily.

"Oh, that. I looked at the walls and they seem to be fine. You just peeled the tile off and destroyed the plumbing and appliances. Cosmetic stuff. We'll find a handyman. Place is solidly built." She shrugged. "Yeah, we'll borrow if we have to. We could do it all ourselves, you know, with a good how-to manual, but we don't have that much free time and a functioning bathroom is kind of a necessity." Seeing him open his mouth, she went on, redirecting the conversation, "Which is why I think we should go to The George."

He blinked at her. "What?" he said, his tone exactly matching her earlier one as, clearly, the gears of his mind had been grinding at a different place.

"I think we should go to The George until the blizzard is past and we get the bathroom repaired. While I don't like the idea of driving in this, we'll have a bathroom at The George. I mean—no place to take showers, though we can probably get a room at the bed-and-breakfast next door for that—but we'll at least have a place to go to the bathroom. The weather—not to mention the neighbors— kind of precludes just peeing in the yard."

Her absurd words managed to bring a smile to his lips, but it vanished very fast. "Yeah. We'll have to go."

"Yes. I know we could just stay at the bed-and-breakfast, but if we're going to be that close to The George, we might as well open too. I'm sure you don't want to spend however long in just a tiny rented room. And we might get a few diners, and it might just pay for that opening. And the bed-and-breakfast. I mean, we could go to one of the emergency shelters, but you and me and an enclosed space with a lot of people . . ." She shrugged. Given what had just happened to him, in the bathroom, she didn't need to draw pictures of a dragon and a panther rampaging amid distressed refugees.

He nodded and took a sip of the coffee. "Okay," he said. "I'll take a sleeping bag. In case we rent a room with only one bed." He got up and headed for his sleeping porch, clearly intent on packing. "And my laptop. Perhaps I can do some of the paperwork that's been accumulating."

"Tom . . ." She didn't want to ask, but she'd have to.

"Why the shift? Was it the storm? You don't normally shift during the day, much less—" She stopped.

He'd turned around, a hand going up to his head, as if to pull back hair that didn't need it—a habit of his when he was nervous. His Adam's apple bobbed up and down as he swallowed. He sighed. For just a moment, it seemed to her, he was concentrating very hard on not shifting. "It was the Great Sky Dragon," he said. "I . . . I don't know how to put this without sounding like a science fiction story, but I heard him in my mind. Without sound." He took a deep breath like a drowning man who has succeeded in getting his head above water for a moment. "I know I sound crazy, but . . . He was there."

She shrugged at him. They were people who could—and did—change into animal shapes with or without wishing to. And still, he was afraid she'd think having experienced telepathy made him sound crazy.

"So you heard him in your mind," she said. "Did he threaten you?"

Tom shook his head. "No, that was the odd part. He warned me. But it wasn't a threat. He said someone he called the Ancient Ones wanted to kill us. That we should beware."

"Right. We'll stay out of retirement homes," Kyrie said, and immediately after, "I'm sorry. It isn't funny. But why should he warn us now, when he went out of his way to almost kill you before?"

Tom shook his head and looked startlingly naked and vulnerable—as if it cost him something to admit this. "I don't know."

The phone rang.

For an intense panic-filled moment, Tom thought it would be the Great Sky Dragon calling him to repeat the vague warnings he'd spoken within Tom's mind. It took a deep breath and remembering the damages to the bathroom to keep him from shifting again right then and there. His back brain equated *dragon* with *safe*. He told himself the phone wouldn't eat him, as he stretched his hand to the phone on the wall and picked it up.

The caller ID window read "Trall, Rafiel" which made him draw a sigh of relief. For all his faults—and there were many—and despite the fact that he still carried a torch for Kyrie, Rafiel was the closest thing Tom had to a friend. He was, with Kyrie, almost the only other shifter Tom was friends with. Almost because an addled alligator shifter who went by "Old Joe" didn't exactly qualify as a *friend*. Not so long as friendship involved more than Tom covering up for Old Joe's shifts and giving him bowls of clam chowder on the side. Kyrie, Rafiel, Old Joe, an orangutan shifter, two now-dead beetle shifters and the dragon triad were the only adult shifters Tom had ever met, period. He guessed there weren't many of his kind in the world. The few, the proud, the totally messed up.

"Yeah?" he said, into the phone.

"Uh," Rafiel's voice said from the other end, as though the phone's being answered were the last thing he could possibly expect. Then, "I'd like to . . . I need to talk to you and Kyrie, when you have a minute."

There was that tone in Rafiel's voice—tight and short—that meant he was on the job. Tom wondered if Rafiel was alone or if he was picking his words carefully to avoid scaring a subordinate. Aloud he said only, " 'Ssup?"

"Murder. There's . . . been . . . well, almost for sure murder. Human bones and stuff at the bottom of the shark tank at the aquarium."

"And?" After all, solving murders was Rafiel's job and he usually managed it without a little help from his friends.

"And I smell shifter," Rafiel said. "All over it."

"Oh," Tom said. "We'll be at The George." And suddenly he felt exactly like a man in the path of an oncoming train.

His dreams had been full of a nightmare about some ancient menace; the Great Sky Dragon had spoken in his mind; and now there was murder, with shifter involvement.

Was the shifter a murderer or the victim? Either way, it could make Tom's life more of a mess than it already was.

"Don't shift! Don't shift! Don't shift!" Kyrie told herself. But she wasn't at all sure she was listening, and she kept looking anxiously at her hands, clenched tight on the wheel. Her violet nail polish was cracked and peeled from her run-in with the bathroom door, so it was hard to tell whether the nails were lengthening into claws or not. Part of the reason she kept her nails varnished was to make sure that she saw the first signs of her nails lengthening into claws. Today that wouldn't work.

Outside the window, in the palm of visibility beyond the windshield, white snowflakes swirled. Past that, the flakes became a wall of white, seemingly streaming sideways, shimmering. Somewhere out there, in the nebulous distance, there were twin glimmers of dazzling whiteness, which were the only indications Kyrie had that the headlights of her tiny car were on.

"Maybe we should have walked," Tom said. He shuffled in his seat and leaned close to the snow-covered windshield, as though he could lend her extra vision.

Kyrie gritted her teeth. Maybe they should have, except that the three steps they'd taken on the driveway, their feet had gone out from under them, and they'd only remained upright by holding onto the car. From which point getting in the car had seemed a given. She slowed down—which mostly meant defaulting to the fractional amount of sliding the car seemed to do all on its own— and twisted up her windshield wipers' knob, not that it did much good.

"How can you see?" Tom asked.

"I can't," she said, just as a sudden gust of wind cleared the space ahead enough for her to see they were at the intersection of their street and the next perpendicular one. And that a massive, red SUV was headed for them at speed.

Don't shift, don't shift, don't shift, Kyrie thought, as a mantra, even as she felt her whole body clench and her muscles attempt to change shapes beneath her skin, to take the form of a panther. *Don't shift, don't shift, don't shift,* as she struggled to keep her breathing even, and bit into her lower lip with teeth that weren't getting any longer, not at all, not even a little bit. She maneuvered quickly with a tire up on the sidewalk, tilting crazily around the corner, even as the SUV went by them and buried them in a shower of slush. Bits of ice rattled against roof and windows.

A moan from Tom reminded her she wasn't the only one worried about panic setting off a shape-shift reaction. "Perhaps," he said, in the voice of a man working very hard to control himself. "I should get out and . . . fly?"

"What? Shift twice without eating? First thing in the morning? And the second time after getting hurt?" she said, and on that, as he moaned again, she realized she'd said the wrong thing. Shifting shapes demanded a lot of energy and, for some reason, it set off a desperate craving for protein. So did the lightning-fast healing of shifters. All Tom had eaten since shifting was half a dozen cookies. And there was no protein at all around. Except, of course, her. She wasn't about to volunteer. And she knew Tom would rather die than eat a person, much less her.

She pushed the gas, taking advantage of a momentary break in the storm that allowed her to see a major cross-roads ahead. Too late, she saw the light was red, but she was sliding through the intersection on the power of her momentum and slamming on the brakes only caused her to fishtail wildly and finally pivot halfway through to the left. Fortunately this turned the car right onto Fairfax, where she was supposed to be. Sliding, she pressed the gas cautiously. Their shifting position caused the snow to seem to shift directions, so that she could now see—more or less—out her front window, but nothing on the side.

I'll never find The George, she thought to herself, and

glared at her nails telling them they weren't becoming claws, no they weren't, *not even a little bit*.

A sudden dazzling purple light to the left made her breathe in relief and confusion. The George's sign was still lit. Thank heavens. Anthony mustn't have closed yet, which meant, of course, that lights and heat would still be on, and less trouble than turning them on again. It also made the diner easier to find.

She brought the car to a minimally-sliding, almost-complete stop and took a deep breath. Normally, turning left into the parking lot of The George from Fairfax involved taking your life in your own hands. Fairfax was a four-lane road, the main east-west artery of Goldport, and it was heavily traveled all the time. In addition, mistimed traffic lights ensured there was no break in the two lanes of traffic across which you must cut to make it into the parking lot.

Today, it involved another kind of risk. She couldn't see at all through the storm, to find out if any traffic was oncoming. Just white blankness. True, there were very few vehicles out, but she'd managed to almost run into two of those few on the way here. Kyrie took a deep breath. There was nothing for it but to turn. And she wasn't going to shift. *Not at all*.

She turned the wheel, fully expecting to go into a spin, but the tires grabbed onto some bit of yet unfrozen pavement and propelled them in a queasy slide-lurch across the other lanes of the road and up a gentle ramp into the parking lot.

The snow didn't allow her to see any other cars in the parking lot, and Kyrie didn't care. Bordered by the blind, windowless wall of a bed-and-breakfast and a warehouse, the parking lot gave on to the back door of The George and, through two outlets, to Pride and Fairfax Streets both. Right now, she waited until the car stopped sliding, then put it in park and pulled the parking brake, and leaned over the wheel, breathing deeply. *You're safe, you're safe. Don't shift.* There was no point even trying to find parking spots in this mess.

When her racing heart had calmed down, she lifted her head and saw the parking lot—as much as *could* be seen. Drifting snow spider-webbed by the light of two street lamps and the purple glare from the diner's back sign obscured everything save for the two large supply vans parked in the middle of the lot. She looked to the passenger side of the car, where Tom was blinking and, she suspected, had just opened his eyes after calming himself.

"We should really—" Kyrie started and stopped. Through the snow she'd glimpsed something, half seen. She thought it was . . . but it couldn't be. Surely . . .

"Was that," Tom said, his voice small, "a dragon's wing?"

"Go inside," Tom said, as he glimpsed the wing again, through the multiplying flakes. "It's a red wing. It's . . ." He didn't say it. He couldn't quite assemble words.

His brain, still fogged from his quick shift into dragon and back, still laboring under the guilt of what he'd done to the bathroom—let alone the terror of the precipitous drive here, which had felt less like driving than tumbling down a chute—could not manage to describe the wing. But he was sure, from his two brief glimpses, that it was a Chinese dragon. An Asian dragon like the Great Sky Dragon and his cohorts.

Feeling for the door handle with half-frozen, still aching fingers, Tom managed to grasp it and throw the door open against resistence of what he hoped was stiff wind, and not a dragon tail or claw, as he yelled over the howling storm at Kyrie. "Go inside. I'll deal with it."

He plunged out of the car, his hair and his unzipped black leather jacket whipping about in the howling storm, just in time for his feet to go out from under him, and to reach, blindly, for the car door for support, and bring himself upright, and stare into . . .

He was big and red. No. As he blinked to keep his eyes from freezing, he thought he wasn't that big. Smaller than Tom himself in dragon form. But he was also horribly familiar—more familiar as Tom focused on the details and noted that the dragon's front left paw was much smaller than the other. He was . . . Red Dragon. Not only was he was one of the Great Sky Dragon's cohorts, but when Tom had last seen him there had been a big battle, and Red Dragon had ended with his arm ripped out at the roots. Or rather, Tom had ripped Red Dragon's arm off, then used it to beat Red Dragon with.

Tom knew—from experience—that his kind was hard to kill. But this was a particular foe he'd never thought to see again; one he was sure had more reasons for vendetta against him than anyone else alive.

He felt his throat close and the panic he'd—barely—

managed to control in the car surged through his body like electric current, seeking grounding. Not finding it, it twisted in a sparkle through his flesh. He felt his bruised, battered limbs wrench, and his body bend, and a hollow cough echoed through his throat mingled with a scream of pain that he could no longer keep back. His mouth opened, and he swallowed an aspiration of snow, cold and suffocating. He knew, absolutely knew, that if he shifted he would attack Red Dragon and probably try to eat him. He was *that* protein-starved. A protein-starved Tom ate uncooked meat and whatever else he could get his hands on. A protein-starved dragon would hunt live prey.

"Run," he told Kyrie with what was left of his human mind and his human voice, already sounding slurpy and hissy as his teeth shifted position. "Run inside, Kyrie."

He could just tell in the periphery of his beclouded vision that she was not obeying. Not even considering it, and he wondered if his voice had already changed too much. If perhaps she couldn't understand him. His body twisted again, the pain of shifting unbearable on his bruised flesh and caked bones, and he kept his eyes on the other dragon, in case he should have any ideas of flaming or striking. Dragons were hard to kill but not impossible. This Tom knew. If you severed the head from the rest of the body, if you divided the body in two. If you incinerated the body. Possibly if you destroyed the brain. Those deaths even a dragon could not overcome.

Tom had to think of how to inflict them on his foe, and he had to protect himself from them. He felt his fingers lengthen into claws and—

"No," it was Kyrie's voice, decisive sounding. And Kyrie—slim, unshifted, very human Kyrie—stood between the two dragons, her dark blue ski jacket making her just slightly bulkier than normal as she yelled at both of them. "No. You're not going to change, Tom. Deep breaths. I'm not having you pass out or worse when you shift. Don't you dare."

There had been a time when Tom had sought out cures for his condition. He'd tried to prevent his shifting with illegal drugs and with will power, with perfect diet and with lack of sleep. He'd visited places where people said native tribes had once worshiped. He'd taken yoga and tried to meditate. None of it had worked.

In times of stress, or when the moon was just right, causing some change in the tides of his being; when panic or excitement overcame him, he would change. And he couldn't control it, any more than a human being can stop sneezing by wishing to stop. But Kyrie standing in front of him and saying "no" tore to the very center of his being and stopped the already started process.

He groaned as he felt his muscles return to their normal position, his bones resume proper human shape. In this state, it was like being filleted, his body sliced by a thousand sharp knifes, but it was needed and he willed it to happen.

She'd made him think even if what he was thinking was that they were both in great trouble. The red dragon had come back to seek vengeance. And, being a triad member and therefore an outlaw, he would stop at nothing. Tom's life, Kyrie's life, their friends, the diner—all of it would be in danger. And behind Red Dragon stood the powerful, mysterious figure of the Great Sky Dragon, who had taken Tom's life only to give it back again, and whom Tom didn't even pretend to understand. But Tom stopped and thought long enough to realize that if he were to shift now he would, probably, as Kyrie had said, lose consciousness. And that would not solve anything. Even if Red Dragon didn't take advantage of his weakness to behead him, an unconscious dragon in the parking lot becoming hypothermic would only add to Kyrie's troubles.

Through clenched teeth he asked Red Dragon, "What do you want?" But Red Dragon only glared and bobbed his neck up and down, waving his head like some deranged bobble-toy, his mismatched limbs rearing, his wings flaring.

"Go inside," Kyrie answered, looking at Red Dragon, but speaking to Tom, impatiently. "Go inside, Tom. We can't have you here. Not weakened. I'll find out what this . . . what he wants."

"But—" Tom said, and stopped as he realized he was about to say "I'm the man. I'm supposed to protect you." He could not say that. Man or not, he was in no state to protect anyone.

Feeling his cheeks heat in shame, he retreated. He retreated step by step, while staring at Kyrie. He walked backwards, through the blowing snow, till Kyrie and the red dragon were no more than outlines of themselves, patterns of shadow drawn on the surrounding whiteness. He felt his heart beat, hard in his chest. He was sure it was beating hard enough that if he looked down he'd see it pound even through the shirt and his black leather jacket. His mouth was dry and tasted vaguely of blood as though the hoarse cough that normally heralded his transformation had stripped it of its lining. He cleared his throat, more because he wanted to remind Red Dragon and Kyrie that he was still there—more because he felt like a coward and a fool, backing away from confrontation and leaving his girlfriend to face evil alone. But he didn't know if the sound carried that far, and besides, what good was it to remind them he was there, when he could do nothing to defend the woman he loved?

Oh, sure, Kyrie was a were panther. Oh, surely, she could defend herself. She had fought these creatures before but . . .

But if he'd not helped Kyrie then, she would have died. And now he was going to leave her alone with one of these—a creature that was bigger than her feline form, a creature that could burn her to cinders. Everything that was Tom—normal and human and responsible—wanted to stay and protect Kyrie. But he knew better, he knew how sensible Kyrie was. And he knew his body would not stand another shift.

He wished there was someone he could call to, but all the shifters he knew for a fact were shifters were a homeless man and Rafiel—who might or might not be inside. Was Rafiel inside? He'd called Tom. Had he had time to get here, yet?

Tom must check. He stepped back faster and faster. He couldn't see so clearly through the snow anymore, but Kyrie seemed to be circling the dragon, or the dragon seemed to be circling Kyrie. It couldn't be good, but at least he saw no flame. That at least was better than it could be.

He stepped back. As he walked into the purple glow of

the sign at the back door he felt the warmth of the diner behind him. Even through the glass door at the back, enough heat escaped that, without looking, he could tell where the door was.

Stepping back towards the warmth, he heard the key in the lock, and then the door opened, right behind him.

He turned. "Anthony!" he said, or rather gasped in surprise, turning back to look and see if Anthony—who had no idea shapeshifters or dragons existed—would see the dragon through the snow before the door closed. But there was nothing out there, just the briefest of shadows, and did he hear Kyrie's car trunk open? What was she doing? Stashing the defeated body of her opponent? Well, it could be worse. If she was opening a car, then she had to be alive. Probably.

"Tom?" Anthony asked. He was slim and Italian or perhaps Greek or maybe some flavor of South American. Or maybe he had all those in his ancestry somewhere. Olive skinned, with curly dark hair, and a Roman nose, Anthony was a local boy, grown up in this neighborhood. He was Kyrie's and Tom's guide to local stores and events. And every small business owner seemed to know Anthony, whose approval counted for more with them than their better-business-bureau rating. He was also the leader of a bolero dancing troupe and newly married. And the one person they trusted enough to let him manage the daytime shift unsupervised.

"Yeah."

"You guys came in."

"You're open."

"I was going to close, but then people started trickling

in and kept coming in. Cold, you know. Or just wanting to see people." He shrugged. "And there's freaky stuff around here, and . . ."

But Tom was listening, wildly, for the sound of the car door, for the sound of Kyrie, for what might be happening out there, in the howling snow.

Kyrie knew this was crazy, but it would be crazier to do nothing. She circled around the red dragon, looking up at the creature, as it circled in turn, to keep her in sight. She could feel her other form itching to take over, but she didn't think that would be the best of ideas. Because the dragon wasn't attacking her. Why wasn't the dragon attacking her?

Truth be told, from what she remembered, Red Dragon had been the least effectual of the triad members. Why would he be the one sent? Unless—she took a look at his shrunken arm—he was trying to avenge himself all on his own.

He opened his mouth and she tensed, ready to hit the snow and roll away from his breath. Instead he made a pitiful sound, low and mournful in his throat.

"What?" she said, as if she expected the creature to speak. Instead, it made the sound again, and then it coughed. The cough was just like Tom's when he was about to change. Or when he was about to flame, of course. She tensed and circled, watching. It moaned and circled in turn. Suddenly, it spasmed. Contorted.

It was changing. Kyrie, who'd thrown herself to the snow-covered ground, looked up to see the creature bend and fold in unnatural ways, seeming to collapse in on itself.

It was shifting. It was becoming human.

But why is he shifting? Wouldn't his dragon form give him the advantage? What could he gain by becoming human?

What he couldn't gain, clearly, was warmth, because in the next moment he stood there, looking like an instant popsicle in the shape of a young Asian male, skinny and very, very naked in the howling storm. He covered his privates with one hand—the other arm being rather too short to allow him to reach that far, and he looked at her with pitiful eyes, even as his skin turned a shade of dusky violet.

"What do you want?" she asked, using all her will power to keep her teeth from chattering. "What do you want? What do you wish from me?"

He shook his head slowly, his eyes very wide. She wondered if he looked like that out of fear of her, and realized it was more likely that it was the cold. "I . . . Must speak. I was sent to speak. To you. I must protect . . . Him."

"Protect the Great Sky Dragon?" Kyrie asked.

Red Dragon shook his head. He had a crest of hair in the front—rumpled—probably a natural cowlick, and in human form, his eyes looked small and dark and confused. "No, not him. He sent me."

He did not speak with an accent so much as with the shadow of an accent—as if he felt obligated to sound

Asian, even though he didn't. It made his words seem stilted. He talked while shivering and the words emerged through short panting breaths. "He sent me to redeem myself. The Great Sky Dragon. Sent me."

"To redeem yourself?" Kyrie yelled as the snow blew into her mouth. She looked at the snow-covered ground for a stone or something with which to hit the enemy. Nothing was visible under the snow, but she must find something. Because she now knew he had come to kill Tom.

And then Red Dragon wrapped his arms around himself, a curiously defenseless gesture. "He sent me to protect the young dragon. He says I must prove I'm worthy before I'm trusted, and this is where he wants me to prove myself. I am to defend the young dragon from the Ancient Ones."

"Defend?" Kyrie asked, her voice a mere, surprised whisper as her mind arrested on the word she could not have anticipated. "Defend? Defend Tom?"

"Tom," Anthony's voice said from behind Tom, as Tom tried to see beyond the light of the diner's back window, beyond where it seemed a dazzle upon a confusion of snow. Beyond all that, he was sure now, there were two human figures. And that must mean . . . Both of them were alive, which he supposed was good.

"Tom," Anthony's voice again. "Look, I don't suppose you and Kyrie are going to stay?"

"We have to," Tom said, still intent on the two people out there in the snow. Why weren't they walking any nearer? He had no doubts that Kyrie could more than hold her own in a fight with Red Dragon, provided they were both in human shape, but all the same, he wished that they would come closer—that he could hear what they must be saying. "We need a bathroom."

It was only as the silence lengthened that Tom thought his remark might be cryptic and he was trying to figure out how to describe what had happened in their bathroom, without giving away that he shifted shapes. A daunting task. "The pipes burst," he said at last, which, of course, was true. He stared into the snow. Were they now, finally, walking towards the diner?

"Oh," Anthony said. "So you two are staying? Because, you know, my wife is alone, and we don't have groceries and if we end up not being able to . . . I mean . . . If we're snowed in for a week or . . . I know I'm supposed to work, but, you see, my wife is not used to Colorado weather, and she's nervous at all the emergency announcements on the radio and—"

Tom looked over his shoulder at Anthony's anxious face, and understood what Anthony hadn't quite said. "You want to go home," he said. "Sure. Go."

"I hate to leave you guys in the lurch, but all the prep stuff is done, and there's a pot of clam chowder and I left a large bowl of rice pudding in the freezer and—"

"Go," Tom said. He was now sure that Kyrie and Red Dragon—in human form—were coming towards him, but they were walking very slowly, and he could not figure out why. Unless Red Dragon was still naked, but Tom knew

Kyrie kept a bunch of spare clothes in her car. Had she been caught short for once?

"There's . . . look, Tom, you're going to think I'm crazy, but . . ."

He had to turn around, no matter how much he wanted to keep an eye on Kyrie. And then he realized all of a sudden perhaps Kyrie was delaying coming inside because she could see Anthony there behind Tom and there was something she didn't want Anthony to notice. Like the fact that she was naked. Or the fact that she could change shapes. It was a strange part of their secretive life to know a person they trusted absolutely with their business and their local connections could not be trusted to know what they truly were. But neither Tom nor Kyrie were willing to risk the reaction.

So Tom turned, away from the door, away from the parking lot, and towards Anthony, who, looking relieved to have Tom's attention at last, held the door open, stepped aside and gestured Tom towards the inside of the diner as he said, "Tom, look. It's . . . oh, this is going to sound stupid, but . . . You see, you might have to call animal control."

"Animal control?" Tom asked, as they walked the long, slightly curving hallway that led from the back door to the diner proper. They passed the door to the two bathrooms on the left, the doors to the freezer room and the two storage rooms on the right, and then found themselves at the back of the diner, looking at the newly recovered brown vinyl booths, the five remaining green vinyl booths that Tom planned to upgrade as soon as possible, and tables newly covered in fake-marble formica. Out of habit Tom counted: five tables occupied here and, from the noise, another five or six occupied in the annex—a sort of large enclosed patio attached to the diner, which had larger tables and which was preferred by college students who arrived in huge, noisy bands.

Tom took off his leather jacket, folded it and stuffed it in the shelf under the counter, then reached to the shelf under that for an apron with The George on the chest. Then felt around again for the bandana with which he confined his hair while cooking—usually to prevent hair falling on the food, though today it would also keep the grill masonry-free, as he was sure his hair was still full of drywall, grout and tile fragments.

"Look, I don't know who deals with situations like this," Anthony said. He frowned. "For all I know it escaped from the zoo or something."

"What?"

Anthony looked embarrassed. "It's an alligator. I know you're going to think I'm completely insane, but I went out there, to throw some stuff away just a few minutes ago. Because, you know, Beth didn't come in, and we don't have anyone to bus, and the kitchen trash . . ."

"Yes." Beth was the new server, and not the most reliable of employees.

"Yeah, anyway, so, I went out there to throw the stuff away, and you . . . Oh. You're going to think I've gone nuts."

"I doubt it," Tom said flatly. He'd just noticed—sitting in his favorite table, by the front window, under a vivid scrawl advertising meatloaf dinner for $3.99—the blond and incongruously surferlike Rafiel Trall. He managed to look like a refugee beach bum, even while wrapped in a grey parka and miles from the nearest ocean. Rafiel looked up at his gaze, and raised eyebrows at Tom.

"Well . . . whatever. If you think I'm nuts, fine, but I swear there was an alligator by the dumpster, eating old fries and bits of burger."

"An alligator?"

"I know, I know, it sounds insane."

And Tom, to whom it did not sound insane at all—Tom, who, in fact, was suppressing an urge to blurt out that it was nothing but a homeless gentleman known as Old Joe, who happened to be an alligator shifter—instead shrugged and said, "No, it doesn't sound insane. You know, people buy them little as pets, then abandon them."

"In restaurant dumpsters?" Anthony asked, dubiously.

"I don't see why not," he said. "People abandon cats here all the time. Why shouldn't they abandon alligators?"

Anthony took a deep breath. "Well . . . sewers in New York, and I've heard of alligators in reservoirs here, but . . ."

"People are weird," Tom said, squirming, uncomfortable about lying to his employee and friend.

"I guess," Anthony said, frowning slightly, as though contemplating alligator-infested restaurant dumpsters were too much for him. He rallied, "Well, be careful when you go back there, all right? I beaned him with a half-rotten cantaloupe and he hid behind the dumpster but I don't think he's gone away."

"Yeah." He hoped Old Joe hadn't gone away. He was totally harmless, and mostly in need of a minder. And that minder, for the time being at least, was Tom.

"And I may go? Home?"

"Yeah." Tom saw Rafiel had stood up and approached

the counter and now leaned behind Anthony, trying to catch Tom's eye. He remembered Rafiel's call had been about murder. "Yeah, go home, Anthony. I've got it covered."

He turned blindly—more on instinct than on thought—to the far end of the counter, where no customers sat, and where the two huge polished chrome coffee machines stood, probably a good twenty years out of date. They shimmered because Tom had taken steel wool to them last month, during a long, slow week, and now they managed to look retro, rather than obsolete.

On the way he grabbed still-frozen hamburger patties from a box Anthony had left beside the grill. He didn't think before he grabbed them, and he didn't think before biting into the first one. It was hard, and the cold made his teeth hurt, but he couldn't stop himself. He needed protein. He desperately needed protein, with an irrational bone-deep craving. If he ignored the craving, then there was a good chance the customers would start looking like special protein packs on two legs. Particularly since his body would be trying to heal the damage he'd caused by shifting in the cramped bathroom.

The third patty in his hand, holding it like a child holding a cookie, and hoping no one was looking too closely, he peered at the coffee machines. The caffeinated side was low, and he thought he should also bring the small backup coffee maker from the back room and use it to run hot chocolate, because on a day like this they should offer a special on hot chocolate. And doing this work at the end of the counter would allow Rafiel to approach him and talk to him without either calling attention or risk being overheard. Which was essential if that murder truly involved shapeshifters. And it probably did, because Rafiel wasn't a fool. Impetuous sometimes and a bit too cocky, but not a fool.

Tom got the spare coffee maker from the back room, and then the good spicy hot-chocolate mix from the supplies room. He darted to the front and wrote on the window with a red dry-erase marker, hot chocolate, 99¢ a cup and was setting up the coffee maker—scrupulously cleaned—to run hot chocolate, when he heard Rafiel lean over the counter. At the same time, he heard steps down the hallway. Kyrie's steps—he'd know them anywhere—and someone else's.

Behind him, Rafiel's voice hissed, suspicious, "What is *he* doing here."

Kyrie should have known that Rafiel would be at The George. As she came in with Red Dragon—in the grey sweatsuit that Tom kept in the back of the car, in case of unexpected shifts—she saw Rafiel ahead and bit her tongue before she echoed his question.

Instead, she shoved Red Dragon ahead of her, hissing as she passed, "Tom, the tables."

He looked around at her, unfocused, and she realized he was holding a hamburger patty in his hand. His eyes still had that odd, semi-focused look they got when he hadn't fully recovered from a shift. She doubted he fully understood what she told him and, anyway, it didn't seem to her as if he'd know what to do with the tables, right now. Hungry dragon. Tasty customers. Perhaps this was not the best of ideas.

"Never mind," she said, and she shoved Red Dragon into a tiny booth covered in tattered green vinyl. Customers never picked it unless the rest of the place was full. It barely fit two people and those people had best be very close indeed. Also, now that Tom had started having some of the booths recovered in new brown vinyl, the older ones, with their cigarette burn marks and the scuffs on the fifties-vintage green vinyl were ignored. That Red Dragon let her just push him, and fell to sitting, like a little kid, reaching out with his shrunken arm to hold onto the table, filled Kyrie with something very close to irritation. "Sit. Stay," she told him.

She ducked behind the counter and picked up her apron—green and embroidered with The George on the chest, atop a little figure of a cartoon dragon.

The pocket still held her notebook and pen. She picked up a coffee carafe and started towards the tables, dispensing warm-ups and taking down orders for this and that, all the while thinking of what might be going on. What on Earth could the Great Sky Dragon mean by sending Red Dragon to *protect* Tom? What could Tom need protection against? What was all that talk of *redeeming* himself? And what could Red Dragon, who could barely challenge Kyrie herself, *do* to *protect* Tom?

She came back to Tom and passed along orders for half a dozen burgers and fries, a platter of souvlaki and a bowl of clam chowder, before ducking behind the counter and assembling two salads. Tom seemed to have finished bingeing on raw beef, and his eyes looked more focused. He also looked vaguely nauseated, as he usually did when he'd just realized he'd eaten something odd.

"What does Rafiel want?" she asked Tom as she worked. Rafiel had gone back to his booth. "I know he called, and said something about a murder, but then we got . . . sidetracked."

"There was a murder," Tom said, in an undertone. She noted that there was now an assembled burger near the grill, and that he was taking bites of it between flipping the burgers on the grill. This was good, because it meant Tom had become himself enough that he wanted his meat cooked, and with mustard and whole wheat buns and lettuce and pickles.

"And he thinks it involves shifters," he said, taking a bite of his burger.

"Oh," Kyrie said. "When it rains . . ."

"Yeah, apparently it pours when it snows too," he said, with a significant look at the windows, fogged with the inside heat and humidity and still being dusted with an ever-thicker snowfall.

He set the food on the counter, neatly grouped by table for her to deliver and said, still in that undertone, "I take it he poses no threat?" He gave a head gesture towards Red Dragon who sat in his booth looking forlorn and as confused as a little kid among strangers.

Kyrie frowned. "Ask me again in half an hour," she said, and delivered all the orders before making her way to Rafiel. She had left him sitting at his table, without so much as taking his order, because he was a friend and, as such, not likely to take offense if she didn't attend to him.

"I'm sorry," she said, as she approached him. "We're very shorthanded today."

He nodded, though his glance went, inevitably, to Red Dragon with his foreshortened arm, as if he suspected her of making a bad joke. "It's okay," he said. "I just came to ask you and Tom to come with me. I need your help. Well . . . I need the help of . . . people I can trust, and I don't want to . . ." He shook his head, and looked at Tom behind the counter. "I don't suppose you could get someone else in, to look after the place? While you come with me? Or could Tom manage alone?"

Kyrie looked up as the bell behind the front door tinkled, and yet another couple came in, muffled to the eyes and sliding on the coating of snow and ice that covered the soles of their shoes. They dropped into seats at a nearby table, and Kyrie said, "I don't know how Anthony managed alone, Rafiel. I don't think we can go anywhere now. Besides, how do you propose to drive in that?"

Rafiel shrugged. "Four-wheel drive and I'm used to this. I learned to drive in this."

Kyrie nodded. Rafiel, like Anthony, was local. "Well, I still don't know how I can come with you. Not with . . ." She waved around at the diner, and nodded towards the new customers, assuring them silently that she could see them and would be with them shortly. "Maybe if one of our employees shows up," she said, doubtfully.

"Yes. Get me a coffee and a piece of pie, please. I'll wait."

She frowned at him, because his willingness to wait meant he was convinced this did indeed involve shifters, and that meant there was no one else he could trust.

Looking towards the booth, she assured herself that Red Dragon was still there, now looking fixedly at Rafiel with a scared expression. Perhaps it was Rafiel that he thought he had to protect Tom from.

She took the order of the new couple—two coffees, which meant they had braved the walk just to be near other people—and went back to grab the pie for Rafiel.

"Chick-pea pie," she announced, as she set it down in front of him—a joke that had developed from the fact that Rafiel never specified what kind of pie he wanted, which led to her inventing more and more outrageous pretended contents to his food. "And your coffee."

"What does he want?" Rafiel asked, looking at Red Dragon and not even acknowledging her joke.

"He says he's come to redeem himself by protecting Tom," she said, and was gratified to watch Rafiel's eyebrows shoot up. She wasn't the only one who found this absurd.

"Kyrie says that you can't manage the diner alone," Tom heard Rafiel say, in barely more than a rumbling whisper. Tom had just moved the furthest away from customers possible, while remaining behind the counter. The sheer pileup of dishes from the tables Kyrie was cleaning demanded that he put them in the dishwasher, which was around the corner from the coffee maker, and almost to the hallway.

He looked up from slamming the dishes down. Rafiel had a slice of apple pie in one hand and his coffee in the other and was standing by the portion of the counter where Tom normally put the dishes for Kyrie to carry away. Past him, Kyrie was cleaning one last table. There remained four fully occupied ones, but everyone had been served, and had gotten their bill, and seemed to be just sitting around, talking, reluctant to face the storm again. "Maybe if it slows down now." "It might, you know?" "It's nasty out."

"I'm surprised there's anyone here," Rafiel said. "At least anyone who doesn't need to be here. What possessed you to come in?"

"I shifted," Tom said, slamming the last few plates into the dishwasher, shutting it and turning it on. "In our bathroom. There's . . . uh . . . no bathroom left."

He looked up, to see Rafiel staring at him, as he half expected, openmouthed. "In your bathroom? Why?"

Tom shrugged. "It will sound very strange."

"Not as strange as deciding to shift in the bathroom. How could you possibly think you'd fit. Or that there would be—"

"Fine," he said. "There was a voice in my head. The Great Sky Dragon's voice."

"The . . . ?"

"Yeah."

Rafiel looked at Red Dragon. "Threatening?"

Tom shrugged. "I thought so at the time. Now I'm not so sure. He was talking about some Ancient Ones or others who were, supposedly, after me."

"I see," Rafiel said, in that way he had that made it clear he did not see at all. He ate his apple pie in quick bites.

"At the time," Tom said, "I didn't even realize the voice was in my head. It sounded like he was talking to me through the bathroom window. Considering the last time I met with him . . ."

"He almost killed you?"

"Yes. Panic had carried me halfway through the shift before I realized he was in fact in my mind, and for some reason this failed to be reassuring."

"Ancient Ones," Rafiel said. "Shifters?"

"I don't know. He didn't say. I just . . . I'd had a weird dream about . . . very old shifters. Some with shapes that . . . well . . ." He felt stupid, but had to say it. "A saber-toothed tiger and all that."

"Stands to reason," Rafiel said. "We're not easy to kill . . . so some of us would be very old."

"Well . . . we don't know if our longevity is any greater. Legends aren't exactly clear on that, are they? Vampires, sure, but shifters . . ." He shrugged. "If we lived that much longer than normal people, wouldn't the world be overrun by us? And wouldn't it be far more obvious that we exist?"

"How do we know there aren't a lot more of us than we thought? I mean, we know shifters are attracted to this place. Do you know how many of your customers are shifters?"

"Yes. You and Old Joe out back, though I'm not sure I'd call him a customer." He added at Rafiel's blank look, "The alligator." He took a quick look around the diner. "Speaking of which. I should check on him. If Kyrie asks, tell her I just went out back and will be right back."

He ducked out into the back hallway, hoping that Old

Joe would still be there. The man seemed to be old and confused enough that he shifted shapes at all sorts of times for any reason or no reason at all. And Tom dreaded the thought of his being naked and lost in the snow, scared away by the cantaloupe that Anthony had thrown at his head.

Rafiel heard Kyrie behind him. No. He smelled her before he heard her—that sharp tang that indicated a shifter, followed by the symphony of scent that was Kyrie herself. She didn't wear perfume—that would probably have covered up all other scents to him—but her smell reminded him of cinnamon and fresh cut apples and the smell of fresh mown grass. All of those were very subtle undertones overlaid on a smell of soap, but they twisted together in a scent that meant Kyrie.

"Tom went outside. Something about an alligator," Rafiel said without turning back.

Kyrie gave what was not even a suppressed sigh, just a slightly longer breath. He could almost hear her shrug. He couldn't tell if it was impatience or exasperation. "Yeah," she said. "He's one of Tom's strays."

There would have been a time when Rafiel would have pursued that hint of impatience with his rival. No matter how much Rafiel might deny it or what he might say, Kyrie remained his dream girl, whom he thought the perfect woman for him. The one he loved and could never have.

For a moment, a nonphysical ache seemed to make

his heart clench, and then he shook his head. "Look, it's just . . ." He shook his head again when he realized he was about to tell her that he couldn't discuss Tom without appearing partial because he still wanted her and wanted her badly. Then he realized he couldn't tell her that.

The problem with it, he thought, repressing an impulse to kick something, was that he liked Tom. They'd saved each other's lives, more or less, a couple of times. They'd fought side by side. There was something in that for men—something older than time, older than human thought. It made them blood brothers; comrades at arms. But beyond all that, he *liked* Tom. Tom was odd and he did things Rafiel couldn't fully understand but then, in a way everyone appeared like that to everyone else.

Tom came in the back door then. Because of the slight curve of the hallway, Rafiel couldn't see him, but he could hear him, talking to someone who answered back in a raspy voice. This presumably meant, Rafiel thought, that Tom was bringing back the former alligator now in human form. Not that he put it past Tom to drag an alligator into the diner. And the fact that he could easily convince everyone in there that this was perfectly normal and nothing unexpected was part of what was unique about the man. Part of the reason Rafiel knew it was no use to try to seduce Kyrie. Not anymore. He had seen his competition and he knew he didn't measure up.

Instead, he turned around, to look at Kyrie, who was staring down the hallway, towards the sound of an opening door. "He keeps old clothes in one of the storage rooms," she said. "For Old Joe. Because he shifts for no reason, and it means he ends up naked a lot."

Rafiel shrugged. "The reason I came," he said, "is that we found an arm. At the aquarium."

"An *arm*?" She looked at him blankly, with a horrified expression. "An *arm*?"

"There was a cell phone ring that came from inside one of the sharks," Rafiel said. "The cleaning divers heard it. They thought, you know . . . the shark had swallowed a cell phone. People lean over—there's an observation area—and they drop things in the water. But then they found the bones at the bottom of the tank. Human bones. That's when we were called in, to determine if they were, in fact, human. They were. A couple of vertebrae. Some toe bones." He waved his hand. For some reason the finding of those fragments of humanity at the bottom of a shark tank affected him more than finding a whole decomposing body, as he often had. They were more pathetic and more anonymous, demanding more of his pity, his outrage—and his justice.

He shook his head, to dismiss the image of the bones—a handful of them, no more. Kyrie looked at Tom, leading Old Joe—a man so old he was almost bent over, and whose skin and hair were not so much white as the curious colorlessness of the very aged—to one of the corner tables, and now Tom was ducking behind the counter and getting a bowl of clam chowder and taking it back to Old Joe.

"So they opened the shark," Rafiel said, hearing his own voice sound toneless. "And they found a human arm, still clutching a cell phone."

"Someone fell in the aquarium?" Kyrie asked, and now Rafiel had her full attention, and Tom had come up and was nearby, his eyebrows raised.

"Was it a shifter?" he asked. "Who fell?"

Rafiel shook his head. "No. It wasn't . . . it's just . . . we went over today, with a team, and did the full work-up, and while we were there, I kept smelling this shifter smell, around the shark tank and up to the little observation area. And then around the offices, too. So I made sure to forget one of my notebooks behind, and I went back to pick it up. There was only one employee there, closing up for the day, really, and she didn't mind having me look around the crime scene." He cringed inwardly, knowing exactly how many violations of procedure he had incurred, but knowing that procedure, somehow, failed to account for shifter criminals and the shifter policemen whose life might be destroyed by them. "If it's even a crime scene, of course."

"And?" Kyrie said.

"And there was a definite trail of shifter-smell winding around the observation area from which the vic could have fallen into the tank."

"But surely," Tom said, "it could also mean that of the many visitors to the aquarium, one was . . . you know, like us."

Rafiel nodded. "Oh, it could mean that. Definitely. And that's the problem. I couldn't smell all around and . . ." He shrugged. "I wanted your noses on the case, as it were. I . . . stole a set of keys while the employee was busy." That she had been busy on a wild goose chase for the wallet he claimed to have dropped somewhere only made him feel slightly guilty. He noted that neither Kyrie nor Tom looked shocked by his behavior, either. Tom chewed his lip and looked like he was thinking. "I truly can't go," he said. "Kyrie is not that good on managing the grill area. It's new. The whole stove is. She's not used to it yet."

Kyrie looked as if she would protest, but was sweeping automatically back and forth across the tables with her gaze, even as she frowned. "Perhaps," she said, "I can come with you if we do it briefly?"

Rafiel looked towards Tom. He knew very well that Kyrie didn't need anyone's permission and, in fact, he was perfectly well aware that Kyrie would resent his openly asking if Tom minded her going with him. Because it would imply Kyrie needed a minder and that she was less than a fully conscious participant in the relationship. Both of which were lies.

So Rafiel didn't say anything, but he looked at Tom.

There had been times, only a few months ago, when Tom would have been very upset at thinking of Rafiel and Kyrie going anywhere together without him. But now he just looked towards the booth where Red Dragon sat and asked, "Can you take him with you?"

Rafiel raised his eyebrow, in mute question, wondering if Tom meant to use Red Dragon as a chaperone. But the look back was guileless and open. "It's just I'd rather not have him around when I already shifted once today. And not in the diner. I don't want to shift again, and I don't want to do it here. And there are two of you . . ."

Kyrie nodded. She had that jutting-lower-lip look she got when she'd determined on a course of action. "Let me talk to him, first," she said, and walked towards the booth, carrying the coffee carafe and a cup, in what might be a gesture of hospitality or, simply, the most discreet weapons she could carry in this space.

Red Dragon was still huddled in the booth where Kyrie had left him, and looked around with huge eyes, as if he expected everyone in the diner to shift shapes and devour him.

And he says he wants to protect Tom, Kyrie thought, and shook her head slightly at the absurdity of it. *It has to be a joke. Perhaps not his joke, but the Great Sky Dragon's.*

She pushed a cup in front of him, and poured coffee into it from the carafe and just as she was thinking that no matter how many packets of sugar Red Dragon put in it, he needed protein and she ought to have thought of it, Tom set a plate in front of Red Dragon, containing two whole wheat buns and what appeared to be a triple hamburger and a whole lot of cheese.

Considering that she knew very well how Tom felt about Red Dragon, Kyrie felt her heart melt. Tom was like that. He would give up his own shirt to clothe someone else, even if it was his mortal enemy. This both scared her and made her think her boyfriend was the best person in the world.

Red Dragon looked sheepishly at Tom who said, "Protein. After shifting."

The young man nodded at Tom and picked up the burger with shaking hands, while Kyrie looked up at Tom and gave him her warmest smile. He looked worried enough, but he winked at her, before returning behind the counter to fool with the grill or start preparations for the next dish, or whatever it was he did back there half the time. Kyrie was quite contented to leave the cooking to Tom, and most of their clientele seemed to approve of the decision.

She turned back to Red Dragon, who was wolfing down the burger.

"I can't call you Red Dragon," she told the creature who faced her, clutching the burger tightly as if he were afraid she'd take it away. "Do you have a name?"

Red Dragon blushed and paused, caught just after taking a bite, his mouth full, the burger awkwardly in his hand. "I'm . . . My name . . ." He blushed darker and looked down at the burger, setting it slowly down on the plate, as he hastily chewed what was in his mouth. "My name is Conan Lung."

"Conan?" Kyrie asked. She didn't know whether she believed it, and she almost laughed at the idea of this man, who was shorter even than Tom, much slimmer, and— definitely—no barbarian hero, being called Conan.

"I . . ." He sighed. "My parents used comic books to improve their English, and they liked Conan."

That he was descended from the sort of people who thought that their son was likely to grow up to be a barbarian hero, might explain his delusional thoughts of protecting Tom. *Might*. She doubted anything *could* fully explain that.

"Right, then, Mr. Lung," she said. "What I want to know—"

"Call me Conan," Conan Lung said, quickly, and in the sort of undertone that implied he expected a rebuff.

"Right then," Kyrie said, thinking to herself she hoped

the creature wouldn't think they were the best of friends, now. In his last foray into their lives, he'd chased them all over town and he'd helped catch and torture Tom. She knew that like all cowards, he could be exceptionally cruel in a fight. And she didn't want to have him at her back in a dangerous situation. In fact, she didn't want to have him anywhere that she couldn't keep a sharp eye on him. "You said you came to protect Tom?"

Red Dragon cast a fearful look at Tom, then another back at Kyrie. "The Great One said that I must come and protect the young dragon," he said, and bobbed a small bow, as though just speaking of the Great Sky Dragon must entail a need to kowtow. "He said I should answer for his life with mine."

Kyrie frowned. Conan sounded terribly earnest and she didn't think just now, scared as he looked, that the man was capable of lying so convincingly. However, having met the vast golden dragon that was master of all other Asian dragons in the West, she couldn't imagine his sending Conan to Tom as a protector.

"You're . . . He told you you're to protect Tom? You're a bodyguard of sorts, then?"

Conan bobbed his head again, then shook it desultorily. "Not . . . a bodyguard. My . . . my fighting is not all that could be desired. But I am one of the Great One's . . . you know? One of his vassals. I'm supposed to . . . to report to him what's happening around . . . the young dragon. To . . . to call him if needed."

"Do you mean," Kyrie started, narrowing her eyes, "that you are spying for the Great Sky Dragon? That if there is any trouble . . ."

"He can be here in no time at all," Conan said. "He tried telling the young dragon to beware, but the young one didn't seem to understand him, so I am here to protect him." A bite of the burger and a fleeting look under his—annoyingly thick and long—lashes at her. "And . . . and you. By making sure the Great One can chase away any enemies before they can harm any of you."

"But protect us from what?" Kyrie asked. She didn't at all like the idea that the Great Sky Dragon had effectively planted a spy among them. She wasn't sure she trusted his intentions or his ideas of what was proper. And she was very sure she didn't trust the Great Sky Dragon, himself. A creature more than a thousand years old—and from what Kyrie understood, the Great Sky Dragon was several thousands of years old—would have seen generations come and go. What would others' lives be worth to him?

Oh, he could have killed Tom, three months ago—killed him in such a way that even the amazing healing power of dragons would not have reversed. And he'd chosen not to. But how did Kyrie know that it was ever a choice? How could she know that under what must surely be an alien honor code, the Great Sky Dragon hadn't been forbidden from killing Tom then? And how did she know that he didn't mean to make up for it now, by setting a trap in which Tom would be caught and killed?

She looked towards her boyfriend, who was leaning on the counter, chatting animatedly with Rafiel, and again felt a sick lurch in her stomach. In place of the family she'd never known, she had a man who loved her and who was—she believed—one of the best people in the world—dragon shifter or no. And she had friends: Rafiel and

Anthony, and a young man named Keith who was, now and again, a part-time waiter at The George.

Kyrie was not willing to give up any member of her chosen family, nor any corner of her domain to shadowy creatures whose life span might be many times as long as hers, but whose moral compass left much to be desired.

"Stay here," she told Conan, as she got up, collecting the carafe. She must talk to Tom and Rafiel and try to figure out what they should do with Conan and what the Great Sky Dragon could be *trying* to do.

Whatever it was, they would be in as much danger as she would be—perhaps Tom would be in more danger, in fact—and she couldn't make a decision for either of them.

"Seriously," Rafiel said, speaking in an undertone to Tom's back, as Tom industriously scraped at the grill. "How many of your clients are shifters?"

Tom gave Rafiel a look over his shoulder, half startled. "I told you. You and Old Joe."

"You know better. You know because of the pheromones the . . . former owners . . . sprayed this place with it, attract shifters. They attracted you and Kyrie, didn't they? Right off the bus. Unless you have a better explanation as to why you and Kyrie found little Goldport, Colorado so irresistible. They attracted me, which is perhaps more easily explainable, since I'm a policeman and I work the night shift. So, failing a really good twenty-four-hour doughnut shop in town . . ." He smiled a self-conscious smile, glad Tom was turning around—spatula still in hand—and answered his joke with a chuckle. "You could say an all-night greasy spoon is the closest thing to my natural habitat. But how can you truly believe we're the only ones?"

Tom shrugged. "I don't know, Rafiel. I don't think there are that many of our kind of people, period. There was an orangutan shifter, back in New York. And of course, the Great Sky Dragon and his brood. And there is, of course, Old Joe and you and Kyrie. But that's out of thousands of people, Rafiel. I don't think there are that many of us to gather here. Or anywhere."

"What you mean is that you don't think there are that many of them in the vicinity. But how far does the call of the pheromones extend? How far will it bring shifters, do you know? How many casual travelers, how many students, will stop here and stay? How many of those do you have as regulars, Tom?"

Tom shrugged. He set the spatula down and leaned over the counter, so that they could talk to each other in a whisper and with a modicum of privacy. "I don't know," he said. "You figured out how to smell shifters before either Kyrie or I did. Can't you smell out shifters in the diner, and tell *me* how many shifters there are here?"

Rafiel shrugged. "Not always. When people wear perfume, or even cologne, sometimes it's hard to tell. When I was in high school—" He stopped abruptly.

"Yes?" Tom asked.

Rafiel shrugged. He'd never told Tom this. He had never told anyone, not even his parents. The incident, secret though it was, had crystalized for him exactly what risk shifters were in, and how their very natures placed them outside the purview of normal legality. Of what other people would see as reality.

Tom was watching him intently and Rafiel sighed and gave in. "When I was in high school, I had a girlfriend. This was around the time I started shifting, but I shifted mostly late at night, and provided I took care not to have dates on full-moon nights, we were okay. She was . . . she seemed very easygoing and was willing to postpone dates and take my less than convincing excuses. Still, when I graduated I went away to Denver to study law enforcement, and it was either break up or get married and, you know, I couldn't get married. Not and risk her figuring out what I really was. So we broke up. Alice stayed behind and worked . . . actually at The George. The Athens as it then was. And then when I came back for Christmas . . ." He shrugged. "Well, you know, being a shifter and all, and the first year at college I had to be in dorms . . ."

"I always wondered how that worked," Tom said.

"Not well. So I was convinced I wanted to quit school, and I came back home for Christmas, and I was going to tell Dad I couldn't be an officer, after all, which would break his heart. Anyway, when I got here I found out Alice was missing. Had been missing for some days. I shifted. I trailed her . . . well . . . her scent. I found her dead. She had been killed because she was a shifter. She was . . ." He looked up at Tom and saw, reflected in the other man's face, the strange, hollow grief he himself felt. "She was a lion shifter. And her new boyfriend caught her shifting and . . . you know . . . killed her. He was scared. I . . ." He shook his head, trying to free himself of memories of the past and Alice's soft brown eyes. "I never knew it. Even though I was with her, every day, I never smelled the shifter in her. She wore a perfume that had the same sort of undertone, and it got lost in the perfume."

He was quiet a while, unable to find words to continue.

"I'm sorry," Tom said, in a low voice.

Rafiel managed a chuckle. "Well, it was a long time ago. Ten years. But you see, if I could smell shifters that well, I'd have *known*. I did not."

"And you became a policeman," Tom said, softly.

Rafiel shrugged. "Someone official needs to be looking out for our kind, which is what this is all about. I didn't count on the diner becoming the center of shifters for miles around." He gave Tom a smile he was sure looked sickly.

"And why are you so interested in how many of our regulars might be shifters?" Tom asked.

"Well, I figure the aquarium isn't that far away, and if there was a shifter . . . well . . . it might have been one of your regulars who was there, and we might be able to tag him on his specific scent. And then I could question him, you know, without seeming to, and if it turned out to just be someone who went to the aquarium for fun or something . . ." He drew to a halt slowly. The truth was he didn't want this murder to involve any shifters. He didn't want to have to lie and skulk and go behind his superiors' backs.

Oh, Goldport was a small enough town, and the police department was somewhat informal and friendly. Rafiel was a third generation cop in the same department. He could get away with a lot. But he didn't like to. He was a policeman because he prized the idea of a justice system based on laws. He didn't approve of anyone defiling it. Not even himself.

"Rafiel," Tom said, laughter at the back of his throat, trying to cut through the words. "Are you truly suggesting we go up to all our regulars and smell them? Half of them are college students or warehouse workers who come here after work. You know what they smell like."

"No. I mean . . . no, I don't think that would work. Perfume and all. But . . . just keep your nose open, okay?"

Tom nodded and opened his mouth as though he were about to add something, but at that moment Kyrie came up to them. "He says he was sent to protect you, Tom. That the Great Sky Dragon said he tried to warn you and you didn't seem to get it."

"Why would anyone—particularly anyone ancient and presumably intelligent—send *Red Dragon* to protect . . . me?" Tom said.

"He says his name is Conan," Kyrie said, looking at Tom, but with an unfocused expression that indicated her attention was on her thoughts and not on their conversation.

"Conan?" Rafiel asked, before Tom could.

Kyrie turned to him. "His parents liked comic books, he says."

"So it stands to reason he should be the hero to protect me? And protect me from what?" Tom said.

"Are you sure you don't remember what the Great Sky Dragon told you?" Kyrie asked. "Perhaps . . ."

Tom shook his head. "It was all very confused." Just thinking back on that precise, booming voice in his head made his muscles clench and made him fear he would shift without warning. "I know he said I had violated old and sacred customs. The laws of our kind . . ." He shook his head, unable to remember.

"Our kind has laws?" Rafiel asked, at the same time that Kyrie said, "That doesn't sound like he wanted to protect you."

"No," Tom said. "It didn't sound that way to me, either, which is why I thought . . ." He clenched his hands on the counter, digging his nails against the hard formica top and making not an impression. If he'd been in dragon form . . . he would have dug his nails right through it. But he would not allow himself to change. Not now. Not today. Not again.

He took deep breaths, trying to forget the voice and the sense of urgency, trying to remember only the words and not the fear they'd induced. "I remember his saying something about Ancient Ones, but I wasn't sure what he meant—the laws or some people who were very old."

Kyrie nodded. "Well, we're stuck with Conan the Wonder Dragon over there, unless you can get rid of him in some way."

Tom looked at her. In some way. It occurred to him it would be very simple to get rid of him the dragon way—flames at twenty feet. When they'd fought as dragons before, Tom had ripped off Red Dragon's arm and beaten him over the head with it. But somehow he didn't think that was what Kyrie meant for him to do. And as for himself . . . well, until proven otherwise, he couldn't really say killing Red Dragon would be in self-defense. The rather pitiful creature, cowering in their smallest booth, warming his hands on a cup of coffee, could be said to be many things, but life-threatening wasn't one of them. Whatever he'd been or done in the past, right now the adjectives that came more readily to mind echoed more of *wet* or perhaps *spineless*.

Tom knew better than to discount the creature just because he cringed and hid around the corners. Tom had lived on the streets and seen many a beggar who seemed meek and mild turn suddenly and go on a rampage. But still, the truth remained he was not openly threatening Tom. If Tom killed Conan now, even in what could be considered a fair duel—as fair as it could be when only one of the duelists was in possession of a backbone—then he would forever feel he had murdered a defenseless being. And murdering defenseless beings would mean that Tom was not just a shifter, but an animal. It would make it very hard to look at himself in the mirror. Which would make shaving a challenge.

He shrugged. Aloud, he said, "Well, the Great Sky Dragon sent him to us for a reason."

"As a spy," Kyrie said. "It seems he has orders to report all we do . . . or at least anything we do that might be dangerous to the Great Sky Dragon. He put it as he can call the Great Sky Dragon and the Great Sky Dragon will come—or at least send help—when needed."

Tom looked at her for a moment, then shook his head slowly. Hadn't she understood the significance of the

Great Sky Dragon in Tom's head? "Kyrie, he can reach into my mind with his voice at will."

"No," Kyrie said. "Conan says that you shut your mind to the Great Sky Dragon, and that's why he sent Conan to us as a spy. To keep an eye on us."

"Perhaps," Tom said. "But then again, if there's going to be a spy among us, is it not better that it be a spy we know? We can keep an eye on him, keeping an eye on us."

"That sounds strangely unhealthy," Rafiel said. "Like one of those situations where you end up being your own grandpa."

"Perhaps it does," Tom said. "But the truth is, you know . . . better the devil we know. And we do know this devil."

"We'll let him stay then?" Kyrie said, doubtfully.

"Better yet," Tom said. "We'll give him a job. That way we can keep an eye on him to make sure he's doing his job and to make sure he's not trying to kill me. All in one."

Kyrie didn't look convinced. "And what if he attacks?"

"Then," Tom said, and graced her with his best, bare-teeth smile, "I attack back. And I'm bigger and faster."

Kyrie sighed, as if conceding a point. "I don't like it," she said.

"I don't either," Tom said, and reached under the counter for an apron to give to Conan at the same time the front doorbell tinkled to let in the tall, thin blond man who usually spent the night in the diner, writing in a succession of cloth-bound journals. They called him the Poet though it was more likely—from the nervous look of him—that he was writing about conspiracy theories. He took his normal table, with his back against the wall. "But we must make the best of a bad situation, and look at it this way, if I get him to serve at tables, you can probably go with Rafiel and be fine. I'll get him a couple of flip-flops from the storage room."

"You're going to make him a waiter?"

"Why not? While protecting me, he might as well hand out some souvlaki," Tom said. Smiling with a reassurance he was far from feeling, he advanced on the small booth. Red Dragon jumped a little when he saw Tom approach, and looked up at Tom with an expression of such abject terror that Tom thought, *Oh yes, if the time comes, I can take him.* But he hoped it wouldn't be needed. He gave Conan a pair of red flip-flops, explaining, "Health regulations." Then he watched the man put on the apron, while he gave him the speech on waiting tables that had been given to Tom himself, when he'd taken a job as a waiter almost a year ago. "Don't be rude to the customers, no matter what they say; write down the orders, no one's memory is perfect." He took a notebook and pencil from the pocket of the apron and waved it at Conan. "And when you go out to take an order always take the carafe with you and give refills to the people who are having coffee." He glanced at Conan's shrunken arm. "You can put the carafe on the tables without damaging them, at least the new ones. And the old ones, who cares? They're all stained and burned, anyway."

Conan nodded, looking as self-conscious as a kid in new clothes, in strange company, and Tom pointed at the table the Poet had just occupied. "There you go. Take his order. It's probably just coffee, but you never know."

Then he turned to look at Rafiel and Kyrie who were both staring at him with a bemused expression. "What?"

he asked in an undertone. "We don't have enough hands on deck today, and if he's going to stick around, he might as well make himself useful." He shrugged. "Besides," he dropped his voice further, "I might as well keep him too busy to think of something creative to do in the way of getting rid of me."

Rafiel shook his head but didn't say anything, and Tom covered up his apprehension with a smile. "Go on. Now Kyrie can go with you for half an hour or so. We won't be leaving the tables unattended."

Kyrie sat down in Rafiel's car, narrowing her eyes at him. "You won't shift while driving?"

Rafiel gave her a blank, puzzled look. "Why would I do such a stupid thing?" He frowned. "It would end up in an accident."

Kyrie shrugged. She'd rather cut her own tongue out with a blunt knife, than tell him how close she'd come to shifting, herself. "I just thought, you know . . . since one shifts when stressed . . ."

He looked away from the windshield past which Kyrie could see no more than a dazzling whiteness of snow, seeming to radiate from the center of the two light cones cast by the headlights. "Why would I be stressed?" he asked. He held the wheel lightly enough to make her want to growl at him—and she was fairly sure that this had nothing to do with an urge to shift.

He put the car in gear and started out of the parking

lot, seemingly perfectly sure of where he was going. How he could be sure, Kyrie didn't know. Perhaps he was flying by instruments. She glared at him.

He looked out the windshield again and drove at what seemed to her a disgustingly high speed towards Fairfax. As the silence lengthened between them, he turned. "What?" he said.

Kyrie was so surprised he seemed to be aware of her disapproval that she felt her cheeks flush and started to open her mouth to justify herself. Before she could, he reached over and patted her arm awkwardly. "I grew up here," he said, in a tone that made it almost an apology. "I learned to drive in winter." He shrugged, as he stopped for a light that was no more than a diffuse red glow ahead. "I'm sure you'll get more comfortable with it in time."

The tone was sympathetic and attempting to be friendly but it felt patronizing and she had to bite back a wish to swat his ears and put him in his place. The image that came to her mind was of a paw swatting at his feline ears. She felt her lips twist upwards, and looked out the passenger window—though she could not see anything more than blinding white snow. "So, how do you think shifters are involved in this?" she asked, in as serious a voice as she could muster.

Without looking, she could sense he'd shrugged. Probably some slight rustle of cloth as his shoulders rose and fell. "I don't know. Not as victims."

"So you think they are . . . ?"

She looked back in time to see him shake his head. "I don't know," he said. "We've already found that some shifters feel the urge to kill in their . . . well . . . their other form. Perhaps that was it."

"Or perhaps just . . . you know, shifters that kill, like other people kill."

He gave a startled bark of laughter. "Oh, yes, very sensible. I should have thought of that, of course. I mean, we're shifters, we're not saints. The animal urge is not necessary to explain killing, is it? As I know only too well from police work."

"Well . . ." Kyrie said.

"No, trust me, it makes sense. Sometimes, with all this, we run the risk of thinking we're completely apart from humanity and different from them, and of course, we're not. We're humans, like all others. Or almost."

"Given a certain tendency to change shapes, yes, exactly," Kyrie said. "Just like all others."

Rafiel slowed down and leaned all the way forward. "I hope this is Ocean Street," he said. "Because I surely can't read that sign."

"So glad to know the superpowers of Colorado natives don't cover everything."

"You should be, otherwise imagine the envy you'd be forced to feel. Everyone would want to be born in Colorado. It would get crowded in the hospitals," Rafiel said. "But what I was saying . . . perhaps I'm foolish to feel guilty for all shifters, or at least to feel I must protect them from . . . you know, the majority of people—like I must . . ." He turned neatly into the parking lot beside a tall cylindrical building with broad rounded windows. "Like I must be the law for our people—those of us who hide amid other people." He looked at her, and for the first time in a long, long time, she detected a look of insecurity about him, as if he were young and not completely confident about what he thought or should be doing. "I guess you think I'm an idiot. I mean, we don't even know how many of us there are, and here I am, trying to keep them safe, as if I knew them personally."

"Not an idiot," she said, immediately, in reaction to his expression more than anything. "You feel a duty to . . . people like us, I guess." A little gurgle of laughter tore through her throat, surprising her. "Frankly, at first, that was why I helped Tom last year, when he found the body in the parking lot. I wasn't sure if he'd killed anyone or not, but I'd never met anyone else like me—you know, never having had a family. So I figured, he was my responsibility to look after. I'd guess you feel something like that."

"Yeah, but I'd feel better, if I didn't have reason to suspect a lot of our people . . . I mean, a lot of people like us have . . . issues controlling themselves."

"Other people do too," she said. And shrugged. "Now, let's go see if I can confirm your supposed shifter-smell. It's unlikely I can help you, since you have a better sense of smell than any of us."

"I just want . . . second opinion," he said. And got out of the car. On the road, behind them, tires squealed.

"Hey, can I help you with the waiting on tables?" a voice asked behind Tom, as Tom prepared a stack of burgers on the grill.

It was a well known voice—that of his friend Keith Vorpal, the only one of the non-shifters who knew shifters existed. Keith was a film student with an unshakeable joi de vivre and an absolute certainty that being a shifter was the coolest thing since being a superhero. He'd gotten embroiled in their affairs and taken part in some life-and-death struggles. Though he'd acquitted himself well enough, he was sure shifters got to have more fun than he did. Sometimes he claimed to be a human shifter. He shifted between a human form and a stunningly similar human form.

However that was, Tom felt strangely grateful that Keith, not a shifter, didn't feel either horrified by them, or forced to turn them in as abominations. And the fact that Keith knew the routines of The George, where he worked part-time, seemed like a godsend right now, when Tom had been doing his job and continuously prodding the hapless Conan to do his.

"Keith," he said, turning around. "Keith."

Keith smiled at him. His tumbled blond hair was in disarray, and his glasses fogged, from having come from cold to warmth. He unwound a bright red scarf from around his neck, as he spoke. "So, you need my help?"

"Yeah, all we have is Conan, and it's his first day." Tom said, and hoped against hope that Keith would have no memory of Red Dragon.

"Conan?" Keith said, as he ducked behind the counter, removed scarf and jacket. Tom heard the sound of Keith sliding the time sheet from under the counter and smiled.

"The new employee. Over there."

"Over . . ." Keith took in breath sharply. "But Tom, he's . . . that is . . ."

Tom was afraid Keith would blurt out loud that Red Dragon was just that, and the enemy besides. And since Kyrie had left, a sudden inrush of customers had come in, ten or twenty in all, all sitting at nearby tables, ordering hot chocolate and burgers and whatnot. He reached over and put a hand on the young man's shoulder, to arrest the flow of words. "It's all right, Keith, truly. I'm keeping an eye on him."

"If you're sure . . ." Keith said, looking confused.

"Yeah, sure about everything but his ability to wait tables. Why don't you go and—" But before he could suggest that Keith should relieve Conan of some tables and give him breathing room, Tom looked up at the booth where he'd left Old Joe. The clothes he'd loaned the old vagrant were still there, but Old Joe was gone. "Shit," Tom said, which made Keith look at him sharply, because Tom rarely swore out loud. "Man the grill, Keith. Just a couple of minutes."

With a suspicion that he knew very well where Old Joe had gone, Tom ducked out from behind the counter and ran down the hallway, just in time to hear the back door creak open, and to see, as he turned the corner, an alligator tail disappearing through the door.

He knew he should have locked it.

The aquarium looked like a cylindrical grain silo—at least if a silo could be massive, made of glass and concrete and rise ten stories into the air. Once you got inside, there were very few staircases where the public was supposed to walk—from the entrance room, outfitted to look like something from *Ten Thousand Leagues Under the Sea*, with rusty-looking ship wheels and riveted panels on the walls, to the restaurant on the other end. Instead, it was all gently sloping floors.

"Surveillance system?" Kyrie asked, looking at the blank screens in the entrance room and wondering exactly what to do if there was one. After all, she was here with a policeman. But policemen—she was fairly sure of this— weren't supposed to break into the scenes of crimes, alone or with civilian friends, after everyone else had departed. She wondered how this would play in court, if it ever came to court. And that was supposing, of course, that the killer wasn't a shifter. Because, if he was . . .

She shivered. She didn't know what to do if the killer was a shifter, and she would bet Rafiel didn't either. You couldn't let a shifter be arrested and end up in a jail, where his secret would inevitably come out. Particularly not if he was the sort of wild, barely contained shifter who would kill without a thought. If you allowed him to be arrested, you might as well confess that you were one too, and let them come for you. Because once the existence of shifters was discovered, then the sort of accommodation, the sort of looking out for each other, covering for each other, that she and Rafiel and Tom all did, would become impossible. People largely failed to see them because they didn't expect them. If one of them were revealed, then all would be.

But what could they do, if a shifter were guilty? How

could they prevent him from being arrested? Cover for him, and allow him to go on murdering? Or take justice in their own hands and kill him? Who knew? The last time, they'd killed the murderer, but that had been self-defense, because he'd been trying to murder them. This time, they might have to make a dispassionate decision.

"Nah," Rafiel said. He'd barely looked at the screens. "First thing we asked was if they had a surveillance system. But they didn't. They said that they've never had issues with break-ins or vandalism. Normally the restaurant is open half the night, you know. So there's people around."

He led her past various incredibly unconvincing concrete caves. "You can shift in the bathroom," Rafiel said. "The ladies' room is there," and he pointed at a little artificial stone grotto amid which a small door opened with the universal symbol of the stick figure in a dress and the words shad roe. It was, Kyrie thought, very good that there was a picture, since she failed to know what either Shad or Roe meant. The only thing she could think was that Shad Roe was the Russian relative of Jane Doe.

She ducked into the bathroom—a utilitarian thing, with metal sinks and beat-up beige-painted stalls. Perhaps it was supposed to evoke a ship, she thought, and resisted an impulse to duck into a stall before shifting. There was no point at all. They were alone here, and besides, her panther self would be utterly confused, dealing with claws and a door lock.

"Right," she told hersel. She removed her clothes swiftly. She concentrated. Shifting was hard, but she'd learned to do it volitionally in the last few months. As she felt her body spasm and shudder, she caught a glimpse of herself in the mirror, her eyes going slitted yellow, her features growing into a muzzle, her teeth into fangs.

She looked away from the mirror, as the image it reflected became a big, black-furred cat. It caught at the edge of her sense, the sweet-tangy scent that the human part of Kyrie knew meant a shapeshifter had been here, and recently too.

Tom ran down the hallway, full speed. He doubted that Old Joe could have run faster than Tom could walk. But the alligator that Old Joe shifted into could. He moved at a frighteningly fast clip, tail swaying. The door slammed shut behind Joe.

Tom hit it a couple of seconds later, the full impact of his body on the cold glass making it swing open. Snow flew into his mouth and stung his eyes, and as he looked around, frantically, all he could see of Old Joe was a trail in the snow, fast becoming covered by the more recent fall.

"Joe?" he said, stumbling along the trail, to where the dumpster stood, surrounded by a brick wall on three sides—presumably to hide from the customers' minds the ultimate fate of their leftovers.

A happy sort of clack-clack sound, not unlike castanets, made him veer sharp left, into the enclosure and almost step on Joe's tail. "There you are," he said, relieved that Old Joe had gone no further. "You really shouldn't wander off like that. You can have warm burgers inside, why are you—"

He froze as he heard a high-pitched animal battle scream and hiss—and almost ran forward, past Old Joe's front paws, to where he could see a little kitten, just inches from Old Joe's happily clacking snout.

It was orange and fluffy and tiny—maybe eight weeks old. Old enough to have open eyes and stand more or less firmly on spindly legs. Tom felt mingled dread and relief. Relief because he'd had other images in his mind, including a helpless baby shifter dragon. Dread, because instead of running, or jumping on the dumpster—if he could jump—the silly little creature stood facing Old Joe, hair fluffed out all on end, blue eyes blazing. As if it thought it could scare away a huge, armored gator. As Tom watched, it emitted another high-pitched battle scream.

Old Joe lunged. Before his teeth could grab the little creature, Tom stooped and picked it up. "No," he told Old Joe. "This is not dinner." He felt the kitten sink all claws into him, even as Old Joe looked up with a look of intense disappointment in his eyes.

Tom absently held the kitten close to him, hoping that the warmth would mollify him. He didn't dare put him down. Even if he had owners—and it was possible he might, and had only wandered in called by the smell of the diner refuse—what kind of owners let a baby this size walk around outside in a snowstorm? Making his voice stern, he yelled at Old Joe, "Shift. Now. Into human form."

The alligator looked up at him with such a sad look that Tom expected it to start crying. A different type of crocodile tears, Tom guessed. He cleared his throat, to avoid showing weakness, and said, "Now. You have no business being out here shifted. You know what kind of trouble Kyrie and I could get into if they found you. Do you want us to get in trouble?"

The alligator shook his head, earnestly.

"Right. Then shift," he said, and averted his eyes from the vagrant's form, as it writhed and twisted, from crocodile to human. "Better," Tom said. "Now stay. Don't you dare shift again or wander off." Aware that the poor creature was naked, he darted inside, grabbed the discarded sweats, and brought them out.

Old Joe put them on, with the expression of a school child obeying an unreasonable taskmaster. He looked resentfully at Tom from under lank clumps of steel-grey hair. "It's tasty. It's been too long since I've eaten an animal."

Tom shuddered. "You're not going to eat this one, either," he said, firmly, holding and sheltering the orange fluffball in his hands. The kitten had started cleaning himself, in affronted dignity, as though to let Tom know he could take care of himself fine, thank you so much.

Old Joe didn't say anything else about it. He gave Tom a half-amused, half-sad look. Though his eyes could be called brown, they had faded as much as the rest of him, so that they looked even more pitiful and washed out. The grey sweat suit—picked up at the thrift store down the street and faded and washed out as it was—looked like a scream of color on the small, short body. As Old Joe stood up, he never straightened to his full five feet or so of height. Instead he stooped forward, bent, and shuffled along.

Tom shifted his hold on the kitten, and held Old Joe's arm, as he led him inside.

"Walk better as a gator," the man said in a raspy voice, tainted with an undefinable accent.

"Undoubtedly," Tom said, maneuvering to open the door, without dropping either of his charges. "But alligators are not native to the Rockies, and if anyone sees you, they'll call animal control. And then what are we supposed to do?"

Old Joe nodded, but Tom wondered how much he understood of his speech. Most of the time Old Joe's hold on reality was thread-thin, no more than a dime's edge worth of awareness. Sometimes, though, when he spoke, Tom glimpsed . . . he wasn't sure what. Perhaps the man that Old Joe had once been—sharp and incisive, bordering on the acerbic. And sometimes, sometimes, he seemed old and wise and world weary, but very much intelligent and capable of logical thought.

The thing was, you just never knew which Old Joe you had. It could be the wise old man or the crazy old codger. His shifting between an alligator and a human wasn't nearly as confusing as that. At least that you could tell. What went on inside his mind wasn't nearly as obvious.

Tom led him inside and to the booth, and said "Stay," then ducked behind the counter, to ask Keith to get a burger started. He cursed himself, inwardly. He'd given the old man clam chowder, because he'd been thinking he'd be cold, of course. But the thing was, he'd just shifted, so of course he'd gone outside, in search of protein. "Make that a triple," he said.

Keith looked at him, as he threw three patties on the grill. "Hungry?"

"Not for me. Old Joe. Bring it to the table when you're done."

"Sure," Keith said.

Tom went back to the booth, where he'd left Old Joe. He didn't want to leave the old man alone too long, for fear he'd shift and escape outside again. At a guess, Tom imagined the only reason he'd managed to get away unnoticed is that there hadn't been anyone seated close enough to him to see him. But three more tables had gotten filled up since then, and while they were too far away to hear him, they had full view of the table. And Tom had no idea how to convince spectators that all twelve people at those tables had hallucinated a man changing shapes into an alligator.

So instead, he slid into the pockmarked green vinyl seat across from Old Joe, who looked up at him, suddenly, with startlingly focused eyes. "They're here, you know?" he said. "They're in town."

"Who is in town?" Tom asked. Through his mind, like a scrolling list, went the names of everyone that Old Joe might be referring to: the Great Sky Dragon's people; whoever had killed the people at the aquarium; some unspecified group that hated shifters.

"Them," he said, and shrugged. "You know, the Ancient Ones."

And all of a sudden, either dredged from memory or created by his mind on the spot, Tom had a comic book cover in his mind, showing the Greek gods in full array and under them the words "The Ancient Ones."

He sighed. "Right." In the morass of Old Joe's mind, who knew what was true and what wasn't. And now the kitten was asleep on Tom's palm, as Tom shielded him with his other hand, so that Old Joe wouldn't see him and get hungry. "Right."

At that moment, Keith dropped the burger in front of Old Joe, who grabbed it as if he'd been lost in a burgerless desert for centuries. "Sorry," Tom said, in an undertone. "I should have remembered you'd need protein. It was stupid of me. No wonder you changed."

Old Joe shook his head, as emphatically as the alligator had, near the dumpster. "That's not why I changed," he said. "It was the Ancient Ones. I can't take them like this. They might kill me, you know?" His eyes gave Tom an appraising look from under the long grey hair. "You know what they're like."

"Actually," Tom said, "I don't." He wondered if Old Joe was talking about something real or something out of his nightmares.

Old Joe devoured the burger, with its bun and pickles, in fast, ravenous bites, all the more surprising because his teeth appeared to be broken and stained, and possibly moss-covered. How old was he? Tom had heard—and had observed in his own years on the street—how hard a life like that could be on people. When you threw in the alcoholism and drug use that plagued people on the streets, how likely was it that Old Joe was no more than middle-aged? Forty. Maybe fifty.

On the other hand, Old Joe was a shifter. So was Tom. And through five years of sleeping outside and roughing it through horrible winters, and working at the roughest manual labor, and shooting up and smoking and eating any amount of drugs . . . Tom had never managed to look his age, let alone unnaturally aged. At twenty-one, he looked closer to eighteen, except for the dark shadow of beard on his face. Even with his five o'clock shadow, he still got carded every time he tried to buy a beer. So Old Joe could not have aged all that fast, could he? Not unless he'd come up with some pinnacle of self-destructiveness that Tom had left untouched. And that, Tom found very hard indeed to believe.

But then again, perhaps alligators aged differently from dragons. How was Tom to know? The problem, he thought, as Old Joe demolished the burger, is that he knew so few shifters. Not enough to give him a statistical universe, truly.

He adjusted his hands, trying to remove one, to rub at his forehead, and stopped short when the kitten emitted a vaguely threatening purr and put out a paw to hold Tom's hand in place. He was so much like Kyrie, asleep, on the sofa, putting out a hand to hold Tom back when he tried to walk off, that Tom smiled. A smile that died quickly, when he heard Old Joe say, in an almost singsong voice, "They want to kill you, you know?"

It was all Tom could do, not to look over his shoulder at where Conan was talking to a customer. "Who?" he asked, instead. "The Ancient—"

Old Joe nodded. "You see, they formed"—he wrinkled his forehead—"many years ago." He waved a hand with short, broken, dirty nails. "To punish those who hurt shifters. And to create a law for shifters. And they know about the deaths. At the castle." His voice was raspy, and he looked one way and another as if to make sure he couldn't be overheard.

"Many years ago?"

"Before cars. Or airplanes or . . . gaslight." His eyes seemed to be looking far away into the past. "Or horses."

"I see."

"I was young, you know? And they said that shifters needed rules and laws to protect them, and to rule themselves, that they needed to defend themselves against the others . . . the ones who would hunt them. And then they formed a . . . a group."

"I see. And why do you think this group is after us? Just because so many young shifters died?"

Old Joe shook his head, then shrugged. "He came to me, when I was outside. Dante Dire did. He came to me. He's the . . . killer for the Ancient Ones, the . . . how do you call it, when someone kills the condemned for a king? The executioner!" He looked very proud of himself for having come up with the word. "That's what he is. He punishes those who hurt shifters. And he came to me and said that many young and blameless shifters had died, and that it was all your fault, and . . . yours and . . . your girl and the policeman. And he wanted to know your names."

"How could he know we did it, and not know our names?"

"He can feel it. Many people can. Well, ancient shifters can."

"And he wanted to know who we were?"

"Yeah. He tried to get me to change," Old Joe squinted. "But I wouldn't. And then, you know, your manager came out, and he went away, but I was hit with a cantaloupe."

Tom tried to think through the confusion of articles, then shook his head. It didn't matter if it was all a dream of Old Joe's. Or rather, of course it did, since dreams couldn't possibly kill them, and real, pissed-off shifters on a rampage could. But . . . but for now, not knowing to which aspect of Old Joe he was addressing himself, he had to treat the thing as if it were deadly serious. "Is there some way they could figure out who we are? Since you didn't tell him? And why did he come to you?"

"He didn't come to me," Old Joe said, somewhat defensively. "He came to the diner because of the smell that attracts shifters, you know. And then he figured this is where all shifters came. And he recognized me. So he asked. I didn't tell him." He folded his gnarled hands in front of him, on the formica table, looking for all the world like a schoolboy who expects a reward, then looked up and smiled a little. "I wouldn't worry. You're safe. I saw Dante Dire again, just a little later. When your girl and that policeman . . . what's his name? When they went out, he got in a car and followed them." He patted Tom's hand, reassuringly. "So, you see, you are safe."

Tom didn't feel at all reassured.

"So . . . what have we learned, children?" Kyrie said, in a singsong voice, as she dressed herself in the chilly bathroom. "We've learned that shifters piss."

She and Rafiel had gone all over the aquarium. Much to her chagrin, she had confirmed Rafiel's smelling of a shifter around the aquarium and up the stairs to the little observation area over the shark tank, where the smell became far more intense, as though the shifter had lingered there.

But that was all she'd learned. The only thing she could contribute—as she walked out of the ladies' room, to meet the again-human Rafiel, outside his bathroom—marked salmon, according to some bizarre logic where all salmons were male, she guessed—was, "I could smell it strongest in the ladies' room."

"Really?"

"Really. So I'm guessing that shifters piss," she said, with an attempt at a smile.

But Rafiel frowned at her, as though lost in intense thought. "And that it's a female."

Kyrie immediately felt like slapping her forehead. That hadn't even occurred to her. "Or that. Or of course, it comes in after hours and isn't sure whether it's shad roe or salmon. Not that I can blame him . . . er . . . her . . . it there."

This got her a very brief smile. "I'm more worried that it lives here."

"What do you mean . . . Oh. You mean one of the sharks?"

He nodded. "I tried smelling the covering to the tank at the top, where they open to feed them and to go in and clean, but couldn't smell anything. Hell, the smell through half of this place is faint. But I think I detect a trace of whatever it is they use to clean the aquariums with, and I wonder . . ."

"But wouldn't they go nuts, staying shifted and in the aquarium the whole time?" Kyrie asked.

Rafiel shrugged. "I have no idea. Truly. You see . . .

sometimes I think that if I lived somewhere in Africa, I'd just walk out one day into the savannah, and become a lion, and never, ever, ever change back."

Kyrie stared at him, shocked. She'd always thought of the three of them, Rafiel was the best adjusted. He had a family who knew what he was and collaborated in hiding him. He had the job he wanted to have, the job he'd dreamed about as a little boy. If anything he'd seemed in danger of being conceited and full of himself, not lost and full of doubt. But as he said those words, she felt as if he'd undressed. His expression had for a moment become innocent and vulnerable, making him look like a confused young man faced with something he couldn't understand nor deny.

"Never mind," he said, and managed a little smile. "It's just sometimes it's so hard being both, you know, living between worlds. I've tried to be human, and I can't—not all the time. And it just occurred to me, if I could *just* be a lion—be a lion all the time and stop . . . stop thinking like a human, stop caring about what humans think . . . it would be easier."

There were many things Kyrie wanted to say. That she understood—though she wasn't sure she did. She relished her rationality too much to let it go in exchange for a promise of simpler thinking. That she felt for him. That she could think of what it all must mean to him. But instead, what came out of her lips, was, "There's always the zoo."

As soon as she heard it, she was afraid he would be offended. And that was a heck of a thing to do to him, anyway. He'd just revealed an inner part of himself—at least she didn't think he was playacting, though with Rafiel, it was sometimes pretty hard to tell—and she'd answered with a joke.

To her surprise, he gurgled with sudden laughter. "Oh, yes . . . But if I couldn't control the changing even then, it could get a little embarrassing, no? Not to mean danger-ous, right there in the feline enclosure."

"Yes," she said. Then changed the subject quickly. "But you think one of the sharks might have done it?"

Rafiel shrugged. "It still doesn't make any sense, does it? I mean, they get fed, as sharks. Why would she . . . or whatever . . . feel a need to come out and push humans into the tank?"

"Perhaps she has a taste for human flesh," Kyrie said. "Or perhaps there was someone who saw her shift, and had to be eliminated."

The refrain in Tom's mind had changed to *oh shit, oh shit, oh shit*, and he jumped up from the seat. Kyrie and Rafiel were being stalked by someone called the execu-tioner for whatever the Ancient Ones were.

He ducked into the storage room and dialed Kyrie on his cell phone. There was no answer. It rolled over much too fast, in fact. He bit his tongue, thinking. Kyrie never charged her cell phone. Which meant, he had to get to her—somehow.

Oh, maybe Old Joe was dreaming it all up, but this seemed a bit complex, and the man's hesitations about time and place were much too realistic, and unless Old

Joe's dreams came in technicolor and surround sound, Tom didn't think it was a dream at all. No. Tom thought that Old Joe was somehow trying to reassure him and claim loyalty points for not having turned him in.

Had he not turned them in? Who knew. Maybe he had. Or maybe he had turned Kyrie and Rafiel in. His primary loyalty seemed to be to Tom, who fed him and looked after him. Everyone else was a distant concern. He might care for Kyrie because Tom did. On the other hand, Kyrie thought that Tom encouraged Old Joe to hang around, and endangered them, and she made no secret of her feelings.

Tom came out of the storage room and dove behind the counter, kitten in hand. "Here," he told Keith, handing over the small, orange fluffball, and ripping off his apron over his head.

"What am I supposed to do with him?" Keith asked, holding the puzzled creature, who was meowing and hissing at having his sleep disturbed. "No matter how much Old Joe wants him, I'm not grilling him."

"No," Tom said. "He's not dinner. Just put him somewhere. I have to go out . . . uh . . . for a few minutes. I'll be right back, I swear."

Keith looked closely at the kitten who was wearing the universal kitten expression that means *let them come, all together or single file. I have my claws.* "How am I supposed to keep him from wandering around? Let me tell you how many health violations—"

"Oh, I'm sure. But if we let him go, Old Joe is likely to eat him. Just tie him up or something. Some sort of a leash."

"A leash? A cat?" Keith asked, in the vaguely horrified

voice of someone who's just been instructed to confront a savage creature.

"Well, something," Tom said. "Please? And mind the place. I need to go out. Truly." He looked doubtfully at the kitten trying to claw at Keith. "Give him some food or something. Cats stay where they're fed, right?" And to Keith's look of incredulity, "Look, just try."

Tom had wanted a pet. The closest he'd come to having a pet was having fish. But those were more like animated swimming plants, as far as he was concerned. From the ages of five to ten, he had spent hours dreaming of various pets, from cats to horses. But his parents' lifestyle did not include time for animals. Truth be told, it barely included time for Tom. So he didn't have much idea what one did with pets, beyond a vague idea you told them what to do and they did it. At least, that seemed to be the interaction of owner and dog that he observed at various parks and in various streets. Except perhaps in the matter of bodily functions, dogs pretty much obeyed. It was all go here, come here, and stay. And by and large, the various mutts did. Surely cats couldn't be that much different. He had a lurch of doubt when he realized that save for a very old lady with a hairless cat on a leash, he'd never seen a cat be walked. "Er . . . just don't let him poop anywhere, okay?"

"Right . . ." Keith said in that tone of voice that indicated that as soon as Tom left the diner, he was calling the men in white coats to go after him. And Tom thought he very well might, but it didn't matter. He ran down the hallway to the back door, and out in the blinding storm where, more by instinct than by sight, he found the car where

Kyrie had parked it. Fishing in his pocket, he found the car keys. He undressed, shivering under the snow and shoved his clothes and shoes into the car trunk, and shut it with a resounding thud, even as he felt his skin bunch and prickle with cold. He hooked the keys to a link in a bracelet that Kyrie had made for him. It was silver, but made of the sort of elastic weave—somewhat like chain mail but not really—that adjusted to his changes in size as he shifted from man to dragon and back again.

A brief thought of Conan came to him, with a sharp stab of annoyance. Don't let Conan see him. Don't let Conan realize he was gone. The last thing he needed, right now, was Conan's intervention, or to have to drag Conan with him on this dangerous expedition. Conan was a complication he didn't need. He wished with all his strength, with everything he could, that the Red Dragon shifter wouldn't realize he was gone until Tom was well away.

And then he forced his body—unwilling and fighting and screaming with pain and begging for more time to recover—into the series of spasmodic coughs and twists that changed the shape of bones and muscles, and made wings grow from the middle of the shoulders.

Wings that spread and flapped, once—twice—powerfully, lifting the dragon aloft in the blinding snow.

"Nasty way of getting rid of your exes," Rafiel said. And shook his head. "Or of course, perhaps we are completely wrong. The smell wasn't continuous. At least for me, it wasn't. You?"

"No, I couldn't follow it from the bathroom to the shark tank. Also, I thought there was a faint trail in the jellyfish and crab area, and all the way to the seafood restaurant." Which she privately thought was the height of bad taste to have attached to an aquarium, though right now, after shifting, those fishies in the tanks were starting to look startlingly like protein packs with incidental fins. "But it wasn't truly contiguous, and it . . . well, it didn't feel quite the same to me. I'd say there were two trails. Maybe three."

It was only as she saw the sudden look of alarm cross Rafiel's face, that Kyrie realized this was probably not the right thing to say.

"Three?" he said. "Are you sure?"

She shrugged. "Rafiel," she said, unable to fully keep her impatience out of her voice. "You know very well that you are the best sniffer of us all, when it comes to shifter-scent. I can only tell you what I smell . . . and it's probably less than you can sniff out."

But he shook his head, and swallowed hard. "No, the problem is that when you said it, it made sense, it clicked. Not one interrupted trail, but three trails. What the hell does that mean? A cabal of shifters, ready to kill people at the aquarium? What are we looking at here? A mob of shifters who have turned on all non-shifters? A shifter religion sacrificing the non-shifters?"

Kyrie shrugged. "Or just, perhaps, three people who happen to be shifters and who walked through the aquarium."

Rafiel grimaced, but nodded. "Oh, perhaps you are right. Perhaps I'm paranoid, but . . ."

"But our situation encourages paranoia?" she said. "Hiding from the world, unable to reveal what we are. Even in this multi-culti time, when every minority gets a pass simply for being a minority, we will never, ever, get such a pass. Because we are . . . dangerous?"

Another grimace that might have been an attempt at a smile. "I was going to say that sometimes paranoia is right, however little we like to admit it."

"Uh." Kyrie shrugged. "I would say we have insufficient data to say."

She started walking away from the bathroom area, and out of the monitors and clearly fake, Victorian-looking submarine hardware area, towards the stairs. The stairs were broad and spiral and surrounded by glass—giving them rather the look of an aquarium designed to contain people.

"Come on, Rafiel," she said, staring out at the blizzard's magnificent raging whiteness. She would guess during one of Colorado's many unclouded days, one would have a magnificent view from here of the city of Goldport, such as it was, sprawling at the base of the Rockies. Now you couldn't even see the office tower across the street. It was just white and more white, blowing and swirling as far as the eye could see.

And just as she thought this, she realized she was wrong—because in the middle of the storm, a flash of green and gold showed, at her eye level, three stories up from the ground.

"What the—" Rafiel blurted out from behind her. "Is that—"

And in the next second, Kyrie was sure that that was indeed her errant boyfriend in dragon form, because Tom, all of him, emerged from the storm, as close to the glass as he could fly and not crash into it. His expression looked alarmed as he stared in at them. If alarmed at his proximity to the glass, or with flying in a storm, or something else, it was hard to tell.

There was just a flash of terrified blue eyes, the dragon's mouth open in silent protest. And then . . . Tom flying away.

"Tell me he didn't just fly here through the storm to check on us?" Rafiel said.

And part of Kyrie wanted to tell him exactly that, except it depended on what Rafiel meant by checking on them. Kyrie was willing to bet that Tom wasn't jealous of their being out, alone, together. She was willing to bet that, because Tom had all but encouraged them to go out, even Tom wasn't that . . . paranoid as to change his mind so quickly. Besides . . . besides, if he didn't know he'd won that contest and won it for good, then Kyrie would give up on the whole relationship right now.

But it had looked to Kyrie exactly as though Tom had been checking up on them. Not in jealousy or fear that they were about to betray him, but in confused fear for them . . . Fear of something happening to them.

Where had he got that idea? And was he right?

Flying in the snow was far easier to talk about than to do. The part of Tom that remained Tom at the back of the dragon's brain was fairly sure that the dragons—if they'd ever existed except as shifters—could never have been creatures of cold climates.

A string of complaints came from the dragon's body, penetrating Tom's mind. Cold might make him ache less, but cold hurt by itself. And he couldn't see. And the wings got no traction against this air laden with snow, which kept accumulating on their broad and outspread surface, thereby multiplying the cold and the lack of movement.

It felt as though the dragon's wings and his toes would presently freeze so absolutely that they would fall off, like so many enigmatic pieces of flesh raining on urban Goldport. Rain of dragon parts. That would be a new one at least. Forget rains of fish.

And yet, Tom's mind, deep within, like an implacable rider on a restive horse, insisted with all his will power that they must—*must*—go to Kyrie. They must protect her. And Rafiel too. The big lump might have been Tom's rival at some point. He was still, doubtlessly, a big lump. Also, generally speaking, a pain in the behind, always appearing so relaxed and laid back and comfortable with himself, while Tom most of the time felt that his personality and mind were sort of like one of those statues kindergartners sculpt: made of itty bits and pieces too mishandled to ever cling together properly, and forming no more than a suggestion of a shape, rather than the shape itself. But still, Rafiel was a friend. Pain or not, he would stand—had stood by Tom—when it was down to kill or be killed. And also, Tom suspected, deep within, Rafiel was a more honorable man and a more noble one than he liked to admit even to himself.

Be it how it may, Kyrie was Tom's girlfriend and Rafiel was one of his very few friends. They would not be allowed to stand alone as they faced whatever and whoever that executioner creature might be.

His purpose impelling him, he flew as fast as he could through downtown, sometimes descending to the top level of the high buildings, where the houses and offices formed a sort of sheltered canyon. He wondered if someone would see him, out of a window or a door—or rather if they'd see the suggestion of a dragon flying in the storm. He wondered what cryptozoology rumors would rise from it—like the Lizard Man in Denver, or all those black panthers and black dogs that appeared everywhere.

By the time he reached the aquarium, minutes later, he'd almost convinced himself that Old Joe had dreamed the whole thing. It was all a nightmare conjured from the old shifter's brain and whatever memories remained in that confused amalgam of personality. There would be no one there with Rafiel and Kyrie, and he would be in trouble with Kyrie for having left the diner for no reason at all. He almost looked forward to that monumental scolding, because if Kyrie was scolding him, that would mean that she was all right. And that all his fears were unfounded.

And yet, dipping towards the parking lot of the aquarium, as he approached, to check how many people might be within and if he might have to shift form and hide, before he exposed them all, Tom saw that Rafiel's big, black SUV was not alone there. Parked just across from it—in what might have been, had the lines under the snow been visible, the immediately opposing space—was a low-slung

Italian sports car.

Tom-the-dragon blinked at the red car, in confusion. It looked like a dormant beast that would, at any minute, fling up and fly or attack. Definitely attack, judging by the look of the vehicle.

Perhaps it is the car of an aquarium employee, said Tom's more reasonable human mind.

Right. Right, Tom's unreasonable human mind answered. *I'm absolutely sure it is. Scientists and fish-feeders often own cars that look like that.*

Well, the place has a restaurant, too. Perhaps it's the car of the owner.

To this, even the doubting Thomas within could not have interposed any serious rebuttal. Instead, it settled into a non-verbal response—a prickling at the back of Tom's long dragon neck . . . a feeling of uneasiness in the pit of his stomach. And it was no use at all his telling himself that he was being silly. He flew around the building and thought he caught a glimpse of Rafiel and Kyrie on the third-floor stairway, but it was not something he could swear to. The glass was thick and curved, and probably designed to ensure the privacy of those within at the expense of the curiosity of those without.

He flew around again, hoping they would come out, because then he could change and warn them. But there was nothing, except a suggestion of movement in a room where the aquariums seemed filled with the spindly forms of crabs. Tom had visited the aquarium with Keith once, a month ago—because one of Keith's would-be girlfriends worked there—and seemed to remember just such a room, right next to the restaurant. He and Keith had joked that the crabs were all probably terminally neurotic and tormented by dreams of drawn butter. But the movement—what seemed like a woman or a small man flitting around a corner was too brief to make sense of.

And yet, he worried. What if the executioner, whoever he was, was already inside, getting ready to ambush Kyrie and Rafiel around the corner of some tank, or push them into the shark tank? What could Tom do from out here?

He decided to land somewhere and shift, then see if he could break into the aquarium. In his misspent years as a transient, he'd often broken into places. Mostly into cars, when he absolutely needed transportation for a short period of time. Sometimes, into garden sheds, carriage houses or garages, in the coldest nights, to get some protection from the weather.

He'd never stolen anything in those break-ins and he'd felt positively virtuous about that, until Kyrie had made him understand the damage he caused, however minimal, still disturbed the lives of innocents.

Still, he had experience breaking into places. Granted, a garden shed was bound to have a flimsier lock than . . . well, a municipal aquarium, even—or perhaps particularly—a municipal aquarium run by a seafood restaurant chain. But all the same, he should be able to break in. And he should be able to find Kyrie and Rafiel. And warn them. Before they got pushed into the shark tank.

He took a half-circle flight away from the windows, looking for a place to land and shift, where he would be less likely to be seen from nearby buildings. This objective was made only slightly more difficult because he could not see into any of the buildings around, and therefore could not tell if anyone might be looking out of a window, and have enough visibility to survey the parking lot of the aquarium. He kind of doubted it, though.

His memories of the location of the aquarium, gathered during his visit, in sunnier—if briskly cold—weather, was that it sat on a corner, bordering two fairly well-traveled streets—Ocean Street, where the aquarium's postal address was—and Congregation Avenue, which led straight to the convention center in less than a mile. On the other side of those roads were office buildings. The chances of anyone being in one of those buildings, on a snowy evening, were very low. In fact, possibly, nonexistent. He'd just land somewhere.

Down below him, in the parking lot, a car door banged. Somehow, in his mind, a voice echoed—not the Great Sky Dragon's voice, but a voice just as immense, just as over-powering—*Hey, Dragon Boy!* it said. *Come and be killed.*

Tom looked down. By the Italian sports car stood a slim, dark-haired man, his head thrown back in defiance. He was naked, but he didn't seem to either realize it or care. He wore his nudity like others wore expensive suits. His head tilted up, he favored Tom with a wide and feral smile. *What is it, little one? Afraid of me? I'll take you in fair combat. As fair as it can be when pitting an adult against an infant.*

Tom wasn't afraid—at least the dragon Tom had become wasn't afraid. The human, locked within the drag-on's mind was not afraid either, or not exactly. He was not afraid of that creature down there, even if he was the vaunted executioner. For all he knew, the man would also change into a dragon, and come after him. And then he might be afraid. And then he might find a reason to kill this creature. But not yet.

And he didn't react to the voice in his head, as he had first reacted to a similar intrusion by the Great Sky Dragon. Finding someone in your mind once—like any other type of event that is supposed to be impossible but isn't—could hurtle anyone into a panic. The human mind was an amazing instrument, though. The second time of someone *speaking* in his mind didn't make Tom feel as violated, or as scared. It was just a voice. Just a voice in his mind. Nothing more.

He took a slow pass over the parking lot, looking down at the person standing by the car. All too human and weak-looking. If Tom was worried about anything, it was not the possibility this person might kill him. No, it was the fear that he might kill this person.

For years, while Tom was a transient, without friends or a fixed place, one fear had pursued Tom relentlessly: the fear that he would shift and lose self-control, and kill someone. It had been his first fear when he'd shifted into a dragon.

And he'd managed to control it—most of the time. The only people he'd ever killed were shifters who were trying to kill him. And even then, if there had been another way, he'd have used another way to stop them. He didn't think he'd ever eaten anyone—not even in the drug-haze days of his past.

He didn't want to kill anyone now. Not even this creature—whether or not he was the executioner that Old Joe had gone on about. Tom swooped again, around the man, slightly lower, trying to think of what to do.

His instincts told him he should leave now, but if he did he would leave Kyrie and Rafiel unprotected. *That* he couldn't do. That would negate his coming here to protect them. He had to, at least, warn them.

He swooped down again, closer. There had to be something he could do, without killing the man. Grab him by an arm and throw him away from the aquarium, perhaps. Then, while he took time to return—or while he shifted into a dragon and came after Tom, Tom would have a chance to warn Kyrie and Rafiel.

But as Tom got close, he saw the man was smoking a cigarette, completely impassive, disregarding the huge dragon closing in on him.

Tom could have bit off his head with a single motion. He could have rent it from his body with his claws. But he couldn't do either, not to a defenseless-seeming human.

Instead, he flew by so close the tip of his wing almost touched the man, but he sheared off, sharply, and executed a circle, coming back, still aware that he couldn't kill the man—that his own self-control wouldn't allow it—but hoping, hoping against hope that the man would be scared.

Oh, are we playing a game? a laughing voice asked in his mind. And suddenly Tom had no control over his body. None. He fell from the sky, like a pebble, unable to stop himself.

Hurtling towards the parking lot, Tom saw the man shift. Not into a dragon. The creature who stood in the parking lot hadn't been seen on Earth for millennia uncountable. Tom recognized it, immediately, from its display in Denver's Natural History Museum, though. It was a dire wolf: tall of shoulder, massive of bone, its teeth huge, unwieldy daggers flashing in the light.

And in that moment he regained control of his body, enough control at least, to tumble to an ungraceful semi-stop, skidding on his tail on the frozen ground.

The creature sprang, with a lightness that belied his size. A sharp pain stabbed into Tom's awareness, and his wing was seized and ripped. He turned, claw raised, ready to strike, but the dire wolf had moved, quickly, more quickly than should be possible, and bit hard on Tom's wrist. Only Tom's last-second recoil prevented him from ripping out Tom's throat. The yellow eyes of the monster shone with unholy glee amid grey fur, and Tom would have flown away— maimed wing and blood-dripping paw. But he couldn't. Kyrie and Rafiel were in there. They could be coming out any moment. What would this monster do to them?

"What the—!" Kyrie said, as she came through the door, and saw Tom being attacked by a creature out of a museum's diorama. For a moment that was all she could think, her mind seemingly frozen on that point—wondering if she was dreaming, if all those visits to the museum had finally affected her sanity, as she told Tom they were bound to. The museum was his favorite haunt, when they took a day off to go to Denver, and sometimes she felt as though she could have drawn every display from memory— including the broken places in the bassilosaurus skeleton.

She heard a soft growl at her side. Rafiel. A look at the

policeman showed him, by touch, without even seeming to notice, stripping off his clothes.

And Kyrie, feeling the shift shudder through her, as she stared at the unlikely creature striking at her boyfriend, thought that this creature moved like nothing she'd ever seen. His movement was like a special effect, where the movie editors cut and pasted frames without regard, so that they displaced someone from one place to the other, without moving them the intervening distance. She was sure this was not what was happening, but the effect was rather as though the creature teleported from one place to the next instantly. And it was biting, rounding on Tom, and slashing, rending, always attacking.

Rafiel, already in lion form—tawny and sleek and large, though not half the size of the creature battling Tom—rushed into the battle, his mane snow-flecked. And Kyrie charged, right behind.

It was folly, her human mind said, sheer folly, to rush like this into battle with a creature that seemed supernatural in its movements. But what else could she do?

The creature teleported towards Rafiel—materializing right in front of him, Tom's blood dripping from the huge dagger teeth, a look of unholy amusement in the slitlike yellow eyes. It lunged at Rafiel and it was clear from the movement that it meant to take Rafiel by the throat, or perhaps to bite his neck in two, killing him in one of the few ways a shifter could be killed.

But as the massive-fanged mouth opened, Tom leapt, and bit the creature sharply on the hind quarters, causing it to close its jaws just above Rafiel's neck, barely touching him with its fangs.

And now Tom was raking what seemed to be a badly bleeding paw across the creature's flanks and making a high, insane hiss of challenge.

And Kyrie, who could see that the creature's eyes were—startlingly—more amused than scared, jumped in, her fur ruffled, growling low in the back of her throat.

The creature rounded on her, ignoring Tom's attack on its exposed flank and pinning Rafiel, casually, beneath a massive paw. It sniffed at Kyrie and the slitted yellow eyes looked more unholy and more amused than ever. *Hello, pretty kitten girl. It would be a shame to kill you, wouldn't it?*

The voice, in her mind, made her jump. She knew it was this creature in front of her, and not the Great Sky Dragon, but she suddenly understood why Tom had reacted as he did to the dragon in his mind. She heard a keen of not quite pain escape the panther's throat and she felt what seemed like a dirty finger rifling quickly through her mind. *Interesting mind, Kitten. Better defended than Lion Boy's.* The feel of unholy laughter. *But not by much.*

And then, suddenly, there was a streak of red from above, and a thing that looked much like a falling boulder through the snow resolved itself into Red Dragon, flying in. .

It roared something that sounded much like "No," or as close to the word "no" as a dragon's mouth could form. And in the next moment it landed in front of the dire wolf. Kyrie expected the wolf to port away or to attack, but he didn't do either. Instead, he stood in place, looking confused.

Red Dragon let out a stream of flame at the dire wolf,

just as Kyrie wondered why Tom hadn't done so. And the dire wolf wasn't there.

What sounded much like "spoilsport," echoed in her mind, and the dire wolf seemed to be quite gone, though they couldn't tell where. Moments later, a sound that seemed disturbingly like human laughter floated from the place where it had retreated.

For Tom it all went too fast. First, he was fighting a creature that seemed to be everywhere at once. His only hope was to take to the sky, but before he could—his bleeding wing, hurting every time he moved, threw off his balance—the creature struck him again. And again. At both front paws, and back paw.

And slowly it dawned on Tom that if the dire wolf could strike him like this, at will, and wherever it chose, then it could have killed him. That it wasn't killing him should have been a relief, but it wasn't. Because he had a feeling that the creature was playing with him the way cats play with mice.

And then there was Rafiel, who seemed to appear out of nowhere, and Tom wanted to yell at him and Kyrie to run, but the dragon throat didn't work properly and he couldn't give them the warning in a way that they could understand. And the only thing for it was for him to intervene and save Rafiel from the dire wolf, even though it probably would mean Tom would die for it. But he'd come to save Kyrie and Rafiel, and he was going to do it, if it was his last action on Earth.

He launched himself at the dire wolf, biting and scratching where he could reach. And then . . .

And then the creature sniffed Kyrie—at least it seemed like that to Tom, through the red mist his vision had become—and then . . . and then there was Conan. Conan had flamed towards the dire wolf, making Tom wonder why he, himself, hadn't. What was wrong with him? He'd sat here and let the creature maul him, with hardly any attempt at defense. Certainly without using his main weapon. Why?

And then the creature fled and there had been a suggestion of mocking laughter in Tom's mind. He stood, under the snow, bleeding, shivering, wondering if the creature was gone for good, or it was waiting for Tom to shift, if it was waiting for Tom to become more vulnerable, if—

"Shift, Tom," Kyrie said. "Now. You can't get in the car as a dragon."

"You left without me—" Conan was saying, clearly already shifted. "You left without me. Do you know what Himself would have done to me if you had died?"

"Shut up, Conan," Kyrie's voice, curt. "Tom, shift *now*."

And Tom realized Conan and Rafiel and Kyrie were in the car, and that they had clothes, and Kyrie was dressing in the backseat, and he blinked, once, twice, once the human way, up-down, then the dragon way, his nictating eyelids flickering side to side, then the human way again, and he groaned out loud as his body twisted and bent and . . . shifted.

His muscles were still writhing to proper shape beneath his skin, his scalp tingling as the bones of his skull adjusted, his vision double as his eyes changed, when he flopped into the back seat of the SUV, falling across the scratchy fabric.

Kyrie, mostly dressed, reached across him to shut the car door. As it slapped shut, Rafiel stomped on the gas. The wheels spun a moment, and then they were hurtling out of the parking lot in a guided slide that careened gracefully around a curve and past a—he was sure of it—red light.

"What if he had come back?" Tom asked. "As . . . as a dire wolf? And killed us while we were human and vulnerable?"

"Was that what that was?" Rafiel asked. Incredibly, he seemed to Tom to be dressing and driving at once, through the blinding white snowstorm. Tom blinked, but the impression remained, as Rafiel put on a sleeve of his shirt, while he held the wheel with the other hand and then presumably steered by the force of his imagination while he used both hands to quickly button his shirt. "A dire wolf?"

"Yes," Tom said, throwing himself back against the seat, and straightening as he felt the pain of open wounds at his back. "Oh, damn, I'm bleeding all over your upholstery."

"Never mind that," Rafiel said. "My uncle has a car detail place. Kyrie, would you look under the seat? There's a first aid kit there, and there should be another pair of pants and a shirt, too, besides the ones Conan got. They'll be long on you, Tom, but it's all I have."

"I left clothes, in the trunk of Kyrie's car."

"Of course. You can change into them there, if you prefer . . . I just thought . . ." Rafiel took another corner in a way that appeared to be skating on two tires. "Kyrie? How badly wounded is he?"

Kyrie had turned Tom halfway towards the window. "Gash across the back," she said. "I suppose that's the tissue your wings extrude out of. Looks vicious but it's mostly skin, and the antibiotic cream is stopping the bleeding, I think."

"Should we go to the hospital?" Rafiel asked.

"Not for this, but his hands . . ."

And Tom, who was aware both his hands stung like mad, but also that he could still use them—he'd checked—growled low in his throat. "No hospital. What are we going to tell them? Animal bite? Leave it alone. You know it will heal fast."

"Dragons heal very fast," Conan said quickly, in the sort of singsong voice that denoted he'd learned this somewhere, by rote.

By touch, almost by instinct, Tom reached into the first aid kit, grabbing cotton wool and hydrogen peroxide and a roll of self-clinging bandages, cleaned away the worst of the wounds and started bandaging his left hand with his right. Kyrie started helping him halfway through, and by the time she'd got his left hand neatly bandaged, and snipped the excess bandage, she said, "He'll do, Rafiel. And it should be all right by tomorrow. Will hurt a bit to use his hands, but . . ."

"You'll go to the bed-and-breakfast next to the diner," Rafiel said. "What is it called?"

"Spurs and Lace," Kyrie said. "It's not as kinky as it sounds. I think they thought it was an allusion to the Old West."

"Whatever. Tom, I want you to go to Spurs and Lace and go to bed. I'll man the diner for the rest of your shift."

"Like hell you will," Tom said. "Don't be stupid. You can't handle the new stove and grill. And you don't know anything about cooking or serving, either. And that is if Keith hasn't set the place on fire in the last half hour, because he doesn't know much more than you do." He set his jaw, and caught sight of himself in the rear view mirror and realized with a shock that he looked much like his father in a mood. "I'll do the rest of my shift, thank you very much. We'll see if Anthony can come in tomorrow morning, and if not we'll call our backups till someone makes it in. There was that woman—Laura Miller?—who applied last week. We could always give her a chance."

Rafiel seemed confused. He cleared his throat. "But you'll be in pain," he said. "And I . . ." He cleared his throat again. "I owe you my life."

Tom shrugged. "So, shut up and drive."

"I think," Kyrie said, "you should at least go to Spurs and Lace for a few minutes and shower. At least if they have a room and they should. They usually have rooms during the week. On the weekend they get all booked up with romantic couples or whatever."

Tom sniffed at himself. "All right," he said, realizing he needed to concede on something, and also that fighting a dire wolf had not improved his rather dubious hygiene from this morning.

"Just don't shift in their bathroom," Kyrie said, as she slapped bandages on his back, then handed him a bundle of clothing. "You might as well wear this and take the other clothes to change." And then, quickly, "Tom, why didn't you just call? I mean, you had my cell number, and Rafiel's. I understand you came over to protect us from this—that you knew this . . . creature was after us, somehow, but . . . Why not just call?"

Tom shook his head. "Your phone battery was out, Kyrie. You never remember to charge it."

"Oh," Kyrie said.

"All right," Tom said again as he slipped the rather loose, long pants on. "Rafiel, I want you to come with me."

"What? To shower?" Rafiel asked. "I said thank you already—"

"Feeble," Tom said, rating the joke. "No. So I can talk to you about what sent me out there, and what I think that creature is. Without anyone in the diner listening in."

"I should come," Conan said. "I should listen in. I'm supposed to protect you."

All three of them yelled "No" at the same time, leaving it to Tom to explain, "No offense, Conan, but you're not exactly a friend."

"You hired me! And I was sent by Himself, I—"

"Himself is not exactly a friend, either," Tom said. "At least he hasn't proven himself one."

Conan frowned, wrinkles forming on his forehead, as though he were trying to understand a very difficult concept. "You're a dragon," he said. "You belong to him!"

"Beg your pardon? I don't belong to anyone but myself," Tom said, his voice echoing his father's iciest tones. "In case you haven't heard there was this guy called Lincoln who freed the slaves."

"No," Conan shook his head, looking forlorn. "You don't understand. You're a dragon. You belong to Himself. Like . . . like family."

"Oh, and if you think that's a recommendation or

reassuring, I should tell you a bit more about my family," Tom said, grinning impishly. Kyrie smiled at him. "I have never gone out of my way to obey them or to belong to them, either."

Conan opened his mouth, as though to reply, but seemed to realize it would be useless, and frowned slightly, as if he were facing a situation for which no one had prepared him.

"Won't it look weird?" Rafiel asked. "My going in with you, when you're going to get a room and shower?"

"I'm going to get a room for myself and Kyrie, for tonight and tomorrow," Tom said. "Probably three nights, actually. I can't imagine us going home before that. Heck, if we go home before a week, it will be a small miracle. I'll explain in detail what happened to our bathroom. But as for why you're going with me to the room, that's obvious." He raised his bandaged hands. "I was in an accident. We'll let them think it was a car accident. And you want to make sure I'm not going to pass out or anything."

"Oh," Rafiel said.

"And then I can tell you about the dire wolf. If I'm not mistaken, he's the person that Old Joe described as the executioner for the Ancient Ones."

"What did you mean 'executioner'?" Rafiel asked. He leaned against a heavy carved rosewood table in Tom's rented room at Spurs and Lace.

Kyrie must have been right about the crazy idea behind

the name. The suite felt like a mashup of Old West and Old Whorehouse. It was bigger than a room, consisting of a bedroom with a queen-size bed, a sofa dripping in velvet and fringe, a dresser that would take five men and a winch to transport, and a hat rack with three cowboy hats on it, and a small sitting area in a projection that was part of a tower, surrounded by windows. The sitting area was outfitted with two too-precious-for-words carved wood armchairs, whose cushions were tormented by a print featuring cowboy boots and roses in random profusion.

Then there was the bathroom, which had a heavy rosewood table facing it. Above the table hung a gold-leaf-framed mirror and above that, on the flowered-wallpaper wall, a pair of spurs.

Rafiel shut his eyes, because you could go nuts trying to make sense of this stuff, and said, "What could he mean by executioner? And why would anyone want to execute us?"

"I think it was the larvae, you know, the ones who died in the fire. Old Joe says the Ancient Ones can feel . . . death on that scale. And that they're looking for the culprits."

"The culprits!" Rafiel heard the sound that came out of his throat, derisive like a cat spitting. "What about the shifters who were being murdered before that?"

"I don't know," Tom sounded exhausted. Rafiel heard the water go off, then the shower curtain close. "Perhaps they think that we did those too."

"And who are they?" Rafiel asked, feeling the anger in his voice and knowing he was projecting his fear into anger and throwing it at Tom. "These Ancient Ones," Rafiel said with less force. "It's pretty absurd to be judged

Keith raised his shoulder sulkily, but didn't say anythi
a while, till he said sheepishly, "I've kept people quie
he returned in what seemed like seconds, to tend to t
l, "by giving them free hot chocolate. I hope tha
y."

"It's fine," Kyrie said.

"Also, of course, there's nothing else open today whi
lped keep them here."

Kyrie took the point, and having finished a plate of gy
eat, she put the plate with the others collected fro
oles, and reached under the counter for her apro
tending to go out to clear the backlog as fast as possibl
only her hands, thrust under the counter, met with some
ing like sharp little needles. On her pulling the hand
ck, the needles withdrew, only to stick her again whe
e reached out once more, only much less further in tha
fore. "What the—?" she said, reaching out.

"Oh, that's Not Dinner," Keith said, flipping a burger.

"What?" she asked, as she knelt to look in the dark shel
here they kept folded aprons to the left and the time
eets to the right. Golden eyes sparkled back at her, and
e looked closer, to make out a little orange ball of fluf
aking his way very fast to lay possessively atop the time
eets. "It's a kitten."

"Yeah," Keith said. "Not Dinner."

"I don't have the slightest intention of eating him,"
rie said, upset, as she reached in and managed to
rieve the apron before the avenging claws got her. "You
ow you can't have your pet here. We're not allowed to
ve animals, except service animals, on the premises."

"He's not my pet."

by people you don't know and whose rules you can't understand. Who are they? What do they want?"

Tom came out of the bathroom, fully dressed, though it didn't seem like he'd have had time. He was limping, and his foot showed red slashes across it. Rafiel remembered the dire wolf biting at Tom's back paw.

Tom limped to the bed, sat down, and started putting socks on. "They're a group. I think they're a group of shifters who have lived very long lives."

"Oh?" Rafiel said. "What's very long? And should we be looking for a group then, or just one man?" Something tickled at the back of his mind, but he couldn't quite pinpoint it.

Tom shrugged. "I honestly don't know," he said. "Because, you see . . . Old Joe . . ." He shrugged again, wincing as he stood tentatively on his wounded foot and looked about for his boot. "Old Joe, you know, is vague. He drifts in and out of reality, and it's hard to tell. He told me that the Ancient Ones were around before horses."

"Before horses evolved? Or before they were domesticated?" Rafiel asked. "Because either way . . ."

"It's unlikely? Yeah. I know. That's why I said he's unreliable. And he said that this creature, the dire wolf, had come to town, that he was their executioner, but he didn't say that the rest of them hadn't come too. Or how many there were. For all I know, and presuming that this story is true—and the executioner thing seems to be— then, you know, it could be that we're looking for anything between a busload of shifters as old as time, and two or three sixty-year-old shifters." He shrugged. "I couldn't tell you."

But his words had tickled something in Rafiel's mind. Two or three shifters. "At the aquarium," he said, "Kyrie and I caught at least two different scent trails. Maybe three."

"Oh?" Tom tensed, looking up. "Any of them our friend the wolf?"

Rafiel shook his head. "I don't think so," he said. "At least the smell wasn't right. Though all the scents were so faded . . ." He shrugged.

"You know," Tom said, "that's the other choice. No Ancient Ones, no conspiracy of shifters. Just Old Joe going senile, and one homicidal dire wolf shifter." He'd found his boots, and was putting them on. "Who knows how many of us are homicidal? It was always my fear that I'd go that way." Tom's boots were work boots, probably picked up second or third hand at some time when Tom was doing manual labor. But even looking vaguely like weapons of mayhem, they were part of Tom.

Rafiel had seen Tom turn back into high danger to recover them. Lacing them as tightly as that had to hurt his injured foot, but who was Rafiel to interfere with his friend's masochism?

"Unfortunately," Tom said, "I don't think that's it. I don't think it's just Old Joe and our dire acquaintance. When has our life been that easy?"

Kyrie shaved broad swathes off the gyro beef roast rotating on its vertical metal spike, and turned her back to the

counter and the customers, to eat with th[...] appetite a recent shift brought on.

The diner had become packed, while she [...] every table filled, even the table at which she'd [...] Conan. A couple was squeezed together into th[...] booth, cooing and billing and holding warm c[...] was working the grill like a pro, though Kyrie [...] he sometimes let things go a little too long, and [...] of omelets were often brown as Tom didn't allo[...] be, and the bacon seemed full of burnt crunchy [...] he was clearly late with the orders.

However, to do Keith justice, that last might [...] much his fault as Conan's. The new waiter, newly [...] amid the tables of the packed diner looked much [...] that had hit the window pane once too many ti[...] was trying to serve everyone clamoring for his a[...] and seemed completely lost. That he only had o[...] arm to hold the serving tray didn't help, as his ot[...] at best, helped stabilize things, but could not help [...] weight, which meant he carried far less per trip o[...] tables than she normally did. The orders were pile[...] counter. As Keith turned and put another one d[...] called out, "Table 23," he seemed to realize the [...] it, saying, "Oh, never mind," and putting five or s[...] on a tray, he rushed out to distribute the platters, [...] than Conan seemed able to.

"That little rat you guys hired left me alone [...] were gone," Keith said. "I don't know where he [...] . . ."

"Don't worry about it," Kyrie said. "He went t[...] We know where he was."

Kyrie took a deep breath, deciding everyone had gone mad, and Keith right now was representative of everyone. What on earth could he mean? That the diner was suffering an infestation of cats, like some places had sudden infestations of rats? It didn't bear probing, not now. Grabbing a tray and filling it with orders, and picking up the coffee pot for warmups, she started among the tables, clearing up the backlog.

Many regulars looked happy to see her, and other people just looked happy to get their orders at last. In a few minutes, she had the main of it taken care of and, having directed Conan to start bussing newly emptied tables, returned to fill the dishwasher, restart the coffee, and pursue the interesting matter of a sudden plague of kittens.

Before she could, though, and while she was bent over the dishwasher, filling it with dirty plates, Tom and Rafiel came in, and Tom made an exclamation of distress and touched Kyrie's arm. "Kyrie, where's Old Joe?"

She looked up. "I don't know. Where was he?"

"I left him in booth number five."

"Well, he wasn't here when I came in," she said.

Tom swore under his breath and, at her startled look, said, "Not your fault. He must have gone alligator again. I hope he's not going to go after one of the customers in the parking lot. And I hope we find him, because we need to talk to him."

As he spoke, Tom reached over the grill, as Keith pulled a stack of cooked burgers aside and said, "I made these for you. I figured you'd need them."

"Great thought. Thanks," Tom said, grabbing the burgers

and eating one after the other, like a kid with candy. "I'll take over the grill in a moment."

"I gave Not Dinner some milk and a few pieces of hamburger," Keith added.

"Not . . . oh. The kitten," Tom said. "Good."

Kyrie noted that Tom seemed to know about the kitten. In fact, she would bet the kitten was Tom's. Tom and his *strays*! Meanwhile, Rafiel had gone out the back door. He returned in a moment, snow glinting in his hair. "He's not out back, Tom. I can't find him. There's no trail I can see."

Tom took over the grill. "Go attend to the tables," he told Keith. "I'll take care of cooking."

Keith hesitated, and Tom was sure that he was hoping to hear what was going on, but he wanted to talk to Kyrie and he didn't want to leave the tables unattended. "We'll let you in on it," he said. "I promise."

"That's not it," Keith said. "I want to talk to you." He spoke in an undertone, and looked worried. "There's someone . . ."

"Right," Kyrie said from Tom's side. "I'll go do those two tables that just came in."

"So?" Tom said.

"It's this girl . . ."

Tom choked on gurgled laughter at the idea that any-one at all would come to him for romantic advice, but he managed to stop and make his features attentive. "Yes?"

"She's . . . she goes to school with me, and she looks

really . . . I don't know how to put this, but I think she's a shifter. That was why I came by today. If I bring her, can you . . . sniff her out?"

Tom looked at him, and felt his brow wrinkle into a frown. "Probably," he said. "Rafiel can for sure. Why do you think she's a shifter?"

Keith shrugged. "I can't quite put my finger on it, but she looks tired in the morning, and . . . you know . . . she talks a lot about strange animals. She had a book on cryptozoology. It just seems . . ."

"Does she change clothes a lot?"

"Not that I've noticed, but . . ." Keith shrugged. "Just a feeling, okay? I've been around you guys enough for that."

"Yeah," Tom said. "Fine." He returned to cooking and, remembering that Rafiel, too, would be having shift-hunger, he grabbed one of the frozen t-bones from the freezer by the grill, and threw it on. His mind was working on the problem he and Rafiel had discussed. The idea of a group or groups of shifters skulking around making decisions about their lives, that they could not possibly anticipate. Did this group have anything to do with the bones in the aquarium? And how could Tom and Kyrie defend themselves from the dire wolf, who seemed capable of teleporting?

They spent the rest of the night watching the door and looking out back around the dumpster, but as far as Tom could tell, both any possible hostiles and the alligator shifter were miles away.

On a normal night there were several lulls, but as the wind howled, fiercer and fiercer outside the diner, rattling gusts of snow against the broad windows and leaving them spattered as if with the spray-snow people used for decorations, customers drifted regularly in and out.

It seemed to Tom, though he didn't look closely at anyone at the tables—kept busy with constant cook orders instead—that some people came in several times during the night. They were probably being kept awake by the wind and the snow, or perhaps the Victorians converted into apartment houses around here weren't exactly airtight and had inadequate heat. Tom remembered staying in many rental rooms and apartments where the temperature, on full-blown heat, never reached above tepid.

The constant stream of orders changed overnight, from burgers to pies and coffee and finally to omelets, eggs and bacon, sausages and hash browns. He felt as if he would never want to smell a cooking egg again in his life, and the pain in his wounded hands—continuously rehurt by his ceaseless work—had gone from a dull throbbing to a barely-keeping-from-screaming burn. He'd sent Kyrie away to rest a couple of hours ago, afraid that if no one else came in to relieve him at the grill he'd have to let Kyrie relieve him, and give her a quick crash course on breakfast dishes on the new stove.

He could have cried with joy when he saw Anthony come in. "It was getting cabin feverish at home," he said, sheepishly. "It's only a one-bedroom apartment. And the wind seems to have died down some, so Cecily fell asleep. You guys can go rest some."

Tom nodded and removed his apron, shoving it under the counter. He was surprised by a sudden feel of pinpricks piercing through his bandages. Looking under the counter, he got a sudden hiss and battle scream from the orange kitten.

He took a quick look over his shoulder at Anthony. He couldn't imagine leaving the kitten behind for Anthony to deal with, so as he grabbed his jacket from under the counter and slipped it on, Tom reached under and grabbed the protesting bundle of kitten and, ignoring the yowls of defiance, slipped it into his pocket.

Kyrie woke up to someone snoring on top of her. In a moment of unique confusion, she thought Tom must have decided to sleep on the bed after all, and he must be snoring, only the snore was so distant and tiny, that it couldn't be Tom. She wondered, momentarily, as she struggled with what seemed to be several tons of gravel on her eyelids, whether Tom could have shrunk, because she felt a very warm and vibrating body—if a very tiny one—laid across the space between her breasts.

Her mind finally added up that these impressions made no sense, and brought her awake with a sudden jar. Her beginning to rise was met with sharp little needles to the chin and, opening her sleepy eyes, she saw a small orange blur. "Uh?" she said, which seemed the height of eloquence just then. She blinked and saw the sun shining fully across the room and onto the bed, and Tom blissfully asleep mostly on and partly off the sofa next to the bed. He had dark shadows under his eyes, and looked paler than usual. He'd taken his boots and socks off in his sleep, allowing her to see the bandage on his foot, and he was sleeping on his side, probably to avoid hurting his injured back.

Kyrie blinked at the kitten on her breasts. "Hello, Not Dinner," she said in a singsong voice. "Are you one of Tom's strays?"

The kitten purred and licked first one paw, then the other. Kyrie had to admit he was handsome, "In a conceited male feline sort of way." She put her hand out to his tiny head and petted it, feeling the curve of the cranium beneath her fingers. "Mind you, you're much cuter than Rafiel and you can tell him I said that." She cast another look at Tom. She was sure she knew how this story went. Her boyfriend had found the kitten out, somewhere, under the snow. And since he couldn't resist strays, be they human or not, he'd brought it in out of the cold.

She wondered if Tom had thought that cats pooped or that he needed to provide himself with a litter box for the critter. "What are we going to do with him?" she asked. "He adopts the most impractical creatures." But, as Not Dinner purred happily and started a kneading motion at her throat, she couldn't blame Tom. And she hoped Tom liked hapless felines. She happened to know that the bed-and-breakfast allowed pets. There was a big sign in the foyer proclaiming four-pawed guests welcome and Kyrie didn't think it meant shifters. And she was sure the lady, a great cat lover, would find her a litter box for the newest member of the family.

Then she must find someone to fix the bathroom so they could return home. She wondered if one of Rafiel's ubiquitous and very useful relatives happened to be a plumber. If Rafiel found them help within his odd family, it would save explaining what sort of cataclysm had happened in that bathroom. Rafiel could make up whatever he wanted or nothing. His family had to know that there was something very strange about their relative, but none of them seemed to mind covering up for him.

"Right," she said, picking up the kitten, as she slipped out of bed, and dropping him atop the sleeping Tom. "You keep the dragon company while I get decent and go about finding you a litter box."

She fumbled in her suitcase for her robe and slipped it on, before opening the door. And then she saw the headline on the local paper laid outside the door. And shrieked.

Tom woke up with Kyrie shrieking, and saw Not Dinner rush towards her and the open door. "Kyrie," he said. "Not Dinner."

Kyrie bent down just in time to stop the tiny animated projectile attempting to run out the door, and grab him in her hand, even as she scooped up the paper with her other hand. She closed the door with her foot and returned to Tom. "Look at this," she said, and turned the paper towards him so that he could read the above-the-fold headline.

The *Weekly Inquirer*—which was a daily paper, a dissonance of nomenclature that bothered no one in Goldport—normally printed city news first page, relegating the national and international news to the middle sections where—it was felt in town—the rest of the world belonged, being far less important than their concerns.

Local news normally consisted of some business moving to town, some business moving out; an event of importance in the life of the mayor; some trial for fraud or embezzlement; a parade; or what Tom referred to as "pretty puppy" news. Today Tom would have expected the big headline to be about the snowstorm. And it was. At least the headline just beneath the title of the paper, in dark blue letters, was "Goldport Slammed by Storm." But above the fold, and in screaming red letters just beneath the newspaper's name was "Strange Animals Seen Around Town." And beneath that "Dragons and Saber-Toothed Tigers and Smoking Squirrels."

"Smoking squirrels?" he said, looking up at Kyrie, whose hand was shaking so much that the newspaper was oscillating before his eyes.

"Whatever. But dragons? Saber-tooth?"

"It wasn't a saber-tooth," Tom said, reasonably. "It was a dire wolf."

"Oh, yes, and I'm sure that the international spotters of extinct animals would care," she said, as she set the kitten on top of him and started reading from the paper. "Last night, amid the howling gusts of the storm—who writes this paper? The Brontë sisters?—a man passing by a building near the aquarium swears he saw in the parking lot a dragon or some other large creature battling it out with what he swears was a saber-toothed tiger. With great presence of mind he snapped a photo with his cell phone." Kyrie stretched the paper towards Tom so he could see an indistinct picture of dark shapes amid white snow. "He took a picture of us." Kyrie said.

If Tom squinted and sort of looked at it sideways, the

dark blobs in the snow did look like Kyrie, the dire wolf and himself. In shifted forms. Or perhaps like three sacks of potatoes. "Kyrie, it's completely fuzzy. No one could recognize a dragon in that."

"No, but . . . if it hadn't been snowing, someone could have gotten a real picture of you and me and the dire wolf."

"All right. I will do my best not to get in fights with homicidal maniacs," he said, and sat up. "At least not when people might get a clear picture of me. Do you have any idea how I should sell this truce to the homicidal maniacs?"

But Kyrie only looked at him with a blank and panicked look. "But they know. Someone knows."

"Kyrie!" Tom said. "How many times do people read this sort of thing, or think they see it, or report it? It doesn't make any difference. Black panthers up in Ohio, I remember reports of that—"

"Yeah, a lot of them when I lived there."

"Oh, really?" he smiled briefly. "Well, I was on the cover of the *Inquirer* once. I mean, the real one, the tabloid. Someone got me, flying over town, with a telephoto lens. No one believed it of course. Not after half the tabloids spent the nineties reporting on the president's alien baby." He put his hand out to her, and held her wrist. "No one will believe it, Kyrie. That picture doesn't look any better than the countless pictures of the abominable snowman. And if it did, people would say it was Photoshopped. Calm down will you? Everything is fine. And look, about the cat, if you don't want it—"

"No, I always wanted a cat and he seems very nice . . . in an insufferable male feline way."

"I don't know if he's a male, I just—"

"Oh, he's a male, trust me. I just know." She grinned, and tossed the newspaper down. "Right, I must go and find him a litter box."

By the time she came back, carrying a small plastic box filled with grey granules, Tom was reading the paper, frowning, very puzzled over reports that a giant squirrel—the size of a German shepherd—had been seen in various locations downtown "wearing a beret and smoking cigarettes," he told Kyrie. "I mean, and you're afraid people will believe the thing about the dragon when they finish with this."

Kyrie looked confused. "Are you sure it's not someone like us? I mean . . . a shifter squirrel?"

"The size of a German shepherd and wearing a beret? What are the chances?"

"Not high," Kyrie said. "But if it's true . . ."

"If it's true," Tom said, feeling as though he had a bit of ice wedged in his stomach, "then he's gone completely around the bend. Which I suppose would make him an ideal suspect for the aquarium murder."

"And perhaps for whoever unleashed the executioner on us," Kyrie said.

At that moment, the phone rang. And Kyrie sprang towards it. "It's Rafiel," she said.

Tom raised his eyebrows at Kyrie, as she pushed the button on the speaker and Rafiel's voice filled the room.

He sounded nervous . . . or perhaps hassled was a better term. "Kyrie?"

"And Tom," Kyrie said. "We're on the speaker."

"Oh? Oh. Good. That saves me telling you stuff twice."

"What stuff?" Tom asked.

"Well . . . this morning, we got a call. At the station. They found . . ."

"Another arm?" Kyrie asked.

"Yes, but in this case, there was a body attached to it. Badly mauled. Aquarium. We're . . . processing it."

"Do you need our help?" Tom asked.

"Processing a body?" Rafiel asked, incredulous.

"No. With . . . anything."

There was a hesitation. Rafiel cleared his throat. "Yeah, but I can't . . ." His car horn sounded. "Did you see the paper, this morning?"

"The squirrel?"

"And the . . . you and the dire wolf."

"And?" Tom asked impatiently, waiting—fearing—what would come next but needing to hear it because until he heard, it was always worse than he thought. Until he heard it, he would think he'd been found, he'd been recognized, he'd been . . .

"And this morning, when we were called in, there were already reporters in the parking lot. From the *Weekly Inquirer.* They were looking for fur or scales, or who knows what. But they got hold of the murder, right at the beginning. And considering, they seem really interested . . . you know, the thing is the *Weekly Inquirer* was bought recently?" He seemed to wait for them to comment and when all that Kyrie and Tom did was exchange a look, he clicked his tongue. "The *Weekly Inquirer* was bought by Covert Corp."

"Covert what?"

"The corp. thing is sort of misleading. I mean, they are a corporation. But they are a family company. They own several magazines. Crosswords, mystery. But the most important property, the one they started with, is called *Unknown*. It's a magazine of cryptozoology."

"Crypto what?"

"Animals that aren't supposed to exist, or animals that aren't supposed to be there. Dragons and . . . that."

"Oh. But if they own many companies . . . What could it mean for the *WI* in particular?"

"The patriarch of the clan, Lawrence Stoneman . . . He's very hands-on, you could say. He seems to keep one of his kids in charge of each place the corp buys. His daughter, Miranda, is in charge of the *Weekly Inquirer*. And she grew up on cryptozoology. I think their interest in the murder is secondary, frankly, as opposed to what interesting animals they might find lurking around. In other words . . ." Rafiel hesitated.

"We can none of us afford to be obvious?" Kyrie said.

"With a maniac stalking us, and a second murder at the aquarium—where there are two, maybe three shifters running around?" Tom said.

"Exactly. So, yes, I do want your help, but I do need to be more careful about getting that help than I've been. I'll come in if I can, tonight. Meanwhile, if you must shift, be careful where you do it, and who might see you. More careful than normal, that is."

"Right," Tom said. And sensing Rafiel was about to

hang up, he added, "Oh, do you have any relatives who could fix our bathroom?" And in response to a scowl from Kyrie, he added, "Not for free. We'll pay. I'd just like to get someone who can start right away, so we can move back home soon, and who won't ask . . . awkward questions." This brought up his deep-seated envy of Rafiel, who not only hadn't lost his family over his shifting nature, but whose family stood ranked behind him, solid, bolstering and protecting him.

Tom had been told that Rafiel's parents knew he was a shifter. This explained—or at least Rafiel thought it did— why Rafiel still lived at home. Tom didn't know how many other members of the extended family knew about it, and he was afraid to ask. In a world where the lack of safety of a shifter meant revealing the existence of them all, he didn't want to learn of the possible issues with Rafiel's security. Rafiel's family seemed to have done well enough with the secret so far, and Tom, who had no personal knowledge of how real families behaved, would not judge.

"Oh," Rafiel said. "I see. Yes, we have plumbers in the family, and one of my uncles can probably do the drywalling stuff or tile or whatever." There was a silence that gave the impression he was trying to think things out. "Yeah, it will do very well. It will give me an excuse to come by the diner later this evening. We'll just have to be careful there."

Rafiel disconnected, and Tom limped towards the shower to wash. He and Kyrie needed to eat something, and one of them should probably go in early to relieve Anthony. Normally, they should have had three shifts. They hadn't, mostly because Tom hadn't had time to even think of hiring a third manager, much less one who was practiced in using the complex new stoves. But they couldn't ask Anthony to do a twelve-hour shift, not when he was newly wed, anyway, so Tom would go in early. He grabbed a change of clothes and headed towards the bathroom, Not Dinner happily winding in and out between his ankles. "I wonder if that Laura person who was supposed to come for an interview yesterday will show up today. Do you think they've cleared the roads enough for traffic?"

Kyrie giggled, and as Tom stared, she said, "I'm sorry, but with everything going on, it's so much like you to be worried about the diner, and getting another manager/cook for the diner."

Tom grinned, seeing her point, but shrugged. "Well, Kyrie, look at it this way—if we survive this, then we'll need the diner in good shape, particularly considering the repairs to the bathroom. And if we don't survive, the fact that I was worried about running the diner won't make a bit of difference."

But Tom found, as he crossed the slush-filled parking lot of The George, that things were not that clear-cut in his mind. It was sort of like telling someone to stop worrying because nothing could be done about a problem. It wasn't in the human mind to stop worrying—to stop looking for the door out of the sealed room; to stop searching for the one true route through the labyrinth. He was sure that if the world were doomed to destruction by asteroid within a day or two, and everyone on Earth were informed of it, at least half of them would go to their graves still frantically looking for an escape from the approaching cosmic collision. In the same way, the sane thing to do, surrounded by problems he couldn't solve, might be to concentrate on the problems he could solve—on the diner, his bathroom, and the fact that his hands—though well enough to go without bandages—still hurt and would probably be sensitive to the heat from the stoves.

That would be the sensible thing to do, and the sane one. Which meant, of course, that his mind insisted on going through everything he couldn't do anything about—the murders at the aquarium; the executioner come to town; whatever the organization might be of old shifters, and beyond that where Old Joe might have gone and whether he was alive.

The weather had done one of those sudden reversals that Tom's almost year of living in Colorado had got him used to—it had gone from several degrees below freezing the day before, and blowing snow and howling wind, to fifty degrees with a very slight breeze which stirred the branches of the icicle-hung trees. All the icicles were dripping, too—from the branches of the trees and the edges of the buildings, a drip drip drip that seemed to be waiting only for a conductor and some rhythm to turn into an animated movie's symphony of thawing and spring.

Only it wasn't spring at all. And tomorrow could very well be freezing again. Or alternately it could be eighties, with everyone wandering around in sandals and T-shirts.

As Tom took a long detour around a melting pool in the middle of the parking lot, he fancied that even the birds on the trees that lined the streets were piping in tones of surprise, as if asking themselves if this was the last of snow or the beginning. He was smiling to himself at the idea of birds driven to Prozac by Colorado weather, but his detour brought him full-face with a poster on the wall of the diner—where it wouldn't have been visible from the back door. That wall was in fact where the storage rooms protruded a little from the otherwise square plan of the building.

The poster was glued at an angle on the whitewashed wall, and it was the sort of poster—printed on cheap paper, in two colors—that normally advertised a dance or a new more or less non-registered nightclub or, alternately, some new band come to town. At first Tom thought it was a new band. It might still be a new band. Only what the words across the top read, in huge bright red type—rodent liberation front. Beneath it was a rant in pseudo-Marxist terms, urging "The downtrodden, the despised who live at the edges of society" to "rise up and take what you want. No more foraging for fallen nuts, no more eating discards. Rise up and take your freedom in your hands. There are more of us than them. Rodents of the world, unite. You have nothing to lose but your mousetraps."

Tom blinked at the page. It was possible it was all allegorical and meaningful and too symbolic for words. They were, after all, not that far away from CUG—Colorado University at Goldport—and since fully half the students seemed to eat at The George any given day—or more typically night—Tom was aware how the minds worked who might be behind this pamphlet. They were the sort of minds that were convinced coming up with a particularly clever image or metaphor excused not having anything new to say.

Without his knowing he was going to do it, his hand reached out and plucked the paper from the wall. It could be a metaphor, a clever image, a college thing to delude themselves that they were doing something to save the world. But in his gut—in a big, insoluble cold lump at the pit of his stomach—he knew it wasn't. He knew it was . . . shifter business. Squirrels the size of German shepherds smoking cigarettes. Crazy. But how crazy did the dragon thing sound to other people as well?

He folded the poster and put it in his pocket, and started walking towards the diner. And heard the splish-splosh behind him of someone stepping on ice, then on water, then falling butt-first into the water. And turned to see Red Dragon—no, Conan. He had to get used to calling him Conan—sitting in a puddle of water, looking very surprised.

Surprised was the least of his problems, though, to tell the truth. He didn't look good. Not good at all. His skin was pale enough to look almost the color of Tom's and he had big circles under his eyes, and to make things worse, he was attempting to get up, but not managing to balance himself enough to do so, because of his shortened arm.

"I shouldn't go to him," Tom told himself. "I truly shouldn't go to him. How stupid can I be? One day I'm going to help someone who is going to kill me."

But in his mind was his sixteen-year-old self, alone, on the streets of New York City in a bathrobe and as lost and confused as any kid could ever have been anywhere. And he'd survived only because the gentleman down the street—an orangutan shifter, though his family didn't seem to notice he was one—who sold roasted chestnuts on the street corner, had seen him and taken him in, and given him a jogging suit, and let him stay there a couple of days, till Tom had caught hold of the idea of day labor and had got a fake ID that said he was eighteen and could, therefore, be hired.

And he was closing the distance to Red Dragon and holding him on the side of his weak arm and hauling him up, even as he looked down at what he was wearing—the jogging suit that Kyrie had given him and a pair of those shoes that you slip your feet into, which have an almost completely smooth bottom. No socks. "You need boots," he said. "For this weather. We'll take you to the thrift store tomorrow or something, okay?"

"I have money," Conan Lung said, in the tone of someone protesting charity. "I brought money with me. In a pouch. I could buy new boots."

"Oh? Good for you," Tom said, not sure whether to be amused or saddened and being, after all, wholly skeptical. If he had money, why grab the elastic shoes? They weren't that much better than the flip-flops Tom had given him. "And you have family in Goldport, too, don't you?" he added, remembering that their past adventures seemed to involve Goldport's minuscule Asian minority.

He shook his head. "Tennessee," he said, and wiped his dripping nose to his sleeve, and looked back, at a bottom that was entirely soaked in runoff from melted snow.

"Oh, now, you're just putting me on," Tom said. "And

don't worry about the sweatsuit. I have a couple others in the storage room. For . . . this sort of situation." He decided he didn't want to talk about Old Joe to the Great Sky Dragon people. "I'll get you one. Socks too."

"I'm not putting you on," Conan said. He sounded aggrieved and tired, and just the slightest bit exasperated— though Tom couldn't tell at whom. "Mom and Dad have a restaurant in Knoxville. People don't all come in to New York City anymore when they immigrate. Planes go everywhere."

"I'm sorry," Tom said, holding onto himself with all his will power to prevent himself from giggling at the fact that Conan had completely forgotten to have an accent. Or completely forgotten to have an Asian accent. Now that Tom thought about it, there was just an edge of a southern twang to his voice. It sounded, Tom thought, like something he'd tried very hard to rid himself of. Something that he hadn't quite managed to leave behind him. And quite out of place in a triad member.

"And I do have money. In a pouch. I wear it on a flexible anklet when I shift," Conan added, sullenly, clearly having caught Tom's disbelief.

"All right. You have money. Couldn't you have got yourself decent shoes, then?"

Conan shook his head. "No," he said. "I got them at the Short Drugs down the block, and this was the best they had. It was this or flip-flops."

"You know . . ." Tom said, leading him towards the back door of the diner and opening it for him. In the hallway, Conan wiped his feet on the mat at the entrance, and duck-walked into the hallway, his cheap shoes squeaking on the concrete. "It might surprise you, but in a list of shoe stores, Short Drugs wouldn't be in the first hundred, being a drugstore and all."

Conan sighed, a sigh half of exasperation, as if Tom were being particularly daft. "I couldn't let you go, could I? I went to Short Drugs because it was just down the block."

And Tom, having closed the door, froze. "Couldn't let me go? As in, you're keeping me prisoner?"

Conan looked back, and now his voice was definitely furious. "No, you fool. I couldn't leave you unprotected." He blushed, hard, whether with embarrassment at proclaiming himself Tom's protector, or with anger, Tom couldn't tell. "What if I left you, and they killed you?"

"Shhhh," Tom said, forcefully, leaning against the wall, finger against lips, concerned most of all with the fact that Conan had yelled, and people might have heard him. "Shhh."

As if on cue, Anthony's worried face peeked around the corner in the hallway. "Tom? Everything all right?"

"Everything is fine," Tom said, talking over Conan's shoulder. "Conan fell in the parking lot. I'm going to grab him some dry clothes, and then I'll come in and you can go home."

"Oh, good," Anthony said. "Because you know Cecily will get worried." He smiled, but still looked somewhat worried, as he looked at Conan. However, he seemed reassured enough that Conan and Tom weren't about to come to fisticuffs.

Tom opened the door to the storage room, and pulled out a sweat suit. "Okay," he said. "You're here to protect me. You've told me this before. But I must ask you—because you never told me—what are you supposed to protect me from . . . ?"

Conan looked back at him. There was naked fear in his eyes, followed by something very much like defeat or humiliation. He took the sweat suit—grey, much washed—that Tom was holding out to him. "I don't know," he said, miserably. "He didn't tell me. Just that they were bad and . . . very powerful. And very large. And knowledgeable and . . . shifters."

"And he sent you? To protect me?" Tom asked. And realizing what he'd just said, and that Conan's hand was clenching hard at the end of his atrophied arm, he added, "I'm sorry, but . . . you're smaller than I in both forms, and with that arm . . ."

Conan shook his head. "You don't understand. You don't understand, okay?" His voice started rising again in a note of hysteria, and Tom pulled him into the storage room and closed the door after them, because the only other choice was pulling him into the bathroom and *that* would look funny. The room was piled high with boxes of paper napkins, potato chips and crackers. All the edibles were sealed in plastic or foil and it shouldn't have smelled, but they still did, so that it was a lot like being locked inside a giant box full of stale crackers.

"What don't I understand?"

Conan clutched the sweat suit in his good hand, clenched his other fist, and spoke through his clenched teeth. "Any of it. I was in high school. I was in the drama club and the choir and . . . and I was in the Latin club, too. And then . . ." He shook his head. "I shifted. And the next thing I know my parents were calling on . . . on Him. And he took me away. Because I was a dragon. I belonged to him. I was his to . . . protect and order. Like . . . like feudal, you know?" His shoulders sagged, despondently. "I was going to be a Country and Western singer. I was . . ." He shook his head.

And before Tom could think of what to say—lost in his own forgotten dreams, though he didn't remember ever wanting to be anything so definite and wholesome as a singer—Conan said, "It doesn't matter." He spoke in a flat tone. "You see, my parents didn't know what else to do with me, and . . . I don't have anywhere else to go. It's all . . . Well, honor and that. I disgraced the Great . . . Himself. I . . . didn't get the Pearl of Heaven for him. So . . ."

Tom remembered the long torture session that Conan and the others had subjected him to. He'd have felt angry, but he didn't know what had been at the back of it. He was just starting to glimpse what drove those he had assumed were crazed gang members. "So you have to redeem yourself."

He almost added that he didn't feel very reassured by the Great Sky Dragon sending Conan, anyway. But he didn't. He was learning that what came flying out of his mouth might hurt other people, even, possibly, people who didn't deserve to be hurt. And besides, he had a feeling—not quite a rational feeling, not even a thought, more of a prickling at the back of his neck that told him that the Great Sky Dragon's plans weren't as simple as they seemed. Instead, they were folded over themselves, more intricately than a highway map. And what he saw might not be all of it. He just wished he could be sure the rest of it was not against him.

"Well," he said, "I'll leave you to change." And escaped out the door of the storage room, to find Anthony in the hallway, looking at him with a very strange expression.

Tom wasn't sure how much Anthony had overheard, or what had caused him to come and look. But all Anthony said was, "I thought you'd have him change in the bathroom. He's going to get mud on the packs of napkins."

Kyrie was dozing on the bed. She would have liked to fall fully asleep again, but this seemed to be beyond her ability while a small creature lay down purring, squarely between her breasts, and punished any attempt at moving with sharp little claws at the base of her throat and a sort of soft "mur" that sounded like an admonition.

So she lay there, on the bed, on her back—which was far from her favored sleeping position—with a patch of sun squarely in her eyes. She tried to move her head just a little sideways. The needlelike claws got her at the hollow of her throat. "Mur."

"Yes, yes, I get it. I'm not allowed to move. I get it."

"Mur!"

She opened a cautious eye, in time to see Not Dinner curl up into a ball. But he remained facing her, and one of his eyes opened just a little.

Kyrie would have giggled, but she was fairly sure that this would have brought the claws out again, so she closed her eyes and tried to get back to dozing. Which was not exactly as easy as it might sound, while her mind kept giving her images of Tom fighting the dire wolf. There was something wrong about that creature. Besides the fact that it should have been extinct long before humans walked the Earth. The way it had moved . . . She shivered, and instinctively lifted a hand to ward off the claws, and the phone rang.

She jumped up and grabbed the bedside phone, but the ringing continued, and she realized what was ringing was her cell phone, and jumped for her purse, which was propped up against the sofa.

The phone showed Rafiel's number. She opened it. "Yeah?"

She remembered, belatedly, that she'd dumped the kitten on the bed and hoped he wasn't hurt. A look at him revealed him angrily licking himself and pointedly ignoring her.

"Kyrie?" Rafiel said. He sounded weird. Detached and breathy as if he had lost his voice and were speaking on echoes alone, unable to put any emotion in his words.

"Yes? What is wrong?"

"Nothing. Everything is fine."

"You sound very odd."

"Oh, got . . . something in my throat. Look, I don't suppose you can meet me at your house?"

"At my house? Why?" she said. And when he didn't answer immediately she said, "Is it about the bathroom?"

"Exactly," he said. "The bathroom. I've got someone to fix it. If you'll just meet me there . . ."

"When?"

"Now?"

"No can do. Must de-stink and put clothes on."

"Oh, why bother? We're only going to take them off."

"What?" She actually removed the phone from her ear and looked at the caller ID, to make sure that it was really Rafiel.

"I'm sorry. Bad joke."

"Very bad joke." Rafiel hadn't said something like this since she and Tom had got together. She wondered if he was trying to revive that rivalry, then realized it was probably just his idea of a joke to break the tension. He'd been with her in the SUV, and he hadn't even looked at her in a suggestive manner. "Okay. Give me half an hour," she said, matter-of-factly. And hung up.

Tom had taken over the grill, and was keeping an eye on Conan as he cooked. He'd found out Conan had camped out on the steps of the bed-and-breakfast all night, which he supposed explained the fumbling way he was moving and how bleary eyed he looked.

The problem, as Tom saw it, was that he could easily get Conan to crash in their house—if their house were operational. But their house was nowhere near operational. And in the bed-and-breakfast, they couldn't exactly offer him the living room floor and Tom didn't feel quite sanguine enough about letting him sleep on the floor of the suite. Inoffensive, he might be, but Tom could hear just the right note of sarcasm in Kyrie's voice if he told her that Conan would be sleeping on their floor. He could tell Conan he could sleep in the storage room, but beyond the fact that this would freak out Anthony, he wondered if Conan would do it.

He'd just settled on offering him the back of one of the diner's vans—in which he and Kyrie did supply runs to the local farmers' markets twice a week in season—and telling him he could park the van in front of the bed-and-breakfast—and look out the window for all Tom cared, when Anthony reappeared from, apparently, making sure Conan hadn't willfully destroyed supplies.

"Everything seems to be fine in the supply room," he said, removing his apron.

"Mmm," Tom said, noncommital, as he turned to shave an order of gyro meat off the hunk slow-roasting.

"Well, you know . . . he's still a newbie," Anthony said. "So, you never know." He folded his apron and put it under the counter. "Keith left today at around ten, said something about bringing a girl to meet you."

"Yeah. Someone from college." Tom shrugged. "Maybe he wants me to give her a job."

"We do need people," Anthony said. "That Laura woman, whom we were supposed to interview, said she would come by as soon as the snow has melted. Something about not having a four-wheel drive." He shrugged. "So, if you're sure you don't need me anymore . . ."

"No, I don't. That's cool, you can go."

"Right. I'll come back late in the afternoon, if you need a break. Just call me. And speaking of calling?"

"Yes?"

"Your dad called."

Tom felt every muscle in his body tense. He might be closer to Tom than he had been in Tom's entire life—close enough that he was closing his New York City law practice and uprooting it to Denver. Of course, Denver—three hours away—was the smallest city that he considered "livable." And Tom wouldn't mind it at all, if it weren't for Edward's seeming conviction that, as the largest city—and capital—of Colorado, Denver must be well known to everyone who had lived in the state for any amount of time. Not only that, but it must be within easy reach of anyone wishing to, oh, look up an apartment for their erratic father.

The other thing was, his dad had his home number and his cell phone number. Why was he calling The George during the daytime? He knew very well his son tended to be awake nights and sleep during the day.

"He said that the cable guy is coming to his loft this week, but he can't fly to Denver till next week, and . . ." Anthony hesitated. "He seemed to want you to go to Denver and wait for the cable guy at his place."

And, though he might try to become closer to his son, Edward remained as self-centered as a gyroscope. "Right," Tom said, ticking up *call Dad* in his long list of things to do and worry about. "I'll deal. I have to explain to him that even if I could normally have gone to Denver over the week—which I doubt, as shorthanded as we are—there's snow all over and the highways are closed."

Anthony seemed to be unsure whether he should say something, but finally it came hurtling out, "Well, I told him the highways were closed," he said defiantly.

"And?" Tom asked, surprised by the tone.

"He said you should fly," Anthony said. "Does he have any idea how small our airport is or how hard it would be to operate in inclement weather?"

"None," Tom said. "Don't worry about it. He's my dad. I'll deal with it. He's not a bad guy he's just . . . you know how it is. Lived his whole life in the Northeast." He set the platter of gyro meat, fries and pita bread on the counter and rang the bell to call Conan's attention. And managed, very nearly, not to grit his teeth. There was no way to tell Anthony that no, Tom's father didn't expect his son to take an airplane. He expected his son to fly as a dragon.

Which was how Edward's mind worked. Once having convinced himself that Tom's ability to shift was not dangerous, he'd become determined to use it as much as he could, and to derive usefulness from it as much as possible. Tom had to remind himself it was, in a way, an endearing quirk, a lot like Keith's absolute certainty that being a shifter dragon would be just like being a superhero. And that his father could have absolutely no idea of the troubles besetting Tom at every side.

He pulled over a huge bowl of peeled potatoes— essential ingredient of The George's famous fresh fries, never frozen proudly advertised in marker on the huge plate glass window up front—and started slicing them into sticks on a broad expanse of cutting board, while he watched Conan give warm-ups and draw up bills for a couple of customers. He'd be just fine.

"Anthony," he said, before the young man turned away. "You didn't . . . see the alligator out back again?"

Anthony blushed. "Oh, geez, about that . . ." He sighed. "I've been thinking about it, and look, it was pretty late last night, and I think I just imagined things. It must have been the shadows, and the snow blowing, you know? I just got a bit goofy."

Tom shrugged. "Okay, just making sure." He hesitated a second. "And you haven't seen Old Joe, either?"

"What? Oh, the old man . . . He's probably downtown at the shelter, you know? The city shelter lets people in when it's this cold, even when they wouldn't let them in regular times. You know, no sobriety check or what have you."

"Yeah. He probably is." And maybe he was, though Tom doubted it. He knew—none better—how shifters felt about crowded rooms, where your roommates could start looking like potential snacks, if you got stressed enough. "Don't worry about it. I just thought, since it's this cold . . ."

"Yeah," Anthony said. "Okay, call me if you need me." He got his jacket from under the counter and put it on, pulling the hood on over his head, till he peered from under a welter of fake fur, like an Eskimo prepared for the arctic.

"Right," Tom said.

And when Conan swung by to drop off orders, Tom grabbed his good arm. "Listen. I was thinking—I know you won't want to sleep in the storage room or whatever because we might go out behind your back. But how about sleeping in the diner van parked in front of the bed-and-breakfast?"

Conan looked startled. "Why?"

"Well, you can't go on sleeping on the steps. You don't look any too awake, just now."

"Oh." Conan sighed. "Look, I have money."

"So you keep telling me."

"If you promise that you won't go anywhere without waking me first . . . I can rent a room at the bed-and-breakfast."

Tom thought about it. It seemed a little odd to have to notify his jailer that he intended to leave. On the other hand, perhaps Conan was a bodyguard, not a jailer. Tom wasn't sure he understood anything anymore. He certainly was sure he didn't understand the Great Sky Dragon. "Well . . ." he said, after a wait. "Yeah. I suppose I can do that."

"Only you have to make sure you do," Conan said. He shot Tom a resentful look. "When you disappeared yesterday and I had to go find you . . . If you'd died, you know . . ." He shook his head. "I was so busy at the tables I didn't see you leave, and let me tell you, Himself wasn't happy."

"How did the Great Sky—"

"Shhh," Conan said.

"How did Himself know?" Tom asked and resisted an impulse to roll his eyes and refer to *he who must not be named*. "Did you tell him?" It seemed to him the height of stupidity for Conan to confess to have lost track of Tom for any time at all, much less to call the Great Sky Dragon and confess his misdeed.

Conan sighed. "What do you think would have happened if I hadn't told him?" he asked. "They're everywhere. Someone would have told him, sooner or later. And then he'd have killed me for not telling him."

"Killed you?" Tom thought how ridiculous it was to

kill someone for such a small offense. Particularly in a creature that claimed to want to protect Tom. He wanted to rebel. He very badly wanted to rebel. But not when Conan would be the one to pay for it. He nodded. "I'll tell you before we go out."

And turned in time to see Rafiel come into the diner.

Sometime between sixteen and twenty, Kyrie had simplified her getting-ready routine. The makeup that had seemed essential at sixteen had now gone by the wayside. The one fussy bit about her appearance was her hair dyeing and that she did once every three months and touched up once a month, and that was about it.

In the bed-and-breakfast, she didn't even have her shampoo or the shower gel she liked to use. Since the bathroom had been obliterated, and all her products with it, all she had was what Spurs and Lace provided, in an artistic little basket lined with lacy fabric. There were three bottles of shampoo, all seeming to belong to some brand that invested a lot in aroma therapy. Vanilla, mint and—bizarrely—coffee. Preferring her coffee on the inside, Kyrie grabbed the vanilla. There were three bars of soap for her perusal, but a look in the tub revealed that Tom had already started a bar that smelled minty fresh. He had also used up a bottle of shampoo labeled chamomile. She was sure he was missing his Mane and Tail, the worst-named shampoo for a dragon to use since the dawn of time.

The shower proved to have a torrential flow of water, and she washed quickly under it, only slightly hampered by the fact that, two minutes into her shower, Not Dinner screeched from outside the shower "Mur?" and patted tentatively at the shower curtain..

"Er," she said. "I'm fine."

"Yow?"

"No, really. We humans don't mind water. Heck, we like it."

A disbelieving "Nahooo?" answered her and she grinned. "I'm only a kitty part of the time, and I refuse to lick myself for hygiene."

"Mur!"

"Yes, I know, quite terrible of me, isn't it?" She finished rinsing and came out of the shower, drying herself briskly, and rubbing her hair almost completely dry with a towel, before combing it. Judging by the drip-drip-drip sounds from outside the bedroom window and the brilliant sunshine which had disturbed her sleep, the weather had turned some sort of corner. Which was very good, because she didn't think she could go outside with damp hair, otherwise. She had vague visions of doing that and having her hair freeze to her head as a large, unwieldy mass.

While she was home, she should grab a couple of hats for herself and Tom, she thought, as she slid into jeans, a red sweatshirt that was probably originally Tom's, but which she'd claimed by rights of laundress, and had been wearing for the last two months. The man never wore long sleeve shirts, anyway. Just his T-shirts under his black leather jacket.

She put her shoes on and told Not Dinner, "Now,

Notty, try to be good. I'll ask the lady to bring you some food, until we can buy you some kitten cans."

"Mur?" he followed her to the door with the dancing step of young, overconfident kittens and seemed terribly disappointed that she wasn't willing to let him follow her outside. An ill-fated last minute rush at the door made her grab him in her hand—where he fit, fairly comfortably, then toss him into the room, as she quickly shut the door.

She asked the proprietress—a large, maternal woman named Louise—to feed the delinquent and informed her that he was a flight risk. It wasn't till she got to the car that she thought she should have asked Louise for a recommendation to a vet. She would need to get Notty his shots, and she should probably have him microchipped, at least if he had wandering paws.

Perhaps she would ask Rafiel, she thought, and smiled absently. He should know everything there was to know about the care of male felines in this town. But her smile died down, as, maneuvering through the mostly-melted streets, she wondered what Rafiel could possibly want. Oh, he'd said that he wanted to meet her at her house. And he'd said it was because of the bathroom . . .

Or *had* he said that it was because of the bathroom? Kyrie couldn't remember exactly. She frowned. Was there another reason? He'd sounded so odd over the phone—as if he'd been not so much talking as making modulated breathing sounds. But no . . . that wasn't right either. It was just as if there were no force of vocalization behind his words. No real sound. He'd said he had something in his throat. Like what? An elephant?

A brief image of Rafiel prowling the zoo and taking a

big bite off an elephant amused her. And she smiled at herself, but as she entered her neighborhood, she went back to frowning. Rafiel's car wasn't parked on the street. This was like an itch at the back of her mind, an itch to which her brain responded by coming up with lots of reasons for the absence—his car had broken down, and he was borrowing someone else's; he had parked in the driveway; he was late.

But if Rafiel's car had broken down, he was likely as not to let her know in advance, so she would know the car to look for. It wasn't the sort of thing Rafiel forgot. Rafiel was a policeman. Details were his life. And he never parked in the driveway, which was a minuscule comma beside the tiny dot of the house and had barely enough space for Kyrie's subcompact. When Tom worked later and had to drive the diner's van home, he had to park on the street. And not just because he didn't want to block Kyrie in, but because there was no way to park two cars in the driveway without one of them having half of its back wheels on the street.

And besides, as Kyrie got to the driveway, it was empty and wet from melting ice. She started to pull in, while the back of her scalp bunched up. *Something is wrong,* an inner voice said. *Something is very wrong.*

But that inner voice was wrong nine times out of ten. Fact was, Kyrie's inner voice was a paranoid patient, and had to be kept carefully locked up in its rubber room, or else she would never hear a sound that wasn't suspicious, she'd never approach a place that didn't feel eerie, and she would spend her entire life running from shadows. Deliberately, she stopped within sight of her kitchen door, and put the car in park, the wheels slightly turned so that—should the car roll down the driveway—it would rest across the bottom of it, instead of slipping out into the street and potentially running into other cars.

Her foot remained on the brake, her hand resting on the keys, her car idling.

Run.

No. No, she wouldn't run. She had run too many times, after she was out of foster care—after she was on her own. Without family or any close friends, with nothing to anchor her down, she had drifted. Convinced she was hideously insane—with her dreams of turning into a panther, her secret fears of eating people—she had kept everyone at arm's length and ran every time someone got too close, every time anyone seemed hostile. Every time a shadow waved in the wind. But now she had a place, she had a job, she had Tom. She had something that was hers, and she wasn't running.

She pushed the parking brake in, relishing the feel of it under her foot, the slight grind of its going in. Then she reached for her purse, from the floor of the passenger side of the car. Where was Rafiel? This was so much like him, telling her to come to the house, and then not being here when she got here. And immediately, she scolded herself, because no, it wasn't like Rafiel at all. He was arrogant, not careless. If he said he would be somewhere, he would be there. He might act put out because she hadn't rushed to meet him, unwashed and in robe and slippers, but he would be there.

She bit her lip. Okay. All right. So something had happened. Could be anything. He was on a murder investigation. Perhaps someone had called and told him he had to be at the morgue now. This minute. Or perhaps . . . or perhaps something else had happened. Perhaps he'd had a fender bender. Or something.

A brief image of Rafiel laid out on a hospital bed made her wince. He wouldn't like that. They all tried to stay out of hospitals as much as possible. Besides being a crowded place, with lots of other humans—it would be a mess to shift in—their healing rate would call too much attention.

She reached for her purse, pulled out her phone. She would call him, figure out if anything had happened to him. Help him, if she needed to.

But the phone was dead. Out of batteries. Kyrie caught herself growling under her breath. She could swear she had recharged it last night. Clearly she hadn't.

She resisted an impulse to throw the phone—with force—across the driveway, and instead put it back in her purse and zipped her purse shut forcefully.

Okay, so Rafiel wasn't here, and she couldn't call him. What then?

She could go back. She could go to The George. It was only five minutes away. She could call Rafiel from there.

But what if he showed up as soon as she drove away? What if it was only a small delay, some administrative thing that kept him back? Then he would be there any second, wouldn't he? And when he got there, he wouldn't find her.

But she could call him.

In five minutes. What if by then he had driven away, furious? Oh, he had no right to be furious. He'd called Kyrie out of the blue. He'd told her to be here. There was no reason at all she should have obeyed him. And he'd said—or at least, he'd agreed—this was about her bathroom. Which meant he wouldn't be coming by alone. He would be with his uncle or cousin, or whoever in his vast tree of relatives was a plumber or a tile layer, or a good enough handyman. And that meant he wouldn't leave in five minutes.

But none of these rational arguments amounted to a hill of beans. After all, Rafiel was all male cat in this one thing, that he could act as capricious as he pleased, and make everyone else seem like they were the irrational ones, the ones who were failing him in some horrible way.

Besides, she realized, she had a phone in the house. Oh, they rarely used it, and in fact Tom had suggested they give it up and go all digital. But his father had protested that it was a number where he always knew he could reach them, even when their cell phones were out of a charge or they were out of range. In fact, it seemed that the phone, on the wall of the kitchen, and possessed of a built-in answering machine, mostly existed to take Edward Ormson's messages.

Which didn't mean it couldn't call Rafiel's cell.

Full of new decision, Kyrie got out of the car and slammed the door behind her. The driveway wasn't anywhere near as icy as it had been the night before, which was good. She should probably shovel the walk while she was here. Although most people in Colorado left their snow and ice on the sidewalk and let it merrily accumulate through the cold days, the law, technically, said that they were supposed to shovel within twenty-four hours of a major snowfall. The snow was melting on the sidewalks across the street, but not here, and Kyrie shuddered at the thought of what might happen if the postal carrier slipped and broke a leg on the way to their front door.

She paused at the door to the kitchen, frowning. The door itself was old, much painted, and starting to peel, a layer of red showing beneath the current decaying layer of white paint. It didn't matter, because it was normally covered by a screen door, which had a glass screen, conveniently slid down for winter. Kyrie was sure—as sure as she was of having charged her phone—that Tom had closed that screen door. She remembered him half-skating back through the ice that then covered the driveway to do it. He'd mumbled that otherwise it would probably fold back in the wind and maybe be wrenched off. So, why was the screen door half open now?

Run.

No, nonsense. Probably some weather-defiant Jehovah's Witness had come and opened the screen door to knock. Or perhaps one of their neighbors, worried about the lack of lights in the house had come to check on them. Most of the people in this neighborhood were elderly and retired and took an inordinate interest in Kyrie and Tom because they weren't and perhaps because they reminded them of their grandchildren.

She got her keys from the pocket of her winter coat, and unlocked her door into the kitchen. The house felt empty. It had that cold/empty feel of a house where no one is.

It should feel empty. They'd never given Rafiel a key. They were friends, but normally they met at the diner.

Right. I'll just call the arrogant lion boy, she thought, as she walked the four steps across the kitchen to the phone. But as she picked it up and before she could dial, a smell rose around her.

It was thick, miasmalike, overpowering. Her throat and nose closed. She gagged. It was like . . . like walking into a closed shed at the zoo, where someone had been housing several hundred wild animals.

And then there was the voice, a voice without vocalization behind it, a voice that seemed to come from the phone and yet not, a voice that seemed curiously devoid of sound, "Welcome, Pretty Kitten."

Gasping and gulping, through the horrible smell, Kyrie turned.

Run.

"Hey, Rafiel," Tom said, as Rafiel walked up to the counter, "I thought you said you'd come by this evening?"

Rafiel shrugged. "I was going to, but I talked to my cousin Mike, and he said that he could go by this afternoon, and I happened to be in the neighborhood, because I have to . . . do some interviews." He looked around. "In relation to the case in the aquarium." Shrug. "So I thought I'd drop by and get the house keys from you."

"All right. If you want to come behind the counter, they're in my jacket pocket under there," he said, as he flipped a couple of burgers. And broke two eggs onto the griddle surface of the new stove. He looked over his shoulder and was amused to see Rafiel gingerly lift the pass-through portion of the counter, as though he was afraid it might be spring-loaded or something. He didn't remember if Rafiel had ever been behind the counter, for all he'd offered to man the diner, just yesterday.

"Yeah," he told Rafiel. "Down there. Just under the edge of the counter. You're going to have to look, because there's Conan's stuff under there too, and there's the time sheet boards. At least there isn't a cat today."

"A cat?"

"Uh . . . Kyrie and I have a cat. I mean, a kitten. He's barely larger than one of the burger buns. Full of himself, though." He heard his own voice become embarrassingly doting, sounding much like the voices of old childless people who dressed their pets in costumes for Halloween and took them out trick or treating. He changed the subject, abruptly, "Hey, why didn't you just go to Kyrie? She's probably awake by now."

"I'm sure she's awake," Rafiel said. "I went by there. The owner—Louise?—said that Kyrie had left to go check on something back home. Yeah, I could have gone by your place, but that was out of my way and this isn't. What?"

The "what" made Tom aware that he was standing there and staring at Rafiel with an idiotic expression on his face. He felt oddly betrayed, and he couldn't have explained to himself why. But the idea of Kyrie going back to their place without telling him made him feel like she had shut him out or something.

Of course, this was very stupid. It wasn't like he and Kyrie lived in each other's pockets, or anything. Sometimes he woke up in the afternoon, and she was gone—gone to the store, or to do laundry or something.

Of course, she always left him a note on the table. Of course, that might also be because when she went she took the only vehicle they normally kept at home, and if she wasn't going to be back in time, it meant Tom had to walk to The George.

"Nothing. I just . . ." Tom said, struggling with the feeling of betrayal, and not knowing what to say. "She didn't tell me she was going to go home, that's all."

"No?" Rafiel said, and frowned slightly, his blond eyebrows meeting up above his oddly golden eyes. "Weird."

"Well, not really," Tom said, almost defensively. "I mean, it's not like I own her, or she needs to tell me where she's going to be, or . . ."

"No, but you'd think she'd tell you anyway."

Tom thought perhaps Rafiel thought this meant he and Kyrie had had a falling out, and he wasn't really ready to be a rival with Rafiel for Kyrie's affections, again. He said, "Look, I don't think she means to dump me or anything, it's just . . . I'm guessing she went home because she realized she missed something. We left kind of in a hurry and didn't bring a lot of stuff." Of course, most of that stuff, like their toothbrushes, hairbrushes and most of their toiletries had, presumably, been ground to dust by his shifting in the bathroom.

"Yeah, but you'd think she'd tell you so you could tell her if you needed anything from home, too."

Tom shrugged. "I can walk there, if I do. It's no big deal. I was just surprised, that's all. It doesn't mean there's anything wrong."

"No," Rafiel said. He was still squatting by the space

under the counter where they put their jackets and where they stored aprons. He had Tom's jacket in his hands, but he hadn't pulled it out yet. "It's just . . . very weird? I mean, I have this feeling it's weird. I know that I don't know Kyrie as well as you do, that I don't know the . . . patterns of your relationship, like you do. But it seems to me she always tells you when she's not going to be where you expect her. How many times have I been here, talking to you—or at home talking to you, for that matter—and you get a phone call from Kyrie saying she's going to the supermarket or the thrift shop, or the bookstore, and do you want anything. Or she tells you if she's going to have the oil changed, and it's going to take a while."

"So maybe she thought it would be very quick and wasn't worth mentioning," Tom said. But he felt it too, the wrongness of it. He just didn't want Rafiel to start thinking along the *Kyrie might be available again and I might have a chance* lines. "Anyway, my keys should be in there, righthand pocket. Yeah, that's it. My house key is the simplest one. Yeah. The keys for this place are way more complicated." He watched Rafiel remove the house key from the ring, fold the leather jacket carefully and push it back under the counter.

Meanwhile, Tom assembled two Voracious Student specials, with the double cheeseburgers and the egg and enough fries to sink a small ocean liner, and set them on the counter ringing the bell and announcing "Eighteen and ten."

Conan scurried towards the counter. He was getting better, Tom thought. He was also learning to carry the coffee carafe in his weaker hand. Tom had no idea how much longer it would take for the full arm to grow in, and it just now occurred to him that they would need to make some explanation to Anthony. He was thinking experimental treatment. It covered a multitude of sins, and most people didn't enquire any further.

Rafiel straightened up, slipping Tom's key in his pocket, and at that moment Keith came in, more or less towing a young woman. Keith was wearing his normal attire when the temperature went above freezing but not over 80—a CUG T-shirt, this one reading "I'm just a CUG in the college wheel," and jeans, topped by an unzipped hooded jacket in sweatshirt material. The girl with him, on the other hand, was dressed as if she thought she was going on a hunting expedition in the arctic wastelands. She was wearing a sweatshirt, a huge, puffy ski jacket in bright shocking pink, and the sort of fuzzy pink muffler that Tom associated—for reasons known only to his psychiatrist, should he ever acquire one—with Minnie Mouse. The rest of the girl's appearance certainly said mousie, if not necessarily Minnie. She was too skinny, the type of too skinny that the nineteenth century would have associated with consumption and a romantically early death, pale and had colorless white-blond hair that seemed insufficient for her head size and age. It was cut in a page boy just at her ears, but it gave the impression of having trailed off of its own accord and stopped growing due to either lack of energy or effort.

And yet, the way Keith looked at her, Tom saw that he seemed to be attracted to her. Who knew why? It made absolutely no sense to Tom, but then very few pairings did. He supposed his was as much of a surprise to everyone as theirs was to him. After all, what on Earth was a cat doing with a dragon? Or vice versa? And what was a nice girl like Kyrie doing with Tom?

"Hey Keith," he said. "Is this the friend you told me you'd bring by to meet me?"

The girl blushed furiously and Keith smiled. "Yeah, this is Summer Avenir, Tom. I've told her this is the best place in the world to get a burger, besides being my own, personal hangout, which, of course, immediately makes it better."

"Of course," Tom said. "Nice meeting you, Summer. And this is Rafiel. He's a friend."

Keith did a double take at Rafiel. "Taking a real job in your spare time, Officer Trall?"

"Nah. Just came by to talk to Tom," Rafiel said, looking embarrassed at being caught behind the counter as though he were an employee. "I'll be going now. Nice to meet you, Summer. Watch out for Keith. He's a troublemaker."

Tom caught Keith's questioning look at him, and frowned. Perhaps it was that he was behind this counter and cooking, with the scent of fresh fries, hamburgers, melting cheese and toasting bread in his nose. Perhaps through all this, it was too much to expect that Tom could smell another shifter. But though he could smell Rafiel faintly—the metallic scent associated with shifters coming through a mask of Axe cologne—there was no other hint of a shifter-scent. At least not close enough for him to track.

As Conan ducked behind the counter, to grab the coffee pot, Tom could smell him too, his scent a little sharper than Rafiel's and not overlaid with anything but soap and water. But, as far as he could tell, there was no other shifter-scent at all.

He would have to ask Keith why he thought this girl might be a shifter.

Kyrie couldn't breathe. Her chest ached and her throat stung and she couldn't breathe. It was all she managed to do not to claw at her own neck in frantic attempts to somehow force herself to get air in, through the miasma that surrounded her. It made no sense, because she knew she was breathing—somehow, she was still breathing, otherwise she would have passed out long since. But at the same time, the stink around her was so prevalent that she felt sure she couldn't be breathing. She just couldn't.

The smell surrounded her, intrusive, offensive. It seemed to her that she was not only inhaling it, but that it was coming through her ears and her pores as well. Pinning her down.

Where are you trying to go, Kitten Girl? Do you think I'd hurt a pretty thing like you?

Kyrie turned around. She wasn't sure why, but she felt as if the thoughts were coming from behind her, as she tried to get to the kitchen door—and somehow couldn't because the stink held her back, held her in place.

As she turned, she saw she was right. He stood in the shadows of the door from the hallway, just off the kitchen, and he seemed to be wearing a shimmery silver turtleneck and tailored black pants. He held a cigarette in his hand.

"We don't . . ." Kyrie said, slowly, because speaking hurt, thinking hurt, assembling thoughts into words seemed a labor worthy of Hercules. "We don't smoke. In the house. We don't approve of smoking. In the house."

She realized how ridiculous she sounded, as she was barely able to breathe and wondering what this . . . creature was and what powers he had over her. They'd determined in the parking lot that it could somehow reach into their minds and touch them. It could change what they were thinking. It was clear even to Kyrie's befuddled mind that it could also cause her to smell what she was smelling. There was no other way anything—human or animal—could smell that strongly, and the creature was or appeared to be in human form, standing in the demi-shadows of her hallway, smoking.

Kyrie hadn't been able to really look at him before—not in the parking lot at night, and under snow. But now she observed him. Was she seeing who he was, or who he appeared to be? And in either case, what could she deduce about him?

He was short for a male. Maybe an inch taller than Tom—she would guess him at five eight or thereabouts, and well built—that much was obvious from his huge shoulders, his muscular arms, his whole posture. The silvery turtleneck shimmered over muscle definition that would have made a gym bunny cry. This was not surprising. In Kyrie's experience most male shifters were built. Something about the animal form and the posture they assumed in their animal form made them exercise as humans normally didn't. In fact, what was strange was people like Conan who seemed to have not one functional muscle in their wiry, stringy shapes.

Beyond that, he was gold-skinned—a tone that Kyrie thought of as vaguely Mediterranean. Anthony's color. Could be anything from the southern regions, from Europe to the Americas. His hair was black, lank, and just a little long in front, falling in smooth bangs over his forehead, though the back seemed perfectly molded to the contours of a well-shaped head.

Other than that there was not much unusual about him—his nose was sharply aquiline, but not remarkably so. His forehead was high, but didn't give the impression of a receding hairline. His lips were broad and seemed sensuous, particularly now when they distended in a come-hither smile. But none of it would have made the man stand out on a crowded street.

None of it but the eyes. His eyes were gold. More gold than Rafiel's, which fell in the outer limits of brown. This creature's eyes were gold to the point of having an almost metallic shimmer to them. And like metal they were cold, unfeeling, blank. A blankness somehow lit from behind, like the screen of an old-fashioned computer.

The result was a look of perfect madness, the look of someone who had gone beyond normal human thoughts, normal human processes. Perhaps beyond thoughts at all.

He grinned at her as though he were a famished wolf and she a particularly tasty morsel of steak. Which might be an analogy much too close for Kyrie's comfort. She backed up, slowly, fighting against the smell, which seemed to hold her in place, to prevent her from moving, to drain her of all energy. It wasn't real, she told herself.

But she still couldn't reason her way to turning around and unlocking the door and running out onto the driveway. And perhaps that was not as irrational as it seemed to be. She didn't want to turn her back on the thing smiling seductively at her. The idea of turning her back on him, made her think of his being on her suddenly, biting into her, savaging her.

She backed against the door, without taking her eyes off him. If she was going to die, she would die with her eyes open. She would face her death without flinching.

Back against the door, she took a deep breath and told herself she was not smelling anything. Nothing at all. It was a smell of the mind, as she fancied Shakespeare might have said. Something that didn't exist. The air in her kitchen would be as untainted as it was when she came in. Cold and clammy, with a hint of disused space, and perhaps the ghost of cookies past, but nothing else.

"What do you want?" she asked the man smiling at her from the shadows. "What do you want from me?"

And the moment she asked, she recoiled, because it seemed to her like inviting the vampire into your home. This gave the creature a chance to say that he wanted her to die. And then, somehow to make it so.

But he laughed, a full-throated and very masculine laughter that she might have found pleasant under different circumstances. He emerged from the hallway and grinned at her. The light from the kitchen window behind her fell fully on his face. It should have made him look less unpleasant or more human. But all it did was gild the planes and features so that he looked like the antique funeral mask of an ancient and cruel emperor. The kind that would have ordered hundreds of thousands of people killed at his funeral rites.

"I just want to know you better," he spoke. It was, she realized with a shock, the first time she heard his voice. Before, he hadn't deigned to speak in audible words, but had tried to reach into her mind. She wondered if this meant that she'd scored a point. She very much doubted it.

Fighting against the smell that surrounded her, fighting against the suggestion that she was a small, frail, young thing at the mercy of this ruthless primeval evil—something she was sure he would like her to believe—she made her voice cutting and as sarcastic as if she were talking to Tom and Rafiel. "The normal way to get to know a woman is to go somewhere she is and introduce yourself. Some of the more polite people might ask her for coffee."

His laughter jangled, pleasant and cultured, but with something just slightly off-key behind it. It was, Kyrie thought, like when you heard thunder overhead, and the glassware in your cupboards tinkled in tune with it. A false note, a strange intrusion in what she was sure he wanted to be a perfectly polished image. She tried to keep this knowledge from her eyes, though, and must have succeeded, because he bent upon her an expression of great amusement—as though she were a particularly clever pet or a favored pupil.

Bending at the waist, hands on his thighs, the red glow of his cigarette end turned outward, he said, "Dante Dire at your service."

"Cute," she said, keeping her voice sarcastic.

"Nothing comes of denying what you are, Kitten. It is better to embrace it."

"I am not 'Kitten.' And I don't care to embrace any-thing." Said primly and with her back to the door and her lips taut.

"Really?" His insane eyes danced with merriment. "Don't you now? Oh, don't worry about it, I'm not going to eat you." He took a pull of his cigarette. "And if I did, you'd enjoy it." Again the mad dance of his insane eyes, followed by, "What do you think I am? Why do you think I'd want to hurt you?"

Because you broke into my house. Kyrie thought. *Because you are using a smell that can only be supernatural to keep me cowed. Because you talked in my mind. Because you attacked and wounded my boyfriend. Because you speak to me as if I were not an adult.*

She kept these thoughts up front, while behind them she ran others. She thought that if he was using his mind power on her, if he'd used some trick of pretending to be Rafiel—she was sure of it now—to lure her, it must mean he didn't want to or couldn't face all of them together. She didn't know why, since he had seemed to do pretty well with it in the parking lot of the aquarium. But it was clear he didn't like it, and didn't care to repeat it. And that was fine. Absolutely fine. But there was more. The fact that he was keeping the smell on her, and feeling that the smell was suffocating her, must mean he was afraid of her thinking clearly, of her thinking what she must do.

The thought sneaked behind her mind, afraid to be seen by whatever mind-scan capacities he had, that she should turn around and open the door. But . . . no. She couldn't do it, even if she tried. Simply couldn't.

"You have nothing to fear from me," Dire said. "I don't

know what you were told about me, but you can think of me as a private investigator. I'm here to find out what is killing our people."

Kyrie made a sound at the back of her throat. "Our people?" she asked. "I am not a dire wolf."

He made a dismissive gesture with his cigarette. "Shifters."

Behind it all her thoughts went on. So she couldn't turn her back on him. It would be just too creepy. Which left her with no other choice . . . or perhaps . . . Like a glimmer, at the back of her mind, came the idea that she could move *towards* Dire, instead of away from him. Move towards Dire, but maneuver so the little folding table and chairs that she and Tom used for their meals would always be between them, and her back too close to the kitchen counter and stove to allow him to teleport behind her. She was sure that there were some rules to this teleportation thing, if teleportation it was and not just an ability to make people forget they'd seen him move through the intervening space. She was sure even if he could instantly magic himself across the room, he couldn't do it when there was a good chance he would end up with a table, a chair, or a fridge embedded in his toned-and-tanned body.

She took a step towards him, and saw his eyes widen in shock, and the stench vacillated for a moment, allowing her to take a breath of the cold, untainted air of the kitchen. The stench returned, of course, but she knew now more than ever that it was fake. Another step, and it seemed to her that a flicker of something moved behind his eyes, as if he, himself, had been on the verge of taking a hasty step back. She sidestepped, then sidled rapidly around the table.

"Why are you afraid of me?" he asked, his voice trembling slightly. "If you're not a traitor to our people, you have no reason to fear me."

Ah! "What is a traitor to our people?" she asked, her voice cutting and slow, though she felt it coming from a shaking brittle place inside her. "I've never had any people. The only one I've ever belonged to is Tom."

"The dragon boy?" the creature asked, and there was real anger behind the words. "He's less than nothing. A larva. Not even a young one. Ignorant. Weak."

Kyrie read something in that, an echoing, resounding jealousy. Jealousy of Tom? Or jealousy, simply, that they had a relationship? What in this creature's past made him so angry at her?

"Tom is the only other shifter who ever took my side. Who ever cared for me."

"All of us care for you," the creature said. "It is the duty of shifter to look after shifter. You should always be loyal to your kin. Your people."

"I have no kin," Kyrie said. "I was adopted."

And before the creature could answer the flip response, she'd managed to reach her objective—the phone hanging on the wall of the kitchen. They should have a mobile phone, she thought. It had never seemed important before, and this phone had been practically free at the thrift shop, but if they had a mobile one . . .

The phone cold in her hand, she pushed the automatic dialing button to get the diner. She saw the creature lunge towards the phone, finger extended, to disconnect her. But if he was afraid to stop her calling for help, that meant help was possible.

With her free hand, she grabbed one of the chairs, and threw it, as hard as she could, at the creature, then, grabbing the other chair, used it to keep him away from the phone, in a move reminiscent of lion tamers at the zoo.

"Put the phone down," the creature said, his voice sounding like sweet reason. "Put the phone down. I only want to talk to you. If you're not a murderer, I won't hurt you."

Oh, sure you won't. And what's a murderer to you, buddy? she thought; at the same time her mind flooded with sheer relief at hearing Tom's voice answer the phone, brightly, "The George, your downtown dining option twenty-four hours a day, seven days a week, how may I help you?"

"Tom," she yelled. "Tom. I'm home. And there's a creature. The dire wolf. Help."

She let the phone dangle before she heard Tom's response. From the other side of the table came growls and fury, as the creature, seemingly giving in to an uncontrollable impulse, shifted into his animal form.

Kyrie grabbed the chair and huddled in a corner holding it—legs out—like a defensive shield. Shifting would earn her nothing but the loss of her clear mind. She might not be able to defend herself this way, but she had to try. And she had to hope she would still be alive when Tom arrived.

Rafiel saw Tom reach for the phone and because Tom had just blocked his obvious path out from behind the counter—not on purpose, Rafiel was sure, but simply by reaching for the phone—Rafiel started going around his friend, to edge behind him and reach over to open the portion of the counter that allowed egress.

He heard Tom give his cheery signature-line response to the phone and rolled his eyes. As if anyone actually would consider a greasy spoon their choice for dining downtown, no matter how many times Tom repeated it. He found Kyrie's "The George" answer far more palatable.

Touching Tom's shoulder with his fingertips, Rafiel expected to cause the other man to step away, however briefly. But instead, Tom stood, frozen. Rafiel became aware that the voice coming teensy and distant through the old-fashioned phone was Kyrie's and that Kyrie sounded hysterical. He didn't remember Kyrie ever sounding hysterical, not even when she thought she was seeing Tom die before her eyes.

The fingers he had prodded Tom's shoulder with, in a very masculine keeping of distance in a friendship type of gesture, now became a full hand laid on Tom's shoulder. "What's wrong?" he asked, as he realized that Tom had gone frighteningly pale, and that his throat was working, his Adam's apple moving up and down, as if he were trying to speak through a great lump in the way.

But when Tom spoke, it wasn't to answer Rafiel. Instead, it was a raw scream, that seemed to have been torn out. "Kyrie!"

People at the nearby tables turned to look, and Conan looked up from a bill he was totaling up. Keith and his girlfriend, too, looked towards Tom, alarmed.

"What—?" Keith said.

But Tom spoke to Rafiel, apparently having totally forgotten that shifter business was secret, or that they might be in as much danger from being overheard as they would be from no matter which arcane shifter might be threatening them or, for that matter, murdering people at the aquarium.

"It's Kyrie," he said, and swallowed. "It's the . . . creature from the aquarium. He . . . I must go. I must go to her."

And as he spoke, he tore from around his head the red bandana which he usually wore, pirate-style, while cooking, and he pulled his apron off.

"Tom," Rafiel said, in warning tones, afraid that his friend would decide to shift, right there in the diner. But Tom, clearly, wasn't that completely lost to reason. He ducked under the pass-through in the counter, and ran towards the hallway.

"Keith, take the grill, please," Tom called over his shoulder, thereby proving that he wasn't completely lost to reason at all, or perhaps that his devotion to the diner outweighed everything else, even his love for Kyrie.

Rafiel didn't stand around to see if Keith took over the grill and stoves. Instead, he ducked under the pass-through on his own, and ran down the hallway after Tom. "Let me go," he said, as Tom, in what seemed to be a blind rush, struggled with the back door. "Let me go. I can go. I can defend her."

"No," Tom said, with a sound like a hiccup. "No."

"You don't think I would fight for her?"

Tom had managed to unlock the door and now pulled it open and walked out into the parking lot, and, after looking around—Rafiel hoped he was making sure that no

one was coming or going close enough to see him—
ducked behind the dumpster, where he would be invisible
from nearby Pride Street.

He started undressing, rapidly, rolling his clothes in a
bundle. "Stay," he told Rafiel. "Give Keith a hand. I'm
sorry if I was too loud in there. She's in trouble. It's not
that I don't think you'd fight for her. But flying is faster."

And like that, Tom kicked his boots aside, dropped his
pants and underwear in a bundle, pulled off his shirt and
writhed and twisted, coughing, once, twice, three times,
as his body changed shapes and textures, the smooth skin
becoming green scales, the head elongating . . .

Before Rafiel could blink twice, Tom was lifting off,
flying across the clear skies of Goldport towards his own
neighborhood.

A curse sounded from the door of the diner. "He swore
he'd tell me." There was a sound of ripping clothes. And
then a red dragon rose, also, following Tom across the
skies.

This was folly, Rafiel thought, particularly while journalists
obsessed with cryptozoology were already suspicious of
the existence of dragons in town. But it didn't seem to
matter, not just now. Nothing mattered, except Kyrie.

Rafiel wanted more than anything to go and save her.
He understood Tom's impulse completely. His body
strained to be in the sky, speeding towards her, ready to
help in any way he could. But Rafiel couldn't fly and Tom
had asked him to stay here and, Rafiel realized, with
Conan gone, following Tom, and Keith at the grill, there
would be no one to wait tables.

There weren't many people inside, but Rafiel was

willing to bet there were more people than Keith could handle on his own, while cooking. *Right.* He ran his hand backward through his mane of unruly blond hair, aware, as he did it, that he would be making his hair stand on end and look more lionlike than ever. Right. Sometimes your duty requires you to be a hero, and sometimes it requires you to wait tables.

He turned to do just that and opened the door to The George. As he stepped into the cool shadows of the hallway, he saw a woman's figure retreating rapidly, ahead of him.

"May I help you?" he asked.

She turned around. It was Keith's blond friend, with her much-too-thick jacket and that look she had of having been dropped headfirst into a fish tank and still not being able to tell the piranhas from the goldfish. "I was . . . looking for the bathroom," she said.

It might very well be. Well—it could be, at least. If she was as confused as she looked, she might have walked all the way to the end of the hallway somehow managing to go by two bathrooms marked with the international icons for stick-figure man and stick-figure woman wearing triangle skirt without noticing them. He would even be willing to understand this confusion if the bathrooms had been marked salmon and shad roe, but since they seemed to be marked restroom it made the confusion less likely.

On the other hand, perhaps she was a shifter. If that was the truth, she might have understood more of the conversation than she'd seemed to, and she might have been in search of further confirmation.

And yet, she still didn't smell like a shifter to Rafiel.

He'd keep a very close eye on her, even as he helped Keith sling the hash or at least the burgers, and prayed with as much faith as he could possibly muster that Kyrie would be all right.

She might not be his—she would never be his—but he was not willing to face a world from which she was gone.

To shift or not to shift. Tom—as a dragon—landed on the driveway, just behind the car. He'd been thinking—as far as he'd been thinking at all—that he wouldn't shift. The dragon was a far more impressive foe than Tom, with all of his 5'6", no matter how strong, no matter how muscular.

But he couldn't even get close to the door as a dragon, let alone enter through the back or front door and go to Kyrie's rescue. A quick look to the house next door, where an elderly couple lived, reminded him too that the longer he stayed here in dragon form, the more likely someone would see him and report him. A vision of journalists with snapping cameras had taken hold of his brain and he was struggling to shift back to human form, as—behind him— he heard a dragon land.

Already in human form, Tom looked back, startled, to see a red dragon on the driveway. Conan. And Tom hadn't called him. But Tom didn't have time to discuss it with Conan, or even to worry about what the Asian dragon might do. Instead, he must go to Kyrie, if Kyrie was still alive, if Kyrie could still be saved. And he didn't even want to consider the possibility of anything else. He plunged through the kitchen door, into a scene of chaos and a gagging animal smell.

"Tom," Kyrie said. She was on the floor, with a chair held as a shield. Across from her, biting and growling and lunging at the chair was the dire wolf, his fur on end, his eyes mad, saliva dripping from his daggerlike teeth.

He can take me in one bite, Tom thought. *He can behead me with a single bite. I'm going to die. But I can't become a dragon here. I can't. It would destroy the room and kill Kyrie, and he'd just port elsewhere.*

Blindly, he reached for the rack of utensils that Kyrie had put on the wall, next to the stove. He rarely cooked at home—both he and Kyrie normally ate at the diner, or else brought home food from the diner. However, Tom was taking cooking courses and on the rare occasions when he did cook at home, he felt the need for semi-decent implements. So Kyrie had tacked up to the wall one of those things with leather pockets normally used in workshops to keep hammers and whatnot. And over the last couple of months, they'd been buying good implements: chopping knives, spatulas, a meat-tenderizing hammer.

Tom saw the dire wolf turn towards him, and he knew he had only seconds, and he knew that he couldn't turn his back on the creature. So he reached with his right hand and grabbed the first handle he could. What he got was a polished, sealed-wood handle, and, from the heft, the meat-tenderizing hammer, with a weighted hammer on one side and a hatchet on the other. Too short to keep the wolf's jaws from closing on his head. He reached again, and brought out . . . an immense skewer. It was Kyrie's latest acquisition, and Tom wasn't absolutely sure what she meant him to use it for. It wasn't a classical skewer as such, but it had a skewer in the center and then four, smaller, metal prongs, on the bottom. Kyrie had said something about a TV commercial for it that mentioned roasting a chicken in a standing position. Since Tom couldn't imagine why anyone would want to do what sounded like a convoluted form of medieval torture—at least if the chicken were still alive—he'd thanked her effusively and set the skewer in the wall pocket, determined to forget it.

Now he realized it was a formidable weapon. He turned to the dire wolf, holding the hammer-ax in one hand, and the skewer in the other, and opened his mouth to say something pithy and challenging on the lines of *make my day*. And the smell enveloped him. It was like the smell of a hundred cats in heat; the smell of a thousand unwashed, wet dogs. It filled his mouth, his nostrils, his every pore. It made it impossible for him to think, impossible for him to move.

"Look out," Kyrie yelled and, rising from her defensive position, hit the dire wolf hard across the back of the head with what remained of her portable chair.

Tom felt the teeth clamp on his leg, and screamed, inhaling more of the smell. He knew what he should be doing. He should be attacking the creature, making him back up, allowing Kyrie to go behind him, allowing them both to escape, with Tom guarding the retreat, towards the car and away.

But no matter how much he thought of it, as the feral mad eyes faced Tom's, as the creature growled and snarled and salivated, all Tom could think was that he couldn't move. That the stench enveloping him was some-how preventing his movement.

"Tom, damn it," Kyrie said, her voice high and hysteri-cal. "Do something. We're going to die."

And at that moment . . . there was a voice. It was the voice that Tom had heard in the shower before, the voice of the Great Sky Dragon. It echoed in his mind, filling up all of his senses, so that it was visible sound and scented words, and seemed to touch him all over, as if in an enveloping blanket.

Mine, the voice said. *Mine. Under my protection.*

Like that—with those words—the horrible gagging smell was gone from Tom's nostrils, from Tom's mind. The feel of the Great Sky Dragon's words still echoing in him—seeming to make his very teeth vibrate—Tom stepped forward, and brought the skewer in hard on the creature's eye, thinking only that if he destroyed the brain it might be the same as beheading. But the dire wolf had jumped backward just in time. The tip of the skewer cut a deep gash down the side of his face, while the ax, which Tom had managed to swing as a follow through, cut across his left ear.

The creature screamed. Blood spurted. And through it all, his voice, less powerful than the Great Sky Dragon's but also echoing inside Tom's head and not outside, as voices were supposed to, sounded, *He must pay. He must pay. And he's not yours. He's not Asian. You can't claim him.*

The stench came back, less overpowering, but back, nonetheless. But only for a second. The Great Sky Dragon's voice sounded again, and clearly he was a creature with a very simple philosophy. *Mine,* he yelled. *Mine. I've claimed him.*

The stench vanished. The dire wolf growled. Tom swung forward, skewer and ax swinging. Making a space behind him. "Go, Kyrie, go," he said. "The car, now."

She got up and lurched, behind him, towards the door, while he moved to block the dire wolf from getting to her. The creature wasn't teleporting or giving the impression of teleporting. Whatever it was that the Great Sky Dragon's voice caused, it seemed to cause the dire wolf to become unable to create what, for lack of better words, one must call supernatural effects.

"Come," Kyrie yelled, as she opened the door, and ran full tilt outside. "Come."

"I will," Tom said, kicking the door fully open with his foot, and backing into the open door, still holding the skewer and the ax.

The dire wolf made a jump—a clumsy jump—towards him. There was no Great Sky Dragon voice, but Tom swung at him, hard with the ax, and cut him across the nose.

Kyrie honked the horn, and now Tom turned, thinking it was the most stupid thing he could do, but also that he ran much faster that way. The passenger door of the car was open, and he more threw himself at the opening than ran into it.

His head on Kyrie's shoulder, he reached to close the door, even as she started the car and backed out of the driveway. The dire wolf came running out of the kitchen and chased them. Kyrie turned abruptly, hitting the wolf with the back left wheel and saying, under her breath, "Sorry, it wasn't intentional."

Tom took a deep breath, two. He straightened, and buckled his seat belt. "To whom are you apologizing?"

"You. Him. I don't know. I didn't mean to run him over. Did I run him over?"

Tom looked back at what looked very much like a bleeding dire wolf still chasing them. "I don't think so. Can you go faster?"

She pressed the gas down, taking these little residential back streets at speeds normally reserved for the highway, and breathing deeply, deeply, as if recovering from shock.

It took Tom a moment to realize that it wasn't breathing, it was sobs. "Kyrie," he said, aghast. He'd never seen her cry. He'd never heard her cry before. Not like this.

"I can't help it," she said. "Reaction." She turned again, seemingly blindly. "I thought I was going to die. And then I thought you were going to die and I . . ."

"I thought you were going to die," a voice said from the back. Conan's voice. He popped from the back seat like a deranged jack-in-the-box, and Kyrie slammed on the brakes hard, stopping them suddenly in the middle of a tree-lined street. "I thought you were going to die. You screamed. So I called Himself. I told him I couldn't go in, but I thought the enemy was in there. And then . . . he aimed for your mind and the enemy's mind."

"What the hell?" Kyrie said. And it was all that Tom could do not to turn around and plant his fist in the middle of Conan's smug-looking face.

Instead, he turned around and said, "What are you doing? What do you think you were doing, hiding back there?"

Conan's expression shifted, from smug to sullen. "I

wasn't hiding from you," he said, in the tone that a kid might use to say it wasn't him who drew on the wall. "I was hiding from the dire wolf."

"Oh, that makes it ever so much better," Kyrie said. "Not."

"Just go," Conan said, "He's going to come for us."

"I don't think so," Tom said, looking behind them. "He's not back there, and besides, he knows where we're going to go, doesn't he?"

"Does he?" Conan asked.

"The diner," Kyrie said. And then, softly, "Hopefully, he's not so brazen as to come and attack us in the diner, in the parking lot, in front of everyone."

"Hopefully," Tom said. "Or we'll be dead. I mean, it's not like we can, realistically, stop showing up at the diner."

"No," Kyrie said. She started the car again, going more slowly. "But perhaps once he calms down, he won't be as dangerous? I mean, I get a feeling we pushed him over the edge, and he didn't very well know what he was doing."

"*We* pushed him over the edge?" Tom said. "*We?* What were you doing at the house, anyway? And without telling me. If Rafiel hadn't told me—"

"You should have asked Rafiel what I was doing at the house," Kyrie said. She drove with jagged movements that caused the car to lurch one way then the other. "He called me and told me to meet him there. Something about one of his relatives repairing the house. And then he wasn't there."

"He called you?" Tom asked. He remembered Rafiel coming into the diner, his confusion at not finding Kyrie in the bed-and-breakfast. He didn't even want to think that Rafiel might be working with the dire wolf. If Rafiel was . . . If Rafiel had betrayed them . . .

"He called me on my cell phone. Told me to meet him at the house ASAP. I thought it was a little weird, but he said he had everything ready to go right then, so I showered and went."

Tom groaned. Either Rafiel was mind-manipulated, or Rafiel had defected to—for lack of better words—the dark side. Either way, it could not be good. "But . . ." he said. "But . . ." And swallowed hard.

"The only weird thing," Kyrie said, "is that his words seemed to have . . . oh, I don't know how to put it . . . no sound. No vocalization."

Tom found his forehead wrinkling in worry before he could think that he was worried. That didn't feel right. Kyrie's purse was at his feet, as it normally was when she was driving. He bent down and picked it up. "May I get your cell phone?" he asked. He didn't like to reach into her purse without an invitation.

"Sure," she said, as she turned onto Pride Street. Five minutes from The George.

He reached into the little pocket on the front lining where she normally kept her phone. He picked it up. "He called you on this cell phone?" he said. It wouldn't turn on, there was no battery. So, he grabbed his cell phone from his pocket, and swapped the batteries. Then he turned the phone on and looked through calls received.

"Yeah."

"When?"

"This morning, almost right after you left, I think. I was

lying in a patch of sun and unable to sleep, and then the phone rang."

Tom looked up and down through the list of numbers. The latest call the phone showed was three days before. He took a deep breath, and waited till she pulled in the parking lot of The George to speak. He wasn't sure what telling her while she was driving would do.

"Kyrie," he said. "There's no record of any such call."

"What?" Kyrie asked. She pushed the parking brake down with her foot, as she reached blindly for her cell phone. "Let me see that."

She pulled the cell phone from Tom's nerveless hands, and went to the menu and calls received, and paged, frantically, up and down the list.

She realized she was shaking violently, and she put the phone down on the seat, very slowly, then very slowly lowered her head towards the wheel, until she rested her forehead on it.

"You mean the whole call . . ." she said, at last. "You mean, he just reached into my mind." For some reason the thought made her physically ill. Reaching into her head to trick her seemed like the worst violation possible. "How could he? How?"

"I don't know. I think he has some sort of mind power," Tom said, hesitantly. He laid his palm gently on her shoulder, as if he were afraid of touching her. But when she didn't protest, he enveloped her in his arms and pulled her to him. "I'm sorry, Kyrie. I think this is worse than anything we faced before."

For a moment, it comforted her, that he held her like that, tightly, against his body. He was still naked—she was quite sure he had forgotten that—and his skin smelled of the hotel's soap overlaid with sweat from fear and fight. It was not unpleasant. His hair was loose—as it always was after he shifted back and forth. He kept a package of hair ties in the glove compartment of the car, in a kitchen drawer at home, and in one of the supply rooms in the diner. His hair brushed her face, softly, like silk.

And for a moment—for just a moment, as her breath calmed down—this felt good and protective and healing. She had a sense that she belonged to him—that she was his, that Tom was somehow entitled to hold her like this and that he—as scattered and lost as he'd been most of his life—he was somehow protecting her. As he'd protected her, or tried to, in that kitchen.

But slowly the thought intruded that he was just looking after her because he looked after everyone—Old Joe, Conan, Not Dinner, and even Keith and Anthony to an extent. Tom seemed to think it was his duty, his necessary place in life, to go through it helping everyone and everything. And this made his arms around her, his soothing voice, the hand now gently stroking her hair and cheek, utterly meaningless.

She shrank back, laughing a little, disguising her embarrassment at having been, momentarily, emotionally naked. "You must put clothes on," she said. "What if someone looks in the car and sees me sitting here with two naked guys?"

"I don't have clothes," Conan said from the back seat, his voice dull and seemingly trying to be distant, as if he were apologizing for being present during their embrace. He hardly needed to.

Tom pulled back. He took a deep breath, as if he needed to control himself, and she didn't look down to see if he needed to control himself in that sense. It wouldn't help to know he'd been embracing her out of automatic pity but that lust had mixed in. She wanted to know he had held her for other reasons—she wasn't even sure what reasons she wanted it to be. Perhaps because he felt so incomplete without her, that he had to hold her and protect her to be able to hold and protect himself. She wanted him to think of them as a unit, she thought. As belonging. And perhaps that was, ultimately, her greatest foolishness, that she so desperately wanted to belong with someone. Not to. She had no fancy to be owned or restricted in that way. For much too long, growing up, she had belonged to the state of North Carolina—had been in effect the child of the state—that she did not want to belong to anyone. But she wanted to belong with someone, to be part of a group. Not at the mercy of passing bureaucrats and their whims, but able to contribute and be taken into account by a group.

She'd thought she was part of that. Even days ago, if you had asked her, she'd have said that she and Tom and Rafiel were just that sort of group. A *you and me against the world* group.

But now the dire wolf could get in her mind and force her own friendship for Rafiel to betray her. And Tom was determined to protect the world and its surroundings. "There's clothes under the seat," she told Conan. "Get some for Tom too. We stuff them there, when we go shopping. We buy extra stuff, I wash it and stuff it down there. From the thrift shop, so they're clean but worn."

"Worn is fine," Conan said, as he passed, over Kyrie's shoulder, a grey pair of sweat pants and a red sweat shirt to Tom.

"I think you should go shower," Kyrie said. "Both of you. I'll go inside"—she made a head gesture towards the diner—"and hold the fort, while you guys make yourselves decent."

Tom frowned a little but then nodded. "If he comes in the diner—" he said.

"I'll call, okay? I don't think he's going to do much in front of every customer at the tables, truly."

"You don't know that," Tom said. "He could reach in and touch your mind. Like he did before. We don't know how many minds he can touch. He could make everyone in the diner ignore him, as he kills you or dismembers you."

"I'll call you. I'll call you as soon as he comes," she said, almost frantically, wanting to go back to the diner, which right now represented routine and normalcy, and to be allowed to go on with life, to forget that someone out there—someone who didn't wish them well—had the power to reach into her mind and make her hear and think things that had never happened.

"I don't know what the owner is going to think, of my keeping going to the bedroom with different guys and coming out in new clothes," Tom said, under his breath, but Conan only gave him this unfocused, uncomprehending look, as if he were talking about some different planet, or something so strange that Conan's mind couldn't begin to understand it.

Tom was fairly sure this was not true. After all, the man had grown up in Tennessee, no matter how strange his parents' culture might have been. He'd watched the same shows, read the same newspapers—generally speaking— and listened to the same music—well, perhaps more country and western—that Tom listened to.

And yet, he genuinely seemed to have no idea why Tom going to his rented room to shower with different guys accompanying him might make the owner of the bed-and-breakfast a little uncomfortable.

"She's going to think I'm running a business," Tom added, under his breath. But it was all pointless: his worrying and Conan's—had to be deliberate—lack of comprehension. They met no one as they walked along the oak-floored hallways of the bed-and-breakfast. The room, when Tom opened it, was as Kyrie must have left it—with the bed coverings thrown half back, and her hair brush thrown on top of the clothes.

Almost by instinct—he certainly had not had time to get used to this—before Tom opened the door fully, he opened it a crack and put his hand in the opening, as if to catch a baseball. Seconds later a furry warm ball hit it, and clung to his wrist with sharp little needle claws. Tom laughed, as he brought the creature up and held him against his chest. "Hello, Not Dinner. Foiled again." Then he opened the door fully, allowing Conan into the room, and closing it and locking it afterwards. "You can shower first," he said. And realized that Conan was barefoot. "Did you leave your shoes . . . ?"

"Somewhere in the parking lot," Conan said, sullenly.

"I left mine in the diner, near the entrance," Tom said, looking down at his toes. "Well . . . I didn't even realize I was barefoot till now. We get used to this stuff."

"Yeah," Conan said, and went into the shower, to emerge, just seconds after, wearing the same clothes but looking far cleaner, his odd crest of hair standing up. Tom realized in losing his left arm, Conan had lost the red dragon tattoo he'd once had upon his left hand. He wondered if the new one would grow in with the same tattoo. No, it couldn't. That would require something uncomfortably like magic. Then would Conan have to go and tattoo the same image on the back of his hand?

Putting Not Dinner down on the bed, where he proceeded to attack some dust mites floating on a ray of light, Tom got up, wondering what part of Conan's belonging to the dragon triad was volitional, and what part was enforced. He remembered his saying that his parents had more or less turned him over to the Great Sky Dragon because he was a dragon and therefore belonged to him. Belonged. What a very strange word to use.

And Tom knew he should be furious with Conan for allowing the Great Sky Dragon to aim for Tom's mind once more. But he'd aimed for the dire wolf's mind. And Tom had no delusions. He knew that if the Great Sky Dragon hadn't spoken in his mind, the chance was good that he'd now be dead. Dire wanted to kill him. And he couldn't defend himself against Dire. That much was clear.

Tom turned the water on high and hot, and opened a new soap from the little basket of toiletries. Stupid as it was, he, who had for so long washed himself with soap from dispensers and with a combination of wet and dry paper towels at an endless succession of public restrooms throughout the land, felt an almost physical repulsion at the thought of using the same soap Conan had used. The soap Kyrie used, sure. No problem there. She was his, he was hers, in all but the legal marriage sense. He couldn't imagine life without Kyrie and he very much hoped she could not imagine life without him.

But the idea that Conan had used that soap and that there were sloughed-off, Conan skin cells in it made his flesh crawl. Which was stupid, he thought, as he washed himself almost vengefully, under water so hot that it made his skin sting. Conan looked clean enough, and he seemed to be a nice guy.

And then Tom realized it was the thought of the intimacy of belonging. Families used the same bathroom, the same soap. He wasn't ready to admit Conan into his family—if he would ever be. Conan belonged to the Great Sky Dragon—that creature that had now made free of Tom's mind, twice, without a welcome mat.

While the thought that the Great Sky Dragon could make free of his mind didn't fill him with the same horror that having her mind manipulated by the dire wolf seemed to fill Kyrie—understandably, because all the Great Sky Dragon had done was talk in his mind, not manipulate him into believing things that weren't true. Also, arguably, because the Great Sky Dragon, at least at this very moment, didn't seem to feel like killing Tom—it made him feel uncomfortable and used.

He'd brought his underwear, jeans, a T-shirt and socks into the bathroom with him. He'd packed—as he always did—a half-dozen rubber flip-flops, bought at the end of summer. He'd wear those till he could get back to his boots. He could lend a pair to Conan, as well. They wouldn't be much worse than his stupid elastic shoes. He dressed in the bathroom and emerged into the bedroom, with words on his lips which summed up the whole issue he had with this situation: "I don't belong to the Great Sky Dragon," he said, defiantly, saying the words aloud—even though he knew it would bother Conan.

Conan had been playing with Not Dinner—or at least submitting mutely to having his sleeve climbed, and his hair and ear played with. He looked up, startled, and frowned at Tom, "You have to," he said. "You're a dragon."

"I'm not a dragon like you," Tom said forcefully, almost viciously. "In case you haven't realized, we don't look at all alike. As dragons. My body type is completely different. *I* am like one of those dragons that Vikings used to carve in the front of their ships. Perhaps there was once some organization I belonged to, like you belong to the Great Sky Dragon. But I don't belong to him. Or to you."

He felt vaguely guilty saying this, as if he were proclaiming the superiority of Nordic dragons over Asian dragons. In truth, he didn't feel like that at all. He was sure the Asian dragons were far more adept at surviving, for one. Look at how they had an organization that looked after them. And look at how their legends had managed to convince people that they were good and righteous—while

all the European dragons had managed to do was simultaneously convince people that they were dangerous and
that they slept on massive hoards of gold. Thereby creating perfect conditions for people to hate them and to steal
from them—to take their valuables and proclaim themselves heros in doing this.

He wondered if the hoard and treasures were true, and
then thought that if shifters really lived as long as Old Joe
claimed—as long as the Great Sky Dragon appeared to
have been alive—then it could very well be true. If you
looked at the panorama of your life as covering hundreds or
thousands of years, then everyone got to live in interesting
times. Every long-lived shifter's life could cover wars and
revolutions and endless upheavals. And gold often saw
you through all of those. So why not hoard?

"It doesn't matter," Conan said. "It doesn't matter if
you are an Asian dragon or not. You are a dragon. You're
a child of the . . . of the G . . . of Himself."

Tom frowned at him. That was what he had wanted to
fend off, he realized. Not the fact that the triad dragons
were Asian—he really couldn't care less about that. What
he wanted to fend off, more than anything, was Conan's—
and seemingly the Great Sky Dragon's—belief that Tom
belonged to him from birth. That Tom had no choice in
this matter.

Tom had never been good at obeying. His inability to
obey his parents, his teachers, his counselors or his
advisors had made his—and probably his parents'—lives
living hell long before he had turned into a dragon and
been kicked out of the house. He always felt like, should
someone tell him to go one way, he must immediately go

the other. It was something deep within himself, something he was aware of but didn't feel he could change without becoming someone else—without dying, in a way.

And now this organization he didn't like or trust, this organization that was involved in criminal activities, and whose code of honor was as quirky as that of any mafia throughout history, wanted to claim him. He shrugged, as if to throw back their imagined weight from his shoulders, and picked up a hair tie from the packet he'd left on top of the dresser. Confining his still-damp hair into a pony-tail, he said, jerkily, "I am not his child. And even if I were, that wouldn't mean I was *his*. That I *belonged* to him."

Yet Conan had allowed himself to be mutely handed over to this organization by his dutiful parents. Tom thought it was better—and more humane—to force your kid out on the street at gunpoint, as his father had done, than to hand him over to the designs and whims of a supernatural creature who probably would care nothing for him.

He saw Conan's small despondent shrug, which seemed to signify he couldn't do anything about either Tom's belonging to the Great Sky Dragon or Tom's stub-bornness, and Tom said, "I am my own."

And in the next moment wondered how that could be true, when the Great Sky Dragon had the ability to enter his mind and make him hear his thoughts.

Rafiel kept his eye on Keith's friend as he moved around the tables taking orders. He'd never really had a job as a waiter, but he had helped Alice sometimes when she worked at this same diner, back when it was The Athens. It was amazing how it came back to him and, except for the fact that Tom's menu was far more elaborate than that of the old Athens, and that he wasn't really desperate to get tips to supplement his income, it was just like being back in time.

His gestures came back, too—the broad wipe at the table before taking orders—the scribbling of orders on his pad, the carrying of the trays, one-handed and perfectly balanced.

As he approached the table where a new customer had just sat, he did a double take. The customer had pulled her—fake-fur fringed—hood back from her face, and was unbuttoning her black, knee-length knit outer coat. Underneath it, it was Lei, from the aquarium, with her long, sleek black hair, her exotic features, and her very shapely body, highlighted by a miniskirt and tight sweater. At least, Rafiel thought, as he ran his gaze over her legs— purely out of concern, of course—she was wearing thigh-high leather boots. He still didn't understand how anyone could, voluntarily, wear a miniskirt in this weather, but then again he couldn't really understand how anyone could voluntarily wear any skirt in cold weather. He'd consider it a peculiarity of the female brain—like inability to feel your legs from the thigh down—were it not for all those proud Scots and their kilts.

"Hello," he told Lei, smiling at her, and giving the table a quick wipe. "How may I help you?"

She was staring at him, openmouthed, just like he had grown a second head, or possibly stood on his head, and it took him a moment to realize in what capacity she had met him, and what she must think of him. A brief, lunatic impulse commanded him to tell her that he was his own underachieving twin, but this he conquered, forcefully. Instead he told her, "I'm just giving some friends a hand for an hour or so. I haven't changed jobs."

Lei turned very red, as though she'd been thinking exactly that, then grinned. "Oh well," she said. "I had been thinking that the police in Goldport must pay very poorly if their officers moonlight in diners."

"Nah. I'm friends with the owners and they had to go out for a little bit." *Please let it be only a little bit.* He gave her his best dimpled smile, which had made weaker women melt. "So, what will you have?"

"Just . . . a hot chocolate," she said, looking at the menu then folding it and returning it to its holder on the edge of the table. "I was just walking by and I felt like coming in." She shrugged. "I guess the aquarium being closed, and my not having to go to work left me with this great need for human company or something."

Rafiel's curiosity peaked at the mention of her having had an impulse to enter the diner. But a deep breath brought him no whiff of shifter-scent. Only the smell of washed female flesh and some perfume that was deep and spicy and hot, and probably cost upward of his salary per ounce and likely sold under some name like Dagger or Treason or something of the sort. And then, after all, people did sometimes feel an impulse to just go in somewhere without being shifters or smelling the specialized pheromones that infused the diner. He shrugged. "Right. I'll bring it to you, right away."

He went back, and drew the hot chocolate, and got a baleful look from Keith. "Do you have any idea how long Tom is going to be? People are ordering souvlaki, and I'm sure he keeps some pre-made, somewhere, but I can't seem to find it."

"No clue," Rafiel said, as he added a dollop of whipped cream atop the cup of rich, dark hot chocolate. "Sorry. But they should be back soon. They said it was only for a few minutes."

"Right," Keith said, but in a tone that implied he didn't believe it. He lowered a basket of fries into the oil, causing a whoosh that seemed deliberate and, somehow, irritated. "You know, I wasn't intending on having to work. I just came in to introduce Summer to you guys, and now here I am, working."

"I know," Rafiel said, trying to be patient. Sometimes it was hard to remember that Keith was younger than all of them. And sometimes it was much too easy. "I know. I'm sure they didn't mean to go out either. Quite sure."

Keith made a sound under his breath. It could probably be translated as "harumph." Rafiel couldn't answer that in any way, so he turned his back, and took Lei her hot chocolate, which she received with a wide smile, as if he had just fetched her fire from the mountain.

"I don't suppose you can sit and talk?" she said.

He looked around, and at the moment there wasn't any customer clamoring for his attention, so he shrugged. "Not sit," he said. "But I suppose I could talk a little. It isn't as though I'm going to get fired. It's just if I stand, at least anyone who needs something knows whose attention to get."

"Oh," she said. And "Yes."

He smiled. "So, what do you need to talk about?" He wondered about her brittle frailty and once more it seemed to him as though she were trying to make a play for his attention—whether his romantic attention or his friendship, he couldn't tell.

All other things being equal, he would have discouraged her. It was often easier to get rid of prospective romantic interest before the first date than after. It saved the girl some hurt feelings and him some of that fury to which hell could not compare.

However, Lei was involved—by working in the aquarium, if nothing else—in the case with the sharks. And Rafiel was never sure when a romantic come-on was just that, or an attempt by an otherwise awkward bystander to tell him something about a case in progress.

"It's not so much that I need to talk," she said, and looked down at her hands, one on either side of the hot chocolate cup. They were nice hands, the nails clean of any polish or shine, but carefully clipped and filed into neat ovals. "I just . . . I was wondering how long till the aquarium is allowed to open again, because, you know, the thing is that . . . Well, I know I'm only an intern of sorts, and I'm there to study as much as to work, but you know, they pay me, and I count on that payment to help make my tuition at CUG."

She looked up at him, intently, pleadingly almost. Her eyes were black, which was something Rafiel had never seen. You always heard talk of black eyes, but you never saw them. Instead, you saw eyes that were deep, dark brown, or something like that, but never that pure black, unreflective.

"We are working as fast as we can," Rafiel said. Except, of course, when he wasn't, like right now, when he was waiting tables, while he should have been visiting people who'd been around the aquarium a week or so before the first human remains were found—around when they'd calculated the first victim had fallen or been thrown into the shark tank. And selling his superiors on the need to do that would be interesting enough—though no one was likely to ask him for a very close accounting of his time for a week or so—because after all it would seem more logical to investigate who had keys to the aquarium, and who might have gone there since it had been closed to the public and in the middle of a snowstorm.

The second corpse—or the bits of it the sharks hadn't eaten—had shown up in an aquarium closed to the public. The suspects should, obviously, be the employees or—if his superiors ever found out that Rafiel had abstracted a key—Rafiel himself.

Only, having found out how easy it was to steal a key, Rafiel could argue—was arguing, with himself, just as he would with his superiors should they call him on it—that other people might have done so. And given his privileged knowledge that there were shifters and that two, maybe three of them, had been to the aquarium around the time of the first crime, he thought it made perfect sense to find out if one of those might have stolen the keys, as he had, and had copies made, and if the crimes were, somehow, being committed as part of a shifter imperative, driven by the animal half of some poor slob with less self-control than Rafiel himself had.

"The police are pursuing enquiries?" Lei said, ironically.

"Well, as a matter of fact the police are," Rafiel said and sighed. "You know"—he wiped at the table in what was more a nervous gesture than anything else—"it's amazing how often those words are true and how often they define most of what I do in my work. We pursue enquiries. We go from place to place and ask questions." He smiled. "All those TV series with heroic detectives who can flourish a gun and threaten a suspect just in the nick of time, or who have the ability to magically assemble pieces of evidence given by some amazing new scientific machine for analyzing skin cells, or whatever, do my job a great disservice. Most of what we do is just . . . patient, slow work. I'm sorry it's affecting your job. I'm sure it affected the job of the poor slob who got killed, also."

"Yes, of course," she said, looking guilty as people had a tendency to when they complained about a murder disrupting their lives and somehow managed to ignore that it had ended someone else's life. "It's just . . ." she shrugged. "Of course I'm very sorry for the man. The TV says he was an out-of-town salesman, or something, but you know, I still need to work and I need a paycheck."

"We will solve the murders as fast as we can," Rafiel said. "Trust me, I don't want some lunatic at large, pushing people into shark tanks."

She looked up at him and her curiously opaque black eyes managed to project an impression of innocence and confusion. "Are you sure that is what happened? I mean, couldn't people just have fallen in? Or . . . or jumped in, even?"

"Oh, sure," he heard himself say. "The first one, maybe. But this one? With the aquarium closed? Are you honestly suggesting that someone took it into his head to steal keys to the aquarium and go in to commit suicide by shark? What kind of person does that? Given how cold it was, it would have made more sense for him to stay outside and let himself die from hypothermia. Alternately, to jump from a very high building. But jump into a tank full of creatures with sharp teeth? Who views that as an easy way out?"

"Well, not easy, perhaps, but quick," she said, hesitantly. "Or perhaps they just were drunk, and dropped into the tank? Who knows?"

"Who knows indeed?" he said, thinking that it was very clear that Ms. Lei Lani knew less than nothing. "Do you often have drunken visitors who take the trouble of copying keys and come in after hours?"

She opened her mouth, then closed it, then opened it again. A blush suffused her cheeks. "I don't know why you keep talking about people stealing keys," she said. "It's not needed, you know. When the restaurant company took over the aquarium, they never bothered to change the locks. They're the same we had when the aquarium belonged to the city and was so poor we had fewer fish than your average pet store—or at least that's what I've heard. I wasn't here, back then. But they never changed the locks and some of the . . ." She blushed darker, a very interesting effect on her tanned cheeks. The more he talked to her, the less he was confident identifying her as a native Hawaiian, and the more it seemed to him she was probably Mediterranean or generic white, who just happened to have dark hair and a generally broad face. "You know, some of the guys who work there, like, some of the ones who clean the aquariums, talk about how easy it is to pick the lock, and about breaking into the aquarium and bringing dates there. I don't know if it's true or if they just talk about it to . . . to tweak me. But I know when we clean that observation area just over the shark tank, we often find . . ." She looked away from him, past him, at the front window and the sparse traffic out there on Fairfax. "We often find used condoms in the planters."

Rafiel raised his eyebrows. "Interesting," he said, while trying to sound, in fact, perfectly disinterested. Not that he was. She might simply be repeating salacious tales her male co-workers told each other. Most of the people who worked at the aquarium were high school or college age, and Rafiel knew better than to put any stock in the stories told by males in that age group. On the other hand, they might very well be true. And if true, they would open a whole other front of investigation into these crimes.

At that moment, he heard Keith say, "Oh, thank God, Kyrie, you're here," and looked up to see Kyrie duck behind the counter, looking like she had been crying but noticeably in one piece.

"Excuse me a moment," he said. "I'll go see if they still need me or if I can go back to my real job."

Kyrie saw Tom's clothes and boots at the back entrance to the diner, just under the overhang that prevented them from getting dripped on by the gutters filled with melted runoff. She picked them up, carrying them in with her. In her mind, she could see Tom shuffling out of them, hurrying to her rescue. She'd seen him do this before, and knew that he always kicked off his boots before he shifted.

He was lucky, she thought, that no one had stolen his boots yet, as likely as he was to leave them in all possible—and some distinctly impossible—locations around town. But the thought that he had been in a hurry to come to her rescue remained, as she stepped into the warm atmosphere of the diner, perfumed with the homey scent of fries and redolent of basil, fennel and mint.

Before they'd taken over, there had been an underlying bad smell to the diner, as though the old grease was never completely cleaned from the various surfaces. As they'd found in their grand cleanup and repainting before reopening under their management, this was by and large true. But now all that you could smell in the diner was the clean aroma of well prepared food. Tom was as fanatic about hygiene as he was about helping people who just didn't seem able to make it on their own. People and animals, she thought, as she remembered Not Dinner. Not that she resented Not Dinner. As someone who had long ago accepted it would be neither safe nor sane for her to have children, a pet might be as close as she came to motherhood.

She put Tom's boots on the lower shelf of the space behind the counter, the shelf into which all of them shoved either uncomfortable or too-heavy shoes on occasion—as well as purses, or bags of purchases. She smiled at Keith's enthusiastic and somewhat shaky salutation, and wondered if Keith had been worried about her, or even knew why Tom had left.

Grabbing an apron from beneath the counter, she said, "Tom will be in in just a second, and then you can go."

"Good," Keith said, sounding even more relieved. "You know, I was supposed to bring Summer here, and introduce her to you guys, and then take her out for a movie, or something. I was not supposed to bring her here, duck behind the counter, and leave her all alone. I don't even know where she's gone now." He cast a panicked glance around the tables—of which only five were occupied, and none of them except the one table with the dark-haired woman who was talking to Rafiel, showing anyone even remotely in Keith's age range.

"What does she look like?" Kyrie asked.

"Blond. Wearing a pink coat."

"Maybe she got bored and went for a walk," she said. Privately, she was thinking that if the girl got bored that quickly and went for a walk instead of, say, sitting at the counter and talking to Keith while he worked, she might not in fact be very interested. But she didn't say anything aloud.

She didn't remember being Keith's emotional age. Chronologically, they weren't that far apart. They were both, roughly college age—but Kyrie couldn't remember a time when she had felt so incapable of standing on her own two feet that she needed the props of a group, or of a friendship, or even of a boyfriend. In fact, until very recently, she had none of those. However, Keith clearly needed friends or a girlfriend or something and even in the months she'd known him, she had seen him assume that people liked him or even loved him on very scant evidence. It would be cruel to disabuse him of it.

Instead, she said as tentatively as she dared, "So this was a date?"

He shrugged. "Something like it. I mean, I told her I wanted her to meet some of my friends, but the idea was that I was going to take her to the morning showing of *Monsters of the Deep* at the Imax at the museum, and then we were . . . you know, going for coffee or something."

Ah, yes, Keith, take the girl to the Nature Museum Imax, why don't you? Dazzle and seduce her. She'll never know what hit her, Kyrie thought. After all, who was she to judge the mating rituals of others. It wasn't like she had a great deal of experience with mating or dating. And Keith, being a confirmed geek, was probably following the right tactic in looking for a girl who could share his obsessions. "Sorry to leave you stuck here," she said. "Maybe she's just outside looking at shop windows or something."

"Maybe," he said, sullenly. "But it's not even that. If Rafiel hadn't offered to help, I don't know how I would have managed both the tables and the cooking."

"Well," Kyrie said. She looked up to see that Rafiel was indeed wearing the red apron of The George, and smiled despite herself. What would the police force think of its officer moonlighting in this way? "I'm glad he stayed, then."

At that moment, Rafiel excused himself and sailed towards her across the diner, notebook in hand, a smile on his all-too-handsome face. "So glad you're here and okay," he said, in an undertone that couldn't be heard by anyone but Keith. "Are the two guys okay, too?"

"Yeah. They're showering," Kyrie said. "They'll be here any moment, or at least Tom will." And then, rapidly,

"Rafiel, Tom says you didn't call me and ask me to meet you at my place?"

"Huh?" Rafiel said. "No, I didn't. I went by the bed-and-breakfast to get the key and when you weren't there, I came here to get Tom's. That's it."

She had known it before, but hearing it now, made her heart sink. Hearing that Rafiel had never called, confirming absolutely that it must have been the dire wolf playing mind games brought on a slight shake, and caused her to reach for the counter for support. She must also have gone pale, because Rafiel said, "What's wrong?"

She told him, rapidly, in just slightly above a whisper. When she finished, she realized that Keith too was staring at her. "You're saying this thing was in your mind? That it made you think things had happened?"

Kyrie nodded.

"Wow," Keith said. "That's like some supervillain. Much worse than the last time." He sounded vaguely fascinated and excited about it.

"You know, Keith," Rafiel started. "This is not—"

"I know, I know, it's not a game or a play. It's the true thing, and it's true for all of you. But the idea . . . It's just cool. So, how are you guys going to defeat him?"

"I don't know," Kyrie said, as she looked over Rafiel's shoulder towards the door, where the bell tinkled indicating someone had come in. Her heart skipped a beat, and it seemed to her that her breath caught in her throat.

The man who had come in was not wearing a silvery turtleneck or black pants. He was rather more elaborately dressed, in an impeccably cut pair of grey trousers and a button-down silver shirt mostly covered by a blazer that must be made of the finest fabric available and fashioned by master tailors. But he was undeniably the same creature who had just fought it out with her and Tom in their kitchen.

"But he has just come in."

Kyrie stared at the dire wolf—Mr. Dire—in his neat attire, as he made his way between the tables, straight at her. Tom's fears came back to haunt her.

What if Dire reached into her thoughts and made her follow him somewhere he could kill her? What if he reached into the minds of the ten or so people in the diner and made them not see or not remember anything as he dragged her off, or even savaged her right here?

She remembered Tom hitting him repeatedly with the meat-tenderizing ax and the skewer, but Dire showed no sign at all of having been cut, or hurt in any way. His skin looked smooth, flawless, with only the shadow of beard marring its otherwise golden complexion. Had he been cut? Had that been an illusion? Or was this the illusion?

The counter had a series of bar stools on the far end, away from the grill and stove. These were rarely used during the day, though they were often occupied at night by single males who came in for their dinner, or by people who couldn't find room at the tables and booths. At this time, just before the dinner rush, they were all empty—a line of chrome and vinyl stools, fixed in a silent row.

Dante Dire flowed into one of these, straddling it. He

smiled at Kyrie, revealing perfectly shaped and perfectly human teeth. She shook herself, realizing that she had been expecting him to reveal the saberlike teeth of his other form. "Could I have a coffee, miss?" he asked, just loud enough for his voice to carry to where she and Keith and Rafiel huddled.

"Don't do it," Rafiel whispered. "I'll take care of it."

But Dire smiled mockingly, and looked straight at Kyrie as he said, "Come on. It's not like I'm going to eat you."

It wasn't as though he was going to eat her, Kyrie thought. He kept telling her that, and perhaps he meant it, or perhaps it was one of those things where people keep denying their deepest thoughts. In either case, what did it matter?

Either he had no intention of killing her—and it seemed to her, now, on cold reflection, that given the time it had taken Tom to come and rescue her, he could easily have finished her before the cavalry arrived—and therefore was merely toying with them, or perhaps giving her some warning of what his true powers were, or he in fact intended to kill her, and had just fallen in the rather bad habit of playing with his food. This last speculation went well with the insanity behind his eyes, and with the resemblance that he seemed to show to some of the crazier Roman emperors, those who thought they were gods and treated all life around them with the suitable disdain of immortals for mere mortal, ephemeral creatures.

So, he either could spirit her away from here, or kill her right here, without suffering any consequences, or he couldn't. In either case, it seemed to her it didn't make any difference to let Rafiel serve him. No difference, that is, except to make him despise her by thinking her a coward. And whether he intended to kill her or not, having him think worse of her would probably make it easier for him to treat her badly.

"No, I'll take care of it," she told Rafiel, as she poured a coffee, grabbed a bowl of creamers and a handful of sugars from beside the coffee maker, and set it on the counter beside Dire.

This—or the fact that despite herself her hand trembled as she set the coffee before him—seemed to amuse him. "Thank you," he told her. "I take my coffee black."

She nodded to him and started to walk away, but he said, "Stay!"

The voice was authoritative enough that she stopped walking and turned around.

"Stay," he repeated. "I think it's time I talked to you and explained what is going on."

"You don't need to," she said, her voice hollow. "You don't have to." She wasn't sure she wanted to know what Dante Dire thought was going on—at any rate she had a feeling his narrative would be highly colored and personal, and not factual or dispassionate.

"I want to," he said. "Look, it's like this . . ." He paused and took a sip of his coffee and his eyes focused to the side and behind her. Kyrie knew, without turning to look, that he was looking at Rafiel and Keith who had, doubtless, abandoned the lit stove and all other duties to come and stand beside her, as if their mere presence could protect her against this ancient and powerful creature. She had to repress an impulse to giggle, as well as an impulse to turn around and shake her head at them for being ridiculous. Instead, she looked at Dire, her eyebrows raised.

Dire looked from one to the other of the men, then back again at her. "Tell the ephemeral one to leave," he said. "This is shifter business. Not his. I want to talk but only to those who might understand it."

Kyrie froze. She heard Keith draw breath, and she knew he was getting ready to make some protest. She was almost relieved when it was Rafiel who spoke: "He's our friend. He has saved our lives in the past. There is no reason for us to banish him from any conversation. We trust him. He's one of us."

Dante Dire looked up. The gaze which he bent upon Rafiel was so coldly calculating that Kyrie felt as if she were frozen by proximity. "He is not one of us," Dire said, letting his eyes drift just enough to indicate he was surveying Keith disdainfully. "He can never be one of us. Nor can he ever truly understand us. Those of his kind who pretend to understand or like our kind, are only waiting to slip the dagger in."

Kyrie opened her mouth, in turn, to speak, but Dire looked at her. "You are young," he said. "The young make mistakes. I am not young and I am not going to suffer for your mistakes."

"But—" Rafiel said.

"We don't really want to hear what you have to say," Kyrie said, finding her voice. "We don't know that you'd tell us the truth. So far you've attacked us, nothing more. We don't see why we should trust you now."

He looked at her, eyes half closed. Slowly, slowly, his lip twitched upwards on the right side, as though she was a particularly clever child saying some interesting nonsense. "I have not attacked you," he said, didactically. "I have tested you. And having tested you, I've decided you are worthy of being told the truth. There are many of our kind," he said. "A great many more born than ever survive to their twentieth birthday let alone their hundredth. Some are killed by their own stupidity and others . . . find ways to die. Few find comrades worthy of them, or fight, as they should, for other shifters and themselves. Those that do are interesting. Interesting enough to deserve to be told . . . some things they should know."

"I don't really care if you find us interesting," Kyrie said, thinking that, on the contrary, she cared a great deal. She could feel his interest in them being exactly the same as the interest of a kid in the bugs he burns with a magnifying glass. And she didn't like it. But she would be damned if she was going to let him see the cold pit of fear in her stomach. "And I don't know what you have to say that we might want to hear."

He toyed with one of the bright pink packages of sweetener that she had left by his side on the counter. He had incongruously large hands, which looked calloused, as if he normally engaged in repetitive manual labor. Agile fingers with slightly enlarged knuckles. Did shifters get arthritis in their old age? And what had he meant about fewer shifters living to be a hundred? How old was Dire, after all? Oh, he changed into a prehistoric, long-extinct animal, but that might not give any indication of how old he himself might be. After all, Tom changed into a mythological being. And it wasn't as though Tom was mythological. Though he often could seem highly improbable.

"You want to hear what I have to say," Dire said. "Because otherwise you'll die from not knowing it. Already, you've broken the rules of our species. You can plead ignorance, and given enough good will, we might listen to you. But you have to show good will. You have to show a willingness to listen."

"So our special circumstances can be taken into consideration?" Rafiel said, ironically. "By a benevolent judge?"

This time Dire's look at him was amused. "Something like that," he said. "You should understand my point. I'm a policeman of sorts myself. And he"—he pointed a long, square-tipped finger at Keith—"is outside my jurisdiction."

"Well, if what you have to tell us is essential to our survival, then shouldn't we wait for Tom to hear it?" Rafiel said, challengingly. And, bringing up Tom before she could, made Kyrie feel guilty that she hadn't done it first.

But Dire shook his head, and shrugged, dismissively. "The dragons look after themselves," he said. "He's a shifter, but not my problem. The old daddy dragon has made it clear that your friend is one of his fair-haired boys and that I can't touch him no way no how, so why bother? He's protected or not, and if anyone does spank him, it will be his own kind. This is what I meant when I said there are things you must learn, before you get in worse trouble. There is nothing—nothing I can do to him, without precipitating a war between dragons and other shifters, the likes of which hasn't been seen on this Earth for thousands of years. I have no wish to see another one of those. The record of the last one still echoes through the legends of the ephemerals. Another one might very well destroy their puny civilization." He grinned suddenly, disarmingly. "And their civilization makes our lives much too comfortable to be allowed to vanish without a trace."

"Uh," Rafiel said, as though trying to figure out what to say.

"Fine, I'll go," Keith flung. "Being ephemeral and all, I'd better make sure that the stove doesn't catch fire. All I have to say is that Tom had better come in and look after it, as I'll still be close enough that I might, accidentally, catch wind of this highly forbidden knowledge, and we can't have that, can we?"

Kyrie wanted to turn around and apologize to Keith, but she also wanted to know what Dire had to say. She was starting to suspect that, biased or not, it would be informative. There did seem to be way too much that they didn't, in fact, know. Like how long their kind lived. Or the story of their relations with the rest of the human race. And it was becoming clear to her, more so than it had been when they'd last tangled with the dragon triad, that there was more to shifters than little groups of them struggling to survive, or loners like Old Joe.

She heard Keith retreat towards the stove, as Dire said, "Now, I'm one of the oldest shifters currently alive—"

Tom came in, followed by Conan, and surveyed the diner with a dispassionate look. Only a dozen people, in all, and all of them eating. "I think table six and eight could use coffee warm-ups," he told Conan, and instinctively looked around for Kyrie, because Kyrie was usually very good with refilling people's coffee and it wasn't like her to ignore the need for warm-ups. He found her and Rafiel behind the counter, at the point they were furthest from the customers at the table. Facing them was . . . He felt his mouth fall open, and the dragon struggle within, attempting to make him shift into his bigger, more aggressive form.

He'd come here, as they'd feared he'd come. He'd come here and tried to . . . He didn't even know what Dire was trying to do, but he was talking to Rafiel and Kyrie, and it seemed to Tom that if this creature was talking to Rafiel and Kyrie, then it must have them under some kind of mind control, because it was impossible that his friends had taken such complete leave of their senses as to listen to him like that. Wasn't it? Shouldn't it be?

He ducked rapidly under the counter, to the other side, and started towards them, but Keith grabbed his arm. "No use, old friend," he said. "That's a conference for non-dragon shifters only. I'm excluded because the bastard says I'm ephemeral, whatever that means. And you're excluded because you're the Great Sky Dragon's pet and the old bastard doesn't want to start a war. Is this the creature who fought you, outside the aquarium? He didn't seem so afraid of causing a war then."

"No," Tom said. "He didn't."

Conan, who had ducked behind the counter also, and was putting his apron on, said, "But then he didn't know Himself was protecting you personally."

Tom bit his tongue, so as not to tell Conan what Himself could do with his personal protection. He suspected if he were to name the exact unlikely anatomical feat he would like to see the Great Sky Dragon perform, it would only cause poor Conan to become speechless. Possibly forever. He couldn't even say the creature's name. How could he possibly hope to resist him? So, instead, he said, "And?" to Keith, instead of to Conan.

Keith shrugged. "He's apparently issuing some sort of warning to them about my kind and your kind, or whatever. He says he's a policeman, so perhaps he thinks he's Rafiel's colleague."

It was clear to Tom that Keith was offended at being kept out of the conference and he wanted to tell him that this was a fraternity he should count himself greatly lucky to be excluded from—that it was better to be excluded than to be claimed by old, amoral creatures. And he was sure if he said it, it would have no more effect than to have told his young, bereft self that it was better to be kicked out of the house with exactly a bathrobe to his name than to be handed over to a criminal, or at best an extra-legal organization by doting and dutiful parents.

So instead he turned, to rummage under the counter. He found his boots there, and wondered whether Rafiel or Kyrie had taken care of that. He put them on, laced them, then put his apron on. Conan was already among the tables, giving warm-ups and taking other orders, or drawing tickets. But he kept looking over his shoulder at Tom, as if afraid Tom was about to do something stupid.

And Tom, who felt a great roil of anger boiling at the pit of his stomach, looked at the three people talking. Talking, as if this were a perfectly normal social occasion, talking as though the dire wolf hadn't tried to kill them just moments before. In the shower, he'd washed and disinfected a wound, halfway up his calf, caused by the monster's teeth. He was sane enough to realize that the creature could have hurt him much worse. It could have bitten his head off. It could have dismembered them all. It could have closed its teeth on his calf, and now Tom would presumably be growing a new foot, just like Conan was growing a new arm, just like . . . But this wasn't rational. This wasn't even sane. He looked at that creature—who showed no sign of their pitched battle—talking to Kyrie, and he wanted to grab another meat-tenderizing hammer and a fresh skewer and renew the wounds he was sure he had made on that impassive, inhuman face.

"I was born a long time ago," Dire said. He looked at Kyrie first, but then up at Rafiel, as though making sure that he, too, was following the story. "It's hard to say exactly when, because, you know, in those days the calendar was different and more"—he flashed a humorless grin—"regional. Limited. The birthday of the god, or the such and such year of the city." Something like a shadow passed across his eyes, as if the visible reflection of all the passing years. "I can tell you it was before Rome. Probably before Rome was founded, certainly before it was heard of in our neck of woods, which was somewhere in the North of Africa—I think. Geography was arbitrary too, and your city, your people, your land, were the only people, the only lands, in the middle of the ocean, where true humans lived."

Rafiel tried to imagine that type of society. He could not. Or rather, he could all too well, but it came from his reading, from movies, someone else's imagination grafted on his own, and he was sure nothing like the real thing. He very much doubted that these people had ever been noble savages, or that such a thing as noble savages existed. On the other hand, he also doubted it was quite as hellish as other movies and books had shown it. In his experience, people were mostly people.

Dire's gaze changed, as though he'd read Rafiel's mind, and so perhaps he had. "I don't know how many shifters there were in the world at that time, but it's been my experience a lot more of us are born than ever survive to reach even human maturity. As I said before, most succumb to the animal desires, when they first change. And then others are the victims of other people's fear, then as now. Now perhaps less, because we are told that shifters don't exist. Back then, they believed we were evil spirits, or the revenge of prey upon their hunters, or other curses, but no one doubted that we existed.

"I was lucky enough to be born in a small village, where my shifting was viewed not as evil, but as a sign of favor from the gods. I was made their priest, and asked to intercede for my people with the wolf gods." He shrugged and again there was that feeling of a dark shadow crossing his eyes, implying to Rafiel that something more had happened.

It would be much like Rafiel saying, "I knew this girl named Alice, and then she died." In the spaces between the words lay all the heartbreak. He found himself feeling an odd tug of empathy towards this man, this creature, who had just declared himself older than time, and he wondered how much of it was true, and how much projected by the mind powers of their foe.

He steeled himself, crossing his arms on his chest, trying to present less of a sympathetic facade, and therefore invite less interference in his thought processes. Kyrie looked impassive, as if she were listening to a story that had nothing to do with any of them.

"It was fine while it lasted, but my people didn't last that long. We were conquered. I think, in retrospect, our first conquerors were Egyptian." He shrugged. "Hard to tell, and I certainly couldn't place it by dynasties. Then there were . . . others." Again the shadow. "And what is a power greatly appreciated in a shaman of the people, is not a quality appreciated in a slave. I shifted. I killed. I ran. I shifted again.

"Through most of history, shifters were neither appreciated nor protected." He showed his teeth in something between menace and grin. "But the truth of it, in the end, is that we scare ephemerals. Our greater powers terrify them. But until we group together there is not much we can do, and we certainly can't exert revenge. Over time . . . we formed such a group. Many of us, most over a thousand years old by the time we met, got together. We formed . . . something like a council of peoples. The council of the Ancient Ones. And we made rules and laws, to defend ourselves. There are many more of them than there are of us, and no matter how long we live, we lack the sheer numbers. So . . . we made rules. One of them is that it is illegal for anyone—even shifters—to kill great numbers of other shifters. Particularly young ones, who cannot have learned to defend or control themselves yet.

"And it is, of course, illegal for ephemerals to go after shifters in any way. These laws are ours." He tapped on his chest. "Our people's. We do not recognize anyone else's right to supersede them or to impose their rules on us."

Rafiel asked. He had to. The memory of those fragments at the bottom of the tank was with him—the idea that his people were causing deaths, causing people to be killed. Shifters like him were killing normal humans. None of Dire's carefully codified laws had anything to do with that. "Can shifters kill . . . other humans?"

Dire laughed, a short, barking sound. "What should we care, then? If our kind kills the ephemerals? Their lives are so short anyway, what should we care if they are shortened a little further. No one will notice and there are too many of them to feel the loss of a few, anyway."

Rafiel saw Kyrie wrap her arms around herself as she heard this, as if a sudden breeze had made her cold, and he said, "And what if the crimes lead the ephemerals, as you call them, to find us, and to go after us? What if the crimes lead to the discovery of the rest of us in their midst? And they turn on us? In these circumstances, you must agree, the security of one of us is the security of all."

"Is it?" Dire asked. "I thought that was why you were a policeman, Lion Boy. Yes, I have investigated all of you— and I thought you were a policeman so that you could keep yourself and your friends safe."

"It's not exactly like that," Rafiel said, and then hesitated, feeling it might not be safe for him to tell the dire wolf that he felt obligated to defend the lives of normal humans as well—that he'd become a policeman because he believed in protecting every innocent from senseless killing.

But before he could say any more, Kyrie spoke up, "You said there was a feud with the dragons? Or a war?"

Kyrie knew Rafiel too well. She knew this dire wolf, this creature talking to them with every appearance of urbane civility, would lose his civility, his compassion, his clearness of mind and word, the minute he thought that one of them wasn't in full agreement with him. She also knew Rafiel's deep-down pride in being a policeman and in his duties and responsibilities to those he served.

He was the third in a family of cops. His grandfather had been a beat cop. His father had been a detective in the Serious Crimes Unit. So was Rafiel. That was the type of tradition that left its mark on the soul and mind. Rafiel hadn't chosen to be a policeman. Rather, he was a policeman, who had simply felt he had to join the force.

And his loyalty to his family—whom Kyrie realized Dante Dire would call *mere* ephemerals—wouldn't allow Rafiel to stay quiet while their lives were deemed expendable by this ancient being who had never met them—and who clearly had no understanding for nor appreciation of normal humans.

She'd heard Rafiel hesitate, and she expected the barrage that would follow. And after that, she knew, it would take axes and skewers again, or worse. She interrupted, blindly, with a question about dragons, which pulled Dante's observant gaze from Rafiel's face, to look at her.

All of a sudden he looked older than he was, and tired. "It was a long time ago," he said. "At first . . . when we formed, dragons were part of our numbers. There were a good number of dragon shifters—in the Norse lands, and in Wales, in Ireland, and all over. And some of them formed part of our council, became Ancient Ones with us.

"I thought your boy dragon was descended from one of these lines—from these great tribes of dragons that lived all over the globe. I thought . . ." He shrugged. "That he was a young one like any other. That he didn't matter."

"And he matters?" Rafiel blurted behind her, still half-bellicose, but at least not openly antagonizing Dante Dire.

Dante shrugged. "Their daddy dragon seems to think he does, even though he doesn't look a thing like his spawn. If he has decided to claim dragon boy, who am I to dispute it? We had a war with them, once, before human history was recorded. Our emissaries ran into his, into his kingdom as he called it. Yes, I see by your eyes that you doubt it, but yes, it was the same being, the same creature. And under him, organized, were the same people—well, some, of course. Some have died, and been replaced. I gather, like the Ancient Ones, he doesn't put much value on anyone until they've proven themselves, only in his case they can't prove themselves until they are over a hundred years old or so. Till then, he counts them as meaning little and being worthless, and he plays his games with them like a child with toys."

"So, is this a game?" Kyrie asked. "That he's playing? With Tom?"

"I don't know," Dire said. He hesitated. "That could be all it is. Your friend could interest him, purely, as a toy, something amusing to play with and to see what he does. Or he could interest him for . . . other reasons. It is not mine to judge. Except that it is clear he's keeping an eye on him through that younger dragon." He pointed towards Conan.

Tom had been on slow boil, anyway, looking at Kyrie sitting there, as if it were normal to talk like a civilized human being with that ancient horror who had been in her mind, who had manipulated her, who had, in fact, violated her thoughts in a far worse way than a violation of her body would have been. He wanted to do something. Like hurl cooking implements at the dire wolf shifter's head. Or perhaps beat him repeatedly with something solid—like, say, the counter top. Or perhaps simply request that he leave the diner.

He crossed and uncrossed his arms, looking towards him—without appearing to—listening to the things he was saying and studiously ignoring Keith's attempts at making Tom take over the stove so that Keith could beg off.

And then he heard the dire wolf say that Conan— hapless, helpless Conan—was not only, as he'd told Tom, an inadequate bodyguard, sent to protect Tom from the

Ancient Ones, but he was, also, somehow, a spy. Or perhaps a listening device. He couldn't stay quiet. He took two steps forward. He put his hand on Kyrie's shoulder, to warn her that he was going to speak, and then he said, "What do you mean he's keeping watch over me? Conan? Yeah, we know Conan is a spy. What of it?"

"Oh, he's more than a spy," Dire said, amused. "He can do things."

Tom frowned. "What can Conan do?"

He saw that Conan, having approached the counter to drop off an order, was standing there, with the order slip in his hand, staring dumbly at Tom and then at the dire wolf, and then back at Tom again.

The dire wolf shifted his attention to Tom and inclined his head slightly, in what might be an attempt at a courteous greeting. Then he looked at Conan and something very much like a contemptuous smile played upon his lips. "Him? I imagine he can't do much. In and of himself. I gather he was recently wounded and those limbs take their sweet time to grow in, when you're that young." His eyes twinkled with malicious amusement. "Who wounded him? You?"

Tom nodded.

"Yes, that would suit the daddy dragon's sense of humor, to send him to guard you, after that. And no, I don't expect he would be any good at it. Certainly no good at all, against someone like me. But unless I'm very wrong, the daddy dragon already has more able forces stationed nearby. He would have sent this creature because he looks helpless and inoffensive, and you, if the thing with the alligator shifter is any indication, have a tendency to take in birds with wounded wings, do you not? So he figured you'd take him in."

"And?" Tom asked, his voice tense as a bowstring, as he shot a look at Conan, who looked ready to drop the order slip on the counter and run screaming into the night. He felt nausea again, the old sense of revulsion at the idea that the Great Sky Dragon knew him; understood him; was playing him.

The dire wolf shrugged and seemed altogether too pleased with what he was about to say. "You see, as you age, you acquire other powers. What a lot of people would call psychic powers, I guess. The ability to enter minds, and to make them think things, or to activate their thoughts . . ."

"Yes, yes, we've gathered that," Kyrie said, mouth suddenly dry.

"I suppose you have," the dire wolf said, and smirked. "But the thing is, you see, that we can also use other, younger shifters, particularly those with whom we have a connection of some sort, as long-distance hearing devices. My guess is that this young one has sworn fealty to the Father of All Dragons, and the Father of All Dragons has, therefore, reached into his mind and made him into his very own listening device. He is listening to us now," the dire wolf bowed courteously in Conan's direction. "I don't know what his game is with you, but I am telling him now that I am staying out of it, and that no harm will come to you through me. None at all. You are his."

Good, the word in the voice Tom had heard before echoed through his head, and suddenly he wondered if that had been what that first touch of the voice, while he was in the shower, had been. An attempt at getting him to admit fealty or subservience to the Great Sky Dragon. Doubtless, that would allow the old dragon to put a spy device directly in Tom's head itself, and not have to bother with Conan. Tom had a strange, sudden feeling that if he had accepted that, Conan wouldn't be alive. He had only crawled back, just in time, to have his boss find himself in need of a pitiful, inoffensive-looking creature. That was the only reason that Conan had been spared.

"Not good," Tom said, making his voice just loud enough to sound forceful, without speaking to the whole diner. "I don't know why the Great Sky Dragon thinks he speaks for me, but he does not. I am not his to either condemn or protect or play games with. You came here to judge me and my friends, and my friends are the only group I owe any loyalty to. If you are going to condemn any of them, Kyrie, Rafiel or Keith, then I demand you condemn me as well," he said. "We are all one. What we did, we did as a group."

He expected . . . oh, he didn't know. Outrage from the Great Sky Dragon. And possibly something more from the dire wolf—rage maybe. Tom could deal with rage right about now, even if he didn't want to have a shifter fight in the diner.

This was not a game. He was not a pawn. And neither was anyone else, here. The sheer denuding of the humanity of everyone, shifter and not, that these old shifters seemed to do, so casually, made Tom want to hit someone. "We are not toys," he said.

There was nothing from the Great Sky Dragon. Not a single word echoed through Tom's mind, and Tom had a moment of strange relief, when he thought he'd set himself free and that the Great Sky Dragon had, somehow, set him adrift. But then the dire wolf threw his head back and laughed so loudly, that a few people turned to look at him.

He brought himself under control with what looked like an effort, reached for a napkin and wiped tears of laughter down his face. "Very funny. Very brave and gallant. No wonder the lady appreciates you, Dragon Boy. You say those things as if you really believed in them. But you know better and I know better. Your elder has claimed you, and in light of your elder's claim, I know you're his, and therefore I am keeping my hands off you. It is not part of my mandate to get people into a war, or to cause trouble for any other ancient shifters. So, I regret to inform you, but you're his, and his you'll remain."

"And what do you intend to do about the rest of us?" Rafiel said. "While there were deaths, as you and the others have felt, they were in self-defense. And as for the young ones who died, it was an accident."

There was a baring of teeth. "I am investigating," he said, slowly. "You know what they say about police work. Most of it is boring and painstakingly slow. I'm going over reports of the case in the local paper. I am looking at the site. I'm making my own determinations." He stood up. From his pocket, he removed the amount of money for the coffee, and carefully laid it on the counter. "I will try to keep shifters from being hurt," he said.

And then he was gone, gliding towards the door, or perhaps teleporting towards it, with a grace so quick and irrevocable that they couldn't have stopped him had they tried.

Tom, on the tip of whose tongue it had been to ask exactly what had happened to the alligator shifter, exactly what this monster might have done to the old friend—the old dependent—that Tom was in the habit of feeding and looking after, was forced to be quiet.

Forced to be quiet, standing there at the counter, looking at his hands slowly clenching into fists. He wanted to scream, or pound the counter. He wanted to shift. And what, with one thing and another, he hadn't taken the time to eat any protein. He hadn't done anything to recover from his last shift. And it didn't seem to matter. He could feel his hands trying to elongate into claws. He could see his fingernails growing.

He stumbled, like one drunk or blind, towards the back door, and outside, stepped into the cold air of the parking lot, suddenly startled that darkness had fallen and that it was snowing again—a steady snowfall, with large flakes. The surprising coldness of the air stopped his fury—or at least acted like a slap in the face, making him take long breaths, and pace a little, stomping his feet, trying to calm down.

He wasn't going to shift. He wasn't going to. As he passed the stove, Keith had called out to him that he needed to go. Tom couldn't leave Keith stuck with this. And while he could, possibly, call Anthony in, if it was snowing again Anthony might be reluctant to come.

He stomped his feet again. There were no windows looking over the parking lot, and the only light came from the two street lamps, which shone, in a spiral of light as though the light were a fracture in the glass of the night, a crack through which something human shone.

There was nothing, Tom thought, blankly. *Only the beast and the night. They resent humans for their light, for their bringing light into the night hours. For their science, for their thought. They resent us. I am human. I might be something else as well, but I'm not one of those. I'm not like them. I am not owned. I don't care if I was born of them. I don't care what unnameable offenses they think they suffered at the hands of those they call ephemerals.*

He stomped his feet again, and walked out to the parking lot, then back again, the snow falling on his head and, he hoped, cooling it. *Shifters are dangerous. Any humans who tried to defend themselves against my kind probably had good reason to. We are dangerous. It's not like we are a harmless and persecuted minority. Oh, there are plenty of those in the world, and the crimes imagined against them are numberless. But no one has to imagine crimes against shifters. No one needs to create grand conspiracy theories to think we control the world or the markets, or even the arts. No. Our crimes are obvious and brutal.*

He put his arms around himself, as he realized he was out without a jacket and that the bitter snow-laden wind was cutting through his sweat shirt to freeze the beaded sweat of anger on his body. *I have met less than twenty adult shifters in my life and half of those were murderers. I cannot, I will not, believe it is wrong for people like Keith to suspect us of intending ill to the rest of them. Clearly this Dire creature intends plenty of ill to normal humans. Clearly. And the others . . .* He shook his head.

"Tom?" Kyrie's voice said, hesitant, from the doorway of the diner. "Tom?"

Rafiel knew a thundercloud when he saw one. He knew that Tom was leaving to deal with anger. He'd been around Tom enough to recognize the signs—as well as the signs that the man was fighting hard not to shift in front of all his customers.

Rafiel could also understand, from the tightening of Kyrie's jaw and the way she looked as if she'd like to bite something in two, as she watched Tom head out the back door, that there might be a storm brewing there.

Had he been an uninterested observer, he might very well have stayed around and convinced both of his friends to act like civilized, mature human beings. He might point out to Kyrie that killing Tom might seem like a really good idea, except that if she should succeed she would spend days not eating and moping about wishing she had him back—and that miracles rarely happened twice. He might point out to Tom that if he wanted a woman with an actual spine he had to allow her to think with her own mind, even if at times her actions seemed strange or ill-advised to him.

But Rafiel wasn't an uninterested observer, and inserting himself into his friends' possible argument seemed to him the worst possible way to bring about a reconciliation. They were all too aware—as he was—that he'd wanted Kyrie for himself. So he would leave them alone and hope they cooled off.

As for Rafiel, he must go interview the people who had signed the guest book at the aquarium the week before the first bones were found. It was probably a quixotic endeavor and a foolish one, to try to find the shifters by following up on the people who had been at the aquarium at one time or another. Surely, it was stupid. He wouldn't have signed that visitors' book, so why should anyone else? Particularly anyone else who was a shifter, who had something to hide and who didn't want to be confronted with the evidence of where he'd been and what he'd been up to.

He wasn't supposed to conduct interviews this late, but then, it was just on five o'clock, the early darkness an artifact of the season, the proximity to the mountains and the impending snowstorm. And these interviews were not, strictly speaking, procedure. In fact, he still wasn't absolutely sure how to justify them to his superiors.

While in his car, heading for the first address listed in the guest book, he dialed his partner at the station. "McKnight?" he said.

"Yeah? Where have you been? We have—"

"Later. I'm following an idea of my own. I was just wondering if you'd do me a favor, and check on the aquarium again. Did anyone do a thorough sweep of that platform above the shark tank?"

"We looked at dirt and prints on the railing and that, yeah," McKnight said. "Well, except the railing seemed to have been cleaned up, but we looked at the floor and all, for all the good it did us. The thing is, you know, it couldn't be just accidental falling in. There's normally a cover there, and it's quite sturdy enough to withstand the weight of an adult falling in. It's only removed to allow the cleaners to get in the tank. At this point, frankly, we're wondering if it's not so much murders as a body disposal system. The coroner hasn't looked at the body yet, so I can't tell you if our boy drowned or was otherwise killed. We might not be able to find out, anyway. Among the things not present seem to be his lungs."

"Yeah," Rafiel said, mostly to stem the flow of words. McKnight was new, and Rafiel was supposed to train him. An endeavor only slightly impaired by the fact that McKnight had just come out of college, with a degree in law enforcement. He was, therefore, to his own personal satisfaction, the highest authority possible on how to solve murders. Rafiel's own training and years of experience were dwarfed by McKnight's learning of the *latest techniques,* the *latest research,* the *latest ways to go about it.*

Which in the end boiled down to McKnight's opinions, nothing else. "This is something different," Rafiel said. "I talked to one of the aquarium employees." Let McKnight think that he had in fact spent the entire day in pursuit of that all-important interview. And let McKnight not guess that he'd been doing double duty as waiter at The George. Though given that he'd interviewed Lei while there, Rafiel thought he could convincingly—if falsely—make a case for having spent his day hiding, in disguise, while he waited for Lei to come in. "And she said not only were the door locks easy to open, but that male aquarium employees were in the habit of bringing dates there. She said that often there were used prophylactics in the planters around that small platform. I don't suppose those have been swept for clues."

McKnight was silent for a moment, which had to count as a miracle in several religions, Rafiel thought. When he came back, it was with less than his normal, self-assured verve. "I don't know about that," he said sullenly. "That platform is actually fairly broad, and the planters are pretty far away from the place where the vic fell or was pushed into the aquarium. So, there's no telling what people might or might not have looked at, that far away."

Rafiel, who had become skilled in the doublespeak employed by McKnight and other young hires, knew what that meant. What it meant, simply put, was that McKnight had been the one in charge of looking all around the area for clues and had decided—from his naturally superior knowledge—that there was no point in looking through the planters. That they were too far away from the area of the crime and that he was, therefore, safe in ignoring them. "I would appreciate it if you'd go over with someone and do a thorough looking over at that area. I don't need to tell you the possibilities it opens, including that of a romantic spat."

"Uh . . . both the vics were male."

"Yes, indeed," Rafiel said, tartly. "And of course, we only know of the male employees using the area as a love nest. However, my information was given to me by a female, and she might not have wished to implicate female employees, don't you think?" He didn't even wish to go into other possibilities with McKnight. "Just go and see what there is to find and how easy the area might be to get into after the place is locked down." And when one hasn't taken the trouble to procure copies of the keys, of course. "I will talk to you again in the morning."

Before he could hang up, McKnight's voice came through, high, upset, "Now? You want me to go now?"

"No time like the present, and you know how it is in these investigations. It might all be hanging on some little fact."

"But . . . but the weather channel says it's going to snow," McKnight said. "They say it's going to snow a lot. Another big blizzard headed our way in fact. I don't want to go out there in a blizzard."

"Well, then," Rafiel said, reasonably. "I would go out there now, before the snow becomes a blizzard."

From the other end of the phone there was something very much like an inarticulate exclamation of protest that, should it be more closely listened to, might translate into a profanity.

Rafiel chose not to listen to it any closer. Instead, deliberately, he pressed the off button of his phone, and turned his attention to navigating the maze of small neighborhoods, the opposite side of Fairfax from the one Tom and Kyrie lived on.

The neighborhoods weren't very different, though. In the early twentieth century, they might have been colonized by Irishmen or Poles, instead of the Greeks that had colonized the area north of them. Yet the houses all looked very much alike. Less brick here, and more the sort of elaborate, architecturally detailed Victorian houses that looked like mansions shrunk down to pint size. These houses often had three floors, but the floors would each contain no more than one room and a landing for the stair leading to the next floor.

They had, at one time, housed the laborers—many of them highly skilled—imported from Europe to build the elaborate mansions of the gold rush millionaires. The men and women enticed over to work for the newly rich had stayed and built their own dollhouse version of the boss's manor. And when the gold had evaporated and the silver lost its value they had stayed behind and added far more solid wealth to Colorado than mere metal could ever bring it.

Now in the beginning of the twenty-first century, the houses were mostly occupied by another kind of skilled laborer. While the neighborhood where Tom and Kyrie rented had never decayed appreciably, it had also never been exactly rehabilitated. Instead, the original Greek settlers had stayed, and the power of family and community supervision had kept the area, as the saying went, poor but honest. And now, when the younger generations were more likely to go to Denver to study, and then out of the state to work, it was mostly the realm of retirees, with no life and immaculate lawns.

The neighborhoods on the other side of Fairfax had been more ethnically diverse, and when the wealth of gold had rushed away from Goldport, there had been nothing there to keep people behind—no family, no weight of tradition. So instead they had moved on, restless, probably to Denver, where there were still mansions to build and money to be made.

In their absence, and with Colorado University right there, a few blocks away, another type of person had moved in. In the sixties, that type of person had often lived fifteen to a two-bedroom Victorian, and grown weed in the basement and generally destroyed the neighborhoods.

And then, recently, the sort of people who liked to buy destroyed properties and improve on them had moved in. Intellectuals, artists, a good number of childless couples with nothing but time on their hands to work on the houses. The houses looked pretty and almost newly built, though after coming across two of them painted in purple and accented with pink, Rafiel wished that these people had never heard the term *painted lady* or that they might have procured a translation of the term *good taste* before engaging in wanton remodeling.

He consulted his planner, and found that all three of the people he meant to see lived in this crisscrossing of pathways, shaded by century-old trees. The first one was on Meadoway, and he turned sharply onto it, admiring the faux-Victorian street light fixtures, and wondering if they were paid for by the neighborhood association or if any-one in the area had friends in city hall.

The first house he was looking for turned out to be one of the smaller ones—a two-floor Victorian with steeply descending eaves and a sort of look of being a Swiss chalet treasonously transported to the middle of Goldport, painted a weak aqua accented with green, and still feeling a little shell-shocked about the whole thing.

When Rafiel rang the doorbell, he was answered by a man who looked as if he could be cast, with no effort at makeup, as a hobbit in *Lord of the Rings*. Well, a rather tall hobbit, since he was about Rafiel's own height. But he had the hair perfectly right, and he was smoking a pipe. He was not wearing shoes, and Rafiel had to keep himself from looking down to see whether his toes were covered in curly hair, as Tolkien had insisted Bilbo Baggins' toes were. Instead, he focused on the amiable face, whose wrinkles showed it to be somewhat past middle age.

The man didn't smell like a shifter, and he'd seen

nothing at the aquarium, and was shocked, shocked—as it turned out by the reports of cryptozoological discoveries in the parking lot of the aquarium and not by the deaths within. Before Rafiel could escape him, he had to be told that the man was a retired used- and rare-book seller, and to be given—he never understand why or how—a lecture on American horror writers of the nineteenth century and the value of their various first editions.

He escaped, gritting his teeth, to follow the winding Meadoway to Mine Street, where the next person lived who'd left both name and address at the aquarium at the time when it was probable the first man had gone for a totally unprotected swim with the sharks. This one was a bigger house, or at least taller, and instead of looking like a Swiss chalet, it looked exactly like a Southern antebellum mansion as it might have looked if Sherman had found himself in convenient possession of a shrinking ray.

The people who lived in it were obviously aware of the resemblance, as they'd painted the house aristocratic white, and had two rocking chairs on the diminutive porch.

Rafiel rang the doorbell twice, but no one answered, even though he could see the blue glow of a television through the windows of the darkened front room. He had visions of people dead in front of a TV screen, but he knew how unlikely that was. Far more likely that they had the sound turned way up and were far too interested in their program to listen to his ringing, or, after a while, knocking on their door. Or it was entirely possible they'd gone out for a burger or something they thought they needed to weather the coming snowstorm, and had left the TV on. People did that.

Before giving up, he sniffed around the door. It was unlikely he would be able to smell a subtle and old shifter smell without shifting, himself. But then again, this was not the aquarium, where shifters might or might not have passed. And even there, he'd picked up the original scent while in his human form and had only needed to shift to pinpoint its location.

In this case, if shifters lived here, it should be much easier. But his sniffing around the house, and around the driveway failed to raise even a vague suspicion of shifter-scent.

So, chances are that it's not here, he thought, and headed for the number three on his list, which was only a couple of blocks down at Skippingstone Way.

The house was yellow and narrow, set on a handkerchief-sized lawn bordered by what, to judge from the pathetic, upward-thrust branches, must be lovely bushes in the spring and summer.

But Rafiel didn't pay much attention to the details, because as he parked his SUV and got out, he got a strong whiff of shifter smell. And the smell only increased as he opened the garden gate and walked up to the porch.

On the porch, a woman stood crying by a pretentious reproduction Victorian mailbox. And she smelled unmistakably of shifter.

Kyrie thought he looked cold. Cold and lonely, with his arms wrapped around himself, standing in the snowstorm. She would have thought he would have come inside, into the warmth. She would have thought he would have come to where they were. And then she thought perhaps he was stopping himself from shifting, and that was all.

But when he turned around to face her, his features bore none of the strange distortions that presaged shifts. His eyes were their normal shape, as was his nose, and his face wasn't even slightly elongated as it seemed to get when he was about to change into a dragon. His teeth, bared, as they chattered against each other, retained their normal human bluntness. But he was pale, and his eyes were veiled—as though they were covered with the nictitating eyelids he grew in dragon form.

He seemed to be glaring at her. "What?" he asked, and his voice was edged with anger, and shimmered with sharp barbs. The signs to stay away were clear, but Kyrie couldn't leave him here, alone and furious.

"I . . . is there anything I can do to . . . help?" Kyrie asked.

"Oh, don't worry," he flung. "I'm not going to shift."

"I didn't think you were going to," she said, trying to keep her voice low and even, because she knew—she knew damn well—that in this mood Tom was like a small child, easily annoyed, easily angered by things he thought she had said, even when she couldn't be further from thinking it. "I just wanted to know why you were out here, alone and . . . and why you look so angry?"

"Why? Why I look so angry?" he asked. "What do you mean I look so angry? I'm being claimed. I'm being owned. By a creature so old we can't even guess at his motives. By a crime boss, Kyrie! And he . . . he uses people as instruments. He used Conan as a spy camera.

And he probably can reach into Conan's mind all the time."

"I know. I realize how it feels, but . . ."

"But you sit there," Tom said. "And you talk to that creature, that . . . that dire wolf, even as he's going on about how he doesn't know what the Great Sky Dragon wants with me. He's talking about how ephemerals and shifters are different, and how our only loyalty is to shifters, and you are there, listening to him!"

"What did you expect me to do?" she asked. "Did you expect me to attack him? In the diner? Besides, he was giving us information we needed."

"Information!" His tone made it sound like the word should be a swear word. "Information! How do you know there is a word of truth in what he said?"

"Does it matter? Clearly there's *some* truth. I mean, I know it's tainted, that it's from his point of view. But, is it to some extent still true? Does it still have some contact with reality? Is it . . . is it going to work for us or against us?"

He was running his fingers through his hair, pulling it out of the bind that kept it in place at the back, scattering around wildly—making it look like a particularly energetic cat had been playing with his hair. "So is it?"

"I don't know," Kyrie said. She again managed to bring her voice down, to control her volume of speech. She knew he wasn't angry at her as such, truly she knew it, no matter how angry he might sound or how much it might seem to her like he was furious at her or perhaps—ridiculously—jealous of Dire. No, she mustn't sound like that. She must be calm and collected so that he would perhaps calm down. "But I know there is nothing we can do."

"Nothing we can do?" he said. "What do you mean nothing we can do? There has to be something we can do—there has to be a way to be free of all of this, hasn't there?" His eyes were wild, almost unfocused.

When Tom had first been hired by The George's erstwhile owner, he'd been addicted to drugs. Heroine, mostly, from what she understood of his stories. The drugs had been a misguided attempt to self-treat the shifting, to prevent himself from changing into a dragon whenever his emotions got control of him. Now, if Kyrie didn't know better, she'd think he was using again. There was a wildness to him, barely restrained and very much full of anger and something else, something seemingly uncontrollable. His blue eyes blazed with it as he said, "Why should I belong to someone? Belong as in be owned? Like a possession? A . . . thing? And only because I was born the way I am? Don't you understand, Kyrie, don't you see how wrong it is?"

Kyrie knew how wrong it was. She also understood, with startling clarity, at a glance, how different her background and Tom's were. He'd been left alone, to more or less raise himself. He might have been as unwanted as she was, as ignored, as disposable to those who were responsible for his existence. But unlike hers, his unsupervised childhood and barely supervised teenage years had been free of the control of strangers. His father might not have known or cared enough to control Tom and to make him follow rules, or even laws. But at least he'd not appointed revolving strangers to have power over Tom's life and determine what he could or couldn't do or say or wear to school.

A ward of the state since she was a few hours old, Kyrie had been passed from one controlling authority to another—foster families, social workers and the sometimes ironically named children advocates, all had passed her from person to person and there was nothing she could do except obey. She tried to convey this to Tom. "You think you're alone in this?" she said. "You think that it's because you're a shifter that strangers have a say over you? I was abandoned by my parents when I was just hours old," she said. "And from then on, I belonged to the state. Which in truth meant that I belonged to whomever the state appointed to look after a group of children. Strangers all, but they could determine everything, including what shots I got, and to what school I went. They could move me around to another foster family, uproot me from the neighborhood, leave me at the mercy of strangers."

He opened his mouth, but didn't answer. Instead, his mouth stayed open, then he closed it, with a snap. He put out a hand, and seemed like he would touch her face with his fingertips, only he let his hand fall before he could do it. "But that doesn't make it better, Kyrie," he finally said, his voice softer, but still seeming to simmer with outrage. "That doesn't make it any better. Yes, your upbringing was horrible, but that is supposed to be over. We're supposed to be our own people, now. We're supposed to be starting over. There shouldn't be anyone who can do this to us." His hand made a gesture in midair, which she supposed symbolized the control that the ancient shifters might have over them. "There shouldn't be anyone who can mess with our minds, our lives, what we are, this way."

Kyrie shrugged. "I didn't say my upbringing was horrible." And then caught herself saying it and thought how strange it was, because by various definitions, it had, indeed, been horrible. "I said that it w—" She shrugged. "It wasn't right. But then neither was yours. Just in very different ways. What I said is that I know this game. There is no point, when people think they own you, in just beating against it like . . . like a trapped bird ripping itself to shreds on the wire of the cage. When people think they own you, the only way you can get away with being yourself, the only way you can keep them off balance enough that they don't actually control you, is to play them one against the other. I think," she rubbed her forehead, as she thought of it. "I think we should do that. I think we should play the Ancient Ones against the dragons, the dragons against the Ancient Ones. I think we should go with the ones who demand least from us and—"

But Tom was shaking his head, making his black, curly hair fly about, like the ends of a whip. "No," he said. "No. We can't. We won't. Any concession we make to these people is like trading away a bit of ourselves and of who we are. Kyrie! Can't you see that they're evil? Can't you see them for what they are?"

"I can see they are very powerful," she said, hearing her voice toneless, and keeping it toneless, because otherwise she too would start yelling and next thing you knew, there would be people gathering to watch their argument. The only reason they hadn't gathered already, as far as she could see, was that it was snowing so hard, and they were in the back parking lot, while most people in The George were gathered up front, near the front entrance. "I can see they have mental and other powers that we lack. I can see too, that having lived so long, they have . . . they can call on contacts, on experience, on people they know. We can't do anything against that, either. So the only chance we have of defeating them, or even of holding them at arms' length, is to play them one against the other."

He shook his head. "There has to be another way. There has to." His hands were curling in fists. He looked at her, again unfocused. His face was contracted, as if in a spasm of pain. "I can't . . ." He shook his head. "They're not good, Kyrie. As people or as shifters. They're not good. We can't let them dictate to us. Ever."

"I'm not saying we should let them dictate to us." And now impatience crept into her voice. "I'm saying that we should use one to combat the other."

"No." He pressed his lips together, in narrow-lipped disapproval. "No."

"Then what are we to do?"

He faced her for a moment. His hands went at his hair again, pulling it back, but in fact snagging it in great handfuls, so that it hung in fantastical disarray around his face, making him look like an extra in a commercial picturing a society with no combs. "I'll figure out something," he said.

And with that the infuriating man started walking away. Kyrie ran after him, slipped on the ice and ended up having to clutch his shoulder to stay upright.

As he turned to look back at her, she said, "You can't go out there like that. Not in a T-shirt. Not . . . like that."

"Yes. Yes, I can," he said. His voice was absolutely flat, now, all emotion gone. "Yes I can. I need to cool off, Kyrie. Don't worry. I'll be back and I'll think of something."

She wanted to scream and shake him till his teeth fell out. It wasn't that she didn't love him. She was as conscious of loving him as she was that he was one of the more infuriating creatures alive—and possibly more infuriating than most dead ones too. Tom had a way of making her want to scream and stomp her foot. Sometimes, she almost understood his father who—trying to justify himself to her at one point—had told her that Tom had brought his disowning on himself, not by changing into a dragon, but because changing into a dragon was the last in a long line of disappointments and infuriating resistence to all normal behavior. His father hadn't disowned Tom because he was a dragon, but because he knew how out of control the human part of Tom was, and that, in a dragon, was terrifying.

But then she realized what Tom was saying. He needed to cool off. He needed to control himself. Which was the other side of the coin, that Tom's father had never seen or never been willing to see. Tom had an almost fanatical need for self-control. The things he'd done that seemed most out of control had more often than not been done to try to get control of himself. It might not be the best survival strategy in the world, but it was his, and who was Kyrie to try and change it? And what good would it do her to try?

Anything else she might tell him—put a coat on, take care of yourself, remember cars slide on ice and could kill you, remember you too might slip on ice—all of it would sound like she was trying to be his mother, and she didn't think maternal authority would go over any better than paternal.

She stepped back and away from him. She shook her head. She turned and walked towards the diner. At the door, she was almost run down by a wild-eyed Conan headed the other way—but she was done with trying to talk sense into dragons for the night, and she wasn't about to even try with this one. She might as well teach table manners to Not Dinner.

Instead, she went into the diner to meet with a sullen Keith protesting that he had to go, that truly he'd never meant to work today.

"Right, right," Kyrie said. "I'll call Anthony in." She wished Tom would give some thought to mundane considerations like the diner and who was cooking for the night, but that would probably be too much to ask for when he was convinced he could find a way for them to win, single-handed, against the ancient shifters.

She snorted.

She wished him luck.

Rafiel walked up to stand beside the woman, who was so absorbed reading something printed on cheap, yellowish paper, that she didn't notice even when he stood right behind her, reading over her shoulder.

The pamphlet was the same he'd seen on a couple of phone poles around the diner. Pseudo Marxist exhortation for the rise of the masses by something that called itself the Rodent Liberation Front. He cleared his throat, causing the woman to jump and turn around.

She was much shorter than he was—all of maybe five-two—and had what was probably a whole lot of mousy-brown hair, which had been enhanced by a wash or a dye or something to have brilliant gold streaks. For something that elaborately dyed, it had not been styled at all, just caught back into a braid that was coming apart at the edges. It made her look curiously inoffensive and childlike. The look was completed by a dark brown over-coat, the neck surrounded with fluffy brown fake fur. She wore white socks and Mary Janes. The visitors' book at the aquarium identified her as a fifth-grade science teacher at Stainless Elementary, just around the corner.

She couldn't have been much larger than her students. And how exactly could she hide the fact that she was a shifter from them?

That was the strongest question on his mind, as she smelled, undeniably, unmistakably, like a shifter. How could she hide it? And why was she crying?

He cleared his throat, and she looked up to see that he was looking at her, looming over her in fact. She let out a squeaky scream and looked up at him in complete alarm. Meanwhile, Rafiel went through and discarded many ways to start the conversation. He thought of asking her if she changed, or if she sometimes felt positively like an animal, or . . . a hundred other, quick-flashing and just as quickly discarded ideas.

The problem with all of them was that he couldn't really say any of them to a stranger. Not even to a stranger who, by smell alone, identified herself as one of his kind. He couldn't tell her he was one of her kind, either. It was one thing to question her, and another, quite different one, to let her hold his security in her hands. Particularly as she looked at him out of brown, tear-rimmed eyes.

"Officer Rafiel Trall, ma'am," he said, instead, as politely correct as he could be. "From the Goldport Police Department."

She squeaked again and put her hand in front of her face. Unfortunately this was the hand holding the Rodent Liberation Front pamphlet, and as it trembled in front of her face, it did nothing to make it easier for Rafiel not to mention that she smelled of shifter. But, objectively, he didn't need to reveal to her that he knew. Not even vaguely. What he needed to do was somehow determine when she'd been in the aquarium and what she'd done. If she'd been there with a large group of children, it was highly unlikely she'd either taken the time to dump an unsuspecting adult male into the tank or to steal the keys of the aquarium so she could come back and do it later. And he could check on her movements during the visit by talking to whoever had been there with her. If these things hadn't changed since his school days, every field trip, even every visit to the park, was facilitated not only by the teacher in charge, but by two or three aides and by a number of mothers who, apparently, lacked enough chaos in their lives and must, therefore, pursue it in these groups.

"I'm sorry if this is not a good time," he told the terrified eyes shimmering with tears. "But this is a very routine enquiry. You signed the book at the aquarium on the thirteenth?"

She blinked, as if this were not what she expected at all, and slowly lowered her hand. It was her turn to clear her throat, because, if he guessed right, she couldn't have spoken otherwise. "Yes, yes," she said. "I took my science class to the aquarium. We're studying environmental biology and the pollution of water courses, and how that affects endangered species of fish." Her voice was pipingly small, but he suspected that's how she normally talked.

"How many children would there be in the class?" Rafiel asked, fascinated by her recital of facts seeming calm enough, even as her eyes looked terrified.

She cleared her throat again. "Oh . . . there were two classes together, actually. I . . . I have them at different periods, you know. So it was forty children. Well, at least not exactly children, they're fifth graders, and they get very upset if we call them children, as they should, since they are, after all, almost teens."

"I see," he said. And he did in fact see that this woman probably lived in fear of her students, most of whom would be her height or probably taller than her. She would do anything rather than upset them or offend them. He wondered how effective that was, as a teaching discipline. He consulted his notebook for her name, which was . . . he squinted at it. Marina Gigio. "So, how many other adults were there to help supervise the . . . er . . . teens, Ms. Gigio?"

"Ms. Braeburn," she said. "And Ms. Hickey. They're teacher aides. And then there were five mothers, but I'd have to look at my paperwork to tell you their names. They vary, you know, with each field trip."

"I see," Rafiel said again. He did. That made eight

adults to forty kids, leaving it on average to each adult to look after five of the kids. Only he doubted very much it worked that way. For one, the mother volunteers, from what he remembered from his own childhood, were far more interested in their own children's safety and behavior than in any other of the kids'. That was probably worse now, since political correctness and a certain paranoia amid parents would have taken its toll. No sane mother would dare scold or even caution another's child. At the end of that lay lawsuits or worse.

So, in fact, five of the adults would be looking after five or at the most—supposing there were a few siblings between the two classes—seven or eight kids. The rest would be left to the teachers and teacher's aides. And the rest, being fifth graders, would be a definite handful. At that age—Rafiel had cousins—they were still capable of most of the idiocy associated with very small children, but to it they had added the creative mischief of teenagers, from stupid pranks to holding hands or kissing when someone wasn't looking. And the world being what it was these days, holding hands or kissing could also lead to lawsuits.

The woman would have had her hands full. Rafiel nodded to her. "Did you see anything suspicious? Anything that . . . well . . . do you remember the shark area, and the point where you can climb stairs to a sort of platform and look down at the shark area?"

She nodded. "I've . . . I've read about it in the paper. Their finding remains there. Thinking that I let all the young people hang on the railing and look down, and they were all playing, you know—nothing vicious—but shoving

each other and saying 'tonight you sleep with the fishes' .
. . I couldn't have imagined how unstable it was. If I'd
known, I'd never have let them up on it. When I think of
what might have happened." She shuddered, or rather
trembled, a trembling flutter that made Rafiel think of
something he couldn't quite name.

"Well, I understand no one knew it was that unstable," he
said. He didn't want to tell her that the area was perfectly
stable, but that the safety cover of the tank had been
removed. As far as he knew—and he would admit he hadn't
looked at the paper much beyond the cryptozoological
report on the front page—the newspaper was still reporting
both findings of bodies at the aquarium as accidents or at
the very worst mysterious deaths. "So you didn't see anyone
else there? I mean, besides the group you took in?"

She shook her head. "No. Just the childr—young people. You know how it is when a school group goes to this
type of place. The other visitors tend to get out of the
way."

"Oh, yes," he said.

"Very considerate of most people, really," she said.
"Giving the children a chance to learn."

"Yes," he said, firmly, not wishing to encourage her
delusions or provoke a flow of stranger explanations.
Instead, he said, "I was just wondering . . . if you saw
anything else suspicious?"

"No," she said, with unusual firmness. She darted a
look—he'd swear it—at the pamphlet she'd received in
the mail, then looked up again. "Definitely not."

If she wasn't lying, then Rafiel would present his shifter
form to the nearest vet for neutering. He frowned. He

didn't want to do it, but something welled up in him—the meaning of her last name, the look of her flutter, and something else . . . a feeling.

He cast about for something he could claim ambiguously had been a guess at what she might have seen, should it fail to hit its mark. "Mouse, right?" he said at last.

She shriek-squeaked, and her hand darted for the door handle.

But Rafiel's hand was there first, holding onto the door handle, speaking in his best soothing, smooth voice, "It's all right, Ms. Gigio. It's all right. This is not about you. I just wanted to tell you I knew, and that it's all right."

But she turned, backing against the door, her back protected by it, and bared little teeth at him. "How do you know? How did you know?"

He didn't answer. He wasn't going to bare his throat that explicitly to her. He wasn't going to tell her in so many words. But he allowed his eyebrows to rise in an expression that was unmistakably *guess.*

"Oh," she said. She dropped the letter and covered her mouth with her hand. "Oh." And then, with something sparking at the back of her eyes. "Are there many of us, then? Around?"

He shrugged. "I know a few. I don't think there're many, no." He had no idea, of course, of how many Ancient Ones there might be. "Less than one percent of the population. Perhaps much less."

"Oh," she said again. "All . . . all the same thing?"

It took him a moment to realize what she was saying, then he shook his head slowly. "Not at all. In fact, I don't know of any two of the same mammals." The closest being himself and Kyrie, for all the good it did them. And Alice had been like him. "There's . . . there seems to be a gamut of shapes, from the most common to the extinct or even mythological."

"Oh," she said again, and let out air, as though deflating, though fortunately she didn't decrease in size as she did it. "I got this letter in the mail. I thought . . ."

"I know," Rafiel said. "I've seen those around the college. I thought they were a student prank."

"I did too," she said. "See them. I saw them outside The George this morning. I often go there for the pesto omelet."

And for the pheromones, Rafiel thought, but didn't say anything. Let her think that her actions were rational and consciously controlled. They needed all the illusions they could hold onto.

"But I thought it was a student prank too," she said.

"It might still be," Rafiel said, though he didn't for a minute believe it. "You know your last name means mouse in Italian. And it's possible."

"Yes, it is," she said, brightening up. It looked like a sudden weight had gone off her. "I mean, it's actually probable. How else would they know? Or . . . Or . . ." She seemed to run out of objections to the idea someone else might know. Rafiel thought this was also an exceptionally bad time to let her know that some shifters could smell out other shifters.

Instead, he just inclined his head, and said, "Will you tell me, then, what you saw at the aquarium? I realize it must have been something you didn't want to talk about to just anyone, perhaps something shapeshifter related?"

She looked up and managed to give the impression she was making complex calculations at the back of her mind. "Well . . ." she said. "Well . . ." And shrugged. "It's just something that could be shifters. I didn't want you to think I was crazy, that is, before I knew . . . you know . . . that . . . that you'd understand."

"I understand," he said. "What did you see?"

"It was in the aquarium area, when it changes over to the restaurant area, you know? It's always really hard to control the ki—young people there, because they always want to stay and eat at the restaurant, no matter how many times you tell them it's an expensive, sit-down place and they wouldn't really be pleased if a bunch of young people—who tend to be rowdier than grown-ups—took over their tables, and, you know . . ." She seemed to realize she was running on and finished lamely, "all that. So I was very busy talking to all of them, and Ms. Braeburn was actually standing by the entrance to the restaurant, herding them past, as it were, to make sure they didn't try to duck inside, and then I saw . . ."

She shook her head. "You know that area has all the huge tanks with the weird stuff? Squids and octopuses, and that huge crab tank, where there's a lens on the bottom, and you can crawl under the bottom and look up?"

He nodded. He hadn't paid that much attention to that area, but he vaguely remembered everything she mentioned.

"Oh, this is going to sound like I'm crazy," she said, and put her hands on either side of her face, as if to keep herself from blushing. It didn't work. A blush showed on her cheeks, on either side of her fingers. It made her, weirdly, very attractive, and Rafiel had to remind himself that when cats played with mice, the result was normally not pleasant.

"I swear, just as we managed to get the kids out of the area, a little naked man came out from under that area—you know, the area where you can crawl to look up and see the crabs and things, as if you were inside the aquarium. He looked Asian—I'd think Japanese. Or at least he looked like the Japanese in movies. And he looked very old. His hair was all white and he was almost bent in double. And . . . well, he was naked, so I looked more attentively." She seemed to realize how that might sound and gasped slightly, before saying, all in a rush, "I mean, I mean, because I'm familiar . . . because I know when you shift suddenly you often find yourself, you know, naked. So I looked, because he didn't look like a streaker or a flasher or any of that kind of person, so I thought, I thought . . . how odd, and maybe he was a shifter. Only it wasn't a real thought, I mean, with words or anything, just an impulse to look more closely at him and see, you know . . . what was wrong."

Rafiel refused to tread in the minefield of innuendo that surrounded that statement. Instead, he said, "And then?"

"Oh, that's the craziest part of all, and I've spent a lot of time wondering if I'd gone around the bend, you know? But this is the thing . . . he winked at me, when he saw me looking. Just winked with all the calm in the world. And then he . . . climbed the tank. He wasn't very big. Shorter than I. And you know the tanks are open at the top, right?

So he climbed the tank and he . . . dropped into it. And then . . . I couldn't see him anymore."

"Do you mean he disappeared?"

She shook her head. "No, I don't think so. It's just as he splashed in, there was all this turmoil and then . . . there were just crabs and anemones there. Nothing out of the ordinary." She looked apologetic. "I hadn't counted the inhabitants of the tank before he dropped in."

"No one would have asked you to," he said, reassuringly.

"I confess," she said. "When I first heard of the bones and the arm found in the tank, I thought it might be a shark shifter, and that he hadn't changed in time . . . ?"

Rafiel hadn't thought of that, and that was a horrible idea, though it would certainly explain the moved-aside cover. And it wasn't like it was completely crazy. After all, sharks ate each other, too. And the remains being as sparse as they were, and having been in the water, how could he be sure the victims weren't shifters? But three shark shifters? All meeting the same fate? Unlikely.

"Thank you for your help, Ms. Gigio," he said. And then, because he felt he owed her something, he added, "I don't expect you'll have any more trouble with those pamphlets, but if you do, give me a call." He handed her one of his business cards. "I'll do what I can."

"Oh, thank you," she said, holding the card close to her chest. "That's so kind of you."

He didn't know what to answer to that, so he merely said, "Good evening, ma'am." And started towards the stairs. At which point, curiosity overtook him. There was something he had never fully understood about shifting. Oh, sure, Tom and Kyrie could go on and on about genes and about crossover from other species—borrowed genes or something like that—and about all this sort of pseudo-scientific stuff, but what Rafiel wanted to know was what happened to the law of conservation of mass and energy when one shifted.

After all, Tom was easily five times his normal size when he shifted. Oh, sure, Tom was a muscular guy, but if you took his mass and distributed it across the bulk of the dragon, the dragon would be lighter than a cloud. Rafiel himself knew he was considerably heavier as a lion than as a man, though the lion was also much larger.

How would those differences in size play themselves over creatures that were much further from human at either end of the scale? What would a mouse shifter look like? Or a crab shifter, for that matter? He kept thinking of the report of the squirrel the size of a German shepherd. That would make finding shifters at the aquarium far easier.

"So . . . how big are you?" he asked. "When you shift?"

She blinked, and blushed, as if he'd asked her a very intimate question. "About . . . ." she said. "Oh, normal size, you know? For a mouse."

And then, as if she'd broached the inadmissible, she opened her door and darted inside, leaving Rafiel rooted to the spot, thinking, *Cat and mouse. Bad idea.*

Tom was all too conscious of having been stubborn, and strange, and that he'd probably annoyed Kyrie—or at least deserved to annoy her. He felt guilty about walking away from their discussion, but he didn't know what else he could tell her, and he was very much afraid he would change into a dragon, right there in the parking lot.

He wrapped his arms around himself, shoving his hands under his arms to keep them warm, as he walked. He relished the sound of his boots against the snow. One of the good things about them was that they had such great traction. He also relished the fact that his hands and arms felt so cold they seemed to burn. Snow was settling all over him. One of the homeless who walked along Fairfax summer and winter was huddled in the recessed doorway of the realtors down the street.

He gave Tom an odd look from under disheveled bangs. "Whoa there, pal," he said. "You won't last long like that. They give coats for free down at St. Agnes. Got me this one." He patted his huge, multipocketed safari jacket. "Really warm."

Tom nodded, but walked on, without even slowing down. Wouldn't last long? How long could he last? How long did things like him live? And what happened to them when they went beyond the limits of normal human life? What did it do to you to live long enough to see all the normal people around you die? And their children, their grandchildren, everyone you could care for? Would it mean that you would come to think of them as ephemerals? As things? Creatures who didn't matter?

If that was true, then Tom didn't want to be a shifter. He didn't want to live to lose touch with everyone he knew—to see Keith's grandchildren get old and grey, and Anthony's great grandchildren die out. To lose all meaningful contact with people.

He stomped his feet, trying to find an outlet for his anger. He didn't want to be owned, he didn't want to owe anything to the Great Sky Dragon. Much less did he want to owe anything to the dire wolf, who had already proven that he had no respect for anyone, not even other, younger shifters—not even older shifters, if Old Joe was any indication.

And Old Joe was something else, working at Tom's mind. Where was he? Where could he have gone? It would be like Old Joe—Tom nurtured no illusions about his charity case—to have disappeared completely at the first sign of a threat. It would be like him . . . but it wouldn't be like him to go more than twenty-four hours without turning into an alligator and coming back to raid the diner dumpster. Particularly in this sort of cold weather when his shifter metabolism would be demanding protein.

Tom backtracked to where the homeless man sat. "Hey," he said.

The man looked back up at him. "Ah, you decided to come back for the coat? But I can't give you the coat, or I'll freeze, see." His speech was more articulate than Tom was used to from the people who would stay in doorways even when the weather turned bitterly cold. The main reason to not go to one of the free shelters was, normally, that they demanded sobriety and this person could not swear to it. "Go to St. Agnes. They will look after you."

"No, no," Tom said, his teeth chattering. "What I want to know is, have you heard of someone called Old Joe?"

"What? The gator?" the man said blinking.

It was Tom's turn to blink and then, in a sudden rush to seem innocent, "Gator?"

"Oh, he says he turns into a gator," he said. "We call him Gator, see?"

"Er . . . have you seen him?"

"Not since yesterday, I think." He shook his head. "He said he was heading out to the aquarium. Don't make no sense to me. The aquarium is closed."

"Er . . . yes, thank you." Tom said, as he started walking the other way again.

"St. Agnes," the homeless man screamed after him. "They'll fix you."

Tom nodded. He walked very fast away from the newly-gentrified area of Fairfax, the area where, since his arrival a year ago, the place had become clean, and all the street lamps worked, and where the businesses were bookstores and movie rental stores, restaurants and clothes stores.

As he walked, the stores changed slowly to "antique" shops, thrift shops, used bookshops, used CD shops, and then another two blocks down, it was down to new age stores, churches advertising free hot meals, and then a bit further on, to where the buildings on either side of the street were warehouses, most of them empty and shuttered against intruders.

Here, in the silence of the surroundings, Tom became aware of a strange sound—like an echo behind him. Feet crunching on snow, almost in perfect rhythm with his. He turned around. Sure enough, following him, at about a half-block distance, was Conan. Keeping him protected, Tom thought. Keeping an eye on him, more the like. A little, sentient spy camera, watching his every move.

"Go away," he yelled, turning around. "I don't need you."

Conan stopped. He looked up. He too had his arms wrapped around himself, only one of his arms was rather shorter than the other, and it made him look even more pitiful. "But . . ." he said. "But . . ." And that was it. His lip trembled.

Tom had spent the last few months taking in every sad sack who stopped by the diner. But this was too much, to expect him to take on a sad sack who also happened to be not just a spy but an instrument used by the Great Sky Dragon. "Don't try it, Conan. You heard. You are a spy device for the old bastard. I don't want him around."

Conan opened his hands. "You don't understand," he said. "I don't have a choice. I was told to follow you, to not let anything happen to you."

"Did you know?" Tom asked. "Before you heard it from the . . ." He came closer, so he could talk to Conan. "From the dire wolf?"

Conan shook his head. He looked miserable. He must have rushed out, because not only hadn't he bothered to put his jacket on, he was still wearing his George apron. "No. He said I was to protect you. I remember being very confused about how I was to do that, considering that, you know . . . you were stronger than I . . . but he said . . ." He shrugged. "I'd just dragged myself back, you know, to . . . well, to the restaurant on the outskirts of town, where . . ."

Tom nodded. Where the point of contact with the triad was. He got that much.

"I expected him to kill me," Conan said. "He punishes failure horribly. I've seen him kill other people for failing."

"But you went back, anyway?" Tom asked. He couldn't understand it. "In your place, I'd have been putting as many miles between me and as many triads as possible as fast as possible."

Conan shook his head. "It's not that easy. First, they are everywhere, truly. When you least expect it, in some small town, some out of way place, you'll meet one of them. And then there's . . . when you first join? I knew they put a tracker in you. I didn't know he could . . . you know . . . see through my eyes or anything. But I knew he could tell where I was. And if I didn't come back, he would send someone for me. And then he would make it really unpleasant."

More unpleasant than death? Tom thought, but was afraid to ask. "So you went back."

"After months, I went back," Conan hung his head.

"I was wondering . . . I mean . . ." He shook his head. "I was almost dead but I came back in a few days, but you . . ."

Conan's eyes were huge. "I was caught in the burning building," he said. "Everyone else died. I must have managed to drag myself out before my brain . . ." He shook his head. "I don't even remember the first month."

"Oh."

"The arm . . ." he shrugged, "is the least of it. I understand bone is hard to grow. They told me . . . in another three months or so it should be normal."

"Oh," Tom said again, and thought that if Conan imagined this made him feel more charitable towards the Great Sky Dragon, he was a fool. All right, Tom might have been guilty of ripping out his arm and burning him, but it had been in self-defense. While the Great Sky Dragon was the one who had sent him after Tom.

"When he sent us out first, he had told us to kill you. Find the Pearl of Heaven, kill the thief. And then all of a sudden, when I came back, he wanted you alive. He wanted you protected." He shrugged. "I don't understand any of it, but I knew it was my chance to . . . to be accepted again. I didn't know he could see through my eyes until today. I thought I had to call him. I called him when you flew away." He sounded miserable. "When you went back to your house because of the dire wolf . . ."

Tom didn't understand it either, but of one thing he was sure. "I want you to go back, now, Conan, all right?"

Conan blinked at him, in complete confusion. "But I have to . . ."

"I want you to go back to the diner, and don't worry about me. Nothing is going to happen to me. Look, it's like this—if you stay here, I'm going to change and flame you. You can't flame me, because you're supposed to protect me, not kill me. If I flame you," Tom kept his voice steady, though he was, in fact, very sure he could never flame the hapless and helpless Conan, "you won't be able to follow me, anyway—and at best you'll have to come back as you did."

"No!"

"The Great Sky Dragon can't blame you for going back."

Conan opened his mouth to protest.

"No, look, I'm not going to get in any type of trouble. I just want to walk around for a while, until I calm down. Nothing will happen to me. I promise. And I won't let you come with me, anyway."

Conan opened his mouth again. "Don't you understand?"

he asked, his voice vibrating and taut with despair. "If you want to flame me, do it. But I can't go back. Himself doesn't tolerate failure and I'm not very valuable to him. Not like you."

In Tom's mind an odd idea formed. If he was valuable to the Great Sky Dragon, then there was only one thing he could use to threaten the creature. "If you don't go back," he said, "I will kill myself. I'll throw myself from an underpass or fling myself under an eighteen-wheeler. I think if I destroy the brain, I won't come back. And I'd rather be dead than owned."

Conan started and looked up at Tom, as if trying to gauge how serious the threat was.

Tom looked back with desperate resolution. He *would* rather kill himself. Particularly if he was going to live millennia. A human lifetime of obeying someone was bad enough. An eternity would be hell on Earth. And then when he'd found out that the Great Sky Dragon could use his people—literally—as instruments . . . That was the worst of all. Tom could not face that. He let his revulsion show on his face, too.

Conan looked panicked, but nodded. He held his hands open on either side of his body, palms towards Tom, in instinctive appeasement. "All right," he said. "I'll go. I'll go."

And he turned around and started down the street. Tom hesitated. Did this mean the Great Sky Dragon was going to leave Tom alone? Or that he had someone else watching Tom?

Tom shrugged. It didn't matter. He continued down Fairfax, now solidly in the office neighborhood, all closed, of course, in the storm. Hands in his pockets, he walked on, under the falling snow. He was shivering, but that didn't matter.

What he wanted to know—what he very much needed to find out—is how he could rid himself from all the creatures who wanted to claim ownership of him, and make his life his own once more. He, who had never obeyed father nor mother, nanny or teacher, would not now turn his life over to more than half mad, dangerous old beings who played under no moral rules he could understand.

From deep within his jeans pocket, his phone rang.

Tom stepped off the road onto a space on the grounds of the aquarium, on the other side of the parking lot. In summer this was a pleasant-enough space with a little bridge over a carefully directed, and probably entirely artificial, small stream, trees, flowers, benches. Right then it was a winter wonderland, with icicles dripping off the trees and slippery ice underfoot.

Tom fished in his jeans pocket, thinking it was Kyrie, and answered the phone, his half-frozen fingers fumbling with the buttons.

"Tom?"

"Dad?"

"Oh, good. I have been delayed at the airport again. Something about flights to Denver being cancelled. Look, I really need you to go there, and to wait in the loft for the cable guy."

"Dad!" Tom turned around, to look at the frozen river.

He had a feeling he'd heard something move or slither down there. It couldn't be water. That would be frozen. So what could it be?

"No. You see, I wouldn't ask if it were just because I want to watch TV, but in the beginning, at least, I'm going to be working from home, and I need the cable connection for the internet."

"Dad, I can't get to Denver," Tom said, drily, keeping his teeth from knocking together by an effort of will.

"Why not? How long would it take you to fly there? It's only a three-hour drive away. Flying couldn't be more than twenty minutes."

"Flying in the current blizzard would probably take about three hours," Tom said. He felt suddenly very tired. "And besides . . . look, I just can't."

"You know, I don't ask you to do this stuff every day," Edward Ormson said, in an aggrieved tone, from the other end of the connection. "It's just that this is really important to me, and I thought . . . Well, I thought our relationship was better these days."

Their relationship was better these days. Tom was very conscious that no matter what bad parents his parents might have been, he had been a truly horrible son, himself. And he owed his father for The George. "If I could at all, I would, Dad. It's just that I'm in the middle of a big mess just now."

"A mess? What type of a mess? Anything legal?"

His father was a corporate lawyer, and clearly, just now, a hammer in search of a nail.

"No," Tom said. "Look, it's just . . . not something I feel comfortable discussing on the phone."

"Did you eat someone?"

Tom dropped the phone. It went tumbling down over the brick parapet of the bridge and hit the river below with a hard thud. Under the bridge, there was that sound as if something had moved or slithered. It was so faint, that Tom couldn't be sure it had happened or if his half-frozen ears were giving him back impossible phantom sounds.

Rafiel got in his truck thinking that while the woman was a shifter, and seemed apparently harmless, yet he couldn't get involved with her. For one, the moment she found out he was a lion shifter . . . He shook his head. Cat and dragon might be one thing—and he still wasn't sure how that would play out in the end—but cat and mouse would be insane. It would require that he lose his marbles completely.

He got his cell phone from his pocket and dialed McKnight's cell phone. "Hey, Dick," he said, using McKnight's diminutive in an attempt to forestall more protests.

The answer from the other side of the phone had almost as much of a squeak as that of Ms. Gigio's, "Yes?"

"So . . . have you done the platform?" he asked.

"Yeah, yeah. We . . . I brought a team over." He spoke with such haste, such obviously tumbling guilt, that it was obvious to Rafiel that he had found something.

"What did you find?"

"We . . . uh . . . I found . . . that is . . . Michelle and I found a couple of used condoms, tied up, in the planters. We will have them processed and . . . and get back to you with the results."

"Thanks, McKnight. Do," Rafiel said, keeping the amusement, but not the forcefulness out of his voice.

He hesitated for a moment, starting the car away from Ms. Gigio's home. Where would he go now? He was dying to know what was happening with those condoms. Well . . . at least Lei had told the truth about that. Maybe.

Getting the phone again, he said, "Dick, can you give me the address of all of the aquarium's male employees? Female, too, while you're at it."

McKnight could. Or at least he could after much hemming and hawing and getting hold of the aquarium records from someone. He cleared his throat, nervously, and in a reedy voice gave Rafiel three male names—John Wagner, Carl Hoster and Jeremy Fry—and three female names—Suzanne Albert, Lillian Moore, Katlyn Jones—and addresses, all within a mile of the aquarium in the area where old Victorians had been converted into apartments, amid a lot of other, mostly cinder-block apartments, of fifties vintage. It mostly housed college students. And they were all close enough to the diner too.

Rafiel was feeling uneasy enough about Tom and Kyrie and whatever their little spat might have devolved into. Some part of him told him that, interested party or not, suspicious or not, he should have stayed around and refereed their argument. They were both younger than him, and both of them had far less experience of relationships.

Not that I can tell them a lot about relationships, Rafiel thought. *After all, I am the master of the love them and leave them.*

"Rafiel?"

He'd forgotten he'd left the cell phone on, and now looked at it in puzzlement, thereby putting his brakes on a little too late for the red light ahead. He hit a patch of ice as he braked and slid through the intersection to the glorious accompaniment of the horns of cars which swerved to avoid him. *Good thing I'm a policeman,* he thought as he took a deep breath, made sure he wasn't about to shift—his nails looked the same size, and there was nothing golden or furry about his hands—and said, "Yeah, McKnight?"

"Are you going to go talk to these people?" McKnight asked.

"That's the idea," Rafiel said.

"In this weather?"

"Well, all the more chance to find them at home, right?" Rafiel said, and hung up before McKnight would actively and loudly worry about his life or his safety or something.

Then he pressed one of his preset dials, and rang up The George.

Kyrie started worrying about Tom almost as soon as he left the parking lot. It wasn't that she was angry at him—or not exactly. A part of her understood that he couldn't bear to be controlled by someone else, much less someone who legally and morally should have no power over him.

Another part of her wanted to tell him to grow up already and that adults knew they couldn't have life all their own way, that they couldn't forever hold at bay the unpleasant parts of reality and those they would rather not deal with. But that part of her, she told herself, was firmly under control. Yes, she was sure that Tom was overreacting. But at the same time he was just as sure that she was underreacting, enduring the interference of the dire wolf in her affairs with excessive placidity and total lack of protest.

Which, she thought, was not really true. She could very easily—and happily, for that matter—allow herself to scream and rant. For all the good it would do.

But she would not allow herself to scream and rant at Tom. Because that would do no good. She was sure he'd gone off to cool off and that he too was trying to hold his temper in check. And she couldn't fault him. She preferred he did that than he shifted and took it out on all those nearby.

Keith was looking intently at her. "Is Anthony coming in?"

"In a few minutes," Kyrie said, keeping her voice calm. In her mind, she was imagining Tom walking blindly into the storm. She wished he had taken his jacket.

"I can't stay, Kyrie. I have to get home," Keith said. "I have no idea what happened to Summer. She must think I'm crazy. I bring her here for a coffee, and the next thing you know, I'm cooking."

"Yeah," Kyrie said. "Anthony is on his way. " He'd

sounded frankly relieved to be called in. Kyrie wondered what exactly his wife had been doing to make him so happy to hear from her. But Anthony solved it himself as he came in. "It's crazy just sitting in the house, watching reruns of *Friends*," he said. "I mean, it's a studio, and it's just snowing outside. And then Cecily is worried about . . . you know . . . the storm and whether the roof is going to cave in. Like . . . we're on the third floor down from the top of the building. If the roof caves in on us, we're in a world of trouble." He looked sheepish for a moment, as he divested himself of his jacket and put on his apron and the hat he wore while he was cooking— which was, granted, not as stylish as Tom's bandana, but served the same purpose of keeping hair out of the food. "She's not . . . I mean, I don't want you to think she's crazy or something. It's just she's not used to going through these blizzards. I guess for people who didn't grow up in Colorado it must look much worse than it is."

"Yeah, it does," Kyrie said. And still, in her mind, she saw Tom walking through the storm. How could he survive it? Could he survive it? She heard Dire saying that most of the young shifters died through their own stupidity and she gritted her teeth and pretended that everything was fine, and got orders, and put them on the carousel of spikes on the counter, for Anthony.

More people came in. Probably people who weren't all that familiar with Colorado, Kyrie thought, and who found it easier to weather the storm in here than alone in whatever tiny apartments they lived in. She kept a smile on her face, and worked as efficiently as she knew how, while Anthony turned out the meals in record time.

She didn't know how long it had been, when she heard the back door open. She set down the tray and the carafe of coffee on the counter, and ran down the hallway. "Tom," she started, with some idea of finishing the sentence with "Tom, I was so worried."

But instead of Tom, it was Conan, coming in. He was a vague shade between blue and lavender. His teeth beat a mad rhythm. His hair was so covered in snow that he might as well have been wearing a powdered wig.

"Where is Tom?" Kyrie asked.

Conan looked up at her, in mute misery. That look made thoughts run through her mind, thoughts she didn't like at all. There had been a fight and the Great Sky Dragon had killed Tom. After all, she remembered, the creature held it his right to discipline those he deemed to belong to him. Or else . . . or else, Tom had been run over. Or simply collapsed and frozen by the side of the road. "What. Happened. To. Tom?" she asked, her voice slow and controlled, even as she told herself that she would not shift. She would never shift. Not in the diner. Shifting wouldn't help anything. Conan already looked halfway between frozen and terrified.

He shook his head. "He is fine," he said, though the words weren't really easy to understand through his chattering teeth. "He's . . . he was fine when I left him."

And then, nerveless, as though his legs had turned to rubber under him and his body wasn't all that much more solid, Conan sank to his behind just inside the door of the diner. "He made me leave," he said. "He told me to leave. He made me leave. What if something happens to him?"

"Tom made you leave?"

A headshake. "No. Himself. He told me to leave. Tom said . . . he said he'd kill himself if I stayed with him, and the Grea—Himself said he meant it."

"Nothing will happen to Tom," Kyrie said. And bit her lip thinking that unfortunately she was growing as weary of the interference of elder shifters as Tom himself was. "It's all right. Come on." She helped him get up—or rather more or less pulled him up, by his arms, by main strength. "Come on. I'll get you coffee or something. You're frozen."

"He's out there, like that," Conan said. "In a T-shirt. What if something happens to him?"

"Tom is a big boy," Kyrie said. "He'll take care of himself. He used to live on the streets. It's not like he's a child whom we must look after."

She was telling herself that more than she was telling it to Conan. And she was so convincing that she almost believed it. At least for the next two hours, she managed to keep herself from freaking out thinking of Tom out there alone and what might happen to him.

It wasn't like the city was safe. There were the Ancient Ones, and whatever was throwing people to the sharks, and the Rodent Liberation Front and the triad. In fact, it was an interesting time to be a shifter in Goldport.

She was very close to losing all self-control, shifting, and loping about in the storm, trying to smell Tom out, when the phone rang.

"Hello," she said. "The George."

"Kyrie. It's Rafiel. Is Tom okay?"

And then, before she could control it, before she could remember that Tom was an adult and should be treated as such, all her anxiety came pouring out of her, "I hope so. But, Rafiel, he walked west on Fairfax two and a half hours ago and he hasn't come back."

"Uh. Does he have his phone with him?"

"Yes. Well . . . maybe. He should have it. But he isn't answering." An hour ago, in a moment of weakness, she'd tried to call three or four times. And another half a dozen times since.

"I see. You two fight?"

"No. Not really. He is just . . . he's mad at the . . . you know . . ."

"Yeah. I imagine." There was a pause, as if Rafiel were trying to think through things. "West on Fairfax?"

"Yeah."

"I see. I tell you what, I'll drive down the road a while and see if I can find him. What was he wearing?"

"What he was wearing when you last saw him. Jeans and a black T-shirt." She felt she needed to defend him against stupidity, even though Rafiel hadn't even paused in a significant manner. "He said he needed to cool off."

"Oh, yes. And I'm sure he has," Rafiel said. "Don't worry, okay? I'll see if I can find him."

Rafiel tried to call a couple of times. No answer. Stubborn dragon, he told himself, about his friend, with something between annoyance and admiration. That Tom wasn't answering Kyrie might or might not make sense. She didn't seem to think they had argued, but Rafiel's experience of women—his mother, aunts and girl cousins included—told him that just because a woman thought that, it didn't mean the man she had emphatically not argued with thought the same.

He drove slowly down Fairfax seeing no movement, let alone movement by someone in jeans and a black T-shirt. Tom had black hair. He should have stood out like a sore thumb.

Unless, of course, he's passed out by the side of the road and covered in a mound of snow, in which case he is pretty much white. Rafiel felt a tightening in his stomach at the thought. How long could a dragon survive hypothermia? In either form? Oh, okay, so they were hard to kill, but was freezing one of the ways they could be killed? He didn't know. And it wasn't as if he was going to go in search of Dante Dire to ask him.

Dante Dire presented the other problem. Because Kyrie hadn't said anything about looking for two people, one following the other, he presumed that Conan hadn't gone with Tom. That meant Tom was out there without his human security cam. What if the bad guys had found him first? While Rafiel had got the idea that Dante Dire was cringingly afraid of the Great Sky Dragon, he didn't get the feeling that he was even vaguely impaired by moral considerations or feelings that he should not kill. Particularly—he suspected—no feelings that he should not kill dragons.

As stupid as it was that Dante Dire, sent to investigate the death of shifters, would end up killing shifters to get them out of his way, Rafiel suspected that this was a *nobody picks on my little brother but me* matter. After all, the Great Sky Dragon, supposed protector of all dragons, had killed at least one of their members in Goldport. The police had processed the body and Rafiel was sure he had been bitten in two in the parking lot of the Chinese restaurant. And the Great Sky Dragon had damn well near killed Tom, too, for all his new interest in protecting him.

Rafiel had now gone all the way to the west end of Fairfax. He turned around and started driving the other way, slowly. A movement from a doorway called his attention. It looked khaki, not black, but considering everything, perhaps with the snow it just looked that way.

Hopeful, he pulled up to the curb, stopped the car, jiggled a little in his seat, just to make sure at least one of his wheels wasn't on solid ice, parked and set the parking brake. "Hey there," he called to the indistinct, blurred form in the doorway.

The form stirred. Almost immediately, Rafiel realized it couldn't be Tom. This was someone older with white hair, probably taller and bulkier than Tom, though that was hard to tell, as he was huddled in the doorway with one of those Mylar space blankets over most of his body save for his shoulders and head. The flash of khaki was from the shoulders, covered in some sort of jacket. He looked at Rafiel from bleary eyes half hidden under unkempt bangs.

"Uh . . ." Rafiel said, jiggling his keys in his pocket. "Do you want a ride to a shelter?"

The eyes widened. "No shelter," he said, with something very akin to fear. He shook his head and rustled the corner of his shiny silver coverings. "I got my blanket."

"Oh. All right," Rafiel said. The man didn't seem drunk, but he seemed as averse to going into a shelter as, say, Tom or Kyrie or himself would have been. Rafiel sniffed the air, smelling nothing, but he wasn't sure he would have smelled anything as cold as it was. He would swear his ability to smell had frozen with his nose. Perhaps, he thought, he should come back and smell the man later. And, as the inanity of the thought struck, he snorted. Yeah, because he really needed to find another charity case for Tom. Old Joe wasn't enough. "Hey," he said, on impulse. "Did you see a guy go by here? About yea tall, wearing jeans and a black T-shirt? Black hair about shoulder long or a little longer?" How was it possible that he was suddenly so unsure of Tom's hair length? He almost sighed in exasperation at himself. Yes, Kyrie was far more interesting to look at, but he should have noticed his best male friend's hair length.

"I told him he needed a jacket," the old transient man said and nodded.

"Uh. You did? Good call."

"Yeah, he was going that way," the man said, pointing west. "If you are looking for him, going that way"—he pointed east, the direction Rafiel was now headed—"won't help."

"Right, but see, I went miles on Fairfax and I didn't—"

"He was looking for Old Joe," the derelict said. "Him that thinks he can be a gator? I told him last I heard Old Joe was headed for the aquarium. I don't know what he meant to do at the aquarium, though."

The aquarium, yeah, that would be like Tom. Let cryptozoology zanies take over the local paper. Let them get pictures of creatures that shouldn't possibly exist fighting it out in the parking lot of the aquarium. Tom, who shifted into one of the creatures, would immediately feel honor bound to go the aquarium. Why didn't I think of it before? "Thanks," he told the old man. "I'll . . . get you a coffee or something."

The man smiled, revealing very brown teeth. "Why, that would be very nice of you."

Back in the car, Rafiel turned around. *The aquarium. What are the odds?*

But it was a few minutes' drive there, at the most, and it wasn't as though he didn't have excuses he could give for being on the grounds. He turned onto Ocean Street and started driving slowly around the parking lot. And caught a flash of a black T-shirt—or mostly black, as it seemed mottled in white—as the person wearing it stepped off the garden path and disappeared from view.

Yeah, Tom, Rafiel thought, with a mix of concern and annoyance. *Because who else would think that late in the evening, in the middle of a snowstorm, is a good time to go explore the garden of the aquarium?*

Still, he wasn't at all sure and couldn't do more than hope that it was indeed Tom, as he parked on the street and jumped out. He ran across the garden, ice and—presumably—frozen grass crackling under his feet. "Tom," he yelled. "Tom."

And then he hit a patch of ice, and his feet went out from under him.

Tom heard Rafiel's voice. He'd walked down the slope towards the river, and he'd looked every place possible his phone might have hit the ice. But it was dark, he didn't have a flashlight and—as far as he could tell—his phone would now be covered by snow, and a lump amid the other lumps resting on the riverbed. While it might be possible to distinguish it from rocks and twigs by its shape, every minute that passed was making it more indistinct, and Tom had no idea how long he'd been looking. He didn't wear a watch—something Kyrie told him was silly. Normally he could rely on the clock on the wall of The George.

And now, between being cold and the snow falling all around muffling sound, he didn't know if five minutes had gone by, or an hour. Or more. Sometimes, the phone rang, but even that didn't make it any easier to find, because it seemed that, just as he had isolated an area the sound might be coming from, the ringing stopped again.

All of this was worsened by the fact that he had to look for the phone from the bank. He didn't think the river was frozen enough to support him. And while the "river" was probably no more than two feet deep, at most, Tom didn't want to get his feet and legs wet. He was cold enough.

On the other hand, he also didn't want to lose his phone. Not to mention that by now his father probably thought that he had eaten someone—instead of just having been startled while his fingers were half frozen. He didn't think, even if his father thought so, that he would feel obligated to call the police and report, but you never knew. For most of his life, Edward Ormson had been a fairly amoral—if not immoral—corporate lawyer. He'd encountered ethics and a sense of responsibility late in life. Like any midlife crisis, it could cause some very strange effects. He might suddenly feel an irresistible obligation to report imaginary crimes.

That's it, Tom thought. *I'll go back to The George and call him from there.* He climbed up from the bank of the river to the path, at least six feet above. Like all such canals, artificial or not, in Colorado, the bed for the little river was deep enough to accommodate a ten-times swollen volume in sudden flash floods.

Though, like the legendary Colorado blizzards, it was something he hadn't experienced for himself, he'd heard of summers when sudden snowstorms up in the mountains sent water thundering down the canyons below, to cause untold damage. So the design of every waterworks in Colorado accounted for those.

He struggled all the way to the road level, and looked towards Fairfax. And then thought that it had taken him probably a good hour to walk here, and that added to the point where he had effectively hung up on his father meant that Edward was probably concocting scarier and scarier stories to tell himself. Right.

Sighing, he started down to the riverbed again. He'd look just one more time. Then there was Rafiel's voice from the garden up there. Definitely Rafiel's. And followed by a thud that indicated the idiot had just taken a header in the snow.

Tom cursed softly under his breath, and started climbing back up the steep bank. He wanted his phone. Badly. But considering the sounds he'd heard from under the bridge, he wasn't absolutely convinced there wasn't something or someone hiding there. Not so long ago, there had been a case in Denver of homeless men being found beheaded.

Tom didn't remember—since at the time he didn't live in Colorado and all he had seen of the affair was the TV news that happened to be playing at a soup kitchen—whether the case had ever been resolved, or if there was still someone in Colorado, perhaps in the smaller towns now, whose hobby it was to kill males foolish enough to be out and unsheltered—and unobserved—in this sort of weather. So it probably wouldn't hurt, before he went down towards the river and made himself invisible to anyone driving by, for him to have backup.

Having made it all the way to the path beside the river, Tom looked in the direction the thud had come from. Rafiel had gotten up, and was dusting off his knees.

"Are you okay?" Tom said.

"I'm fine," Rafiel said, and glared at him. "You?"

"I'm great," Tom said. "I just dropped my phone. Down on the river." He paused a second. "Right after my father asked me if I'd eaten someone."

"Oh," Rafiel said. He looked uneasy. Had his parents ever asked him if he'd eaten someone? No. Never mind that. Probably not. Though Tom had yet to meet Rafiel's mom, Rafiel had brought his dad over for lunch at The George a couple of times.

An older, sturdier version of Rafiel, his hair white and giving less the impression of a leonine mane than his son's wild hair, Mr. Trall had impressed Tom as eminently sane. And eminently sane parents didn't leap to the conclusion their sons went around eating people, not even when the sons happened to have another, more carnivorous form. Which didn't help Tom at all, because his father wasn't sane.

Rafiel was fishing in the pocket of his jacket. "Here, why don't you call him on my phone?"

"Oh," Tom said, surprised the idea hadn't occurred to him, though considering how much ice he felt on top of his head, his brain was probably frozen solid. And not being a silicon-based life-form, this didn't help his thought processes at all. He took the phone and started dialing his father's number, all under what he couldn't help feeling was Rafiel's stern scrutiny.

"Hello? Dad?" Tom said, as the phone was answered on the other side.

"Tom. Oh. Good. I was . . . er . . . I've been worried."

Tom tried to grit his teeth, which was pretty hard, as they insisted on chattering together. "No, Dad, I didn't eat anyone."

"Oh." Pause. "Well, I didn't think you had. I was just . . . er . . . worried."

Please, don't let him have gone to the police, Tom thought, as he watched Rafiel turn on his heel and head back towards the truck. Tom had a vague moment of panic at the thought that Rafiel was just going to drive back. Well, at least he'd left him with the phone. But the slog back to The George seemed suddenly like too much of an effort to make. Tom was very cold and very tired, and maybe he should just lie down here and—

"So what sort of trouble are you in?" Edward Ormson asked, over the phone. "I notice you're using someone else's phone. Isn't that your policeman friend? Tom! You've been arrested."

Damn, damn, damn, damn, damn! His youthful antics had included several arrests, for vandalism, for joyriding, for possession. His father had bailed him out countless times. But did this justify—five years later—his father assuming he'd been arrested, just because he was using a policeman's phone? *Well, okay, yeah, it probably kind of does,* he thought.

"I'll get someone to come post bail as soon as—"

"I wasn't arrested, Dad. It's . . . hard to explain over the phone. Do you remember the pearl?" He raised his eyebrows and had trouble concentrating on the flow of conversation, as Rafiel was making his way back, a bundle of fabric swinging from one hand.

"You didn't steal it again?"

"No, I didn't steal anything. Ow." The last sound was because Rafiel was roughly and very matter of factly putting a hooded sweat shirt over Tom's head and dressing him in it without so much as a "by your leave." It involved pulling Tom's hands through the sleeves, as if he'd been a child or a mental patient. "Ow, all right. I can dress myself, Rafiel."

"What?" Edward asked.

"Nothing. Rafiel has decided I'm not properly attired for the weather and is making me put on a hoodie." He glared at Rafiel.

"Seems sensible to me, if what I'm seeing on the weather channel is any indication," Edward said. "So, you were saying about this pearl."

"Not the pearl. The . . . owner of the pearl. He seems to think I belong to him. Because of who I am, you know?"

"Because you're my son and I worked for him?"

Sheesh. His dad could be surprisingly dense. "No,

Dad. No. Because I am . . . you know, like him and his relatives."

"Oh. What is he doing? We could file a—"

"Father." Despite his annoyance Tom almost laughed. At least his father was trying to help. Which was, all things considered, not bad. "I am sure he wouldn't be the least intimidated by a legal order of some sort. He eats lawyers for breakfast. Probably literally."

Rafiel pulled the hood up over Tom's head. Tom said into the phone, "Look, I have to go. I'll call you from The George when I get there."

Right now the diner, with its warmth and warm coffee and food seemed to Tom like a vision of lost paradise. He hung up and gave Rafiel the phone. And then he noticed that Rafiel had a flashlight in his hand. One of the larger ones of the type people said the police often used as a weapon in a pinch. Tom stepped back. But Rafiel said, "Come on. Let's go look for your phone one last time."

"Kyrie will be worried," Tom said.

"Just a minute. We'll look for your phone and if we don't see it, with the flashlight, then we go back. And, you know, Kyrie is probably not that worried. She knows I'm looking for you."

Tom bit his tongue to avoid saying that of course that would calm down anyone's anxiety, because who could ever doubt that once Rafiel was on the case everything would turn out for the best? But considering that Rafiel had found him, and gone out of his way to try to help him, his sarcasm would be misplaced. "All right," he said.

Seeing Tom subdued always frightened Rafiel a little. He'd been through law enforcement courses. He knew Tom's type.

Tom was the kind of person who usually had to be dragged away from whatever incident had just happened, still kicking and screaming and throwing a fit. The sort of person who could never get a traffic ticket without adding resisting arrest to the charges. The sort of person, in fact, who wasn't subdued unless he were very sick or very scared. Since Tom didn't look either, Rafiel had to assume freezing did something to shifter dragons.

Reptiles. Cold blood. Can't they die if they get cold enough? He didn't want to think about it, and besides, he'd given Tom a hoodie. Granted, it was Rafiel's size, and therefore a bit long on Tom, but that was good as it would go over Tom's hands.

Rafiel started towards the river, and then started, slowly, down the slope. His knee still hurt from banging it on the path when he had fallen and he had no intention of taking another header.

"Here," Tom said, stepping up beside him and offering him a hand. "My boots are sturdier than yours."

Rafiel took Tom's hand for support, half afraid that the very cold-feeling fingers would snap off under the grasp of his hand. He was sure—more than sure—that a normal person would have hypothermia from this adventure. But it always came back to . . . they weren't normal, were they?

They made it all the way to the bottom, where the frozen river glistened two steps from them. Unfortunately, it only glistened in the spots not covered up by snow. The rest was an amorphous, lumpy mess. He turned his flashlight on, and pointed it at the river and at that moment, Tom's phone rang. This helped Rafiel pinpoint the roughly rectangular snow-covered lump. "There," he said, nailing the shape with the beam of his flashlight. "Right there. Can you get it?"

Tom looked out speculatively. "I don't know if the ice will hold up. But if the ice breaks under me and I wet my feet, it's okay, because you'll give me a ride back to the diner, right?"

"Right," Rafiel said. Had the idiot thought that Rafiel was going to just come out, then leave him to freeze out here? "If parts of your body start breaking off from the cold I'm fairly sure Kyrie would kill me," he said, and grinned sheepishly at his friend. "So, yeah, I'll give you a ride back, you idiot."

Tom nodded and edged cautiously on top of the frozen river, with the sort of duck-footed waddle of someone trying to neither slip nor skate on the surface. In the middle of the river, he picked up the phone, then, as he was straightening, dropped it again.

"Would you stop that?" Rafiel asked impatiently. "The idea is to get back into the car and back to The George. Not to stand here and play find the phone."

But Tom shook his head, and bent, and picked up the phone again. He walked back close enough that he could whisper and Rafiel would hear him. "There's something in the tunnel under the little bridge, Rafiel. I saw a tail disappear that way."

A tail. Great. Rafiel was going to assume that, no matter how much Rafiel might want it to be otherwise, Tom didn't mean he had seen the friendly, furry, potentially wagging tail of a kitten or puppy. "Uh . . . a tail?"

"Reptilian. Dragging."

Rafiel frowned in the direction of the bridge and the shadows under it. It seemed to him, as he concentrated, that he did hear something very like a rustle from under there. But . . . a tail? "Perhaps the Great Sky Dragon sent one of your cousins to look after you."

"They're not my cousins."

"Whatever," Rafiel said, feeling an absurd pleasure, as if he'd scored a point. "They think they are."

"I'm hardly responsible for people's delusions."

How could someone like Tom, who didn't so much get in trouble as carry it into the lives of everyone around him, sound so much like a New England dowager?

"Yeah, but anyway, maybe he sent one of his underlings to look in on you?"

Tom shook his head. "Well, he did. Conan. But I sent him back his merry way. Or not merry." Tom frowned. "Besides," he whispered, "the tail looked like an alligator's."

"An alli—" Rafiel resisted an urge to smack his own forehead, and, shortly thereafter, an urge to smack Tom—hard—with the flashlight. "You mean Old Joe? The homeless guy said he told you he was at the aquarium."

"Yeah," Tom said. "I figure he's hiding out here, in alligator form."

"Is that why you're whispering? Look, what do you want with Old Joe, anyway? So he's hiding here, as an alligator. Perhaps we should leave him alone?"

Tom shook his head, which was par for the course. Of course he didn't think they should leave Old Joe alone, because that would be the life-preserving, not-getting-into-worse-trouble solution.

"Okay," Rafiel said. "So what do you want to do?"

"I figure he knows something," Tom whispered back. "And I want to find out what it is."

"Uh . . . what he knows is probably the best places to sleep when a storm threatens, and, Tom, you aren't even that with it. You ought to be indoors." And watched. By a nursemaid. Or a psychiatrist.

Tom shook his head again. Snow and ice flew from his dark hair. He frowned at Rafiel. He'd become alarmingly pale in the cold, so that he looked like he was wearing white pancake make-up, from which his lips—a vague shade of blue—the tip of his nose—a lovely violet—his dark eyebrows and his blue eyes emerged looking vaguely unnatural in all their chromatic glory. "Look, he knows something. And it's something that might help us. He knows about the Ancient Ones."

"Okay, even supposing he knows," Rafiel said impatiently, "what do you propose to do about this? And why are we whispering? If he didn't hear the cell phone ring, and doesn't know we're here, then he's way too addled to help us."

"That's not it," Tom said. "I don't want him to know we're about to go after him."

"We are? Into a sewer tunnel? After an alligator?"

"I don't think it's a sewer," Tom said, looking into the shadows under the bridge. "At least, I don't think the city would have an open sewer through a recreation area. I mean, I'm well aware that they're all crazy, but all the same, there's a difference between crazy and loony."

Not from where I'm standing, buddy. Aloud, Rafiel said, "Look at it this way—that connects to a drainage pipe somewhere. And that drainage pipe is connected, somewhere, to the Goldport sewers. You have heard of people flushing baby crocodiles, right?"

Tom made a sound of profound exasperation. "Yes, in New York City. Some science fiction writer or another wrote a very unpleasant story about it. But it's an urban legend, you know. No pet stores have sold crocodiles, that I remember. So it mustn't be legal anymore."

"Doesn't matter," Rafiel said, pragmatically. "It was legal back in the fifties. And crocodiles live forever."

"And migrate from New York City to Goldport, Colorado?" Tom shook his head. "Rafiel! Next thing you know, you're going to tell me we'll find Denver's lizard man from Cheeseman Park under there. Come on. Just come here, shine your flashlight under there. I promise I won't make you actually go under there and look amid all the dangerous animals."

He gave Rafiel one of his more irritating smiles.

"Oh, all right," Rafiel said, grudgingly.

For all that Tom had cajoled Rafiel into shining his light under the bridge, he was somewhat scared of what it might uncover. What if Rafiel was correct, and it would show a bunch of dragons under there, all of them spying on Tom?

Choking back a laugh at the absurd image, Tom told himself he was getting worse than his father. Any moment now, he'd start asking himself if he'd eaten people.

Rafiel slip-skated to stand beside Tom, closer to the center of the river, and shone his flashlight searchingly into the space beneath the little arched bridge.

It was cozier under there than Tom expected—or at least, there was none of the trash he'd come to expect in that sort of place. He'd slept in that sort of place, sometimes, and it seemed never to be empty of a few rusting cans, a couple of unidentifiable, shredded cardboard boxes and perhaps the rotting body of a road-kill racoon. But under this bridge, it looked pretty clean. A couple of branches and some leaves, and other than that, just the clean shine of ice.

"Fine," Tom said. "I guess there isn't—"

But at that moment he heard the clack-clack-clack of alligator teeth that seemed to be Old Joe's way of laughing. It was faint and muffled, but definitely there. Tom grabbed Rafiel's wrist and aimed the flashlight at the place the sound had come from. There in the dark, Old Joe was squeezed under the place where the bridge came down to meet the bank and where it was, therefore, almost impossible to see.

Tom heard himself make a sound that was much like that of a steam train stopping. "Come out," he said, peremptorily. "Come out now."

He didn't know what he expected. Old Joe had obeyed him in the past, but in the past he'd caught Old Joe raiding The George's dumpster, and therefore he was, technically, trespassing on Tom's property. This time, Tom half-expected him to turn tail and run very fast, which, Tom understood, could be very fast indeed for an alligator.

Old Joe must have thought it too. For a moment there was a rebellious light in the tiny eyes, in the reflection of the flashlight. Rafiel must have thought of worse things, because he tried to pull the flashlight away from Tom and started to say, "Enough. You know—"

But Tom said, in his best voice of command, "Don't you dare. Don't you even think about it. I thought you were dead. I've been worried sick for days. Now, you'll come out here, shift, and explain yourself."

Old Joe slithered forward, swinging his tail from side to side. Rafiel must have been still pretty unsure about what the creature meant to do, because he took a step backwards. But Tom stood his ground and Old Joe gave him a sheepish look, as if sorry that he had tried to scare him, or perhaps simply sorry that he hadn't managed to scare him.

He shifted, right there on the snow, and stayed sitting down on his butt on the ice, his hands around his knees. Rafiel made a sound and said, "I have clothes. In my car."

Old Joe gave him an indulgent, almost amused look, the sort of look grown-ups give cute little children. "No need," he said. "I will shift again, after you're gone." He looked up at Tom. "And now, what do you want? Why did you think I was dead?"

"Because of the dire wolf," Tom said. "You said he had talked to you and you clearly knew him, so I thought . . ." He felt as though he'd lost some of his capacity to command and his righteous indignation too, now that Old Joe was treating him as if he had been silly and alarmist.

Old Joe shrugged. "Yes. Dire is a bad person," he said. "He and his council of ancients, always dictating the way in which people are supposed to live, the way in which shifter people are supposed to be people, and whom we should respect and whom we shouldn't." He shook his head. "He's a very bad person." He looked up at Tom, intently. "You stay away from him."

"I have every intention of staying away from him," Tom said, hearing his own voice sound sullen, like an annoyed little boy's.

"You stay away from her, too."

"Her?" Tom said, with some strange notion that Rafiel had paid Old Joe to warn him against Kyrie.

"The girl that came to the aquarium, in the car," Old Joe said. "Just a little while ago."

Rafiel cleared his throat. "I know he spends more on his hair product than most third world nations produce in one year, but that wasn't a girl. It was my subordinate, McKnight. Though he might have had a girl with him," he said, vaguely remembering something about Michelle, one of the part-timers.

"No. Not the police people!" Old Joe looked aggrieved, like they were both very dense. "The other woman. She came by, after the police left, with a guy. She left without the guy."

"You mean . . ." Rafiel took a step towards the aquarium, but Tom held his wrist. He couldn't say anything. He wasn't about to cast aspersions on what Old Joe was saying right in front of Old Joe, but he held Rafiel's wrist and said, "Wait."

Then to Old Joe, he said, "And you haven't seen Dire

again? He hasn't talked to you again? Tried to find out things about us?"

That embarrassed look that he suspected meant Old Joe was lying, flitted across the alligator's face again. "Well," he said. "He came and he did ask me some questions. Like, what had happened at the castle, and all, but he . . ." He shrugged. "I didn't tell him anything that could hurt you. I swear I didn't. And then I ran away so I didn't have to tell him anything else." He looked at Tom, a look much like a glare from under his fringe of hair. "That's all I know. Can I go now?" And without waiting for permission, he shifted, and ran—in alligator form—back under the bridge, in a clacking of teeth, much like a fugitive snicker.

"We've got to go to the aquarium," Rafiel said.

Which meant, Tom thought, that he wasn't thinking at all. How was he going to get in? And if he did, how was he going to justify going into the aquarium to look for a body just now? Tom was fairly sure his friend hadn't thought this through.

"Wait. Let's go to your car and discuss this first," he told Rafiel.

"But—"

"Wait."

In the car, Rafiel turned on the gas to start warming up the motor, so they could have heat soon.

"Rafiel, you can't go in there," Tom said. "You just can't."

"What do you mean, I can't?" Rafiel said. He reached

for his phone, ready to call McKnight and ask him to come and process the scene.

"I meant, you can't." Tom looked very grave and slightly sad, which was very odd. If Rafiel didn't know him better, if Rafiel weren't sure this was one dragon who didn't go about pushing people into aquariums . . .

"Why not?" he asked belligerently, while behind his rational mind, there ran thoughts he wouldn't even acknowledge, much less express, such as that dragons were aquatic creatures and that, as aquatic creatures, they might have some craving or other relating to water and pushing people in it. "You know it's my duty. I'm a policeman. If there's a body in there—"

"*If*," Tom said. "But beyond that, Rafiel, how are you going to tell them you heard about it? Who are you going to say informed you? And how are you going to say you got in?"

Rafiel tapped his fingers on the seat beside him. "But . . . time is of the essence," he said. "If there is a corpse, the more complete it is, the better the picture we will get. I mean, with the other ones, we don't even know if they were already dead when they were dumped in. And if we're dealing with shifters . . ."

"Yes. Of course. Perhaps an anonymous phone call? From one of the phone booths remaining, at a convenience store not on Fairfax?" Tom said. "One of the ones in the less busy areas? You can park at the back, or even farther away than that, and I can call and tell the police that there is a corpse in the aquarium. But it has to be to the central station. And I can't be identified."

"Yeah," Rafiel said, thinking. "So long as you don't stay

on the line. They'll try to keep you on the line, so that they can get to you. You must not do that. Say your piece and .run, and we'll get out of there fast." As he spoke, he thought of the convenience store to go to, on Fer de Lance Street. Between the local pioneer museum and a high school, the place was guaranteed to be deserted today.

He started off, headed that way, by the shortest route possible. "Well, at least what Old Joe says," Rafiel said, "sort of narrows it down to a female employee of the aquarium. I had a list of names of male employees to interview, but now . . ."

"No," Tom said, seriously. His features were set in such a way that they seemed to be carved, and a muscle played on the side of his face, giving the impression that he was about to have a nervous breakdown or something. "No, don't be so sure. What you're not thinking about, Rafiel, is that . . . well . . . Old Joe is not the best of witnesses, you know? He often . . ." He shrugged.

"He often what? Drinks? Does drugs?"

Tom shook his head, emphatically. "No. Nothing like that. At least, not that I know, and I think I'd have been able to tell. No. But he sometimes seems to be . . . not quite anchored to reality, if you know what I mean?"

Rafiel quirked an eyebrow. Sometimes he wondered how anchored to reality they all were. Considering what they were, and what they could do, it would be a wonder if they didn't sometimes feel unmoored and adrift. "Okay," he said.

He pulled up behind the store, on Fer de Lance. Actually behind and on the other side of the street, so that no one associated him with the phone call. There wasn't anyone around, in any case. The high school was closed, as was the pioneer museum. The rest of the block had the sort of empty feel that areas of town had that aren't flourishing. Like the last houses that had stood there had just been bulldozed, and they hadn't come up with anything else to replace them. The vacant lots didn't even have trees or proper plants. Just a sort of scrubby grass, now completely covered by snow.

"What are you doing?" he said, realizing Tom was throwing himself over the front seat and towards the back.

Tom, now fully in the back seat, gave him a grin. "Getting out on the driver's side," he said. "It's towards the school, and that's firmly closed, so no one will see me."

He had the hood firmly pulled over his head, and started to open the door, then stopped. "Do you have a quarter? Because I can't use a credit card on this. It would be way too obvious."

Rafiel grabbed a quarter from the drink holder, where he normally kept parking-meter fodder. He flipped it at Tom, who grabbed it out of the air. Good to know he was getting the feeling in his hands back.

He watched Tom get out of the car, very quickly, cross the high school campus semidiagonally, so that any witness would say he came out of the school. Sometimes—he thought, as he watched Tom cross the street and run, hell-bent for leather, towards the convenience store, so fast that he wasn't any more than a brief dark blur amid the snow—it was easy to believe the things Tom told him about his teenage years. Casual juvenile delinquence would impart that sort of knowledge. How to trick the police, 101.

In less time than seemed possible, for what he needed to do, Tom was back, coming into the car through the back door and saying, "Drive, drive, drive."

Rafiel drove. "Who answered?"

"I think just the receptionist or dispatcher, or whatever. She told me she would transfer me to someone else, but I hung up." He grinned at Rafiel, a feral grin, and leaned forward on the seat. "I grabbed the phone with my sleeve. And I wiped the coin before putting it in."

Rafiel sighed. "Probably overkill," he said. "We are not exactly the most advanced scientific police in the world." He took a bunch of turns, very fast, not so much seeking to be physically far away from the convenience store, as seeking to be in a place no one would associate with the convenience store. In no time at all, it seemed, he was driving through an upscale neighborhood of the type that used to be a suburb in the days when the main form of commuting was the trolley car. Eight blocks or so, in a direct shot from downtown Goldport, this neighborhood was all shaded, set-back, two- and three-floor houses, which managed to look much like Christmas cards under the snow. "As long as they don't catch you in the act of putting the coin in, or dialing them up, that's pretty much it. Oh, if it's anyone but McKnight, they'll exert due diligence, too, by going to the clerk and asking if they saw someone call."

"Unlikely," Tom said. "I was at the back of the store the whole time. Unless he can see through brick walls . . ."

"Yes," Rafiel said, and then, because the way that Tom was leaning forward over the seats was starting to give him visions of suddenly hitting a tree and ending up with Tom splattered all over his dashboard, "You know, we have laws about seat belts, in this state. As a policeman—"

Tom didn't answer. He just leaned back and buckled the seat belt. Then he made a sudden startled sound. "Kyrie," he said. "I haven't called Kyrie."

Kyrie was bargaining with fate. She was working, steadily, as if nothing had happened, but behind her smile, her ready quips at the customers, she was bargaining with fate.

She had started from the point of view that if Tom were to walk in, right then, she would only tell him how worried she'd been. She wouldn't make a big deal at all out of it. But since then, as the minutes passed and she heard neither from him nor from Rafiel, she'd started bargaining.

Okay, okay, if Tom walks in right now, she told herself, *I'll just smile and tell him how glad I am that he's alive.* Aware that she'd actually paused to listen for the sound of the back door opening up, she let out a hiss of frustration at herself. It wasn't sane, and it wasn't rational, but the thing was that she'd been expecting Tom to come in in response to her silent concession. She sighed at her own stupidity, and looked at the wall. Okay, he'd been gone more than two hours. What if he was frozen by the side of the road?

She could call Rafiel. She should call Rafiel. But what if Rafiel hadn't found him, yet? Or worse, what if Rafiel had found him? And he wasn't alive? In that case, the longer she took to find out about it, the better, right?

No. No. She was being stupid. It was unlikely he'd be dead, and if he was ill or severely hypothermic, of course she wanted to know. Needed to know. She set down the latest batch of orders and nudged Conan, who was getting much better at tending tables, but who, despite lots of coffee, looked like death warmed over.

"Take over my tables for a little while, okay?" she asked.

He nodded. His gaze turned to her, said what he could not say in full voice. And it was something that Kyrie simply didn't want to hear. *What if he's dead? What if I left him and then the Ancient Ones killed him?*

Kyrie shook her head at him, slightly, denying her own misgivings as well as his. And then she stepped behind the counter and reached for the phone on the wall, trying to figure out how she could ask Rafiel questions without either giving away the shifter thing, or alarming Anthony, who was looking at her curiously. She was sure he had decided that she and Tom had had a spat. He was giving her that look of concern and gentle enquiry friends give you when they don't want to stick themselves in the middle of your marital disputes.

She took a deep breath. She could just ask Rafiel how it was going.

The phone rang, so suddenly and loudly that it made her jump. She fumbled for it, almost dropped it, managed to get it to her ear and say, "Hello?"

"Is that how you answer the phone for a business?" Tom's gently teasing voice was such a relief to hear that Kyrie felt her knees go weak, and tears sting behind her eyes.

"Idiot," she said.

"Um . . . that's also not the approved . . ." Tom said. She could see him grin as he spoke. And then, as though realizing he could only push his luck so far, he said, "Look, everything is okay. Sorry to take so long to call back, but we found Old Joe—"

"Old Joe?" Nothing could be further from her mind than the transient alligator shifter. She saw Anthony give her an odd look. Clearly that had also not figured in his speculation.

"Yeah. I'll explain when I get back. Look, it might be easier . . . if you can leave Anthony and Conan in charge and join us in the room at the bed-and-breakfast?" He chuckled softly. "I'd like to add girls to the repertoire of odd visitors I shower with."

"Idiot," she said again, very softly.

"Yes, I am. Conan made it back okay, right?"

"Yeah. Conan is fine. He's getting better at waiting tables, too." Again, Kyrie was conscious of Anthony's baffled look at her. She did her best to brazen it out, as she asked, "So you met Rafiel?" At least she assumed so, unless he had now taken to using the royal we.

"Yeah. He'll be coming back with me. We're going by a doughnut place first, though, apparently."

"What?"

"I don't know," Tom said. Kyrie could hear another voice in the background, that she had to assume was Rafiel talking. "He says they have a tracker in his car, and if he doesn't go by a doughnut place at least once a week they kick him out of the force."

"Ha ha," Kyrie said.

"Yeah, I told him it was lame, too, but at least he's making an effort at making fun of himself. A few more years and he should be human. Hey. Stop hitting me. Police brutality. So, do you think you can make it to the room? In about fifteen minutes?"

"I'll manage," Kyrie said.

"All right. And, listen . . . I'm an idiot. Sorry if I worried you."

She tried to deny that he worried her at all, but her mouth refused to form quite that big a lie. "It's okay," she said, instead, because she had bargained with fate, and she'd promised not to kill him, not to maim him even slightly, and finally that she wasn't even going to yell at him. "It's okay."

Tom thought the place must have been a Dunkin' Doughnuts in a previous life, but it had now become—according to the sign hastily painted on a facade in which the Dunkin' Doughnuts name was still readable from the too-white shadow of the letters that used to cover it—Good Morning Doughnuts.

The whole place had the sort of look of someone in limited circumstances and hiding out under a false name to avoid embarrassing the family. On the door, a hand-lettered sign read *cash only please*, which gave the impression that the people running it were planning to escape to South America at any moment, taking their ill-gotten gains with them.

But inside, it was surprisingly cozy, with aged but well-scrubbed formica tables, around which gathered bevies of retirees and housewives. This was clearly a gathering spot for a working-class neighborhood.

Behind the counter, a Chinese family made Tom tense, before he scolded himself that race had nothing to do with it. Yes, most dragon shifters might be Asian. But he clearly wasn't. And the dire wolf was just as bad as the Great Sky Dragon's triad. Perhaps worse, as at least it could be claimed that the Great Sky Dragon tried to protect all dragon shifters—while the dire wolf seemed to have very few loyalties but to himself. Tom wondered if Dire was representative of the Ancient Ones at all. Perhaps he'd just chosen to claim the role. There was no telling.

Rafiel was clearly known here. He ordered a dozen doughnuts, rapidly choosing the flavors, and grinning at Tom's bewildered expression. "I told you. We're required to visit these places. At least once a week."

Tom shook his head, smiling a little.

"Do you want coffee?" Rafiel asked. And when Tom nodded yes, he proceeded to order three. "I owe one to a guy in a doorway on Fairfax. He told me where to find you."

"The guy in a khaki jacket?" Tom asked.

"Yeah. He didn't seem to want to go to a shelter at any cost, and he had one of those Mylar blankets." Rafiel shrugged. "I wondered . . ." But never said what he wondered as he handed the bills over to the lady behind the counter.

Later in the truck, Tom said, "I wondered too. But he didn't smell of shifter."

"I know," Rafiel said. "Though to be honest, as cold as I was, I don't think I could smell anything."

"That's possible," Tom said. He bit his lip. "But I think I or you would have smelled something . . . even just a hint."

Rafiel nodded. He put a hand into the doughnut box, nudging it open in a way that bespoke long practice. He wedged a doughnut in his mouth, as he shifted into gear with his free hand. Then, with the doughnut still in his mouth, he backed out of the parking lot of the doughnut shop and onto the road.

"Why a dozen doughnuts?" Tom asked. "Seriously. Don't tell me they'd kick you out of the force. Why a dozen doughnuts?"

Rafiel took a bite of his doughnut, dipped into the box again for a napkin and wedged the napkin-wrapped doughnut into the cup holder on the dashboard, all while driving with one hand, in a way that Tom had to admit, given the snow and what looked to him no more visibility than about a palm beyond the windshield, seemed a bit cavalier.

"Energy," he said. "I think I'm going to have a long night of it. I don't think I can go and interview the male employees now, of course. But if Old Joe was right, and if there really was a body at the aquarium, I should get a call any minute now. And that usually means a few hours securing the scene, sweeping for evidence and all that. It's not a five-minute job."

"Right," Tom said.

"But first," Rafiel said, in all seriousness, "we must take the coffee to Khaki Guy, whom we'll do our best to sniff out, if he is a shifter. And then we must meet Kyrie. There's a meeting I'm not looking forward to."

"Why?" Tom said, surprised.

"Because I didn't call her as soon as I found you." He grinned wider and added, with every appearance of enjoying the thought, "She's going to rip my balls off and beat me with them."

Kyrie was glad they arrived at the room almost exactly fifteen minutes later. She had just the time to pick up Not Dinner, who, being a cat, and faced with a surfeit of stuffed furniture and other comfortable sleeping surfaces, had chosen to fall asleep in the bathtub. But he'd woken up when she first came into the bathroom, and scrabbled up her petting arm, until she held him under her chin and petted him, while he purred ecstatically.

She'd managed to get to the bed, with him trying to climb into her shirt, under the neckline, and install himself on her left shoulder, when she heard the key in the lock, and then Tom came in.

He still looked like nothing on earth, with his hair floating around him, in a wild dark cloud. He was wearing a hoodie she'd never seen on him, and which must be Rafiel's, since it was dark grey and said "Policemen Do It More Forcefully" across the chest. He was also carrying a doughnut and a cup of coffee. And he stood, just inside the door, grinning sheepishly at her, while Rafiel came in, behind him, and closed the door.

The weird thing, she thought, was that Rafiel looked scared, while Tom didn't. Tom looked more embarrassed, as if he'd done something horribly stupid. Which, of course, in a way, he had.

"Sorry," he said. "I still can't understand how you could take it so calmly." A blush climbed his cheeks. "But I guess you're more grown-up than I am. You've always been."

And she, who only a couple hours before was thinking exactly the same, shook her head. "No. I don't think it's a matter of being more or less grown-up. Truly. I think we're just . . . very different people." And then, for fear he'd interpret this as breaking up with him when, in fact, over the last hour or so she'd come to the conclusion she *couldn't* live without him, even if she tried, she added, "And that's okay. I mean, we're supposed to be. It would be very weird to fall in love with yourself, wouldn't it?"

Tom looked slyly at Rafiel and for just a moment, Kyrie thought he was going to say that Rafiel managed it fine. But instead, he shrugged a little, and that, Kyrie thought might in fact be a function of growing up. He'd learned not to bait the policeman.

"So . . . you said you needed to talk to me? Tell me . . . something?"

Tom nodded. "At least right now," he said, "I don't need to shower." And smiled. "I keep thinking I'm going to catch one of those horrible diseases you catch from washing too much. A fungus or something, because I destroyed the normal balance of the skin."

He walked to the vanity, and grabbed his hairbrush and started vigorously brushing his hair back, tying it neatly again, in his normal ponytail. While he did so, he talked.

He told her of walking out—of thinking about a lot of things, though he wouldn't specify what those things were—of hearing that Old Joe might be at the aquarium and of wandering there. Then he told her about the phone, and how his father had thought he'd eaten someone.

Kyrie had to clench her hands into fists at this point, and make an effort not to speak out loud. Because she who never had parents, at least had an idea of what parents were supposed to be. And what they weren't. And she was fairly sure they weren't supposed to be like Edward Ormson. Oh, surely, his son was a strange creature. An enigma that they couldn't quite solve. But he should know Tom enough to know he wouldn't—couldn't—murder anyone. Much less eat him or her. Yes, she knew that Tom claimed to always be afraid of that also. Which was silly. Perhaps she knew him better than he knew himself, but she was quite aware that he would never do anything like that.

Thinking this she met his eyes in the mirror and they smiled at each other. He stepped back, slowly, to sit by her side on the bed, and hold her hand. "I shouldn't have gone away," he said. "Yes, I needed to cool off. But I needed to be with you as well. As is, I made you worry needlessly. Is . . . is Conan all right?"

"Very worried about you," Kyrie said. "He kept thinking the Ancient Ones might get you, and then the Great Sky Dragon might come for him."

Tom smiled, this time ruefully, and squeezed her hand a little. "I figured it was something like that."

"Okay, my story now," Rafiel said. He had sat backwards on the vanity chair, facing them, his arms around its middle, his chin resting atop of it. Despite his obvious grown-up proportions, the width of his shoulders, the glint of a five o'clock shadow in a tawny color that matched his leonine mane, he looked much like a truant boy. He told them, clearly, and doing the expressions and the voices of both himself and his interlocutors about his three interviews with aquarium visitors. "The thing," he said, "is that she told me there was another shifter, in the aquarium. She thought he was one of the spider crabs." He sighed. "So maybe that was the other shifter we smelled." He explained about his earlier interview with Ms. Gigio.

"Do you think she's the woman that Old Joe was warning you about?" Kyrie asked. "I mean . . ."

"I don't even know if Old Joe hallucinated the whole thing," Tom said. "Until there is proof to the contrary, I'd like to withhold opinion as to whom he was talking about."

Kyrie nodded. Rafiel looked up and shrugged a little. "She doesn't smell like a shifter. If she's only a crazy person who is pushing people into the shark tank . . . then she's not my problem."

"Rafiel!" Kyrie said, before she realized that she was going to say it, a note of indignation in her voice. "I can't believe you'd say that. What do you mean she's not your problem? You sound like . . . Dire . . . with all his talk about how ephemerals don't matter, how only shifters do."

Rafiel shook his head, even if a slight amount of color appeared over his high cheekbones. "You misunderstand me," he said. "That's not what I meant at all. Only that it won't require anything special from me—just police work, which I would do for any other case. It's not my problem as a shifter; I don't have to skulk and lie and find a way to make it all come out right. Only . . . only make sure that we find the culprit and she has a proper trial. Or he, if it's not Lei, but it's still not a shifter. It's the shifter angle that has me worried. Right now, the more I hear and the more I probe into this, the more I get worried that there is a shifter angle—it could be anyone, from Dante Dire, to this unknown spider crab shifter to . . ." He shook his head. "I don't think it could be Ms. Gigio. But it could definitely be the Rodent Liberation Front, whoever they are. Any rodent shifters crazy enough to try Marxist theory must be ready for everything."

"And crazy enough for anything," Tom said ruefully.

At that moment, Rafiel's phone rang. He picked it up and answered. From their side, the conversation bordered on cryptic. Rafiel said, "Yeah, yeah, yeah. Right. I'll be there." And hung up, and got up to go.

"They found a corpse?" Tom asked, his body as taut as a bowstring, his tension seemingly communicating itself to Kyrie via the hand he held.

Rafiel nodded. "Yes. He's . . . He was almost not eaten at all—they'd . . . the sharks had just started on him, and they fished him out. Well . . . I don't know about not eaten at all." He looked a bit green and swallowed, as if the images his words evoked were getting to him, as well. "But he still has a face and lungs. And . . . well . . . they figure that they will be able to identify him, and look for signs that he was pushed into the tank while still alive. Or not."

Kyrie nodded.

"Glad I got the doughnuts," Rafiel told Tom. "It's going to be a long night. I'll call you guys or come by when I'm off."

And, with Kyrie holding tightly onto Notty, to prevent

the orange fuzzball making a dash for the door, Kyrie and Tom stood up, to say goodbye to Rafiel, as he opened the door to leave.

And stopped, staring at the newspaper outside the door. It was one of the many peculiarities of the *Weekly Inquirer* that it was usually delivered late on the night of the day it was dated, sometime between eleven and midnight. Probably because it had started as a weekly paper, and there was less emphasis on the news being up to the minute, than on it being wittily or interestingly reported.

Only this time, none of them looked to see whether the news was properly reported. Instead, the three of them stared aghast at the headline, in screaming red, marching across the top of the front page: *Local Diner Haunted by Dragons.* Beneath it was a picture far clearer than any that zoological papers and magazines had ever boasted. It showed Tom and Conan both flying in dragon form. Tom was somewhat more distant—and therefore a little more blurred—but Conan was in the full glare of a very good electronic camera that had captured every scale and every fold of his skin in all its glory, as well as his mouth, open, the fangs parted, as if to roar.

"Wha—" Kyrie said in shock.

Rafiel swore under his breath. And then Notty took off, running down the carpeted hall. And Tom took off after it.

Tom caught the cat just short of the stairs. It required throwing himself headlong, his hand extended as if for the great baseball catch. What he caught was a tiny handful of spitting fury, that he held very firmly, while bringing it up to his chest, and standing up. He registered, distantly, that he'd just hit his knee hard, and that the wood beneath the carpet had far less give than he expected.

Holding Not Dinner, he limped back to the bedroom. Rafiel was still standing, holding the paper. "I have to go," he said, in a little, squeaky voice.

"But how . . ." Kyrie said.

Rafiel blushed. "I should have told you."

"What should you have told us?" Tom asked. "You saw someone take that picture?"

"Well . . . not quite that . . . But that Summer girl that Keith brought in? Right after you and Conan took off—" He turned to Kyrie. "This was when they were trying to rescue you, you know. Anyway, right after they took off, Keith's girlfriend was right there, at the back door, and I thought it was very weird. She said she'd got lost looking for the bathroom, but you know, it's not like it's all that hard to find, or like it's not properly marked, and right there . . ." He frowned. "I remember at the time thinking that something was wrong, and even more so when she disappeared right after. But then Dante Dire came in, and it just made me forget all that stuff."

"Yeah," Kyrie said. "I think he has that effect."

And Tom had to admit he did. "I'm sure," he said, feeling like his voice was constricted, "that it is all a matter of priorities. I mean, the dire wolf could kill us. What is the worst this woman could do? Make me move on?" He shrugged, attempting to look completely unaffected by this. "How bad would that be? I've moved so much, from town to town, and . . . all over." But he didn't want to move, and his heart was breaking over even the possibility of doing so. He didn't want to go anywhere. Let alone that he had Kyrie and a home, even if it was just a rented house, and apparently, now, a kitten.

He didn't want to leave the diner behind. It was the first time in his life that he felt invested in a place. He owned The George—half of it. It was his. He had shaped it already and would shape it more, make it something uniquely his, his own diner.

"I don't think it will come to that," Rafiel said. He stepped inside the door and flung the paper towards the bed. "At most, we'll say it's a good Photoshop job. I mean, Tom, who is going to believe in dragons? Seriously? If they'd caught me or Kyrie, it might be worse . . ." He shrugged. "Let's just take care that this doesn't happen again, okay?"

But how to make sure it didn't happen again was something completely different, Kyrie thought, as they got back into the diner, and Tom got the report from Anthony on what was prepared and what not. He tried to send Anthony home because it was best if Anthony went back and slept and came back in the morning, to relieve them when they would definitely need to rest, supposing there would be any rest that day.

They had barely got into the swing of their shift when Tom's phone rang, and he pulled it from his pocket. "It's

Rafiel again," he said. And then, asking a puzzled Anthony to cover for them another five minutes, he pulled Kyrie with him into the storage area and put Rafiel on speaker.

"Hi," Rafiel said, between munching that indicated he was doing justice to the doughnuts he'd bought. "Look, I just came out to the car, with the excuse that I needed a doughnut."

"News on the body?" Kyrie asked.

"Well . . . yeah, kind of. But . . . the thing is . . ." He cleared his throat. "I got a phone call, from our medical examiner who was examining the . . . er . . . prophylactics they found in the planters."

Kyrie rolled her eyes. "You can say condoms, Rafiel. I know the word." An impish grin. "I've heard it a time or two."

A sound very much like a raspberry from the other end of the phone. "The medical examiner called it prophylactics. Of course, he also called the stuff inside genetic material, which he says exactly matches that of the first two vics."

"What, both of them?" Tom asked, sounding absolutely shocked.

"Well . . . no, one each. And no, there is no indication . . . I mean . . . the condoms were definitely used for . . . er . . . heterosexual sex. I mean . . . there were vaginal . . . secretions . . ." He paused in what seemed to Tom like an excess of embarrassment, like he had suddenly choked on it and couldn't go on. Tom grinned and waited, and eventually, after a noisy throat clearing, Rafiel came back on. "So it would seem that the male employees are not in fact a problem . . . though I can tell you, one of them, who apparently lives nearby and who dropped by to see if we needed him to show us or tell us anything, is definitely a shifter. His name is John Wagner. College student. Nice guy. Body builder. Works here part-time. I don't know what his shifted form is, but he . . . well . . . I'm fairly sure he doesn't have vaginal secretions."

"Unless his shifted form is as a woman," Tom said, wryly. ·

"Uh . . . I don't think so. You know, the other thing, the other part of the exam . . . of the . . ."

"Condoms," Kyrie said.

"Yeah. The other part of it is that it showed . . . well . . . The medical examiner thought this was from salve or cream, possibly a traditional medicinal one and that it should be easy to trace because of the exotic ingredient, but I'm not so sure. You see, there were . . . other cells on the sample. On the outside . . . They appear to be . . . Sharkskin cells. The examiner also thinks, possibly, because that was the shark tank, it might be someone who handles the sharks on a regular basis, although I don't even want to think what he imagines the handlers do with the sharks to get the cells in that particular region of their bodies."

Kyrie shrugged. "I bet you he thinks it's poor hygiene. And it might be."

"Oh, yes," Rafiel said. "It might be. On the other hand . . ."

"On the other hand, it could be something completely different," Kyrie said.

"Like someone who turns into a shark and back," Tom said. Because there was the very definite feel that the shift was never as complete as it seemed in either direction. More than once, Tom had shaken out his boots to find dragon scales inside them, even though he'd never worn them while a dragon and usually stepped well away from them before he shifted. And sometimes, when he washed his hair in the shower, one or two green and gold scales fell out.

"Yeah," Rafiel said. "That's what I'm very much afraid it is."

"In which case," Tom said, listening to Rafiel munch, "it's not so much a matter of maliciously pushing her— we'll assume her, since Old Joe said so—victims into the tank. It's more like your buying your doughnuts. A little snack to see her through the night."

The munching stopped. "Ew. Not like my doughnuts."

"Well, of course not," Tom hastened to say. "Unless you eat cannibal doughnuts." And then seized with sudden inspiration, "You know, Kyrie, we could do those next year for Halloween. Fill them with raspberry, or something, and put names on them . . . you know, like Joe or Mike, and call them cannibal doughnuts."

"Sure, we could," Kyrie said. "If our objective were to totally gross out and drive away our clientele. Besides, we can't do doughnuts properly. Not without a dedicated fryer."

"Maybe there will be enough money by the fall to buy another fryer," Tom said.

"Uh," Rafiel interrupted, "before you guys start arguing domestic arrangements, the other thing is, that I tried to find Old Joe, because, you know, since he was right about the last corpse—by the way, the name was Joseph Buckley; he was a software salesman—I thought he might be able to give me details and pinpoint who the woman might be he was talking about. But I can't find him anywhere."

Tom sighed. "He's very, very good at hiding. I think he's been doing it for centuries. If he's right about having been alive since before horses . . ."

"Yeah. Probably. Anyway . . . I can't figure out where he's gone, so if you hear something let me know."

And then he hung up, leaving them in the storage room, staring at each other.

"I wonder if John Wagner is a member of the Rodent Liberation Front," Tom said, biting the corner of his lip, in the way he did when he was thinking of something unpleasant. "I think he's one of our regulars. I remember the description, and also processing credit card bills for John Wagner."

Kyrie nodded. "Yeah, he is. He usually comes in for breakfast on Wednesday. And he's very fond of sweet bread, you know, Hawaiian bread. He always asks for a toast of that. Something about growing up in Hawaii."

"Interesting."

"Why interesting?" Kyrie asked.

"Because . . . if I remember correctly—and mind you, this is me remembering some cheap book or other that I read at some shelter for runaway teens, years ago—but if I remember correctly, Hawaii is the only place that has legends of shark shifters." He frowned. "Well, the Japanese might too. But Japanese shifter legends are very difficult to understand. I mean . . . they're not Western in structure. So even though I was very interested in all stories about shapeshifters, I don't think I remember any Japanese ones."

Kyrie nodded, but she felt her forehead wrinkle. "You know . . ." she said. "I . . . I don't know. I can't understand why I never smelled John Wagner. I mean, I serve him every week. You'd think I'd have sniffed him out."

Tom frowned. "Rafiel and I were talking about that, because of sniffing out Khaki Guy, you know. Both of us tried and neither of us could get a scent, but really . . . it's so cold, and then, the thing is . . . I've been homeless, but I washed. At least once a day. He clearly doesn't. There were smells, you know, of food and stuff, which I'm sure he's dropped on his clothes. And there was a smell of tobacco, too, and it was really hard to make out his smell amid all those, much less in the cold. So we don't know if he's a shifter, or just paranoid about shelters and closed-in situations. Which lots of people are, for reasons that have nothing to do with being shifters."

"Obviously," Kyrie said. "But John Wagner washes. I'm sure of it. He usually looks squeaky clean."

"Yes, but then when does he come in? Early early morning, right, before six a.m.? Before we quit. And I bet you he works days. So at six a.m. or before that, he's freshly washed, and probably has deodorant and after-shave on. Mix that with the smells of the diner—from fries to eggs and bacon—and you'd need to be looking for the smell of shifter to identify him. Or any other shifter."

"Yeah," Kyrie said. She nodded. "Well, I'm going to be looking for it, from now on. In just about everyone. Rodent Liberation Front and Ancient Ones and triads!" she said in a tone of great exasperation.

"Oh, my," Tom said, and smiled apologetically.

The aquarium was probably noisier than when it was open to the public, Rafiel thought, as he stood back, watching the frantic activity around him. People were snapping shots of the tank area and McKnight, with remarkable efficiency, probably born of the fact that Rafiel was frowning vaguely in his direction, was directing three people—three of Goldport's part-time officers, more used to breaking up drunken brawls among students than to doing crime scene processing—in combing through everything around there, including the planters by the side of shark tank.

And Rafiel, having quietly gotten away from the thick of things, had managed to sidle up to John Wagner, who was leaning against the far wall, under the plaque that explained the sharks' habits—unpleasant—and habitats—more extensive than Rafiel was comfortable thinking about.

He was a young guy, light-haired. Probably in his twenties, and he looked like he devoted serious time to body building. His file, as well as the brief conversation that Rafiel had had with him, indicated that Wagner was in college. Rafiel wondered what he majored in. Perhaps physical education or sports medicine?

Rafiel leaned beside him, casually. He noted that the man gave him a brief, amused, sidelong glance, and he returned a friendly smile. "So," he said, trying desperately to sound as if he was just making casual conversation, "you work out?"

The amused glance took him in again, and a lip curled ironically on the side. "A bit," the young man said. "Now and then."

And then Rafiel decided to go for broke, with the type of question that, should his interlocutor refuse to understand it or to respond, could be passed off as a joke of some sort—and which would certainly sound like a joke to anyone overhearing it. "In human form?" He had figured that Wagner's was the shifter-smell all around the shark area.

If he expected Wagner to be discomposed, he missed his mark. The smile only became a little broader, and he said, "Sure. The other one isn't really conducive to it. Unless I wanted to work on my ear muscles. And then there's all the drool."

"What?" Rafiel asked, unable to help himself. He cast a quick glance at the other people in the room, who were all surrounding something and taking pictures of it.

Wagner cackled, in unbecoming satisfaction. He muttered something under his breath that sounded disturbingly like "dumb ass," then added, "If you can smell me, what makes you think I can't smell you?"

"Oh," Rafiel said, now totally out of his depth. "Oh." He turned around to look at Wagner fully. The young man was grinning at him.

"Do you . . . do you know many of your . . . of our kind?" Rafiel asked. He'd never before interviewed anyone fully aware of what he himself was.

Wagner shrugged. "A couple. A friend back home, and then one more in college."

"Oh. What . . . are they?"

"Uh?"

"What forms do they take?" Rafiel said, his eye still on his subordinates and colleagues to make sure no one approached to hear this very strange conversation.

"Oh. My friend, Keith Kawamoto, back home was a bear. Which was very weird in Hawaii. Oh, sure, we had lots of fun roaming the beach late at night in our shifted forms. And he used to hang out in the Aiea Loop Trail. Weird-ass reports to everyone who would listen—and a lot of people who wouldn't—by the tourists. But who is going to believe tourists talking about a bear and a dog walking along the beach at low tide? Or a bear just hanging out? There was some enquiry once, to see if a circus that was passing through had lost a trained bear, but that was about it."

"And then here?"

Shrug. "There's a guy in the dorms who turns into a unicorn. Weird-ass thing to turn into, and of course no one believes it even if they see him. Sometimes we get reports of a white horse hanging about, is about it. It's assumed to be a prank." He shrugged. "After I smelled him out, we became pretty good friends. I keep telling him he's a unicorn so he can go in search of virgins, but he doesn't look like he'll ever have the courage, if you know what I mean." He waggled his eyebrows. "Engineering student and a bit of a dumb ass, but a nice guy."

His matter-of-fact approach to the situation and the way he seemed to have co-opted Rafiel as a buddy, whether Rafiel wanted to be one or not, were disconcerting enough that it took Rafiel a moment to collect himself. "So . . . you don't . . . I mean . . . I've had reports from . . . from another shifter . . . of a spider-crab shifter here in the aquarium. So I take it that's not true. I mean . . ."

"What? Because I didn't include him in my count? Nah, I didn't count him because I don't really know him. I know of him, but I don't know him. I think everyone in the aquarium—well, everyone who works here after-hours—has seen him. Weird-ass old Japanese guy, you know, all wrinkly and stuff. He looks like the Japanese guys in those reports they used to do where they found some old World War II soldier, who had been defending the same island in the Pacific for fifty years, ready to expel anyone who tried to land, only no one ever did."

"Uh . . ." Rafiel said. "So, you've talked to him?"

Wagner shook his head. "Nah. He doesn't talk to anyone. I don't even know if he speaks English, or if he was brought here in crab form." He shrugged. "I know he's been here for about ten years. It must be weird, you know, to have a form where if you shift you have to be near or in water. I don't know what I'd do if that were my problem. I mean, you can't always control when you shift."

Rafiel nodded. He couldn't imagine it either.

"So no one has talked to him?"

"Not that I know. Of course, the other people don't know he's a shifter. Anyone who is not expecting it, and who sees a little old man climb the side of an aquarium and plop inside, and disappear, thinks they're just seeing things, you know. So they talk about him as a ghost. If you go on-line, this aquarium is in Colorado's list of most haunted places. Just because of the old Japanese man. And they've made up all sorts of weird-ass shit about him.

You know, that he was eaten by sharks here or some shit like that." He shrugged. "But as far as I know he's never talked to anyone. He just sits there and watches."

"I see," Rafiel said, wondering whether he was being lied to, and if so why. *Professional disinformation,* he thought. *You always wonder if they're lying to you. And if they are, why.* "So . . . did you smell him? The crab shifter? Is that why you know he's not a ghost?"

John Wagner looked startled. "You can't smell them. Not the water ones. Keith Kawamoto says he knows a dolphin one, and he said that, too. They don't smell like the rest of us. Why should they? Their signals will go over water, not air—"

"But—" Rafiel said. "How do you—"

"I've seen him shift. Watched him. I know what that looks like. Don't you?"

"Yeah . . . but . . . he doesn't smell? Of shifter?"

John Wagner shook his head. "And that's what worries me, you know? There could be others, in here." He gestured broadly at the tanks all around. "We'd never know. So . . . how could I find them if I can't smell them?"

"And do you have any idea?" Rafiel asked.

"Oh, sure," Wagner said. "You know, how when you shift you're always dying for a protein snack?"

Rafiel thought of Tom stuffing down pepperoni and cold cuts once, in a convenience store in the middle of Arizona. He thought of himself, dropping into the diner for bacon and eggs in the middle of the night, after a shift. He thought of sharks . . . "You mean?" he said, his voice sounding thick and queasy to his own ears. "You mean the sharks?"

John Wagner nodded. "Oh, yes," he said. "The sharks. And you know . . ." He shrugged. "Ah, hell. You grow up with legends about this stuff, you know? In Hawaii it's the beautiful girl who goes swimming with you at night and becomes a shark." He frowned slightly. "One of my college profs said it was a gynophobic fantasy like the vagina dentata. Dumb ass."

Rafiel, not sure he got the point, cleared his throat. "A girl," he said, "who turns into a shark. A girl from Hawaii? Like Lei Lani?"

Wagner shrugged. "Eh. Don't quote me on that. I have nothing against Lei. She's okay by me. Pretty easy on the eye too. Besides, I'm not too sure she's from Hawaii."

"What do you mean you're not too sure? I thought she was interning here, from the aquarium there or something?"

"Heard something like that too. 'Course, I didn't look at her resumé or anything, you know. But . . ."

"But?"

"But I, well . . . At the end of the day I told her, you know, *Eh tita, pau hana?*"

"You told her tit what?" Rafiel asked, flabbergasted.

"Exactly. And she said just that. And she thought I was getting fresh or something . . ." He frowned. "And no Hawaiian girl would. That phrase is . . . eh . . . *so, strong sister, quitting time? Tita* is . . . a strong woman. When a Hawaiian *tita* comes after you, you run. Very strong personality. But she didn't get that at all. And anyone from Hawaii would *know.*" He paused. "And she didn't know *tako* is a squid. And . . ." He shook his head. "She's just not right."

Kyrie saw him hanging around, outside the door. Dire. He was wearing a dark suit, and he was smoking, outside, pacing between the door and the side of the enclosure, where the diner had been expanded over what, in pictures from the thirties, had once been a covered porch.

She wondered if he was pacing out there because he, thanks to the latest Colorado laws, couldn't smoke inside. Or if he was pacing out there because he didn't want to come in.

She followed his movements with her gaze—watching the dark silhouette, the trail of red cigarette end. He looked nervous in his pacing, she thought as she wiped down a just-vacated table. Or perhaps he looked like a predator about to pounce. She'd gone to the zoo once, when she was about five, with the family she was staying with at the time. She remembered they had the tigers in altogether too-flimsy-looking enclosures. And she remembered a particularly large tiger pacing like that, while staring at her, as if she were next on his list of minimum daily requirement. Fifty pounds of skinny little girl. That was what Dante Dire's movement reminded her of, and she could feel his gaze almost burn through the window at her.

She looked over, as she took the tray back. Tom was cooking, his back turned. She was fairly sure he hadn't seen Dire. If he had, he'd say something.

And there was tension in each of Tom's muscles, in

each of his movements. She wondered what he was thinking about. The murders? The newspaper article? The problems with Dante Dire? Or the semi-eternal, nearly all-powerful dragon who claimed ownership and full control of Tom, simply because Tom had been born with the ability to shift into a dragon.

She watched Tom flip a burger, and then he turned around to look at her. He raised an eyebrow, enquiringly. "Yes?"

"Nothing," she said, blushing a little, and disguising it by setting down the tray and ducking behind the counter to set the carafe back in its place so it could refill. "Nothing. I was just thinking that . . . as bad as things are, I don't want to lose this. I don't want to let this go. This is . . . what . . . us . . . our place. The George. It's . . ." She looked at him and was met with what looked like incomprehension, and blushed again. "It's the only home I've ever had," she said.

He looked blank a moment longer, and she realized, suddenly, that it wasn't incomprehension. It was Tom controlling his expressions and his emotions. Perhaps he thought she'd seen his naked emotions too often? Perhaps he thought she had come to his rescue once too often? Perhaps . . .

Or perhaps this was beyond thought and feeling. Perhaps it was just what men did. They didn't melt into tears at every turn. They didn't want women to feel they had to hold their hands and protect them. Kyrie saw it with sudden, distinct clarity. Oh, perhaps, in this age of the sensitive male, it was an ideal honored most often in the breach, but Kyrie could see it. From the earliest times of mankind, men had protected women, right? Women had been weaker, or at least more vulnerable while pregnant. It was a physical thing. For women, security and reproductive success had depended on having someone big and strong to protect them. But that meant that women often had to hold the someone big and strong together emotionally. And it meant that the someone big and strong didn't want to appear emotional to a prospective mate.

Tom swallowed. He managed to look perfectly impassive, but unbent a little as he said, "I know. I know. Me too. I don't want to lose this. But I keep thinking, and I don't know what to do. I can't . . . Kyrie, I can't ask the Great . . . I can't ask the creature to protect us. And I don't care if that's what he thought he was doing when he sent Conan to us. If we accept . . . if we ask his help . . . I'll never be able to call my own soul my own." He frowned and spoke, urgently, in what was little more than a whisper. "It would be the same as admitting I belong to him. If I'm his to protect, I'm his to order around."

"Yeah," Kyrie said. "Yeah. We'll think of something." She was thinking of something. She was thinking that if anything was going to be done about Dire, she would have to do it, and that she wasn't going to be able to tell Tom about it.

Oh, she could get angry about it. She could talk about stupid male pride. But what would it accomplish? She could see that he couldn't ask for help in this, not without bartering his—for lack of a better word—soul in the bargain. She wasn't even sure it was a male thing, but she was sure the male thing complicated it. Tom had to feel that he could defend home and woman. That much was obvious. He could not trade down on it.

"I'm going to take a break," she said. "For a moment. Conan has the tables and there's not that much."

"Okay," Tom said, and turned back towards the stove. Which, by itself, was a mark of his being worried, concerned, not thinking straight. Because, normally, he would have glanced back to make sure that Conan did have the tables and that the work wasn't overwhelming him. Kyrie didn't think it was. Maybe when Conan was starting, but this was his third night. His third night. Seemed like a month, at least.

She went by Conan on the way out, asked him to cover her tables. At the very least, she thought, she had to go out there and get rid of Dire before Tom saw him. Tom was tense enough already and not much could be gained from making him even more nervous.

She slipped out the front door, and only as the cold air outside hit her, did she think that Dire could kill her, out here, and perhaps make sure no one could see. But then again, she thought, that was one of those things she couldn't control, wasn't it? If he was going to kill her and mind-control people not to see her—as he would have to on a public street which, even in this snow day, had traffic, albeit foot traffic—then he could do it in the diner too. Or in her house. Or at the bed-and-breakfast. There was no safe place.

And if there was no safe place, there was no reason to be especially afraid of any place. She took a deep breath and looked up. Straight into Dire's eyes.

He smiled at her, a slow, welcome smile, and took a drag of his cigarette. "Hello, Kitten," he said, very softly, as though he were an older man, flirting with a younger girl in a cheesy movie from the seventies.

Kyrie felt a finger of unease crawl, coldly, up her spine. But he only smiled at her, a broader smile at what must have been her momentary, pinched look.

"You shouldn't be here," she said. "I mean, outside here. It will make our customers nervous to see someone roaming around outside, I mean . . ." She faltered. She couldn't explain why it would make the customers nervous. There was something, of course, to his step, to his look, that indicated he was on the prowl, that he was dangerous. But would normal people know that? Or did she see it, because she feared it?

"I'm not going to eat your customers, Kitten," he said, amused. He glanced at the diner then across the street, at the other, closed buildings. Down the block and across the street, white Christmas lights swung forlornly from the front of the hastily closed used bookstore. They normally turned them off when they left for the day, but they'd forgotten.

For some reason, those swaying lights were one of the saddest images Kyrie had ever seen. Dire lingered on them, then looked back at her. "To quote Bette Davis," he said, and smiled a little. "What a dump." He threw his cigarette on the ground and stepped on it. "What's a girl like you doing in a joint like this?"

She tightened her lips, mentally willing Tom not to look outside. She maneuvered, slightly, so that they were in the blind spot between the door to The George and the side enclosure. "In case you haven't noticed," she said, "I own the dump. Or at least half of it."

"Ah, yes, the diner named after the dragon slayer. Your boytoy has a weird sense of humor, doesn't he?" He looked at Kyrie. "Was he bragging that he kills other shifters? Was he actually proud of this?"

Kyrie thought of the painting of St. George and the dragon that Tom had hung over the back corner booth on the day they'd taken possession of The George. She remembered his words, "Because we have to be both the beast and the slayer."

She knew what Dire's opinions on this would be, and she'd be damned if she was going to give Tom up to some sort of insane punishment. She shrugged. "He has an odd sense of humor," she said.

"Ah. I see. Loyal." Dire said, and frowned slightly. "But I have a problem, you see? I was given a mission. As I told you and your friends, I'm sort of like a policeman, except the law I operate by is only the law of our own people. We don't"—he looked around with distaste—"recognize ephemeral law. But our law is nonetheless enforceable for applying only to us, and I'm the one sent to enforce it." He grinned, suddenly. "In other words, Kitten, I must find someone who is guilty. And I must deliver him to them. I was thinking your boyfriend might serve. But Daddy Dragon would get upset, and he can be a total bastard when he's pissed. So it would be better if it were that nice policeman."

"The—" Kyrie felt anger rise in her, and tried to keep it down. Getting furious at someone much more powerful than her wouldn't solve anything and it certainly wouldn't help anything. "What do you mean deliver him to them?"

"As the guilty one, you know?" Dire said, clearly

unaware of the storm of emotions she was feeling. "I must find the guilty party, but they are not here, and they'll never know if it's the real guilty party, if you know what I mean. I could tell them it was." He shrugged. "So, your boyfriend or the policeman?"

"What?" she asked. And then the anger grabbed her. She glared at the ancient—and amoral—creature. "I don't think so. Not Tom. You wouldn't dare. Not Rafiel. Not even Conan. No. None of them is guilty. Not one. No."

"Well," he said, completely unconcerned by the rising tone of her voice. "It would be easier if it's not the dragons. Though if I told the Ancient Ones that it's the dragon boy, your boyfriend, they couldn't do anything, anyway, and . . ." He shrugged. "He might have to run away, true, because some of our members are less than sane and might want to strike anyway. But I would never. There's the daddy dragon. There's a treaty of sorts between our kinds. And I'm not stupid."

He shook his head. "No, I'm not stupid at all. I'm fine with telling them it was him, but he'd have to run, and if they came here and got you by accident . . . well . . . that would be a waste, wouldn't it?"

His gaze traveled lazily up and down her figure. "Wouldn't it? So, how about this? We work together. We pick a likely guilty party. Or a fall guy. It's all the same to me. I've asked enough, and I've gone to the site, and what I think happened is that these shifters were killing other shifters to serve their purposes." He shrugged. "This happens, right? It's one of the ways in which our kind can be very stupid. And why not everyone lives to be a full adult shifter. But then . . . then you came on the scene.

And you played heroes. Okay. You're allowed to be heroes, I suppose. And they *were* preying on shifters. But then you killed a lot of innocent young ones. I'm not sure how it happened. Self-defense, or perhaps accidentally. I'm not going to ask. I'm just going to tell you that death on that order of magnitude requires a culprit, and I'll have to find one."

"Not here you don't have to find one," Kyrie said, sternly. She felt very angry. In fact she felt as though she could throw lightning bolts out of her eyes, she was so mad. "We already have the Great Sky Dragon to deal with. We have some reporter taking pictures of our shifted forms. We have the Rodent Liberation—"

"What?" Dante asked, his eyes very intent.

"Rodent Liberation Front. They—"

"No. The reporter part."

"Oh." Kyrie shrugged. "Front page of the *Weekly Inquirer* this morning."

He glared at her. "You let a reporter photograph you *shifting*?"

"No," she said. "We didn't let . . . she came to the diner, she—" Kyrie stopped short of saying that Keith had brought her. She didn't even know why, but her tongue just stopped short of it, as though a red light had gone on in her mind. "We found she'd taken pictures of Tom shifted. And Conan too." She paused and tried to bite her tongue, but it wouldn't stay still. "They were going to my rescue when you . . . were threatening me."

Dante Dire glared at her. He threw his head back. "I can't believe," he said, "that you thought you needed their help. I can't believe they are so foolish as to allow themselves to be photographed. And I can't believe that dragons—dragons!—would shift where they could be seen. This is all a big muddle, and I will end up having to sort it out."

Kyrie, who felt weirdly grateful he had at least moved on from demanding that she choose a sacrificial victim for him to turn in to the Ancient Ones, started telling him not only didn't he have to sort it out, but this had nothing to do with him. "I don't think you—"

"Kyrie?" Tom had opened the door of the diner and stood looking at her and Dire. He nodded to Dire, as if he were a casual acquaintance and not an ancient horror who could destroy them all. "I wonder if you could come back from break," he said.

"Yes. Yes, of course," Kyrie said, walking away from Dire and practically scurrying towards the open door. "Of course."

She followed Tom in, and half expected to hear Dire come in behind them, but instead she heard something like a soft chuckle behind her. She didn't turn. She didn't look.

She followed Tom all the way past the areas of the counter that customers sat at. All the way to the cooking area, at the other end.

He smiled a little at her, as he turned to put a few burgers on the grill.

"Look, I didn't want to talk to him, but I thought—"

"That you didn't trust him out there, lurking, scaring our customers," Tom said. He smiled over his shoulder. "I got that. I was worried too."

"Yeah. He . . . was saying more of the same. That he needed to . . . to throw someone to the Ancient Ones."

"Or to the wolves," Tom said.

"Metaphorically," Kyrie said. "Look, it's just . . ."

"I know. I just went to rescue you. I wasn't sure you would get rid of him otherwise."

"Thank you," she said. And wondered if Tom had seen the dire wolf before she had, if he'd made plans . . . This wasn't the time to ask him. "Maybe you should go and get some sleep. I could get Anthony in early. And that would get you here for . . . for a little while longer than I am . . . You know . . . so we . . . so the diner is not without us."

The look he gave her over his shoulder was worried, this time. "Perhaps that would be better, yes," he said.

And she knew that he had understood what she couldn't explain. That she felt responsible for the customers in the diner. That a lot more of them than John Wagner and the mouse-teacher might be shifters. And that Dire might very well decide on one of them as a scapegoat. And she couldn't live with it.

Rafiel parked behind the diner, and pulled out his cell phone. "Yeah, McKnight?" as soon as McKnight answered.

"Yeah?" McKnight answered, cautiously.

"Two things. Look up any records for John Wagner and also . . . I don't know how you can do this, but . . ." He reasoned quickly that, of course, Dante Dire might have used another name. But he couldn't fly, so he presumably had to use some means of transport—airplanes. Even if private. And he would rent places. And while he could use another name, it was Rafiel's guess that most people didn't change all that often. Most shifters, either. They got comfy with a name and kept it, he guessed. "Check up on Dante Dire," he said. "Particularly anything having to do with Hawaii, and also when he might have come to town. Any place in Colorado he might have been."

"Dante . . . ?"

"Dante Dire," Rafiel spelled it.

"Who . . . ?"

"Just someone who's been around a lot, and I wonder . . ." He had a moment of fear. What if McKnight stumbled on something that—He stopped. That what? Tipped him to the fact that there were shapeshifters? Not likely. Rafiel suspected that for the average person it would take having their noses rubbed in it. In fact, they would have tumbled on to what was happening long ago if it weren't so. "He's just suspicious," he said, "Nothing definite, so don't break any laws, but check up on him, okay?"

There was a sound from the other side that might have been assent, and Rafiel said, "Right. I'll call back." And hung up. He cut his ignition and got out of the truck. Halfway through stepping down, he saw something through the snow.

He would never be able to swear to what it was. A dog, a bear, something rounding the building, or just—perhaps—a shadow. But he thought Dire, and having thought it, he followed the suspicious shadow around the building to the front.

And stopped, because in front of the building, leaning against the lamppost was the blond girl from the newspaper. There was something odd about her, but he couldn't put his finger on it, and he said, "I beg your pardon, you—"

And then it hit him. His human nose, not as sharp as his lion nose, was nonetheless acute enough to catch the smell of blood—the smell of death. Closer, closer, he saw that the girl was pale, dead—her eyes staring unseeing straight ahead. But she'd been propped up against the lamppost, and her clothes had been put back on. And she couldn't have been dead very long, because there was a steady drip-drip-drip of blood down the front of her clothes, from beneath her ski jacket.

For a moment he stood horrified, but his mind was working, behind it all. Dire. He was sure Dire was involved. Oh, he couldn't have done it now. No way that could have happened. But he had to be involved—somehow.

In his mind it all added up. Dante had killed the girl earlier, then . . . Then led him here. Like a gigantic joke. A joke perpetrated by an unfeeling, uncaring, ancient creature.

Like the shark murders—it would be just Dire's idea of a joke, to set it up, somehow, so that he could push into the tank guys who had been dallying with one of the female employees. The first time they'd seen him was around the aquarium. Perhaps he had a way in all along. Why shouldn't he? Rafiel had managed to get keys easily enough. And it would amuse some *thing* like Dire to create the impression of a shark shifter and see how they reacted.

With numbed fingers, Rafiel had—somehow— retrieved his phone from inside his jacket. He hit the redial button, staring at the corpse of the blond girl.

"McKnight. Send the meat wagon and . . . and come along. There's been a . . . death. In front of The George. And get someone to check the visitor book at the aquarium. Find out if Dante Dire was there . . . anytime in the last month."

Tom woke up with the phone ringing, and a panicked Notty digging needle-sharp claws into his underarm, where he'd been nestling.

"Ow," he said, grabbing the furry body blindly in his right hand, then looking for the phone on the bedside table with his left. One of the good things of this split sleeping schedule was that he got the bed when Kyrie wasn't here. And her pillow still smelled like her, too.

"Yeah," he said, turning on the phone, and fully expecting it to be Kyrie telling him about some emergency at the diner. Before he heard any sound from the other side of the phone, he'd already covered the possibles in his mind. She might have run out of paper napkins. Or it could be the beef. Did he order more beef? Perhaps it was the dishwasher flaking again. They needed to buy a new one soon. "Yeah?"

"Oh, damn," Rafiel's voice. "Damn, damn, damn."

Tom sat up, setting Notty down beside him on the bed. "What?" His relations with Rafiel had been less than cordial at one point, but even back then, Rafiel had never called him for the purpose of cursing at him.

"Tom?" Rafiel said, as if surprised to hear him.

"You called me."

There was a silence on the other side, a silence during which Rafiel seemed to be taking several deep breaths. "Oh, shit, Tom, we're in so much trouble."

"What happened?" Tom said, jumping out of the bed and looking around for his clothes. He'd showered before going to bed, so he could probably skip it this time. Truth be told he had a shower problem—he enjoyed so much being able to shower when he pleased that he had a lot of showers even when not shifting back and forth. Unfortunately they did not have support groups for the hygiene-dependent. "Rafiel, what happened?" he repeated when no answer came.

"We found . . . a corpse," Rafiel's voice was distant, like he was holding the phone away from his mouth, or perhaps speaking in a tiny voice. "Just outside the diner. I'm calling you while McKnight is talking to Kyrie."

"Outside the diner!" Tom said. "In the parking lot again?"

"No, corner of Pride and Fairfax. By the lamppost. She was . . . propped up. Leaning against the post . . ."

"She?" Tom's mind went immediately to the woman whom Rafiel had found, the woman who was a mouse shifter.

"The . . . Summer Avenir. The reporter for the paper? The one that Keith talked to or brought in?"

"The one that published dragon pictures?"

"Yeah, we're going to have to talk to Conan. And the . . . whoever the triad members are in this area."

"She was killed by a dragon?" Tom asked.

"Well, she was killed by something with really big teeth," Rafiel said, in the tone of a man who has come to his rope's end and still has quite a bit to climb. "And then she was propped up. This is putting a damper on our normal story of attacks by wild animals, you know? It's clear"—he took a deep breath—"very clear it was one of us." He lowered his voice. "I can smell shifter all over the scene, still. I thought I'd seen Dire before, but . . . I don't know."

Tom moaned and dropped onto the bed, to put his socks on. His feet and in fact all his wounds from the encounter with the dire wolf were completely healed and the very faint scars would soon vanish. "We must make sure he stops."

"Who?" Rafiel said.

"Dire."

"Uh . . . yeah. I'd say that's a given. The question is how."

"I don't know," Tom said.

"You could"—Rafiel cleared his throat—"talk to the Great Sky Dragon."

Tom stopped, his hand on his sock, his mouth on the verge of uttering an absolute no. Instead, he took a deep breath. "You must see we can't, Rafiel. You must see we *can't.*"

"Why not? If they are rival organizations, both ancient, why can't you talk to the Great Sky Dragon and make him deal with Dire? I mean, I know that Dire said he had a non-aggression pact with the triad, but it doesn't seem to me as if that pact is much good. How could it be? Otherwise he wouldn't have gone through all that trouble to make sure the triad knew he didn't intend to kill you."

Tom heard himself make a sound that was half annoyance and half anger. "I still can't ask for their help,

Rafiel. If we ask for the help of a criminal organization, how can we, in the future, hold ourselves able to stop them? If we ask for the help of an organization that deals in drugs, that kills, that basically seems to view other humans—what did Dire call them?—ephemerals, as mere cattle to be milked, then how can we hope to stand for justice among our kind? Or anywhere?"

There was a long silence. Tom had the impression that Rafiel was running several arguments through his own head and discarding them just as fast as he thought them up. Finally he made a sound somewhere between a huff and a sigh. "Tom, we can't be so pure as the driven snow. I understand what you're saying. And standing for justice is very well—don't get me wrong. I'm as fond of graphic novels as Keith is. And justice and truth and all that, but Tom . . . I'm afraid he's going to kill one of us. I don't even know, you know . . . if he might not have set up the aquarium murders. He's . . . cunning, and he has an . . . odd sense of humor. Look at how he conned Kyrie into going to the house. At any point he could turn and decide to hold one of us—or all of us—responsible for those deaths and just kill us." Pause. "You know, it's quite likely it was him who killed this woman, without so much as a thought."

"Well, she did publish pictures of dragons in the newspaper," Tom said.

"But it could have been Photoshop. I mean, even if she had caught you mid-shifting, do you think that it couldn't be Photoshop? No one will take it seriously. Look at all the pictures of the alien that the tabloids keep following up on and publish. Do you believe he exists?"

"No," Tom said. "And no, I don't think anyone paid undue attention to the pictures. But they are pictures of our kind and . . . well . . . Dire is very old. At least assuming it was him. Though, frankly, the Great Sky Dragon is very old too, and I don't think any of his younger subordinates would have dared point out to him that times have changed."

"No," Rafiel said. "I'm sure they wouldn't. So . . . they killed this young woman. Without a thought. Because she was . . . an ephemeral."

"No, because she was an ephemeral they thought was threatening shifters." Tom found his mind going down the dangerous path that he knew these people's minds must take every time. He said matter of factly, "Think of it from their perspective, how it must have been throughout history. The discovery of a shifter would lead to a hunt for others. Death was always the end. Of course they would kill anyone that was a remote threat."

"Of course? You sound as if you approve."

"No. Understanding is not approving. There is a qualitative difference." He felt suddenly very tired. "You know, when I was on the streets, they had all these programs where you were supposed to mingle with the other runaways and empathize and understand them. Sometimes that's what you had to do for a meal. And the counselors always seemed to think that if you understood someone, you'd like them . . . and you know? It's not true. Sometimes the more you talk to a teenage habitual liar and drug pusher, the less you like them. But . . . but I do understand how they got to be the way they are. And at the same time . . ." He took a deep breath. "I understand how we could go that way. From the best of motives. Protecting ourselves and our friends. I understand how we could start deciding that . . . killing the occasional ephemeral meant nothing. Or even that we should kill a few every now and then, out of the blue, to keep the other ones in fear. I understand them, Rafiel. And it scares me. That's another reason not to ask for the Great Sky Dragon's help. That, and I'd like to continue being able to call my soul my own."

Rafiel huffed again and when he answered he was peevish. "Very well," he said, in a tone that implied it wasn't very well at all. "But I hope you know what to do, because this can't go on. With the deaths at the aquarium—and by the way, the latest one, Joe Buckley, had water in his lungs, so it wasn't a body disposal, it was murder by shark—and now some mysterious animal going around town killing people, not to mention what my colleagues are convinced is some madman who just propped up the body afterwards . . ." This time the sound was just a sigh. "I don't know how to cover up all of this, Tom. I just don't. And I'm an officer of the law. The killings must stop. And I think there's more than an even chance that it's all Dire. I'm . . . following up on it, but I really think there's a good chance he came to town before, you know, when they felt the deaths, and he set all this up. And we must stop him."

"I understand," Tom said and he did, and in this case he could even empathize. "I'll think of something. Look, I'll come down and help you talk to Conan, okay?"

After Rafiel hung up, Tom started tying his boots, a task made more complex by the fact that Notty was trying to help. "I'd better think of something, eh, Notty?" he said, as he petted the little round kitten head. "Or we are in deep, deep trouble."

Notty looked up at him with guileless intensely blue eyes that seemed to say he had every confidence in Tom's ability to make it all right. Tom wished he did too.

Every shifter could be a target, Kyrie thought. And even as she was thinking this, she had to put up with being interviewed by a young man with sparse red-blond hair and the slightly bulging blue eyes that always give the impression their possessor is desperately looking for a fairytale to believe in. He, somehow, seemed absolutely convinced that Kyrie must have a wild animal stashed somewhere, and must have deployed it to kill this woman journalist.

If only you knew, Kyrie thought, but just looked placidly at the man. "No," she said, in a firm voice, while she kept an eye on Conan who was dealing with the tables. She stood with her back to the counter. On the other side of it, Anthony was cooking orders. He'd been interviewed, but his interview had been very brief, since he hadn't left the stove since he'd come in at about four in the morning. And no, he hadn't seen any dead woman against the lamppost, though, frankly, if she'd been propped up and looked natural, he might not have noticed. After all, he'd been running in, and he'd been working what very much amounted to double shifts because of the weather and their being shorthanded. And now he had to go back to the stove before it went up in flames; did Officer McKnight mind?

Officer McKnight could not persist against Anthony's push to get back to work, and therefore he was now absolutely determined to make life difficult for Kyrie. Kyrie looked up and resisted an urge to smile. She wondered if she was supposed to cry into the table-wiping rag she was holding and confess that yes, she'd done it all.

She decided against it on principle. The man looked like he'd had his sense of humor surgically removed at birth and he might very well take her at her word. Instead, aloud, she said, with increasing firmness, "No, I was not mad at her for publishing the dragon pictures. Why should I be?"

"Well . . ." McKnight said, and looked at her with those bulging eyes, making her think he was going to dart an improbably long tongue out and catch a fly or something. "The thing is Ms. . . . . Smith, you and your . . . partner, Mr. Ormson own this diner half and half, right."

"Right," Kyrie said, wishing if he was going to pronounce Smith that way he would add "if that is indeed your real name."

"And this woman published pictures of dragons in the paper and said she'd seen them at the back door of your diner. Now . . . wouldn't you think people might be afraid to come here? That it might ruin your business?"

"What?" Kyrie asked, completely puzzled. "Are you truly asking me if I think that people are afraid of *dragons*? Are you afraid of dragons, Officer?"

"Well . . . that's neither here nor there, is it? I mean, I know that dragons are imaginary and I . . ." He shrugged.

"But this is not about what I believe. Don't you think that people out there on the street might think that there are really dragons and that they might get attacked, if they come here?"

Kyrie shook her head. "No. In fact, considering all the recent movies and stories with good dragons, I think that if they were to believe dragons existed—and frankly I don't think even a lot of our college student clientele believes any such thing—they would be thrilled. If anything, that picture in the paper might bring us droves of customers." She realized as she said it that this was true, though certainly that was not how she and the others had first thought of it.

McKnight clearly hadn't thought of it that way either. He said, "But—" and then repeated "But, but," like it was the sound his brain gave off while sputtering and trying to start. "But you have to understand," he finally said. "Not everyone might have felt that way. And what if they were scared and stopped coming here. Wouldn't you have hated that reporter? Wouldn't you have thought of doing . . . something to her?"

"Something?" Kyrie said. She frowned. "What exactly are you suggesting? That I roamed the streets looking for a wild animal, whom I then convinced to chomp on this journalist, when she was conveniently just outside our door?" She glared. "Because a death by wild animal attack will, of course, hurt our business far *less* than rumors of dragons."

"Well, no, but you might . . . you might not have thought of that, as you were, you know . . ."

"Looking for a wild animal to kill her? Tell me, was it a

mountain lion or a bear? And how did I keep it from killing me? My extrasensory powers?"

McKnight looked confused. Or rather, he looked more confused than normal. "But . . . but . . . if you had . . ."

"And what if I had grown wings and flown?" she asked. *Which I can't do. Though my boyfriend can.* "Do I have to answer hypothetical questions on that too?" She glared at him. "Given an ability to find wild animals disposed to kill inconvenient journalists at the drop of a hat, and supposing I had the superpowers to prevent them killing me, I still wouldn't have killed the journalist."

"Oh? Why not?"

"Because she was a person. A human being. And she'd done me no noticeable harm. Do you often kill people because they're annoying or sensationalist, Officer?"

"Me? Well, no, of course . . ." He seemed to finally realize he wasn't going to win this argument no matter how hard he tried. "Right," he said. "Right. Thank you, Ms. Smith. I will . . . I will go and ask your customers if they've seen anything."

Yes. Do, why don't you? Because that won't affect business at all, she thought irritably, as she ducked behind the counter, and found Anthony's gaze trained on her, half amusement, half awe.

"What?" she said.

"I think you have a bit of policeman caught between your teeth," he said.

"What?"

"Metaphorically speaking. I think that's what Tom calls biting off someone's head and beating them to death with it."

"Well," Kyrie said, deflated, as she got the carafe from the coffee maker and put the latest round of prepared orders on a tray to take out. Conan had been half handling all the orders, but she was fairly sure the breakfast crowd would prefer their eggs before they got all cold and rubbery. "He's dim."

"Yeah. I wonder why Rafiel didn't ask us the questions himself."

"Dunno. Dealing with some administrative stuff, I guess," Kyrie said, and started towards the tables, carrying the tray. She smiled and joked with her regulars. But her mind wasn't in it.

No, her mind was carefully processing the input of her nose. How many shifters were there in the diner? They knew for a fact that the diner had been soaked—some years ago—in pheromones designed to attract shifters. It had called her all the way from the bus station, in response to something—she wasn't sure what. For all she knew it had called her all the way from Cleveland where her last job had been. How many more people did it call? And what were their forms?

She didn't think they were implicated in the death of the journalist, Summer Avenir. She didn't think so, but you never knew. After all, the Ancient Ones weren't the only ones who could lose their heads when faced with something like pictures of shifters on the front page of their local paper and just outside their favorite diner. While Kyrie and Tom had no wish to associate wild animal attacks with their diner, some customer who just wanted to stop a threat might have more direct views of how to do so.

She saw Tom and Rafiel come in through the back door, poor Tom looking very pale and cranky, which made perfect sense, since he'd slept all of two and a half or three hours at most.

At the moment she saw them, she was standing by the front door and away from most of the occupied tables. She stood her ground, ostensibly waiting for them to go by her, so she could move freely.

But as they came close enough, she asked Rafiel in a whisper, "The teeth that killed the woman . . . They weren't alligator teeth, were they?"

Rafiel had a headache. No, it wasn't a headache as such because headaches were natural occurrences that came and went without much provocation. *This* headache was like a living thing, compounded half of pain, half of fear and mostly of anger. It sat on his brain, seeming to squeeze all rationality out of it.

He wanted to be mad at Tom for refusing to even consider calling the Great Sky Dragon and the triad to their aid. What was he doing? Did he think they could play heroes all by themselves? Who were they against this ancient shifter group that permeated all nations and was a law unto itself? If the group decided whom to kill and whom to let live, to whom could they speak out against it? How could they when they were part of it too?

To some extent Dire was right when he told Rafiel and Kyrie that in the ancient times there had been many deaths, that in those days shifters were viewed as dangerous, as things to be eliminated.

But then again, weren't they dangerous? So many of them seemed to have a lust for killing and a total disregard for those outside their group.

Rafiel stood in the brightly lit parking lot and squinted against the light, and watched Tom walk from the inn, around the thawing slabs of ice in the parking lot. The sun was out, things were melting. Probably only to freeze again this night, but for now, ice was in retreat.

Rafiel squinted at Tom and thought to himself that if shifters were known, and if they were known for what they were, those creatures that Dire called ephemerals would be more than justified in exterminating them all, root and branch, the guilty with the innocent. But then . . . but then he and Tom and Kyrie were innocent.

And if we want to remain so, we'd best find a way to control those among our kind who aren't—those who are a danger to the society we live in. From there it followed that Tom had been right. They could not call on the Great Sky Dragon. They couldn't call on any of the old, corrupt organizations that looked down on the society amid which they lived and from which they derived the benefits of civilization. *No. It must be us. Me and you and me against the ancient shifter world. And Keith too, if he's willing.*

The ridiculous thought of the four of them facing down the Ancient Ones, much less the Ancient Ones, the triad and whatever was killing people at the aquarium—if it wasn't Dire or the crab shifter—made his head throb all the worse. The Rodent Liberation Front might be more their speed.

Tom, who always looked like heck when he was tired, now looked tired and grumpy and ill-awakened, with shadows under his eyes, and the sort of expression that suggested he was about to face a firing squad by the early dawn light.

He stomped across the parking lot towards Rafiel and greeted him with a grunt. They walked across the parking lot together, presumably, Rafiel thought, to talk to Conan. What Tom expected to get from Conan, if not the help of Conan's patron, was beyond him.

And then, as they got into the diner, and went close by Kyrie, he found his arm grabbed and Kyrie asked, "The teeth that killed the woman . . . They weren't alligator teeth, were they?"

Tom snorted behind Rafiel and said, with certainty. "It wasn't Old Joe."

But Kyrie was looking at Rafiel with those bright eyes of hers, that inquisitive all-attentive gaze she so rarely turned towards him. "Was it, Rafiel?"

He shook his head slowly. "Not so far as the examiner on the scene thought. He said bear or dog"—he shrugged—"only much, much bigger teeth. I could imagine, by a stretch of the imagination, its being a dragon, but not an alligator, no."

While he talked to Kyrie, Tom had gone behind both of them and into the glassed-in annex, where Conan was cleaning a table. Tom cheerfully helped him put the menus and condiment bottles back. Then he grabbed the wrist on Conan's good arm. Rafiel had no idea what he said to the man. Tom spoke in too low a voice to be heard. But Rafiel saw Conan pale, and then Tom shook his head and said something else, and Conan looked at him half in fear, but seemed calmer and nodded.

Rafiel wished he could hear it, but doubtless, through this headache, he wouldn't make any sense of it, in any case. Aloud he told Kyrie, "Looks like you'll have to take over all the waitressing. I think we're talking to Conan." He watched Tom take Conan to the table nearest the window—the one where the two sets of glassed-in walls met, and fortuitously the corner nearest the lamppost around which the dead woman had been wrapped.

"I won't seat people near there," Kyrie said, and turned to meet a couple who had just entered. Which left Rafiel with nothing to do but go talk to Conan.

Conan was sitting across from Tom, and as Rafiel approached, Tom got up. Before Rafiel was fully settled, Tom came back with three cups of coffee, a bowl full of the little packaged creamers, and a container of sugars. Conan hesitated and looked almost guilty taking the coffee. Or perhaps he just looked guilty. He looked guilty most of the time, a sort of cringing general-purpose guilt that made Rafiel's headache worse.

Tom looked at Rafiel as though expecting him to start the questioning, and Rafiel sighed. "The dead woman, out there?" he said.

"Yes. You asked me earlier," Conan said. "I didn't see anything."

"Really?" Rafiel asked, with withering sarcasm. "Were you waiting on people in this annex, then? Was there no one seated here?"

"Oh. Well, of course people were seated here. But . . . but it's dark out there. I didn't see anything." And then, as if with sudden inspiration. "Kyrie attended to people here too, and don't you think she would have spoken up if she'd seen something?"

Tom jerked forward, and Rafiel, fairly sure that he was going to come to Kyrie's defense, perhaps in a violent way, put a hand forward to stop him. "I'm sure she would have," he said. "I also know that these . . . creatures, whatever they might have been, from whichever side, have defenses that we can't begin to fathom. I'm fairly sure that Dire doesn't actually teleport, for instance. And if he can fake a phone call and make Kyrie actually hear my voice as if it came from her cell phone . . ." He shrugged. "It's possible they made themselves invisible.

"But you, Conan, aren't just one of us, one of the young shifters, are you?"

This brought him a wide-eyed glance from Conan, not an admission of guilt, not even, Rafiel thought, with an inward groan, an admission that Rafiel had somehow penetrated a deception. No. All that fish-eyed glare was pure shock, combined almost for sure with a calculation on Rafiel's mental health or lack thereof. "Of course I'm one of you," he said, in outraged protest. "What else would I be? I am twenty-three years old, and I was born in Tennessee. Knoxville. Mom and Dad own the Good Fortune Restaurant there. I was president of the Latin club in high school. Check it out. I'm in the yearbook."

"That's not what I meant," Rafiel said. *Though I worded it vaguely enough to catch something else, should it be there.* "What I mean is that the Great Sky Dragon sent you here to protect Tom. He has a link to your mind. Surely he wouldn't be fooled by whatever mind tricks Dire might be using. Surely, he would see whatever was happening. Did you not see anything? Sense his alarm in some way?" *Mind tricks. What if he convinces the victims of shark to just jump IN to the aquarium? Surely he can do it. Damn. How can one check that? Prove that? He probably doesn't even need to be there. Look what he did with Kyrie's phone.*

Conan shook his head. He looked miserable and on the edge of sniffling like a lost child. "I never . . . I didn't see anything. But . . . but before, when he spoke through me? I didn't see anything either. I wasn't . . . aware that he was doing anything."

Rafiel took a deep breath and drank a sip of hot, black coffee to fortify himself. "And could you have done it, Conan?"

This time he got the wide eyes and a look of almost panic. First Conan shook his head, then he opened his mouth. He looked like he was about to scream or run, but he did neither. Instead, he put his head in his good hand, and Rafiel fully expected him to show a tear-streaked face when he looked up. It wasn't. His face was perfectly dry, though his eyes looked reddened.

"Look, do you think I haven't asked myself this?" he asked. And, as though driven out of his voice by stress, the pseudo-Asian accent was gone, replaced by just the faintest hint of a Southern twang. "Ever since she was discovered I've asked myself this. He spoke through my mind. Could he also . . . do other things through my mind? I don't know. I don't know." He shook his head. "I don't know if he could have had me change and attack the girl. I think not, because if he could have, then when we were hunting Tom"—he looked at Tom—"why would he not do the same? Why would he leave us to our own devices?" He shrugged. "On the other hand, I think, why would he not have put a listening thing in our heads then as he did now, so he could advise us when we ran into trouble?" He shrugged again. "I don't know. I just don't know."

"Perhaps he didn't think it was worth it for just me," Tom said. "After all, I was just a young shifter, right? While here he knows he's up against the executioner sent by the Ancient Ones, right? So it would be more important. And he would send you, of course."

Conan started to shake his head, then shrugged again. "You might have been only a young one, but he was . . . By the end of it, we were all in full hunt for you. Though to be honest . . ." he looked pensive, "he only ever sent the young ones of us, never the old, experienced ones. Why, I don't know, just as I don't know why he wants you protected now." He looked suddenly embarrassed. "Only I'm kind of glad he does, because you're a nice guy and I don't want to be ordered to attack you."

"Would you, if he ordered you?" Tom asked.

Conan looked at Tom. And Rafiel felt as though he was seeing several thoughts flicker through Conan's mind. *No.* And then *yes* and then . . . Conan shrugged. "I'd like to think I wouldn't," he said, opening his hands on the table-top, as if to show the absence of weapons. "But the thing is, if he ordered me, and I didn't obey, then I would be left . . ." He sighed. "With the absolute certainty of my own death. I belong to him. He's in my mind. Still, the prospect of waking up with myself, day after day, year after year, after killing someone who has become a friend

. . ." He made a face. "Death might be preferable. On the other hand"—disarming smile—"I think I've proven I'm a coward and very attached to life. So . . . I don't know. The Great Sky Dragon would tell me to tell you that no, of course I wouldn't kill you, but I'm telling you the truth."

He seemed inordinately proud of it, and Rafiel who could feel the same gears turn in Tom's head that were turning in his—*what does he mean he doesn't know*, and *this is not a free man*—said, "It's always good to tell the truth. So, you don't know if you killed this woman or not?"

"I don't think I did," Conan said. "The thing was, see, we were fairly busy all night. Yes, there was a lull around four, but it wasn't a lull *in* the restaurant. It was just that no more people were arriving, not that the ones that were already here were leaving. A bunch of people came in and sat from three to five or so, just . . . here. Ordering more stuff, you know? So Kyrie and I were both very busy, all that time. I think Kyrie would have noticed if I'd left my tables unattended for any of that time. She would have asked me. You know she keeps an eye on me all the time. And I asked her . . . I asked her right after I heard. Just a quick question. And she said I'd been here all the time, helping with the tables."

"So it's improbable it was you," Rafiel said. "I presume that you don't have a way to cast the same sort of mind-invisibility thing that Dire does?"

"Not that I've ever heard of. And I've never heard of any of the senior dragons doing it . . . not even Himself. He usually appears in perfectly normal, reasonable ways."

"Except flying, yes," Rafiel said. "So you know of no reason why the Great Sky Dragon would want this woman dead? Wouldn't seeing dragons, one of them you, on the cover of the *Weekly Inquirer* unnerve him or enrage him?"

Conan shook his head. "I'm sure it wouldn't," he said.

"Why?" Rafiel asked.

"Because if it had I would have heard from him, or from one of the other ones, in the town, you know? Someone would have come to me and told me . . ." He seemed to run out of words or perhaps of imagination as to what they'd tell him.

"That you'd been a very naughty dragon?" Tom asked, seeming suddenly amused.

Conan nodded once. "That. I'm sure they would have. And he didn't. Which means he wasn't mad about the picture. Wasn't mad about showing myself. He is not . . ." A sudden lopsided smile. "I know it's playing into a stereotype a little, and perhaps it is wrong, but you know we Asians are supposed to be good with technology? Well . . . Himself is. He really is. He's very, very good with it. And he would have thought what I thought. That the dragons could be a Photoshop job, and that no one living in the world today would think they were real, unless they were shifters or already knew shifters themselves."

"But then . . . that leaves . . . Wait. What if she had gone after those you call senior dragons? I assume there are some of those here in town?"

Conan nodded once. "The Three Luck Dragon Restaurant where we . . ."

"Where I almost got killed?" Tom asked.

Conan's eyes opened wide. "You did? Was it there? I heard about it through the organization after I . . . came back. But I didn't know it had been done there, right at the center of our operations." Then to Rafiel: "That's where we met in the parking lot."

"And I assume the owner is one of you," Rafiel asked, and seeing the expression on Conan's face, hastened to add, "You don't have to answer that."

"She might have gone there," Conan said. "Yes. And harassed someone. But the thing is . . ." He shrugged again, an expressive, eloquent shrug that was almost a word in itself, a word that combined lack of knowledge with ability to acquire any. "The thing is that I don't think Himself would do it this way. For some reason he wants you protected." He gave Tom a look. "To be honest, it might be simply because you impressed him. Or Kyrie did. And because he is afraid that the Ancient Ones will take you out without his protection. I don't know. You don't ask that sort of question. But, anyway, if he wants to protect you, the last thing, the very last thing he would do was to come here, to leave the dead woman this close to your diner, and therefore call attention to you, right? He'd never do that. He's not stupid."

Rafiel didn't think the Great Sky Dragon was stupid at all. And even through his headache, he had to concede Conan's logic. He didn't see the Great Sky Dragon leaving a corpse that close to Tom, not if he wanted to protect him, at any rate.

His headache was worse. "Damn," he said. "That means it was probably Dire."

Conan nodded, sagely.

"Which means we need to figure out a way to deal with him."

"Deal with him?" Conan said. "You can't. Not alone. That's why Himself sent me, so that . . ."

Rafiel looked at Tom. Tom shook his head at him, but said nothing.

"Right," Rafiel said. "I think I'll take my headache and go see if I can come up with any new ideas."

Tom smiled at him, suddenly. "Where are you going to take your headache?"

"I don't know," Rafiel said. He had a savage need to be mad at someone and to be rude to someone, and he didn't want to do it here, and he didn't want to be mad at Tom. "I don't know. Maybe I'll drive in circles for a while till I think of somewhere to go."

The quizzical half-amused look he got back didn't really help his mood or sense of humor any. Nor did hearing Tom tell Conan—clearly, in answer to a question he didn't hear, "No, I don't want you to help. I don't want the Great Sky Dragon involved in this. It's between me and my *friends*. If the Great Sky Dragon gets involved I'll make sure to die. And then all his work and meddling will be for nothing."

Kyrie was worried and she didn't like to be worried. Or rather, she tried to minimize the time she spent being worried, tried to minimize the time she devoted to feeling stress. She much preferred, by far, to work on solutions than to turn over in her mind things that couldn't be helped.

But she was sure that it had been Dire who'd killed that

poor woman. She remembered her own words to him—in haste and rage, and mostly wanting to get rid of him—about the reporter and the paper. Oh, she should have known better than to say that sort of thing to a psychopath, but she didn't feel guilty. Not exactly.

She had simply not been brought up with the idea that whatever she might say to someone might cause that person to go off and take it into his head to kill someone else. Though she'd grown up in foster homes, and some of her foster siblings had been less than stable, she'd never met with that level of volatility. Now she had. And she'd take it under advisement in the future. It had perhaps been stupid of her to speak of the poor girl. But Kyrie hadn't intended her death, and nothing could be served by castigating herself over crimes she hadn't meant to commit.

And yet, she felt a nettle of guilt and a nettle of worry as she went about, waiting on tables. She would swear she smelled at least two shifters, perhaps more, though it was hard to tell through the smell of bacon and eggs and fresh-grilled pancakes.

However, when she stopped by the Poet—who had come in unusually late, and was clearly staying for breakfast—she could smell him—she was sure of it—the sharp tang of shifter around him.

She stopped long enough to refill his cup, and she could feel the smell rising from him, and then she noticed something else. What he had written on his notebook, in tiny, obsessively-neat block print, was "A modest proposal for a rodent revolution."

Rodents, Kyrie thought, moving away as he looked at her, and before he could realize she'd read over his shoulder. A Rodent Liberation Front. She wondered how real that was. It had seemed to—pardoning the pun—ferret out that school teacher rodent. Perhaps it had spies?

She shivered at the idea of an army of rodents spying on people. It reminded her of the movie *Ratatouille*, which she'd thought Tom would like, because, even though it was an animation for children, it was about a rat learning to be a chef. And since Tom had started culinary classes and was invested, heart and soul, in cooking the best he could for The George, Kyrie had thought this would be the perfect movie. Only the scene of the rats, flowing like a furry tide to take over the restaurant and do everything in it at night, had made Tom jump up and say, "Turn it off." Kyrie herself had felt pretty uncomfortable, too, though perhaps not as much as Tom, who'd said that all he could think was of a similar tide of rats taking over The George. The juxtaposition in his mind of rats and cooking surfaces just seemed to drive him crazy.

And yet . . . wouldn't such a furry tide of rats—such a group of shifters—have power? Shouldn't she be able to get help from them? She knew Tom didn't want to ask for help from the Great Sky Dragon. She understood it, even. But this was a diner customer.

The thought lasted all the walk back behind the counter, to replace the spent carafe and take up the filled one. Tom was behind the counter also taking over from Anthony and listening to Anthony's instructions on what was cooking and at what stage.

"I'll be back by six, right?" Anthony said. "Is that early enough for you? Because, you know, these double shifts are killing me, though Cecily says we could use the money because she wants a large screen TV. Where she plans to put the large screen TV in our apartment, I don't know, though doubtless I'll find out."

"You'll find out she wants to move to a bigger one," Tom said, in an amused tone, and Kyrie was surprised and admiring at once, that he could keep this calm and joke with Anthony like that, with everything that was hanging over their heads.

Anthony shrugged. "Ain't that the truth. But she's worth it. She's a great cook. Her steak is almost as good as yours. And I'm sorry, Tom, you're a good-looking man, but Cecily is much prettier."

Tom chuckled at that, and Anthony, putting his jacket on, ducked out of the counter and off towards the hallway. And Kyrie turned to Tom and said, "What about the RLF?"

Tom blinked at her. "Beg your pardon?"

"What about the Rodent Liberation Front?" Kyrie said. "What if we asked their help?"

"You're joking, right?"

"Well, they are a group of shifters, and they seem to be . . ." She looked up to see Tom's lips tremble. "Well, all right, the idea of an army of rats is somewhat creepy."

"Creepy isn't the half of it, and what I fear is not an army of rats," Tom said, "it is an army of rats, mice, gerbils, squirrels and guinea pigs."

"But . . . surely they could . . . do things?"

"Like what, nibble people to death?" Tom asked. Then shrugging, "Oh, I grant you they could probably be very useful in spying and that sort of thing, but . . ." He shook his head. "I don't know, Kyrie. All these organizations seem to come with their own, for lack of a better word, agenda: their own assumptions about who's in and who's out. I'd prefer to just be human."

Kyrie had to giggle at that. "Ah. Well. So would I, but we're not."

Tom shook his head. He frowned. "No. But perhaps we must be? I mean, I'm not going to deny, I can't deny, that I'm also something else, but we live in a society of humans and our parents . . . well . . . at least mine," he had the grace to blush, as if just remembering that she had no clue who or what her parents were, "are human. We owe humanity something . . . Even if we owe our kind something too." He looked annoyed, as though he'd just noticed that his tongue had got him hopelessly tangled. "Look, if I saw someone go after a . . . a mouse shifter, simply for being a mouse shifter and because the difference scared them, of course I would defend him or her. We owe each other that. But . . ."

"But if you found a mouse shifter nibbling on human babies at night and counting it as not mattering because he thought himself superior and more human than them . . . You'd eat the bastard?" Kyrie asked.

Tom flashed a smile. "Kill. Despite my dad's imagination, I do try very hard not to be a cannibal."

Kyrie chuckled. She could no more imagine Tom being a cannibal than she could imagine him being a mass murderer. Shifter or not, she knew her boyfriend held himself to a very stern standard. And would not, could not deviate. Not and remain himself. Which meant he couldn't ask for help. And that she would have to be the guarantor to the Great Sky Dragon that Tom wouldn't kill himself. She thought she could do that, if she had asked for help—and not him. If it were her debt.

A couple came in, and Kyrie went to seat them at a table by the window and take their order. The problem, when it came right down to it, was that Kyrie was also not absolutely sure that Tom could kill Dire even presuming he found a way to defeat his mind powers, no matter how much he thought Dire was dangerous to humans. She knew Tom. She thought Tom's own scruples would stop him. He would only kill when cornered. He would kill to protect his friends. But, given Dire's abilities, when Tom found himself cornered it might be too late.

Dire might not kill Tom. Kyrie wasn't sure how the truce of the Ancient Ones with the dragons would hold given an attack on a dragon. But she knew that he would hurt Tom. And wreak havoc on the rest of them.

And she saw no way out of it, she thought, as she set the two orders for French toast on the counter. They had to get rid of Dire, but Tom wouldn't let her ask for the help of anyone who might defeat the creature.

Rafiel didn't drive in circles. He drove through streets where people were making their cautious way to work—some of them for the first time in three days. It was slow going, and very broken progress, as he had to stop often to avoid ramming into the car in front of him, or else slow down for groups of schoolchildren slipping, sliding and giggling across an ice-patch on the crosswalk.

He stopped by a friendly doughnut shop—not his normal one—and grabbed two crullers and a tall cup of coffee, before retreating to the car parked in front of the shop, sparing just one grateful thought to his shifter metabolism that—thank heavens—allowed him to eat as much as he pleased of what he pleased.

The shop was in a neighborhood of small, remodeled townhouses and apartments. It had either been there since the middle of the twentieth century or someone had gone through a whole lot of trouble to make sure it looked as though it had. Though it had no tables, the interior had that green-formica and chrome look of the Fifties, and the sign over the shop blinked in pink and green neon good doughnuts. Which they were, or at least the crullers were—soft and moist. And the coffee was just as it should be, black as a murderer's soul, hot as hell and strong enough to peel paint—or stomach lining.

Rafiel's phone rang. He saw McKnight's cell number and took the phone to his ear with a "Yeah?"

"That guy you had me check on?"

"Dante Dire?"

"Yeah, I left a couple of the part-timers dealing with the data stuff. They didn't want to see the body."

"Yeah." *Smart part-timers.*

"Well, we didn't find signs that he was in the aquarium, but . . . well, his movements are kind of hard to check. He's all over. But he . . . well, he's been in Colorado for a couple of months. Also . . ."

"Also?"

"He made a killing in the stock market. Several times. He's either an amazing gambler, or he is crooked as hell."

Or he can read minds, Rafiel thought and shivered. "Thanks, McKnight."

Rafiel drank and ate in his car and considered his options.

He was about five blocks away from the aquarium. In the bewildering way towns in the west had of turning from residential to commercial and back again, this neighborhood became all offices as soon as you crossed under the expressway to the west. And then the aquarium was right there. He should go back to the aquarium. Oh, it was only one of the cases on his plate right now, but it was—arguably—the one he could actually do something about.

Whatever Tom and Kyrie had to say, he couldn't figure out how he could do anything about the dire wolf. And he certainly couldn't do anything about Conan and the Great Sky Dragon. He felt sorry for Conan, poor bastard, but that was about it. He didn't know where, if at all, the alligator fit in all this, and he'd be damned if he understood, even mildly, what was going on with a shifter crab. But whatever was going on at the aquarium he had to solve. There had to be a female involved, which seemed to rule out the old Japanese shifter. Unless, of course, the Japanese shifter disapproved of immoral behavior in his aquarium. Who knew? Morals had changed a lot, hadn't they even in the last couple decades, let alone from whatever old era this shifter came from? And then there was always Dire. Dire's casual disregard for life. And even if they didn't find a trail showing he'd been in town, he might have been. And he might have mind-controlled those victims into jumping in the tank. To . . . make their life difficult? Keep them on their toes while he investigated their other alleged misdeeds?

His motives were almost impossible to fathom, except that it was pretty sure they weren't good. He seemed to take relish in casual emotional torture.

Or it could be a female at the aquarium.

He became aware that someone was knocking enthusiastically on the passenger side window, and looked away from pink and green neon to see Lei Lani's face surrounded by fluffy grey fake fur on a red ski jacket hood. She tapped the window again, and smiled.

Hello, suspect number . . . well, many.

He reached for the control on his door handle with a sugary hand and lowered the window. She smiled at him. "Officer Trall," she said. "I just came in for a coffee, and I saw you parked here. Nothing wrong in the doughnut shop, is there?"

He shook his head. "No. Just having breakfast. I'm afraid I was up all night and was starting to flag. But I am about to head back to the aquarium, to look at a few things."

"Oh, good. May I go to the aquarium now? I won't come near the crime scene. I know you guys have it all taped up and everything. I just want to go to the office and pick up some reports on shark health that I've been looking at which are urgent." Suddenly, her happy expression dimmed. "Well . . . if we don't end up having to kill half of them because we need to recover parts of people, and have the others shipped to parts unknown. I mean, who's going to come and look at our sharks, if they know they've eaten people?"

Rafiel shrugged. A tingle ran up and down his neck. His dad, now retired from the Goldport force had first told him about these *feelings*. The sense that *something* was wrong.

There was something to Lei Lani, to her talk, that made him suspect she knew something.

He doubted she could be *the* shark shifter, if there was one, because how did she convince her victims to go swimming in there? She didn't look strong enough to *push* men over. Unless she got them to lean over the tank somehow.

But she knew something, and she was trying to get him not to notice.

"Lots of people will come, probably," he said. "People do." He reassured her. "Why do you think they like sharks? Because they're fascinating marine creatures? No. Because they eat people. And this is their best chance at seeing them confined and safe, you know . . ."

She looked at him a moment, with huge, incredulous eyes, then blinked. "Perhaps. I guess being a shark expert, I have a soft spot for them. I don't think of them as . . . man-eaters."

And right there, Rafiel decided he needed to talk to Ms. Lani. Everyone thought of sharks as predators! And being, as they were, on semi-informal terms right now, it would probably be easier. But he'd like to reconcile what he'd heard from John Wagner about her with her comment that the male employees often had sex by the shark tank, and that, again, with the fact that the condoms found had vaginal secretions.

"Why don't you hop in?" he said. "If you're going to the aquarium, I might as well give you a ride." And because he had no intention of letting her go near the aquarium alone.

"Oh, thank you," she said, suddenly acting shy. "I could walk, you know? It's only a few blocks." She gestured vaguely across the way. "I live just over there. Normally I walk."

"Judging from the pedestrians I saw on the way here," Rafiel said, "there's quite a bit of ice on the sidewalks. I might as well give you a ride."

She got in, gingerly, and put her coffee cup on the dashboard as she sat down and buckled herself in, before picking the cup up again. "Thank you, really."

Rafiel backed out of the parking space and into the flow of traffic, while his passenger remained absolutely quiet. It wasn't till they were a block away that she said, still in that oddly shy tone, "So, I suppose I shouldn't ask you if you have made any progress? You said you don't discuss your investigations."

He answered with a shrug. "Well," he said, "we have made some progress. As you told us, there were some condoms discarded in the planters by the water." He watched carefully for her reactions, while seeming to ignore her.

"Oh?" she said, and raised an eyebrow. "I told you, I heard the guys at the aquarium talk, and that John Wagner? He's the worst. He has this . . . imaginary friend or whatever that he calls 'the drool'—you know, like it's a part of him, or a mobile, sentient weapon. If people displease him, he'll say 'fear the drool, I am basset,' and everyone laughs and all, and you know, he talks about how he used to own a basset and how much they drooled. But . . . it feels creepy somehow. And he keeps saying things like 'I'd never say anything impolite. Now the drool, he's a

brazen bastard.' Like . . . like he's schizophrenic or something."

Rafiel was so horrified by the vision the words conjured,
of the ebullient John Wagner turning into—of all things—
a basset hound, that he could barely trust himself to
speak. While silence lengthened, he caught himself
thinking, *But . . . he can't be a shifter basset, can he? I
mean I can imagine dog shifters, but would they be a
particular breed?*

His limited knowledge of dog fancy told him that the
current breeds favored as pets in the U.S. must all be of
fairly recent creation. Recent, at least in evolutionary
terms. And surely, surely, being relatively recent they
couldn't have gotten enmeshed with human genes, could
they? It seemed to him all the shifters he'd seen so far
changed shapes into species and breeds that had been
very long on the Earth. Some longer than humans. But
then again, they had no idea how the shifting mechanism
worked. Was it truly genetic? Or was there some other
mechanism at work? Rafiel was hesitant to say it was
magic, but then, wasn't magic just a name for a process no
one understood yet? And after all, as far as they knew,
dragons had never even existed.

"I'm sorry," Lei said, sounding distant, and somehow
worried. "I didn't mean to cast aspersions on John. I
mean, he's a nice guy and all. A little . . . extroverted, you'd
call it, and he makes some jokes that could border on
sexual harassment, but I'm sure he means well."

Oh, I wouldn't be sure of any such thing, Rafiel
thought. Much as he'd liked the guy—and he realized
with surprise that he had liked the guy, which was odd,

considering that John Wagner appeared to consider him a dumb ass—he was quite sure it was part of Wagner's fundamental approach to the world to put the cat among the pigeons as much as humanly possible.

Which was why Rafiel was loathe to think of what he'd said about Lei as meaning anything at all. For all he knew, Lei had simply made that sort of prissy comment about John Wagner being sexist, and John had it in for her. Oh, not consciously. He didn't seem like the sort of guy who— fully aware of what he was doing—would be either vengeful or petty. But he might very well view casting doubt on her credentials and sending the police to look into her background as just a bit of fun and mischief. "No," he said, speaking to Lei. "That isn't it, you know. I didn't think you were particularly paranoid about John Wagner. I met him while we were processing the scene. He said he dropped by to see if we needed any help." Which, of course, was also the typical behavior of mass murderers, as Rafiel well knew. "He seems like a nice guy. Ebullient. But . . . but he didn't threaten me with the drool."

He was rewarded with a ladylike giggle and a small headshake. "I'm sure he only does that to his friends or people he works with and knows. I'm wondering if it was him . . . I mean, by the pool."

"No," Rafiel said decisively. "It couldn't be any of the men at the aquarium."

"Why not?" she asked. "I mean, did you—?"

"DNA test them? No. The semen in the condoms belonged to the last two victims, so you see, it couldn't be—"

"But, Officer!" she said and seemed within a breath

of pointing out to him that they, after all, lived in the twenty-first century.

"No," he said, cutting her off. "You see, the outside of the condom had vaginal secretions." Now she looked surprised, staring at him. "And something else. Our analyst says that the outside of the condom also had minute fragments of sharkskin."

"Shark?" she asked, now looking truly surprised. "How do they know it's shark and not some other fish? I mean, I know there are preparations"—she blushed—"people use, to facilitate sex or heighten pleasure or . . ."

"No," Rafiel said. *Curiouser and curiouser. What does she know that requires this much enthusiasm to hide?* "This was shark. There is something in sharkskin called denticles. Our examiner says that they were on the outside of this condom. And please, don't ask me how. I wouldn't begin to be able to explain it." Which was true, he thought. *Not because I can't begin to explain, but because I wouldn't. If these shark particles are like the bits of hair and fluff I find on my bed after a shifted night, or the scales that Tom is forever shaking out of his stuff, then it would indicate that the shark itself is a shifter. Herself, presumably, given the vaginal secretions. But how would a small woman get her victim in before she shifted?*

"Uh," Lei said. She unzipped her ski jacket to reveal that underneath she wore a semitransparent white blouse. Not semitransparent in a way that would necessarily look racy or provocative, but just as though a nice business blouse had been made out of too thin a material and therefore allowed a vague translucence to let forth the golden hues of her skin, the whiter tones of her bra, and a pinkish spot in the middle, between her breasts which was probably one of those rosettes with which bra manufacturers adorned bras, for reasons Rafiel—who usually concerned himself far more with the removal of their product than its purchase—couldn't understand. He glanced sideways and into her black eyes, as she said, "I think it is possible, isn't it, that they could have . . ." She shifted uncomfortably in the seat. "You know . . . put stuff on the condom to throw people off?"

Rafiel shrugged. He wasn't going to laugh the hypothesis off. Mostly because once you got shifters involved in a crime scene, the improbable was not only, often enough, possible, but it was, strangely, often the most likely solution. After all, if you started with the impossibility of someone changing shapes into an animal, then wouldn't it follow that every other impossibility would be true? *My disbelief was suspended from the neck until dead,* he thought. But still, he spoke as if he were a normal policeman, and as if he didn't very well know that all this involved shifters. "If that were the case," he said, "wouldn't it have made much more sense to have tossed the condoms away, out of the vicinity of the aquarium? And which of the . . . stuff, do you suggest they put on the condom? The vaginal secretions or the sharkskin?"

She seemed surprised, and squirmed some more, as he pulled into a parking spot at the aquarium—which was still closed to visitors and whose parking lot therefore remained empty. "I . . . I guess both?" she said, at last, hesitantly.

"Um . . . okay. I could grant you both, at least if there were no woman involved . . ." He neglected to say that unless it was manual sex there would have been other traces. "Throwing in vaginal secretions might change our perception of the crime. But why the sharkskin? They can't have meant to throw suspicion on a shark. Unless," he said, as an idea occurred to him, "some woman at the aquarium is a craftswoman specializing in sword and knife handles made of sharkskin. They do those, don't they? I don't remember what they call it . . . Oh, yes, I do. Shagreen, isn't it?"

She shook her head. "I don't know," she said. "There are so many ways in which humans exploit the beautiful creatures." And then, as though catching sight of his shocked expression, she added, "Well, they are, you know, truly. Though my professor at college said that the natural historian always identifies with their subjects. Or at least, there is no other way to account for otherwise rational beings suddenly becoming misty-eyed over monitor lizards."

It might be true. "So, you went to college in Hawaii?" Or perhaps her lover was a were shark and she fed him . . . who knew? Perhaps all that stuff about John Wagner was because they were accomplices?

"University of Hawaii," she said. "Easiest thing, you know . . . I mean . . . it was my native state."

"You were born there?"

She laughed lightly. "Born and raised. I don't know when my first ancestors came to the isle. But since I'm a bit of a mix, I guess they all came at various times, over the course of history."

"Well . . ." he said, wondering if he too would get tagged with sexual harassment. "It's a very pleasant mix."

There was something wrong here, something off to Lei's approaching him like this. What game *was* she playing? In these circumstances Rafiel often found it useful to give someone enough rope.

She seemed startled and blushed. "Thank you."

"Go and deal with your paperwork, or whatever you're going to do," Rafiel said. "I have to look at some things here on the grounds." The "some things" mostly applied to Old Joe. But he didn't want to tell her that. He doubted he could get much of rational value out of Old Joe. If anyone could do that, it would be Tom, and Tom was, alas, not around just now. But Rafiel was hoping to get . . . something. "I'll come and see if you're ready afterwards."

He was sure Lei was up to something too. It would be easier to play along till he found what it was. He could check on old Joe, then drop in on Lei, suddenly. Perhaps he would catch her kissing a shark or something. He repressed a chuckle at the idea.

First, he hoped Old Joe could give him some inkling of whether Dire was likely to be afraid of anyone. And second, some idea of whether Old Joe knew the crab shifter at the aquarium. For neither of those conversations did he wish to have the curvaceous Lei around, particularly since Old Joe was probably going to be in his shifted form.

He knew his colleagues on the force had locked and sealed the shark chamber the night before after it became obvious that they were in fact dealing with murder. She wouldn't have the key to that, surely. McKnight was supposed to come in with the employees later on and supervise them while they fed the sharks and the other fish, so that no fish in those rooms would starve. But he didn't see anything wrong with letting Lei go and do whatever paperwork she needed to do. At least not if he could drop in on her unannounced.

He watched her go towards the aquarium and only as he saw her go in, did it occur to him that she'd never told him she had a key. Did she have a key? Surely interns wouldn't. Or did someone come to open the restaurant or aquarium at a designated time? Well, he'd find out. If she couldn't get in, she couldn't do much.

Getting out of the car, he ambled down to the stream. But it was flowing now, the water gurgling amid the remaining ice floes. Rafiel thought he saw what might have been a pair of alligator eyes and the snout of an alligator peeking from beneath the water, but he couldn't really tell.

"Come on," he said, speaking to the still air and wondering if he'd gone nuts. Surely anyone who heard him would think he had. "Come on, now. Old Joe? I need to talk to you. Tom's safety might be at stake."

Was that swishing sound an alligator's tail churning the stream? Or was it just the normal gurgling of the water augmented by his hopes?

He waited. But no snout broke the water, no alligator came towards him. No, it would not be this simple, Rafiel thought. No one was about to hand him the solution. He'd have to figure it out himself.

Kyrie waited till there was a lull early in the afternoon, when the diner was almost empty. Tom busied himself with those things he did when his cooking expertise was not needed—scrubbing the cooking surfaces, marinating meat, bringing out frozen dough and setting bread to rise. The bread was one of the few things Tom didn't make himself, from scratch. The woman, Laura, who had applied here some days ago, had offered baking skills, which, of course, would be a great help. Kyrie hoped she would show up for an interview as soon as the weather permitted it. For one, with the addition of Conan and the seeming disappearance of the unreliable waitress Beth, she was now the only woman on staff. For another, she wasn't sure how much longer Keith would want to continue working for them.

He had only ever been a part-time employee, because of his studies, but since he'd discovered Summer had taken pictures of Tom and Conan, he hadn't been back at all. Kyrie didn't know if he was upset with them, or if it had just finally been borne upon him how difficult and dangerous their position was. Probably both. She would have left them and herself far behind, by now, if she could. At least . . . she couldn't leave Tom. Any more than she could walk away from herself. But she would have left their shifter condition far behind.

As she walked towards the annex, she found herself daydreaming of a life in which neither she nor Tom were shifters. How peaceful the days would be and how devoid of unusual events.

Of course, she knew in her heart of hearts that the daydream was great foolishness. Because, if Tom hadn't been a shifter, he'd be living somewhere in New York City. Or perhaps he would have been sent to those Ivy League colleges where the wildest behavior is excused if the family pays enough. At any rate, he would never have crossed paths with her.

And besides, things were the way they were, so she must do what she must do. She felt a twinge of fear at the idea of exactly what she must do. Tom would disapprove. In fact, Tom would be very, very upset. If he ever found out. She didn't want to keep secrets from him. But sometimes people had to be kept in the dark for their own good. And in this case, Tom had to be kept in the dark for the continued ability to call his soul his own.

She approached Conan as he finished wiping a table, and spoke in an undertone, her ears listening for any sounds of approaching footsteps, which might be Tom coming to check on them. "Conan, do you have a way to contact the representatives of the dragon triad, here in town?"

She'd obviously been so careful that Conan himself had not heard her approach. He dropped the tray he'd been holding, and bent to retrieve it, his gaze fixed on her, his eyes big as saucers.

Seeing him open his mouth, and very much fearing how much noise he might make, she put her finger in front of her lips. He nodded and it seemed to her he looked a little pale, but when he straightened up, he whispered back, "Well, you know that Himself can take over my mind and . . . and listen in, but . . ."

"I don't mean like that," she said. "I mean, do you have a phone number to call or something? I presume that I could still approach them outside the Three Luck Dragon?" she asked.

"Inside," he said. "The owner. Yes."

"Then would you call whatever number you need to call and tell them I come in peace, but I want to talk to their leader?"

Conan gave her a long and analyzing stare, before giving her a very curt nod. "When?"

"After Tom goes back to the bed-and-breakfast to sleep," she said, "which I figure will be around six, because that's when Anthony will come in again."

"Oh," Conan said and then, "you haven't slept at all yourself."

Kyrie shrugged. "No. I can go twenty-four hours without sleeping. It just makes me more susceptible to shifting, but . . ."

He nodded. "I assume you . . . have a plan? And that you want our—the dragons' help with it?"

"Yes. Well . . . I want their help. I don't have a plan yet, but I'm sure one will emerge. Only, I must find out if they can help me, and then I must do what I can . . . I mean . . . I'm sure we can't fight this fight alone. And Tom won't ask for help." She saw him nod. "And Tom must never know of this."

Conan shrugged. "He won't learn it from me," he said. "Of course, the other dragons have their own . . . approach to honesty and promises."

"Meaning you can't promise me anything?" Kyrie asked, with alarm but not really surprised. She'd already once met the Great Sky Dragon's idea of morality. She wasn't sure he cared even for shifters that weren't his own kind.

After Anthony had come in, and Tom had gone back to the bed-and-breakfast to sleep, she went outside and—

with trembling fingers—dialed the number Conan had given her. A heavily accented woman's voice answered, "Three Luck Dragon! How may I help you?"

Momentarily mute, Kyrie wondered if there was a polite way to say, May I speak to the boss dragon? Instead, she cleared her throat and said, "May I speak to the proprietor?"

The woman rattled something off, very fast, that appeared to be some Cantonese dialect, and Kyrie said, "Conan Lung told me to call. He said that the owner of the restaurant would speak to me."

There was a long silence, followed by the sound of cutlery and a rattle of plates and a voice saying something in an Asian language. Kyrie took a deep breath. Her thumb moved towards the disconnect button on the phone.

"Hello," a male voice said. It was a resonant voice, with almost no trace of an accent.

Caught off guard, Kyrie cleared her throat, nervously and said "Am I speaking to the owner of Three Luck Dragon?"

"Speaking," the voice said.

"Oh. Oh. Good. I wanted to talk about . . . about the owner of the diner . . . The George."

For a terribly long moment, while the speaker on the other side was silent, she thought he was going to ask "Who?"

But instead, when he spoke, he said, "The young dragon? The one whom Himself . . ."

"Yes." Kyrie hastened, not wanting to know if the man was about to say "the one whom Himself almost killed" or "the one whom Himself is protecting." That she didn't know which one the man was about to say betrayed her ambivalence about this being and about the step she was taking.

Was she doing the right thing? Or was she about to betray Tom's trust in her for nothing?

"I assume," the man said from the other side, his voice even more impersonal, colder, as though he were a receptionist talking to a stranger about some abstract transaction. "I assume that you do not wish to speak of this over the phone?"

Kyrie did not wish. No matter that Anthony was busy at the grill. No matter that she could go outside and attempt to talk from there. What she had to say was bound to make more than a few clients or passersby get curious. And then there was the fact that Summer might have friends or relatives coming around to see her place of death. There was already a clutter of flowers around the base of the pole, and one pink teddy bear clutching a heart. Summer's friends were bound to be journalists. Considering the paper was obsessed with cryptozoology, how would they react to hearing Kyrie talk of dragons. "It would be better if I may speak in person," she said. She remembered the parking lot, and the Great Sky Dragon in it. And all the other dragons around. Had this man—dragon—been there too? There was a great deal she'd rather do than see one of these dragons again. All else aside, they were a criminal organization and one populated by shifters, who could destroy her and Tom several times over. But she didn't have any choice. She'd run out of all choices.

"Come to the restaurant," the man said. "I'll be here. Ask for Mr. Lung."

Mr. Lung? Was he related to Conan?

Rafiel opened the door to the aquarium. It had been unlocked. The smell of fish and bleach—combined—hit his nostrils as well as damp air that seemed hot compared to the frosty air outside. He stepped into the shadows, lengthened since all the lights in the aquarium were off. He almost called out to Lei, except he remembered the offices were far enough around the corner that he was sure she couldn't hear him. He walked past the sealed door to the shark room, up a short flight of service stairs, now the only way to get past the shark room, to where the light of the floor-to-ceiling windows made the room with the anemones and crabs much brighter than the one belowstairs. He walked past the aquariums, looking curiously at the spider crab one. He wished he could tell that one of the giant, long-legged crabs—some of them looking as weathered and beaten as though they'd escaped from the mother of all clarified butter dishes—was a shifter. They all had moss growing on them. He squinted, reasoning that a shifter crab would have less moss, wouldn't it? Surely the moss sloughed off when the crabs shifted to human then back? Surely . . . But all of them seemed to have an even covering of the green stuff, and Rafiel started wondering if John Wagner had hallucinated it all. Perhaps for his own amusement. The man seemed to have a very odd sense of humor.

Normally he could have cut through the shark room to the office area, but now he had to make it across the silent restaurant, and then down another set of stairs, to the back.

As he got to the bottom floor, he saw light shining out of the office and called out, "Ms. Lani?"

She stuck her head out of the office, for just a moment. "I'll be ready in just a moment, Officer Trall."

"Oh. All right," he said. *Now what are you up to?*

"You may come in." Her voice sounded vaguely amused.

He ambled out of the hallway and into the cramped offices he had visited and searched before. On the wall, on a pegboard were the keys he had stolen and gotten copied, as well as several other sets of keys, which he assumed were to either other areas of the aquarium—areas he'd found no need to explore—or to the utility parts of the aquarium. At least he assumed that electrical circuits and such would be locked behind panels and couldn't be accessed by just anyone.

Other than that, the office consisted of a very long, narrow room, which might have, in some previous incarnation, been a hallway. It had no windows, and only two rows of desks, six on each side against the walls. While Lei Lani rummaged through the desk nearest the door, Rafiel walked up and down the rows of desks, to the small fridge set against the narrow far wall, and the coffee maker on top of the fridge. The coffee maker had coffee in it, and, inside, some blue mold over a residue sludge that might very well be sentient in itself, or perhaps even a shifter.

Rafiel eyed it dubiously. He was well aware, no matter how much he pretended not to be, that Tom and Kyrie thought there was something wrong with him, since he still lived with his parents, and he was the first to admit that perhaps he had leaned on parental protection too long. Until he'd met Kyrie and Tom, he had never seen other shifters manage for themselves, without normal people to cover up for them. But whatever his staying with his parents might betray about his character, it did not betray a lingering, overlong adolescence. To the contrary. Rafiel kept his area of the house neat, and had even acquired the reputation of a neat freak at the police station. If this coffee machine, or anything like it, were in the station, he'd be taking it out, rinsing it, washing it, then giving all his subordinates a lecture on keeping foodstuffs around as they molded. With a rueful smile, he thought that McKnight and the others must think he was a pure bundle of joy.

To distract himself from the machine, he turned his attention to the desks, once more. Above them were corkboards, with the usual family pictures and the like, showing that most people who worked here were pretty ordinary. One of the corkboards was ornamented with groups of young men standing around drinking beer and an inordinate number of pictures of a simpering blond in different bikinis. Rafiel presumed it was a young man's desk and, in fact, looking at the various groups in the pictures on the wall, quickly narrowed down the user of the desk to a tall, disheveled blond who looked like a football player. He was the youth who appeared in every picture and Rafiel had a vague memory of seeing him among the other employees the police had cursorily interviewed. Judging from the attention given to beer and girls amid the man's favorite memories, it wasn't hard to imagine him bringing girlfriends to the shark area to impress them. But then, the pictures were all of the same girl, and she didn't look like she'd be that much into sharp-toothed creatures.

Next to that desk was another one, whose remarkably neat and empty corkboard showed only two pictures. One had a soulful-eyed, sad-looking basset. The other, which was clearly a bought postcard, showed a donkey about to cross a busy highway and said, in yellow letters across the top "dumb ass." Rafiel thought the desk might as well be labeled as John Wagner's, and resisted a momentary impulse to look through the drawers. He truly had no reason to suspect John Wagner of anything, no matter how much he had—and he undoubtedly had—upset Lei. At least, judging from her comments on him. But then, Rafiel thought, those two would rub the other one the wrong way, wouldn't they? Lei Lani with her careful image, her nice clothes and manners, and John Wagner who seemed to believe his job was to repeatedly poke the universe in the eye.

He moved on to the next desk, and perked up because it was so obviously a woman's. Or perhaps he was letting his assumptions show, but he truly could not imagine any man, no matter his sexual orientation, adorning a desk with a collection of pretty kitten mugs, and owning a notepad in pink ornamented with butterflies. Besides, the collection of smiling kids in various stages of tooth loss and toothiness on the corkboard seemed to clinch the matter. They were all the same kids, he guessed, at different stages of growth. Or at least, the entire horde were redheaded and blue-eyed and had disturbingly vacuous expressions. "I guess she has what? Eight children?" he asked, more to distract himself from the contemplation of such a thing than to talk.

"What?" Lei said, the rustling of papers momentarily stopped.

"I said your . . . colleague seems to have eight children?"

She looked across and smiled. "Suzanne isn't married," she said, and, as though realizing that really didn't mean much in context, added, "She doesn't have any children. Those are her nephews and nieces."

"Oh," Rafiel said, embarrassed. He stepped across the other way, to look at the desk next to Lei's, which had pictures of what appeared to be bodybuilders on the corkboard, a note saying "Call me" and the number, and a collection of pink notebooks on the desk. He had just resolutely decided he wasn't going to say anything, much less ask it, when he noticed that Lei was staring intently at him, and blushing slightly.

He raised his eyebrows at her. It wasn't as if he could ask her why she was staring at him, of course, but raising eyebrows was surely allowed. She sighed and colored deeper, and looked down at her hands, which were resting on a pile of papers, from which protruded a couple of plastic baggies.

"Look," she said, "I was . . . curious . . . you know . . . after what you told me about what you found on the outside of the . . . of the preservatives."

"Yes?"

"Well . . . I looked in Lillian's desk . . . and . . . well . . ." She reached over and slid open the drawer in the middle of the desk.

Rafiel looked down at a welter of pencils and pens, a forlorn nest of paper clips, a confusion of rubber bands. Lei seemed to lose patience with him. She reached down and picked up a tube of something and put it on top of the desk.

Rafiel looked closer. "Petroleum jelly?" he said.

"Well . . ." Lei said. "You know, it's used for . . . you know . . . sex . . ."

"Yes, I know," Rafiel said. And, he imagined, for a dozen other things. He had a vague idea that it was also used for some sorts of closures that must resist water, like, say, wetsuits, which he knew were used when divers went in to clean the tanks.

"But that's not what . . . what made me . . . I mean . . . why I think I should tell you," Lei said. "It's this." She showed him some grey adherences to the slightly greasy outside of the tube. "I thought . . . it might be sharkskin." And then, looking up at his face, she looked like she was trying very hard not to give a sigh of exasperation. "We use petroleum jelly around the . . . you know . . . around the aquariums, on seals and valves and such, and I thought, she might have got sharkskin on it. We collect the skin for samples and such, you know, and that she . . . you know . . . then used it for . . . for other things."

Rafiel shrugged. He took the tube and reached for the end of one of the baggies under Lei's pile of papers. It came out from under the papers, scattering grey flakes as it was pulled away. It was full of what looked like white and grey dandruff.

"Oh," Lei said. And then. "Not that." She pulled the baggie away and put it on her desk. "Those are some samples I meant to send to the lab, for sharkskin diseases. Of course, now I don't know if our sharks . . ." She shrugged and looked pained.

"I need a plastic baggie, if I'm going to send this to analysis," Rafiel said. "And I must put a label on it, then seal it. And you must be willing to say I didn't tamper with it." Though of course, that didn't mean Lei Lani hadn't tampered with it, Rafiel thought but didn't say. Her finding this in the desk seemed very odd, and oddly convenient.

She primly got him a plastic baggie from her own desk, where she had a pile of them folded together. "We use them for samples," she said, as she handed him one.

"Curiously," he said, "we do too." Sealing the bag, he wrote on it with a marker from the desk drawer, saying what he had found and where. This would never hold up in a court of law, of course. There were so many ways in which it might have been tampered with. But at this point Rafiel was not operating on the assumption the matter would ever come to a court of law. Instead, he thought, this would end up in the court of Rafiel and it was for himself that he must collect evidence. And he wondered how stupid Ms. Lani thought he was.

Kyrie parked in front of the restaurant and got out of her car, shivering at the sight of the facade, at its cheery sign saying three luck dragon above another sign that proclaimed for your health, we don't use msg in our cooking.

Kyrie pulled her coat tighter around herself. She had

very bad memories of this parking lot. Without meaning to, she looked toward the sky, afraid of a flapping of large wings, the sudden appearance of the Great Sky Dragon in all his golden and green glory. But the skies were empty and a sound somewhere between throat-clearing and a cough made her turn to look.

In the slightly open door of the restaurant, stood a middle-aged Asian gentleman, with impeccably cut salt-and-pepper hair and a big white apron. She took a deep breath. Three steps brought her close to him, and she had a moment of surprise, at noticing that he was wearing a shirt and tie under his apron.

"Ms. Smith?" he said, extending his hand.

She hesitated only fractionally before she shook it. It felt slightly cool to the touch. Not abnormally so. It was the same way Tom's skin usually felt, as if he'd been holding a glass with a cold drink all the time. Maybe it was something about the metabolism of dragon shifters, though Kyrie would bet the dragons were not actually cold-blooded.

The man held the door open to her. "Please come in."

He led her past the counter, manned by a small lady who was watching TV and doing accounts at the same time, then past the dining room where only three people sat at tables, and into a door that led into busy, noisy kitchen. Before she had more than a moment to recoil from the sound of pans banged together, the clash of plates, the way people yelled at each other across the room, she felt Mr. Lung's cool hand on her elbow, and saw him pointing at yet another, narrower door.

She went through it to find herself in a very small room. There was only one table, long and narrow, covered in an immaculate white tablecloth. Three chairs, one on either of the longer sides of the table, and one at the end. At one corner of the table, the tablecloth had been pulled back, to reveal a cutting-board surface. That area was covered in cabbage and there was a cleaver amid it. On the other side sat a pile of papers that looked like account books, but which Kyrie could not presume to decipher, given they were written in Chinese ideograms.

Mr. Lung smiled and waved her to one of the chairs on the long side of the table, then sat himself on the facing one and took up the cleaver. "I hope you don't mind," he said, "if I work while we talk? I find it helps me concentrate. Also, we are a family operation. I don't cook, but I help with the preparation for the cooking. And then I take off the apron and serve at tables." Judging from his smile, one would think this was a pleasant social chat.

"You . . . know my name . . ." Kyrie said.

"Of course," he said, equably. "We met before. I mean, I've seen you. And I knew who you were. I was not . . . in my human form."

Kyrie thought of the assembly of dragons, of the Great Sky Dragon and of Tom—as she then thought—getting killed. She felt as if her throat would close.

Mr. Lung seemed to notice her discomfort. He set the cleaver down again, amid the chopped cabbage, gently, as if he were afraid the blade might scare her. "I know what it must have seemed like to you," he said. He joined his hands and rested them on the edge of the table, but kept his spotless shirt sleeves away from the cabbage. "But even then, I knew . . ." He shrugged. "He doesn't tell us much. He doesn't need to. He's like . . . the father of the family, and the father doesn't owe explanations to anyone, does he?" He smiled suddenly. "Well, now your attitudes here are different, but where I grew up the father could do as he pleased and didn't need to tell wife or children anything." For a moment it seemed to Kyrie as though he glanced across endless distances at a time she couldn't even imagine. "But we don't question him, and I haven't. I do have my suspicions, but I'm not so foolish as to share them, and besides, I might be quite wrong. But I can tell you he didn't mean to seriously punish the young dragon. If he had . . ." Mr. Lung shrugged.

He picked up the cleaver again, and resumed chopping cabbage. "If he had, you wouldn't be worried for the young dragon now, because he would be dead. Himself can be quite ruthless when he chooses. I don't think he has it in him to mind what other people feel or think." He shrugged again. "But he treated the young dragon very gently, particularly for someone who had just led him on a chase and defied him the way—what is his name? Mr. Ormson?—had."

Kyrie heard herself sniffle skeptically. "He had given people orders to kill him before."

Mr. Lung narrowed his eyes at her. "This is where I can't give you more detailed explanations, Ms. Smith. Partly, because they are only my conjectures. But I think . . . I think Himself found out something about Mr. Ormson when he met him in the flesh. And that's when he decided he could not kill him."

"Found out what?"

Mr. Lung shrugged. "I can't tell you that. All I can say is that the dragon triad looks after its own."

"But he's not . . . an Asian dragon."

"Sometimes the differences are smaller than you think," Mr. Lung said. "And not everything is as black and white as it appears. For now . . ." He chopped cabbage with a will. "Let's establish that it matters to Himself—in fact, it's important to him—that nothing should happen to the young dragon. So, anything I can do to help you with this . . ."

"He'll never join you, you know?" Kyrie felt forced to warn. "He just can't. He would . . . he will never give anyone that sort of authority over him."

Mr. Lung nodded. "I talked to his father," he said, as if he were admitting to a distasteful encounter. "I know all about Mr. Ormson's hatred of authority. All I can say is that he's very young."

Kyrie opened her mouth and almost said it wasn't the authority, it was the feeling of belonging absolutely to someone, and the fact that the triad was, after all, a criminal organization. But she realized in time that nothing could be gained from antagonizing the people she needed to help her, and almost smiled. It would be such a Tom thing to do, after all. Perhaps Tom was contagious. Instead, she closed her mouth. And when she opened it again, it was to say, "There's a dire wolf shifter in town."

"Ah, the executioner. We've . . . heard." The nimble fingers plied the cleaver impossibly fast, chopping exact, neat strips of cabbage. "We have . . . a pact with the Ancient Ones."

"I know. I don't know if Dante Dire intends to violate it," she said. And watched his eyebrows go up, as the cleaver stopped.

"What do you mean 'violate it'?" For just a moment,

Mr. Lung's urbane mask seemed to slip. He set his mouth into what would have been a grin, except that it displayed far more of his small, sharp teeth than any natural grin could display. "He wouldn't dare."

Kyrie could swear she saw an extra pair of nictitating eyelids close, then open from the side, but she knew it couldn't be true. She looked away from him, hastily. "I don't know," she said. "I know the following: he's a sadist. He's not as much in control of himself as he thinks he is. He seems to have decided he likes me, or at least is not willing to hurt me, for now. And he's looking for a scapegoat for the deaths that brought him here."

"He should be more concerned," the dragon said, "with the other deaths. The ones that originally got you involved."

"Yes," Kyrie said. "But he doesn't seem concerned with searching out the true culprits or investigating anything. He wants to protect himself, and get out of here with his . . . reputation undiminished." Mentally she added to herself that at least she hoped he wanted to get out of there. The idea that he had a thing for her and that he might stick around to make himself agreeable to her was driving her insane. In the long list of suitors she'd rejected, Dante Dire was something she'd never met. Something she didn't need.

She started telling the dragon about her encounters with Dire and more, about what she sensed and feared from the creature. When she was done, Mr. Lung swept the cabbage into a mound, and looked at her over it. "So, you fear he might inadvertently kill the young dragon? While baiting him?" He looked skeptical. "We are not that frail, Ms. Smith. Nor that easy to kill."

"No," she said. "That is not what I fear at all. What I

fear . . ." She shook her head. "You know Tom, such as he is." She smiled a little. "Hatred of authority and all, he insists on looking after those he thinks he's obliged to protect. To . . . to keep them from harm. As such, he's . . . well . . . he doesn't want me hurt. And he doesn't want Rafiel hurt, nor Keith, nor anyone in the diner. That girl reporter getting killed just outside the diner scared him. He thinks it's up to him to save us all. And I'm very afraid he's about to do something stupid."

Mr. Lung was quiet a long time. When he spoke, it was in measured tones. "I would say he will do something stupid. That sense that he must do something he's completely unprepared to do . . . I've seen it before. He will get hurt."

"Yes," Kyrie said, feeling a great wave of relief at being understood. "That's what I thought. He will get hurt."

"No," Mr. Lung said, with great decision, his face setting suddenly in sharp lines and angles. "No. Himself would not want him hurt. I will do what it takes. What is your plan?"

"Right," Rafiel said over the phone as he drove away from the doughnut shop where he had dropped off Lei Lani. "And I want you to check the backgrounds of the aquarium employees," and to McKnight's protests answered, "No, nothing special, okay? Just basically their resumé. But check with the places where they're supposed to have studied and all."

"You . . . suspect one of them is an impostor?" McKnight asked.

"I don't know what I suspect," Rafiel said. "I just want to check it out."

"Oh," McKnight said. "Now?"

"Now would be good," Rafiel said, as sternly as he could. "Call me as soon as you have anything."

He hung up before McKnight could formulate an answer, and set a course towards the laboratory to drop off the petroleum jelly. He was fairly sure the petroleum jelly would have sharkskin in it. He was also fairly sure that the skin had come from the scrapings in that baggie Lei had on her desk. It had taken all of Rafiel's self-control—plus some—to avoid giving away how obvious all this was. Except that he could feel a theory assembling, like an itch at the back of his brain. If he had to bet, he would bet that Lei Lani was the shark shifter. And he would bet she took her dates to the aquarium and then . . . made a snack out of them.

The problem was, even if it proved that she hadn't gone to the University of Hawaii, even if it could be proven that she wasn't who she said she was . . . how could he be sure she was a shark shifter? And even if he were sure she was a shark shifter, how could he be sure that she was committing these heinous crimes? Or that she was committing them on purpose? Or that she knew what she was doing?

In a normal crime, you knew. And if you didn't know— if you weren't absolutely sure that the criminal knew right from wrong, or that he was in full possession of his faculties, you had the courts. Rafiel's job was supposed to be to provide a case to the courts. Not constituting himself judge, jury and executioner. That would make him no better than Dire.

No . . . he needed to go and talk to someone. He looked at the clock on the dashboard. Middle of the day. Normally both Kyrie and Tom would be at home and awake. He wasn't sure how the strange schedule was affecting things. He also knew they wouldn't be home. Rafiel had left their key with his father, who said his uncle would have the bathroom repaired in the next two or three days. But for now, Kyrie and Tom would be at the bed-and-breakfast. Or at least one of them would be. Almost for sure.

Rafiel parked in the back of The George. A quick look inside revealed Anthony at the grill, which meant Tom at least was off. The tables seemed to be attended to by Conan and Keith. That meant . . . maybe both Tom and Kyrie were off.

Turning away from The George, Rafiel crossed the parking lot, went up the broad stone steps flanked by sickly-looking stone lions—or perhaps dogs—and up to the front door of the bed-and-breakfast. The sign on the door said do come in, and Rafiel did. In response to a light tinkle from the bell affixed to the back of the front door, the kindly-looking, middle-aged proprietress came from the back of the house, wearing a frilly apron and smelling vaguely of vanilla.

"Hi," Rafiel said. "I'm here to see my friends, Mr. Ormson and Ms. Smith?" *And don't I sound like I have a truly interesting social life, the way I keep visiting Tom and Kyrie in their room.* He felt himself blush but smiled at the woman.

"Oh, sure. Just a moment," she said, heading to the antique mahogany desk in the middle of the room. "I'll just give them a ring to make sure they are decent and want to see you." Her smile somehow managed to soften the implication that he was an interloper or trying to disturb their privacy under false pretenses. She pressed some buttons, put the phone to her ear. "Mind you, I think only Mr. Ormson is in. Ms. Smith—" She stopped abruptly and her voice changed to the mad cheerfulness that people reserve for barely awakened males and slightly dangerous dogs, "Oh, hi, Mr. Ormson! Your friend, Mr.—" a pleading look at Rafiel.

"Trall."

"Mr. Trall is here. He would like to see you. Is it okay if I send him up?"

A series of rasps answered her and she said, "All righty, then. I'll send him up." And then, in her normal voice, to Rafiel. "He says to go on up. You know where the room is, I presume?"

"Oh, yes. I've been there before," Rafiel said. *Not that it would surprise anyone at the station to hear this. They would think that, at one stroke—so to put it—both my aloofness to my dates and my odd changes of clothes midday are explained.* The idea amused him, but it still made him blush, which he was fairly sure made him look very guilty.

He more or less ran up the stairs, all the way to the top floor, where he knocked lightly on Tom's door. There was the sound of steps approaching the door, and then a disheveled, unshaven Tom, in his underwear—and had Kyrie bought him jockey shorts with little dragons on them? Either that or Tom's sense of humor was worse than Rafiel had anticipated—holding a flailing kitten in one hand, opened the door.

"Hi," Rafiel said, walking in. "Sorry to disturb you. I can see I woke you."

" 'Sokay," Tom mumbled, followed by something that might have been "Never mind." He closed the door and set the orange furball gently on the floor. " 'Scuse me a moment?"

Rafiel nodded and Tom ducked into the bathroom and closed the door. Rafiel heard flushing and the shower running, then splashing of water. In what seemed like less than three minutes—spent mostly in pulling Not Dinner off Rafiel's pants, which he seemed to believe were the climbing part of a jungle gym—Tom opened the door again and emerged, wrapped in a white robe, with his hair in a towel.

"Nice turban," Rafiel said.

Tom glowered in response. He had shaving things out on the marble-topped vanity. A spray-on shaving cream can, and one of those razors that seemed to come with an ever-increasing number of blades. Even so, it all looked very Tom-like and unnecessarily difficult to Rafiel who, knowing Tom, was only surprised he didn't shave with a straight razor and use a brush to apply lather to his face. "I use an electric razor," he blurted out.

Tom, in the process of swathing his face in shaving cream, so that he looked like a turbaned Santa Claus, gave Rafiel a questioning look, then shrugged. "You're light-haired," he said, speaking in a weirdly stilted manner, almost not moving his lips—probably to avoid getting shaving cream in his mouth. He rinsed his hands. "To get my beard properly shaved, I need to grind the electric razor into my skin, and then I end up with burns.

Besides," he shrugged, "when I started shaving, I was homeless. They have hand razors in those little kits shelters give away as charity. Electric razors not so much."

The idea that Tom had been homeless for years seemed insane, Rafiel thought, as Tom shaved a strip of cream off his face, rinsed the razor and looked at him. He had unearthly blue eyes, very intense in color. They looked like nothing so much as the blue on the type of pioneer enamelware often sold at touristy shops. It was disturbing to find himself under scrutiny by those sharp, bright eyes.

"Talk," Tom said.

"Hey, I'm supposed to say that," Rafiel said. "I'm the policeman."

He sat down on the one loveseat from which he had an unimpeded view of the bathroom. Tom, who had shaved another strip of cream and beard, shrugged. "If you didn't have something to talk about you wouldn't be here waking me."

"Well," Rafiel said. "I do need to talk to someone and you and Kyrie"—he shrugged—"are practically the only friends I have. At least the only friends I have that I'm not related to. And that I can . . . you know . . . be frank with."

"Right."

"But it's not like I know anything. It's more like I need to figure things out." Not Dinner, having ascended the heights of Rafiel's lap, was climbing under Rafiel's shirt. "What's he—?"

"Notty does that," Tom said, in a resigned tone. "Crawl under your clothes, I mean. He's a baby. Cold."

"I suppose," Rafiel said, though frankly, if he was going to have a feline getting in his clothes, he'd much rather—by far—it were Kyrie. "All right. Well, these are my suspicions." He proceeded to lay out the case against Lei Lani, such as he could make it out. Her half-truths, her exaggerations. As he was talking, the phone rang.

"Boss?" McKnight's voice.

"Yes?"

"That woman, Lei Lani?"

"Yes?"

"She doesn't seem to have graduated from the University of Hawaii. The aquarium there never heard of her, either."

"I see," Rafiel said. "Do a full records search, would you?" he said and hung up before McKnight could protest. He related the knowledge to Tom, who raised his eyebrows.

"But the fact she didn't attend the University of Hawaii," Tom said, as the blade went swish-swish across his face, rinse-rinse under the faucet, and then swish against his face again, "doesn't mean that she is a shark shifter."

"No," Rafiel said. "And that's what's making me uncomfortable. Look . . . I wish I could smell her out, but I can't. John Wagner says that aquatic shifters have pheromones you can only detect in water, which makes sense, of course, except that it makes it really hard to figure out who they are."

"Yeah," Tom said, rinsing the razor and setting it aside and then rinsing his face and drying it. He removed the towel from his hair, and started brushing the hair out vigorously. "The thing is—"

"The thing is that she might just have been taking

boyfriends there, and when her boyfriends were found dead in the aquarium, she panicked and decided to put the guilt on someone else. It's entirely possible," he said, "that someone else is a shifter—shark or otherwise, and responsible for getting the victims in the tank once Ms. Lani is done with them. For all I know, the Japanese spider crab shifter—if there really is one—shoves people in the tank because he disapproves of fornication in the aquarium."

"Wouldn't the Japanese spider crab have done that before?" Tom said. "I mean, from what you said, he's been at the aquarium for years, right?"

"But we don't know that Ms. Lani or someone like her has been having fun at the aquarium for that long," Rafiel said. "This could be a response to something perceived as a new wave of immorality."

"I guess," Tom said nodding. "Which, of course, leaves us up a creek without a paddle, because we can't prove that Lei Lani is a shifter. And even if we could, how could we prove that she's the one getting them in the shark tank?" He crossed the room to where his tote bag was open on the floor, and retrieved underwear, jeans and a red T-shirt, then retreated with them all to the bathroom, closing the door till the barest crack remained open to allow the sound through. "I mean, the victims are dead. They can't exactly tell us what went on."

"The problem," Rafiel said, as Notty climbed the rest of the way inside his shirt and installed himself on his shoulder, under his shirt, his little orange fuzzy head protruding from Rafiel's collar and making a sound reminiscent of a badly tuned diesel engine, "is that if shifters weren't a secret, and I could tell my medical examiner what to look for, I'm sure they could find traces of whatever happened, maybe enough to tell us if we're looking for a crab shifter, a shark shifter or none of the above."

"Unless your medical examiner is a shifter himself," Tom said, emerging from the bathroom, and tying his hair back. "I wouldn't recommend it. If you're lucky, he'll recommend a psychiatric evaluation. If you're not, he might believe you"

Rafiel sighed. "I know. But we still have to figure out something."

"Yes," Tom said. "Yes, we do." He turned around to face Rafiel and smiled a little. "Nice second head, by the way."

Rafiel petted Notty's head protruding from his shirt. "Yeah, I think it will make me a veritable chick magnet."

"Not advisable. Notty would eat the chicks."

"Probably. But you know two heads . . ."

"Think better than one. Yes. Which reminds me . . . Could you . . . I mean, you have the keys to the aquarium, right? I mean, that's how you took Kyrie there before?"

Rafiel nodded.

"Well, then I think I might have an idea. We'll need to go by my house but I think there's something we can do."

Kyrie's head was whirling. Mr. Lung had believed her, when she said that Tom would not kill himself, provided it wasn't his independence that had been compromised. And he'd told her to let Conan Lung—whom he assured her was no relation, except in the way that all dragon shifters were supposed to be descended from the very first dragon—in on whatever the plan was. He promised that so long as Conan was with them, or where he could see them if they got in trouble, help would be instantaneous. So now, the question was—how to trap Dire?

And did she want to entrap him? Did she truly want to kill him? Despite everything that she'd told the owner of the Three Luck Dragon, she felt squeamish at the thought. After all, he hadn't tried to kill her. If that was what he wanted to do, he would have done it long ago. He'd pursued her, and tried to scare her and hurt her, but he had not actually sought to kill her.

Should she kill someone who wasn't trying to kill her? To say that he was a sadist—which, of course, he was—and was trying to terrorize her and hurt her just didn't seem enough reason to kill him. As she drove into the parking lot of The George and noted Rafiel's car parked where he normally parked when he was visiting, she sighed. It stretched the definition of self-defense to kill someone merely because they were psychopaths.

Oh, she was quite sure that Dire had killed plenty of people in his time. Well . . . she was almost sure he had killed Summer, the journalist. But horrible as that crime was, it was almost certain that he had done it to protect them. To keep them secret. Yes, of course it could be argued that by keeping their secret, he kept his own. But he could just as easily have killed them, and he hadn't. She opened the door of the car and got out onto the cool parking lot almost deserted in the after-lunch lull.

"Hello, Kitten Girl," a familiar voice said.

She spun around to see Dante Dire—in human aspect,

wearing a well-tailored black suit, standing just steps from her. Her stomach knotted. Her heart sped up. She tasted bile at the back of her throat. He could read thoughts. Had he been reading her thoughts the last few minutes?

If so, he seemed in a strangely good mood. "I want you to know I've solved all our problems," he said, grinning at her. "I want you to know you don't have to worry anymore."

Our problems? What can he mean?

He laughed at what was, doubtlessly, her very confused expression. "Ah, I see you don't know. Well . . . it's like this. You know I came here to decide on who had killed a great deal of young ones, right? I was to do preliminary investigations, and then tell the council what I had found and wait for their decision. They'd probably send three or four more to verify my conclusions, and you know . . ." He put his hand in his pocket and made a sound of jingling, probably with change. "The truth is if they probed the problem, they would find that it was of course you and your friends . . . If it were just your friends, I wouldn't mind denouncing them. I don't know why the daddy dragon has an interest in Dragon Boy, but I'm sure—Dragon Boy not being one of his own nestlings, see?—that if push came to shove, he would let Dragon Boy go. And I could fulfill my mission and go back to my normal life."

As he spoke he approached her, and somehow his voice became lower and more seductive. "And let me tell you, my normal life is the sort of life anyone would dream of. I have my own private plane. I have bank accounts in every country. I've lived long enough to allow me to accumulate more money than I know what to do with. When I arrive somewhere, even if I arrive naked," he flashed her a smile,

"I can always be properly attired and in a brand-new car within an hour."

He came very close, until his face was almost touching hers, and his voice descended till it was just a purr. "You can share that life with me, Kitten Girl. I can show you the world and everything beyond. Come on. You were made for better things than this dinky little diner."

Kyrie knew that he was doing something to her mind, even as he spoke, in that low seductive voice. She could feel her mind not so much changing as being changed for her. All of a sudden, as if she were looking through Dante Dire's eyes, the diner did look small and dinky—almost decayed, in fact, though they'd remodeled it extensively when they'd taken over three months ago.

Why do I want to do this? Is this really what I want to do with my life, serve hash and soup to students and people who are making barely more than minimum wage? Is this really how I want to spend every day? All of a sudden the place where she had at last felt she belonged seemed tacky—a squat of concrete, a glare of neon. And Tom, who was like the other half of her heart, seemed like a boring young man with curiously foreshortened ambition. All he wanted to do was take cooking classes and spend his life incrementally improving food and service at The George until it was the best diner in Colorado. In his free time, he did accounts or researched recipes. The most exciting thing they'd done in the last three months was take a weekend off and go to Denver to visit the *Titanic* exhibit at the Natural History Museum. Truth be told, Tom was a very boring man. And her life with him would be a very boring life.

In her mind's eye the years with Tom stretched endlessly, never too flush with money and forever living on the outside of all fashionable or even exotic entertainment. Nothing would ever happen, nothing ever break the routine.

"That's it," Dire said, softly, his face so close she could feel his warm breath on her skin. "That's exactly it. He'll kill you with boredom, Kitten Girl. He'll be the death of you.

"Or . . . you could come with me," he said. Through her mind there flashed, in succession, images of her in various designer clothes, images of her on a Mediterranean beach. Images of her eating in fine restaurants and taking airplanes. By Dire's side. And in her mind, for whatever reason, she was madly in love with Dire.

Kyrie didn't love Dire. In fact, she couldn't imagine being in love with any psychopath. She shook her head. "You're in my mind," she said, speaking through her clenched teeth, against the waves of love and attraction washing through her brain. "And you weren't invited."

He chuckled softly, in amusement. She raised her knee and hit him between the legs. Hard. The images vanished from her head. Before he could recover, before he could shift, before he could climb into her mind again, she ran, like mad, into the diner. She knew it wouldn't afford her much protection—or at least she thought it wouldn't—but she didn't care. She wanted away from that cold, dark mind.

She ran into the diner through the back door, and ran down the hallway into the diner itself. Anthony, who was peeling potatoes, turned around to give her a very puzzled look.

"I'm sorry," Kyrie said, ducking behind the counter. "I thought you'd need me. That I was away too long."

"No, you're fine. As you see, we don't have that many tables occupied."

"Yeah, I see," Kyrie said, as she put the apron on.

"Oh, Keith came in," Anthony said. "He says he can use the cash."

"Oh good," Kyrie said.

Anthony chopped the potatoes into sticks. "Well, with him here, rush hour wasn't really a problem. And Conan is getting better, despite that arm."

"Yeah. He's fairly smart," Kyrie said. Anthony said something about Conan singing really well, too, but Kyrie wasn't thinking of that. She was thinking of Dire, out in the parking lot. She didn't want to kill him. Not if she could help it. But she wasn't sure she could.

In Rafiel's car, Tom called Kyrie on the cell phone. Or rather he called The George, but it was she who answered, as he expected.

"Hi, Kyrie," he said.

She seemed faintly surprised and oddly suspicious. "Who is this?"

Had he slept such irregular hours that he still had sleep-voice? He didn't think so, but he cleared his throat all the same and said, "Me," with, he realized afterwards, the kind of confidence only a boyfriend would have in being recognized from such a syllable.

It seemed to work. Or at least she said, "Oh. I didn't expect you to be awake." She took a deep breath. "You know, *he* has impersonated Rafiel before . . ."

Tom took a look at Rafiel who was driving while tapping his fingers on the steering wheel in rhythm with some very strange song about never growing old. "Yeah. But only over the phone."

"We are talking over the phone!" Kyrie said, as if he'd taken leave of his senses.

"Oh . . . you mean . . ." Tom took a deep breath. "Well, I'm not going to ask you to go anywhere or anything, just wanted to know if Anthony is okay staying till six or so? Because it will be till then before I come back."

"All right," Kyrie said. "A long shift but . . . he's been pulling those."

It seemed very strange to Tom that she didn't ask him why or where he was going, or even what he was intending to do. It wasn't that Kyrie was overly inquisitive or determined to have him live in her pocket. It wasn't even that she demanded to know where he was at all times. But when he called to tell her he was going to be late for something, she asked why. Normal human curiosity. He thought of what Kyrie had said about Dire. "He has impersonated Rafiel before." But surely Dire wouldn't say that about himself if he was impersonating Kyrie. Besides, Tom remembered the description Kyrie had given of how Rafiel sounded over the phone—all breath, no voice . . . Kyrie didn't sound that way. And, on yet the other paw, Kyrie sounded exactly like she did when she was harassed and shorthanded.

"I'm sorry if I am putting you in a bind," he said.

He'd discovered nine-tenths of a good relationship was preemptive apologizing even if you didn't know—sometimes he would say particularly if you didn't know—what you had done wrong. He'd found that his social skills, blunted by looking out only for himself for much too long, sometimes missed fine points of the effects his actions might have on Kyrie.

"You're not," Kyrie said. "I'll manage. Anthony was planning on staying at least that long, and Keith has come in. We're okay."

"Oh. I'm just . . . I'm with Rafiel. I'm helping him run an errand."

"All right. Call if you're going to be later than six. Or I'll worry."

"Right," Tom said, and hung up.

Rafiel, pulling into the parking lot of the aquarium, gave Tom a quizzical glance. Perhaps it was just Tom's expression—there was more amusement than there should have been. "She upset about you staying out late?"

Tom did his best to glare at Rafiel. He was fairly sure this was wasted effort. All his efforts to glare at the policeman before—glare him into silence; glare him into being sensible—had met with chuckles. This time was no exception. Tom shook his head. "If you're going to tell me 'better me than you,' even I am not stupid enough to buy that."

"Uh . . . no, dude. I'd rather it were me, but I didn't know she kept the shackles quite that tight."

"She doesn't." Tom frowned. He tried to think of how to explain what had disturbed him about the call. While he thought, Rafiel drove around the aquarium to the back, the overflow parking lot. They were all empty, but Tom imagined that the front parking lot, visible from Ocean and Congregation, was not the best choice for stealthy work. And they must be stealthy. Or at least not stupidly obvious. "It's . . ." He tried to figure out how to explain it. "It's more that she didn't seem her normal self."

"Oh?" Rafiel said, and for once there was no smirk behind his expression. "Do you think something is wrong?"

"It's quite possible," Tom said. "But she's at the diner, so . . ."

"So she's either safe, or there's nothing you can do to make her so."

"Yeah," Tom said. He didn't like it, but it was the truth. "If it's something that can happen in front of a whole bunch of people, my being there won't stop it."

They got out of the car and Rafiel led them to a side door, where, after trying a variety of keys, he found one that clicked the door open. Rafiel was carrying the cardboard box they'd gotten from Tom and Kyrie's house. It contained a surveillance system that Tom had been meaning to install around the diner.

"I must need to get my head examined," Rafiel said, as they stepped into the warmer, dark interior of the aquarium. "This is so many levels of illegal."

"Stealthy," Tom said. "Many levels of stealthy. We must make it stealthy. I mean . . . we can't solve this in the open. I mean, if you wanted to, what could you tell your assistant, what's his name? McQueen?"

"McKnight." Rafiel said with an odd sort of groan.

"What are you going to tell McKnight? That you

smelled something funny while you were a lion? They'd have you committed. So . . . we have to do things . . . in creative ways."

"Right," Rafiel said. He gave the impression of speaking through clenched teeth. "Creative. Right."

Rafiel took them past banks of gurgling aquariums filled with fish. "Who feeds the fishies?" Tom asked. "Or do they eat each other or something?" He squinted at the label on the nearest tank, which said piranhas. The sound track of some nature program he must have watched, and forgotten, in childhood, ran through his head. Something about piranhas skeletonizing a cow in a matter of minutes. Tom had never been able to understand what a cow would be doing in the water, and he very much hoped that no one at the aquarium dropped a mooing heifer into the tank.

Rafiel waved a hand dismissively. "People can come in and feed them," he said. "That's not an issue. We only sealed the room with the sharks, but I understand it's open and McKnight comes in, when needed for personnel to clean the tank and feed the sharks, then he seals the room again." He looked over his shoulder. "At least that's the plan. I don't think it's happened yet."

He stopped outside a sealed door, and took out something very much like an exacto knife, with which he pulled—deftly—the police seal off the door and the handle. "I'm going to hell," he said under his breath.

"Well," Tom said. "If you're a believer, you know, it's a good question whether our kind has normal souls or if—"

"Tom, that isn't helpful."

"Well, I'm not a believer, myself, but it's a fascinating

idea. Are we judged by the divinity of humans, or by some . . . you know, animal god?"

Rafiel pulled the door open. "Not right now it isn't a fascinating idea. I'm facing the problem of living with my guilt about breaking police regulations. I don't even want to *think* of anything else."

They were in the big dim room that Tom had heard described several times, but never seen till now. Walls and ceilings had been sculpted to look like the inside of a cave, stalactites and stalagmites delineating paths. Though, Tom thought, it was expecting rather too much of suspension of disbelief to think that the stalagmites had formed benches by natural processes. And the speckled-cement stairs with their metal railings, leading up to an observation platform— probably nine by nine feet wide—also with metal railings and planters with curiously plastic-looking flowers, just about killed that natural structure feel.

Rafiel went up to the platform and looked around nervously. He looked as if he expected doom to fall at any moment. Like . . . he thought his superiors would be psychically warned or something. And Tom, who'd been a juvenile delinquent and delighted in breaking rules long before he'd known he was a shifter, could only smile at him.

"It's not funny," Rafiel said. "I could be fired if anyone finds out about this." He clutched the grey box of surveillance equipment against his chest, as though it were a shield of righteousness. "Good lord, I could be *arrested.*"

Tom didn't realize he was about to cackle till the sound bubbled out of his lips despite his best efforts. "Sorry, sorry," he said, to Rafiel's glare. "It's just I was thinking . . .

we could be killed. We could be discovered as shifters—
and ultimately killed—and you're worrying about being
arrested. I mean . . . if they came for you, what's to stop
you taking off in lion form?"

"What? Other than losing my identity, my family,
everything I've worked for?"

Tom sobered up. He too could leave. At any moment,
he could just go. It was easy. Take to the wing, and forget
Kyrie and The George, and Keith and Rafiel and Anthony
and Notty. No. What good was it to save yourself by losing
everything that was important to you?

"Exactly," Rafiel said, softly, having read Tom's expressions
without need for words. He shrugged. "But your point is
taken too. In the maze of dangers we face, risking being
arrested is not so very bad. And then I doubt we will be
arrested, or even found out. At least with a bit of luck." He
looked above himself, then around at the walls of the fake
cave. "But we forgot something, Tom. Neither of us is an
electrician. How are we going to put these up?" He waved
the package containing two cameras and a mess of electrical
stuff.

Tom grinned. "Well . . . you know . . ."

"Oh, don't tell me you used to wire cameras in people's
houses while you were homeless. There are things I don't
want to know."

This time Tom's gurgle of laughter poured out, without
his ability to control it. "No. But when we had The George
remodeled, the electrician didn't have an assistant. Nice
man, but . . . you know, semi-retired. Did it cheap. One of
Anthony's acquaintances."

"And?"

"Well, he needed help. Holding this, twisting that. Third hand kind of stuff. And I didn't have anything better to do. I was recovering from . . . near death. And he liked to talk . . . Seventies, you know, and no one wants to listen to him most of the time."

"So he taught you electrical stuff?"

"A bit. Jackleg stuff," Tom said. He brought out the little set of tools he'd slipped into the pocket of his jacket earlier, and grinned as Rafiel looked surprised. Just now and then he liked to upstage Mr. Unflappable Trall and be better prepared. He looked up and pointed to a light. "I think we'll tap that light," he said. "It's close enough to the stalactite and the plastic plants, that we can sort of run the wire behind and no one will know."

Rafiel looked at the light in turn. "Any idea how you'll reach it?"

"Oh, sure," Tom said. "I stand on the railing."

"Uh . . . I see. And if you fall?"

"I won't," Tom said.

"Really?"

"No. Because you're going to hold my ankles."

Rafiel looked up at Tom, who'd propped himself up, with a foot on either of the intersecting metal railings. He looked doubtfully down at the railings, which he wasn't even sure should be able to support that weight, then up again at Tom, who was fiddling with the light cover, and doing something underneath. After a while, Tom trailed a wire down, and pulled it, so it followed, kind of behind one of the cement stalactites that dropped down from the ceiling and around the edge of the railing.

"How much wire do you have?" Rafiel said.

"Enough," Tom said. "Right. I'm going to jump down now."

"Not while I'm holding you," Rafiel said, and stepped back.

Tom's feet wobbled on the railing, he started tilting forward. Rafiel reached up. Grabbed his wrist. Pulled. Something at the back of his mind said it was better for them to fall on the platform than on the tank. They toppled to the floor. Rafiel hit his elbow and his head, and gathered himself up. "Are you all right?" he asked Tom who had fallen in a heap, and was pale and shivering.

"Yeah," he said. "Yeah. Only . . ." He shook his head and scrambled to his knees and, on his knees, across the platform, to the planter, the box was tilted up against. Fishing in the box, he brought out the camera, which was about the diameter of a dime, and about as thick. He stuck it to one of the planters, well hidden in the foliage, the wire behind it. Then, as he seemed to make sure that the camera lens was unobstructed, he said, "When I was little, we had goldfish. At least, I wanted a pet, but you know, we lived in a condo. No place for pets, really, so my dad got me a bowl with goldfish. He also started calling them Schroedinger fish, because—well, I wasn't very interested and it wasn't in my room—it was in this passage between my room and the walk-in closet, and I didn't always remember to feed them. So Dad said every time we checked on them, it was not sure if they were alive or dead till we actually saw them. I remember this one time I forgot to feed them for like"—he narrowed his eyes with thought—"five days? When I came back to feed them, they all congregated in one spot, you know, clearly waiting for food.

"The sharks looked like that," he said and, for the first time, looked up to meet Rafiel's gaze. "Just like that. As if they were pet fish, used to being fed by people, you know?"

Rafiel sighed. "I'd say they are. I just wish we knew by whom."

"Well . . ." Tom said, and gestured towards the camera. "That will tell us, right?"

"Yeah," Rafiel said. "If they come in, of course. I mean, what with . . . you know . . ." He shrugged. "The room is sealed. Or will be again, once we leave. If it's a casual thing, if she just brings her boyfriends in, and someone . . . like the crab shifter, doesn't like it . . ."

"But if it's not," Tom said, "then we'll get it. The camera is motion-activated and it connects to my laptop, which is at the bed-and-breakfast. It will sound an alarm . . ." He gave an impish smile. "At least as soon as I install the program."

"Right," Rafiel said, but the idea didn't please him. There had to be another way around it, some other way to make things work. He didn't like the idea of just sitting down and waiting for some poor sap to be thrown in the shark tank. Not the least of which, because the poor sap would then be doomed. "So, why did you think you needed a surveillance system for The George?"

Tom stood up and dusted off the knees of his pants, as if this would fix the dust all over his clothes from having fallen headlong onto the observation platform. "I thought, you know, with the stuff that was happening at the back before . . . murder and all . . ." He shrugged. "I thought if a bunch of shifters were coming to the place, called by pheromones, we'd do as well to have early warning and proof if any of them had . . . control issues."

Rafiel, raising his eyebrows, reasoned that his friend trusted other shifters about as much as he did. They climbed down the stairs. Rafiel opened the door to the shark room, waited till Tom went by, then sealed the door again, initialing it once more, and putting in the date and time on the destroyed seal. "I'm going to hell." This time Tom didn't seem disposed to argue.

They walked quietly side by side along the deserted hallways, past the concrete trunk filled with plaster coins and Rafiel wondered if even very small children were fooled by it. He didn't remember ever being small enough to fall for that kind of fakery.

And then he wondered what they were going to do with the camera. While it had seemed like a good idea to set the camera in place, he now wondered how sane it was. Tom had been all enthusiastic about it, but it was probably just his happiness at getting to wire something. "Hey," he said, softly. "The other camera? Where do you intend to put it?"

Tom looked surprised. "Nowhere, really, I don't—"

He shut up abruptly, and Rafiel realized he had heard a sound, just before Tom stopped talking. Something like a soft footstep to their right. They were at the top of the stairs that led down to the aquarium with crabs and to the restaurant. For a second, he thought that it would be the crab shifter, emerging from his aquarium. Perhaps they could interrogate him.

But the person who came walking out of the shadows

was Dante Dire—lank hair falling over his dark eyes, and his dark eyes sparkling with fury. "What are you doing here?" he asked.

Rafiel drew himself up and tried to hide the quiver of fear that ran through him on seeing the creature. Because he was not a fool, he remembered—all too well—that this creature could reach into his mind and change his thoughts; the idea paralyzed him. He could have endured any form or amount of physical torture, but the idea that someone— something—could change what he thought and how he felt . . . that he could not stand. "It would be better to ask what you are doing here," he said, keeping his voice steady. He was aware of Tom's having done something—he didn't know what. But Tom had been behind him as they walked, still in the shadows, Rafiel presumed, and now when Tom stepped forward there was nothing in his hands. He'd put the camera box down somewhere. And immediately Rafiel made himself stop thinking about the camera, and think only that they were there to gather evidence against the murderer who'd been throwing people into the shark tank. He put that thought in front, as it were, and hid all the rest—even his fear—behind it.

Dire's face hardened. "You have no business," he said, "trying to entrap innocent shifters."

"Innocent," Tom said, calling attention away from Rafiel—and presumably his thoughts. Rafiel felt as though something had been pressing against his thoughts, and the pressure now lifted, leaving him free to think clearly for a change. "Why do you think we're trying to entrap any shifters, innocent or otherwise?"

Dante Dire straightened up and stared, right over

Rafiel's shoulder, at Tom. "Ah! You think I'm stupid and don't read the paper? I do. And the paper says there have been murders in this place. And then, and then, I see you here, skulking, looking for clues. His mind," he pointed at Rafiel, "makes it clear enough he's looking for clues against someone he thinks is a shifter." He crossed his arms on his chest. "It's you or me, pretty Kitten Boy. We're going to have this out now. The way I told it to the girl, I need to kill someone who can plausibly be accused of having killed the young shifters. You will do as well as any."

Rafiel felt as though his heart had skipped in his chest. He felt fear surging through his veins, demanding loudly that he shift. "I have to investigate," he said. "I have to. It's my job."

"Bah. A job paid for ephemerals. A job in which you obey ephemerals. A job"—he spat out the word as if it were poison—"where you demean your nature for money. Money is easy, Kitten Boy, when you live almost forever. As you'd already have figured out, if you were made of stronger stuff. But you're not, and now you'll die for it." He glared at Rafiel. "Are you going to shift, or do I kill you as you are?"

And not all the forces in the hell he claimed awaited him could have kept Rafiel from shifting.

Tom felt as if he'd frozen in place. He'd thrown the box with the remaining camera behind some plastic bushes at the edge. He hoped he'd managed it before Dire saw it.

He must have managed it, because Dire hadn't said anything about the box, just challenged their right to be there and announced that he was planning to kill Rafiel.

Stunned at the idea, Tom started to speak, but nothing came out of his mouth. It seemed to him that this was a duel. At least Dire had challenged Rafiel to a duel, challenged him to shift. If the intent were only to kill Rafiel, why not kill him as a human, without bothering with the lion form?

Except, of course, that Dire was a sadist. And the lion would, of course, provide him with a better fight, he thought, as lion and dire wolf stood facing each other, in this incongruous setting—tanks bubbled on either side, fish swam looking incuriously onto the scene. And Tom retreated until his back was against the concrete wall, while his brain worked feverishly.

His first thought—that Dire was doing this to gratify his sadistic impulses—was confirmed when, instead of going for the jugular, the huge prehistoric beast jumped at Rafiel and grabbed him by the scruff, much as a mother cat grabbing a baby. Only, it then lifted him off the ground and shook him, and threw him, sending him sprawling against one of the tanks.

For a moment, Tom, heart thumping at his throat, thought that Rafiel was already dead—that the dire wolf had broken his neck with that shake and toss. He heard something like a hiss come out of his mouth, and he realized what was about to happen. As he pulled off his shirt and dropped his pants—barely ahead of the process already twisting his limbs and covering his skin in green scales—he thought that he didn't want to fight the dire wolf. As ill-matched as Rafiel was against Dire, Tom was no better. He remembered the fight in the parking lot. He remembered that the dire wolf had almost killed him then. Why should now be any different?

But Rafiel was the closest thing he had to a best friend. If Tom stood by and watched the dire wolf finish Rafiel off in order to blame him for the deaths of hundreds of newborn shifters, just a few months ago, Tom would never be able to live with himself. Nor—he thought, ruefully, as his body contorted, in painful acrobatics, bending and twisting in a way it wasn't meant to, and as wings extruded from his back—would Kyrie want to live with him.

Dire was concentrating on Rafiel and hadn't seemed to notice Tom's shift, yet. Dire had swung the lion again, this time against the piranha tank. Tom flung himself into the fight, blindly. In the tight confines of the aquarium building, flying was no advantage, but he flung himself, aided by his wings, at the dire wolf and bit deep into what he could grab, which happened to be an ear, while letting out an ear-splitting hiss-roar that translated all his anger and frustration at this unreasonable ancient creature.

The dire wolf looked shocked—he turned a bloodied muzzle towards Tom, his eyes opened to their utmost in complete surprise. And Tom, instinct-driven, slashed his paw across the face, claws raking the eyes. Blood spurted. The dire wolf screamed. And the part of Tom that remained very much human was aware that this was a momentary advantage. The creature would recover. Eventually it would regrow its eyes. Until then, it might very well be able to look through their eyes. He couldn't allow it time to recover.

Leaping across the room, he grabbed Rafiel by the

scruff even as Rafiel, dizzy and battle-mad tried to grab at him. But grabbing the scruff seemed to paralyze him, and Tom—fairly sure that in normal circumstances he'd have a hard time lifting Rafiel and trying to hold as gently as possible so he didn't wound Rafiel more—ran down the stairs with his friend held between his teeth.

Down the stairs and at a run through the aquarium—was that a Japanese man hiding in the shadows? and had he winked at Tom?—and turning sharply left; down a narrow corridor between tanks and . . .

Tom hit the exterior door with his full body weight. As he hit, he thought Dire might have locked it, but the door was already opening, letting them out into the cold air, where Tom dropped Rafiel and concentrated on changing. The dragon argued that Rafiel would make a really good protein snack, but Tom forced his limbs to shift, decontort. Before he could fully form words, he said, "Now, Rafiel, shift." The words came out half roar, half hiss, with only the barest vocalization behind them. And then Tom's eyes cleared and he realized Rafiel was already human, trying to walk to the car on a leg that bent the wrong way.

"Your keys?" Tom said.

Rafiel looked at him, his eyes full of pain, but reached for a bracelet at his wrist—metal but of the sort of links that stretched, so that it stayed with him through his shifts. He pulled the key and handed it to Tom, who opened the car, climbed in, and flung the passenger door open, just in time for Rafiel to climb in. He saw Dire's car parked next to them.

"Drive, drive, drive," Rafiel said. And Tom was driving, as fast as he knew how, down the still-half-iced streets, breathing deeply, telling himself that residual panic didn't justify shifting, that he would not—could not—shift. He tasted Rafiel's blood in his mouth, from the wounds the dire wolf had made at the back of Rafiel's neck, and it didn't help him keep control. Not at all.

It was a while—and Tom had no clue where he was, having driven more or less blindly—before Rafiel said, softly, "Thank you."

"What?" Tom asked, hearing his own voice ill-humored and combative. "Why?"

"Well . . . you . . . saved my life."

"As opposed to just letting you die? What do you think I am?"

"Brave. I know that creature scares the living daylights out of me. I don't know if I'd be able to make myself intervene in a fight between him and you."

"Don't worry about it," Tom said, hoping his dismissive tone would stop the conversation. He'd never learned to take compliments, and he wasn't ready for gratitude for doing what he had to do—what was clearly required of him as a human being. He just wanted to get back to the bed-and-breakfast and have a shower and—

"Damn," he said.

"What?"

"I left my boots in the aquarium."

Rafiel laughed. It was weak laughter. Not so much amuse-ment, as a reflex of relief. He remembered Tom, once, running naked down the street, save for his all-prized jacket and his boots.

"It's not funny," Tom said.

"Yes, it is. You have an unnatural attachment to those boots."

"They're mine, and I like them," Tom said. Still driving like a maniac, he turned to glower at Rafiel. "I haven't had many things in my life that I could hold onto, you know? Things that were mine, I mean."

"Yes, but why in the name of all that's holy would the things you want to hold onto be items of apparel when you are a shifter?" Rafiel asked, smiling.

Tom shrugged. "It was all I had before settling down. All I had were the clothes on my back."

"Right. Well, it's unlikely the creature knows how attached you are to your boots, so you'll probably be safe," he said. "Meaning he won't piss in them. And if he does, I'll buy you new boots."

"Thank you. I like the ones I have."

"Unnatural," Rafiel said. "But I'm not going back to get them. Not even for you, my friend."

"Ah, look, the dire wolf will probably be gone and besides we can't leave them behind. Someone will go to the aquarium. Someone will know we broke in."

Rafiel looked at him, disbelieving. "You have to be joking."

"No, I'm not. It's my boots, and they'll figure out they're mine, and next thing you know, they'll be talking about my pushing people into the shark tank or something."

Rafiel groaned, seeing what he meant. "Oh, okay, fine. But if the car is still there, I'm not going in. I'm just not.

And I suspect we left blood all over the floor and isn't that enough to show I was there? What do the boots matter? I'll just have to try to divert any investigation that—"

"Rafiel, you were shifted. They'll find lion's blood." He gave Rafiel a sideways look. "On the other hand, unless I'm wrong, you also left your cell phone and your clothes and your official identification there. So you'll have to have a really good story to explain having been in there . . ."

"I could tell them I lost them this morning, when I was there with Lei."

"What? And your clothes? Shredded as if you'd burst out of them?"

Rafiel groaned and heard himself swearing softly. "Fine, we'll go back. I'm trying to figure out how the day could get any worse."

Which was a stupid thing to say, he realized, as he heard the siren behind him, and saw the flashing lights in the rear view mirror. "Don't worry," he told Tom, as Tom smashed his foot on the gas. "I'm a policeman."

"What, naked, in the car, with another man, in public? How much authority will you have, Officer Trall?"

"They . . . uh." Naked in public was the problem. They'd bring him up on an indecency charge so fast. He looked back. "We could get dressed."

"Fast enough? Before he comes up to the window?"

It might have been possible if they were being followed by a police car. The cop would have had to park way behind them, and then approach them carefully. But Rafiel could see that there was a motorcycle cop in hot pursuit. "We can't outrun it. He probably already has my license plate and—"

"Right," Tom said. "There's only one thing to do. But afterwards, you have to get me a burger. No. A dozen of them."

"Sure thing," Rafiel said, not absolutely sure what Tom meant to do and not caring either. "I have money under the seat, with the clothes. We don't even have to wait till we get my wallet." At this point, anything Tom could do to get them out of this fix was worth it.

"Right." Tom said. "But you have to drive. Can you drive?"

"Sure. I'll use my left foot."

Tom pulled over and stopped. Something to the way he clenched the wheel, the way his nails seemed to elongate slowly, the way his bone structure appeared to change, made Rafiel want to scream, *Don't shift in my car.* But when Tom was already this much on edge, all the scream would do was cause him to shift immediately. He bit his tongue and held his breath.

Tom rolled down the window, then grasped the handle. His voice all hissy and slurpy, as if his dental structure had already shifted, he said, "The moment I get out, drive. Just drive straight. I'll catch up."

"Tom . . . don't—" He was going to tell him not to eat the man, but didn't have time.

There was a voice from the open window. "Sir, you were doing . . . What—"

Tom opened the door and leapt out, while shifting—so that the effect was rather like a kernel of corn popping—bursting and exploding into a massive, much larger form, as it escaped the confines of its skin.

There was a strangled scream from the policeman, and

Rafiel switched seats and closed the door and drove straight ahead. He was on Fairfax, he realized. The world's longest, straight thoroughfare. It was listed in the *Guinness Book of World Records* as such. He hoped it was long enough to allow Rafiel to still be on it whenever Tom caught up.

"Don't eat him," Rafiel yelled and rolled up the window, as he drove. He didn't know if Tom had heard him.

Perhaps ten blocks ahead, as Rafiel entered a definitely seedy area of abandoned warehouses and graffitied over-passes, he saw a shadow fall over the car. A shadow such as if a really large dragon body had flown overhead. And then, in front of a warehouse, Tom stood, extending his thumb in the universal gesture of the hitchhiker.

Rafiel stopped and unlocked the door. As Tom got in, he looked for signs of blood around his mouth or something. Trying to keep it light, he said, "You know, hitchhiking naked is a felony. And we don't even go into what eating a policeman might be. The force disapproves of it."

Tom stopped, in the middle of buckling his seatbelt. "I didn't eat him," he said. "He started screaming for mercy as soon as I was fully out of the car. I just flew away after that. I figure there's no way he's going to tell anyone what happened, and your license plate will never be mentioned."

"You sure?" Rafiel said.

"I'm sure. If I'd eaten him, you wouldn't look so tasty right about now."

Rafiel wasn't absolutely sure whether Tom was joking, but then again, he also wasn't willing to tempt fate. "Clothes are under the seat. We should put something on before we go to a drive-through," he said.

"And afterwards?" Tom said.

"Afterwards," Rafiel said, "we go get your damn boots."

When they got to the aquarium, Lei Lani was just ahead of them, opening the door on the restaurant side. Rafiel tried to remember whether they might have left it unlocked—whether they might—perhaps—have left via that entrance. He couldn't remember. Clearly, being concussed and dangling from a berserker dragon's jaws did something to the memory. But it didn't matter, he thought. After all, Dire might have left the door open, too.

She was in the process of opening the door as they came up behind her—wearing tracksuits and looking rather disheveled and, in Rafiel's case, limping, but seeming much more respectable than they'd been before. Tom, who had inhaled five burgers in the ten blocks here, even had a little color and seemed reasonably human. At least, Rafiel hoped so, because if he had looked tasty to Tom, then Lei must look positively tender.

Still, she turned and looked at them, seeming puzzled. "Oh, Officer Trall . . ." she said. "I . . . didn't expect to see you. I realized there was another report that I left behind."

Or perhaps another colleague to try to implicate. Or,

Rafiel thought, not quite sure why, but catching something shifty about her eyes, a look of discomfort. *Or perhaps you've decided it's too late to cover things up, and so are going to leave without a forwarding address.*

He was fairly sure this last wasn't true. Not unless McKnight had been so clumsy in his prodding that she now knew, or suspected, that the police had found the lies about her background. *McKnight? Incompetent? What are the odds?* he thought, sarcastically, and barely suppressed a groan. A look at Tom revealed an expression so full of distress and a gaze desperately attempting to make several speeches, that Rafiel almost groaned again.

He wished he could mind-talk to Tom and inform him that, yes, yes, he had realized they needed to retrieve their things before Lei Lani found them. Meanwhile he would have to hope she didn't notice they were wearing identical stretch-shoes.

She didn't seem to. When he said, "I forgot my wallet," she merely gave him a wry look and said, "You seem to do that a lot."

Rafiel shrugged. "I drop it," he said. "I need bigger pockets or a briefcase or something. But then, if I had a briefcase, I'd probably leave it behind."

She smiled and didn't comment on that, and turned right, to go to the office. Rafiel turned the other way, towards the piranha room, his heart accelerating. The dire wolf would be there, right there, ready to jump out at him.

But the room was quiet and empty, except for the gurgling of the tanks and the sound the piranhas made swimming back and forth. Tom's clothes and boots were where he had left them, by the tank. Rafiel's were quite shredded, so he transferred his wallet and ID and cell phone from the shreds, then bundled them up.

He looked up to see Tom standing, holding his own clothes and the box for the cameras. "Here," he told Tom, thrusting his bloodied, shredded clothes at him. "Take this to the car, okay?"

He got raised eyebrows in response.

"I'm going to go ask Lei Lani for a date," Rafiel said.

"What?" Tom's voice came out louder than the half whisper in which they'd been speaking, like a small outburst of sudden indignation. "Excuse me?"

"Shhh." Rafiel said, gesturing down with his hand. "It's not what you think," he said, in a whisper.

"Isn't it? This is a heck of a time to work on your social life, Rafiel," Tom said, but he lowered his voice to a whisper as well.

"It's not my social life," Rafiel said. "It's . . . you know how . . ." He concentrated on listening for the slightest sound. His hearing was more acute than normal human, but he heard nothing. Not close enough for Lei Lani to hear. And yet, he didn't feel comfortable. He sighed. "Come to the car."

Tom shrugged and followed him to the car. Rafiel threw his shredded clothes in the back. Tom sat on the passenger side and started changing. Rafiel, his gaze sweeping the parking lot to make sure they were quite alone, explained. "I've been worried," he said. "About the camera and how all this was going to work."

Tom frowned at him. "Duh. Whoever it is brings a date there, and then the computer sounds the alarm, and then—duh—we catch her. Or him."

"No," Rafiel said, very patiently. He loved Tom like the brother he'd never had. Truly, he did. But elaborate plans were not the man's main strength. His greatest act of heroism had been on the spur of the moment. Most of what Tom did seemed to be on the spur of the moment. "Yeah, we will have footage of whatever happens. It's even possible we'll know who it is, and what they're doing. If they're shifters, we could go and kill them in cold blood, and stop the deaths. Of course, then we'll have Dire on our tails, but that's something else again. But . . . Tom, the poor sap who is brought here will die. There is no way we can get to him in time."

"Oh," Tom said. "Unless we're expecting it?"

"How can we be expecting it, if it's a stranger?" he said. "By the time the camera beeps, they'll already be in the aquarium. There is nothing we can do. Except collect the remains."

Tom frowned. "Damn. I hadn't thought that through. I don't think it's going to be that easy to sit there, waiting, you know, while . . . some poor sap . . . Damn, Rafiel, I don't even think I can do it. I mean, I know he'd probably die anyway, whether this is part of our trap or not. But I don't want to be . . . I'd feel like an accomplice."

"No, it wouldn't work," Rafiel said. "Which is why I'm going in there and ask Lei Lani for a date."

Tom frowned at him. "Because you think she's the murderer?"

Rafiel shrugged. "Not exactly. But I think there is a good chance she might be. I think it's quite possible she's a shark shifter. Which might or might not mean anything. I've also found she's never attended the University of

Hawaii, at least not under this name." He shrugged. "All of it might have other, innocent explanations, and if this were a normal investigation, where I could share my suspicions with my colleagues, it wouldn't be the time for a desperate gamble. But it isn't a casual investigation—it's a life-and-death one. And . . . other people will die. Plus, Dire seems to have settled on me as the sacrificial victim for him to execute."

"Dire will just be furious," Tom said, "if we go after Lani and she's a shifter."

"I think Dire is furious now. There is one thing I know we can't do, Tom, and that's face Dire, the triads and the aquarium murderer all at the same time. For the last week I've walked on eggshells, afraid one or the other of those are about to give us away. I can't go on like that. Let's start taking the enemies down one at a time. The aquarium murderer, at least until further notice, is not more powerful than us, so let's take that one on first. Then we'll figure out some way to get Dire. And then the triads . . ." He shrugged. "Perhaps they'll just go away."

"Fat chance," Tom said.

Rafiel shrugged again. "One at a time. So, I'm going in and asking Ms. Lani out."

"But . . . like that?" Tom asked. "You are all bruised, have two big gashes on the back of your neck, and you probably broke your ankle."

Rafiel shrugged. "So, I tell her I got in a fight in the course of duty. You know there is little that a woman loves better than a hero."

Tom stared at him for a long time, then sighed and

shook his head. "The worst part, Mr. Hero, is that you'll probably pull it off."

Rafiel gave him a feline grin. "Of course I will."

Kyrie looked from one to the other of the men, her mouth half open, as though all the words had escaped her and weren't coming back. Rafiel looked like he'd been put into an industrial threshing machine. His forehead was scratched, his arm showed blood through the shirt. He was walking as if he had—at the very least—a seriously bruised ankle.

Tom looked hungry. In fact, despite the fact that he'd announced to her, up front, that he'd already eaten, and even though his story made it clear he'd had something like ten hamburgers, he looked starved, and sniffed the air as if trying to inhale calories through sniffing in stray particles of cooking meat.

And yet, both of them looked as happy, as full of themselves as boys who had pulled off a really good prank. It had to be one of those male things, because she couldn't begin to imagine what was going through their minds. "And you went back?" she said. "For the boots and the ID?"

"And the clothes," Rafiel said, enthusiastically. "My clothes. Well, the shreds of them."

"I see," Kyrie said.

"It wasn't a big deal," Tom said, as his head swivelled to follow a gyro platter carried by Keith. "Dire wasn't there when we went back."

Yes, of course, that made it all right, Kyrie thought, as she sighed and despaired of explaining to these overgrown boys that, after all, Dante Dire had the power of messing with their minds. He might have made it seem that there was no one there. He might have jumped them from a dark corner. He might still be waiting to—She couldn't say any of it, certainly not in the diner, although the three of them were occupying the corner booth, under the picture of the dragon slayer, and there were no other occupied booths in this part of the diner.

Keith stopped by and dropped a plate entirely filled with gyro shavings and souvlaki in front of Tom, who looked up at him, surprised, "How did you know?"

Keith shrugged. "Meat-seeking behavior," he said. "I've come to know it." He looked from Rafiel to Tom. "What have you two been doing with yourselves?" he asked. And then paused, and bent over towards the table, his hands on the formica. "It isn't about Summer Avenir, right? I mean . . . is there some big fight going on that you guys haven't told me about?"

Kyrie sighed and shifted further into the booth. "Come. You can hear about it."

But Keith shook his head, and looked around at the tables. "Nah. Conan went to take a nap, he said, and that would leave the tables unattended."

Kyrie frowned. This sudden reluctance to run away with the shifter circus was not like Keith at all. A look at the young man showed her dark circles around his eyes and a general impression of being less than healthy. "Huh," she said.

"It's nothing, okay?" Keith said. He shrugged. "It's just

that, you know, you guys always said that being a shifter was no picnic, that there was stuff . . . but you know, for me, it was all about fighting and . . . well, it was like being a superhero."

"Yeah, so you told us," Tom said.

"Only, then . . . Summer turned out to be the grand-daughter of the newspaper owner, and to have been after cryptozoology stuff, and she endangered you and got herself killed . . . and now I know it's not . . . "—he looked at them, intently—"I assume it wasn't one of you. I wouldn't have come back if I thought it had been one of you."

"No," Kyrie said, shocked. "No. It's . . . one of the people we're fighting."

"People!" Keith said. "Somehow, no, I don't think it's people."

Kyrie felt shocked as if she'd been punched. "What about us?"

Keith sighed. "I want to say of course you're people . . ." he said. "I want to say it . . . but . . . ." He looked away. "It would help if Tom didn't look like he could happily take a chunk out of a passing diner."

Tom, finger-deep in gyro meat, looked up. "Hey!"

"No . . . I know you're not like that," Keith said. "And of course you can trust me, and all. But . . . these . . . creatures, like the ones we fought against before . . . It's not like a computer game, and it's not like a comic, and it's not like being superheroes."

"We never said . . ."

"I know you didn't. But I'm an idiot, okay . . . and I thought . . ." He shrugged. "I thought a whole lot of stupid things. But it's not fun anymore. It's serious. And the things you guys fight, they're really serious too. I take it the . . . . creature you're fighting is the one who was in here the other day talking about how I was just a transitive or something and—"

"Ephemeral," Tom said. "Because you live less than we do, and he—"

"Yeah. I got the gist. Anyway . . . I take it that's the big bad, and I wish you luck and all, but I want no part of it. I . . ." He took a deep breath. "I might as well tell you that I've applied for a scholarship to do the last two years of college abroad, in Italy. I was accepted. I'll be leaving at the end of the month. That's my two-weeks' notice."

They all looked at him, stunned. Oh, Kyrie understood what he was saying. In fact, they'd been the first to tell him that it wasn't fun, it wasn't like being a superhero, it wasn't anything of the kind. But Keith had been, in a way, the one normal human admitted to their fraternity, the one they could trust.

The one, Kyrie thought, *who reassures us that we're still human.*

"Sure," Tom said, sounding deflated. "Sure. I just . . . tell me the exact date and I'll make sure you have your check a couple of days in advance so that you can cash it before you fly, okay?"

Keith looked startled. Had he forgotten that Tom tried to take care of people no matter what? "Okay," he said, as he walked away.

And he couldn't be that mad at them, Kyrie thought, at least not consciously, because having seen Rafiel eye Tom's food jealously, he brought him a plate of meat as well, and silverware for both of them. "Anthony thinks you have a tapeworm," he said, walking away. "Both of you."

"You know," Rafiel said, "Dante Dire would say we need to kill Keith, to ensure our own safety."

Kyrie shook her head, feeling vaguely impatient. Dire could say whatever he wanted. Keith could say whatever he wanted for that matter. She could understand Dire's point about how hard it was to consider as people and as equals, people who didn't consider you human. But she was sure of something and that was that Dire was far more dangerous to Keith than Keith ever could be to any of them. The other thing was that Kyrie was fairly sure people were just . . . people. It was just that shifters had so many more means of causing harm than people who didn't at the drop of a hat grow claws and fangs. "You still didn't tell me," she said with a trace of impatience, "what you were doing at the aquarium today?"

"Oh," Tom shrugged and looked sheepish, managing to look much like a kid caught with his hand in the cookie jar. "We were installing a camera."

"Installing a what?"

"A camera. In that platform area where, clearly, there's been screwing going on."

"Why?" Kyrie asked. The idea was unfathomable. "So you guys could have your very own private porn channel? Isn't it kind of gruesome? I mean considering . . ."

"No," Tom said. "It's for an alarm. I've already installed the software in my laptop. You and I are going to keep watch on it. By turns. It beeps, you see . . . when someone moves in front of the camera and activates it."

"We're going to keep watch on it by turns?" Kyrie asked. "And what exactly do we do about The George,

Tom? You still need to cook, and without Keith, or with Keith on reduced hours, I still need to wait tables. What do we do about that?"

The minute she said it, Tom's face fell, and she felt as though she were the most horrible woman alive. "Look, I can see where it's important, but . . ."

Rafiel cleared his throat. "You're right, Kyrie," he said. "That's why I have a plan. We couldn't just wait, see?"

Tom nodded. "So, Rafiel came up with something. Rafiel says, and he's right that we'd start with the weakest enemy and move on towards the strongest, because, you know, we can't fight all of them at the same time."

"No," Kyrie said. "But I don't think this will help us fight at all."

"No, it will," Rafiel said. "I think that the Lani chick likes me. Oh, I don't mean she's in love with me or anything," he answered Tom's knowing smile. "That's not it at all. But the thing is, she has sort of come on to me and hinted since she first met me. If she's the aquarium killer, and if she is a shark shifter, perhaps I look tasty."

"Officer Mignon," Tom mumbled.

"Something like that. But in any case"—Rafiel shrugged—"she has tried to, you know, hint that she would be okay going out more than once. And in fact, you know, she came up to my car outside the doughnut shop, when I didn't even know she knew my car . . . so . . . I think, particularly if she's guilty and is worried about it—

but even if she isn't guilty and her boyfriends just keep taking headers into the shark tank through no fault of her own . . ." He stopped and looked lost.

Kyrie said, "No." Tom made some indeterminate sound.

"No, really," Rafiel said. "I've gone on dates with women before. Truly. Some people don't seem to think I'm that horrible."

"I didn't mean that," Kyrie said. "It's more, I'd prefer you don't run that risk."

Rafiel looked towards Tom who was eating, oblivious to them. So he assumed Tom wasn't jealous. Which was good, because he didn't think Kyrie meant it in any other way than as a caring friend. "How much more of a risk is doing nothing?" Rafiel asked. "I almost died today, and I wasn't doing anything I thought was dangerous, except maybe to my moral health."

"Well, you were trying to solve the aquarium murders," Kyrie said. "And if anything, this is more likely to bring Dire on you, since he said that you should not investigate these murders."

"Yeah," Rafiel admitted. "But you see . . . that only makes it obligatory that I do something. How am I going to live with myself, knowing that I stopped an investigation because someone who doesn't consider humans as such told me to stop? How can I go on? And besides, Kyrie—"

"And besides, Kyrie," Tom said. "Even if we don't do anything at all, Dire will end up killing us. Or at least, he will kill one of us so he can blame all of the deaths on that one person and skip off back to his affairs, his reputation as executioner untarnished. He doesn't care whom he blames. After what I did to him," Tom's voice became rueful as he said this, "it's very probable that the pact with the dragons won't even hold him back anymore."

"So we'll do something about the aquarium murders," Rafiel said. "And then we'll figure out some way to get Dire. Because we have to. It's him or us."

"And through all of this," Tom said, "we'll try to keep Conan safe. Frankly, we shouldn't even let him know what we intend to do. Conan shouldn't cross the street by himself, much less get involved in intrigue and conspiracy."

"So," Rafiel said, "I asked Lei Lani out tonight. And she said yes."

The expression of complete surprise on Kyrie's face was totally worth it.

Kyrie bit her tongue hard. Listening to Rafiel's plan, she realized that it made the perfect trap for Dire. She couldn't imagine how the two men kept imagining they would be allowed to deal with each of the threats in turn—without more than one of them imposing themselves upon their notice at the same time.

It was clear, to her, at least. Dire had been watching them. Dire had been watching the aquarium. Dire knew they wanted to catch and punish the aquarium killer. They were not going to be allowed to do it without interference. It would never happen.

And they couldn't simply go after Dire in cold blood, anyway. If they went after Dire in any way that couldn't be construed as self-defense, and if they went to the triads for help, the only thing that would happen would be that the Ancient Ones would accuse the dragons of murder, and a war would break out. Mr. Lung had warned Kyrie against that.

So the best thing was to get Dire to come after them. Which the aquarium trap seemed like the perfect setup for.

But that meant that Kyrie had to arrange the night shift, somehow, so Conan could be free, without Tom knowing. First, she thought, she would go to the bed-and-breakfast and talk to Conan. And then, if he could perhaps pretend to be sick . . . then Kyrie would have an excuse to ask Keith to work.

"If you guys get in the car," Rafiel said, "and wait in it, perhaps a block from the aquarium, then you can get me in time. Not that I should need help. I mean . . . I've fought other shifters before, but . . . I'd prefer to have backup."

"Of course," Tom said. "But not in our car. In the supply van."

Kyrie saw Rafiel give Tom a surprised look and Tom sighed, long-suffering. "You can see into the car. But the old supply van, the one without the George logo, we can sit in the back—well, we can sit in the back once I throw in a couple of cushions—and no one will see us. Or even know we're there. Just an anonymous van parked by the side of the road."

"Oh," Rafiel said. "Right. That will work."

Kyrie knocked at the door to Conan's room, which was in the bottom floor, just off the entrance. There was a sound of shuffling, from inside, and then Conan's voice, "Yes?"

"It's Kyrie," she whispered. She'd left Tom taking care of her tables, with the excuse that she had to go take a shower to wake up, since she hadn't slept in . . . much too long.

Conan opened the door, and looked at her, somewhat surprised. "Kyrie?"

"I need to talk to you. May I come in?"

"Yeah, sure." He threw the door open into a room that was about a quarter the size of theirs—just a little bigger than the destroyed bathroom at home. It had a daybed against one wall, a small dresser and a desk opposite. At the end of it the door opened into a tiny bathroom, where she could just see the glass door of a stand-up shower, with what looked like a pair of underwear drying draped over it.

Without meaning to, she looked down. Conan was wearing pants—or rather shorts and a baggy white T-shirt. "Is anything wrong?" he asked her.

"Yes and no," she said. She closed the door, then leaned against the desk while he slumped on his bed, and looked at her. And she explained. She explained everything. What had happened, what the plan was.

"But, Kyrie, I can't," he said. He put his hands on his head, grabbing a handful of his straight black hair on either side. "I can't do that. He told me he'd kill himself, and the Great Sky Dragon said he meant it."

"He would kill himself," Kyrie said. "If he had to be . . . beholden to the Great Sky Dragon, yes. But don't you see in this case he doesn't have to? Even if he finds out I asked for help, I'll be the one he's mad at, you see. I'll be the one who is indebted to the triads. He's not."

Conan looked at her, blinking, and it took her a moment to realize he was fighting back tears. "I'm not sure he's not right, Kyrie," he said, pitifully. "If I had any choice, now—which I don't—I'd choose not to belong to the Great Sky Dragon, too." And seeing Kyrie flinch, he must have realized what she'd thought, because he smiled. "I don't know if he's still listening to me, no. He might be. Or he might have turned off when Tom told him he wouldn't allow me to follow him around." A small frown. "I don't think so, though, or Mr. Lung would have told you that you needed to do something else to get his attention, than just have me around. He didn't, so I guess . . . Himself is watching. And he now knows I'd prefer not to belong to him, which is fine. I would. If he didn't know that before . . ." Conan shrugged. "I don't think he cares. I'm not *important* like Tom and I never had a choice."

Kyrie sighed. In her mind only one thing mattered right now. She didn't want to appear callous towards Conan. She even liked Conan in a way, though he was definitely one of the strays that Tom was so prone to picking up. But she didn't have time or patience, just now, to discuss his philosophy of life. "Does this mean you won't help?" she asked.

"No," Conan said. "It doesn't. I'll help, of course. It's not like I have a choice, you know. I have to help. Or die. And I'm not ready to die."

"I was going to suggest you take my car, because—"

Conan shook his head. He looked very sad. "If I know how my people work, I expect there will be a car brought to me in the next hour, a car that Tom won't identify. And just tell Tom I have a cough and decided not to work because I might be contagious. The only thing I want to know . . ." He paused.

"Yes?"

"Is what they intend to use me as, other than possibly bait. It's not that I mind. It can't be much worse than all the other things I've had to do. I just wish I had more of an inkling of what will happen than 'Conan will watch, and then we'll intervene.' " He looked very tired. "Doesn't matter. I'm sure better minds than mine will handle it."

Kyrie was caught between a desire to bitch-slap him and a desire to free him from his vassalage.

Kyrie hoped that Dante Dire had the place under surveillance of some sort. She had to—simply had to—arrange for him to follow them that night. She wasn't quite sure how to do it, except, of course, by managing to pretend that the last thing she wanted was for him to follow them.

There was a good chance she wouldn't need to do anything to get him to follow them. She suspected he had gone after Tom and Rafiel after seeing them leave the bed-and-breakfast. If that was the case, any of them going near the aquarium was likely to cause Dire to follow. She just wished she could be sure. She also wished she could be sure that Tom hadn't blinded him for a few weeks. Because if Tom had, then it was going to be very hard to entrap him.

While Tom was busy at the grill and Keith was keeping up with the tables, in the brief post-dinner lull, and before Anthony came in to spell Tom, she took the time to go outside, into the parking lot, looking for Dire's car.

Instead, she found Dire himself, standing outside the back door, smoking. His dark eyes, she noted, looked fine.

He grinned at her, as if he knew what she was looking at. In the next few words, he proved he did. "Well, Kitten," he said, "you and your boyfriend are very rude." He shrugged. "Not that I resent it from you. I like my women with a bit of spirit."

"I am not your woman," Kyrie said.

He grinned again, flashing white between taut lips. "Oh yes," he said. "I know that. But you know, shifters' lives are long and all that might yet change. Your boyfriend is too dumb to know what's good for him, so he's not likely to make old bones."

"I think my boyfriend is perfectly fine," she said, snappishly. And meaning the snap, too, because Dire annoyed her—besides putting a chill up her spine—and because she thought he would expect her to react this way.

Dire shrugged. He took a pull on his cigarette, making the tip glow bright. "I'm sure you do. You're both very young. Young as ephemerals. But he doesn't understand that, when needed, one must sacrifice a friend . . . or two." His gaze on her was speculative, and she felt as though she were being considered as a "sacrifice."

"And have you sacrificed many *friends*?" she asked, wrapping her arms around herself.

If she expected him to flinch or look guilty, she would have been sorely disappointed. He threw his head back and laughed. "One or two . . . dozen. But I'm still here, aren't I?"

"Yes," Kyrie said, and judging the time to be right, added, "In fact, I wish you weren't here so much. What are you doing here, all the time? Are you following us?" Mentally, she projected the feeling/idea that tonight of all nights she didn't want him around.

She watched his eyes quicken, but nothing more in his gaze gave away that he'd caught on to something. His voice was quite disinterested and amused as he said, "I find you entertaining."

Tom felt awkward and stupid. Which, he supposed, in many ways he was. At least when the many ways involved human interaction. He felt very strange taking time off and getting into the supply van with Kyrie. Kyrie drove till they were outside the aquarium, about the time that Rafiel would be starting his date. It was unlikely, of course, that Lei Lani would be dragging Rafiel to the aquarium at the beginning of the date—even if Rafiel was right in his suspicions. Even if she intended to drag him there later.

But they didn't want to be too far away to intervene if she did take him there. The time was quite likely to be too short, then. And the idea was not to have Rafiel get himself killed. For one, even if they got the woman immediately afterwards, the police tended to get religious when one of them got killed. They would leave no stone unturned. And when it came to murders committed by shifters, Tom would very much like to let mossy stones lie. And for another . . . Tom liked the lion bastard. Life wouldn't be nearly as much fun without a friend in the police, he thought. Why, they might not get pulled into whichever murder was going on, on the vaguest suspicion that a shifter might be involved.

So, they'd taken the laptop—still quiescent—and driven to a block from the aquarium, where they'd parked on a darkened side street. The van smelled of old cabbage and—strangely, since Tom didn't remember carrying any in it—stale crackers. It had only two seats, since the back was normally filled with crates and boxes of supplies for the diner. In summer and fall, he and Kyrie had taken the van to the farmers' market early every morning, when Anthony came in to relieve them. They'd got better deals, and better produce too. Though Tom had probably gone overboard on the apricots, which was why they had about a hundred jars of jam in the cold room at The George. Which would come in really handy the minute he learned to make homemade bread.

But because he and Kyrie rarely got to go out alone, because he didn't want them to sit in the front seats and be obvious, and because he was a fool, he'd made sure the van was clean and he'd brought a blanket to spread on the metallic floor that had long since lost its carpet, if it had ever had one.

He'd also brought two very large throw pillows from their room.

It was only when Kyrie had looked at the blanket and the pillows, and turned an inquisitive glance towards him, that he realized how it might look. "What?" he said. "What? I thought it would be more comfortable than the bare floor and all, while we wait."

She had smiled just a little, an odd, Mona Lisa smile. "I'm sure it will be," she had said all soft and breezily.

And now they were parked on a side street, less than a block from the aquarium. It was a narrow street and at this point pretty much deserted, with what looked like an empty—with broken windows—house on one side, and a park on the other. They left the front seats and went to the back, where they sat primly on the pillows across from each other, and they put the laptop up, its back against the front seats. The laptop had been a gift from Tom's father and, until now, he'd never used it for anything more exciting than doing the accounting for The George.

But the laptop wasn't being exciting either. A blank screen with a field of stars streaming past—his screen saver—stared back at them. Tom looked at it, then looked at Kyrie. The laptop was supposed to beep if it caught anything, and just now, Tom was disposed to let the laptop do its thing and not give it undue attention. Because, after all, if you couldn't trust your laptop, what could you trust?

Instead he looked over at Kyrie. He was dating the only woman in the world who could look like a goddess in worn jeans and a utilitarian brown sweat shirt. The brown brought out the olive tones in her skin, and went seamlessly with the layer-dyed hair which was her only concession to vanity. Well, she had one other, but he wasn't sure whether that was due to vanity or to her belief that this was her good-luck charm, much like his boots were his—but she was wearing her red feather earring, dangling from her ear, jewel-bright against her dark hair. It seemed to highlight her dark-red lips, which were jewellike enough even without the benefit of lipstick.

He longed to trace with his hands the outline of her breasts under the sweat shirt. His lips ached for her lips. It had been . . . a week, maybe more, since he had so much as hugged her. And he wondered if she now thought he was a perfect idiot, since he'd shifted in the bathroom. He wondered if he'd ruined her respect for him, and if now it would be only a matter of time before she told him they couldn't go on like this.

"I'm an idiot," he said. And as she turned to look at him, he went on, honestly. "If I had half a lick of sense, when I knew I'd be spending at least an hour, and probably more in a van with the most beautiful woman in the world, I'd have had the good sense to bring champagne and chocolates, or something."

"We couldn't have champagne," she said. "We can't afford to be tipsy."

"Apple cider then," he said. "Something to make you feel as special as just being near you makes me feel."

For a moment he thought he'd upset her. Her mouth opened in an "Oh." and her eyes widened, as though surprised. And then, unaccountably, she was in his arms, her body warm against his. He frantically searched for her lips and found them, kissing her desperately, as if he could only draw breath through her mouth. "Kyrie," he said. "Oh, Kyrie."

Halfway through dinner, Rafiel found himself hoping that Lei Lani wasn't the murderer, whether or not she was a shifter. And he wanted her to be a shifter. He really did. Because then she would understand him—and he could maybe even marry her.

He didn't know what it was exactly, and he'd have been hard pressed to say, but he felt happy in her presence. Very happy. Almost on the edge of drunk.

Tuscany Bay, the fashionable restaurant to which he'd decided to take her, despite the nonsensical name, turned out to be a very decent Italian place, with dancing and a jazz band that played softly melodic sounds. And being around Lei seemed to erase Rafiel's pains, so that, after a dinner of grilled salmon, he could stand on his bruised ankle, and lead her in a heartfelt—and possibly slightly obscene—slow dance.

They danced one song, two, and Rafiel was conscious that most people in the place were staring at them, and he was sure—absolutely sure—that everyone of them was envying him. Lei was wearing a simple—almost severe—black and white dress, and the cutest little fedora tilted sideways on her head. Beneath it, her hair was loose, brushed till glossy and dark as sin.

After the second song, she said, "I think we should go out. You know, for a walk."

And he was fine with that. He'd have gone anywhere with her. At the door, when they picked up their coats from the coat check, the coat check lady whispered to Lei, "Don't let him drive," and Rafiel could not understand why. Did she think he was drunk? How could he be? He had drunk iced tea all evening.

But it didn't matter. As they walked outside, the cold air did feel invigorating. Lei put her arm in his. Above the skies had cleared and a million stars seemed to sparkle in the deep black velvet of the night.

He was a little surprised when they got to the aquarium and she opened the door. There was something about the aquarium. Something he was supposed to remember. But he had no idea what. And he was sure it couldn't be very important. After all, he was lucky. He had Lei Lani, right there.

Tom had just said, "Oh, I'm such an idiot," against the soft depths of Kyrie's tapestry-dyed hair, when the alarm sounded. For a moment, for just a moment, he thought it was ringing inside his head. Reminding him there was a reason he didn't usually allow himself to lose control, that he might at any moment lose control of himself and shift, which would work about as well in the van as it had in the bathroom.

He tried to tell the alarm to stuff it, but it continued to ring, quite oblivious to his opinions, and it dawned on Tom that it was the sound from the laptop at about the same time that Kyrie pulled away and said, "Damn, the laptop."

"Yeah," Tom said. "Yeah." It wasn't the most coherent response in the world, but it was the one he had, and he was going to stick to it.

Kyrie touched the button that made the screen saver stop scrolling by and brought the transmission from the camera to them in vivid, bold color. Tom remembered, irrelevantly, his father going on about how he'd picked that laptop because of the wonderful movie screen. All the same it took him a moment to figure out what he was looking at.

"Oh, good lord," Kyrie said. "Is he crazy or stupid?"

And then Tom realized he was looking at Rafiel and Lei Lani, without clothes, in what used to euphemistically be called a moment of passion. He jumped to the front seat and out. He had gone five steps before he realized that Kyrie hadn't been as fast. And it took him only two seconds to see a dire wolf round on him, from outside. It was growling in a low tone, and of course there were no words in its growl. But Tom would swear it was saying "Payback time, Dragon Boy."

Kyrie removed her earring, and then her clothes and leapt from the van even as she shifted. As a panther, she interposed herself between Dire and Tom. She growled, a fierce, loud growl that meant that he wouldn't be allowed to touch Tom, and she willed Tom to go past her. Willed it with all her mind.

There was Dire, standing in front of them, blocking the access to the aquarium. How long before Lei Lani took it into her head to drown Rafiel? They'd been naked and . . . um . . . Tom had no idea how long it was supposed to last. Movies had given him a range of times from a couple of minutes to hours, and he had no idea which one was closer to the truth.

But he knew, or at least he suspected that when the fun and games were done, it would be the final swim for Rafiel, a swim from which he would not return.

He could tell from the way Kyrie—in panther form, her fur velvet-dark—interposed herself between him and Dire, that she meant for him to go past. But how could he go past when Kyrie's life was at risk? He remembered what Dire could do. And he wasn't willing to see him treat Kyrie as he'd treated Rafiel.

Oh, Dire might want Kyrie, or at least he might think so. But did he want her more than he wanted to fulfill his *duty* and return, once more victorious, to his cosmopolitan lifestyle? And Kyrie would make as good a sacrifice to Dire's lifestyle as Rafiel.

Tom realized his body had made the decision for him because while he thought, he had stripped bare and untied his boots. He now stepped out of his boots, and spoke, in his slurpy almost-dragon voice, "Attack me, you prehistoric horror. Or can you only defeat girls?"

And then he shifted.

Damn the man, Kyrie thought, a passenger in the back of the panther's mind, even as Dire lunged at her and tossed her aside, while he rounded on Tom.

Kyrie landed heavily on a scruffy front lawn, and tried to get up. And couldn't. At first she thought she must be paralyzed, and then she realized Tom wasn't moving either. After issuing his challenge and leaping, he'd landed heavily, as if he couldn't control his paws, and now was half lying on the street, while Dire circled around him, growling, with every appearance of enjoyment.

He was going to kill Tom, she realized. He was in their minds. He was controlling them. And he was going to kill Tom. And then probably kill her.

Don't be silly, Kitten Girl, his voice said in her mind, with a suggestion of indecent laughter. *That would be a waste.*

She wanted to get up. She tried with all her mind and heart to get up. But she couldn't. She couldn't move.

And then, from above, came the flap of wings.

Tom heard the flap of wings. His eyes—about the only part of him not paralyzed—turned upward in time to see huge wings, descending. He wanted to protest, to say no. He hadn't asked for help. Even there, at death's door, he hadn't asked for help.

Let Dire kill him, but at least he would die free, and not owe his life to a criminal dragon.

Laughter filled his mind, and then a voice he remembered all too well. *Commendable*, it said. *Or perhaps crazy. Never mind. Go now. You are free. Go take care of your friend.*

And suddenly Tom could move, and he could see Kyrie move too. She was leaping towards the aquarium ahead of him. So she'd heard the golden bastard in her mind as well. And the golden bastard was interposing himself between Tom and Kyrie and Dire. The dire wolf screamed a sound of pure fury and Tom, who hadn't wanted the Great Sky Dragon's help, nonetheless hoped the Great Sky Dragon was doing to Dire what he did to them, and rifling through his mind, and using it. He hoped so, as he lurched, as fast as he could towards the aquarium.

Kyrie hit the aquarium door first, full lope, and rebounded back, shocked. Locked. The door was locked. The cat in whose mind Kyrie was couldn't understand it, even as Kyrie forced it to try to turn the knob. Until she felt a dragon claw rest, gently, on her shoulder, moving her aside.

The cat felt threatened and wanted to fight, but Kyrie was in control and she forced the body to step aside. And felt it recoil in terror and put belly to the ground and growl softly, as the dragon faced the door and opened his massive jaws, and let loose a stream of white-hot flame.

The door cracked. The outer lining of metal melted and ran. The inside layer of wood charred. The door fell inward, and Kyrie forced the great cat to leap in, over the smoldering door, and down a hallway, to where a door stood open with a seal ripped in two, and Kyrie lunged up the hallway, and loped up the stairs to the platform, in time to see . . . Rafiel, in human form, leaning over the railing and getting a push, and falling, falling headlong into the shark tank.

He made a sound of panic as he fell, and his shape blurred and changed. It was the lion that hit the water with a loud splash. The cover of the tank, removed, stood to the side.

A woman laughed, and turned to Kyrie. "I see. Why don't you join your boyfriend?"

Tom wanted to scream "No," but what came out of the dragon's mouth was a long, incoherent growl, as he rushed in, past Kyrie and almost past the woman on the platform.

The thought in his mind was that he must go and rescue Rafiel. He must. But he had a moment to think that if the woman stayed where she was, she might find a way to push Kyrie in. And he couldn't allow that, so he did what seemed all too logical to the dragon, and grabbed at the woman, pulling her in with him, as he plunged in after Rafiel.

The sharks hadn't started on Rafiel, who was trying to swim, his lion body quite adept at swimming, but not so much at reaching up to the edge of the tank lid and climbing out. He growled softly, whenever he tried and failed. And he looked—the human in Tom's dragon mind thought—very much like a drowned cat.

He thought all this as he plunged in, hitting the water

with a great splash and going down-down-down, drawing a deep breath scented with what seemed like intoxicating perfume, and realizing he was breathing under water.

He came up beneath Rafiel, lifting him, pushing him up with his own body, till the lion's paws touched the edge of the opening, and then the dragon gave the lion a little shove, pushing him out.

And he felt a shark—skin rough as sandpaper—touch his back paw. Something from a nature program about sharks turning, or circling or something before biting crossed the dragon's mind, and the dragon did what came instinctively. It snapped downward and it bit at the shark. Hard. The shark flopped. Blood poured out. Other sharks rushed in.

Feeding frenzy, Tom's human mind thought and pushed, with all its might, at the dragon's body, impelling it, mind over matter, to the opening, its wings unfurling, half jumping, half flying out of the tank.

On the way he picked up the lion, who had been cowering on the edge of the tank where the covering rested, and lifted him all the way to the platform.

And before he could shift and talk or look around for Kyrie, he heard an unholy growl.

Dante Dire, Kyrie thought. And—through the panther's mind, confused, blurred—went the thought that he'd escaped the Great Sky Dragon. Somehow. She would hate to imagine how.

And then she was plunging after him, madly. She felt him bite her, attack her, too ravening to care who she was, too maddened with rage to care whether he could just mind-control her instead.

From the shadows a dragon emerged. No. Two dragons. One of them red and with a foreshortened arm. And a very wet lion. They all fell on Dire, and Kyrie couldn't honestly say who was attacking what, except that Dire seemed to be everywhere at once, his teeth biting and his claws scraping, but never enough to get hold of them.

And then he seemed to regain control. Suddenly, the horrible smell she remembered from her kitchen when he'd attacked her there, surrounded them. And into their minds poured Dire's voice, *If you are done now, I can kill you.*

But at the same moment, two other voices sounded. "I don't think so," said a tremulous voice and, looking over, Kyrie was surprised to see Old Joe standing, for once, very straight. Next to him was an old Japanese gentleman, looking faintly amused.

You! Dire said. *You. You're weak. You can never face me.*

"We're not weak," the Japanese gentleman said. His accent was, clearly, the real thing, but not that incomprehensible. "We are free. We would have nothing to do with your council and your rules. We told you before it was wrong to separate yourself from humanity."

"We told you it would come to no good," Old Joe said, his voice clearer and more firm than it had ever been, at least that Kyrie had heard it.

"No good, uh?" Dire had shifted. He was human, looking at them with scornfully curled lip. "I am the executioner.

Even the Daddy Dragon couldn't face me. He cares too much for his whelp to use his form too long. He was afraid I would hurt the body he was borrowing." He grinned. "And I won. Because I don't care for anything but myself. Come," he said, and shifted, in a single, fluid movement. *Come now, we'll see who is stronger.*

It all happened too fast. There were suddenly an alligator and a giant spider crab. And they shifted, and the crab was stabbing at the dire wolf, while the alligator seemed to be everywhere at once, biting and slicing. The dire wolf's teeth closed on hard carapace and armored back. The alligator's teeth clack-clacked in what sounded like laughter.

There was a howl, a growl of pent-up fury, and suddenly the dire wolf was not there.

"He will come back," Tom said softly. And Kyrie realized he had shifted, and so had she, and they were both naked, hugging on the top step of the platform.

Before she could answer, a dripping-wet Rafiel walked around the shark tank, below them, and halfway up the stairs. "I'll be damned if I can explain all the trace on the scene now," he said, ruefully. "They're going to find scales, and blood of at least three different animals. But," he said, "I don't think that the murders will go on." He looked incredibly tired and somehow defeated, even as he announced good news. "She . . . shifted as she died. They will find human remains in the tank this time. Female."

Tom, pulling Kyrie against him, shuddered. And Kyrie said, "Why did you let things get that advanced?"

"I don't know. It could be some form of pheromones," he said. "Or else, she put something in my drink." He looked up, his golden eyes very sad. "I know that it was all delusion. I know she just wanted a snack. But for a moment, it was like being a kid again, back when I was in love with Alice." He shrugged and sat on the bottom step of the platform, and leaned against the railing. "I guess time never winds backwards."

And Kyrie who remembered something from the fight, looked to the other side of the steps, where Conan sat, looking just as dejected as Rafiel. "Conan," she said, "what was it Dire said, about the Great Sky Dragon borrowing your form?"

Conan shook. He looked up at her, seeming drained and pale. "He . . . he didn't . . . I mean, he can't be everywhere at once, but just like he can listen through his underlings . . . he can make us take his form. With all of his powers. Only if he does it for long, we die."

Kyrie blinked at him. "He made you take his form?"

"Just . . . just for a moment. Then he realized I couldn't stand it . . ."

"And he realized he cared for you?" Tom said, skeptically.

Conan shook his head. "No. He realized he cared for *you*. And he thought . . ." He sighed. "He thought you wouldn't forgive him if he killed me. Even when . . . even if it was to kill Dire. So he . . . let me go. He told me . . . in my mind, that I was now yours. That I'm to do what you tell me."

Tom coughed. "Mine?" Something like a choked laughter escaped him. "No offense, Conan, you're a nice guy. But the only person I ever wanted to be mine was Kyrie, and it wasn't in that sense. If he gave you to me, I give you to yourself. You're yours."

"I was afraid of that," Conan said, dolefully.

"Afraid," Kyrie said.

Conan shrugged. "Yes. I don't know how . . . not to belong to someone. I've taken orders from someone since before I was an adult. I'm not used to being my own person."

"Try it," she said, not without sympathy. "You can get used to it. And you still belong to us. Just as a friend, not a . . . possession."

"Truly?" he asked. "And I can . . . still work at The George?"

Kyrie felt Tom tremble with silent laughter. "If you want to. But I thought you were going to sing for your supper."

Conan blushed. "Maybe someday. But for now, I'm just glad to have a job."

"And on that, gentlemen and lady," Tom said, "I'm starving, and I think we should go to The George for some food. Because, you know it and I know it, that the old bastard is going to come back and try to kill us and right now another shift might kill *me*."

"Maybe he won't try to kill us," Old Joe said. He was standing alone. The crab shifter was nowhere to be seen. "Maybe he's afraid now?"

"I very much doubt it," Tom said, drily. But he added, "And Joe? Thank you. You saved our lives, I think."

Old Joe shrugged, but blushed and said, "You do what you have to."

"Yeah," Tom said. "At any rate, let's go eat something. What about your friend? Does he want to come?"

"Who? He? No. He never does. He doesn't feel very comfortable as a human, anymore. All he wants is his aquarium and to watch life go by."

Two weeks later, Tom woke up from sleep in his back porch, at his and Kyrie's house, looking up at the ceiling some past occupier had painted a deep pink. The bathroom had been repaired. The house was silent. Kyrie's breathing wasn't audible from her bedroom, and neither was what he was sure must be Notty's quite industrial-sized purr.

He wasn't sure what had wakened him, but Dire was on his mind. He hadn't seen Dire or heard from him for two weeks, and he wanted Old Joe to be right. He wanted it to be that Dire had gone away forever.

And just as he thought this he heard the voice in his mind. *Hey, Dragon Boy, come and be killed!* With the words came a flash—the view of Dire, in his animal form, waiting, down the street from Tom, in a little park, where pine trees covered in snow stood silent guard over a gazebo and stone boulders. In summer, the park was frequented by everyone in the neighborhood. But in winter no one ever went there, and the little lake in the middle was iced over—though not enough for anyone to skate on it.

It was the perfect place, Tom thought, for a duel. A shifter duel. But he was thousands of years younger than Dire. And he knew he couldn't fight the mind powers.

Or did he? There was something Dire had said, about how the Great Sky Dragon himself had been defeated because he cared too much for his subordinate. Perhaps he was right. Perhaps the way to fight with the mind, the way the Ancient Ones did, came from not caring.

Yes. It does, Dante Dire said in his mind. *It comes from us having seen the generations unfold and caring for nothing. You love life, that's your weakness. While we love only death, even our own, if it comes to that.*

And something in Tom's mind beat against the words. Denied them. He didn't care if they were true. He would not accept them. That was no way to live.

He got up, undressed silently. On his way out the door, he opened Kyrie's door a crack—enough to see her sleeping, under the moonlight, on her side, her face supported on her arm. Notty was nestled in her hair, purring. They looked peaceful. Domestic.

And Tom went out, into the cold dark night.

On his front porch, after closing the door carefully behind himself, he shifted.

He flew into the park. Dante waited for him, shifted, in the deepest dark, near where the trees clustered, just by the lakeside.

So good of you to come and die, he said. And Tom could

feel him casting cold binds of domination and power over his mind. Nets of cold control.

But Tom held on to what he knew was true. To what he loved. The image of Kyrie and Notty, sleeping in the moonlight. The George, shining like a neon jewel through the snow. Anthony at the grill. Conan tending tables. The images burned within him like warm fires. Like home fires, calling to his heart.

Mine, mine, mine, he said, and while he caught Dire trying to hold on to these images, to threaten them, to tell Tom they were weaknesses, he couldn't hold them.

Tom's love for his family, his friends, his diner, shone through, warming his soul, and Dire's cold thoughts slipped off. He had only hatred and barrenness to offer. And those were never very strong weapons.

After that, it was easy. The dragon, after all, could fly. The dire wolf couldn't. He looked almost small, in the dark, amid the trees and the snow.

The vicious teeth tried to rend Tom's wing, as Tom approached, but Tom flipped over, suddenly, and bit the dire wolf's neck. Hard.

Tom grabbed it by the neck and shook it, as Dire started to shift, under his jaws—guessing Tom would have more trouble killing a human than an animal. A pitiful human fist hit the dragon's scales. A forlorn human scream echoed. Again and again, Dire tried to cast his cold uncaring spell upon Tom's mind—Tom pressed harder.

He tasted blood, and recoiled from it, but forced his jaws to close. The taste made him gag, but he persisted. Bone crunched. Dire's head and body fell, two separate parts.

It was truth that Dire loved death and pain—or causing them. But Tom loved life. And while Tom lived he would keep those he loved safe. Which meant Dire must die.

Afterwards, Tom took the head, and the body, and swam with them, deep into the cold, dark lake—after breaking the ice covering on it. He found that there were caves, on either side of the lake, leading quite deep under the city, perhaps to what had once been mines and were now flooded. He put the head and the body in separate tunnels, and blocked the entrance with large stones. He didn't want either ever found.

And then, half frozen, he swam back, and walked home.

After a shower, after rinsing his mouth with mouthwash, again and again, and again, Tom put his robe on and went to the kitchen, where he put paid to two packages of sandwich ham while the dozen eggs they had just bought boiled enough to not be repulsive.

When the craving for protein abated, still feeling chilled, Tom opened the door to Kyrie's room and called, softly, "Kyrie?"

She opened her eyes, and Notty's head shot up. "Yes?"

"Do you mind if I sleep here? Just sleep? I mean . . . I just . . . want to be with you."

Kyrie sat up in bed. "What's wrong?"

"Nothing. I'm just . . . I'm very cold."

"Are you coming down with something?"

"I don't think so. I'm just . . . I just need company."

She shifted to one side of the double bed, taking Notty with her, leaving him space. Tom climbed in, and curled up on the mattress, looking at Kyrie and Notty, who was now parading back and forth between the two of them and purring, the contented purr of a cat with two body servants.

"Kyrie," Tom said, wanting to talk, wanting to explain this feeling that wasn't regret or guilt, but had shades of both. He'd taken a life. He'd killed someone who'd lived thousands of years. He'd had to do it. None of them would be safe till he was dead. So why was it that this thing he'd done made him feel so cut off from the rest of humanity?

He moved fractionally towards Kyrie. "Listen," he said.

Notty jumped up, back arched and hissed towards Tom. His pose was so possessive of Kyrie that Tom laughed aloud. "Yes, yes, your girl cat, Notty. I'll behave."

He petted the ruffled kitten till Kyrie said, softly, "What is it?"

He looked at her. Her eyes were half closed. He smiled. The talk would wait. Tonight was not the night to try to explain what he'd done or how he felt. He wanted more than anything to hold Kyrie, to love her. But tonight was not the night for that, either.

Let the night close itself upon its horror. Let wonders unfold another time. "Nothing," he said quietly.

He petted Notty till he passed from wakefulness into a dream where he was holding Kyrie in the midst of a field of snow. And it was very warm.

When they got into The George, in the evening, they found Conan and Anthony sitting at the back booth, in front of what looked like a veritable mound of bread. Sitting across from them was a young woman with brown hair, hazel eyes and a blade of a nose. She looked towards them and extended a hand and spoke, in a pleasant contralto, "Hi. I'm Laura Miller. You must think I'm the most unreliable person alive, but I simply couldn't come in before. I had to take care of some family matters . . . But I'm here now, and I'm free to interview for the job, if you still want to consider me. And I brought some samples of my baking with me."

"Consider her," Anthony said. He picked a roll from the confusion of bread. "She makes this Italian bread . . . My mom would weep, I tell you."

Tom, grinning, turned towards her. "Well, as you can see, I have to consider you. And we were taking care of family matters, too. I have no idea how to interview you, just now, my mind is still in a whirl. So . . . is there anything you want to tell me?"

The woman blinked at him, then looked toward Kyrie, then, perhaps having decided that if they were crazy they weren't, at least, unpleasant, rattled off quickly, "I can do gourmet cooking, but really, I don't like it as much as a variety of good plain cooking. I truly do need to bake, though. Cookies, biscuits, breads, muffins, scones, pies, fancy pastries, whatever. I like making breads and pies and biscuits and muffins most of all, though. Cornbread's fun to make, both Northern and Southern. So's gingerbread. With or without rum sauce. Fresh pitas are like a miracle, puffing themselves up like little balloons. Stews and soups and prep cooking are satisfying, too. But not as good as baking. But I can get the bucket of scrams ready for morning rush, and get the onions and peppers for morning and lunch rush, and chop the salad, and mix up the tsatsiki.

"I can do a lot of prep cooking. I can do quantity cooking. I can run an industrial dishwasher. But I really love baking. Just don't ask me to do gourmet dinners where everything needs to be perfectly plated. My idea of decorative plating is to put the juice with the cherries and onions over the pork loin rather than beside it. And maybe to have carrots and green beans by the pork loin instead of potatoes and corn. But fancy plating with everything all pointing in perfect directions and swirled sauces? It all tastes the same in the mouth, anyway. And unless it's someone's birthday, I don't frost cakes fancy. Just tasty. I like to do one-offs, but that's why I don't like fancy frosting every day. Special should be special. And pies are either lattice, pierced, open, or have a couple of shapes out with tart cutters. If The George wants Martha Stewart, you can hire her. But I do use my grandma's pie crust recipe. And she won blue ribbons." She stopped, giving the impression that she'd run out of breath.

And Kyrie looked at Tom and found him looking at her. And she wondered how the woman would do with shifters and madness, but, hell, Anthony seemed to do well enough even while being totally clueless. And frankly, the list of breads was enough to make her want to drool.

She winked at Tom. He winked back and they said at the same time, "You're hired."

Just at that moment, she thought she smelled a vague shifter's scent beneath the smell of all the baking. Was their new employee a shifter?

But Tom was saying, "We'll discuss terms, okay? But we're flexible, since one of the really important qualities I wanted was someone who could bake." He'd somehow got hold of a little curlicue of a roll sprinkled with what looked like cheese, and was eating it, merrily. "And you certainly can do that."

Laura smiled, and at that moment the bell behind the front door tinkled. Edward Ormson, whom Kyrie always thought looked like an older and better-dressed version of Tom, came in. He was pulling a flight bag, and looked up at the group of them with a quizzical smile. "Oh, good," he said, to no one in particular. He looked at Tom, "I assume everything is well and you still haven't eaten anyone?"

Did Laura's eyes widen just a little? Kyrie couldn't tell, and Tom was laughing. "No, Dad. I haven't. And yeah, everything is fine."

"First day they opened the passes, so first day I could get here. I will go and check in at the hotel later, but I thought I'd come and see how you were doing, and make sure everything was okay."

Tom felt . . . oddly amused and tender. His father had driven here, as soon as the snow stopped for two days and the mountain passes opened, to make sure everything was okay. He could have called. He could have asked someone else to check on them. But no. Edward Ormson, who hated making himself uncomfortable, had driven a mountain road that would still have patches of ice and which was probably crowded with long-delayed travelers, to come here and check on his son.

They'd all come a long way.

But Tom still had no idea whatsoever how to express his affection for his father. So he did the only thing he knew how to do. He stepped behind the counter, and took off his jacket, putting it on the shelf under there. Then he put on his apron and his bandana, and said, "Okay, Dad. I'll make you dinner before you go to your hotel. What would you like?"

His dad grinned. "Noah's boy."

"We don't eat people," Tom said. "I thought we'd established that."

"No, no. See, you have all the diner slang in the menu, so I went and studied it, on-line. 'Noah's boy' is ham. You know. Ham. In the Bible."

Kyrie giggled, and Tom gave her an indulgent smile. "Um . . . I don't think we have that in the menu, but sure. I'll make it. One Noah's boy, coming up. And then I'll discuss your pay and hours, Laura."

A look over his shoulder showed him that Laura was made of uncommonly resilient stuff. She was smiling a little and had sat down at the booth.

The front door tinkled, to let in the dinner rush hour, and Kyrie put her apron on, ready to go attend to the tables.

The Poet came in and sat at his table, with his notebook. Tom wondered if the Poet truly was a member of the Rodent Liberation Front, and, if so, if he was the squirrel that shifted to the size of a German shepherd and smoked cigarettes. Anything was possible, he guessed. But he hoped the Rodent Liberation Front would be still now for a while, and let them have at least a little peace.

Kyrie was still behind the counter. Before going back out, she touched his shoulder with her warm hand. It wasn't even a public display of affection. But it was enough.

And The George's neon signs shone softly, while a fresh snowfall started—big, fluffy flakes, blanketing Goldport in quietness and cold.

The Following is an excerpt from:

DARKSHIP THIEVES

SARAH A. HOYT

Available from Baen Books
January 2010
hardcover

✧ONE✧

I NEVER WANTED TO GO TO SPACE. Never wanted
see the eerie glow of the Powerpods. Never wanted to
visit Circum Terra. Never had any interest in discovering
the truth about the darkships. You always get what you
don't ask for.

Which was why I woke up in the dark of shipnight,
within the greater night of space in my father's space
cruiser.

Before full consciousness, I knew there was an intruder
in my cabin. Once awake, I couldn't figure out how I knew
it. The air smelled as it always did on shipboard, as it had
for the week I'd spent here—stale, with the odd tang
given by the recycling.

The engines, below me, hummed steadily. We had just
detached from Circum Terra—a maneuver that involved
some effort, to avoid accidentally ramming the station or
the ship. Shortly we'd be Earth bound, though slowing

down and reentry let alone landing, for a ship this size, would take close to a week.

My head felt a little light, my stomach a little queasy, from the artificial grav. Yes, I know. Scientists say that's impossible. They say artificial gravity is just like true gravity to the senses. You don't feel a thing. They are wrong. Artificial grav always made me feel a little out of balance, like a couple of shots of whiskey on an empty stomach.

Even before waking fully, I'd tallied all this. There was nothing out of the ordinary. And yet there was a stranger in my cabin.

Years in reformatories, boarding schools and mental hospitals, had taught me that the feeling I woke up with was often the right one. Something had awakened me—a door closing, a step on the polished floor.

Now, why? Knowing the why determined how I dealt with it.

Three reasons that came to mind immediately. Theft, rape, murder. But all of them were impossible. The space cruiser belonged to Daddy Dearest and there was no one aboard save Daddy Dearest, my charming self—his only daughter—and his handpicked crew of about twenty five, half of whom were his bodyguard goons and half maintenance-crew of one description or another. Far more than I thought it would take to run a ship this size, but then what did I know about ships?

Now, whatever I thought of my father, the Honorable Patrician Milton Alexander Sinistra of the ruling council of Earth, I neither thought him stupid nor stupidly inclined to trust people. His goons were the scum of the Earth—only because there were no real populations on any other planet—but they were picked, trained, conditioned and, for all I knew, mind-controlled for loyalty. Hulking giants all, they would, each one of them, have laid down his life for my father. Not the least because without Father they'd only be wanted men with no place to hide.

As for his other servants and employees, they were the best Father could command, in any specialty he needed.

None of them, nor anyone who had ever seen Father in a white hot rage would ever do anything against Father or his family. Well . . . except me. I defied Father all the time. But I was the sole exception.

There were no crimes at our home in Syracuse Seacity. There weren't even any misdemeanors. No servant had ever been caught stealing so much as a rag from the house stores. Hell, no servant broke a plate without apologizing immediately and profusely.

So the three reasons I could think of for an intruder to be here didn't apply. No one would dare steal from me, rape me or murder me under Father's roof. And no one— no one—who had even heard rumors about me would do so absent a fear of Father.

Without opening my eyes, I looked through my eyelashes—an art I'd learned through several sojourns at various institutions—and turned in bed. No more than the aimless flailing of a sleeper seeking a better position. The cabin was dark. For a moment I could see nothing. I could turn the lights on by calling out, or by reaching. But either of those would let the intruder know that I wasn't asleep.

And then, my eyes adjusting, I saw him standing out of the deeper darkness,. It was a him. It had to be a him. Broad shoulders and tall. He stood by my bed, utterly still.

My heart sped up. I tensed. I didn't know who he was, nor what he was about to do, but it couldn't be good. No one with good intentions would come in like that, while I was asleep and then stand there, quietly waiting. As if to make sure I really was asleep.

Then I thought it might not be one of Father's people at all. Our security was good. Really good. But we'd just been on a four-day-long state-visit to Circum Terra, where the population were the top scientists in their field. Smart people. Smart people who had been isolated for a couple of years. Smart people who had stared and sighed when I walked around and attended parties and was my most flirty self in the clothes that were one of the few perks of being Father's daughter.

If one of those people had sneaked aboard . . .

Moving slowly, in the same seemingly aimless movements, I clenched my hands on the blanket about an arm's length apart, and made fists, grabbing handfuls of the stuff. I'd have preferred to twist it around my wrists, so it wouldn't come loose, but that would be way too obvious.

The man in the dark took a step towards me. He was good. If he was a scientist, he must have been a cat burglar in a previous life. If I hadn't been awake, he surely wouldn't have awakened me now.

I sprang. I hopped up to the edge of the bed. The ceramite bed-rail gave a better surface for bouncing. I bounced, on my tiptoes and flew up, blanket stretched between my hands.

There is this state I go into when in fear or anger. It seems as though I can move faster—and be stronger— than normal people. At least enough to take everyone by surprise. It had seen me through countless battles in boarding schools, hospitals, detention centers. I never understood why people didn't match it. They didn't seem able to.

As time seemed to slow for me, I wrapped the blanket over the head of the intruder and pulled, with the blanket still held in both hands. A blanket is the worst garotte possible. I much prefer a scarf or a rope. But even I couldn't have everything. Where would I put it? Who would polish it?

As my prey started to flail, I knew that however much slower than I he was, he was stronger. And bigger. I pulled the ends of the blanket I had grabbed, as tight as I could around his neck. It wasn't pliable enough. I needed something big and heavy to crash over his head. But— damn the space cabin!—everything was locked behind drawers and doors. And he was thrashing, struggling, groping for my arm.

I did what comes naturally in these circumstances. I lifted my foot, aiming with my heel because bare toes aren't very effective, and kicked. Hard. Right at the center of his manhood. He screamed and let go of my arm.

Just long enough for me to find, on the floor, the boots that, according to my bad habit, I had taken off and left by the side of the bed. I mustn't have been asleep very long, since my maid hadn't picked them up yet. This meant that most of the people on board should be awake still.

As I thought this, I grabbed the boot. It was more fashionable than practical, a boot designed for walking indoors and looking good. Fortunately at that time looking good—in the short silk dresses I normally favored—demanded a fairly high heel, plated all around with a thick layer of silver. And chunky, according to current fashion.

I had just time to weigh it in my hand. My uninvited guest was trying to pull the blanket off and calling out some nasty words that good scientists shouldn't pronounce.

When hitting someone on the head it's all a matter of knowing the point where it will do the most good. Or harm. Long experimentation had told me the point above the ear would work, only, of course, he was moving around too much to make it exact. I did try.

I visualized my hand going through his head—because otherwise the blow would lack the needed force—pulled back, to gain momentum, and brought the heel of the boot hard on his head. As hard as I could from the disadvantage of a lower height. If he hadn't been half-bent, trying to unwrap the blanket, I'd never have managed it at all.

As it was, the first hit made him pause. Just pause. He didn't fall and I thought I hadn't hit hard enough, so I hit again, harder.

He made a sound like choking and went down. The blanket, which he'd managed to loosen most of the way by the time he fell, came off his face.

"Lights on," I said, and jumped back, holding my boot, because if he came back at me I was going to hit him again, and this time I wanted to be able to see where.

But as the soft glow shone on his pale face, I recognized Andrija Baldo, the head of my father's goons. And he was very still.

His square face was pasty gray. The brutal lips another shade of grey. There was a drop of blood running from beneath his hair. I wondered for a moment if I had killed him, and exactly how mad Father would be if I had.

Then I realized his chest was rising and falling minimally. So, still alive.

And in his right hand, firmly clutched, was the oval shape of an injector. I knew the color too. There was only one medicine they packaged in those piss-yellow injectors.

Morpheus. The strongest knock-out juice in the universe.

PRAISE FOR
LOIS McMASTER BUJOLD

What the critics say:

The Warrior's Apprentice: "Now here's a fun romp through the spaceways—not so much a space opera as space ballet... It has all the 'right stuff.' A lot of thought and thoughtfulness stand behind the all-too-human characters. Enjoy this one, and look forward to the next."   —Dean Lambe, *SF Reviews*

"The pace is breathless, the characterization thoughtful and emotionally powerful, and the author's narrative technique and command of language compelling. Highly recommended." —*Booklist*

Brothers in Arms: "...she gives it a genuine depth of character, while reveling in the wild turnings of her tale... Bujold is as audacious as her favorite hero, and as brilliantly (if sneakily) successful."   —*Locus*

"Miles Vorkosigan is such a great character that I'll read anything Lois wants to write about him... a book to re-read on cold rainy days."   —Robert Coulson, *Comics Buyers Guide*

Borders of Infinity: "Bujold's series hero Miles Vokosigan may be a lord by birth and an admiral by rank, but a bone disease that has left him hobbled and in frequent pain has sensitized him to the suffering of outcasts in her very hierarchical era.... Playing off of Miles's reserve and cleverness, Bujold draws outrageous and outlandish foils to color her high-minded adventures."   —*Publishers Weekly*

Falling Free: "In *Falling Free* Lois McMaster Bujold has written her fourth straight superb novel.... How to break down a talent like Bujold's into analyzable components? Best not to try. Best to say: 'Read, or you will be missing something extraordinary.'"
—Roland Green, *Chicago Sun-Times*

The Vor Game: "The chronicles of Miles Vokosigan are far too witty to be literary junk food, but they rouse the kind of craving that makes popcorn magically vanish during a double feature."   —Faren Miller, *Locus*

MORE PRAISE FOR
LOIS McMASTER BUJOLD

What the readers say:

"My copy of *Shards of Honor* is falling apart I've reread it so often.... I'll read whatever you write. You've certainly proved yourself a grand storyteller.

—Lisa Kolbe, Colorado Springs, CO

"I experience the stories of Miles Vorkosigan as almost viscerally uplifting... But certainly, even the weightiest theme would have less impact than a cinder on snow were it not for a rousing good story, and good story-telling with it. This is the second thing I want to thank you for... I suppose if you boiled down all I've said to its simplest expression, it would be that I immensely enjoy and admire your work. I submit that, as literature, your work raises the overall level of the science fiction genre, and spiritually, you work cannot avoid positively influencing all who read it."

—Glen Stonebreaker, Gaithersburg, MD

"'The Mountains of Mourning' [in *Borders of Infinity*] was one of the best-crafted, and simply best, works I'd ever read. When I finished it, I immediately turned back to the beginning and read it again, and I can't remember the last time I did that."

—Betsy Bizot, Lisle, IL

"I can only hope that you will continue to write, so that I can continue to read (and of course buy) your books, for they make me laugh and cry and think ... rare indeed."

—Steven Knott, Major, USAF

What do you say?

Cordelia's Honor

pb • 0-671-57828-6 • $7.99

Contains *Shards of Honor* and Hugo-award winner *Barrayar* in one volume.

Young Miles

trade pb • 0-671-87782-8 • $17.00
pb • 0-7434-3616-4 • $7.99

Contains *The Warrior's Apprentice*, Hugo-award winner *The Vor Game*, and Hugo-award winner "The Mountains of Mourning" in one volume.

Cetaganda

0-671-87744-5 • $7.99

Miles, Mystery and Mayhem

hc • 0-671-31858-6 • $24.00
pb • 0-7434-3618-0 • $7.99

Contains *Cetaganda*, *Ethan of Athos* and "Labyrinth" in one volume.

Brothers in Arms

pb • 1-4165-5544-7 • $7.99

Miles Errant

trade pb • 0-7434-3558-3 • $15.00

Contains "Borders of Infinity," *Brothers in Arms* and *Mirror Dance* in one volume.

Mirror Dance

pb • 0-671-87646-5 • $7.99

Memory
hc • 0-671-87743-7 • $22.00
pb • 0-671-87845-X • $7.99

Miles in Love
hc • 1-4165-5522-6 • $19.00
trade pb • 1-4165-5547-1 • $14.00
Contains *Komarr, A Civil Campaign* and "A Winterfair Gift" in one volume.

Komarr
hc • 0-671-87877-8 • $22.00
pb • 0-671-57808-1 • $7.99

A Civil Campaign
hc • 0-671-57827-8 • $24.00
pb • 0-671-57885-5 • $7.99

Miles, Mutants & Microbes
hc • 1-4165-2141-0 • $18.00
pb • 1-4165-5600-1 • $7.99
Contains *Falling Free* "Labyrinth", and *Diplomatic Immunity* in one volume.

Diplomatic Immunity
hc • 0-7434-3533-8 • $25.00
pb • 0-7434-3612-1 • $7.99

Ethan of Athos
pb • 0-671-65604-X • $5.99

Falling Free
pb • 1-4165-5546-3 • $7.99

1634: The Baltic War
by Eric Flint & David Weber
1-4165-5588-9 ◆ $7.99

1634: The Galileo Affair
by Eric Flint & Andrew Dennis
0-7434-9919-0 ◆ $7.99
New York Times bestseller!

1635: Cannon Law
by Eric Flint & Andrew Dennis
1-4165-5536-6 ◆ $7.99

1634: The Ram Rebellion
by Eric Flint with Virginia DeMarce
1-4165-7382-8 ◆ 7.99

1634: The Bavarian Crisis
by Eric Flint with Virginia DeMarce
1-4165-4253-1 ◆ $26.00

1635: The Dreeson Incident
by Eric Flint with Virginia DeMarce
1-4165-5589-7 ◆ $26.00

Also by Raymond E. Feist

MAGICIAN
SILVERTHORN
A DARKNESS AT SETHANON

FAERIE TALE

PRINCE OF THE BLOOD
THE KING'S BUCCANEER

SHADOW OF A DARK QUEEN
RISE OF A MERCHANT PRINCE
RAGE OF A DEMON KING
SHARDS OF A BROKEN CROWN

KRONDOR: THE BETRAYAL
KRONDOR: THE ASSASSINS

With Janny Wurts:

DAUGHTER OF EMPIRE
SERVANT OF EMPIRE
MISTRESS OF EMPIRE

Raymond E. Feist

Krondor
❖ Tear ❖
of the Gods

BOOK THREE OF THE RIFTWAR LEGACY

HarperTorch

An Imprint of HarperCollins Publishers

This work is based on the game "Return to Krondor" published by Pyrotechnix, Inc.

A hardcover edition of this book was published in Great Britain by Voyager, an imprint of HarperCollins Publishers.

HARPERTORCH
An Imprint of HarperCollins*Publishers*
10 East 53rd Street
New York, New York 10022-5299

Copyright © 2000 by Raymond E. Feist
ISBN: 0-380-79528-0

First HarperTorch paperback printing: June 2002
First HarperTorch international printing: May 2001
First Eos hardcover printing: March 2001

HarperCollins ®, HarperTorch™, and ❤ are trademarks of HarperCollins Publishers Inc.

Printed in the United States of America

Visit HarperTorch on the World Wide Web at www.harpercollins.com

10 9 8 7 6 5 4 3

Acknowledgments

As with other projects, I am in debt to many people, but more
so with this than almost any other work I've undertaken. That
was due in significant part to the evolution of the game, "Return
to Krondor," the core story of which also serves as the core of
this novel. I would be lax in my crediting those responsible for
that project, upon which this rests, if I did not point to the work
of many people, some who will go uncredited upon the game itself, for dealing with dozens of potentially terminal problems,
distractions, and delays.

Literally hundreds of hands touched "Return to Krondor"
in its evolution, too many to single out here. Knowing this list
is incomplete, I would like to thank:

Andy Ashcraft, Craig Boland, Chuck Mitchell, Susan
Deneker, Leanne Moen, and Michael Lynch who at various
times had to listen to my opinion when they probably would
rather have been working.

Scott Page, who found himself unexpectedly dealing with
other people's messes, but who stayed the course.

Bob Ezrin, who was the Father of Us All during very trying
times at 7th Level, who had to clean up an impossible mess
made by other people who betrayed his trust, and who held my
hand and kept the company alive when he rather would have
been in the studio making music.

St. John Bain, who inherited a mess, and who with good
humor and determination made someone else's vision his own;
indefatigable is the only word that describes his commitment to
Krondor.

Steve Abrams, old friend and partner-in-crime, whose con-

tributions to my work over the years have often gone uncredited, but never unappreciated.

Jonathan Matson, my agent, for all the usual reasons, and in this case, for all the unusual reasons.

My daughter, Jessica, and my son, James, for making every day spent with them better.

Jennifer Brehl and Jane Johnson, my editors in New York and London, for so much more than the job description requires.

On a personal note: This book was produced during a very difficult time for me personally, the end of my twelve-year marriage, and there are people out there who helped me through that period, people who did not have anything directly to do with the production of this novel, but who, by keeping me relatively sane during that period, helped me finish the project.

So, special thanks to Steve Abrams, Andy Abramson, Jim Curl, Jonathan Matson, Rich Spahl, and Janny Wurts for keeping me together early on, and being there for the long haul. There have been others, but the aforementioned went above and beyond the call. Words cannot express my gratitude. I am blessed beyond belief by friends of special quality.

And to the "gang" at Flemming's in La Jolla, the best steak house and wine bar in California, for giving me a place to hang.

Raymond E. Feist
San Diego, CA
August 30, 2000

For Bob Ezrin,
who else?

Contents

Prologue
Attack

The weather worsened.

Dark clouds roiled overhead as angry lightning flashed, piercing the night's blackness on all quarters. The lookout atop the highest mast of the ship *Ishap's Dawn* thought he saw a flicker of movement in the distance and squinted against the murk. He tried to use his hand to shield his eyes as the salt spray and biting cold wind filled them with tears. He blinked them away and whatever movement he thought he had seen was gone.

Night and the threat of storms had forced the lookout to spend a miserable watch aloft, against the unlikely chance the captain had drifted off course. It was hardly possible, considered the lookout, as the captain was a knowledgeable seaman, chosen for his skill at avoiding danger as much as any other quality. And he knew as well as any man how hazardous this passage was. The Temple held the cargo's value second to none, and rumors of possible raiders along the Quegan coast had dictated a hazardous tack near Widow's Point, a rocky area best avoided if possible. But *Ishap's Dawn* was crewed by experienced sailors, who were now closely attentive to the captain's orders, and each was quick to respond, for every

man aloft knew that, once upon the rocks at Widow's
Point, no ship survived. Each man feared for his own
life—that was only natural—but these men were chosen
not only for their seamanship, but also for fealty to the
Temple. And they all knew how precious their cargo was
to the Temple.

In the hold below, eight monks of the Temple of Ishap
in Krondor stood around a most holy artifact, the Tear of
the Gods. A jewel of astonishing size, easily as long as a
large man's arm and twice as thick, it was illuminated
from within by a mystic light. Once every ten years a new
Tear was formed in a hidden monastery in a tiny secret
valley in the Grey Tower Mountains. When it was ready
and most holy rites completed, a heavily armed caravan
transported it to the nearest port in the Free Cities of
Natal. There it was placed upon a ship and carried to
Krondor. From there, the Tear and an escort of warrior
monks, priests, and servants would continue on, eventually reaching Salador to then be taken by ship and transported to the mother Temple in Rillanon where it
replaced the previous Tear, as its power waned.

The true nature and purpose of the sacred gem was
known only to the highest ranking among those serving
within the Temple, and the sailor high atop the main mast
asked no questions. He trusted in the power of the gods
and knew that he served a greater good. And he was being
handsomely paid not to ask questions as much as to stand
his watch.

But after two weeks of battling contrary winds and difficult seas, even the most pious man found the blue-white
light which shone every night from below, and the
monks' incessant chanting, nerve-wracking. The duration
of the unseasonable winds and unexpected storms had
some of the crew muttering about sorcery and dark

magic. The lookout offered a silent prayer of thanks to
Killian, Goddess of Nature and Sailors (and then added a
short one to Eortis, who some said was the true God of
the Sea) that come dawn they would reach their destination: Krondor. The Tear and its escort would quickly
leave the city for the east, but the sailor would remain in
Krondor, with his family. What he was being paid would
allow him a long visit home.

The sailor above thought of his wife and two children,
and he smiled briefly. His daughter was now old enough
to help her mother around the kitchen and with her baby
brother, and a third child was due soon. As he had a hundred times before, the sailor vowed he'd find other work
near home, so he could spend more time with his family.

He was pulled from his reverie by another flicker of
movement toward shore. Light from the ship painted the
storm-tossed combers and he could sense the rhythm of
the sea. Something had just broken the rhythm. He peered
through the murk, trying to pierce the gloom by strength
of will, to see if they might be drifting too close to the
rocks.

Knute said, "The blue light coming from that ship
gives me a bad feeling, Captain."

The man Knute addressed towered over him as he
looked down. At six foot eight inches tall he dwarfed
those around him. His massive shoulders and arms lay
exposed by the black leather cuirass he favored, though
he had added a pair of shoulder pads studded with steel
spikes—a prize taken off the corpse of one of Queg's
more renowned gladiators. The exposed skin displayed
dozens of reminders of battles fought, traces of old
wounds intersecting one another. A scar that ran from
forehead to jawbone through his right eye, which was

milky white, marked his face. But his left seemed to glow with an evil red light from within and Knute knew that eye missed little.

Save for the spikes on his shoulders, his armor was plain and serviceable, well oiled and cared for, but displaying patches and repairs. An amulet hung around his neck, bronze but darkened by more than time and neglect, stained by ancient and black arts. The red gem set in its middle pulsed with a faint inner light of its own as Bear said, "Worry about keeping us off the rocks, pilot. It's the only reason I keep you alive." Turning to the rear of the ship, he spoke softly, but his voice carried to the stern. "Now!"

A sailor at the rear spoke down to those in the hold below, "Forward!" and the hortator raised one hand, and then brought its heel down on the drum between his knees.

At the sound of the first beat, the slaves chained to their seats raised their oars and on the second beat they lowered them and pulled as one. The word had been passed, but the Master of Slaves who walked between the banks of oars repeated it. "Silently, my darlings! I'll kill the first of you who makes a sound above a whisper!"

The ship, a Quegan patrol galley seized in a raid the year before, inched forward, picking up speed. At the prow, Knute crouched, intently scanning the water before him. He had positioned the ship so it would come straight at the target, but there was one turn that still needed to be made to port—not difficult if one reckoned the timing correctly, but dangerous nevertheless. Suddenly Knute turned and said, "Now, hard to port!"

Bear turned and relayed the order and the helmsman turned the ship. A moment later Knute ordered the rudder amidships, and the galley began to cut through the water.

Knute's gaze lingered on Bear for a moment, and then he returned his attention to the ship they were about to take. Knute had never been so frightened in his life. He was a born pirate, a dock-rat from Port Natal who had worked his way up from being an ordinary seaman to being one of the best pilots in the Bitter Sea. He knew every rock, shoal, reef, and tide pool between Ylith and Krondor, and westward to the Straits of Darkness, and along the coast of the Free Cities. And it was that knowledge that had kept him alive more than forty years while braver, stronger, and more intelligent men had died.

Knute felt Bear standing behind him. He had worked for the enormous pirate before, once taking Quegan prize ships as they returned from raids along the Keshian coast. Another time he had served with Bear as a privateer, under marque from the Governor of Durbin, plundering Kingdom ships.

For the last four years Knute had run his own gang, scavengers picking over wrecks drawn upon the rocks by false lights here at Widow's Point. It had been the knowledge of the rocks and how to negotiate them that had brought him back into Bear's service. The odd trader named Sidi, who came to the Widow's Point area every year or so, had asked him to find a ruthless man, one who would not shirk from a dangerous mission and who had no aversion to killing. Knute had spent a year tracking down Bear and had sent him word that there was a job of great risk and greater reward waiting. Bear had answered and had come to meet with Sidi. Knute had figured he'd either take a fee for putting the two men in touch, or he might work a split with Bear in exchange for use of his men and his ship. But from that point where Knute had brought Bear to meet with Sidi, on the beach at Widow's Point, everything had changed. Instead of working for

himself, Knute was now again working as Bear's galley-pilot and first mate—Knute's own ship, a nimble little coaster, had been sunk to drive home Bear's terms: riches to Knute and his men if they joined him. If they refused, the alternative was simple: death.

Knute glanced at the strange blue light dancing upon the water as they drew down upon the Ishapian ship. The little man's heart beat with enough force to make him fear it would somehow break loose from within. He gripped the wooden rail tightly as he called for a meaningless course correction; the need to shout diverted into a sharp command.

Knute knew he was likely to die tonight. Since Bear had expropriated Knute's crew, it had simply been a matter of time. The man Knute had known along the Keshian coast had been bad enough, but something had changed Bear, made him far blacker a soul than before. He had always been a man of few scruples, but there had been an economy in his business, a reluctance to waste time with needless killing and destruction, even if he was otherwise unfazed by it. Now Bear seemed to relish it. Two men in Knute's crew had died lingering, painful deaths for minor transgressions. Bear had watched until they had died. The gem in his amulet had shone brightly then, and Bear's one good eye seemed alight with the same fire.

Bear had made one thing clear above all else: this mission's goal was to take a holy relic from the Ishapians and any man who interfered with that mission would die. But he had also promised that the crew could keep all the rest of the Ishapian treasure for themselves.

When he heard that, Knute had begun to make a plan.

Knute had insisted upon several practice sorties, claiming that the tides and rocks here were treacherous enough in the daylight—at night a thousand calamities could be-

fall the unprepared. Bear had grudgingly acquiesced to the plea. What Knute had hoped would happen did: the crew learned to take orders from him once Bear gave over command of the ship. Bear's crew was made up of thugs, bullies, and murderers, including one cannibal, but they weren't terribly intelligent.

Knute's was a daring plan, and dangerous, and he needed more than a little luck. He glanced back and saw Bear's eyes fixed on the blue light of the Ishapian ship as they bore down on it. One quick glance from face to face of his own six men was all Knute could afford, and then he turned back to the Ishapian ship.

He gauged his distance and the motion, then turned and shouted past Bear, "One point to port! Ramming speed!"

Bear echoed the command, "Ramming speed!" Then he shouted, "Catapults! Ready!"

Flames appeared as torches were quickly lit, and then those torches were put to large bundles of skins full of Quegan Fire oil. They burst into flame and the catapult officer shouted, "Ready, Captain!"

Bear's deep voice rumbled as he gave the order: "Fire!"

The lookout squinted against the wind-driven salt spray. He was certain he saw something shoreward. Suddenly a flame appeared. Then a second. For a moment size and distance were difficult to judge, but the sailor quickly realized with a surge of fear that two large balls of fire sped toward the ship.

Angry orange-red flames sizzled and cracked as the first missile arced overhead, missing the lookout by mere yards. As the fireball shot past, he could feel the searing heat.

"Attack!" he shouted at the top of his lungs. He knew

full well the entire night watch had seen the fiery missiles; nonetheless it was his task to alert the crew.

The second fireball struck mid-decks, hitting the companionway that ran from below to the foredeck, and an unfortunate priest of Ishap was consumed in the sticky flames. He screamed in agony and confusion as he died.

The sailor knew that if they were being boarded, staying aloft was not a good idea. He swung from the crow's nest and slid down a stay sheet to the deck below as another ball of flame appeared in the sky, arcing down to strike the foredeck.

As his bare feet touched the wooden planks, another sailor who shouted, "Quegan raiders!" handed him a sword and buckler shield.

The thudding of a hortator's drum echoed across the waves. Suddenly the night came alive with noise and cries.

From out of the gloom a ship reared, lifted high by a huge swell, and the two sailors could see the massive serrated iron ram extending from the galley's prow. Once it slammed into its victim's hull, its teeth would hold the rammed ship close, until the signal was given for the galley slaves to reverse their stroke. By backing water, the galley would tear a massive hole in Ishap's Dawn's side, quickly sending her to the bottom.

For an instant the lookout feared he would never see his children or wife again, and hastily uttered a prayer to whatever gods listened that his family be cared for. Then he resolved to fight, for if the sailors could hold the raiders at the gunwale until the priests emerged from below, their magic might drive off the attackers.

The ship heaved and the sound of tearing wood and shrieking men filled the night as the raider crashed into the Ishapian ship. The lookout and his companions were thrown to the deck.

As the lookout rolled away from the spreading fire, he saw two hands gripping the ship's gunwale. The lookout gained his feet as a dark-skinned pirate cleared the side of the ship, and boarded with a leap to the deck, others following.

The first pirate carried a huge sword, curved and weighted, and he grinned like a man possessed. The lookout hurried toward him, his sword and shield at the ready. The pirate's hair hung in oiled locks that glistened in the light from the flames. His wide eyes reflected the orange firelight, which gave him a demonic cast. Then he smiled and the lookout faltered, as the filed pointed teeth revealed the man to be a cannibal from the Shaskahan Islands.

Then the lookout's eyes widened as he saw another figure rear up behind the first.

It was the last thing the lookout saw, as the first pirate swung his sword and impaled the hapless man, who stood rooted in terror at the sight before him. With his dying breath, he gasped, "Bear."

Bear glanced around the deck. Massive hands flexed in anticipation as he spoke. His voice seemed to rumble from deep within as he said, "You know what I'm after; everything else is yours for the taking!"

Knute leaped from the raider's craft to stand at Bear's side. "We hit 'em hard, so you don't have much time!" he shouted to the crew. As Knute had hoped, Bear's men rushed to kill the Ishapian sailors, while Knute signaled to the handful from his old crew, who headed toward the hatches and the cargo nets.

An Ishapian monk, climbing up the aft companionway to answer the alarm, saw the pirates spreading out in a half-circle around him. His brothers followed after. For a

moment, both sides stood motionless, as they measured one another.

Bear stepped forward and in a voice like grinding stones said to the first monk, "You there! Bring me the Tear and I'll kill you quickly."

The monk's hands came up and moved rapidly in a mystic pattern while enchanting a prayer to summon magic. The other monks took up fighting stances behind him.

A bolt of white energy flashed at Bear, but vanished harmlessly just inches before him as the ship heeled over and started to dip at the bow. With a scornful laugh, Bear said, "Your magic means nothing to me!"

With surprising speed for a man his size, Bear lashed out with his sword. The monk, still recovering from the shock of his magic's impotence, stood helpless as Bear ran him through as if cutting a melon with a kitchen knife. The pirates let loose a roar of triumph and fell upon the other monks.

The monks, though empty-handed and outnumbered, were all trained in the art of open-handed fighting. In the end they could not stand up to pole weapons and swords, knives and crossbows, but they delayed the pirates long enough that the forecastle was already underwater before Bear could reach the companionway leading below decks.

Like a rat through a sewer grating, Knute was past Bear and down the companionway. Bear came second, the others behind.

"We've got no time!" shouted Knute, looking around the aft crew quarters; from the abundant religious items in view, he judged this area had been given over to the monks for their personal use. Knute could hear water rushing into the hole below the forecastle. Knute knew ships; eventually a bulkhead between the forecastle and

the main cargo hold would give way and then the ship would go down like a rock.

A small wooden chest sitting in the corner caught his eye and he made straight for it, while Bear moved to a large door that led back to the captain's cabin. Movement was becoming more difficult as the deck was now tilting, and walking up its slick surface was tricky. More than one pirate fell, landing hard upon the wooden planks.

Knute opened the small chest, revealing enough gems to keep him in luxury for the rest of his life. Like moths to a flame, several raiders turned toward the booty. Knute motioned to two other pirates close by and said, "If you want a copper for all this slaughter, get up on deck, help open the hatch, and lower the cargo net!"

Both men hesitated, then looked to where Bear struggled to open the door. They glanced at one another, then did as Knute instructed. Knute knew they would find two of his men already at the hatch and would fall in to help. If Knute's plan were to work, everyone would have to do his part without realizing that the order of things on the ship had changed.

Knute unlatched a trapdoor in the middle of the deck, and let it swing open, revealing the companionway leading down into the cargo hold. As he stepped through the opening toward the treasure below, the ship started to take on water, and he knew she was fated to go down quickly by the bow. He and his men would have to move fast.

Bear was smashing himself uphill against a door that obviously had some sort of mystic lock upon it, for it hardly moved under his tremendous bulk. Knute cast a quick glance backward and saw the wood near the hinges splintering. As he lowered himself into the hold, Knute looked down. He knew that there was enough treasure below to make every man aboard a king, for the odd man

named Sidi who had told Bear about this ship had said that ten years' worth of Temple wealth from the Far Coast and Free Cities would accompany the magic item Bear was to bring him.

Knute regretted having met Sidi; when he had first met him, he had no idea the so-called trader trafficked in the magic arts. Once he had discovered the truth, it was too late. And Knute was certain there was far more to Sidi than was obvious; Sidi had given Bear his magic amulet, the one that he refused to remove, day or night. Knute had always stayed away from magic, temple, wizard, or witch. He had a nose for it and it made him fearful, and no man in his experience reeked of it like Sidi, and there was nothing tender about that reek.

The cargo hatch above moved, and a voice shouted downward, "Knute?"

"Lower away!" commanded the little thief.

The cargo net descended and Knute quickly released it. "Get down here!" he shouted as he spread the large net across the center of the deck. "We're taking on water fast!"

Four sailors slid down ropes and started moving the heavy cargo chests to the center of the net. "Get the small ones first!" instructed Knute. "They'll be gems. Worth more than gold, pound for pound."

The sailors were driven by two goals: greed and fear of Bear. The massive captain was smashing through the door above with inhuman strength, and everyone in the crew knew as well as Knute that Bear was becoming more violent by the day. Even his own crew now feared to be noticed by Bear.

One of the men paused to listen to the fiendish shout as Bear finally smashed through the door. A half-dozen pirates, finished with butchering the ship's crew, descended the ropes from the deck above and looked questioningly

at the pilot. Knute said, "The captain said everything else was ours for the taking if he got that damn stone the priests were guarding. You going to let all this sink?"

They shook their heads and set to, working in pairs to move the larger chests and sacks into the nets, although Knute could see the doubt on their faces. But they hurried and got most of the booty in the net and tied it off.

"Haul away!" Knute shouted to the men above.

Pirates grabbed small chests and sacks and attempted to get back to the forward ladder. The ship was now heading down by the bow, picking up speed and rocking slightly from side to side. "Tell them to back water!" shouted Knute, as he negotiated the ladder to the upper deck, clutching the small wooden chest as a mother would a baby. He saw a brilliant light coming through the captain's cabin door and his eyes widened. Bear stood outlined against the glare, obviously struggling through the water as if engaged with a foe of some kind. "Get out!" shouted Knute. "You're going to drown!" Not that Knute would shed a tear if that happened, but if Bear somehow came to his senses and made good his escape, Knute wanted to appear convincing in his role as loyal and concerned pilot.

Knute hurried to the gunwale and nimbly leaped atop it. Glancing at those behind him who were sliding across the deck, trying for the boat below, he called, "Hurry!" The galley was backing away, and water rushed quickly into the hull of the Ishapian ship. Knute knew that, had he not given the order to back the galley, the weight of the dying ship might have pulled its bow under the waves.

A longboat bobbed on the water a few yards below and he muttered, "By the gods, I've gotta get out of this business."

He glanced upward and saw the cargo boom with the net loaded with treasure being lowered to the deck of the

galley. With a quick prayer to every god he could remember, Knute leaped from the sinking ship, hitting the water while he clutched the small chest with all his might. Weight pulled him downward and he struggled, and finally his head broke the surface as voices echoed across the water. With his free arm he struck out for the longboat, reaching it quickly. Strong hands reached over the side and pulled him aboard.

"The ship sinks!" men yelled as they leaped from the deck into the foam.

"Leave the rest!" shouted a man holding what appeared to be a large sack of gold coins. He hit the water, and after a minute his head broke the surface. He struggled mightily to get the sack aboard Knute's boat.

"No! Noooo!" came Bear's anguished cry from the bowels of the sinking ship as Knute helped the pirate aboard the boat.

"Sounds like the boss is having a problem," said the drenched pirate.

"Row," instructed Knute. The sailor complied and Knute looked over his shoulder. "Whatever the boss's problems, they're no longer ours."

"You going to leave him?" said one of Knute's men.

"Let's see if that cursed amulet keeps him alive on the bottom of the sea."

One of the pirates grinned. Like the rest of his brethren he had been obedient out of fear as much as any loyalty to Bear. "If it does, he's going to kill you, Knute."

"He's got to find me first," said the wily pilot. "I've sailed with that murdering lunatic three times, which is two too many. You've been his slaves long enough. Now it's our turn to live the high life!"

The pirates rowed. One of Bear's crew said, "If he does make it out alive, he'll find others to follow him, you

know that? Why shouldn't I cut your throat now and gain his favor?"

"Because you're greedy, like me. If you cut my throat, you'll never get that galley safely out of these rocks. Besides, even if Bear lives, it'll be too late," said Knute. "We'll all be safely gone."

They reached the galley and quickly climbed aboard, other longboats and a few swimmers reaching the ship at the same time. The ship creaked as the longboats were hoisted aboard. Men scrambled up ropes while others lowered nets to haul the riches taken from the Ishapian ship. The crew moved with an efficiency rarely seen, spurred on by equal shares of avarice and the fear that Bear would suddenly appear. Finally they lashed the cargo to the center deck and Knute said, "Get underway!"

"Where are we going?" asked one of the pirates who had rowed Knute to the galley.

"To a rendezvous down the coast. I've got some men waiting for us who will offload this cargo, then we row this galley out to sea and sink it."

"Why?" asked another man as the crew gathered around Knute.

"Why?" echoed Knute. "I'll tell you why, fool. That ship we took was the property of the Temple of Ishap. In a few days the entire world is going to be looking for the men who sank it. Bear's got that ward against priests, but we don't. We'll divide up our shares and go our separate ways, tonight!"

"Sounds good," said one of the sailors.

"Then get to the oars! The slaves are half dead and I want us split up and every man on his own by sunrise!" shouted Knute.

Just then, Bear's voice cut through the storm. "It's mine!! I had it in my hands!"

All eyes turned to the sinking ship, and against a lightning flash they could see Bear standing at the rail. Slowly, he climbed atop it, shook his fist at the retreating galley, and leaped into the water.

Like a spur to a horse, the sight of Bear plunging into the water as if to swim after them caused the sailors to spring to action. Below, the hortator's drum began to sound as slaves were unchained and pushed aside by frantic pirates. Knute paused a moment to look where Bear had stood outlined against the lightning flashes. For an instant Knute could have sworn Bear's eye had been glowing red.

Knute shuddered and turned his mind away from Bear. The man was terrible in his anger and his strength was unmatched, but even Bear wouldn't be able to storm into the Prince's city and find Knute.

Knute smiled. The men waiting for him were expecting a ship full of riches and a dead crew. Poisoned wine and ale waited below, and Knute would pass it out minutes before reaching the rendezvous. By the time the cargo was offloaded and aboard the wagons, every pirate and slave below would be a corpse. His own men would also be departed, but that was an unfortunate circumstance he couldn't avoid. Besides, it meant more for him and those driving the wagons.

All his life he had waited for an opportunity like this and he was going to be ruthless in taking advantage of it. None of these men would lift a finger to help Knute, he knew, if his life was at risk, so what did he owe them? Honor among thieves might exist with the Mockers, where the Upright Man's bashers ensured honorable behavior, but on a ship like Bear's, the rule was strictly survival by strength, or by wits.

Knute shouted orders and the ship heeled over as it

turned against the waves, striking for a safer course away from the rocks of Widow's Point. Soon the ship was clear of the last of the underwater rocks, and the rowers struck a steady pace. The little pilot moved to the stern of the galley and looked over the fantail. In a brief flash, for an instant, he thought he saw something in the water. It was a swimmer, following after the ship with a powerful stroke.

Knute's eyes strained as he peered through the darkness, but nothing more was glimpsed of the swimmer. He rubbed his eyes. It must be the excitement, he thought, the chance to at last be rich and out from under the heel of men like Bear.

Turning his mind to the future, he again grinned. He had made deals before. He would pay off the wagoners, have them killed if necessary, and by the time he reached Krondor, every silver coin, every golden chain, every sparkling gem would be his.

"Where are we going?" asked a pirate.

"*Captain,*" said Knute.

"What?"

"Where are we going, *Captain,*" Knute repeated, coolly.

The pirate shrugged, as if it didn't matter, and said, "Where are we going, Captain? How far down the coast are your men?"

Knute grinned, knowing that this man—like every other man in the crew—would happily let him play at command up to the minute they'd cut his throat if they thought he would make them rich. He played along. "We're meeting a gang at the beach north of Fishtown, outside of Krondor."

"Fishtown it is!" said the man, quickly adding, "Captain!"

* * *

Throughout the night the crew rowed, and when dawn was less than two hours away, Knute called one of his most trusted crewmen over. "How are things?"

"Bear's men are nervous, but they're not smart enough to plan anything if they think they might lose out on what we've taken. But they're still jumpy. You don't cross someone like Bear and sleep soundly."

Knute nodded, then said, "If everything's secure, there's some wine and ale below. Break it out."

"Aye, Captain," said the man, his grin widening. "A celebration, eh? That will take the edge off."

Knute returned the grin, but said nothing.

Within minutes the noise of celebration emanated from below. For hours all Knute had heard was an ominous silence punctuated by the sound of rhythmic rowing, oars groaning in their oarlocks, wood creaking as the hull flexed, and the rattle of tackle and blocks in the rigging. Now the murmur of voices arose, some joking, others surprised, as men made the rounds of the rowing benches with casks and cups.

One of the pirates looked at Knute across the deck and Knute shouted, "See that those aloft go below for a quick drink! I'll take the helm!"

The pirate nodded, then shouted aloft as Knute made his way to the stern of the ship. He said to the helmsman, "Go get something to drink. I'll take her in."

"Going to beach her, Captain?"

Knute nodded. "We're coming in a bit after low tide. She's heavy as a pregnant sow with all this booty. Once we offload, when high tide comes in, she'll lift right off the beach and we can back her out."

The man nodded. He was familiar with the area near Fishtown; the beaches were gentle and Knute's plan made sense.

Knute had chosen a slow-acting poison. As he took the helm, he calculated that he'd be coming into the beach by the time the first men began to pass out. With luck, those still alive would assume their companions were insensible from drink. With even more luck, the wagoners he had hired out of Krondor wouldn't have to cut any throats. They were teamsters working for a flat fee, not bully boys.

Knute had piled one lie atop another. The wagoners thought he was working for the Upright Man of Krondor, the leader of the Guild of Thieves. Knute knew that without that lie he would never control them once they saw the wealth he was bringing into the city. If the teamsters didn't believe a dread power stood behind Knute, he'd be as dead as the rest of the crew come morning.

The sound of the water changed, and in the distance Knute could hear breakers rolling into the beach. He hardly needed to look to know where he was.

One of the pirates came staggering up the companionway from below and spoke. His speech was slurred. "Captain, what's in this ale? The boys are passin' . . ." Knute smiled at the seaman, a young thug of perhaps eighteen years. The lad pitched forward. A few voices from below shouted up to the deck, but their words were muffled, and quiet soon descended.

The oars had fallen silent and now came the most dangerous part of Knute's plan. He lashed down his tiller, sprang to the ratlines and climbed aloft. Alone he lowered one small sail, shimmied down a sheet, and tied off. That little sail was all he had to keep him from turning broad to the waves and being smashed upon the beach.

As he reached the tiller, a hand descended upon Knute's shoulder, spinning him around. He was confronted by a leering grin of sharpened teeth as dark eyes studied him. "Shaskahan don't drink ale, little man."

Knute froze. He let his hand slip to a dagger in his belt but waited to see what the cannibal would do next. The man was motionless. "Don't drink ale," he repeated.

"I'll give you half the gold," Knute whispered.

"I take all of it," said the cannibal, as he drew out his large belt knife. "And then I eat you."

Knute leaped backward and drew his own knife. He knew that he was no match for the veteran killer, but he was fighting for his life and the biggest trove of riches he would ever see. He waited, praying for a few more moments.

The cannibal said again, "Shaskahan don't drink ale." Knute saw the man's legs begin to shake as he took a step forward. Suddenly the man was on his knees, his eyes going blank. Then he fell face forward. Knute cautiously knelt next to the man and examined him. He sheathed his knife as he leaned close to the cannibal's face, sniffed once, then stood.

"You don't drink ale, you murdering whore's son, but you *do* drink brandy."

With a laugh Knute unlashed the tiller as the ship swept forward into breakers. He pointed it like an arrow at a long, flat run of beach and as the ship plowed prow first into the sand, he saw the three large wagons sitting atop the bluffs. Six men who'd been sitting on the shore leapt to their feet as the ship ground to a halt in the sand. Knute had ordered the wagons not be brought down to the cove, for once loaded they'd be sunk to their hubs in sand. The teamsters would have to cart all the gold up the small bluff to the wagons. It would be hard, sweaty work.

No sooner had the ship stopped moving than Knute was shouting orders. The six wagoners hurried forward, while Knute pulled his knife. He was going to ensure no one below recovered from too little poison, then he was going to get that treasure to Krondor.

There was one man in the world he knew he could trust and that man would help him hide all these riches. Then Knute would celebrate, get drunk, pick a fight, and get himself thrown into jail. Let Bear come for him, thought Knute, if by some miracle he had survived. Let the crazed animal of a pirate try to reach him in the bowels of the city's stoutest jail, surrounded by the city watch. That would never happen—at the very least Bear would be captured by the city guards; more likely he'd be killed. Once Knute knew for certain Bear's fate, he could bargain for his own life. For he was the only man who knew where the Ishapian ship had gone down. He could lead the Prince's men and a representative of the Wreckers' Guild to the site, where the Wreckers' Guild's mage could raise the ship and they could offload whatever trinket it was that Bear had been after. Then he'd be a free man while Bear rotted in the Prince's dungeon or hung from the gibbet or rested at the bottom of the sea. And let everyone think the rest of the treasure went down with the pirate ship in the deep water trench just a mile offshore.

Knute congratulated himself on his masterful plan, and set about his grisly work, as the wagoners from Krondor climbed aboard to offload "the Upright Man's treasure."

Miles away as the dawn broke, a solitary figure emerged from the breakers. His massive frame hung with clothing tattered and soaked from hours in the brine. He had tossed aside his weapons to lighten himself for a long swim. One good eye surveyed the rocks and he calculated where he had come ashore. With dry sand under his now bare feet, the huge pirate let out a scream of primal rage.

"Knute!" he shouted at the sky. "By the dark god I'll hunt you down and have your liver on a stick. But first you'll tell me where the Tear of the Gods is!"

Knowing that he had to find weapons and a new pair of boots, Bear turned northward, toward the secret temple at Widow's Peak and the village of Haldon's Head. There he would find some men to serve him and with their help they would track down Knute and the others. Every member of his crew who had betrayed him would die a slow, agonizing death. Again Bear let out a bellow of rage. As the echoes died against the windswept rocks, he squared his shoulders and began walking.

One

◆

Arrival

James hurried through the night.

As he moved purposefully across the courtyard of the Prince's palace in Krondor, he still felt the odd ache and twinge, reminders of his recent beating at the hands of the Nighthawks while he had been their captive. For the most part he was nearly back to his usual state of fitness. Despite that, he still felt the need for more sleep than usual, so of course, he had only just settled into a deep slumber when a page came knocking upon his door and informed James that the overdue caravan from Kesh had been sighted approaching the city. James had gotten up and dressed despite every fiber of his being demanding that he roll over in his warm bed and return to slumber.

Silently cursing the need to meet the arriving magician, he reached the outer gate where two guards stood their stations.

"Evening, gentlemen. All's well?"

The senior of the two guards, an old veteran named Crewson, saluted. "Quiet as the grave, Squire. Where're you bound at this ungodly hour?" He motioned for the other guard to open the gate so that James could leave the precinct of the palace.

Stifling a yawn, James said, "The Prince's new mage has arrived from Stardock, and I've the dubious honor of meeting her at the North Gate."

The younger guard smiled in mock sympathy. "Ah, you've all the luck, Squire." He swung the gate wide to allow James to depart.

With a wry smile, James passed through the opening. "I'd rather have a good night's sleep, but duty calls. Fare you well, gentlemen."

James picked up his pace, as he knew the caravan would disband quickly upon arrival. He wasn't worried about the magician's safety, as the city guard would be augmented by caravan guards coming off duty, but he was concerned over the possible lapse in protocol should he not be there to greet her. While she might be only a distant relative of the Ambassador from Great Kesh to the Western Court, she was still a noble by rank, and relations between the Kingdom of the Isles and Great Kesh had never been what one might call tranquil. A good year was one in which there were three or fewer border skirmishes.

James decided to take a shortcut from the palace district to the North Gate, one that would require he pass through a warehouse district behind the Merchants' Quarter. He knew the city as well as any living man, and had no concerns about getting lost, but when two figures detached themselves from the shadows as he rounded a corner, he cursed himself for a fool. The out-of-the-way route was unlikely to be host to many citizens abroad on lawful business at this time of night. And these two looked nothing like lawful citizens.

One carried a large billy club and had a long belt knife, while the other rested his hand easily upon a sword. The first wore a red leather vest while his companion wore a

simple tunic and trousers. Both had sturdy boots on, and James instantly recognized them for what they were: common street thugs. They were almost certainly free-booters, men not associated with the Mockers, the Guild of Thieves.

James pushed aside his self-recriminations for taking this shortcut, for the matter was now beyond changing.

The first man said, "Ah, what's the city coming to?"

The second nodded, moving to flank James should he try to run. "It's a sad state of affairs. Gentlemen of means, wanderin' the streets after midnight. What can they be thinking?"

Red-vest pointed his billy club at James and said, "He must be thinkin' his purse is just too heavy and be hopin' for a helpful pair like us to relieve him of it."

James let out a slow breath and calmly said, "Actually, I was thinking about the foolishness of men who don't recognize a dangerous mark when they see one." He drew his rapier slowly and moved the point to halfway between the two men, so that he would be able to parry an attack from either man.

"The only danger here is tryin' to cross us," said the second thug, drawing his sword and lashing out at James.

"I really don't have time for this," James said. He parried the blow easily and riposted. The swordsman barely pulled back in time to avoid being skewered like a holiday pig.

Red-vest pulled out his belt knife and swung his billy club, but James ducked aside and kicked out with his right leg, propelling the man into his companion. "You still have time to run away, my friends."

Red-vest grunted, recovered his balance, and rushed James, threatening with the billy club while holding his knife in position to do the real damage. James recognized

the man's outrage—this was no longer a simple mugging; these two men now meant to kill him. He ignored the billy club, dodging toward it rather than away, and sliced at the man's left wrist. The knife fell to the stones with a clatter.

While Red-vest howled in pain and fell back, his companion came rushing in, his sword cocked back over his shoulder. James danced backward for two steps, and as the man let fly with his wide swing—designed to decapitate the young squire—James leaned forward in a move he had learned from the Prince, his left hand touching the stones to aid his balance and his right hand extending out. The attacker's sword passed harmlessly over James's head and he ran onto the point of James's rapier. The man's eyes widened in shock and he came to an abrupt halt, looked down in disbelief, then collapsed to his knees. James pulled his sword point free and the man toppled over.

The other brigand caught James by surprise coming over the shoulder of his collapsing friend, and James barely ducked away from a thrust that would have certainly split his head. He took a glancing blow on his left shoulder, still sore from the beating he had taken at the hands of the Nighthawks, and gasped at the unexpected pain. The hilt of the knife had struck, so there was no blood—his tunic wasn't even ripped—but damn it, he thought, it hurt!

James's training and battle-honed reflexes took over, and he turned with the attacker, his sword lashing out again as the man went by, and stood behind him as he too went down to his knees, then toppled over. James didn't even have to look to know his sword had cut Red-vest's throat in a single motion.

James wiped his sword off on the shirt of the first man

he had killed and returned it to its sheath. Rubbing his sore left shoulder, he shook his head and muttered, "Idiots," quietly under his breath. Resuming his journey he marveled, not for the first time, at humanity's capacity for stupidity. For every gifted, brilliant man like Prince Arutha, there seemed to be a hundred—no, make that a thousand—stupid men.

Better than most men in the Prince's court, James understood the petty motives and narrow appetites of most citizens. As he turned his back on the two dead men, he acknowledged to himself that most of the population were decent people, people who were tainted by only a little larceny, a small lie about taxes owed, a little shorting of a measure, but in the main they were good.

But he had seen the worst and best of the rest, and had gone from a fraternity of men bent on trivial gain by any means, including murder, to a fellowship of men who would sacrifice even their own lives for the greater good.

His ambition was to be like them, to be noble by strength of purpose and clarity of vision rather than by accident of birth. He wanted one day to be remembered as a great defender of the Kingdom.

Ironically, he considered how unlikely it was that that would ever happen, given his current circumstance. He was now commissioned to create a company of spies, intelligence men who were to act on behalf of the Crown. He doubted Prince Arutha would appreciate him telling the ladies and gentleman of the court about it.

Still, he reminded himself as he turned another corner—glancing automatically into the shadows to see if anyone lurked there—the deed was the thing, not the praise.

Absently rubbing his right shoulder with his left hand, he noted how it had been overstrained by the swordplay.

The little exercise with the two brigands was reminding him he wasn't fully healed from his recent ordeal in the desert at the hands of the Nighthawks—a band of fanatic assassins. He had been up and around within days of returning to Krondor, but he was still feeling not quite right after three weeks. And two sore shoulders would continue to remind him of it all for a couple of days, at least.

Sighing aloud, James muttered to himself: "Not as spry as I once was, I fear."

He cut through another alley that brought him around the corner to the street leading to the North Gate. He found himself passing the door of a new orphanage, recently opened by the Order of Dala, the goddess known as "Shield to the Weak." The sign above the door featured a yellow shield with the Order's mark upon it. Princess Anita had been instrumental in helping to secure the title to the building and funding it for the Order. James wondered absently how different his life might have been had he found his way to such a place when his mother had died, rather than ending up in the Guild of Thieves.

In the distance he could see two guardsmen speaking with a solitary young woman. He left off his musings and quickened his pace.

As he approached, he studied the young woman. Several facts were immediately manifest. He had expected a noblewoman of Kesh, bedecked in fine silks and jewelry, with a complement of servants and guards at her disposal. Instead he beheld a solitary figure, wearing clothing far more appropriate for rigorous travel than for court ceremony. She was dark-skinned, not as dark as those who lived farther south in Great Kesh, but darker than was common in Krondor, and in the gloom of night, her dark hair, tied back in a single braid, reflected the flickering torchlight with a gleam like a raven's wing. Her eyes,

when they turned upon James, were also dark, almost black in the faint light.

Her bearing and the set of her eyes communicated an intensity that James often admired in others, if it was leavened with intelligence. There could be no doubt of intelligence, else Pug would never have recommended her for the post as Arutha's magical advisor.

She carried a heavy staff of either oak or yew, shod at both ends in iron. It was a weapon of choice among many travelers, especially those who by inclination or lack of time couldn't train in blades and bows. James knew from experience it was not a weapon to be taken lightly; against any but the most heavily-armored foe a staff could break bones, disarm or render an opponent unconscious. And this woman appeared to have the muscle to wield it effectively. Unlike the ladies of Arutha's court, her bare arms showed the effects of strenuous labor or hours spent in the weapons yard.

As he neared, James summed up his first impression of the new court magician: a striking woman, not pretty but very attractive in an unusual way. Now James understood his friend William's distress at the news of her appointment to the Prince's court. If she had been his first lover, as James suspected, William would not easily put her behind him, not for many years. Given his young friend's recent infatuation with Talia, the daughter of a local innkeeper, James chuckled to himself as he surmised that William's personal life was about to get very interesting. James didn't envy him the discomfort, but knew it would no doubt prove entertaining to witness. He smiled to himself as he closed upon the group.

One of the two guards conversing with the young woman noticed James and greeted him. "Well met, Squire. We've been expectin' you."

James nodded and replied, "Gentlemen. My thanks for keeping an eye on our guest."

The second guard chimed in. "We felt bad, I mean, her bein' a noble and all, and havin' to wait so long, but we didn't have enough men to send with her to the palace." He indicated the other pair at the far end of the gate.

James appreciated their dilemma. If any of them had left his post, for whatever reason, without permission, the guard captain would have had their ears. "Not to worry. You've done your duty."

Turning to the young woman, James bowed and said, "Your pardon, milady, for making you wait. I am Squire James of Krondor."

The young magician smiled and suddenly James reevaluated his appraisal. She was very pretty, if in an unusual fashion for the women of the Western Kingdom. She said, "It is I who should apologize for arriving at this unseemly hour, but our caravan was delayed. I am Jazhara, most recently of Stardock."

Glancing around, James said, "A pleasure to meet you, Jazhara. Where is your entourage?"

"At my father's estates on the edge of the Jal-Pur desert. I had no servants at Stardock and requested none to travel here. I find that the use of servants tends to weaken the will. Since I began studying the mystic arts, I have always traveled alone."

James found the availability of servants one of the key attractions of the Prince's court; always having someone around to send on errands or fetch things was very useful. He was also now embarrassed to discover he should have ordered a squad of soldiers to escort Jazhara and himself back to the palace; her rank required such, but he had assumed she'd have her own bodyguards in place. Still, if she didn't bring it up, neither would he. He merely said,

"I quite understand. If you are willing, however, we can leave your baggage under the watch of the guards, and I will arrange to have it brought to the palace in the morning."

"That will be fine. Shall we go?"

He decided to avoid shortcuts and keep to the broader thoroughfares. It would take a bit longer to reach the palace, but would afford them safer travel. He suspected that in addition to knowing how to use that staff to good effect, Jazhara probably had several nasty magician's tricks at her disposal, but the risk of an international incident to save a few minutes' walk wasn't worth it.

Deciding that being direct was his best course, James asked, "What does your great-uncle think of this appointment?"

Jazhara smiled. "I do not know, but I suspect he is less than happy. Since he was already unhappy that I chose to study at Stardock—over my father's objections—rather than marry a 'suitable young lord,' I fear I've likely put him in a dark mood."

James smiled. "Having met your great-uncle on a few occasions, I should think you'd want to stay on his good side."

With a slight twist of her lips, Jazhara said, "To the world he is the mighty Lord Hazara-Khan, a man to be dreaded by those who put their own interests ahead of the Empire's. To me he is Uncle Rachman—'Raka' I called him because I couldn't manage his name when I was little—and he can deny me little. He wanted to marry me off to a minor prince of the Imperial House, a distant cousin to the Empress, but when I threatened to run away if he sent me south, he relented."

James chuckled. They rounded a corner and headed

down a large boulevard that would eventually lead them back to the palace.

After only a few minutes, James found himself enjoying the company of this young woman from Kesh. She was quick, observant, keen-eyed, and witty. Her banter was clever and entertaining without the acerbic, nasty edge one found so often among the nobles of the Prince's court.

Unfortunately, she was too entertaining: James suddenly realized he had turned a corner a few streets back without thinking and now they were in the area he had planned on avoiding.

"What is it?" Jazhara asked.

James turned and grinned at her, a grin that could barely be seen in the faint glow of a distant lantern hanging outside an inn. "You're very perceptive, milady."

"It's part of the trade, sir," she replied, her voice a mix of playfulness and caution. "Is something wrong?"

"I just got caught up in our discourse and without thought turned us into a part of the city it might be best to avoid at this hour."

James noticed a very slight shift in the way she held her staff, but her voice remained calm. "Are we in danger?"

"Most probably not, but one never knows in Krondor. Best to be alert. We shall be at the palace in a few minutes."

Without comment, they both picked up the pace slightly, and hurried along, each watching the side of the street for possible assailants in the gloom, James taking the left, Jazhara the right.

They had rounded the corner that put them in sight of the palace district when a sound echoed off to James's left. He turned and as he did so he recognized the trap: a pebble being tossed from the right.

As he turned back toward Jazhara, a small figure darted from the shadows. Jazhara had also spun to look in the same direction as James and was slow to recover.

The assailant darted close, a blade flashed, and suddenly a child was running down the street clutching Jazhara's purse.

James had been prepared for an attack, so it took an instant for him to realize that a street urchin had robbed Jazhara. "Hey! Stop! Come back here!" he shouted after the fleeing child.

"We have to stop him," said Jazhara. "Besides a few coins, my purse has items which could prove fatal to a child."

James didn't hesitate.

He knew the city as well as any man, and after a moment's pursuit, he slowed. "What is it?" asked Jazhara.

"If memory serves, he just ducked into a dead end."

They turned into the alley after the cutpurse and saw no sign of him.

"He's gone!" Jazhara exclaimed.

James laughed. "Not quite."

He moved to what looked to be some heavy crates, and reached around behind them, pulling away a piece of cloth tacked to the back. With a quick motion, in case the young thief was inclined to use the blade to defend himself, James snatched a thin arm.

"Let me go!" shouted a young girl who looked no older than ten, dressed in rags. She dropped her blade and Jazhara's purse on the cobbles.

James knew it was a ruse to get him to release her arm and pick up the purse, so he held firm. "If you're going to be a thief, you must learn who to mark and who to leave be."

He turned to block her path if she tried to run and held

her arm loosely. Kneeling so that he was at eye level with her, he asked, "What's your name, sweetheart?"

Quickly sensing that this man and woman weren't trying to harm her, the girl relaxed slightly. "Nita," she said with a tiny hint of defiance. "Mommy called me that after Prince 'Rutha's wife, 'Nita."

James couldn't help but smile. He knew Princess Anita would be flattered to hear of that tiny honor. "I'm Squire James, and this is Jazhara, the court mage."

The girl seemed less than reassured at being confronted by two members of the court. "Are you going to take me to jail?"

"James," said Jazhara, "you're not going to put this child in jail, are you?"

With mock seriousness, James said, "By rights I should. A dangerous criminal like this preying on innocent people at night!"

The child's eyes widened slightly, but she stood unafraid and didn't flinch. James softened his tone. "No, child. We'll not put you in jail. There's a place we could take you, if you like. It's called the Sign of the Yellow Shield. They take care of children like you."

The reaction was instantaneous. "No! No! You're just like the other men. You're just like the bad men!" She struck at James's face with her free hand, and tried to pull away.

James hung on. "Hold on! Hold it! Stop hitting me for a minute."

The girl ceased hitting him, but still kept tugging. James slowly let go of her arm and held up his hands, palms out, showing that he was not going to grab her again. "Look, Nita, if you want to stay here that's fine. We're not going to hurt you," he said softly.

Jazhara asked, "Who were you talking about, Nita? Who were the bad men?"

The girl looked up at the mage and said, "They say they're like the Yellow Shield, and all good children go with them, but they hurt me!" Her eyes started to fill with tears, but her voice was firm.

James asked, "How did they hurt you?"

Nita looked at the former boy-thief and said, "They took me to the big house, and they locked me in a cage, like all the other children. Then they told me to dye cloth for Yusuf, or else they'd beat me, and some of the other children, the bad children, they took and they never came back and there were rats and squirmy things in our food and—"

"This is horrible," said Jazhara. "We *must* act on this 'Yusuf,' but first we must care for Nita."

"Well, I suppose we could take her to the palace," began James, turning to look at Jazhara.

It was the chance the girl had waited for. As soon as James looked away from her, she was off, sprinting down the alley toward the street.

James stood and watched her turn the corner, knowing that he could probably chase her down, but deciding not to. Jazhara stared at James with an unspoken question in her eyes. James said, "I told her she could stay with us if she wanted to."

Jazhara nodded. "Then you will do something about this?"

James leaned down to pick up Jazhara's purse. He dusted it off and as he handed it to her he said, "Of course I will. I grew up on these streets. This isn't about duty; it's personal."

Jazhara turned away from the palace and started walking back the way they had come.

"Hey!" said James, hurrying to catch up. "Where are you going?"

"Unless this Yusuf lives in the palace, we need to go deeper into this poor section of the city, I am guessing."

"Good guess," said James. "There's a dyer named Yusuf up in what's called 'Stink Town,' to the north—it's where all the tanners, slaughterhouses, and other aromatic businesses are housed. But now?"

Looking at James with a resolute expression, Jazhara said, "We can't start any sooner, can we?"

"Apparently not," replied James. Then he grinned.

James kept his eyes moving, peering into every shadow, while Jazhara gazed resolutely forward, as if fixed upon a goal. As they walked purposefully through the Poor Quarter of Krondor, Jazhara said, "Do you expect trouble?"

"Constantly," answered James, glancing down a side-street they were passing.

The rising stench in the air told them they were close to their destination, the area of the Poor Quarter given over to those businesses best kept downwind. "Where do you think this Yusuf resides?"

James said, "The cloth-makers are all located at the end of this street, and along two others nearby." Turning to look at Jazhara, he said, "You realize, of course, that the place will almost certainly be closed for the night?"

Jazhara smiled. "Which will give us an opportunity to look around unnoticed, correct?"

James smiled back. "I like the way you think, Jazhara."

Several times along the way they passed individuals hurrying by; the city was never truly asleep. Those who passed cast appraising glances at the pair, either as potential threats—or as possible victims.

They reached an intersection and glanced in both directions. Off to the left, all was quiet, but to James's sur-

prise down the street to the right a few places were still obviously open for business. "The dyers' trade must be very profitable for these establishments to be conducting business all night."

"Or they're paying nothing for their labor," said Jazhara as they passed one such open establishment. The door was ajar and a quick glance inside indicated there was nothing suspicious taking place; a dyer and others— obviously members of his family—were busy preparing a large shipment of cloth. Most likely it was to be delivered at dawn to tailors who had ordered the material.

They moved along the dimly-lit street until they reached a large, two-story building, before which stood a large man with a sword at his belt. He watched with a neutral expression as James and Jazhara approached.

James asked, "What is this place?"

The guard answered, "This is the shop of the honorable Yusuf ben Ali, the illustrious cloth merchant."

Jazhara asked, "Is he in?"

"No. Now, if that's all, you'll excuse me." Since the guard showed no sign of leaving, it was clear that he expected James and Jazhara to move along.

James said, "I find it odd to believe your master is out at this late hour, and you are merely standing here guarding a workshop in which no one is working." He moved to stand before the man. "I am Prince Arutha's squire."

Jazhara added, "And I his newly-appointed court mage."

At this the guard's eyes flickered over to her for an instant, then he said, "My master is indeed within. He is working late on a shipment that must leave tomorrow on a caravan and wishes not to be disturbed by any but the most important guest. I will see if he considers you to be important enough." He turned his back on them, saying, "Follow me to my master's office, but touch nothing."

They entered the building and discovered a brightly-lit
display area, showing finely-woven cloth dyed in the
most marvelous colors. A bolt of crimson silk was allowed to spill from a rack, the best to show off its scintillating color. Surrounding them was indigo and bright
yellow linen, cotton of every hue, all waiting for potential
buyers. A door to the rear of the showroom was closed,
and a narrow stairway ran up along the left wall to a single door. A large chandelier ablaze with a dozen candles
hung from the ceiling.

Beyond the viewing area, huge vats of dye stood, while
large drying racks held freshly dyed cloth. James saw two
children, no older than ten years, moving a rack aside to
make way for another being pushed by another pair of
children. The youngsters were dirty, and a few appeared
to shiver beneath their thin ragged clothing. Jazhara noticed one little girl, who looked to be about seven years
old, yawn, struggling to keep her eyes open as she pushed
the heavy drying rack. Two guards stood watching the
children.

The guard who had accompanied them inside said,
"Wait here. I will fetch my master."

James asked, "Isn't it late for the children to be working?"

The man said, "They are lazy. This order must be ready
by noon tomorrow. Had they finished at dusk, they would
be asleep in their beds now. They know this. Do not talk
to them; it will only slow them down. I will return with
my master."

The man hurried across the large room and disappeared through the rear door. A few minutes later, he and
another man returned. The newcomer was obviously a
merchant, yet he carried a curved desert sword—a scimitar. He wore Kingdom tunic and trousers, but elected a

traditional desert man's head cover, a black cloth wound as a turban, its length allowed to drape below the chin, from right to left, the end thrown across the left shoulder. He had a dark beard and the swarthy looks of Jazhara's countrymen, a fact confirmed as he reached them and said, "Peace be upon you," the traditional greeting of the people of the Jal-Pur.

Jazhara replied, "And upon you be peace."

"Welcome to my workhouse, my friends. My name is Yusuf ben Ali. How may I serve?"

James glanced back at the laboring children. "We've heard how you work around here. This place is being shut down."

If the man was surprised at this pronouncement, he didn't show it. He merely smiled. "Oh, you've heard, have you? And what exactly did you hear?"

Jazhara said, "We've heard about your working conditions and how you treat children."

Yusuf nodded. "And let me guess, you heard it from a young girl, perhaps less than a decade in age? Or was it a young boy this time?"

"What do you mean?" James asked.

"My dear sir, it was all a lie. My competitors have taken to paying children to accost guardsmen and other worthy citizens. They ply them with stories of the 'horrors of Yusuf's shop.' And then they vanish. My shop is then closed down for a few days while the Prince's magistrate investigates, and my competitors flourish."

Jazhara said, "But we've seen the working conditions inside."

Ben Ali glanced over at the ragged youngsters and shook his head slightly. "My dear countrywoman, I may be unable to provide for the children as I would like, but even I have a heart. They have a roof over their heads, and

hot meals, and clothes. It may not be the extravagance
that you would be used to, but, as the wise men taught us,
poverty is food to a righteous man, while luxury can be a
slow poison." He inclined his head toward the children.
"We work late tonight. This is not unusual in my trade,
but I assure you most nights these children would be
safely asleep. When this shipment is done, I shall send
them to their beds and they will be free tomorrow to
sleep; then, when they awake they shall have a day of rest
and play. What else would you have me do? Put them
back on the streets?"

Children working to support their families were nothing new in the Kingdom. But this smacked of something
close to slavery and James wasn't convinced this man
Yusef was what he seemed. "What about up there?" he
asked, pointing at the stairs.

"Ah, the second floor is under construction—we make
improvements. It is not safe at present to see, but when it
is done it will expand our capacities, and will include better quarters for the children."

James was about to speak, when Jazhara said, "James,
may I have a moment alone with this gentleman?"

James was surprised. "Why?"

"Please."

James glanced from Jazhara to Yusef, then said, "I'll
be outside."

When he was gone from the building, Jazhara lowered
her voice and said, "You work for my great-uncle?"

Yusef bowed slightly. "Yes, kin of Hazara-Khan, I do.
And I wished to speak to you alone. You did well sending
our young friend away. A Kingdom nobleman is a complication. Does he know your great-uncle's position?"

Jazhara smiled. "As Governor of the Jal-Pur, or as head
of Keshian Intelligence in the north?"

"The latter, of course."

"He may suspect, but what he knows is not the issue. This place is what matters. Is what the young girl said true?"

"The Imperial treasury hardly provides enough support for this operation," said Yusuf. "I must supplement my means; this shop is very successful, primarily because the labor is almost free." He looked at her disapproving expression and said, "I'm surprised at you. I expected a great-niece of Hazara-Khan to value practicality over misguided morality. Deceit, after all, is the first tool of our trade. What I do here aids me in my work."

"Then what the girl said was true. Does my great-uncle know about this?"

"I have never bothered to inform him of the details of my operation, no. But he appreciates my results. And now that you are here, they will be greater than ever!"

"What do you mean?"

"It is well known of your falling out with your family and your choice to study magic at Stardock. Only your great-uncle's power has shielded you from those in the Imperial Court who think you a potential risk. It is time for you to grow up and face your responsibilities. You are a child of the Empire, a citizen of Great Kesh. Your loyalties must lie with them."

"My loyalties also lie with this court, and the Prince. I am the court mage, the first to be appointed to this position."

Yusuf studied the young woman's face. "Sometimes the ties of blood must be held above the ties of hollow words."

"I am not a spy!"

"But you could be," insisted ben Ali. "Work for me; grant me secrets from the lips of Krondor's courtiers and

make your family proud!" His expression darkened. "Or disgrace your country, your family, and continue as you are. Your great-uncle can provide only limited protection if you swear that oath to Arutha." He paused, then added, "These are harsh choices, Jazhara. But you are now an adult, and the choice, as ever, must be yours. But know that from this point forward, whatever choice you make will change you forever."

Jazhara was silent for a long moment, as if considering the merchant's words. Finally she said, "Your words are harsh, Yusuf, but your actions have shown me where my loyalties lie."

"Then you will help me?"

"Yes. I will honor his teachings and the ideals of my nation."

"Excellent! You'd best leave now, before your friend becomes suspicious. Return again when you're settled into the prince's court and we shall begin."

She nodded and walked toward the door. She passed the still-laboring children, one of who looked up at her with eyes dulled from lack of sleep. In those eyes, Jazhara noted a flicker of fear. When she reached the door, she glanced over her shoulder at the smiling spy and the three guards who stood nearby.

James waited at the end of the alleyway. "Well?" he asked as she approached.

"Yusuf is a spy for my great-uncle."

James could barely conceal his surprise. "I don't know which I find more astonishing; that he is what you say, or that you've told me."

"When I left my father's court and trained at Stardock, I set aside my loyalty to Great Kesh. What my great-uncle does, he does for the betterment of the Empire." With a nod of her head to the entrance to Yusuf's shop, she added

with a steely edge to her voice, "But this one seeks to line his pockets with gold from the suffering of children, and his service to the Empire is of secondary concern, I am certain. Even were I in service to Kesh, I would not long abide his continued existence." She gripped her staff and James saw her knuckles go white. Although he'd known the court mage for but a few hours, he had no doubt she was not making an idle threat; no matter where Jazhara's loyalties might lie, she would see Yusuf pay for his crimes against the children.

"What do you propose?" he asked.

"There are but three guards. You are, I assume, a competent swordsman?"

"I am—" began James.

"As I am a competent magician," interrupted Jazhara. "Let's go."

As they strode back toward the dyer's shop, James felt the hair on his arms stand up, a sure sign magic was being gathered. He had never liked the feeling, even when he knew someone on his side was employing it. Jazhara said, "I will distract them. Try to take Yusuf alive."

James pulled out his rapier and muttered, "Four to one and you want me to try to keep one of them alive? Wonderful." Jazhara entered the shop ahead of James, and Yusuf turned as she did so. "What—?" he began.

Jazhara pointed her staff at him and a loud keening sound filled the air as a ball of blue energy exploded off the tip of the staff. It struck the merchant, doubling him over in pain.

James rushed past the magician, quickly scanning the room for a sign of the children. They were gone. The three armed guards hesitated for a moment, then sprang into action. James was about to strike the guard on his right when the energy ball caromed off Yusuf and struck

the guard to James's right. James quickly switched his attack to the center assailant.

James had fought multiple opponents before, and knew there were certain advantages. The most important thing he had found was that if his opponents hadn't practiced as a unit they tended to get in one another's way.

He lunged and took the center assailant under his guard, running him through. As he withdrew his blade, he leapt to his right and as he had hoped, the man on James's left stumbled into the dying man in the middle.

Yusuf's sword suddenly slashed the air near James's head. He had recovered from the magic Jazhara had thrown at him and was now on James's right, his scimitar expertly slicing the air.

"Great," James muttered. "The spy has to be a master swordsman."

The two remaining thugs had regained their feet and were a danger, but Yusuf was the true threat. "Jazhara! Keep those two off me, if you please."

Jazhara advanced and another burst of energy shot across the room, this time a red blast of lightning that caused the air to crackle as it struck the floor between James and the two guards. They quickly retreated as smoke began to rise from the wooden floor.

James didn't have time to appreciate the display, for Yusuf was proving a formidable opponent. It looked as if there would be almost no chance of keeping the Keshian spy alive, unless he got lucky. And given a choice, he'd rather keep himself alive than spare Yusuf and die in the process.

James used every trick he knew, a lethal inventory of combinations and feints. Twice he came close to cutting the Keshian, but twice in turn Yusuf came close to ending the struggle, too.

James circled and the turn brought Jazhara and the other two thugs into view. One had left the magician and was coming to help his master finish off James, while the other approached the magician warily, as Jazhara stood ready with her iron-shod staff before her.

James didn't hesitate. He feigned a blow to Yusuf's right hand, and as the Keshian moved to block, James spun to his own right, taking him away from the Keshian spy. Before Yusuf could recover, James was standing at his exposed left side, and all the merchant could manage was to fall away, avoiding a killing blow. This brought James right into the reach of the approaching guard, who lashed out high with his sword, a blow designed to decapitate the squire.

James ducked and thrust, running the man through. He then leapt to his right, knowing full well that Yusuf would be coming hard on his blind side. James hit the floor and rolled, feeling the scimitar slice the air above him. As he had hoped, Yusuf was momentarily slowed as he tried to avoid tripping over the falling corpse of his guard, and that afforded James enough time to regain his feet.

Off to one side, James could make out Jazhara and the other guard locked in combat. She wheeled the staff like an expert, taking his sword blows on hardened oak and lashing back with the iron tips. One good crack to the skull and the fight would be over, and both James and Jazhara's opponent knew that.

Yusuf came in with his sword point low, circling to his right. James glimpsed bales of cloth and display racks to his own right and moved to counter Yusuf. The spy wanted James's back to possible obstructions, so he might cause the squire to trip.

James knew it was now just a matter of who made the first mistake. He had been in struggles like this before,

and knew fear and fatigue were the enemies most to be avoided. Yusuf's face was a study in concentration: he was probably thinking the same thoughts.

James paused as if weighing which way to move, inviting Yusuf into committing himself to an attack. Yusuf declined. He waited. Both men were breathing heavily.

James resisted the urge to glance to where Jazhara struggled to finish off her opponent, knowing that to do so would invite an attack. The two men stood poised, each ready for an opening, each waiting for the other to commit.

Then James had an inspiration. He intentionally glanced to the left, at Jazhara, seeing her block a blow from the guard; she took the tip of the staff inside the man's guard, and James saw her deliver a punching blow with the iron end of the staff to the man's middle. He heard the man's breath explode out of his lungs, but didn't see it, for at that precise moment, James spun blindly away to his left.

As he had expected, Yusuf had acted the moment James's eyes wandered, and as he had also suspected, the attack came off a combination of blade movements. A feint to the heart, which should have caused James's sword to lash up and out, to block the scimitar, followed by a looping drop of the tip of the scimitar to a low, inside stab, designed to impale James in the lower belly.

But James wasn't there. Rather than parry, he had spun to the left, and again found himself on Yusuf's right hand. And rather than dance away, James closed. Yusuf hesitated for an instant, recognizing he was over-extended and needed to come back into a defensive posture. That was all James needed.

His rapier struck out and the point took Yusuf in the right side of his neck. With a sickening gurgling sound,

the spy stiffened. Then his eyes rolled up and his knees gave way and he fell to the floor.

James pulled out his sword and turned to see Jazhara break the skull of the last guard.

The man went down and Jazhara retreated, glancing around to see if any threats remained. Seeing only James standing upright, she rested on her staff as she tried to catch her breath.

James walked to her and said, "You all right?"

She nodded. "I'm fine."

James then looked around the room. Bolts of cloth were overturned and had been sent every which way, and many were now stained with crimson.

Letting out a long breath, James said, "What a mess."

Two

◆

Schemes

James sheathed his sword.

"Where did the children go?"

Jazhara looked around, then glanced up the stairs. "I'll look up there. You see if they are hiding in that office," she instructed, and pointed to the door at the rear of the shop.

James nodded, with a half-smile. No point in making an issue out of who was in charge, he thought, turning to comply with her instructions. She was, after all, a princess by birth. Then as he reached the door he wondered, *does* a court magician outrank a squire?

He opened the door, sword at the ready, in case someone else lurked within. He entered a small office at the center of which stood a writing table. Two burning lamps lighted the room, and a large chest stood against the far wall. The chest was apparently unlocked, its hasp hanging open, but James had received too many harsh lessons about trusting appearances, and so he approached the chest with caution. He glanced first at the papers spread across the writing table and saw several in a Keshian script he recognized. Most of these were orders for dyed cloth. Other letters in the King's Tongue were also

business-related. Then he spied two documents in a script he did not know.

He was examining the chest for traps when Jazhara appeared in the doorway. Through clenched teeth she said, "The dog had the children caged."

James turned and looked through the door and saw a dozen frightened children, ranging in age from five to ten, standing mute behind the magician. They were dressed in filthy rags, their faces streaked with grime. James let out a slow sigh. Poor children in Krondor were nothing unusual; he had been an "urchin" himself before becoming a thief. But systematic abuse of children was not part of normal Kingdom practices. "What do we do with them?"

"What was that place you spoke of earlier?"

"The Sign of the Yellow Shield. It's an orphanage established by the Princess and the Order of Dala."

One of the children drew back at mention of the place, and James remembered Nita's reaction. James called into the main room, "You, boy, why does that frighten you?"

The lad just shook his head, fear written across his face.

Jazhara put a reassuring hand on his shoulder. "It's all right. No one will hurt you. Why are you frightened?"

A girl behind the boy said, "These men said they were from the Yellow Shield and if we came here they'd feed us."

James rose, left the office, pushed past Jazhara to where the nearest thug lay in a pool of blood. To an older boy he said, "Run outside and find a city watchman. You should find one two streets over by the Inn of the Five Stars. Tell him Squire James requires two men here as soon as possible. Can you remember that?"

The boy nodded and ran off, leaving the street door open behind him. James glanced after him and said,

"Well, if he doesn't head straight for a hideout somewhere, help should be here in a few minutes."

Jazhara watched as James turned the dead Keshian over and looted his purse. "What are you looking for?" she asked.

James held up a ring. "This." He rose and handed it to her to examine.

She turned the ring over in her hand. It was a simple iron ring with a small painted yellow iron shield fastened to it. "Those who serve the Order of Dala wear a ring similar to this. I suspect these men showed this to the children to lure them here, claiming they were taking them to the orphanage."

Jazhara glanced toward the children, several of whom nodded. "That would explain why Nita was so adamant about not going there," she said.

James returned to the office and looked again at the closed chest. He hesitated, then opened it. Inside were more documents. He removed a few and asked, "Jazhara, can you read these? They appear to be in a form of Keshian I don't understand."

Jazhara took the proffered documents and glanced at the topmost. "I can read them, but it's a desert script, from the area around Durbin, and not from the interior of Kesh."

James nodded. He could only read formal court Keshian. Jazhara's eyes widened. "Filthy traitor! Yusuf has been using my great-uncle and his resources, setting Kesh against your Prince, and your Prince against Kesh!"

James looked perplexed. Finding out that Yusuf was a Keshian agent was hardly a shock. Discovering he was also betraying his master was. "Why?"

Jazhara held out a single page. "To serve someone named 'the Crawler.' "

James rolled his eyes heavenward, but stayed silent. The Crawler had been a thorn in the side of both the Prince and the Mockers for months now and James was no closer to establishing his identity than he had been the day he had first heard his name. Hoping for some clue, he asked, "What else does it say?"

Jazhara finished reading the document, then looked at the next. "This Crawler is someone of note, someone who rewarded Yusuf handsomely for his betrayal. There are references to payments already made of large amounts of gold and other considerations."

She hurried through several other documents, then came to one that caused her to stop and go pale. "This cannot be . . ." she whispered.

"What?" asked James.

"It is a warrant for my death should I choose not to serve Yusuf. It bears my great-uncle's signature and seal."

She held it out with a shaking hand and James took it. He examined the paper closely then said, "It isn't."

"Isn't?" she asked softly.

"You said it cannot be and I'm saying you're right. It isn't real. It's a forgery."

"How can you be certain?" she asked. "I've seen my great-uncle's script and seal many times and this appears to be from his hand and ring."

James grinned. "It's too flawless. I doubt that even your great-uncle could order the death of his favorite niece without some noticeable trembling in his hand. The letters are too perfect. I can't read the words, but I can see the handwriting and it's a clever forgery. Besides, even if the handwriting displayed that slight agitation I'd expect, there are two other reasons."

"Which are?" she asked as the sound of approaching footsteps reached them.

"Your great-uncle would never be stupid enough to sign his own name to a death warrant on any Keshian noble, especially one in his own family. More to the point, we've seen a fair number of documents bearing his seal in the palace over the years and there's a tiny imperfection in his signet." James pointed. "Look here. Where the long point of the star touches the bottom of the seal there should be a fine crack, as if the ring has a tiny fracture. This seal doesn't have it. The ring wasn't his."

"Then why?" asked Jazhara. As she spoke, a small company of the city watch appeared outside the door.

"Because," said James, striding toward the door, "if the new court mage in Krondor dies and someone in the Imperial Court starts casting around for someone to blame, who better than the head of the Keshian Intelligence Corps? Someone in the Empress's Palace might wish to see him removed and replaced with his own man."

"The Crawler?" asked Jazhara.

James turned and nodded.

"Then he is someone of importance," she said. "To threaten my great-uncle is to risk much. Only a man with his own power base within Kesh would dare this."

At the door, a guard of the watch said, "One of these children came to us and we hurried here as quickly as we could, Squire. What can we do to help?"

James replied, "There are some bodies inside that need to be removed, but otherwise everything's under control." He glanced at the children who hovered around them in a circle, as if ready to bolt should the alarm go up. "You'd better take charge of this lot before they scatter."

"Where shall we take them?"

James said, "To the Shield of Dala Orphanage the Princess helped found, over by the Sea Gate. Last I heard they had plenty of beds and hot food."

Several children started to inch away, as if getting ready to flee. Jazhara crouched and reached out as if to gather the fearful children to her. She said, "They are not like the men who have hurt you. There you will truly find food and warm beds."

Confronted otherwise with the prospect of a cold night with only stones to sleep upon and an empty belly, the children remained. The guard looked around. "Well, then, if you're all right getting back to the palace without a guard, Squire, we'll get this bunch moving. Come along, children," he said, trying not to sound too gruff.

The children left with two of the guards while the remaining pair peered into the building. "We'll have these bodies gone by morning. What about the building?" one of them asked.

James replied, "It'll be looted five minutes after you leave, so I'm going to poke around a little more and take anything important to the prince. Once we're gone, get rid of the bodies and let whoever wanders by take what he wants. If the previous owner has any heirs, I would welcome them coming to the palace to complain."

The watchman saluted and James and Jazhara reentered the dyer's shop. Jazhara thoroughly examined every paper in the chest and James inspected every likely spot that might harbor a secret hiding place. After an hour, James announced, "I don't think there's anything else."

Jazhara had been carefully reading the papers found in Yusuf's office. "There's enough here to warrant a full investigation from my great-uncle's end," she said. "This attempt to have my death placed at his feet in order to discredit him . . . it would have created a virtual civil war in the north of the Empire, for the desert tribes would know it to be a false accusation."

"But the Empress and her council in the City of Kesh might believe it."

Jazhara nodded. "Whoever this Crawler is, he seeks to benefit from confrontation between our peoples, James. Who would gain from such chaos?"

James said, "It's a long list. I'll tell you sometime. Right now, we should get to the palace. You have barely enough time to take a short nap, change into clean clothing, eat, then be presented to Prince Arutha."

Jazhara took a final long look around the room, as if searching for something or trying to impress details on her memory, then without comment she lifted her staff and moved purposefully toward the door.

James hesitated for a half-step, then overtook her. "You'll send word to your great-uncle?" he asked when he caught up with her.

"Certainly. This Crawler may be Keshian and what occurs here in Krondor may be but a part of a larger scheme, but it's clear that my great-uncle is at risk."

James said, "Well, there's the matter of the Prince."

"Oh." Jazhara stared at James. "Do you think he would begrudge my great-uncle a warning?"

James touched her shoulder lightly. "It's not that. It's only . . ."

"Matters of politics," she finished.

"Something like that," James said. They turned a corner. "It may be there's no problem in communicating this discovery to your great-uncle, but Arutha may request you leave out certain facts, such as how you got the information."

Jazhara smiled slightly. "As in not revealing we know Yusuf was ostensibly an agent working on behalf of Great Kesh?"

James grinned. "Something like that," he repeated.

As they continued to walk, she added after a while, "Perhaps we could simply say that while dealing with an illegal slavery ring, we discovered a plot to murder me and pin the blame upon my great-uncle, to the purpose of having him removed from his position as Governor of the Jal-Pur."

"My thinking exactly."

Jazhara laughed. "Do not worry, my friend. Politics are second nature to Keshian nobles not born of the True Blood."

James frowned. "I've heard that term once or twice before, but must confess I'm vague as to what it means."

Jazhara turned a corner, putting them on a direct path back to the palace. "Then you must visit the City of Kesh and visit the Empress's court. There are things I can tell you about Kesh that will not make sense until you have seen them with your own eyes. The True Blood Keshians, those whose ancestors first hunted lions on the grasslands around the Overn Deep, are such. Words would not do them justice."

A hint of irony—or bitterness—tinged her words, and James couldn't tell which, but James decided not to pursue the matter. They crossed out of the Merchants' Quarter and entered the palace district.

As they approached the palace gates, Jazhara glanced over to the large building opposite and noticed the solitary guardsman there. "An Ishapian enclave?"

James studied the sturdy man who stood impassively at his post, a lethal-looking warhammer at his belt. "Yes, though I have no idea of its purpose."

Jazhara looked at James with a wry smile and a twinkling eye and said, "There's something occurring in Krondor about which you're ignorant?"

James returned her smile. "What I should have said is that I have no idea what its purpose is—*yet*."

The guards came to attention as James and Jazhara reached the gates and the senior guard said, "Welcome back, Squire. You've found her, then?"

James nodded. "Gentlemen, may I present Jazhara, court mage of Krondor."

At this, one of the other guards began to stare at Jazhara. "By the gods!" he exclaimed suddenly.

"You've something to say?" James inquired.

The guard flushed. "Beggin' your pardon, Squire, but a Keshian? So close to our Prince?"

Jazhara looked from one to the other, then said, "Set your minds at rest, gentlemen. I have taken oath and I will swear fealty to Arutha. Your prince is my lord, and like you, I shall defend him unto death."

The senior guard threw a look at the outspoken soldier that clearly communicated they would be talking about his outburst later. Then he said, "Your pardon, milady. We are honored to have you in Krondor."

"My thanks to you, sir," replied Jazhara as the gates were opened.

James followed, and as the gates were closed behind them he said, "You'll have to excuse them. They're naturally wary of strangers."

"You mean, wary of Keshians. Think nothing of it. We would be equally suspicious of a Kingdom magician in the court of the Empress, She Who Is Kesh. When Master Pug entrusted me to this position, he was very clear that my appointment is *not* to be political."

James grinned. Nothing in the court was not political, but he appreciated the sentiment. He regarded the young woman again. The more he knew her, the better he liked her. Mustering up his best courtier's tone, he said, "A woman of your beauty and intelligence should have no trouble with that. I myself am already feeling a great sense of trust."

She laughed. Fixing him with a skeptical expression, she said, "Your compliment is appreciated, Squire, but do not presume too much, too quickly. I'm sure your Prince would be upset were I forced to turn you into a toad."

James returned the laugh. "Not half as upset as I'd be. Forgive my impertinence, Jazhara, and welcome to Krondor."

They paused at the main entrance to the palace, where a page waited. "This boy will escort you to your quarters and see to whatever you need." Glancing at the sky, James added, "We have two hours until dawn, and I will attend the Prince an hour after he breaks fast with his family. I'll have someone come fetch you to court for the presentation."

"Thank you, Squire," said Jazhara. She turned and mounted the steps to the palace doors. James watched her go, appreciating just how nice her retreating figure looked in her travel clothes. As he took off in the direction of his own quarters, he muttered to himself, "William's got good taste in women, that's for sure. Between Talia and this one, he's got his hands full."

By the time he reached a small gate near the palace wall, on the path leading to the rear servant's entrance, his mind had already turned from exotic beauties from distant lands and was wrestling with mysteries more deadly, such as who this Crawler was and why was he trying so hard to plunge the Kingdom into war.

Arutha, Prince of Krondor and the Western Realm, second most powerful man in the Kingdom of the Isles, looked at his squire and said, "Well, what do you think of her?"

"Even if Duke Pug hadn't vouched for her, I'd be inclined to trust her, to take her oath of fealty as heartfelt and genuine."

Arutha sat back in his chair, behind the desk he used when conducting the more mundane daily routines of ruling the Western Realm. It was his habit to take a few minutes there to ready himself for morning court, before the conduct of his office was taken out of his hands by de Lacy, his Master of Ceremonies.

After a moment of reflection, Arutha said, "You must be tired. If loyalty were even a remote issue, Jazhara would not be here. I mean, what do you think of her as a person?"

James sighed. "We had . . . an adventure, last night."

Arutha pointed to the documents upon his desk. "Something to do with a dead cloth-dyer of Keshian ancestry who appears to be working for Lord Hazara-Khan, no doubt."

James nodded. "Yes, sire. She's . . . remarkable. As much as I've been around magic in the last ten years, I still know little about it. But she seems . . . I don't know if powerful is the correct word . . . adept, perhaps. She acted without hesitation when the need arose and she seems capable of doing considerable damage should that be required."

"What else?"

James thought. "I think she's able to be very analytical 'at a full gallop' as they say. I can't imagine her being rash or foolhardy."

Arutha nodded for James to continue.

"We can deduce she's educated. Despite the accent, her command of the King's Tongue is flawless. She reads more languages than I do, apparently, and being court-born will know all the protocols, ceremonies, and matters of rank."

"Nothing you've said is at variance with Pug's message to me concerning this choice." Arutha indicated an-

other piece of parchment on his desk. "You have a nose for smelling out things even a magician of Pug's puissance might not recognize."

"In that, Highness, she's what you require in an advisor on things magical, I would wager."

"Good." Arutha rose and said, "Let us go and meet her, then."

James hurried to reach the door and open it for his prince. While no longer Senior Squire of the Court of Krondor, he was still Arutha's personal squire and usually attended him when he wasn't off on some mission or another for Arutha. James opened the door.

On the other side, Brion, the newly-appointed Senior Squire, awaited Arutha's appearance. Brion was the son of the Baron of Hawk's Hallow in the eastern mountains of the Duchy of Yabon. A tall, rangy, blond-headed lad, he was a hard-working, no-nonsense sort, the perfect choice for the tedious work of Senior Squire, work James had to admit he had never fully embraced with enthusiasm. Master of Ceremonies de Lacy and his assistant, Housecarl Jerome, were thrilled with the change in assignments, as they had both been forced to compensate for James's absences when he was out and about on Arutha's behalf. James glanced at Brion as he followed Arutha, leaving James with the other squires awaiting the duties of the day. When Arutha was seated, Brion nodded to Jerome, who moved to the large doors that would admit today's court to the Prince's presence. With a dignity James still found impressive, the old Master of Ceremonies moved to the middle of the entrance, so that as Jerome and a page opened the doors, those outside would first see de Lacy.

With a voice still powerful, the Master of Ceremonies said, "Come forth and attend! The Prince of Krondor is upon his throne and will hear his subjects!"

He turned and walked toward the dais, while pages led members of the court to their assigned places. Most of those in attendance were regular members of Arutha's court and knew exactly where they should stand, but a few newcomers always needed a boy nearby to instruct them quietly in matters of court protocol. And Brian de Lacy was a stickler for protocol.

James saw several officers and nobles of Arutha's staff enter and take their customary positions while petitioners who had convinced someone on the palace staff they needed to speak personally with the Prince followed. Jazhara was first among those, since she would soon make the transition from newcomer to member of the court.

James was impressed. Gone was the dusty, efficient travel garb, and now she wore the traditional formal raiment of her people. From head to foot she was dressed in a deep indigo silk, and James had to acknowledge that the color suited her. She wore far less jewelry than was customary for a woman of her rank; but the pieces she did wear—a brooch which held her veil pinned to her shoulder, which in her homeland would be worn across her lower face in the presence of strangers; and a single large bracelet of gold embedded with emeralds—were of the highest quality. The former thief suppressed a smile as he considered what they'd fetch if sold to some of the less reputable gem dealers in Krondor.

Master de Lacy intoned, "Highness, the court is assembled."

With a slight inclination of his head, Arutha signaled for court to commence.

James glanced around to see if William was present. As a junior officer of the Prince's guard he had no particular reason to be here, but given his history with Jazhara, James thought it possible he might put in an appearance.

De Lacy spoke: "Highness, we have the honor to present to you Jazhara, newly come to Krondor from Stardock, recommended to your favor by Duke Pug."

Arutha nodded for her to come close and Jazhara approached with the calm, effortless poise of one born to the court. James had seen more than one previously confident petitioner stumble while under the Prince's gaze, but Jazhara reached the appropriate spot and bowed, a low, sweeping gesture, which she executed gracefully.

"Welcome to Krondor, Jazhara," said Arutha. "Duke Pug commends you to our service. Are you willing to undertake such?"

"With my heart and mind, Highness," answered the young desert woman.

De Lacy came to stand halfway between Jazhara and the Prince and began the oath of service. It was short and to the point, to James's relief; there were far more tedious rites that he'd been forced to endure in his years of service to the crown.

Jazhara finished with, "And to this I pledge my life and honor, Highness."

Father Belson, a priest of the Order of Prandur, and Arutha's current advisor on issues concerning the various temples in the Kingdom, approached and intoned, "Prandur, Cleanser by Fire, Lord of the Flame, sanctifies this oath. As it is given, in fealty and service, so shall it be bound, in protection and succor. Let all know that this woman, Jazhara of the House of Hazara-Khan, is now Prince Arutha's good and loyal servant."

Belson conducted Jazhara to her appointed place in the court, next to his own, where both would be available should Arutha need their opinion on some issue concerning magic or faith. James glanced at the remaining company and realized court would be blessedly short this

morning. There were only two petitioners and most of the regular court staff appeared anxious to be elsewhere. Arutha was a ruler who, to everyone's relief except perhaps de Lacy's, preferred efficiency to pomp. He left grand ceremony, such as the monthly galas and other festive occasions, to be overseen by his wife.

Jazhara caught James's eye and gave him a slight smile, which he returned. Not for the first time, James wondered if there might be something more in this than merely a collegial gesture, and then he mentally kicked himself. James's view of women was quite outside the norm for men his age in the Kingdom: he liked them and wasn't afraid of them, though he had been from time to time confused by them. Still, while he enjoyed intimacy with a woman as much as the next man, he avoided complicating liaisons. And a relationship with one of the Prince's advisors was only slightly less complicating than one with a member of his family; so he shunted aside such thoughts. With a slightly regretful inward sigh he told himself, *it's just that she's exotic.*

When court was over and the company dismissed, Arutha rose from his throne and turned to Jazhara. "Are you settled in?"

"Yes, Highness," she answered. "My baggage was delivered to the palace this morning and all is well."

"Are your quarters adequate?"

She smiled. "Very, Highness. Master Kulgan told me what to expect, and I believe he was having some fun with me, as they are far more commodious than I had expected."

Arutha smiled slightly. "Kulgan always possessed a dry sense of humor." Motioning for James, he said, "Squire James will conduct your tour of Krondor today, and should you need anything, he will ensure you get it."

"Thank you, Highness." With a grin, James said, "As you know, we had a bit of a tour last night, Highness."

Arutha said, "I saw the documents this morning." To Jazhara and James he said, "But first, you two, in my office, please."

Brion hurried to open the door and Arutha led Jazhara and James into his private office. As he was about to step through, Arutha said, "Squire Brion, see what Master de Lacy has for the squires this morning."

"Sire." Brion bowed and departed.

Arutha sat. "Jazhara, allow me to begin by saying that had I a moment's concern regarding your loyalty to our court, you would not be standing here."

Jazhara inclined her head and said, "Understood, Highness."

"James, as soon as possible, please familiarize our young magician with everything we know so far about the Crawler. That will require, I suspect, a fair amount of personal history, since his confrontation with the Mockers is significant in understanding his motives. Be frank. I have the impression this young lady doesn't shock easily."

Jazhara smiled.

Arutha fixed a solemn gaze on both of them. "This Crawler has had his hand in no small amount of mischief over the last year or so. He was indirectly involved in one of the more threatening attacks on our sovereignty and created a situation that put a great strain on our relationships with a neighboring nation to the east. The more difficult he is to find, the more I worry about him." Addressing James he said, "Be thorough. You needn't return to the palace, unless I send for you, until you feel Jazhara has seen all she needs to see."

James bowed. "I will be thorough, Highness."

Jazhara bowed as well and followed James out of the Prince's office into a side corridor, where James asked, "Where to first, my lady?"

Jazhara said, "My quarters. I'm not traipsing around Krondor in this gown. And I feel only partially dressed if I don't have my staff in my hand."

James smiled. "Your quarters it is."

As they walked through the palace, Jazhara said, "I haven't seen William yet. Is he avoiding me?"

James looked at her. Frank, indeed, he thought. He said, "Probably not. While he's a royal cousin, he's also a junior officer and has many duties. If we don't run into him during our travels, I know where we'll be able to find him this evening."

Jazhara said, "Good. We need to talk, and I'd rather that occurred sooner than later."

James noticed she was no longer smiling.

Three

Vow

Che watchman saluted.

James returned the acknowledgment, while Jazhara took in the sights of Krondor. She was wearing her travel garb once more. She carried her iron-shod staff, and her hair was tied back. She looked . . . businesslike. James found it interesting to contrast how she looked now, and how she had appeared at court earlier that morning. Two very different women . . .

They had begun early in the day, visiting the shops and markets of what people commonly referred to as the "Rich Quarter" of the city, a place in which shops displayed items of great beauty and price to buyers of means. Jazhara had lingered at several shops, much to James's chagrin, for he had never enjoyed the pastime of looking at goods he had no interest in buying. He had several times been assigned to the Princess's shopping expeditions, mostly to keep Elena out from under her mother's feet as much as to guard Arutha's wife. It was perhaps the only time in his life when he hadn't particularly enjoyed the Princess's company.

James had then taken Jazhara through the so-called "Merchants' Quarter," where the traders and captains of

commerce had their places of business. The center of this district was dominated by a coffeehouse. They had paused to enjoy a cup of the Keshian brew, which Jazhara pronounced as fine as any she had tasted at home. This had brought a smile from their server, a young man named Timothy Barret, the youngest son of the owner. Businessmen flocked to Barret's to conduct business, mainly the underwriting of cargo ships and caravans.

After leaving the Merchants' Quarter, they had visited one working-class district after another. It was now past sundown and the evening watch was making its rounds. "Perhaps we should return to the palace?" James suggested.

"There's still a great deal of the city to be seen, yes?"

James nodded. "But I'm not certain you'd care to spend time there after dark."

"The Poor Quarter?"

"Yes, and the docks and Fishtown. They can be pretty rough even during the day."

"I think I have shown I am capable of taking care of myself, James."

"Agreed, but I find it best to keep the opportunity for trouble to a minimum; it has a habit of finding me anyway."

She laughed. "Perhaps more tomorrow, then. But what about William? You said he would likely be off-duty this evening."

James pointed to a side street. "Let's cut down there. William is almost certainly at the Rainbow Parrot."

"A soldiers' tavern?"

James shrugged. "Not particularly, though many of Lucas's patrons are old friends who served with him in the Riftwar. No, it's just the place William prefers to frequent."

Jazhara glanced sidelong at James. "A girl?"

James felt himself flush and decided a simple, direct answer was appropriate. "Yes. William has been seeing Talia, Lucas's daughter, for several weeks now."

"Good," said Jazhara. "I feared he was still . . ."

As she paused, James supplied, "In love with you?"

Without looking at James she said, "Infatuated, I think, is a better word. I made a mistake and . . ."

"Look, it's none of my business," James said. "So if you don't want to talk about it, fine."

"No, I want you to know something." She stopped and he turned to look at her. "Because you're his friend, I think."

"I am," said James. James had been something of a mentor to William since he had arrived at Krondor.

"And I would like for us to be friends, as well."

James nodded. "I would like that too."

"So, you know, then, that William was a boy who followed me around for years once he was old enough to become interested in women. I was a few years older and to me he seemed an eager puppy, nothing more." She paused and stared down at the street, as if recalling something difficult to recount. James, too, stood still. "I became involved with an older man, one of my teachers. It was not a wise thing to do. He was Keshian, as I was, and he shared many of the beliefs I do on magic and its uses. We drifted into a relationship without too much effort.

"Our affair became . . . awkward, for my family would not have approved of any such liaison, and rather than dictate to me, my great-uncle got word to my lover that he was to cease his involvement with me." She began to walk slowly again, as if it helped her form her thoughts. James accompanied her. "He rejected me, and left Star-dock, returning to the Empire."

"And to a small reward, I'm sure."

"At the least. Perhaps it was nothing more than wanting to spare me a confrontation with my own father or perhaps he was afraid—my great-uncle's reach can be very long, even into a place such as Stardock."

"And?" James prompted.

"William was there. I was hurt and frightened and alone and William was there." She looked at James. "He's a lovely young man, honorable and kind, strong and passionate, and I felt abandoned. He helped me." Her voice trailed off.

James shrugged. "But what?"

"But after a while I realized it was as wrong for me to be his lover as it had been for my teacher to be mine. William was the son of the duke, and had another destiny before him and I was . . . using him."

James suppressed the quip that almost sprang to his lips about it not being a bad way to be used, and said instead, "Well, he wanted . . . I mean . . ."

"Yes, but I was older and should have seen the problems to come. So I broke off our affair. I fear I may have tipped the balance in his decision to leave Stardock and come to Krondor."

They turned into a street and headed toward an inn displaying a large parrot with rainbow-colored feathers on a sign over the door. "Well, I've known Will for a bit now, and I think you can put aside that concern," James said at last. "He was set on becoming a soldier, one way or another, all his life, from what he's told me."

Jazhara was about to reply, but before she knew it, James was drawing his sword and saying, "Guard yourself!"

She brought her staff to the ready and hurried after him. She saw that the door to the inn was partially open

and that there was a dead soldier lying before it; and now she could hear the sound of fighting coming from within.

James kicked the door wide and leapt through, Jazhara behind him, staff at the ready. A scene of carnage greeted them. Two armed men lay dead on the ground, mercenaries judging by their dress. Several bar patrons also lay dead amidst the broken furniture. A young woman lay near the fireplace, blood pooling about her head.

In the corner William conDoin, cousin by adoption to the Royal House of Krondor and Lieutenant in the Prince's Household Guard, stood ready with his large sword held two-handed before him. Three men advanced on him.

William, seeing the newcomers, called, "James! Jazhara! Help me! Talia's been hurt!"

One of the men turned to engage the squire. The other two attacked William, who barely had room to deflect both strikes with his larger sword. A devastating weapon in the field, the hand-and-a-half or "bastard" sword was a liability at close quarters.

Jazhara lifted her hand and a nimbus of crimson light erupted around it. She cast it at the closest of William's opponents and watched as the light harmlessly struck the ground near his feet. "Damn," she muttered. She hefted her staff and stepped forward, leveling a jab with the iron base at the side of the man's head.

The intruder sensed or saw with his peripheral vision the attack and ducked aside. Whirling to face his new foe, he made a wicked slashing attack at Jazhara, causing her to fall back.

But she had freed William to concentrate on one foe only, and he quickly killed his man. James also dispatched his opponent, then used his sword hilt to strike Jazhara's attacker at the base of the skull. Rather than

stun the man, it served only to distract him, and he turned as Jazhara lashed out again with her staff. The sound of breaking bones was unmistakable as the iron heel of the staff crushed the back of the man's head.

James looked around the room and said, "What black murder is this?"

William had thrown down his sword and was kneeling beside Talia, cradling her head in his lap. The girl's face was pale and her life flowed out by the second. "Oh, William . . ." she whispered, "help me."

William looked down despairingly. He glanced at James, who shook his head slightly, regret clearly showing in his expression. William then looked at Jazhara and entreated, "You were one of my father's finest students. Can you perform a healing?"

Jazhara knelt beside the young soldier and whispered, "I'm sorry, William. Her wounds are too severe. Even if we were to send for a priest . . . it would be too late."

James knelt on the other side of the girl. "Talia, who did this?"

Talia looked up at James. "They were after Father. I don't know who they were. The leader was a huge bear of a man." She coughed and blood trickled from her mouth, staining her lips. "He hurt me, William. He really hurt me."

Tears streamed down William's cheeks. "Oh, Talia, I'm sorry . . ."

Suddenly the girl's distress seemed to ease. James had seen this before in those on the verge of death. For a moment their eyes brightened, as if the pain had vanished, as if the dying stood upon the threshold of entering Lims-Kragma's Hall. At this moment, they saw clearly in both worlds. Talia whispered, "Don't worry, William. I swear by Kahooli, I will have my vengeance!"

Then her head lolled to one side.

"No . . . Talia!" William sobbed. For a moment he held her, and then slowly he placed her on the floor, and gently closed her eyes. At last, he rose and declared, "They must pay for this, James. I'm going after them."

James looked toward the doorway of the inn. If the intruders had been seeking Talia's father Lucas, that was the way the old man would have bolted. He said, "Wait, William. The Prince will have my head if I let you go off alone. You'll have your revenge and we'll be there beside you. Now, tell us what happened."

William hesitated a moment then said, "Right. Martin and I had just ended our shift. We headed over here for a drink, just like always, and that's when we saw them run out of the building. Half a dozen of them, with that big bastard leading them. Martin tried to halt them, and they attacked us without so much as a word. If you hadn't come along, I'd no doubt be lying alongside Martin." He gestured toward the dead soldier.

James inspected the carnage. In addition to Talia, they had slaughtered everyone else in the inn. The other barmaid, Susan de Bennet, lay sprawled on the floor in the corner, her head severed completely from her body with what looked to have been a single blow. Her red tresses fanned out around her head, which lay a foot away from her body, her blue eyes still wide in shocked amazement. The other patrons were likewise hacked to pieces.

"Why?" asked James. "Why charge in and kill everyone in sight?" He looked at William. "Did the big man go after Lucas?"

"No. Some other men went out through the back. Once those five murderers backed me inside the inn, the big bastard and some others fled down the street."

"Do you have any idea where they were heading?" asked James.

Before William could answer, the building seemed to rock as the night was torn by the sound of a thunderous explosion. James was first out the door, with William and Jazhara close behind him. To the west, a fountain of green flames rose into the night as rocks shot up into the air. As the sound of the explosion diminished, the rocks began to rain down. James and his companions ducked beneath the overhanging roof eaves, and waited.

When it was clear that the last of the rocks had fallen, William said, "Listen!"

In the distance they could hear the clash of arms and the shouts of men. They hurried toward the noise, and turned the corner that led to the city jail. As they ran toward the jail, another explosion ripped through the night and they were thrown to the ground. A tower of green fire again reached into the darkness, and James shouted, "Get under cover!"

Again they hugged the walls of a building as more stones rained down upon them. William shouted, "What is that? Quegan Fire?"

James shook his head, "No Quegan Fire I've ever seen was green."

Jazhara said, "I think I know what it was."

"Care to share that intelligence with us?" asked James.

"No," she answered. "Not yet."

As the clatter of falling stones quieted, James leapt up and they continued running toward the jail. They reached a junction with two other streets, and sprinted left. A short distance further on they came to another intersection, and it was there they saw what was left of the jail. A gaping hole in the wall stood where the wooden door had once been, a few flames could be seen inside, and smoke rose from the maw. Nearby, an overturned wagon served as cover for two guardsmen and Captain Garruth, com-

mander of the city watch. James, William, and Jazhara approached the wagon in a running crouch, keeping the wagon between them and the opening, for crossbow bolts and arrows were flying from the hole at those behind the wagon.

Glancing back, Captain Garruth motioned for them to stay low. When James came alongside, the captain said, "Astalon rot their black hearts." He nodded to the two young men he knew and said, "William. Squire James." Without waiting for an introduction to Jazhara, the guard captain continued. "As you can see, we've a bit of a problem."

"What happened?" asked James.

"Bloody brigands! They've blown out the back of the jail, and cut down half my squad."

"Who are they?" asked William.

"Your guess is as good as mine, lad. The leader's a giant of a man, bald, with a thick beard. He was wearing some sort of bone amulet, and he swung a mean sword."

William said, "That's the one, James."

"Which one, boy?" asked the captain as another arrow slammed into the underside of the wagon.

James glanced at William. "The one that killed Talia, the barmaid at the Rainbow Parrot."

Garruth let out a slow breath then said heavily, "Lucas's girl. She is . . . was . . . such a sweet thing." He glanced at William. "My sympathies, Will."

With cold anger, William replied, "I'll have his heart, Captain. I swear I will."

Garruth said, "Well, now's your chance, lad. They've got us pinned down, but maybe the two of you can creep back down the way you came and circle behind the jail."

"Where's the sheriff?" asked James.

Garruth inclined his head toward the jail. "In there, I

expect. I was due to meet with him when everything went to hell."

James shook his head. He had little affection for Sheriff Wilfred Means, but he was a good and loyal servant of the Prince and his son Jonathan was one of James's agents. He would discover if the younger Means was still alive later, he supposed.

"If the sheriff and his men were inside when the bastards blew up the jail, we won't see help here from the palace for another ten or fifteen minutes," said James.

Garruth said, "Aye, and that gives them time for whatever bloody work they've got in mind. Never seen anyone try to break *into* a jail before, so there must be something in there they want."

James said, "No, there's some*one* they want."

William said, "You think Lucas went to the jail?"

"Maybe," said James. "But we won't know until we get inside."

Garruth said, "You'd best leave the woman here until the palace guards arrive."

Jazhara said, in a dry tone, "I appreciate your concern, but I can handle myself."

The captain shrugged. "As you will."

They crouched low and returned the way they had come, until they reached the big intersection, safely out of firing range of the jail. All three stood and began to run.

They quickly reached the rear wall of the jail, in which another gaping hole could be seen. "The second explosion?" asked William.

"The first," said Jazhara. "They blew this one out to catch men eating and sleeping there"—she pointed through the hole to a table and overturned bunks—"then when those in the front of the jail ran back to aid their

comrades, they set off the explosion on the other side, through which they almost certainly attacked, catching whoever was inside from the rear."

James said, "We'll not find the answer out here."

He ducked low and ran toward the hole leading into the guardroom, expecting a volley of arrows at any moment. Instead he found only two men looting the corpses on the ground. One died before he could draw his sword and the other turned on James, only to be struck from behind by William. James held up his hand for silence.

From the entrance come the sound of arrows and quarrels being fired, but all was still in the guardroom. James motioned for William to take the left side of the door into the front room, and for Jazhara to stand a few feet behind James. Then he moved to the partially opened door. He glanced through. A half-dozen men, four with bows and two with crossbows, were spread in flank formation, patiently shooting at anything that moved outside the hole in the wall. It was clear they were merely holding Garruth and his men at bay so someone inside could accomplish his mission.

James glanced at William and Jazhara, and then toward an opening in the floor with stone stairs leading down to the underground cells. He knew there was a staircase in the front room leading to offices and the sheriff's apartment above. Which way had the big man gone? Up or down? James decided that either way they'd need Garruth and his half-dozen guardsmen to deal with the big man and his crew. So the six bowmen ahead must first be neutralized.

James held up three fingers, and Jazhara shook her head emphatically. She tapped her chest, indicating that she wished to make the first move. James glanced at William, who shrugged, so he looked back at Jazhara and nodded.

She stepped forward, raising her right hand high above her head, while grasping her staff in the left. Again the hair on James's arms stood on end as magic was gathered. A golden light enveloped the woman, accompanied by a faint sizzling sound, then the light coalesced into a sphere in the palm of her hand. She threw it as if it was a large ball and it arced into the room, landing between the center pair of bowmen. Instantly they dropped their weapons and twitched in wild spasms. The two next to them on either side were also afflicted, but held on to their weapons and managed to regain control of their movements almost immediately. The two crossbowmen—one of either side of the flank—were unaffected. Fortunately for William, the man he charged had just fired a bolt and was moving to reload his weapon.

The other man turned and fired wildly, the bolt striking the wall high above James's head. Suddenly the balance shifted. The archers dropped their bows and drew daggers, for the projectile weapons were useless at close range. James had one man wounded and down before his neighbor had freed his dagger from his belt. William's large sword was menacing enough that one of the mercenaries threw down his crossbow and attempted to leap over the desk and dash through the gaping hole in the wall.

Seeing the man attempting to flee from within, Captain Garruth and his men sprang forward and the man was down in moments. Inside, the others threw up their hands and knelt, the mercenary's universal sign of surrender.

Garruth indicated that two of his six men were to guard the prisoners. To James he said, "There are more of them than these six. I'll take my men to the basement, if you three will check upstairs."

James nodded. "Who's supposed to be up there?"

"Just the lads sleeping until their mid-watch shift, and

a scribe named Dennison. The sheriff and his men sleep up there." Glancing at the hacked bodies, he said, "I doubt any of them are alive." He scratched his beard. "It was a perfect raid. They knew exactly when to hit. The company was at its lowest complement and least able to defend itself, and reinforcements were unlikely to get here quickly." He started toward the stairs leading down to the cells, and two of his men followed cautiously.

James motioned to William and Jazhara to accompany him and they made their way to the stairs leading to the upper floor of the jail. As they reached the steps, they ducked reflexively as another explosion came from above.

While smoke and stone dust poured down the steps, Captain Garruth shouted, "He's heading for the North Gate!"

James didn't hesitate. "Come on!" he bellowed, and ran through the gaping hole just a few feet away.

Looking down the crowded street leading to the North Gate, James could see the head and shoulders of a large man towering above the throng, shoving his way through the curious onlookers who had gathered to see what the commotion at the jail was. James, William, and Jazhara raced after him.

As they neared the crowd, James glanced back and saw that Garruth's men were engaged in a struggle with about a half-dozen mercenaries. To William and Jazhara, he shouted, "We're on our own!"

People who had been shoved aside by the big man found themselves being pushed aside once more, this time by James and his companions. "Out of the way! Prince's business!" he shouted.

In the din of voices he could barely be heard and finally James let William, who was stockier and stronger

than James, take the lead. People jumped aside as they recognized the garb of the prince's personal household guards, when he bellowed, "Stand aside in the name of the Prince!"

Still, precious moments had been lost, and the big man was out of sight. As they neared the intersection with the road that emptied out through the North Gate, another mighty explosion could be heard, followed instantly by screams and shouts.

They reached the corner and saw a large, two-story building in flames. Smoke billowed from the lower windows as flames climbed the outside wall.

"Gods," said James. "He's fired the orphanage."

From the main door four women and a man were ushering out children, many of whom looked stunned and disoriented, coughing from the heavy smoke. James ran to the door.

The man turned, saw William's garb and shouted, "Someone's burned the orphanage! They threw a bomb through that window." He pointed with a shaking finger. "Flames erupted and we barely got out alive."

Jazhara said, "Are all the children out?"

A scream from upstairs answered her.

The man coughed and said, "I tried to go upstairs, but the fire near the stairs is too intense."

"How many are up there?" asked William.

"Three," said one of the women, who was crying. "I called the children for supper, but they were taking their time coming down . . ."

"I may be able to help," said Jazhara.

"How?" asked James.

"I have a spell which will protect you from the heat unless you touch the flame itself. But it lasts only a short time."

The man said, "Then weave it quickly, woman. Their lives are at stake."

William started to strip off his armor, but James said, "No, I'm faster than you." He also had no armor to doff. He handed his sword to William and said, "Ready."

Jazhara said, "The spell will protect you from the heat, but you must be careful not to breathe the smoke too deeply as it will kill as fast as a flame." She pulled a handkerchief from the hands of one of the nearby women and handed it to James. "Hold this over your mouth and nose."

She closed her eyes, putting her right hand on James's arm and the back of her left hand to her forehead. She made a short incantation and finally said, "There. It is done. Now hurry, for it will last but a short time."

James said, "I didn't feel anything."

"It's done," she repeated.

"I usually feel magic when it's—"

"Go!" she said, pushing him toward the door. "Time is short!"

"But—"

"Go!" she repeated with a strong push.

James tumbled head-first through the door, and ducked at the sight of flames licking the ceiling above. To his surprise, he felt no heat.

The smoke, however, caused his eyes to water and he blinked furiously to clear them. He wished he had thought to wet the cloth he held over his nose and mouth. He made for a stairway, following a serpentine route around flaming tables and burning tapestries.

He quickly reached the top of the stairs and did not have to ask if the children were still alive. Three tiny voices split the air with their screams and coughs. James shouted, "Stay where you are, children! I'm coming to get you!"

He hurried toward the shouts at the other end of the room, a barracks of sorts where the children obviously slept. Bedding was smoldering and flames climbed the walls, but he found a straight path to the children.

Two boys and a girl huddled in the corner, terrified to the point of immobility. James quickly decided that trying to guide them through the flames was pointless. The older of the two boys appeared to be about seven or eight years of age. The other boy and girl he guessed as being closer to four.

He knelt and said, "Come here."

The children stood up and he gathered the two smaller children up, one under each arm, then said to the older boy, "Climb on my back!"

The boy did, clamping his arm over James's throat. James put down the other two children, almost gagging. "Not so hard!" he said, prying the boy's arm from across his windpipe. "Here," he said, placing the boy's arms across his chest. "Like this!"

Then he scooped up the other children and hurried back to the stairs. He moved quickly down the steps and saw the flames had closed around the landing. "Damn!" he muttered.

There was nothing for it but to run. He leapt as far as he could through the flames and instantly understood Jazhara's warning. The heat itself hadn't been noticeable, but the second the flames touched him he could certainly feel it. "Oooh!" he shouted, as he landed in a relatively clear patch of wooden floor, while the planks on all sides smoldered and burned.

The roof above was making alarming sounds, creaks and groans, that told James the support timbers were weakening. Soon the upper floor would collapse on him and the children if he didn't move. The smoke was mak-

ing the children cough and James's eyes were tearing to the point of being unable to see through the smoke. Taking in a lungful that caused him to cough, he shouted, "Jazhara! William!"

William's booming voice answered from slightly to his left. "This way!"

James didn't hesitate. He leapt forward, trying as well as he could to avoid the flames, but by the time he came spilling out the door with a child under each arm and one across his back, he was burned on both legs and arms. The children were crying from their burns, but they were alive. He collapsed onto the cobblestones, coughing.

Two women took charge of the burned and frightened children, while Jazhara knelt and examined James's burns. "Not serious," she judged.

James looked at her through watering eyes and said, "Easy for you to say. They hurt like the blazes!"

Jazhara took a small jar out of her belt pouch and said, "This will make them stop hurting until we can get you to a healer or priest."

She applied a salve gently to the burns and, true to her words, the pain vanished. James said, "What is that?"

"It is made from a desert plant found in the Jal-Pur. My people use this salve on burns and cuts. It will keep wounds from festering for a while, enabling them to heal."

James stood up and looked toward the gate. "He's gotten away?"

William said, "I expect so. Look." He pointed to the other side of the street where members of the city watch were moving citizens back from the fire so that a chain of men with buckets could start wetting down the nearby buildings. It was clear that the orphanage was doomed, but the rest of the quarter might be saved. William

sounded defeated. "Those men are from the gate watch, so I suspect the murderer got out of the city just by walking through."

Jazhara said, "What sort of monster would set fire to an orphanage to create a diversion?"

James said, "The same sort who would break into a jail at sunset." He coughed one more time, then said, "Let's go back and see if we can find out who he was after." He started walking back toward the jail.

Soldiers from the palace had arrived to augment the surviving city guards at the jail. James had just learned that Sheriff Wilfred Means and all but six of his men had been killed. The sheriff's son, Jonathan, stood in the main room surveying the damage. James had recently recruited the young man to work secretly for him in the Prince's burgeoning intelligence network. The squire put his hand on Jonathan's shoulder and said, "I'm sorry for your loss. Your father and I were never what could be called friends, but I respected him as an honest man who was unstinting in his loyalty and duty."

Jonathan looked pale and could only nod. Finally he controlled his emotions and said, "Thank you."

James nodded. "For the time being, you and the other deputies report to Captain Garruth. Arutha will need time to name a new sheriff and you'll be undermanned for a while."

Jonathan said, "I need to go home if that's all right. I must tell my mother."

James said, "Yes, of course. Go to your mother," and sent the young man on his way. Jonathan was an able man, despite his youth, but he doubted Arutha would willingly elevate him to his father's office. Besides, having Jonathan tied to a desk wouldn't help James's

plans. He put aside those thoughts and went looking for Garruth.

The captain was directing workers and soldiers as they started making repairs on the jail. "Didn't catch him?" he said when he saw James and the others.

James held up one of his burned arms and said, "Bastard set fire to the orphanage as a diversion."

Garruth shook his head. "That one is a mean piece of work." He inclined his head to the stairs leading to the cell below. "You should take a look at what he did down there. I'd not want to be on this one's bad side."

James led the others down the steps to the lock-up. The jail was a holding area for minor criminals waiting to get justice from Arutha's magistrates, or for prisoners waiting to be transferred to the palace dungeon or the prison work-gangs.

The jail comprised a large basement divided by bars and doors into eight cells—two large general holding pens, and six smaller cells used to isolate the more troublesome prisoners. At any hour of the day, drunks, petty thieves, and other troublemakers would be found locked up.

A city watchman saluted when he saw James and said, "It's not pretty, Squire. Only one man left alive here, in that far cell."

James couldn't believe his eyes. Guardsmen were carrying bodies from one of the two large cells. James instantly saw what had likely transpired. The large man had come down, perhaps with henchmen, perhaps alone, and had found two cells occupied, six empty. The small cell across the way had been ignored, while he had opened the large cell. The door lay on the floor, and James wondered what sort of man could pry it off its hinges.

Three men lay dead in the cell, and a fourth was being

carried out. Three of these men had died by the blade,
killed quickly from the evidence before James's eyes, but
the fourth man look as if he had literally been torn limb
from limb. Eyes fixed wide in pain and terror, the
wizened-looking little man lay with his left arm ripped
off at the shoulder, his right leg smashed and broken in
several places, and his left leg severed below the knee.
His blood had splattered the walls across the room.

James glanced at Jazhara and saw her looking at the
corpse without flinching. William looked pale, though he
had seen dead men before. The young lieutenant said,
"Who could do such a thing?"

"Someone who could kill barmaids and fire orphan-
ages," answered Jazhara.

James knelt beside the corpse and said, "I know this
man. His name is Knute. Pirate working up the coast,
used to come down from time to time to fence stolen
property. Clever bastard, but obviously not clever
enough."

"What do you mean?" asked William.

"I have an idea, but I'm keeping it to myself until I get
more information," said James. With a slight smile he
glanced at his companions and added, "Don't want to
look too stupid if I'm wrong."

He stood and turned to the guard. Pointing at the other
cell with the single living man in it, he asked, "What's his
story?"

The guard shrugged. "Can't get much out of him.
Local drunk, I'm guessing, Squire. Scared to madness,
I'm thinking."

James motioned his companions to come with him. He
crossed to stand before the drunk, who stood gripping the
bars as if afraid to let go. His hair was gray and his face
drawn and pale, damaged from too many nights lying

drunk in the gutter. His eyes were tightly shut and he muttered, "Gods, gods, gods! Calm, calm, try to be calm. They'll be along soon. Any moment now, they've got to come soon . . ."

James said, "Scovy?"

The man opened his eyes wide, and tensed as if ready to leap away. Seeing James he said, "Jimmy! Dala bless you! You've come to save me!"

James said, "Not so fast, old man. Did you see what happened?"

Words came tumbling from Scovy's lips. "Oh, yes, yes, I saw it! Would that I had gone to Lims-Kragma's Hall before seein' what was done to that poor soul!"

"You mean Knute?"

Scovy nodded vigorously. "Knute it was. Pirate from up near Widow's Point. Smug he was, saying he wouldn't hang. Said the Prince himself would sign his pardon once he heard the secret Knute was keepin'."

"What secret?" James asked.

"Blast if I know, Jimmy. Knute wouldn't say. I'm thinking treasure. Knute probably had it hid . . . that's what all this fuss is about."

Jazhara said, "Tell us what happened tonight."

Scovy looked at Jimmy and said, "Get me out?"

James nodded. "If I like what I hear."

Scovy said, "Well, first this sound comes from above, like the gods' own thunder was shaking the building. Twice it rocked the building. I was sitting down, but I damned near hit my head on the ceiling I jumped so high. Scared me sober, it did. Then this man comes down the stairs. Huge fellow, with a beard and a scar through one eye, murder in the other. Knute called him 'Bear.' "

"What then?" asked William.

"Well, Knute's about to piss himself, swearing to all

the gods he didn't betray Bear. The big man seems to believe him, then he reaches over and rips the door right off the cell. Calm as you please he walks in, draws a long dagger and kills those other three sods in there. Then he tells Knute to follow him, and Knute takes a step forward, then Bear's grabbing him by the throat and lifts him clean off the ground.

"Knute's kicking and squealing like a pig heading for slaughter, and Bear keeps asking Knute where 'it' is. 'Where did you hide it?' he keeps asking. 'What did you do with it?' "

Jazhara said, "And then?"

"Knute just keeps screaming he hadn't done nothing . . . Bear says Knute's a liar and starts cutting into him, slicin' him apart piece by piece. He wouldn't even wait for an answer. He only stopped when he heard fighting upstairs. Then he screams like an animal and rips what's left of Knute into pieces." Lowering his voice, he said, "I'm only alive because this Bear ran out of time, I'm thinking. He was insane, Jimmy. Something about him . . . it's not right. I've seen strong men, but nothing like this one. I've seen crazy men, but this man is the craziest ever." His lips quivered as he finished his story. "Get me out?"

James nodded to the guard and said, "Release him."

The guard produced a key and opened the door. "Thanks, Jimmy. I won't forget."

"See that you don't, Scovy."

The prisoner hurried up the stairs and James turned to his companions. "Any ideas?"

Jazhara said, "This Knute betrayed Bear?"

James nodded. William said, "Whatever 'it' is, this Bear must want it very badly to risk so much mayhem and murder to recover it."

James let out a slow breath. "My thinking too." Turning toward the stairs upward, he said, "Let's see if Garruth has uncovered any more information in that mess. But one thing I know for certain."

"What?" William and Jazhara asked simultaneously.

"Arutha is not going to be happy."

Four

◆

Secrets

A soldier descended the staircase.

"Captain, we found someone alive. It's Dennison," he said.

James glanced at Garruth, who nodded that the squire should investigate and James signaled to Jazhara and William to accompany him upstairs.

Up there, they found the rooms in as much disarray as the ground floor. Through a door in the far end of the hall, they could see another hole blown through the wall that was obviously the way the man called Bear had exited the jail.

Sitting on a stool with a cold wet rag pressed to his head was the jail's scribe, Dennison. The scribe looked up and said, "Thank Dala, who protects the weak and the pious. Who knows what horrors they'd have inflicted upon me had you not shown up."

William looked around the room. "What happened here?"

"I was knocked to the ground by a thunderclap, then rendered almost senseless by a second. This stool upon which I sit fell atop me, striking my head here." He rubbed at a nasty bump on his forehead. "I had blood

upon my brow when they arrived, so I feigned death. They killed all the guards in the barracks room." He pointed to the door leading into the largest room on the top floor. "Someone with a powerful, deep voice gave the orders, but I kept my eyes closed so I can't tell you what he looks like. But I did catch a glimpse of one of his men."

"Did you recognize him?"

"I think so. I've seen him before. He's rumored to be the bosun's mate for Sullen Michael, the pirate."

James's eyes narrowed. He'd met many liars in his day, and this man was a particularly bad one. "Sullen Michael? How would a law-abiding servant of the Crown, such as yourself, know this man?"

The scribe blinked and said, "Ah, I have been known to drink . . . from time to time . . . and occasionally I find myself in the less savory taverns . . . down by the docks." His speech became more rapid as he said, "Ah, maybe I'm wrong. Everything was happening so fast, and I only caught a glimpse before I closed my eyes again. I mean, it could have been someone else . . ." His voice trailed off as he looked around the room uncomfortably.

James glanced at Jazhara and William, and William inched over to the stairs, while Jazhara took up position between the scribe and the hole in the far wall. James said, "Given how thorough they were in killing just about everyone else, why do you think *you* were left alive?"

The color drained from the scribe's face and he stammered, "As I said, sir, I feigned death."

"Odd they didn't check more closely," Jazhara offered coolly.

James nodded to William, then the squire stepped forward and grabbed the slender scribe by the shirtfront. "It's more than passing strange that every man in this jail

was killed—every man except you and the drunk down-stairs."

"And the drunk only survived because he was in a different cell," William observed.

James shoved the scribe so his back was to the wall. "The raiders knew exactly when to hit this jail. Who knew the schedule?"

Going even paler, the scribe sputtered, "The sheriff! The deputies!"

"And you!" said William, pressing in close to the man. "There's a girl lies dead because of those mercenaries, a girl I loved! I think you know more than you're telling, so you'd best be out with it before I spill your blood."

The scribe was shaking with fear as he held up a placating hand and he looked beseechingly from William to James to Jazhara. "Truly, masters, I've no idea."

William whipped out his dagger and put the point against the man's throat. A thin trickle of blood snaked down Dennison's neck. "You lie! Say your prayers!"

"No, wait!" screamed the scribe. "I'll tell. I'll tell. Just don't kill me!"

James moved slightly, as if to pull William away from the scribe, and in even tones said, "Did you know this man Bear?"

Dennison nodded, looking defeated. "We did a bit of business. He used to slip me a few crowns in exchange for information regarding the jail and the guards, and on occasion I'd lighten a few sentences here and there when his men were picked up. I'd cut them loose; no one noticed. I don't know what Bear was doing with that pirate Knute, but he was mighty upset when Knute got picked up."

"What secret was the pirate keeping that would lead Bear to murder?"

The scribe let out a bitter laugh. "No one needs to *lead* Bear to murder, Squire. He finds it whenever he wants. It's why I could never say no to him all these years. He'd have killed me without even blinking that one good eye of his. I don't know why he was after Knute. I just found out that Knute had a room at Ye Bitten Dog, but I've not been able to let Bear know yet, and I wasn't about to sit up and tell his men when they were killing everyone in sight."

"Well, you're not going to tell him now," said William, as he reversed his dagger and slammed the hilt into the base of the scribe's skull.

The scribe collapsed and William said, "I'll ask the captain to get this one to the palace and keep him under close watch."

James nodded. "He speaks to no one."

William picked up the limp scribe and hoisted the dead weight over his shoulder, and carried him down the steps. Jazhara shook her head and said, "A mystery."

James said, "Whatever secret Knute hid, Bear wanted it badly enough to be named the most wanted man in the Western Realm. If I know Arutha, by tomorrow there'll be a price of at least ten thousand golden sovereigns on Bear's head. Every mercenary will give long thought as to whether they should serve Bear or turn him in."

"What do we do now?"

James glanced around and cocked his head toward the scribe's desk. "First I write a note to Arutha. Then we search every paper here, just in case our friend downstairs left something useful. And then I propose we start looking for two things."

Jazhara held up one finger. "Number one: Knute's secret."

James nodded and held up two fingers. "And number

two: Lucas. Talia's father." Thoughtfully, he said, "And I'm not going to be surprised if finding one doesn't lead us to the other."

Ye Bitten Dog was as run-down a tavern as existed in Krondor, and that was no mean feat. James shook his head. "Not my favorite drinking hole."

William indulged in a rueful chuckle. "From what I've heard, James, you used to frequent worse."

James grinned and pushed open the door. "There are no worse places. Keep your wits about you; we'll not be welcome here."

He entered, the others close behind, and instantly it was apparent what he meant. Every eye was fixed upon William, or rather upon the tabard he wore: that of the Prince's Household Guard. The blood splatters and burns didn't escape notice, either.

At the far end of a long common room a band of men huddled around a high circular table, designed so that one could drink while standing up. Their garb and bare feet identified them as sailors.

Three other men, apparently workers, stood before the fireplace, and they also stared at the newcomers.

Near the door two heavily armed men had ceased their conversation upon William's entrance.

For a long moment, silence reigned in the tavern, then slowly voices could be heard as men started speaking in low murmurs. James spied the tavern keeper and moved to the long bar.

"What the hell do you want?" was the barkeep's welcome.

James smiled. William recognized that smile. It meant trouble was coming.

"Drinks, for me and my friends."

The tavern keeper was a dark-haired man, with a thick thatch that appeared as if it hadn't been visited by a comb in a year. His chin was covered in stubble and his heavy jowls and deep circles under his eyes gave the impression of one who sampled his own ale far too regularly. He placed three full flagons on the bar and growled, "That'll be six coppers. Drink up then shove off; we've no love for stooges of the court in here."

"Charming," muttered Jazhara as she sipped at the ale. It was thin and bitter, so she placed it upon the bar and stood back to watch.

James said, "You the chap they call Lucky Pete?"

The puffy face split into a smile. "Ay, Lucky Pete, on account o' me skills with the fair sex." He winked at Jazhara and said, "Come see me later, darlin', and I'll show ya me peg leg."

He put his hand over hers. She smiled, leaned forward, and whispered, "You'll have two to show me if we don't find what we're looking for." She removed his hand.

Pete grinned and chuckled, which did nothing to improve his appearance. "Got fire, do you? I like fire in me women."

William said, "We heard a fellow named Knute lodges here."

Pete cocked his head. "Knute? Did you say Knute? I'm hard of hearin', you know, an' me memory ain't what it used to be, lad." He made a show of cupping his hand behind his ear.

James glanced around and saw others in the room were quietly watching the conversation. He had been in enough dives like Ye Bitten Dog to know that if they tried to bully Pete there would almost certainly be a brawl in short order. He reached into his belt purse, pulled out two gold coins, and placed them on the counter.

Pete's expression brightened. "Ah, yes, me hearin's improvin' by the moment!" He lowered his voice. "Yeah, I knew ol' Knute. Jes' a small-time pirate, but he did all right for himself for the most part. At least until the bloody guards caught up with him." He glanced at William. "No offense, of course."

"None taken . . . yet," William replied. "Did Knute say anything unusual over the last few days?"

Pete said nothing. After a long silence, James put another coin on the bar. More silence and James pulled out a fourth coin. Pete gathered up the gold pieces and said, "Ha! He drank so much, who could tell? I know I've never seen him so jumpy an' the funny thing of it was, when the guards nicked him, he seemed relieved; almost like he was aimin' to get nicked. Started a tussle right outside that door, he did." Pete pointed to the front door. "Most fellows like Knute, well, they jus' go to lengths to avoid jail, you know what I mean?" James nodded. "But ol' Knute just started a fuss an' then hung around 'til a watchman comes along, then he throws a drink in the lad's face, kicks him in the shins, all manner of dotty nonsense. Knute's not a scuffler, if you know what I mean. He's a thinker, but this time he was right off his head, from what I could see."

James said, "Can we see his room?"

Pete made a display of indignation. "You must be daft! I can't be lettin' folks wander through me guest's belongin's!"

James slid two more coins across the bar. "Your guest lies dead, hacked to pieces."

Pete swept up the coins. "Well, in that case, I guess he won't be mindin'. Go along. Got the key right here." He slid it across the bar. "Left door at the top o' the stairs. You can look, but make it quick, an' don't be botherin'

me other guests. An' bring the key back directly, else I'll send me friends t'see ya!"

They climbed the stairs and found themselves on a small landing, with four doors, two ahead, and one to the left and one to the right. James turned to the left door and inserted the key.

As he turned the key, James heard a sound from within. He stepped back, drew his sword in a fluid motion, and kicked the door open. Inside the room a large man was rummaging through a chest placed atop an unmade bed. He turned, pulling out a large knife as the door slammed open.

James shouted, "Drop that blade!"

The man reversed the dagger, holding it by the point, drew back his arm, and threw it at James. James shouted, "Down!" and went limp, dropping to the floor. The blade flew through the door inches above James's twisting body.

James heard the sound of glass shattering as the man hurled himself through the small window overlooking the rear courtyard of the inn. William leapt over James and was at the window before James could rise.

"Damn," said William as he looked through the opening.

James came up behind him and said, "What?"

William pointed and James looked out. The man lay sprawled upon the cobbles below, his neck obviously broken from the angle at which his head was twisted.

James said to William, "Look around and see what's here, while Jazhara and I examine our friend below."

James and Jazhara hurried downstairs and past Lucky Pete, who asked, "Where's me key?"

"William will bring it when he's done," said James. Pointing at a door next to the bar, he asked, "That the way to the rear courtyard?"

"Yes, why?"

"Because you've got a corpse back there," James replied, pushing through the door.

Pete put his elbows on the bar and said, "Happens all the time, lad."

James reached the body and knelt next to it. A small pouch was still clutched in the man's hand. He pried open the man's fingers and removed it, examining the contents. Inside was a simple key.

"What do you think it's for?" asked Jazhara.

"I'm not sure, but there's something familiar about this key."

William appeared. "Nothing up there worth stealing. Just some clothes."

"There's this," said James, holding out the key.

William examined it, then said, "Come over here into the light."

They moved to the rear door of the inn, where a single lantern burned, and William took the key from James and indicated a mark on it. "See this symbol?"

James took it back from him and peered more closely. "That's Lucas's key! The one that unlocks his passage to the sewers!"

Jazhara said, "Then this must be what that villain was looking for. What does it mean?"

James tapped the key against his cheek. "Lucas has a secret entrance to the sewer, in the storage room behind the bar. He used to charge people for the use of the key, *this* key."

William said, "So Knute has been using Lucas's slip-me-out to get into the sewers."

James nodded. "Yes. Probably so he could hide the treasure from his last raid, the booty he was talking about to that drunk Scovy. The one that would buy him Arutha's pardon."

"Do you think he stole the key from Lucas?" asked Jazhara.

"No, they must be in this together. Knute's murderer wanted to know where 'it' was; I wager 'it' is the treasure."

William said, "So Lucas must have escaped into the sewers when Bear attacked. But then why hasn't he contacted you or the Prince?"

Jazhara said, "Perhaps he can't."

James shook his head. "Lucas is the only man who is not a member of the Mockers who knows the sewers as well as I. He'll have several places to lie low." James's voice got lower as he thought about it. "He must know what sort of man Bear is. And he must know that if he's been involved in piracy, even just fencing stolen goods, Arutha would be unlikely to afford him significant protection. Lucas has spent his life walking a fine line between lawlessness and legitimate business, but this time he's crossed that line."

William spoke bitterly, "And his daughter paid the price."

James put his hand on William's arm. "And Lucas will have to live with that for the rest of his life."

Jazhara said, "Which will not be long if Bear finds him. Our task is clear; we must find Lucas—and quickly."

James nodded agreement. "Pray we get to him before Bear does."

"Where do we start?" asked William.

James gave his friend a wry smile and pointed downward. "The sewers."

Blood still stained the floors of the Rainbow Parrot Inn, but the bodies had been removed. A soldier stood beside the door as James, William, and Jazhara approached.

"Simon!" said William as he recognized the soldier. "How goes it?"

"Quiet, here, Lieutenant. Got the bodies out and taken to the Temple of Lims-Kragma, so's they can be properly sent on their way."

"Where are the other guards?" asked James.

"Well, Jack's at the back door, and that's it, Squire. Sergeant Tagart had the rest of the lads take the bodies to the temple. I guess the sergeant didn't think much of anyone trying to rob an inn that was already ransacked. A couple of lads will relieve us at the end of our shift, then we can go down with the others."

"Down where?" asked James.

"Why, the sewers. Ain't you heard, Squire?"

James said, "Heard what?"

"Some bloke was cut loose from the jail a few hours ago. He got someone to stand for drinks at an alehouse in exchange for telling why the jail was attacked."

James winced. "Scovy."

"Could be that's the fellow," said the soldier. "Anyway, there's been rumors aplenty. Pirate treasure in the sewers. Mountains of jewels and gold. Says a pirate named Bear hit the jail because someone there knew where the treasure was."

"So the sewers are now crawling with treasure hunters," said William.

"That's a fact, Lieutenant," said Simon. "Heard from one of the city watch who passed by a few minutes before you got here that a band of blokes came hobbling out of the big grate near Five Points, all cut up and bleeding. Word is the Mockers are trying to keep everyone else out of the sewers so they can find the treasure themselves."

James sighed. "Well, I wonder what else could happen to make finding Lucas more difficult."

"Well, someone said there's a monster down there, too, Squire."

James looked at Simon and said, "You're joking, right?"

"On my honor, Squire," said the soldier. "Seems two nights ago they found a body floating in the bay, all chewed up the way a cat does a mouse. Then they heard some fellow over at Ye Bitten Dog heard from another bloke that a band of smugglers was attacked by something that was big as a bull, with long arms and big teeth."

Jazhara asked James, "And you want to go down there?"

"No," answered the former thief, "but we have no choice. If we're going to catch Bear, we need to find Lucas before he does. I have an idea where Lucas may be lying low."

William nodded. "Even if Bear doesn't find Lucas; if Lucas was in cahoots with Knute and is sitting on that treasure, anyone else who finds it before we do will probably kill Lucas."

James said, "No more delays. Come on." To Simon he said, "When your relief shows up, tell the duty sergeant that we're in the sewers hunting the killer. I want word sent back to the palace asking the Prince to send a company down after us to help clear out these treasure hunters."

"As you say, Squire." Simon saluted.

James started to turn away, and Simon added, "One other thing, Squire."

"What is it?"

"There's a rumor surfaced a bit ago." He glanced around as if ensuring no one else was listening. "Seems a bunch of drunken lads from up Fishtown way came out of the sewers over near Five Points, dragging some fellows with them. They were pretty messed up."

"Mockers?" asked James, wondering if the fishermen might have run into the Guild of Thieves.

"No, not Mockers, Squire." He lowered his voice. "They said it was that monster I was telling you about. Went over to the Temple of Dala and had to give the priests every copper they had just to keep their friends from bleeding to death."

"The monster again?" William looked dubious. "Stop that nonsense."

Simon shrugged. "Just telling what I heard, Lieutenant. Some sort of . . . thing, bigger than a man by half. One fisherman said it just showed up in the tunnel with them and started breaking bones and biting off fingers."

"Great," said James. "Just great." Shaking his head, he led his companions into the back room and to a wall lined floor to ceiling with shelves full of dry food, extra crockery, and bottles of wine. He produced the key they had found in Knute's room and moved aside a bag of dried beans. Behind it was a keyhole large enough to accommodate Knute's key.

He inserted the key and turned it. A soft rumbling sound and a loud click followed, then James gripped the side of the shelves and pulled it to the right. It slid effortlessly to the side, revealing a half-height passage and steps leading down. "You've got to duck a bit to get down these steps," he said. "William, go fetch us a light."

William returned to the inn's common room and reappeared a moment later with a lantern. James said, "We could enter at any one of a dozen places, but picking up Lucas's trail might be easier here."

He motioned for the lantern, took it from William's outstretched hand, and led them into the darkness.

" 'Ware the drop," James whispered, as he jumped three feet down from the tunnel from Lucas's inn to the sewer floor. He turned and offered his hand to Jazhara,

who took it, and using her staff for balance jumped nimbly down. William leapt after her and landed on something that squished under his boot.

"What a stench!" William complained as he scraped his boot on the stones rising above the inch-deep liquid.

James turned to Jazhara and said, "I'm afraid this isn't exactly what I meant by a tour of the city. But duty calls . . ."

She asked, "Do you truly think your friend Lucas has fled down here?"

James peered around through the gloom. After a moment he said, "He knows these sewers almost as well as the Mockers do." He peered at the walls and floor as if seeking a sign of where to begin. "Back at the time of the Riftwar, Lucas worked with both the Mockers and Trevor Hull's smugglers. He built up a lot of goodwill with the Mockers and so they leave him alone down here. Not many can claim that. This is where he'd go if he were in trouble."

William said, "We've a lot of ground to cover, so we'd best get started. Which way first?"

James pointed. "That way, downstream."

"Why?" asked Jazhara.

"There are some old smugglers' hide-outs that Lucas knows. Not many, even in the Mockers, know exactly where they are anymore. I'm betting Lucas is holed up in one of those secret rooms."

"You know where they are?" asked William.

James shrugged. "It's been years, but I sort of know their general location."

William let out his breath in an exasperated way. "Sort of?"

Jazhara laughed. "Better than no idea, it seems to me."

They made their way through the sewers, the sound of

their passage masked by the drips, splashes, and gurgles of the water echoing off the stones. Every so often, James would raise his hand to halt them, and listen.

After nearly a half-hour of careful movement, they entered a large tunnel. The sound of rushing water came from ahead. James said, "The center of the sewer system lies up there. A half-dozen large tunnels empty into it, and it leads out to the south end of the bay. From there we will take another tunnel to the old smugglers' landing. The outflow is big enough for a boat to enter, which is why the smugglers had their landing at the opposite end, near the eastern wall of the city."

William said, "Anyone using it these days?"

"Besides Lucas? I don't know. There aren't many alive today who have been down there who aren't in the Prince's service. Maybe the Mockers have discovered those storage rooms."

They entered a larger conduit and the sound of rushing water grew louder. "Walk carefully here," warned James.

They entered a large rotunda, with six tunnels branching off, like spokes on a wheel. Above them, smaller pipes emptied out into the circular area and filthy water splashed down below them. They moved cautiously in single file on the narrow walkway along the wall, for the stones around the deep hole were encrusted with slippery filth. As they passed the second of the larger tunnels, William asked, "Where do these lead?"

"Each leads to a different portion of the city," said James. He paused and pointed to one of the tunnels on the opposite side of the gallery. "That one over there leads back toward the palace. Some prince, years ago, decided to make the sewers more efficient, I guess. There's an old cistern up there"—he pointed upward to the darkness—"and it was supposed to release water every night to help

flush out the sewers. Don't know if it ever worked the way it was supposed to, but . . ." He resumed walking. "I don't know anyone who remembers it being used. Lots of merchants just dig their own tunnels to the sewer when they start up their shops. The royal engineers have maps, but most of them are outdated, useless." Almost to himself he added, "That would be something worth doing, updating those maps and requiring people to inform the Crown when they make changes."

They entered the third large tunnel and James said, "Be cautious. We're entering Mocker territory."

A short time later this tunnel emptied into a smaller circular area, with two more tunnels entering a third of the way up on either side, forming a "Y" intersection. An old man stood near the intersection, holding a long stick that he used to poke at floating debris.

William began to draw his sword slowly, but James reached back and stayed his friend's hand. "It's just an old toffsman, named Rat-Tail Jack."

"Toffsman?" whispered Jazhara.

"He scavenges for items of value. You'd be amazed at what can turn up down here."

Slowly James walked into view and said, "Good day, Jack."

The man turned. "Jimmy, as I live and breathe. Been some years."

Upon closer inspection, the man was of middle age, stoop-shouldered, and slender. His hair was matted and filthy, of indeterminate color. He had a receding chin and large eyes, and they were fixed upon James and his two companions.

"Playing lookout, I see," James said, flashing a grin.

The man stopped the pretense of poking at the sludge. "You know the trade too well, me old son."

"What's up in the wind?"

"Bloody murder and a bunch of lunatic treasure hunters. Been a handful of lads taken to the temples for healing already. Word's been passed to shut down the Thieves' Highway."

Jimmy said, "So I guess that means I'm supposed to turn around and go back."

"Even you, old son." The man pointed to the other two tunnels. "Bashers are waiting. You'd best go no further. That's Mockers territory. The big 'rats' down there will have you for supper, they will."

"Not for old time's sake?"

"Not even that, Jimmy me lad. You got the death mark lifted, I hear, but you're still not one of the Dodgy Brotherhood and when the Thieves' Highway is closed, only Mockers can pass."

William whispered, "Is there another way?"

James replied, "Too long. We'll have to try to talk our way past whoever's ahead."

"And if that doesn't work?" asked Jazhara.

James said, "We fight." He turned back to Jack. "We're looking for Lucas. Seen or heard anything from him?"

"He's hiding out, boy, somewhere down here, but I can't lead you to him."

"What about Bear?" asked William. "Any word of him?"

"There's a bad one," said Jack. "He was down here a few days ago looking for something. Killed a few of the boys. We put the death mark on him."

"He's marked by the Crown, as well," said James.

"Still don't make the Mockers and Crown friends, old son," said Jack.

James said, "Who's in charge over there?"

"Bosun Mace."

James shook his head. Bosun Mace had been a sailor

in the King's Fleet who had been whipped out of service for thieving. He had joined the Mockers to put his talents to more profitable use. He was a bully, short tempered, and had never liked James when the boy had been a Mocker. He had been one of the few men who had been friends with Laughing Jack, a Basher whom James killed for making a failed attempt on the Prince's life.

"It's going to be a nasty fight," said James to his companions.

Rat-Tail Jack said, "Doesn't have to be, lad, if you use that fabled wit of yours. There's always something that can be traded for, old son."

"Such as?" asked Jazhara.

Jack said, "Go talk to Mace and when he starts to threaten you, ask him who's been chewing up his lads. That'll get his attention."

"Thanks, Jack," said James. He motioned for his companions to move forward. They took the tunnel to the left and as they did so, Jack let out a shrill whistle.

"What was that?" asked William.

"Jack's taking care of himself," said James. "If he didn't call out the alarm, the Bashers would think he was in league with us."

A short distance later they reached a widening of the tunnel and from along both sides of the wall men stepped into view, surrounding the trio. There were a half-dozen of them, all armed. A large gray-haired man in front stepped forward into the torchlight.

After a moment he smiled. It wasn't a pretty sight. Jowls covered with stubble hung from a head that seemed a size too big for anything human. His eyes looked as much like a pig's as a man's. A bulbous nose that had been broken too many times to recall was the centerpiece of his malformed visage.

"Well, Jimmy the Hand," said the large man, slapping his left hand with the long sap he held in his right. "You looking for some pain, boy?"

"Looking to talk, Mace."

"I always thought you talked too much, even when you was one of us, you little snot." With that he shouted, "Get 'em, lads!" and swung his billy club at James's head.

Five

◆

Monsters

(J) ames ducked.

The billy club split the air above his head as he shouted, "Mace! Wait! We need to talk!"

Jazhara had her staff at the ready and William brandished his sword, but both held off from engaging the approaching thieves until a blow was delivered.

"I'll talk to you," answered Mace, swinging again at the elusive former thief, "with this!"

"Who's been chewing up your Bashers?" shouted James as he avoided a third swing.

The large man stopped, holding his club high above his head in preparation for another blow. "What you know about that, boy?"

James kept his distance. "I hear things."

Suddenly the man looked worried, and James knew that something grave must have occurred, for as long as he had known Mace the Bosun, the man had never shown fear or doubt. Mace lowered his billy and held up his free hand to signal the other thieves to stop their advance.

"All right, then," he said at last. "What have you heard?"

"Just that someone—or something—has been grab-

bing your men and leaving them . . ." James was bluffing. He knew no details, but reckoned that what Rat-Tail Jack had referred to was in some way connected to the "monsters" Simon had described at the Rainbow Parrot. And the old toffsman's advice about bringing up this topic had proved accurate so far.

"Mangled," said one of the other thieves.

"Mangled," repeated James.

"It's fair disgustin'," said another thief. "Looks like they'd been gnawed on, like a dog does wit' a bone, you know, Squire?"

Others nodded.

"Where?" asked James.

"That's the thing," said Mace. "One place, then another—there's no rhyme or reason to it. You never know."

"How long has this been going on?" asked James.

"Fair close to a week, now," said Mace.

James said, "You let us go by, Mace, and I'll find out what's killing your men and get it dealt with."

"How you going to do that if some of my toughest men can't face this thing, whatever it is?"

Jazhara held up her hand and a globe of light sprang forth.

"Blind me eyes!" exclaimed one of the thieves. "A bloody magician!"

"The Prince's bloody magician," corrected James.

Mace waved his billy at Jazhara. "You know the Mockers have no truck with magic!" he shouted. "Prince's squire and all, you still know the Mockers' Law!"

Jazhara closed her hand and the light vanished. "Look the other way for a while."

"Or else let me call down a few squads of the Prince's regulars," said William. "A couple of hundred armed men might flush the thing out, don't you think?"

The thought of soldiers invading the Thieves' Highway was obviously more odious than a magician, for after a moment Mace said, "All right, you can pass. But if any more of my lads gets killed, Prince's squire or no, the death mark will be back on you, boy. You have my word on that."

James bowed theatrically, and said, "Your warning is heard. Now, if we may go?"

Mace waved them by. "Tread lightly, Jimmy the Hand. There are them about who ain't members of the Guild."

"Noted. What's the password?"

" 'Lanky boy,' " answered Mace.

They left the Mockers and continued down the passage. When they were safely out of earshot, Jazhara said, "I understand many people fear magic, but why are the Mockers so averse to it?"

James said, "Because thieves thrive on misdirection and subterfuge. You ever hear of a thief stealing something from a magician?"

Jazhara laughed. "Only in stories."

"That's the point. If Arutha wanted to rid the city of thieves, he could for a while by having you, or someone like you, ferret them out with magic."

Jazhara peered around the tunnel. "I think they overrate our abilities. I could create some problems in a limited area for a small number of them, but once I had left, I suspect they would return, like rats."

James chuckled. "Almost certainly, but no one said a fear has to be based in reality."

Jazhara glanced at James. "Squire, I know you by reputation to be a man of some accomplishments for one so young, but to find you to be a deep thinker is impressive."

Now it was William's turn to chuckle, leaving James to wonder if the remark was a compliment or a barb.

* * *

Twice they halted to hide as bands of armed men came by. After the second group had safely passed, James said, "That lot had been in a tussle."

William nodded as he relit the lantern. "Two of them aren't going to make it if their companions don't carry them."

"Which way do we go now?" asked Jazhara.

"Where they came from," said James.

They continued on, deeper into the sewers.

The sound of lapping water heralded the existence of another large waterway.

"This is the original river sluice," said James. "One of the early princes built it. I've been told that this was originally above ground . . . maybe designed as a small canal for barges from the river."

William knelt and inspected the stonework. "Looks ancient." He stood and glanced around. "Look there," he said, moving over to examine something on the nearby wall. "This doesn't look like the usual tunnel wall. It's more like a fortification wall." He indicated the size of the stones and the almost seamless way in which they were set.

"No foot- or handholds," James agreed.

"How did it come to be so far below the ground?" asked Jazhara.

James shrugged. "People build things. They fill in the spaces between them to make roads. At least a dozen of the sewer tunnels look like old roads that have been covered over, and that central spillway we passed earlier was almost certainly a cistern ages ago."

"Fascinating," she said. "How old do you estimate?"

"Krondor's four hundred years old," said James. "Give or take a week."

Jazhara laughed. "By Keshian standards, a young city."

James shrugged and began walking. "This way."

As they turned a corner into another passage that ran parallel to the main watercourse, something darted across their field of vision halfway down the tunnel, at the edge of the lantern light.

"What was that?" asked William, bringing his sword to the ready.

"It was big," said Jazhara. "Larger than a man by half."

James had also drawn his sword. "Cautiously, my friends."

They moved carefully down the passage until they came to the intersection where the figure had vanished. Ahead lay a long corridor leading to the right, while to the left a short passage led back to the edge of the canal. "If the thing moves through the water," said William, "that would explain why it is hard to find."

"And why it could move about from place to place quickly," observed James. "That way," he said pointing to the left.

They walked slowly, and after a dozen steps spied a faint green light wavering in the distance. Jazhara whispered, "My hair stands on end. There is magic nearby."

James said, "Thanks for the warning."

Jazhara removed something from her belt pouch. "If I give the word, fall to the ground and cover your eyes."

William said, "Understood." James nodded.

They inched toward the light, and saw a door set in the stone wall. It was open. When they reached the portal, they halted.

James attempted to make sense of what he saw. Human bones lay strewn about, along with the bones of rats and other small animals. Rags and straw had been fashioned into a large circular pallet, in which rested several large

leathery objects, each as long as a man's arm. They pulsed with a sick, green inner light.

Jazhara gasped. "By the gods!" Suddenly James made sense of what they beheld. Within the leather sacks, as he thought of them, figures were visible.

"They're babies!" the magician cried, horrified. She closed her eyes and began a low incantation. At last, her eyes snapped open and she said, "This is the darkest magic. This place must be destroyed. Shield your eyes!"

Both men turned their backs to the door as Jazhara hurled the object she'd taken from her pouch. A flash of white light illuminated the area as heat washed over them.

In the sudden brilliance the far end of the corridor was revealed. There stood a misshapen, hunchbacked figure, a creature seven or more feet tall. Atop its frame sat a massive head, its visage a caricature of a human face with a protruding jaw exposing teeth the size of a man's thumb. Beady black eyes widened in shock at the burst of light. Its arms hung to the floor, and instead of hands, large callused flippers bore the creature's weight.

After a second, the monster roared and charged.

James and William stood ready as Jazhara turned.

The thing was almost upon them when James threw his dagger with his left hand, a short, deft cast, catching the creature in the chest. The monster barely hesitated, but it let out a roar of pain.

The light coming from the fire behind them revealed gaping wounds upon the creature's body. The fights with other groups in the tunnels had left the thing weakened, James hoped, and now he knew it was mortal, as blood seeped from several of the gashes.

William's sword snaked point first over James's head, and he braced to let the creature run up onto the blade.

The creature slowed, and rather than impale itself, it lifted what James thought of as arms rather than forelegs. With a sudden backhand slash, the flipper-like hand sliced through the air, and James barely avoided decapitation. The flipper struck the stones with a solid crack; James knew there must be a hard callus or bone ridge along the flipper's edge that would likely cut through flesh.

Jazhara chanted a spell and held up her hand. A point of searing red light appeared upon the creature's head and suddenly it howled in pain. Both flippers came up as if to shield its head, giving William an opening.

The long hand-and-a-half sword shot forward. A short man, William was nevertheless powerful of arm and shoulder and he drove his sword home with all his weight. The blade struck deep. The creature wailed.

James shot past his companion and struck for its throat with his rapier and in seconds the thing lay upon the stones, dead.

"What is it?" asked William, panting heavily.

"Nothing natural," said Jazhara.

"Someone made it?" asked James, moving cautiously around the still corpse.

Jazhara knelt and touched a flipper, then ran her hand across the brow above the blankly staring eyes. Finally she rose, wiping away a tear. "It was a baby."

William almost gagged. "*That* was a baby?"

Jazhara turned and started walking down the tunnel. "I need to be away from here," she said, her voice choked with emotion.

James and William hurried to overtake her. "Wait!" James cried.

Reaching the intersection, Jazhara halted. Before either William or James could speak, she turned and said,

"Some magic is evil beyond imagining. There is a branch of the Lesser Path, called by some 'Arcane Vitrus' in the old language. It means 'the hidden knowledge of life.' When used for good, it seeks to unravel the reason people sicken and die, or to find cures for deformity or illness. When used for evil, it can fashion creatures such as these."

"Babies?" William asked.

Jazhara nodded. "Children stolen or bought hours after birth, placed within those 'egg sacs' to be refashioned and twisted against any reasonable nature by malignant arts."

"So this monster was the first to hatch?" James asked, shaking his head.

"That poor child was no monster," said Jazhara. "Whoever created it is the monster." She looked to James. "Somewhere in Krondor is a magician who makes black mischief. Someone who wishes great turmoil in the Prince's city."

James closed his eyes. "As if Bear wasn't enough." He sighed and said, "One problem at a time. Let's find Rat-Tail Jack and Mace and then Lucas."

They turned and began retracing their steps, back the way they had come.

As they walked Jazhara said, "That creature can't have been down here long."

James looked thoughtful. "Mace said the trouble first started a week or so ago."

William said, "Maybe whoever created it wanted to see if the magic worked, then when it did, planned to make more."

"I think you're right," Jazhara said. "Which means the magic is very powerful, for not only does it twist the human design, it works quickly, perhaps in a few days or a week."

"So the creature really was a baby," said James. "In both senses."

"Yes, and in pain." Jazhara's voice was bitter. "This is the sort of horror that turns people against those of us who practice the mystic arts. It is why magicians are shunned and hated. I must send word to Master Pug and let him know a rogue magician of powerful arts is in Krondor."

James said, "Ah, I'd leave that to the Prince. Arutha tends to prefer a more direct approach. If he feels the need to inform Stardock, he will."

Jazhara said, "Of course. I will merely advise His Highness to send word to Master Pug."

They continued on in silence, occasionally pausing when the sound of others in the sewers reached them. Eventually they returned to the spot Mace and his gang had halted them. William said, "Are they gone?"

James kept walking. "They're nearby; trust me."

They moved to the large canal and found Rat-Tail Jack still picking over the sewage floating by. As they approached, he looked up. "You're alive? Guess that means we need to be rewarding you, Squire."

James said nothing, but looked quizzical.

"How about we don't kill you for breaking oath with the Mockers and entering the sewer without our leave? That reward enough for you, Squire?"

All James said was: "Lucas."

"Monster's really dead?"

"Yes. Now, what do you know about Lucas?"

Jack stopped poking at the floating detritus. "We was keepin' an eye on Lucas. He's an old . . . business associate from way back, but we was figurin' he was handling some business that rightly was ours. One night three boats rowed by some grim-looking lads came up the main canal from the harbor. Couldn't get close enough to see

which of the old smugglers' hideaways he used, but we'd have found it sooner or later. Lucas went up to his inn.

"Then he drops right down among us yesterday and offers us his inn if we just let him pass. Well, for that nice little inn of his, we said 'pass,' and he scurries off. Knows the sewers, does old Lucas, 'cause the lad set to tail him got shaken before he reached the smugglers' landin'. Still, enough, we figure we'll get around to findin' him, 'cause the lads checkin' around up top hear rumors of pirates and gold. We figure Lucas knows where their treasure's hid. That's why he was free with his inn and all. So we figure we'll send a couple of Bashers on him but then this monster shows up and all them treasure hunters start running through the tunnels . . ."

"Where is he now?"

"We have a good idea of where he was, Squire, but you know how it goes with us Mockers. Always misplacin' things. Of course, for a price, anythin' can be found."

"We killed the monster," said William.

"And for that you get free passage, nothin' more," replied Jack.

"What's your price?" asked James.

"One favor, from you and your new friends, to be named later."

"What?" William exclaimed.

"Why?" asked James.

Jack said, "It won't be asked soon, maybe never, but we think there's trouble comin'. Big trouble. That monster was just the tiniest bit of it. And we need all the friends we can get."

"You know I can't break my oath to the Prince and do anything illegal for you," said James.

"I'm not askin' for that," said Jack. "But we need friends, don't we, Jimmy the Hand?"

James pondered the request, then said at last, "That we do, Rat-Tail Jack. You have my oath."

"We think Lucas is near the basement where old Trevor Hull hid the Princess when you were a boy. There are a couple of cellars from torn-down buildings that you can still get into, large enough to hide some treasure, and close enough to the water to get it there."

"I know the area," said James. "We'll be out of the sewers by sun-up."

"See that you are. We can't control every murderin' dog down here."

James motioned for Jazhara and William to follow him and they continued along their way, heading for the central canal.

The trio moved silently and slowly. In the distance they could hear the low murmur of men's voices.

James and his companions made their way cautiously to a point near an intersection of the main canal and another large waterway. Crouching low in the darkness, their lantern shuttered, James, Jazhara, and William waited.

Six men, all wearing black, were consulting with one another, speaking very softly. Jazhara's intake of breath behind James told him she recognized them. James and William already knew them for what they were: Izmalis. Keshian assassins. More than a dozen had turned up in the desert fortress of the Nighthawks that Prince Arutha had destroyed just months earlier.

James had no illusions: if Jazhara could strike with some magic spell that would incapacitate two or three of them for a few minutes, then he and William stood a chance. In an open fight without the advantage of surprise, it would take a miracle for the three of them to survive.

James turned and tapped Jazhara on the shoulder, pointing to the six men, and then he put his lips next to her ear. In his softest voice he asked, "What can you do?"

Jazhara whispered, "I can try to blind them. When I tell you, close your eyes tightly."

She whispered the same instructions in William's ear. Then she rose from her crouch and began an incantation, her voice soft. Something—a too-loud word, a rustle of cloth, the scrape of a boot against stone—alerted one of the assassins, who turned to peer into the gloom. Then he said something to his companions, and at one they ceased their discussion to look where he indicated.

Slowly they drew weapons. James whispered, "Do it now!"

Jazhara said, "Close your eyes!" and let loose her spell. A shaft of golden light sprang from her hand and exploded in a searing-hot, white flash. The six assassins were blinded instantly. Jazhara shouted, "Now!"

James sprang into action, with William just a step behind him. Jazhara uncovered the lantern, throwing the tunnel into stark relief. The young squire struck the first man with the hilt of his sword, knocking him into the canal. "Take one alive if you can!" he shouted.

William struck down one man, but almost got run through when he found his next opponent in a defensive posture, ready to respond to the sound of an attack. "Think I'll try to stay alive, first, James," he said, using his long sword to get over the blinded man's guard and kill him.

Jazhara came up next to William and struck another assassin across the face with the iron-clad butt of her staff. The man crumpled to the floor.

James found the next two Izmalis had regained some of their sight and were poised for attack. As James knew

from experience, multiple opponents often got in one another's way, but these two looked practiced at fighting in tandem. "I could use some help," he said to Jazhara.

As soon as he spoke, both men launched a coordinated attack, and only his preternatural reflexes saved him. The first man struck out, the curved blade of his scimitar slicing at James's mid-section, while his companion struck a half-beat later, coming in where James should have been standing had he made the expected response to the initial attack.

Instead, James had blocked to the right with his blade, and instead of retreating he had pressed hard on his own weapon, forcing the first assassin to continue moving to his left. With his left hand, James gripped the Izmali's right elbow and threw his weight into the man, sending him spinning into the canal.

Suddenly the second assassin facing James was alone, with Jazhara bearing down with her staff, ready to strike, and James was now on his off-hand side.

William engaged his last opponent and called, "I've got this one cornered!"

The Izmali facing Jazhara said something in a language James didn't understand, then raised his left hand to his mouth, and toppled to the stones. William's opponent did likewise, falling into the canal with a splash.

"Damn!" shouted James, grabbing the collapsing assassin before he hit the stones. As he expected, the man was already dead.

Jazhara looked at the assassin James had knocked into the canal and said, "He floats face-down."

"What happened?" William asked.

"Nighthawks. They've taken their own lives. Fanatics." Addressing Jazhara, James inquired, "Did you understand what he said?"

"I think he ordered his companions to die, but I did not recognize the language. It is said the Izmalis have their own tongue, that no one outside their clan may learn."

William said, "We found some like these when the demon was summoned at the abandoned fortress in the desert."

"Demon?" Jazhara asked.

"I'll tell you back at the palace," said James. "But it's clear the Nighthawks numbered Keshians in their bands."

"Which makes them a threat to the Empire as well as to the Kingdom."

James regarded the young woman for a long moment, then said, "It might be wise to send some specific information to your great-uncle."

"Perhaps," said Jazhara, leaning upon her staff, "but as you've observed, that's for the Prince to decide."

James grinned. "Let's check the bodies."

They examined the four assassins who hadn't ended up in the canal and came away with nothing. The only personal items they wore were the Nighthawks' amulets around their necks.

"I thought we'd seen the last of these in the desert," said William.

"We hurt them, certainly, and we destroyed one nest, but there are others." James stood up and tucked an amulet into his shirt. "I'll give this to the Prince. He won't be pleased."

"What were they doing down here?" asked Jazhara.

William said, "Searching for the treasure, I expect."

"If they're to rebuild their nasty little empire, they'll need gold," agreed James. He glanced around. "We came in time, I think." He moved to a large wall with two iron rings set into it and turned the one on the left. After a moment, a deep rumble started and the stones moved aside.

"Lucas!" he shouted. "It's James. I've come from the Prince with help!"

From deep within the darkened passage a voice called, "Jimmy! Thank the gods it's you. They've been searching for me all over, trying to kill me."

James motioned for Jazhara to bring the lantern and the three of them entered the tunnel. A dozen feet in, Lucas stood holding a crossbow, and as soon as he recognized the two young men, he laid it down, relief on his face. "The thugs of that madman, Bear, have been after me for an entire day."

"They're not the only ones," said William. "Treasure hunters and assassins and thieves as well."

"Damn," said Lucas. "Knute said his men were hand-picked, and would keep silent, but I suspect the fool couldn't keep his own gob shut."

"What is it Bear's after?" asked James.

"Damned if I know, James," replied Lucas. The old man sat down on a water cask. "I was going to help Knute fence the booty from his last raid. I guess Knute double-crossed Bear, because Bear and some of his men showed up at my inn and started killing everyone in sight. I barely got out alive myself after telling Talia and the others to flee through the kitchen."

James and William exchanged glances. In a soft voice James said, "Talia's dead, Lucas. Bear caught her and tried to get her to tell him where you were hiding."

Lucas seemed to collapse from within. His face turned gray and his eyes welled up with tears. "Talia?" His chin fell to his chest. For a long while he sat silently, then said with a sniffle, "I lost my sons in the war, but never thought that Talia . . ." He sighed. After another long silence, he said, "This deal with Knute would have set me up. She wouldn't have had to be a barmaid anymore. She

would have had a proper dowry for a proper young man." He looked up at William.

William also had tears in his eyes. "You know I cared for her, Lucas. I swear to you we'll find Bear and Talia will be avenged."

Lucas nodded sadly. "All this trouble, all this black murder, and now it's pointless. I should just return the booty to Knute."

"You haven't heard about Knute?" asked James.

"I heard the guards picked him up night before last. He's in jail."

"Not anymore," said William. "Bear broke into the jail and cut Knute to pieces."

"By the gods! He's gone mad," exclaimed Lucas.

"We'll deal with Bear," William avowed.

"Thank you, William," said Lucas, "but mind your step. Talia may be gone, but you're still with us, and I'd prefer it if you stayed that way. This Bear is dangerous, and he's got magic on his side."

Jazhara said, "What kind of magic?"

"Dark powers, milady. Knute was terrified after he saw Bear work magic. That's why he broke with him." He shook his head. "You want to see what the bastards were after?"

James nodded. "I am a bit curious."

Lucas rose and led them to a stout wooden door. He threw aside the bar on the door and pulled it open. Jazhara stepped forward with her lamp, and even James had to let out an appreciative low whistle.

The small room was filled knee-deep in treasure. Sacks of gold coins were piled atop several small chests. Solid gold statues and piles of jewelry were strewn about. Lucas stepped into the room and opened one of the chests. Inside was more gold, and a small statuette. Jazhara reached

down and picked it up. "This is Ishapian," she said softly. "It is a holy icon of their church, the Symbol of Ishap."

James's eyes grew wide. "They hit an Ishapian vessel! There couldn't be a more dangerous undertaking for a pirate, by my reckoning."

Lucas said, "Most men would say foolhardy. Bear wanted something off that ship, something specific. Knute was certain that, whatever it was, it wasn't among the loot he'd stashed down here."

Jazhara asked, "How did he know that?"

"Knute told me that Bear flew into a rage when the ship went down, despite having taken all this." He waved his hand. "It's one of the reasons Knute left Bear to drown. He was afraid Bear blamed him for the ship going down too fast."

"A reasonable fear, considering what Bear did to him," observed Jazhara.

William looked confused. "How does this help us? We still don't really know who we're chasing, and what he's searching for."

Lucas opened another chest, one that looked different from the others. It was made of dark wood, much older, and appeared never to have been cleaned. It was stained and the hinges were rusty. He pulled out a rolled-up parchment and handed it to James. Then he handed a battered, leather-bound book to Jazhara. "It's all there. These papers list every ship that Knute's crew have sunk over the years, including this last job with Bear."

James looked at the map. "This will tell us where the Ishapian vessel was hit."

"Knute was thorough, I'll say that for the little gnoll," admitted Lucas.

"It still doesn't tell us what Bear is after," observed Jazhara.

William said, "Could we bait him into coming to us if we spread a rumor that we know what he's after?"

James said, "Maybe, but first things first. I must go to the palace first and report to the Prince." He turned to Lucas. "You stay here with William. I'll send Jonathan Means and some deputies down here to take charge of all this gold."

"What will you do with it?" asked Lucas.

James smiled. "Give it back to the Ishapians. We may not know what Bear was after, but I'll wager a year's income they do."

Lucas's shoulders sank slightly, but he nodded.

Jazhara and William followed James out of the room, and they returned into the sewers. As they hurried down a corridor toward the nearest exit, they heard the secret door to the old smugglers' hideout closing behind them.

Six

♦

Intrigues

Arutha waited for the page to leave.

When the youngster had departed from the Prince's private office, the ruler of the Western Realm of the Kingdom of the Isles looked at James. "Well, this is a far worse mess than we had imagined, isn't it?"

James nodded. "Much more than a simple hunt for pirate loot, Highness."

Arutha graced the magician with his half-smile, and his dark eyes studied the young woman. "You've gotten quite an unusual reception in our city, haven't you, milady?"

James quipped, "Given our recent history, Highness, it may be more usual than either of us likes."

Jazhara smiled at the casual banter between the two men. "Highness, my instructions from Duke Pug were simple: Come to Krondor and help you in any fashion I might, relative to issues of magic. To those ends, I am here to serve, even if it means having to practice the more bellicose side of the art in defense of your realm."

Arutha sat back and made a tent with his fingertips, flexing them in and out a little, a nervous habit James had observed in him since the first day they met. After a mo-

ment, he said, "We have two such topics of discussion, both of which may require, as you put it, 'the more bellicose side' of your arts."

"The creature," supplied James.

Jazhara nodded her agreement. "Highness, the presence of that monstrous child and the quality of evil magic required for such an undertaking indicate that malignant forces of great power are involved."

"Indeed," said the Prince. "Is there any reason you can imagine for someone to practice such horrific magic within the city itself? Certainly the chance of discovery was high, even in an abandoned corner of the sewers."

Jazhara said, "If the purpose was to create chaos in your city, Highness, then such a choice makes sense. For any other reason I can imagine, no; it is a choice that defies understanding.

"So, assuming the intent was to create chaos, then the potential reward would have been worth the risk of early discovery." Jazhara hesitated, then added, "The creature formed from the evil magic used upon those babies would no doubt have grown in power. The one we destroyed had killed or injured more than a dozen armed men in the course of a few days, by all reports. It was weakened when we fought it. Moreover, it was immature, still an infant by any measure. In a few more weeks, I suspect it would have been quite powerful. A host of those things loose in your city . . ."

"You draw an unattractive picture," said Arutha. "But your argument is persuasive." He leaned forward. "Since the arrival of the moredhel renegade Gorath we have been wrestling with a series of seemingly inexplicable events, but throughout those events there has been one constant: someone who seeks to plunge Krondor into chaos."

"The Crawler," said James.

Arutha nodded. "I agree."

"Who is this Crawler, sire?" asked Jazhara.

Arutha nodded to James, who said, "We don't know. If we did, he would have been hanged long since. He first appeared over a year ago, running a gang that attempted to dislodge the Mockers in Krondor. But at the same time, he appears to be working the docks, interfering with commerce. Further, we've ascertained that he had a major relationship with the Nighthawks. In other words, he's a thoroughly bad fellow."

Arutha said, "And potentially far more dangerous than we had thought initially. He seems to have had a hand in the attack on the Duke of Olasko and his family."

"The man moves in many circles," said James.

"And then there is the matter of the Ishapians," said Arutha, pointing to the statuette Jazhara had carried to the palace. "I have sent word to the High Priest of the Temple here in Krondor and I expect we'll be hearing from him soon."

"Does this have anything to do with that house across the square from the palace, Highness?" asked James.

Arutha's half-smile returned. "Not much gets past you, does it?"

James merely smiled and made a half-bow.

"Yes," said Arutha, "but I will wait upon the presence of the High Priest or his agent before sharing that intelligence with you. Go and rest, both of you, but be ready to return here at a moment's notice. I doubt the Ishapians will be long in answering my summons."

Arutha was correct. Jazhara and James were not even halfway back to their respective quarters when pages overtook them, informing them that the Prince required their immediate presence in the throne room.

They returned to find the High Priest of Ishap, along

with two other priests and a warrior monk in attendance. The High Priest was an elderly man, scholarly in demeanor with closely cropped snow-white hair. Like their superior, the two priests were also bareheaded, and wore their dark hair cut short. Unlike other orders, the Ishapians tended to favor plain fashion. The priests were dressed in brown-trimmed white robes; the monk wore armor and carried a helm under his left arm. A large warhammer hung at his belt.

Prince Arutha sat on his throne, and while there were only two other officials of the court in attendance—Duke Gardan and his scribe—James realized that Arutha wanted to conduct this interview from a position of power.

The Ishapians were long thought to be the most mysterious of Midkemia's religious orders, not courting converts as the other temples did. James had encountered them before, at the old Abbey at Sarth, and knew there was a great deal more to the Ishapians than commonly believed. They held a kind of supremacy among the orders; other temples avoided conflicts with them.

The High Priest said, "Highness, your message carried a note of the imperative and I came as soon as I received it."

"Thank you," said the Prince. He motioned to Gardan and the old Duke's scribe produced the statuette, handing it to the High Priest for inspection. "Where did you get this, Highness?" the High Priest asked, traces of surprise and worry in his voice.

Arutha signaled to James, who said, "It was discovered earlier today in a cache of stolen goods. Booty from a pirate raid."

"Booty?" said the High Priest.

Arutha said, "We both know, Father, what is due to

occur this year. I need to know if that item came from the ship due into Krondor this month."

The High Priest said, "These are matters which cannot be discussed in open court, Highness."

Arutha nodded to Gardan and the duke dismissed the scribe. The High Priest looked at Jazhara and James and Arutha said, "The squire is my personal agent, and Jazhara is my advisor on all things magical. The duke has my trust beyond question. You may speak freely."

The High Priest looked as if a burden had been placed upon him, for his shoulders sagged visibly. "*Ishap's Dawn* was due in Krondor a week ago, Highness. We have sent ships out to search for her, all the way back to the Free Cities. Perhaps she is disabled or . . ." He looked at James. "A pirate raid? Is that possible?"

James said, "Apparently. A madman named Bear, aided, it seems, by dark magic, appears to have taken your ship. Guards are bringing the rest of the booty to the palace so that you may reclaim it, Father."

A glimmer of hope sprang into the High Priest's eyes. "Tell me . . . is there a large box . . ."

James interrupted. "According to his first mate, whatever it is that Bear wanted sank with the ship. It was the cause of some considerable friction between them. Bear tore the man apart with his hands trying to learn the location of the sunken ship."

The warrior monk kept an impassive face, but the High Priest and his two other companions appeared to be on the verge of fainting.

"Then all is lost," whispered the High Priest.

Arutha leaned forward. "The ship carried the Tear of the Gods?"

The High Priest said, "Yes, and all the other treasure accumulated over the past ten years by every temple from

the Far Coast to the Free Cities. But all the gold and gems"—he brandished the statuette—"are meaningless without the Tear."

James caught Arutha's eye. The Prince said, "When I first came to this throne I was told something of the Tear's importance, yet you have kept its secret from the Crown. Why is this artifact of such great value?"

The High Priest said, "What I tell you, Highness, only your brother the King in Rillanon, and a very few of our order, know. I must have your vow·that what I tell you here will not leave this room."

Arutha glanced at Gardan, who nodded, then to James and Jazhara, who also agreed. "We so vow," said the Prince.

"Once every ten years, a gem is formed in a secret location in the north of the Grey Tower Mountains. The origin of this gem is lost to us; even our most ancient tomes do not reveal how our order first came to know of the existence of the Tear of the Gods.

"But this we do know: all power from the gods to men comes through this artifact. Without it, we would all fall deaf to the words of the gods, the gods would not hear our prayers."

Jazhara couldn't help herself. She blurted, "You'd lose all contact with the gods!"

"More than that, we fear," said the High Priest. "We believe that all magic would fade, as well. For it is by the grace of the gods that man is allowed to practice the arts of magic, and without divine intervention, we soon would be just as other men. Soon the existing Tear in our mother temple in Rillanon will fade, its shining blue light will go dark. If the new Tear is not in place before that happens, we will lose our link with the heavens."

"Won't there be another Tear in ten years?" asked James.

"Yes, but can you imagine ten years of darkness? Ten

years in which man has no commune with the gods? Ten years in which no healing can be done? Ten years without prayers being answered? Ten years without any hope?"

James nodded. "A grim picture, Father. What can we do?"

Arutha said, "We do have the location of the sunken ship."

Once again, a spark of hope appeared in the High Priest's eyes. "You do?"

"Within a fairly confined area," said James. "We have a map, and if the ship went straight down, we should be able to locate it."

"We have magic arts that can do many things, sire," said the High Priest. "But to enable a man to breathe underwater and search out the wreck is beyond our gifts. Is there another way?" He looked pointedly at Jazhara.

Arutha appreciated the gravity of the question; the temples, more than other institutions, were wary of magic they didn't control. Jazhara would be an object of suspicion at the best of times; and this was hardly the best of times. The Prince said, "Do you know another way, Jazhara?"

She shook her head. "Regretfully, Highness, I do not. I know of those in Stardock who are capable of such feats, but few of them are what you might call robust men. For such a task you'd need a strong swimmer, and a source of light."

James said, "That won't work."

Arutha raised an eyebrow. "Oh?"

James grinned. "Highness, I've lived my life near the sea. I've heard what sailors say. Once you go below a certain depth the water weighs down upon you and even with a magic spell to help you breathe, withstanding such pressures would likely prove impossible. No, there's another way."

"Tell us," said the High Priest.

"The Wreckers' Guild," said James. "It's their trade to raise sunken ships. They can bring them up long enough to be salvaged. In some cases they can repair a breach and tow a once-sunken ship safely to port for refitting. I've seen it done more than once."

"But they would have to be told of the Tear," said the High Priest. "And we cannot tell anyone of this."

James shook his head. "No, Father. All we need tell them is to raise the ship. Then someone trusted by the Crown goes into the ship, finds this artifact, and returns it here to Krondor."

The High Priest indicated the silent warrior monk to his left. "Brother Solon here should be that person. There are mystic safeguards around the Tear, so even had this creature Bear reached the Tear, he might not have been able to retrieve it. Brother Solon will be able to remove the safeguards so that the Tear can be recovered."

James looked at Arutha. "Sire, if this man Bear doesn't know the exact whereabouts of the Tear, wouldn't it be likely he'd be close by, looking for an Ishapian expedition heading for the wreck site? Logically he would wait until the artifact was recovered, then strike."

The High Priest said, "We have means of defending the Tear."

"No offense intended, Father, but from what Lucas told us of the pirate Knute's account of things, Bear has some sort of powerful protection against your magic. Otherwise how could he have taken the ship to begin with?"

The High Priest looked troubled as Jazhara said, "An amulet, I believe he said, something with the power to shield the wearer against priestly magic."

Arutha looked at James. "You advise stealth?"

"Yes, sire," said James. "We must find a way to divert Bear's attention. If we can distract him enough to keep

him away from the site while we raise the ship, retrieve
the artifact, then return here before he realizes he's being
distracted . . ." He shrugged. "We might have a chance."

The High Priest said, "Highness, I would prefer a large
armed force—"

The Prince held up his hand. "I realize the care of the
Tear is the province of the Temple of Ishap, Father, but it
was my jail that was destroyed, my wife's orphanage that
was burned to the ground, my constables who were
slaughtered; that makes it the Crown's business to ensure
nothing like this occurs again.

"If, as is reported, Bear and his mercenaries are immune to your magic, it would seem force of arms may be
needed to recover the Tear. How many fighting monks
can you muster within a day?"

The High Priest looked defeated. "Only three, Highness. The majority of our warrior brothers were on
Ishap's Dawn, guarding the Tear of the Gods."

James ventured, "Father, given how many were slaughtered here in Krondor, my best advice is to retrieve the
Tear and get it safely on its way to Rillanon before Bear
realizes it's not still at the bottom of the sea."

Arutha was silent for a moment, then said, "I will ac-
cede to James's plan." To James he said, "As for that 'distraction': order the Pathfinders out immediately, to find
Bear's trail. Have William muster a full patrol of Household Guards to follow swiftly after them. From what you
report, William has ample motivation to press Bear and
harry him through the wilderness. Bear may be resistant
to magic, but I warrant he might be troubled enough by
two dozen swords to keep moving. And tell William that
should he overtake Bear, the death mark is on this man
and he may deal with him as he sees fit. That should be
'distraction' enough."

"And the Tear?" asked James.

"You and Jazhara go to the Wreckers' Guild and secure enough members to raise a ship. Gather them quietly at some point outside the city, leaving the city in twos and threes, then meet at one of the villages on the way to Sarth. Then ride quickly to . . ."

"Widow's Point," supplied James.

"Widow's Point," repeated Arutha, "and get on with recovering the Tear."

James bowed and said, "How many shall we take with us?"

"I want you, Jazhara, and whoever you get from the Guild, along with Brother Solon, to depart at first light tomorrow. I will send a patrol the next day, and have them go to . . ." He looked at Gardan. "What's the nearest town to Widow's Point?"

Without looking at a map, Duke Gardan said, "Haldon's Head. It lies upon the bluffs overlooking the Point. It's a refuge for scavengers who pick over the wrecks there, but for the most part is a sleepy village."

"Too close, sire," said James. "If Bear has agents near the wreck, they will almost certainly be in Haldon's Head. Our arrival alone will cause a stir, unless we depart within a day or so. It's certain the appearance of an unscheduled patrol will alert Bear's men."

"What is the next village to the south?" asked Arutha.

"Miller's Rest," said the duke.

"Then station them there. As soon as you get the Tear, James, hurry south to Miller's Rest and the patrol will escort you back to Krondor. If you encounter more than you can handle, send someone down to Miller's Rest and the patrol will ride to your relief. Is that clear?"

"Yes, sire," said James, bowing.

To the High Priest, Arutha said, "Father, go and make

whatever arrangements you must and have your man meet James outside the gates two hours after first light, at the first crossroads.

"James, you take those men from the Wreckers' Guild, and leave with half of them at first light. Jazhara and the others from the Guild will leave one hour after that. You should all blend in with the normal traffic leaving the city at dawn." Looking at James, the Prince added, "Need I stress caution?"

With his almost insolent grin, James said, "Caution it is, Highness."

Arutha pointed an accusing finger. "We have seen much together, James—more than most men in a dozen lifetimes—but this task is equal to any set before you. Acquit yourself well, for the fate of us all rests in your hands."

James bowed. "I will, Highness."

To Jazhara, Arutha said, "I trust you will remind our young adventurer of the gravity of this task."

She bowed as well. "If need be, Highness."

"Then go, all of you, and may the gods smile upon your efforts."

Outside the throne room, James held Jazhara back until at last Duke Gardan emerged from the room. "Your Grace?" James said.

The duke turned, his dark features creased like old leather, but his eyes still bright and alert. "What is it, Squire?"

"Could I prevail upon you to send word to the Officer of Stores that we'll be down to equip ourselves for this journey?"

"Some problem?" asked the duke.

James grinned sheepishly. "My credibility of late has suffered, as I have used the Prince's name a little too often—"

"Without Arutha's knowledge," finished Gardan. He returned the smile. "Very well, I'll send word at once."

James said, "When do you finally retire? I thought your departure was agreed upon."

"I was due to leave for Crydee in a month; now I do not know," he answered with an almost theatrical sigh. "When *you* stop bringing crises to the Prince, I think."

With an impish grin, James said, "I think if that's the case, you'll still be here in another ten years."

"I hope not," the duke said, "but I will most certainly be here when you return. No one is spared duty until this crisis is resolved. Now, go about your business." To Jazhara he bowed, and said, "Milady."

"Your Grace," they said in unison.

After the old duke had departed, Jazhara said, "What now?"

James said, "To the Sea Gate and the Wreckers' Guild."

At mid-morning, the Sea Gate was bustling. Cargoes being unloaded in the harbor and transported into the city spawned dozens of carts and wagons that moved slowly down the street toward the Old Market and beyond. Sailors just arrived from long journeys hurried off-ship to find inns and women. Above the docks, sea birds squawked and wheeled in flight, seeking out the debris from dropped cargo that comprised a major part of their diet.

Jazhara suppressed a yawn as they walked. "I'm so tired that watching all these people dash about makes me feel as if I'm sleepwalking."

James smiled. "You get used to it. One of the tricks I've learned in Arutha's service is to nap whenever I get the chance. My personal best is four days without sleep.

Of course I had the help of a magic potion and once its effects wore off I was good for nothing for a week . . ."

Jazhara nodded. "Such things must be employed with caution."

"So we discovered on the trip home," said James, now also stifling a yawn in response to Jazhara's. "Whatever fate awaits us, I hope it involves at least one good night's sleep before we depart."

"Agreed."

They reached the Wreckers' Guild, a fairly nondescript two-story building a block shy of the Sea Gate. Several men were gathered outside, next to a large wagon. Two of them climbed atop the wagon as another pair began to walk away, lugging a large chest.

James stopped and tapped one of the men on the shoulder.

Without turning to see who stood behind him, the man snarled, "Shove off!"

Tired, and in no mood for rudeness, James said, "Prince's business."

The man threw him a quick glance. "Look, if you're here about the Guild Master, I just told everything I know to the Captain of the Watch."

James took the man firmly by the shoulder and spun him about. The mover's large fist pulled back to strike James, but before he could, the squire had his dagger at the man's throat. "Indulge me," he said with more than a whisper of menace in his voice. "Perhaps you could spare a moment and go over it once more. What exactly did you tell Captain Garruth about the Guild Master?"

Lowering his fist, the man stepped back. "It doesn't take the brains of an ox to know he was murdered."

One of the other movers, watching the exchange,

shouted: "It was Kendaric what did it! He cost us all with his greed."

The first man motioned toward the Guild entrance. "If you want details, you'd best talk to Jorath, inside. He's the journeyman in charge, now."

James put away his dagger and motioned for Jazhara to accompany him. They entered the Guild Hall, where several men stood in the corner deep in discussion. A young man, barely an apprentice by the look of him, stood nearby. He was tallying various items of furniture and personal belongings and recording figures in a ledger. James approached him. "We're looking for Journeyman Jorath."

The boy didn't stop counting, but merely pointed over his shoulder with his quill at a door leading to a room in the rear.

James said, "Thanks," and moved on.

He and Jazhara entered a room occupied by a large desk and several chairs. Standing before the desk was a middle-aged man, with dark hair and a short, neatly-trimmed beard. He wore a plain blue robe, similar to what one might expect on a priest or magician. Glancing up from the document he was studying, he said, "Yes?"

"I'm from the palace," said James.

"I assume that since I've already answered questions, you're here to tell me you've made some progress." His tone dripped arrogance.

James narrowed his gaze for a moment, then let the irritation pass. "We are not part of the Guard. We need a ship raised."

"I'm afraid you're out of luck. The Guild is closed. Evidently you haven't heard, but the Guild Master has been murdered."

"What happened to him?" asked James.

"No one knows, exactly. There was some sort of struggle, apparently. He was found dead in his room, with his possessions scattered about. He put up a good fight, but it seems his heart gave out."

James asked, "Why is the Guild closing down?"

"The Guild Master and Journeyman Kendaric were the only members of our guild capable of leading the ritual necessary to raise a large ship."

"Well, we need to speak to the Journeyman right away."

"Quite impossible, I'm afraid. Kendaric is the prime suspect in the Guild Master's murder, and he seems to have gone into hiding. With both him and the Guild Master gone, we're out of business." He let out a soft sigh. "Which is probably not so bad, all things considered."

"What do you mean, 'all things considered'?" asked James.

Jorath put down parchment he had been consulting. "Confidentially, the Guild has been losing money for several years now. The Guilds of other cities, Durbin and Ylith, for example, have developed new techniques that enable them to work more efficiently. They've been winning all the contracts."

James was silent for a long moment. Then he said, "How do you know it was this Kendaric who killed the Guild Master?"

Jorath picked up another scroll and glanced at it. "They fought constantly. At times they seemed near to blows. Abigail, the woman who cleans the Guild House, heard Kendaric and the Guild Master arguing the night of the murder."

"That's not proof," said Jazhara.

"No, but he's been missing ever since the body was found, so it's a good bet he's guilty."

Jazhara was about to say something, but James shook his head slightly. To Jorath he said, "May we look at the Guild Master's and Kendaric's rooms?"

Jorath shrugged. "Help yourself. The Guard have already been up there, but if you think you can do some good, be my guest." He turned back to his scrolls and left James and Jazhara to show themselves upstairs.

Jazhara waited until they had climbed the stairs. When they were alone, she asked James, "What?"

"What, what?"

"What didn't you want me to say to Jorath?"

"What you were thinking," said James, heading for the first of three closed doors.

"What was I thinking?" asked Jazhara.

Looking over his shoulder as he opened the door, James said, "That Kendaric might also be dead. And that someone doesn't want anyone raising a certain ship off Widow's Point." He glanced down, and said softly, "Someone's forced this lock."

He cocked his head, as if listening, motioned for silence, then held up his hand. "There's someone inside," he whispered.

Jazhara took up a position beside James and nodded. James stepped back then kicked hard against the door, shattering the lock plate as the door swung open.

The old woman inside jumped back and let out a shriek. "Heavens!" she exclaimed. "Are you trying to shock an old woman to her grave?"

"Sorry," James said with an embarrassed smile. "I heard someone inside and saw the lock had been forced—" He shrugged.

"When I couldn't raise the master," said the old woman, "I had two of the apprentices bring a bar and force the door. I found the master, there, lying on the

floor." She sniffled, and brushed at a tear with the back of her hand.

"What can you tell us?" asked James. "We're here on behalf of the Prince."

"The master was a wonderful man, but he had a bad heart. I used to fix hawthorn tea for him for his chest pain. It did him no good to be constantly arguing with Journeyman Kendaric."

"What was Kendaric like?" asked Jazhara.

"He was a poor boy from the streets, without family or friend. The Guild Master paid his admission fee to the Guild, because Kendaric was so poor. But the old master knew the boy was brilliant, and it would have been a crime to deny him because of poverty. The master was right, as the boy grew to be first among the journeymen. He would have been the logical choice to be the next Guild Master, except . . ." Her voice trailed off as more tears welled up in her eyes.

"He was brilliant, you say?" Jazhara prodded.

"Oh, he was always coming up with new ways to do things. He was working on a spell that would allow a single guildsman to raise large ships by himself. He thought the Guild would be more prosperous with his new spell, but the Guild Master wanted to preserve the traditional way, and they fought about it. He used to say that he argued with Kendaric to train him, to make his mind sharp, to make him tough enough to take over the Guild when he passed on. That's what makes it a bit odd."

"What's a bit odd?" asked Jazhara.

"Well, I just think it's odd that Kendaric killed him. Despite all their arguing, I would have sworn that Kendaric truly loved the old master."

Jazhara mused, "Everyone seems convinced that Kendaric is the killer, but isn't it just speculation?"

The old woman sighed. "Perhaps. But I heard Kendaric and the Guild Master arguing on the night of the murder. They always fought, but this time was the loudest I'd ever heard. I found the old master dead the next morning when I came to bring him breakfast. As I said, it took two apprentices to force open the door. Kendaric must have hit him and when the master's heart gave out, Kendaric must have escaped through the window. I said as much to the guards when I called them. They told me I was awfully clever to have figured it out the way I did."

James could hardly keep from rolling his eyes, but simply said, "We'll look around a bit, if you don't mind."

They realized quickly that anything of importance had been taken from the room by the Guards. "What are the other two rooms?" asked Jazhara.

Abigail said, "Those are the journeymen's quarters."

"And Kendaric's room is which one?" asked James.

"The next over," replied the old woman.

James returned to the hallway and opened the neighboring door. Instantly he dropped to the floor, narrowly avoiding a searing blast of heat that shot through the doorway. Behind him, Jazhara did likewise, although James couldn't tell if she had managed to evade the flames. He didn't have time to check, as the magician who had thrown the blast of fire at him stepped aside to allow a warrior in black to charge at the spot where James lay.

The Izmali lifted his sword and sent it plunging down toward James's head.

Seven

◆

Conspiracy

James rolled to his right.

The Izmali's sword came crashing down where James's head had been a moment earlier, and the assassin raised it to strike again, with incredible speed.

James had no time to draw his own sword, so he kicked out with as much strength as he could muster. His action was rewarded by the sound of a kneecap breaking and a muffled cry of pain from the black-clad murderer. The Izmali stumbled, but did not fall.

James rolled again as the warrior fell, and came to his feet with his sword drawn in a single fluid motion.

Jazhara unleashed a spell, but the scintillating ball of red energy shot off to one side and struck the floor near the enemy magician. Despite being missed, the magician appeared alarmed to discover he faced another magic-user. He turned and fled, jumping through the open window to the street below.

Jazhara turned her attention to the assassin as James closed on the man. She raised her staff above her shoulder, the butt end aimed at the man, ready to attack high if James retreated. James lashed out with his blade, a move designed to force his opponent to retreat and put weight

on his injured leg. The man was an experienced swordsman, and he shifted his weight to risk a dangerous near-
miss by James's blade rather than strain the injured knee.
He quickly returned with a quick inside thrust that almost
removed James's head.

As James retreated, Jazhara thrust her staff forward
and forced the assassin further into the room. Wisely, he
took up a stance just inside the door, so that James and
Jazhara would be forced to attack him one at a time.
Without taking his eyes from the assassin, James said,
"Jazhara! Get downstairs and see if you can find any hint
of his magician friend. I'll take care of this murderous
swine."

Jazhara didn't debate the order, but turned and hurried
down the stairs. From below came shouts of inquiry
about the sounds of struggle that could be heard.

James appraised the situation. Neither he nor the assassin was going through that door willingly. Whoever
advanced was certain to be attacked the instant he stood
in the portal, the frame of the door jamb limiting his
choices of response. The attack was almost certain to require moving sideways. They were locked in a stalemate.

Then James stepped back, lowering his sword point, as
if inviting attack.

The Izmali stood ready, his blade point circling warily,
refusing to take the invitation.

James said, "Help will soon be on the way. I doubt
you'll try jumping through the window with that broken
kneecap." He glanced down at the injured leg. "I admire
your strength. Most men would be lying on the floor,
screaming in pain."

The assassin took a tiny step—not more than two
inches—closer.

James continued to speak. "I've met a great many of

you Nighthawks over the years. The first one I killed was trying to assassinate the Prince, many years ago. I was but a lad, then. Threw him from the rooftop."

Another inch forward.

James let his sword point touch the floor and took a deep breath, as if relaxing. "Nothing compared to that bunch down in the desert. I doubt you've heard, since you were probably up here. I mean, had you been down there, you'd be dead like the rest of them, correct?"

And another inch.

"I still don't see why your brotherhood has allowed itself to be manipulated by a bunch of religious zealots. All it's done is get most of your clan killed. The Crawler can't have that much control over the Nighthawks, can he?"

The assassin tensed.

James paused, and let his weight fall a little toward his sword, as if he were leaning on it. "Funny to find you here, really. I thought I'd left the last of your kind rotting in the sun, waiting for the buzzards."

The Izmali tensed as the shouts from outside heralded the arrival of some city guards. Then he raised his sword and lashed out at James; but James was moving the instant he saw the assassin's sword come up.

As James had hoped, the assassin had been so distracted by James's banter, he had failed to notice James's slight movement toward the door. The tip of his scimitar struck the lintel overhead and was deflected, just as James fell toward the swordsman while bringing his own blade upward. The man's weakened knee betrayed him and he stumbled, half-falling onto James's outstretched sword point.

James threw his weight behind the lunge and the assassin stiffened as the rapier rammed home. James recov-

ered and pulled back his blade as the Izmali slumped to the ground.

Jazhara and a pair of city guardsmen reached the hallway a moment later. "The magician escaped," said the Keshian noblewoman. "These guardsmen were at the gate and I called them to come help."

Looking down at the dead assassin, one of the guardsmen said, "Looks like you weren't needin' much help there, Squire."

James knelt and examined the dead assassin. "Hello, what have we here?" he said, withdrawing a small parchment from the man's tunic. "Usually these lads carry nothing." He glanced at it, then handed it to Jazhara. "Can you read this script?"

She scrutinized it. "Yes, it's similar to the desert script used in the message to Yusuf. *Retrieve the scroll, eliminate the witness in the alley, then return to the dog.* There is no signature, nor is there a seal."

"Witness in the alley?" asked the senior guard. "That'd have to be Old Thom. He's an old sailor without a home."

"He's got a couple of crates in the alley back of this building he calls home," added the other guardsman.

James said, "Jazhara, let's see what these lads were looking for." Then he addressed the guards. "One of you stand by." He motioned to Jazhara to follow him into the room.

They looked around and nothing appeared out of the ordinary. James shrugged. "I was a little too busy to notice where those cutthroats were standing when we opened the door."

"They were in front of this desk, James," Jazhara said.

James inspected the desk, which at first glance seemed ordinary enough.

"What do you think 'return to the dog' means?" Jazhara asked.

James continued his inspection. "Probably some sort of code for a person or place." Something caught his eye and he pulled out a drawer. With a practiced eye he measured the depth of the drawer, then said, "There's a compartment behind this drawer or my name wasn't Jimmy the Hand." He knelt down and reached back. There was a click of a small latch, and a tiny door fell open, revealing a small red velvet pouch that he extracted.

He weighed it in his hand. "It's heavy. Feels like stone." Deftly, he untied the silk cord that secured the pouch and turned it over, allowing the object to fall into his other hand.

A stone of shimmering green and white, carved to look like a nautilus shell, rested in his palm.

"This is a Shell of Eortis!" Jazhara exclaimed.

"What is that?" asked James. "I met some adherents of that god when I visited Silden a while back, but I know little of their beliefs."

"I've seen one such artifact at Stardock." Jazhara held her hand over the object and closed her eyes, muttering a brief enchantment. Then she opened her eyes wide. "It is genuine! It is an old and rare item that aids water-magic. You'd have to know someone like the Masters of Stardock or the High Priest of the Temple of Eortis the Sea God to even hear of one. To possess one . . . this must be part of the secret of the Wreckers' Guild."

"But why wasn't this in the possession of the Guild Master?" James mused aloud. "Is this more proof that Kendaric had a hand in the death of the Guild Master, or did the master give it to his favorite student for safekeeping?"

"And why were the Nighthawks looking for it?" pondered Jazhara.

"Could you use this to raise a ship?" asked James.

"No, but you could use it to make the weather favor-

able for such an undertaking, had you the right spells to employ."

"Do you think this is what they sought?"

Jazhara thought for a moment, then said, "As it will not raise a ship, probably not."

"Then let us continue to look." He examined the other side of the desk and found another false drawer, this time one that was discovered by reaching up inside the desk from underneath.

"Very clever," James said, as he removed what appeared to be a box. "But not clever enough."

The box was roughly a foot wide, half as deep, and three inches thick. There was no apparent lock or latch, and the top was inlaid with a mosaic of stones. James tried the simple approach and thumbed back the lid. It lifted without difficulty, but the box was empty. "Nothing," he said.

Jazhara said, "No, there is something. Close the lid and open it again."

James complied and Jazhara said, "It's a Scathian Puzzle. It's a lock."

"To what? The box is empty. And the sides are too thin to contain another secret compartment."

"It's an enchantment. Its nature is to camouflage whatever is inside until it is unlocked."

"Can you unlock it?"

"I can try." Jazhara took the box and closed the lid, then set it down upon the desk.

She studied the mosaic on top of the box, then put her finger upon a tile. Its color changed from red to green to blue, and for a brief instant James thought he saw a blurred image wavering upon the tile's surface. Jazhara repeated the gesture quickly, touching a neighboring tile; again, the tile's colors mutated, and another image appeared on the tile.

Working deftly she moved the tiles around, for they slid where she directed. James was fascinated, for disarming traps and locks had been a career necessity in his days as a thief, but he had never encountered one quite like this. After a while, his eyes widened, for he realized that the tiles would fade back to their original pattern if she hesitated too long in moving one. And the closer she got to the end of the puzzle, the quicker they faded.

Jazhara's fingers were flying now, rapidly moving the tiles until at last a picture of a ship at sea was formed. Then there was an almost inaudible click, and up came the lid.

The box was no longer empty. Lying flat within the box was a single parchment. James reached in and retrieved the document. He glanced at it, and said, "Nothing I can read."

Jazhara took the parchment and studied it. "I believe *this* is the spell they use to raise the ships."

"How does it work?"

Jazhara scrutinized it even more closely. Then she whispered, "Incredible." In her normal speaking voice she added, "With this scroll and some other components, a single guildsman can raise a ship on a mystic fog!"

"What's so amazing about that?"

"Guilds like the Wreckers, who practice limited magic, usually possess only a few minor spells that are passed from generation to generation, and it usually requires several guildsmen to accomplish anything. Whoever wrote this knows a lot more about magic than the rest of the Guild." She paused, then added, "I'll wager this Kendaric never realized he was a Lesser Path Magician!"

"Then this spell must be worth a fortune to the Guild."

"Undoubtedly," said Jazhara. "Any Lesser Path Magician with an affinity for water-magic could eventually uti-

lize it. I suspect Kendaric is the only one who can use it as written."

"Then we must find Kendaric." Pointing to the scroll, he said, "Hide that." He turned and left the room. Jazhara secreted the parchment within a compartment in the pouch at her waist, and followed James a moment later.

Glancing down at the dead Nighthawk, James said to the guard, "Keep an eye on this corpse, and if it starts to move, call me." To Jazhara he said, "Let's investigate the alley."

As they sped down the stairs, Jazhara said, "If it starts to *move*?"

With a rueful smile James glanced back over his shoulder and said, "The Nighthawks used to have an irritating habit of not staying dead."

He led her outside the building and around to the back, where, behind the building, they found a long, dark, twisting alley. While still early in the day, the gloom of the place provided a dozen shadows in which anything could hide. Reflexively, James drew his rapier. Jazhara clutched her staff and made herself ready as well.

They moved through the alley until they reached a position below the open window through which the magician had leapt. James pointed. "He must have landed here, and then run"—he glanced in both directions—"that way." He indicated the way they had just come. "I'm almost certain the other end is blocked."

"If he reached the street and simply started walking he would just be another citizen out on his morning's business."

James nodded. "It's why I love cities and hate being alone in the wilderness. So many more places to hide in a city."

Glancing into the darkness as they continued, Jazhara

said, "I know many of my countrymen would disagree; they find hiding in the desert easy."

"You may have noticed I'm not a desert man," James observed.

They came to a pile of boxes, and James pushed one aside. The stench that arose from it caused Jazhara to step back. Inside were a dirty blanket, some rotting food and a few personal items—a woolen cap, a broken comb, and a dirty tunic. "Nobody home," said James. He glanced around. "Old Thom must be out begging or thieving. We won't find anybody here until after dark."

"I find it hard to believe that people actually sleep like that."

"It's not hard once you get used to it. The trick is to use the trash to keep the guards away." He looked around the alley once more. "Let's go."

"Where?"

"Back to the palace. Let's get some rest, then after sundown we'll come back and have a chat with Thom. I think he's seen something that someone else doesn't want him talking about, and if we can find out what that is, we might make some sense out of all this."

"It's obvious someone doesn't want us raising that ship."

"Yes," said James. "And while William is chasing Bear around the wilderness, there's someone else arranging for the murder of Guild Masters and beggars."

"The Crawler?" asked Jazhara.

James said, "That's my guess. Come on, let's return to the palace and get some rest." They walked quickly out of the darkness into the daylight of the busy street.

William signaled for his patrol to halt, while a lone rider hurried down the trail toward him. They were less

than an hour out of the city and following marks left by a pair of Royal Pathfinders. The rider reined in and saluted. It was Maric, one of the Pathfinders. "Lieutenant."

"What have you found?" William asked.

"A half-dozen men left the city on foot through the fields to the northeast of the North Gate. They took no pains to hide their passage. One of them was a big man, a heavy man, probably the one called Bear. His prints are wide and deep. At the edge of the fields they had horses waiting for them and rode hard up that trail. Jackson is following them. He'll leave signs."

William signaled for the men to ride on. Maric fell in beside the lieutenant. The Pathfinders were legendary, men who were descended from the first foresters and wardens of the earliest Princes of Krondor. They knew the surrounding wilderness as a mother knows the features of her children and they tended to be an insular lot who only grudgingly took command from officers outside their company. Their own captain was rarely seen in the palace, save by the Prince's orders, and they didn't socialize with the garrison's regulars. But they were among the finest trackers in the West and no man in the Armies of the West doubted their skills.

After a few moments of silence, William asked, "What else?"

"What do you mean, Lieutenant?" replied the Pathfinder.

"What is it you're not telling me?"

The Pathfinder glanced at the young officer and gave him a small smile and a nod. "These men take no pains to hide their passage. They are not afraid of being found. They hurry for another reason."

"They need to get somewhere fast," William observed.

"Or need to meet someone," suggested Maric.

"Ambush?" asked William.

"Possibly," replied the Pathfinder. "If they appear to be anxious to get down the trail, then suddenly turn . . ." He shrugged.

"Jackson would warn us."

Without emotion, Maric said, "If he's alive."

They rode on in silence.

If the alley had been gloomy in the daytime, it was inky at night. James uncovered a lantern he had secured at the palace.

After sleeping through the late morning and early afternoon, James and Jazhara had dined with the Prince and his family. It had been Jazhara's first dinner with the royal family, a privilege of her new position, and she had enjoyed the opportunity to meet and chat with Princess Anita, the Princess Elena, and the twin princes, Borric and Erland. James had apprised the Prince of their progress thus far, and Arutha had approved of James's investigation of the missing journeyman, Kendaric.

Once again dressed in her practical travel garb, Jazhara walked a step behind James as they traversed the dark alley. As they neared the crates, James signaled for silence and Jazhara touched him on the shoulder to indicate that she understood.

As they approached the crates, they heard a voice shout out, "No! No! Old Thom didn't tell a soul!"

"Thom, I'm not going to hurt you," James called out. He turned the lantern on the crate and the light revealed an old man, dressed in rags, huddling inside. His nose was misshapen and red, from repeated breaks in his youth and hard drinking in his later years. His front teeth were missing, and what little hair remained was almost white, spreading around his head like a faint nimbus.

Red-shot, watery blue eyes regarded them as he said, "You're not here to hurt old Thom?"

"No," said James, kneeling and putting up the light so that his own face would be revealed. "I'm not here to hurt you. Just to ask some questions . . ."

"Ah, a Prince's man, are you?" said the old beggar. "Fate is kind. I thought it was them murderers come back to finish Old Thom."

"Why would they want to finish you?" asked Jazhara, coming up behind James.

Thom glanced at Jazhara, then answered. "I 'spect it's 'cause I was here the other night when they broke into the Guild House."

"When was that?" asked James.

"The night the Guild Master died. A pair of 'em, all in dark cloaks, climbed right up the wall and into his room, they did."

"Nighthawks," James said. "They were going to come back, Thom, but we got to them before they could find you."

"You're a good lad, then. My thanks to ya."

"You're welcome," said James with a smile. "Did you see anything else?"

"Well, before them dark cloaks went inside, they was talkin' to somebody down the street a ways."

"Did you see who?" asked Jazhara.

"Old Thom couldn't rightly see, 'cept he was wearing Guild colors."

James said, "He had a torque?"

"Yes, that colored thing some of 'em wear around their neck."

"Could it have been Kendaric?" asked Jazhara.

Old Thom said, "Aye, the fella what was always arguin' with the old Guild Master? I seen him the night of

the killin', I did. He left the Guild House early that night; never did come back."

"Could it have been Kendaric who was with the Nighthawks?" asked James.

"Coulda been," replied Old Thom. "Or maybe not. He wasn't wearin' colors when he left."

James sat back on his heels. "There are only two other men who would wear colors: the master and Jorath. The Guild is closed for the night, but tomorrow we will return to visit Journeyman Jorath."

James fished in his pouch and came up with two gold coins. He handed them to Old Thom and said, "Get yourself a decent meal and a warm blanket, my old friend."

"Thanks, son," said the old fisherman. "Old Thom thanks you."

James and Jazhara left the old man in his crate and returned to the city streets.

Morning found James and Jazhara once again at the Wreckers' Guild office, but this time they entered to a much quieter scene than they had the previous day. When they came in they found Jorath in the main office, reading documents. Looking up, he said, "Again?"

"We have a few more questions, Journeyman," said James.

"Very well."

"We have uncovered a few things, but obviously this case will not be put to rest until we've located Journeyman Kendaric. What can you tell us about him?"

Jorath said, "He was the oldest journeyman in the Guild, the only one senior to myself. There are two others, both out of the city at present. Kendaric was a man of unusual talents, and had the potential to be prime among us, perhaps even the next Guild Master. Unfortunately he

was also greedy and arrogant, probably because of his half-Keshian ancestry."

Jazhara kept a straight face, but James saw her knuckles turn white as she tightened the grip on her staff.

James asked calmly, "Do you really think his ancestry matters?"

"Without a doubt," replied Jorath. "He's always been arrogant, but ever since he had to give up his engagement to a Kingdom girl, he's had it in for us. Her parents didn't want a Keshian marrying their daughter, and who can blame them?"

Jazhara said, "I take offense at your obvious prejudice toward Keshians, Guildsman."

Jorath inclined his head slightly. "Lady, I am no bigot, but as a scholar of some skill, I can tell you that Keshians, and half-breeds in particular, are generally unable to control their emotions."

Jazhara leaned forward and with an icy smile said, "As the newly-appointed court magician of Krondor, and as a great-niece of Abdur Rachman Memo Hazara-Khan, Ambassador of Great Kesh to the Prince's court, I can tell you that you are gravely mistaken. Were I not able to control my emotions, you would now be a slithering worm."

The blood drained from Jorath's face and he stammered, "I apologize most sincerely, milady. Please forgive me."

Hiding his amusement, James said, "Tell us about this woman Kendaric was engaged to."

Jorath appeared glad to change the subject. "A local shopkeeper, if I remember. I don't know the girl's name."

James looked hard at the journeyman, and said, "Thank you. If we have more questions, we'll return."

As they left the office, James glanced up the stairs. He

motioned for Jazhara to be quiet and they crept up the stairway. At the top of the stairs, James indicated the third door: Jorath's room.

"What are you doing?" Jazhara asked.

"Our friend downstairs is a little too sanguine about all that's gone on. He's hiding something."

"I agree. Given that his world seems to have been turned upside down, he seems almost . . . relieved."

James deftly picked the lock of the room and they entered. The chamber was neat, with nothing obviously misplaced. "Tidy fellow, our Journeyman Jorath, isn't he?" James observed.

"Indeed."

James went to the desk while Jazhara investigated the contents of a chest at the foot of the journeyman's bed. In the desk, James found some documents and a ledger. He took them out and had started reading them when Jazhara exclaimed, "Look!"

James glanced over. Jazhara was holding up a ledger identical to the one James had in his lap. "This was hidden under some clothing."

James took the second ledger and put it beside the first. After a few moments, he said, "Well, there it is. Our friend Jorath has been embezzling funds from the Guild. With the Guild Master dead, no one would inspect the records."

"And if he could find Kendaric's spell-scroll, he could restart the Guild with himself installed as master, with a clean record," said the magician.

James nodded. He continued his reading, tossing aside scroll after scroll, then he stopped. "Look at what we have here," he whispered. He handed the parchment to Jazhara.

She read aloud. "Guildsman. You've made the right de-

cision in coming to us with your plans. We've received the gold you promised. Show the bartender this letter and you'll find him very cooperative. My people, who will be waiting for you at the dog, will deal with final details and future payments. Orin."

"At the dog," James said.

"A place?"

James put the other scrolls away. "Yes, Ye Bitten Dog."

Jazhara said, "Ah, of course. The bartender. Lucky Pete."

"Things are now starting to come together," said James, taking the two ledgers and the scrolls. "I think we need to have another chat with Journeyman Jorath." He wrapped the ledgers and scroll in a tunic he pulled from the chest.

They hurried down the stairs and entered the office, where Jorath was still reviewing documents. "Yes?" he said looking up. "Again?"

James said, "You know who killed the Guild Master."

Jorath stood up slowly, and arranged the scrolls on the desk in an orderly fashion. "Amazing. I would have credited the Prince's servants with far more intelligence than you're currently evidencing."

Jazhara said, "We know you've been dealing with the Nighthawks."

Jorath seemed untroubled by the accusation. "Even had I the inclination to consort with criminals, who I meet with outside the Guild is my own business, unless you can prove I conspired in a crime.

"Besides, my entire life is wrapped up in this Guild. Why would I choose to jeopardize it all by killing the Guild Master?"

James unwrapped the ledgers and the scroll and said, "To prevent being caught out as an embezzler."

Jazhara added, "And there was Kendaric's new spell. With him out of the way, you could claim it as your own."

"If you could have found it," James went on. "Obviously, you needed the Nighthawks for both tasks."

"An interesting theory," said Jorath, slowly backing away. "Well thought out and complete. Tell me, if you had not interfered, do you think I could have gotten away with it?"

Before James or Jazhara could answer, the Guildsman pulled an item from the sleeve of his robe and cast it into the air. A brilliant light erupted and James found himself momentarily blinded. Reflexes took over and he instantly stepped back, knowing that he was likely to be attacked while he couldn't see.

He felt the blade just miss him as he blinked furiously, while drawing his own sword. Again he stepped back, and without hesitation lashed out, a move designed to keep Jorath back or, with luck, land a blow.

He heard the journeyman retreat and James knew he had almost succeeded in hitting him. James had fought in the darkness more times than he cared to remember, and he closed his eyes, knowing that darkness would be less distracting than the blurred images and lights that danced before his eyes.

He sensed that Jazhara had moved away from him, her own protective reflexes taking her away from possible danger. James threw a wild high blow and felt the shock run up his arm as Jorath's sword blocked his.

Without hesitation, James slid his blade down Jorath's, moving forward rather than retreating. James hoped that the guildsman was not a practiced swordsman, for if he was, James was almost certain to be wounded.

As he had hoped, James heard a startled exclamation from the guildsman as James threw his weight forward,

reaching out with his free left hand to grip Jorath's right wrist. He slammed upward with his own sword, and with a satisfying crack felt the hilt of his sword smack into the man's chin.

Jorath slumped to the floor as James blinked away tears. His vision was slowly returning, enough to see that the journeyman was now lying unconscious on the floor. Jazhara was also blinking furiously, trying to clear her own eyesight.

"It's all right," said James. "He's out."

"What'll happen to him?" asked Jazhara.

"Arutha will almost certainly hang him, but he'll be questioned first."

"Do you think he's involved in the search for the Tear?"

James shook his head slowly. A Guild apprentice appeared at the door and looked down at the fallen journeyman. His eyes widened in alarm. James shouted, "Get the city watch, boy!"

The youngster hurried off.

James looked at Jazhara and said, "I think he was merely a convenience for the Nighthawks and the Crawler." Shaking his head at how little he knew, James added, "Or whoever else is behind all this madness." He sighed. "I think the Nighthawks and whoever is employing them wanted to ensure no one could raise that ship but themselves. If I'm to guess, there's someone up in Ylith who's arranging for a team from their Wreckers' Guild to head down to Widow's Point—or there will be soon." Pointing to the belt pouch in which Jazhara had Kendaric's scroll, James added, "Finding that scroll would simply have made things easier for the Nighthawks. They would have promised Jorath whatever he wanted, gotten him to raise the ship, then killed him." Glancing down at the unconscious journeyman, James

shook his head in disgust. "Either way, he ends up a dead man. What a waste."

"So what now?" asked Jazhara.

"We visit Lucky Pete and see if we can uncover this last nest of the Nighthawks and stamp them out. Then we find Kendaric. I think it's safe to say he's no longer a suspect."

"How do we find him?"

"We look for the woman he was engaged to; perhaps she will know somewhere to start the search."

"Jorath said he didn't recall who she was."

James grinned. "Maybe the journeyman didn't, but I bet someone around here remembers. Probably old Abigail knows. Gossip like that doesn't say hidden long."

Jazhara said, "I'll go ask her."

James nodded. "I'll wait for the city watch."

A few minutes later Jazhara returned just as two city watchmen arrived with the apprentice. James instructed them to take Jorath to the palace and told them what to say to Duke Gardan. The watchmen saluted and carried off the still-unconscious guildsman.

After they left, James asked, "Did you get a name?"

Jazhara nodded. "Her name is Morraine. She runs a shop called The Golden Grimoire."

James nodded. "Just your kind of place. An apothecary shop with a bit of magic for sale, according to rumor. It's in the nicer part of town." He glanced around and said, "We're finished here."

"Where to first?" asked Jazhara as they strode toward the door.

"First, to the palace to collect a half-dozen or so of the duke's best swordsmen. Then back to Ye Bitten Dog."

"You expect trouble?" asked Jazhara.

James laughed. "Always."

Eight

◆

Kendaric

J ames signaled.

The squire and Jazhara surveyed their surroundings as they walked toward Ye Bitten Dog. Six of the Prince's Royal Household Guard waited at the intersection of the two streets nearest the entrance of the inn, hiding in the shadows as night fell upon the city. In addition, a young constable, Jonathan Means, was positioned across the street. He was the son of the former sheriff, Wilfred Means, and despite no direct order from the Prince, he was acting in his father's stead. James had also recruited him as one of his first confidential agents in what he hoped one day would be the Kingdom's intelligence corps. Young Means would wait fifteen minutes, then enter the inn. Alternately, at any sign of trouble, he would signal to the squad of soldiers and they would rush the building.

James and Jazhara wanted to see what sort of information they might weasel out of Lucky Pete before resorting to threats. And if there were Nighthawks in residence, it would be useful to have a riot squad close at hand.

James pushed open the door. Inside, the night's revelries were starting to pick up, as whores and dockworkers

on their way home from a day's labor lined up three deep at the tables to carouse.

Glancing around, James realized they had caught the attention of a worker near the door who was looking at James and Jazhara's fine clothing. "What have we here?" he said loudly.

His companion turned. "Looks like a court boot-lick and his Keshian pet, to me."

Without bothering to look at the man, Jazhara said, "Careful, my friend. This pet has claws."

The man so addressed blinked in confusion, but his friend exploded into laughter.

"That's enough," James said. "We seek no trouble." He took Jazhara's elbow and guided her through to the bar at the rear of the room, where the owner was filling tankards and handing them to a bar-boy to carry to the tables.

As they approached, Lucky Pete looked up. "What do you want now?"

James said, "Just some information, Pete."

The boy took the flagons and hurried off, and Pete wiped up a puddle of spilled ale with a filthy bar rag. "It'll cost ya. Like always."

"Did you hear about the troubles at the Wreckers' Guild?"

Pete shrugged. "Maybe."

James slid a coin across the rough-hewn planks of the bar.

"Okay, I heard something."

James slid another coin, and Pete remained silent. After a moment, James slid a third coin across the bar, and Pete said, "Seems some journeyman couldn't wait for the old master to die so he could replace him and hurried the old fellow off to Lims-Kragma's Hall. Fellow named Kendaric."

"So we've heard," replied James. "Any idea where we might find this Kendaric?"

Pete said, "This answer's for free: No."

James considered for a moment whether Pete might be lying, but rejected the notion, given Pete's appetite for gold. If he were to lie, it would be to get more gold, not less. James glanced at Jazhara and she gave him a slight nod, indicating that she, too, thought this avenue of questioning was a dead end.

James lowered his voice. "I could also use some information on obtaining some 'special' services." He slid another coin across the bar.

"What sort of 'special' services?" asked Pete, sweeping it up.

"I need the skills of some men with . . . muscle."

Pete shrugged. "Bashers are a copper a dozen in Krondor. Find 'em at the docks, the markets . . ." He narrowed his gaze. "Of course you know that already, don't you?"

James slid yet another coin across the bar. "I had heard this was the place to get in touch with a special breed of nocturnal birds."

Pete didn't touch the coin. "Why would you want to talk to these 'birds'?"

"We want to offer them a well-paying job."

Pete was silent for a moment, then picked up the coin. "You've got balls, boy, but have you the cash to back 'em up?"

James nodded. "More gold than you've ever seen, if you've got what I want." He placed another coin on the bar, then quickly put four more carefully atop it, to make a small, neat stack.

Pete swept up the coins. "First payment, only, Squire." He grinned, displaying discolored teeth. "Aye, lad, you've come to the right place. Go 'round back, if you would.

There's some gentlemen in the rear room you ought to speak to." He tossed James a key, then gestured with his hand toward a door behind the bar. "You'll be needin' this, lad."

James caught the key and started toward the indicated door. He unlocked the door and glanced over his shoulder at Jazhara, who looked ready for trouble. James estimated they now had about ten minutes before Jonathan Means entered the inn. James's instructions had been clear; if he and Jazhara were not in sight, Jonathan was to bring the squad.

James and Jazhara entered a corridor as the door to the barroom clicked shut behind them. Three more doors lined the hallway before them. A door on the immediate left revealed a pantry, and James spared it only a cursory glance. The first door on the right, once opened, revealed a miserable-looking bedroom, filthy and strewn with clothing and remnants of food. James whispered, "Must be Pete's room." He looked back over his shoulder at the door that led back into the common room and added, "Can you do something dramatic with that door, something loud enough to bring young Means and the guards in a hurry?"

With a slight smile, Jazhara nodded. "I have just the thing if I'm not otherwise distracted."

"Good," James said, opening the last door. They entered a small room, furnished only with a single table, behind which sat two men. The one closest to James, on the right, was a bearded man with dark hair and eyes. The other was clean-shaven and blond, with his hair falling to the collar of his jacket. Both wore black tunics and trousers. Each had a blade at his hip, and wore a heavy black gauntlet.

Both men looked up at James and one said, "Yes?"

"Pete said we could find someone here who might provide us with a solution for a particularly bothersome problem."

Both men moved back in their chairs, a seemingly casual move, but one that James knew gave each of them a better chance to stand and draw his sword. "What do you want?" the second man asked.

James produced the letter he had found in Jorath's room. "We know about your arrangement with the Wreckers' Guild. For a small price, we'll make sure no one else does."

The two men glanced at each other, then the blond man spoke. "If you're looking to line your pockets with gold, you should be warned that you are dealing with the Guild of Death. Those who try to blackmail us tend not to live as long and comfortably as they otherwise might. Unless, that is, you're offering some other sort of arrangement?"

James smiled. "That's exactly what I was thinking. Here's my idea—" Leaping forward, James suddenly overturned the table onto the blond-haired man, at the same time kicking out with his boot to shove the chair out from under the bearded man. "Jazhara! Now!"

Jazhara turned and pointed her staff toward the far door and uttered a few syllables. A bolt of white energy exploded from the staff, fired down the short hallway, and blew the door off its hinges with a deafening sound.

James had his sword in hand. He grinned. "That should bring them running." The first swordsman was scrambling backward, away from James's blade, while awkwardly trying to draw his own. The blond man used the overturned table as a barrier, so that he could retreat an extra couple of feet to the wall, gaining space to pull out his sword.

James had to leap away to avoid a lunge from the blond man, aimed at James's left side. Jazhara struck down with her staff at the swordsman's arm, striking his wrist with a numbing blow. The blond man yowled in pain as he dropped his sword. As he attempted to pull his dagger out with his other hand, Jazhara struck him on the temple with the iron-shod butt of her staff. The man dropped to the floor.

James heard shouts and confusion from the front of the building, and knew that Jonathan Means and the guards were now in the common room. Unless there were other Nighthawks there, the dockworkers and other laborers would be unlikely to challenge armed guardsmen.

James lashed out with his sword, slicing the hand of the bearded man on the floor, who was still struggling to pull out his sword. It had the desired effect, for the man let go of the hilt. James touched the tip of his sword to the man's throat. "I advise you not to move if you want to keep breathing."

Jazhara turned toward the door, readying herself in case whoever came through it first wasn't friendly.

The bearded man shifted his weight slightly and James pressed the blade into the man's skin until he cried, "Ah ah!" Deftly, James flipped the man's collar aside with the sword's point, and slipped it under a chain around the man's neck. Then, with a flick, he drew the chain over the man's head. An amulet slid down the blade.

As the point rose in the air, the bearded man made a frantic grab for his own sword. Without taking his eyes off the amulet, James kicked with his left boot, taking the man on the chin and knocking him unconscious.

At this point, Jonathan Means broke through the door at the end of the hall, followed by two of the Prince's Household Guard. They were frog-marching Lucky Pete

between them, his peg leg slamming against the floor in a most comic fashion.

Jonathan said, "Most of the lads in there started clearing out when Jazhara blew the door off the hinges." He smiled at her and said, "I assume it was you and not some other magician, milady?"

She nodded and returned the young man's smile.

The acting sheriff continued. "Most of the rest of them fled when they saw the seven of us rush in. That one"—he pointed at Pete—"and a couple of others tried to fight, but we had them under control in a few minutes." He glanced at the two unconscious figures on the floor. "What have we here?"

James turned his sword to Means and let the amulet slip off the blade. "False Nighthawks. Part of that band sent into the sewers to cast blame on the true Guild of Death a few months back if I don't miss my guess."

"How do you know them to be false?" asked Jazhara.

"No poison rings, and they didn't try to take their own lives," answered James. "The Nighthawks are fanatics about not being taken alive." He sheathed his sword.

"What is the significance of these being false?" asked Jonathan.

James said, "That remains to be discovered when we question these two. I suggest you get them to the palace dungeon and hold them for questioning. With the Old Market Jail gone, it's either the palace or the jail at the docks."

Means nodded. "The palace it is, Squire."

Means called for help and another four guards came in to carry the unconscious "Nighthawks" away. James turned to Lucky Pete and said, "Now, it's time for us to have a talk."

Pete tried to smile, but his face was an exercise in

panic. "Now, Squire, I don't know nothin', really. I just rented some rooms and the basement to these lads."

James's gaze narrowed. "The basement?"

"Yes, through that trapdoor there and down the stairs," he said, pointing to a spot on the hallway floor.

"Damn," said James, pulling his sword out once more. To Means he said, "Leave a man here with Pete and follow me."

James pulled up the trapdoor and scrambled through it without waiting to see who was behind him. He ran down the stone stairs, which led down to a small landing halfway down, then doubled back to the basement floor below. From above, Jazhara said, "James! There is something very wrong here!"

Turning to look up at her, James said, "I feel it, too."

Energy crackled in the air which indicated that magic was being gathered nearby, and James's experience told him it wasn't anything good. The hair on his arms and neck rose as he reached the bottom steps and confronted a door. He waited until he knew that Jazhara, Means, and another guard were behind him, then said, "Ready!"

He kicked open the door and found himself in a large room carved out of the soil beneath the tavern. Near the middle of the room stood three men, two dressed in the same way as the two men upstairs, in black tunics and trousers, black gloves and with swords at their side. The third man wore robes and James recognized him as the magician they had seen at the Wreckers' Guild.

But what drew James up short and made him gasp was the figure forming in the center of the room, inside a complex design drawn on the floor in a white substance. "A demon!" he shouted. The creature was coalescing into solid form, substantial from head to waist. Its head was misshapen, with two curving horns that arched down and

forward from its brow. Glowing red eyes regarded the intruders and it bellowed like a bull, its massive shoulders flexing as it attempted to reach out to them.

The enemy magician cried out, "Hold them! We are almost done!"

The two black-clad swordsmen drew their weapons and charged the short distance that separated James from the demon. Jazhara attempted to cast a spell, but had to break her concentration in order to avoid being struck by one of the two men.

James parried the other attacker as Jonathan Means and a guardsman burst into the room.

"Gods!" shouted Means. "What is that thing?"

"Kill the magician!" James cried.

The guardsman didn't hesitate. Rather than risk approaching the magician and coming within reach of a demon that was almost completely solid, the soldier pulled a dagger from his belt and with a powerful throw sent the blade spinning toward the magician.

The dagger struck the magician in the heart, knocking him backward as the demon gained solid form. The demon bellowed in rage and tried to attack, but the lines upon the floor seemed to form a mystic barrier, preventing him from reaching James and the others.

James saw Means rush to Jazhara's side, and concentrated upon his own foe. The man was an expert swordsman and James was conscious of the enraged demon he could see over the man's shoulder. The assassin was also aware of the demon behind him, for he took a moment to glance back before focusing on James. James sought to press his advantage, but the swordsman anticipated it.

James moved to one side, shouting, "Jazhara! Can you do something about that thing?"

Jazhara was attempting to disentangle herself from the

second swordsman, in order to allow the guardsman or Jonathan Means to engage with him, but the room was too crowded to allow an easy transition. "I'm occupied at the moment, James," she called.

Means cried, "Let me past!" and Jazhara instantly drew her staff toward her, holding it upright as she turned and suddenly Means was past her, lunging at the swordsman, who was forced to back away.

Jazhara looked at the demon and said, "I know almost nothing of such creatures, James!"

James beat back a high attack by the assassin he faced and attempted to back him into the demon's reach. "I'm turning into something of a expert, I'm sorry to say," he retorted. "This is the third of these creatures I've run into in my life."

"One thing I do know," Jazhara shouted. "Don't cross into that diagram and don't break the lines."

"Thank you," said James. He thrust out with his blade, managing to nick the assassin in the leg. "I'll keep that in mind," he added as he pulled back.

Jazhara saw the stalemate between her companions and the two assassins, and stopped to catch her breath. She closed her eyes, recalling an incantation, then when she had it firmly in mind, she slowly began to cast her spell. When she was finished, a crimson bolt of energy flew from her outstretched hand and struck the face of the assassin attacking James. The man cried out and dropped his sword. Clawing at his eyes, he screamed in pain and staggered backward.

Too late, he suddenly realized he had backed inside the inscribed design on the floor. He tried to retreat, but the demon seized him. Picking the assassin up from behind like a father might pick up a baby, the twelve-foot-tall demon tossed the man high into the air, literally bouncing

him off the dirt and stone ceiling. Then as the assassin fell, the creature slashed with its bull-like horns, impaling him on the points. The man screamed once and died.

James ignored the gore and turned his attention to the second swordsman, reaching over Means's shoulder to slash at the man's throat. A liquid gurgle sounded as the assassin dropped his blade, a stunned look in his eyes as the blood began to flow from his mouth and nose. He made a daubing motion with his left hand at his throat, as if trying to staunch the wound, then he fell forward and expired.

James turned to confront the demon, which had finished tearing apart the assassin who had lain upon its horns. Body parts littered the room and the creature bellowed in rage as it confronted James and his companions.

"What do we do?" asked Jonathan Means, shaking now that he realized the nature of the monster they faced.

"It cannot cross out of that space," said Jazhara, "unless he who summoned it gives leave. But it will remain there for a long time unless we banish it or kill it."

"Those things are hard to kill," said James. "I know."

Jazhara turned to the guardsman. "Send word to the palace. Summon Father Belson and tell him we have a demon to banish."

The guardsman glanced at James, who nodded.

James said, "Let us back out of here and wait for the good father to show up."

Time seemed to drag as they waited for the arrival of Prince Arutha's religious advisor. James stood just the other side of the door, watching the evil creature as it raged and glared at him, full of malevolence. Several times it feigned an attack, but always it pulled up at the mystic barrier.

"What's this nonsense about a demon?" shouted a voice from above.

James turned to see Father Belson appear. The slender, black-bearded cleric arrived in a hurry, minus his usual purple and scarlet robes. Instead he wore a woolen nightshirt over which a heavy cloak had been thrown. "This idiot," he said, pointing back at the guard, "wouldn't even grant me leave to dress—" Then he glanced past James and caught sight of the demon. "Oh, my," he said softly.

"I'll get out of the way and let you go to work, Father," James said.

"Go to work?" Father Belson replied, blinking in confusion. "Work doing what?"

"Getting rid of the demon. That's why we summoned you."

"Get rid of the demon? I can't do that," said the priest of Prandur in horror.

James blinked like an owl caught in a sudden light. "You can't?"

"Demons are creatures of the lower realms, and as such often consume fire energy. My service to the Lord of the Flames prevents me from having any skills with the sorts of magic that can possibly harm the creature." Looking again at the demon, the priest added softly, "Best I can do is irritate him, and at worst make him stronger."

"What about exorcism?" asked Jazhara.

Glancing at the Keshian magician, the priest said, "That's not something my temple does. You'd have to find a priest of Sung, and a powerful one at that, or an Ishapian."

James sighed. He turned to the guard who had originally brought Father Belson and said, "Hurry to the Temple of Ishap and tell the High Priest we request the services of one who can banish a demon—and quickly. Use the Prince's name. Go."

The guardsman saluted. "Squire." He turned and hurried off.

To Father Belson, James said, "Sorry to have awakened you."

Not taking his eyes off the creature, the priest said, "Oh, I wouldn't have missed this for anything."

"Good," said James. "Then keep an eye on the thing just in case, while I go interview a prisoner."

James returned to the upper room. Pete was sitting in a chair with a guard at his side. James said, "Now, before we were so rudely interrupted . . ."

Pete looked close to panic. "I tell you, Squire, I don't know nothin'. Just some lads throwin' gold around for me to know nothin'. So I looks the other way when they want to use the down-below, and the pass-me-through to the sewers. You know how it is."

James nodded. He knew all too well how it was. To the guardsman he said, "Take him to the palace. Lock him in the dungeon, and we'll see what else he knows at our leisure."

The guard grabbed Pete roughly under the arm and said, "Come with me, little man."

The peg-legged former sailor squawked at being manhandled, but went along peacefully.

It took almost an hour for the Ishapians to arrive, a grayhaired priest of some significant rank and two armed warrior monks. Once James acquainted them with the situation below they agreed it had been a wise move to summon them.

They hurried down the steps to the basement and the Ishapian priest said to Father Belson, "You may depart now, Servant of Prandur."

Belson bowed slightly. "As you wish."

As he passed, James said, "You're leaving?"

With a wry smile, the priest said, "I know when I'm not wanted."

James was puzzled. There was a great deal about the politics of the Kingdom that James had come to understand during his tenure at Arutha's court, but the relationships among the temples was a complex knot of intrigues he had scarcely been aware of before then, and one he had had little reason to investigate.

The priest of Ishap turned to James and said, "How did this come to be?"

"That man," James said, pointing at the dead magician lying on the floor near the far wall. "He summoned the creature."

The priest looked across the room, then observed, "If he were alive it would be easier to return the creature to the plane of hell from which it was summoned."

Dryly, Jazhara said, "Unless, of course, he ordered it to attack first."

The priest glanced at the magician, but did not respond to her observation. Turning to James, he said, "So be it. Let us begin."

The two monks came to stand on either side of the Ishapian priest and began a low chant. After a moment, James felt a distinct cooling in the air, and heard the priest's voice rising above the others. The language was tantalizingly familiar, but one he could not understand.

The demon glared from behind the barrier erected by the mystic symbols on the floor, helpless. From time to time its bovine features would contort and it would bellow a challenge, but finally it was done. James blinked in astonishment as one moment the creature stood there, then an instant later it was gone, the only evidence of its passing a subtle shift in the pressure of the air around them and a slight sound, as if a door closed somewhere nearby.

The priest turned to James. "The Temple is pleased to

help the Crown but it would be better for all of us if you returned to the critical task set before you, Squire."

"We were going to leave this morning, sir, but things have proved less convenient than I would have liked. We'll go as soon as possible."

The priest nodded impassively. "Brother Solon will be waiting for you at the gate at dawn tomorrow." He turned and left the room, followed by the two monks.

James sighed. "Arutha won't be pleased if we have to wait much longer."

Jazhara said, "We have but one task left before we can go."

"Find Kendaric," James said. "And I think I know where to start."

The Golden Grimoire was a modest but well-appointed shop. It was an apothecary store of sorts, but Jazhara recognized at once the contents of many jars and boxes to be ingredients a magician might employ. A sleepy looking young woman had let them in only upon James's insistence they were on the Prince's business. "What do you wish?" she asked once they were inside, suspicion in her voice.

James regarded her. This must be Morraine, he thought, the woman to whom Kendaric was engaged. She was slight in build, with a slender face, but pretty in a way. He thought that when fully dressed and awake, she probably looked a great deal more attractive.

James produced the shell and said, "Can you tell us what this is?"

Morraine raised her eyebrows. "Place it there, please." She indicated a green felt cloth upon the counter next to which a lantern burned. James did so and she studied it closely for a bit. "This is a Shell of Eortis, I'm certain. It

has powerful magic properties. There are only a few reputed to exist. It is an artifact of incalculable value to a sea captain or anyone else who must voyage across the ocean." She looked at James. "Where did you get it?"

James admired the woman's ability to maintain a calm demeanor. She would be no mean gambler, he thought. "I'm certain you know where we found it, Morraine," he said.

Morraine held his gaze for a moment, then lowered her eyes. She betrayed no surprise at hearing her name. "Kendaric. We were lovers for a while, but my family forbade us to wed. I gave it to him as a gift. It was my dearest possession." Then, almost defiantly, she added, "I haven't seen him for a long time."

James smiled. "You can stop lying. You don't do it well. Kendaric is innocent and we have proof. It was Journeyman Jorath who had the Guild Master killed to mask his embezzlement of Guild funds."

The woman said nothing, but her eyes flickered from face to face. Jazhara said, "You can believe us. I am Jazhara, the Prince's court magician, and this is his personal squire, James. We require Kendaric's presence for a most critical undertaking on behalf of the Crown."

Morraine said softly, "Come with me." She picked up the lantern from the counter and led them to a far wall, where several volumes rested upon shelves.

Jazhara glanced at the titles and saw that many of them were herbalist guides and primers on making remedies and potions, but that a few dealt with magical issues. "I shall have to return here when time permits," she muttered.

Morraine removed one large volume, and the shelf slid aside, revealing a stairway going up. "This goes to a secret room in the attic," she said.

She led them up the stairs and into a small room,

barely able to hold a single bed and table. Upon the bed sat a man in a green tunic. He wore a goatee and mustache and had a golden ring in his left ear. "Who are these people?" he asked Morraine in a concerned tone, staring at James and Jazhara.

"They are from the Prince," said Morraine.

"I didn't do it!" exclaimed Kendaric.

"Calm yourself," said James. "We have proof it was Jorath who had the Guild Master killed."

"What about those men in black?" asked the journeyman of the Wreckers' Guild. "They were trying to kill me! I barely escaped them."

Jazhara noticed a slight hint of a Keshian accent in his speech, from one of the northern cities. "They've been dealt with, as well," she said.

Kendaric sprang to his feet and hugged Morraine. "This is wonderful! I can return to the Guild. Thank you for this news."

Jazhara held her hands up. "A moment, Guildsman," she said. "We have need of your services."

Kendaric said, "Certainly, but perhaps it can wait for a day or so? I have much to do. If Jorath is guilty of murder, I must return to take charge of the apprentices. It will take a while before order is restored to the Wreckers."

James said, "Ah, unfortunately we need your help now. The Prince needs your help. And considering it might have been the Nighthawks that found you first, but didn't because of our efforts, you owe us."

"I didn't ask for your help, did I? I must get back to the Guild! All those debts to pay!"

"Kendaric!" Morraine said, sharply.

"Yes, Morraine?" he answered, meekly.

"You are being ungrateful and rude to people who have saved your life."

"But the expenses, my love—"

"We'll work something out. We always have." She turned to James. "He'll help you, Squire. He's a good man at heart, but sometimes he lets his personal desires lead him astray."

"Morraine!"

"I'm sorry, dear, but it's true. That's why you have me to set you straight."

Jazhara said, "You plan to defy your parents, then?"

With a tilt of her chin and a brave smile, Morraine said, "We shall have a wedding as soon as Kendaric has returned from whatever mission you have for him."

Looking defeated, the guildsman said, "Very well."

"Please watch out for him. Kendaric sometimes overreaches himself."

Jazhara smiled. "We'll take care of him."

"Thank you for restoring his good name."

They walked down the steps to the door. James and Jazhara went out into the street and waited as Kendaric bid Morraine good-bye. When the journeyman emerged from the shop, Jazhara said, "You should count yourself lucky to be so well loved."

Kendaric said, "Luckier than you know. I shudder to remember the bastard I was before I met Morraine. Her kindness saved my life, but her love saved my soul."

James glanced at the starlit sky. "We have three hours to first light. Time enough to get back to the palace, report to the Prince, and meet Brother Solon at the gate."

As they walked toward the palace, James said, "Do you ride?"

"Badly, I fear," said the journeyman.

Laughing, James said, "By the time we reach our destination, you'll be an expert."

Nine

◆

Diversion

William waited patiently.

His horse pawed the ground, anxious to be moving again, or to find something to graze on. Either way William had to keep a firm leg and short reins on the animal.

The day had turned cold and he could see his own breath before him as night fell. The patrol had halted in a small clearing in the woods, large enough for a camp. The men behind him were silent, avoiding the casual small talk and muttering that was common during a standstill in the ranks. They knew the enemy was close.

As evening approached and the gloom of the woods deepened, everyone was on edge. They could almost feel a fight approaching. Swords were loose in their scabbards and bows near to hand as the men kept their eyes moving, watching for any sign of trouble.

Then from ahead two figures appeared on the trail, emerging from the murk. Maric and Jackson rode at a slow canter, and instantly William relaxed. If the enemy were near, they would more likely be coming back at a gallop.

Without waiting for their report, William spun his horse around and said, "We'll camp here."

The sergeant in charge of the patrol, an old veteran

named Hartag, nodded and said, "I'll post the sentries first, Lieutenant."

As the sergeant barked his orders, the two Pathfinders reined in. Maric said, "We lost them."

"What?" William swore.

The other Pathfinder, Jackson, an older man with almost no hair remaining above his ears, but with a long flow of gray hair down to his shoulders from what fringe remained, nodded. "They suddenly turned among some rocks and we lost the trail. We'll find it again in the morning, but not in this light."

William could barely hide his frustration. "So they know we are following."

"They know someone follows," said Maric. "But we can't be certain they know who and how many."

"How far ahead?"

"Two, maybe three hours. If they press on later today than we do, it'll be half a day before we find their trail."

William nodded. "Get something to eat and go to sleep early. I'll want you out as soon as you think it's light enough to pick up that trail again."

The two Pathfinders nodded and dismounted.

William rode down the trail for a few yards, as if he might just see something in the distance. The horse demanded fodder, and using his empathic talent for mental communication with animals, William sent him a reassuring message: *Soon.*

He dismounted and rubbed the horse's nose, causing its lip to quiver. He knew the animal liked the touch. All the while, he kept looking into the darkening woodlands, thinking that somewhere out there Bear was waiting. But at last he turned the horse around and headed back to the clearing. He could see fires were already being started and the men had their bedrolls out.

He found a spot close to where his sergeant stood and nodded greeting. William undid his own bedroll and tossed it to the ground, then led his horse to where the picket had been staked out. He unsaddled and removed the bridle, then haltered the beast and tied it to the picket line. Finally, he gave it a nose-bag of oats, then sent a re-assuring *Grazing soon* to all the horses. Several snorted and sent back mental images that William could only equate to human sarcasm, as if they were saying: *We've heard* that *before*.

That brought a smile to William's face. A moment later he realized it had been his first smile since Talia's death. He glanced heavenward and silently told her, *Soon you'll be revenged*. As he returned his attention to his men, William wondered how James and the others were faring with their quest.

James was leading his horse. They had dismounted a few minutes earlier to rest the animals, but had kept moving. The journey from Krondor had been uneventful thus far, and James wished to keep it that way. They should reach the village of Miller's Rest in one more day, and Haldon Head another day after.

James had decided to slip out of the city with a small caravan, mixing in with the guards and merchants. At a small fork in the road, he and the others had slipped away onto a path that led to a lesser-used road headed north. They had traveled for a week, avoiding detection as far as they could tell, and James was praying that they would reach a small inn before nightfall.

The inn would be where, if all went according to plan, they'd make contact with one of Prince Arutha's agents in the field, and James hoped to incorporate that man into the network he was establishing. Presently, the man, who

went by the name of Alan, was simply a minor court official whose office was that of estate manager for several of the Prince's personal holdings to the north of the Principality. Unofficially, he was a snoop and gossip who often sent important information south to his ruler.

Kendaric and Brother Solon had been silent for most of the journey. James judged the monk of Ishap a quiet man by nature, who rarely volunteered information, preferring to answer questions with simple yes-or-no answers. James had tried to engage the monk in conversation a couple of times, simply to relieve the boredom, and also out of curiosity. Solon had a slightly strange accent, which James found vaguely familiar, but the monk spoke so rarely that James couldn't place it.

Kendaric had just been sullen for most of the way. He had claimed confidence in his ability to raise the ship with the spell Jazhara had found in Kendaric's room, but he objected to the necessity for travel by horseback. He was an unskilled rider and the first few days had caused him a great deal of soreness and discomfort, although by now he was, at last, starting to sit his mount with some grace and his complaints about his aching back and legs had diminished.

Jazhara had been James's most voluble companion, though even she often lapsed into deep, thoughtful silences, occasionally punctuated by a question about their whereabouts; she found the terrain north of Krondor fascinating, the cool woodlands being new and alien territory to a desert-born noblewoman. James continued to be impressed by her intelligence and her interest in everything around her. He had decided that not only did he like her, but that she was a great addition to Arutha's court. And he now understood why she had held such a powerful attraction for William when he had lived at Stardock.

James shared little of those feelings, apart from a man's appreciation of a striking woman, but he recognized how another man might easily be smitten.

Finally, Brother Solon said, "Doesn't the road ahead look ripe for surprise?" His obvious concern caused him to utter the longest single sentence James had heard from him since the day they met.

The warrior monk rolled his "r's" and said "fer" in place of "for." James halted and looked over his shoulder. "Now I recognize that speech!" he said. "I've spent enough time with dwarves to know that accent." Glancing upward, above Solon's head, in exaggeration of the man's height, he said, "You're the tallest damn dwarf I've ever encountered, Solon!"

"And you're the dimmest lad ever to serve a prince, if you think I'm a dwarf," responded the monk. "I grew up on a farm near Dorgin, with naught but dwarven lads with whom to play. So, that's the reason for my manner of speech. Now, don't change the subject." He pointed. "Do you ken what I'm sayin' about the road ahead?"

Kendaric said, "A few bushes and a wide spot in the road worry you?"

James shook his head. "He's right. There's someone hiding in the trees ahead."

"And doin' a right poor job of it, too," added Solon.

Jazhara said, "Should we double back?"

The monk handed the reins of his horse to Kendaric and said, "I think not, milady. I'll not skulk along this path like a coward!" He called out. "You who are hidden are now revealed, by my faith. Stand and face the might of Ishap or flee like the craven dogs you are!"

After a moment of silence, a small band of men emerged from concealment. They were dressed in clothes only slightly better than rags, with an oddly mismatching

assortment of armor and weapons. Two bowmen stayed behind, while two other men hung to the flanks. The small band moved onto the road, and approached, stopping a few feet away from Solon.

The leader took a step forward, a gawky man of middle height with an impossibly large nose and Adam's apple. James was struck that he looked as much like a turkey as any human he had seen. He half-expected the man to gobble.

Instead, the man smiled, revealing teeth so decayed they were mostly black. "Your pardon, sirs," he began, with a clumsy half-bow, "but if you'd see the day safely to your destination, you'd be wise not to begrudge us some silver for safe passage. After all, these are rough hills indeed."

Solon shook his fist at the man. "You'd dare to rob a priest?"

The leader glanced back at his friends, who seemed uncertain as to what to do. Then he turned back to Solon. "Your pardon, sir. We wish no trouble with the gods. You are free from our demands and may go as you will. But they must pay." He pointed at the rest of the group from Krondor.

"They are under my protection!"

The bandit stared up at the towering monk and then looked again to his companions. Attempting to look resolute, he said, "They don't wear any holy vestments. They're under no one's protection but their own."

Solon stepped up close to him and said, "If you'd tempt the wrath of my god, you'd better have a very good reason!"

James said, "Let's just kill them and get on with it."

Solon said, "No bloodshed if we can help it, James." Then with astonishing speed for a man of his size, the

warrior monk swung one mighty fist upward, catching the bandit leader squarely under the chin. The slight man was lifted right off his feet and flung backward. His ragtag band of companions scrambled to catch him as he fell. Solon glared out from under his gold-colored helm and said, "Any other of you daft twits think you can extort silver from us?"

The men glanced at one another, then as two of them carried their unconscious leader, they hurried off, while those on the side of the road vanished into the brush.

When the road appeared empty once more, Solon returned to his horse. "I thought not," he said.

James and Jazhara exchanged glances, then both started to chuckle. James mounted his horse and declared, "Let's go."

The others followed suit and soon they were again riding cautiously through the darkening woodlands.

As night fell, they turned a bend in the trail and spied light ahead. James signaled for caution and they slowed to a walk.

As they approached the light they discovered they had chanced upon an inn, nestled close to the road in a small clearing. A single two-story wooden building with a large shed behind for horses, the inn was marked with a cheery glow from within, smoke rising from the chimney, and a sign depicting a man with a rucksack and walking stick.

"This must be the Wayfarer," said James.

"Then the Prince's agent should be waiting for us?" asked Kendaric. "This man Alan?"

James nodded. "Before we go inside," he said to Kendaric, "remember, don't be too free with who we are or where we're going. Bear may have agents here as well."

Kendaric said, "Look, I don't care about any of this intrigue. I just want a bed and a hot meal. Is that too much to ask?"

James looked at the guildsman. Dryly, he answered, "Unfortunately, it often is too much to ask."

They dismounted and James shouted for the hostler.

Quickly a lackey arrived from the shed behind the building and took the horses. James spent a few moments instructing the boy on the care he required for the mounts. When he was satisfied that the horses would be well-tended, he motioned to the others to follow him into the inn.

James pushed open the door and they entered a tidy, though crowded, taproom. A merry fire burned in the hearth, and travelers and locals mixed easily as they ate and drank.

James led his companions through the taproom to the bar. A stout-looking man behind the counter looked up and with a broad smile said, "Sir!" Then spying Jazhara and the other two men, added, "Lady, and gentlemen, I'm Goodman Royos, the innkeeper. How may I be of service?"

"For a start, a round of ale for weary travelers."

"Certainly!" With practiced efficiency Royos quickly produced four large pewter jacks of ale. As he placed them on the bar, he asked, "Where are you heading?"

"North," James answered. "So, what's the news in these parts?"

"Oh, everything's been pretty quiet of late, although Farmer Toth's wife just rode through for Krondor. She seemed quite upset."

"Any idea why?" asked Jazhara.

Royos shrugged. "Can't say. She and her husband have a farm ten miles or so this side of Haldon Head. They

usually stop here for a bite on their way to the city or coming back, sometimes spend the night under their wagon out back where I keep the horses. Nice folks."

Kendaric said, "You said something about Haldon Head. We're heading there. Is it far?"

Jazhara rolled her eyes. "Kendaric . . ."

Royos said, "Haldon Head? No, just another couple of days. I don't want to scare you folks, but rumor has it that Haldon Head is cursed with witchcraft!"

Jazhara said, "What do you mean by 'witchcraft'?"

Royos said, "Now don't get me wrong. I'm not superstitious myself, but ships have sunk off Widow's Point ever since men began sailing these waters. Some say it's a curse, but I figure it's just the reefs and shoals when the tide is tricky."

Brother Solon said, "You say lots of ships go down there?"

"For hundreds of years. Some fall prey to their captains' ignorance of the reefs and the tides, others are taken by pirates. There are pirates who know this shoreline like the backs of their hands. They'll run ships aground, then board them while they're helpless."

James said, "You sound like you know what you're talking about."

Royos laughed. "I wasn't always an innkeeper . . ."

James nodded. "I'll not ask what you were before."

"Wise choice," said Royos.

Solon said, "So what's up at Haldon Head to be superstitious about?"

Royos chuckled. "Well, some say the area is haunted by the ghosts of all the dead sailors." He shook his head. "It's probably just the fog that lingers offshore."

"That's all?" asked Solon.

Royos frowned as his demeanor turned a little more se-

rious. "Well, lately I've heard tales about some folks gone missing up there, and cattle getting sick and the like." Then, returning to his cheery mood, he said, "Still, cattle are always getting sick, seems to me, and people do wander off from time to time."

Kendaric said, "We're also looking for a fellow named Alan."

Royos said, "That's Alan over there in the corner to your right. He regularly stops by when passing through." Lowering his voice, the innkeeper said, "I think he does some business for the Crown, though he's not much of a talker." Leaning back, he added, "But he's a wonderful listener. Never once saw him walk away from a yarn or tale."

James threw Kendaric a black look, then turned and crossed through the crowd to the opposite corner. A solitary man occupied a small table there, watching the room with his back to the wall. James said, "Alan?"

"I'm sorry. Do I know you?"

"I don't think you do. We're from the 'Citadel.' "

Alan waved James closer. "Glad to hear it. 'Uncle Arthur' sent word you'd be coming by."

James sat at the only other chair at the table, with Kendaric and Jazhara standing behind. Solon looked around the room to ensure they weren't overheard.

"What's the word on William's quest?"

"He's doing fine. He and his friends are hunting up in the mountains. Word was sent back they've found 'bear tracks.' "

Lowering his voice, James asked, "What have you heard from Haldon Head?"

"I haven't been up there for a while. That town seems to be under some sort of curse. I've heard about sick people, sick farm animals, missing children, and there are ru-

mors of dark creatures roaming the night. I don't know what's true, but I've met a lot of people on the road who are getting away from there in a hurry. They say it's witchcraft."

Jazhara said, "I hate that word! What do you mean?"

Alan glanced up at Jazhara, and while he had never seen her before he must have deduced she was the Prince's new magician, for he said, "Begging your pardon, milady. There's an old woman living at Widow's Point who the local villagers in Haldon Head go to with their common ailments. They've always tolerated her, even welcomed her when they were ill, but with the strange goings-on of late, they've taken to calling her a witch."

Jazhara said, "Perhaps we can be of some assistance when we reach Haldon Head."

James said, "Where are you off to next?"

"I'm hurrying down to the garrison at Sarth. Word is we've got goblins raiding to the east of here. Likely there's a camp nearby."

"They going to be a problem to us in reaching Haldon Head?" asked James.

"I don't think so, but it's best to stay on the road during daylight. So far, I've only heard of them hitting farms for food animals." Looking around the crowded room, he said, "I'd best slip out now. I've got a small patrol camped down the road. Thought it best not to call attention to myself. I should rejoin them and start out for the south at first light." He rose. "One last thing, the patrol sent to aid you hasn't reached Miller's Rest yet. They could be there by the time you pass through, or show up later. Best to stay out of trouble at Haldon Head until you know they're in place."

James thanked Alan and the agent departed.

Kendaric asked, "Can we get something to eat?"

James nodded. "And some rooms." He stood up and returned to the bar to arrange it with Goodman Royos.

William waited patiently for the return of the Pathfinders. He had stopped his patrol at a small clearing near a brook. A tree had been blazed with the agreed-upon cut, a symbol that meant "wait here."

He could feel the tension in the pit of his stomach. The only reason for making such a mark was that they were closing in on their quarry. Time dragged as he waited for the return of the scouts. He considered his options. He had been trailing Bear for over a week now. Several times he had waited while the Pathfinders had lost the trail only to pick it up again a few hours later. On two occasions, it was clear that Bear had met with other men. The Pathfinders deduced that he was recruiting mercenaries. Twice, other riders had left Bear's group to ride off on errands of one sort or another. Three times they had come across signs of goblins in the area, and William had even dispatched one of his riders back to Krondor to carry word of their possible incursion into the Principality. William prayed this was just some tribal migration to better hunting grounds, and not a gang of raiders. He wanted to concentrate his energy on Bear and his men, not a group of nonhuman troublemakers looking to steal cows and children. He knew that if he did encounter a raiding band, he'd be honor-bound to attempt to drive them back up into the mountains and that to do so would risk losing track of Bear. As much as he wanted to avenge Talia's murder, he couldn't abide the thought of a human child being sacrificed in one of the goblins' magic rites.

Finally, one of the two Pathfinders appeared. It was

Jackson who came into the clearing, leading his horse. "We've spotted a band of mercenaries, Lieutenant."

"Bear's men?"

"Maric thinks so, but we saw no sign of the man himself. From the description, he'd be a hard one to miss. Maric's staying close. They're camped in a little clearing about a mile up the road. Best if we slip half the company around them, then hit them from both sides."

William considered the plan. He disliked the idea of splitting his forces while on the march, yet he knew that if he came at the mercenaries from one side only, they might break and flee into the woods. He needed intelligence more than dead bodies. At last he nodded. "How long?"

"We can be in place in an hour."

William glanced at the late afternoon sky. They would attack the mercenaries as it was getting dark. "Good. Be ready at sunset. Don't attack until you hear us coming, then hit them hard."

"Lieutenant?"

"Yes, Jackson?"

"I recognize this company. They're the Grey Talon, up from Landreth."

"Landreth?" asked William. "Valemen."

Jackson nodded. "Tough bastards. Last I heard they were fighting down in the Vale for a trading concern against Keshian raiders. They sometimes come up to Krondor to spend their gold, but usually we don't see them this far north."

William pondered the significance of this. "They must have been in Krondor when Bear was there, and Bear's agent must have gotten word to them to head north."

"Something like that," agreed Jackson.

"Which means Bear doesn't have many of his original crew left."

"Fair guess," agreed Jackson. "But these lads will not cry quarter unless they're seriously beaten. I know that from their reputation."

"Still, it means they won't have any personal loyalty to that monster. If we can capture . . ." He turned and signaled for Sergeant Hartag. "What's the lie of the land? On foot or horse?"

"Foot, I think, Lieutenant. Too noisy getting the horses in place in the evening, and if we get close before we spring the attack, we have a better chance of taking charge of the fray."

"On foot, then," agreed William. "Take half the men and go with Jackson. Picket the horses and get as close to the other side of their camp as you can. Deploy your archers to one side. They'll signal when they're ready. We'll need their covering fire to make sure that none of these ruffians escape. If you get into trouble, lead them toward the trees, then disengage and let the archers cut them down.

"Wait until you hear us attack from this side of the trail and then go in fast and hard. But remember—I want at least one of them taken alive." To Jackson he added, "Go now, tell Maric to meet me at the trail, then get these men into place."

The Pathfinder nodded, mounted his horse, and rode off. In moments the sergeant had all the men mounted, and the company divided into two squads, and he led the first up the trail to rendezvous with the Pathfinders. William waited until they were well along the trail, then gave the order for his own squad to follow.

Riding into the gloom of the woodlands, William could

feel his anticipation mounting. Soon he would know where Bear was hiding, and then he would face him.

The men waited for the signal. William had inspected the enemy camp and was forced to admit that the men he faced were seasoned professionals. There were about thirty of them, and while they had elected to sleep on the ground, they had still picked the most defensible site in the clearing, atop a small hillock, with clear lines of sight in all directions. The good news was that they hadn't bothered making any sort of defenses. Even a rude earthen berm fortified with cut stakes would have proven a hindrance for William's men. These men were obviously in a hurry, making camp just before nightfall, probably planning on breaking camp at first light. They would set sentries, and those would be vigilant.

William waited until the sun had set low enough past the distant hills to throw the entire landscape into a chiaroscuro of dark gray and black. He devised a plan and relayed his orders to his archers. Five of the dozen men with him would hang back.

William motioned with his sword, and walked out into the clearing, seven men walking easily alongside him. He had covered a dozen yards when a voice called out from the camp. "Who goes there?"

"Hello, the camp!" William shouted, continuing to walk casually. "I seek the Grey Talon company."

"Well, you've found them," came the response. "Come no closer!"

William stopped. "I bring a message for Bear." The agreed-upon signal to the archers was the word "Bear."

As the sentry was about to answer, five arrows shot overhead and William shouted, "Now!"

The archers had picked their targets well, and before

they realized they were under siege, five of the mercenaries were down. More arrows flew from the other side, and William realized Sergeant Hartag had his own bowmen ready.

From both sides of the camp, soldiers of the Kingdom appeared, while the Grey Talon mercenaries grabbed their weapons and made ready to answer the attack. William charged the nearest sentry, who raised his shield to take the blow from William's large hand-and-a-half sword. William started to swing downward, then turned the blade in an elliptical swing that brought the huge blade crashing into the side of the shield, knocking it aside, and turning the soldier so he couldn't return the blow, since his sword-arm was now away from William. As the sentry turned to strike, William swept his blade downward from the shield, slashing the back of the man's leg, hamstringing him. The man went down with a cry and William kicked him over with his left leg. The mercenary wasn't dead, but he wouldn't be fighting. William wanted prisoners. William wanted to know where he could find Bear.

William's men had the advantage of surprise, but the Grey Talon mercenaries were a hard and experienced bunch. The struggle was bloody and only the fact that a half-dozen mercenaries had gone down early enabled William's men to carry the day. After William's third kill, he glanced around, expecting to see mercenaries asking for quarter, but he was surprised to find they were still fighting, even though there were now two of the Prince's soldiers facing each mercenary.

"Keep at least one alive!" William shouted, even as he remembered the man he had hamstrung, lying somewhere on the ground in the midst of the carnage. He turned to see how his own command was doing. The

archers had put up their bows, drawn their swords, and were now entering the fray. The mercenaries continued to resist and several of William's men were down, either dead or seriously wounded. "End this!" William shouted to a retreating mercenary who was desperately attempting to keep two Krondorian soldiers at bay.

The man ignored William and kept looking for an opening. William swore in disgust as another mercenary was killed. He circled around behind one of the last remaining mercenaries, and struck him from behind across the helmet with the flat of his blade. "Don't kill him!" he shouted to the two men who were about to run him through. The man staggered, and one of William's soldiers leapt forward, grappling with the mercenary's sword-arm. The other stepped inside and struck the mercenary hard across the face with the hilt of his sword, stunning the man.

Then it was over. William looked around and shouted, "Sergeant!"

Hartag hurried over and said, "Sir!"

"What's the damage?"

"Six men down, sir. Three dead, two more likely to join them, one who might survive if we get him to a healer quickly. Several others wounded, but nothing to brag about."

"Damn," muttered William. That left him with eighteen men, not all of them fully able. "What about the mercenaries?"

"Damnable thing, sir. They wouldn't ask for quarter. Fought to the death. Never knew mercenaries to do that. Usually they're smart enough to know when they're whipped."

"How many alive?"

"Two," answered Hartag. "One's bleeding to death

from a deep leg wound and won't be with us much longer." William nodded, realizing this must be the man he'd hamstrung. Hartag continued. "The other's that fellow you banged across the head. He should be rousing soon."

The mercenary came around after a few minutes and William had him dragged over. "Who are you? Are you one of Bear's men?"

"Not anymore. Name's Shane McKinzey. Currently—" He glanced around. "Used to be with the Grey Talons. We was contacted by Bear's agent so we came to join up. We met with this Bear, and he told us what to do."

"Why the fight to the death?" asked Hartag.

"Orders." He rubbed the back of his head. "Seems our captain"—he motioned toward a corpse being dragged to a makeshift funeral pyre—"he got the word that Bear had some sort of magical powers. Said he'd hunt down and eat the soul of any man who betrayed him." He blinked, as if trying to clear his vision. "Man, I've been hit before, but nothing like that." He shook his head. "Anyway, Capt'n, he says a clean death and fast ride to Lims-Kragma's Hall is better than bein' sucked dry of blood and havin' your soul captured by some hell's spawn."

"Why were you camped here?"

"We was left to kill anyone following him. This was our first job for him. Looks like it'll be our last."

"Where's Bear now?"

"Don't know. We were supposed to camp here and kill anyone coming this way, then meet him on the morning of the new Small Moon, at Two Fangs Pass."

Hartag said, "You're lying."

"Maybe, but since you'll have to kill me anyway to keep me from warning Bear . . . why should I be honest?"

"Since we'll kill you anyway," said William, "maybe

you ought to come clean and help us get the man who set you up."

Shane looked at William, and said, "I've been a mercenary for more years than you've carried a sword, boy. I don't fear dying, but I can see you're afraid of killin' in cold blood."

William pointed to where his men piled the dead. "Take a look at the rest of your men and tell me again that I'm afraid. Still, you could live if you're honest. You've never worked for Bear before, right?"

"What of it?"

"Then you don't need to share in Bear's punishment. Tell us what we want to know and my men will escort you back to Krondor. From there you can take a ship to wherever you like. I suggest back down to the Vale."

The mercenary rubbed the back of his head as he weighed his options. "Well, I guess I've not much of a company left. All right, you've got a deal. I was lying about the killing-anyone-who-followed part. We were supposed to make it look easy to attack us—damn we did make it too easy—bleed a little, then run like hell. Bear's setting a trap for you at Two Fangs Pass. We were supposed to lead you to it. If you hurry, you can beat him there."

"You made the smart choice. Thanks." William beckoned to a nearby soldier. "You and Blake take Mr. McKinzey here back to Krondor with anyone else who's too badly wounded to go any further."

"Yes, sir!" came the answer.

Hartag spoke softly. "You think he's telling the truth this time, Will?"

"Yes. He's got no reason to lie, and getting as far from Bear as he can is obviously his best choice." William's eyes seemed to light up as he continued, "We have him.

Get the men ready to ride. We're pushing through this night, and the next if need be, and we'll get to Two Fang Pass before Bear."

"Sir!" said Hartag, and he turned to carry out his orders.

Ten

◆

Goblins

Ⓙ ames awoke.

Something was wrong. He leapt to his feet and kicked at the foot of Kendaric's bed. The guildsman sat up with a sleepy expression and mumbled, "What?"

"I smell smoke."

James hurried to the next room, where Jazhara and the monk were sleeping, and pounded on the door. The hall was already blue with smoky haze and the acrid smell of burning wood stung his eyes. "Get up!" he shouted. "The inn's on fire!"

Doors up and down the hall flew open as the handful of other guests looked out to see what the fuss was about. James repeated his warning as he buckled on his sword and grabbed his travel pack. Jazhara and Solon appeared a moment later and hurried after him and the others down the stairs.

In the common room, it was obvious that the fire had been started near the front door, for now the entire wall around the exit was engulfed in flames. "The kitchen!" James shouted. He hurried through the door behind the taproom bar and saw Goodman Royos and a young woman drawing buckets of water. "Stay calm!" shouted the innkeeper.

James grabbed the man by his shirt. "Don't even try. You'll never put that fire out with buckets of water. Get out while you can!"

The man hesitated for a moment, then nodded. He ushered the girl out of the kitchen into the backyard as the last of the guests fled through the rear door.

Screams alerted James to the fact that something even direr than a fire was at hand.

He and Solon had their weapons at the ready when they emerged from the rear of the building, only to discover a band of goblins trying to untie the horses from their picket line beneath the run-in shed.

James counted quickly: there were a dozen of the creatures nearby. The goblins stood shorter than men, and were smaller across the shoulders, but not by much. Sloping foreheads terminated in heavy brows of thick black hair. The black irises of their yellow eyes caught the firelight, seeming to glow in the darkness. James had fought goblins before and realized at once that this must be an experienced raiding party. Three of the warriors wore tribal topknots complete with feathers or bones in their hair, signifying that they were chieftains or priests. They all carried bucklers and swords, and James was only thankful that they didn't appear to have archers with them.

There were three other armed men emerging from the inn, so including Solon, himself, and a few of the guests, James counted eleven warriors. Jazhara could handle herself, he knew, so he shouted to Royos, "Get the girl behind us!"

The goblins charged, and Jazhara unleashed a ball of fire at the center of the group. It struck square on. Flames immediately consumed three goblins, while another three off to one side were badly burned.

The remaining six goblins came forward at a howling run, swinging furiously. Out of the corner of his eye, James saw Solon wield his heavy warhammer deftly, caving in the skull of one goblin before the creature could dodge away.

One more down, five to go, thought James.

Kendaric came into James's view awkwardly waving a short blade, and suddenly James realized that the journeyman had no skills whatsoever to defend himself. James leapt to one side and kicked at the goblin who had overrun his position, sending the creature sprawling. He then leapt to his right, and with a spinning blow, cut at the goblin who menaced Kendaric, slashing him across the back of the neck.

The panic-stricken wrecker stared at James with wide-eyed terror. James yelled, "Get over there by Royos!"

Kendaric seemed unable to move, and James barely avoided being struck by a sword-blow from behind. He only sensed the attack at the last second and ducked to his left. Had he ducked to his right, he thought, he'd have been a head shorter.

James spun and saw that he had been attacked by one of the burned goblins. This one's entire right side was still smoking, his eye swollen shut, so James immediately moved to his own left, attacking the goblin's blind side.

Jazhara unleashed another spell, a searing red beam that struck the face of one of the goblins approaching Kendaric. The creature screamed, dropped his sword and clawed at his eyes. The other turned toward the source of the attack, and hesitated.

Kendaric used the distraction to turn and flee, leaving the goblin isolated. Brother Solon and another man from the inn appeared in Kendaric's place and both attacked the goblin at the same instant. The goblin saw

Solon's huge warhammer coming at him and dodged, while the other man attempted to strike out with his sword. The two attacks confounded each other, and the goblin turned and fled.

Suddenly the remaining goblins were all running for their lives. James gave a half-hearted lunge at one who managed to elude his sword-point, then stood up and surveyed the damage.

The inn was now completely in flames, and Royos and the young woman were watching it, holding onto one another. The stable-boy stood near the horses, his eyes wide with fear.

A half-dozen goblins lay on the ground.

James shook his head. "What brings goblins so close to the coast?" he wondered aloud.

Brother Solon came to stand beside James. "Goblins tend to be a stupid lot, but not stupid enough to raid for horses unless they've a camp nearby."

The young girl approached and said, "Farmer Toth's wife rode through on her way to Krondor, sir, looking for soldiers to come save her baby girl."

"Maria!" exclaimed Goodman Royos. "You weren't supposed to hear of such things."

"Father," the girl replied, "do you think you can shield me from every trouble in the world?" She turned to look at the burning inn. "Is my home not destroyed before my eyes?"

The innkeeper put his arms around her shoulders. "I forget that you are growing up, daughter."

The other guests, two men with swords, and another with a large hunting knife, as well as two women gathered around. Royos said, "My thanks for all that you did in driving off the goblins."

James nodded. "I wish we could have done more."

"You saved lives," said Royos. "Inns can be rebuilt. Customers are much harder to come by." He kissed the top of Maria's head. "As are daughters." Royos and Maria turned back toward the inn, to arrange a bucket brigade to douse the remaining flames.

"Aye," said Solon. "They were a'waitin' for us to come out so they could butcher us."

James scratched at his ear. "Why such a blatant raid? They have to know there'll be a patrol up in the hills after them soon . . ."

Jazhara said, "To draw a patrol away from somewhere else?"

James looked at the young magician and motioned for her to walk with him. When they were out of earshot of the others, he asked, "Bear?"

"Perhaps. It would certainly suit his cause if soldiers were not near Widow's Point and Haldon Head when he attempted to claim the Tear of the Gods."

James said, "If we knew how he planned on getting to the Tear, then we'd have a better notion of where he is likely to be."

"Were I this Bear, and failing to gain Kendaric's spell, I would wait for Kendaric to appear and capture him."

"Or wait for us to do the work, then take the Tear from us once we're back on dry ground."

"Either way, I would allow Kendaric to reach Widow's Point," finished Jazhara.

James said, "I don't wish to wait, but I'm reluctant to attempt this without the reserves down in Miller's Rest." He glanced over to where the others waited, and called out, "Brother Solon! You seem to have some knowledge of goblins. How large a camp do you judge they'd have nearby?"

The warrior monk paused to consider, then said, " 'Tis

hard to judge. The daft creatures do not think as you and I think. Perhaps three companies such as this one. One to hold the camp while the other two raid. They numbered chieftains and priests in this party, which is somewhat unusual."

"To what end?" asked Kendaric, now sufficiently recovered from his fright to follow the conversation.

"Ah, that is as plain as can be," said Solon. "They've taken a baby." He glanced at the sky, where Small Moon was waning. "They'll sacrifice the wee one in two days when the moon is dark, an offering to their god. So, these aren't bandits out lookin' for plunder. This is an all-out ghost-appeasement raid. Their ancestors are tellin' them to come down and spill human blood, take human slaves and horses, then come back. 'Tis a very bad business."

Jazhara said, "We must do something. If they're going to kill the child in two nights, the soldiers will not be here in time."

James said, "As loath as I am to think of a child dying in such a fashion, we have more pressing business elsewhere."

Jazhara grabbed James by the upper arm and in a low, angry tone, growled, "You'd leave a baby to be butchered like a food animal?"

James rolled his eyes and shook his head. "I'm not going to win this one, am I?"

"No. I'll go alone if I have to."

James pulled his arm free of her grip. "You have your duty."

"And you've already said this may have been done to draw away our soldiers. We will have to wait anyway, James, if you won't move to Haldon Head before the patrol gets here. If we can rescue the child and return her to her family, we lose only a couple of days, and when the soldiers following us arrive here, they can move straight on to Miller's Rest."

Sighing in resignation, James motioned for Solon and Kendaric to approach. "Solon, could these goblins be working for Bear?"

"I think not," said the monk. "Though he could be influencin' them. A few weapons or a bit of magic, as gifts, some intelligence on safe places to raid, some jars of wine or ale, they might think plunderin' down here was their own brilliant idea."

Kendaric said, "Is this Bear everywhere?"

James answered, "No, I don't think so. I don't think Bear is behind this. I think he's working for another."

"Why?" asked Jazhara.

"I'll tell you as we travel." He glanced up at the sky. "Dawn will be here in a couple of hours and we have to be ready to ride."

"Where are we going?" asked Kendaric.

With a wry smile, James said, "We're hunting goblins."

Kendaric was complaining, again. "This is not at all wise!"

James shook his head, ignoring him. To Solon he said, "They're not taking pains to hide their tracks, are they?"

The warrior monk was leading his horse as he followed the goblins' trail. "No, they're a wee bit damaged, and in a hurry to get back to their healers, I'm thinkin'."

James pointed ahead. In the distance the hills rose and behind them the peaks of the Calastius Mountains. "You think they'll be up in the rocks?"

"Almost certainly," answered the monk. "They'll have found a defensible position, maybe a box canyon or small meadow, but it'll be hell to pay to dig them out of it."

"And the four of us are going to 'dig them out?' " demanded Kendaric.

Running out of patience, James said, "No, we're not

going to dig them out. We're going to hold the horses and send you in to destroy them."

Kendaric stopped his horse, looked down with a stunned expression. "Me?"

Jazhara couldn't contain herself and started to laugh. Even the taciturn Solon allowed himself a chuckle.

James shook his head. "Don't worry. I have a plan."

He turned away from Kendaric, who was now falling farther behind, allowing Jazhara to lean over and say, "You have a plan?"

James whispered back. "No, but I will have by the time we get there and I look around. And maybe he'll shut up until then."

Jazhara smiled and nodded. They rode on.

At last, Solon signaled a halt. "I'm not a proper tracker, it's true, but you'd have to be a blind man to not see this." He dismounted and pointed at the ground where James could see heavy boot-prints in the dirt.

"He's in a bit of a hurry, apparently," said the monk.

"Who is it?" asked Kendaric.

"Unless someone here has the gift of future sight," said Solon, "it's only guessing, but I suspect we're lookin' at the tracks of that farmer, come to fetch home his bonny girl."

"Good guess," said James, pointing ahead. In the distance they saw a solitary figure cresting a hill. He had been hidden from sight by a closer rise, but now they could see him marching purposefully down the trail. "We'd best catch up with him before he gets himself killed."

Solon mounted and they urged their horses into a fast canter. They overtook the farmer quickly. The man turned and regarded the riders with suspicion. He held a scythe like a weapon, across his chest, ready to block or swing.

"Hold," said James with his right hand held up palm outward. "We're on the Prince's business."

"Finally! I was beginning to think help would never come. How is my wife?"

James said, "I believe you've mistaken us for others."

The farmer asked, "What?! You mean Becky didn't send you from Krondor? I thought you had come to rescue my daughter!"

Solon said, "Be calm, Farmer Toth. You are in Ishap's grace now. We know something about your child. Please, tell us what happened to your daughter."

The man seemed to relax. "It's been almost a week, now, since my friend Lane and I were out hunting. We were in the foothills east of here, when at night we heard flutes and drums.

"We went to see what it was, and in a canyon not too far from here we came upon a band of goblins. They had a little boy, and then they . . . oh, gods . . . they cut the child in two. Sacrificed him! I cried out . . . I couldn't help myself, and they came after us. We managed to escape, but then the day before yesterday they fell upon us back at my farm. Lane and I tried to hold them back, but there were just too many. They got into the house . . . and they took my daughter! Lane's a tracker and went after them, and I sent my wife Becky to Krondor for help, and then followed after Lane. Now you've shown up."

James asked, "Which way did Lane go?"

"Back to the canyon, I'm almost certain. He left small signs for me to follow. I was going to wait for the soldiers . . . but I couldn't bear the thought of them sacrificing my little girl."

"She's safe until the dark of the next moon," said Solon.

"It was the dark of the Middle Moon the night we saw

the boy killed," agreed Toth. Then he became concerned. "Tomorrow night is the dark of the Small Moon!"

"We must act quickly," said Jazhara.

"It's all that witch's doing," said Toth.

"Witch?" asked Jazhara.

"There are rumors of witchcraft up at Haldon Head— that accursed witch must have had my daughter stolen for her foul spells!"

Jazhara's eyes narrowed. "Did you see the 'witch' when the goblins killed the little boy?"

"Well, no, but . . ."

"It is of no matter now," injected Solon. "If we are to help, we must move quickly."

"I beg you do!" said Toth. "Please help me find my daughter."

Solon glanced around. "Camp here, good farmer. We shall have to strike this night, else the bonny child is lost."

James nodded. "Let's get moving."

They led their horses along the road while the farmer looked around for a place to wait. James glanced back and saw the man's face. Clearly all his hopes rode with them.

"Looks like Toth's friend Lane ran into some trouble," said James. A short way down the trail they had followed for the last hour lay a small mound of corpses. Beyond that another pair of goblins lay across a still, human form.

"He made the bastards pay," growled Solon.

Kendaric said, "But at what price? The man is dead!"

"Calm yourself," said Jazhara.

"Calm, she says," Kendaric muttered, shaking his head.

"I think that body just moved," said James, jumping from his horse and hurrying over. He pulled the two gob-

lins off the pile and examined the man. "Bring water!" he instructed.

Jazhara hurried over with a waterskin while James cradled the man's head, watching as the magician poured a little water onto the man's face, reviving him.

Blinking, Lane said, "Goblins . . . they took my friend's daughter. I found their camp, but . . . there were too many . . ."

"Don't worry, we'll find them," said Jazhara.

"They're close. The box canyon, north of here. Please. Don't let them kill that little girl."

James started to ask a question, but Lane's eyes rolled up into his head. James put his ear near the man's mouth and after a minute, said, "He's gone."

Solon said, "He'll not die in vain. We'll see justice done."

James gently rested the man's head on the rocks, and stood. Glancing upward, he said, "It's going to be dark in less than two hours. Let's see if we can find that box canyon." He motioned for Solon and Kendaric to dismount. "We'll walk the horses and leave them at the mouth of the canyon. When we return, we'll give Lane a proper burial."

It took them less than an hour to reach the entrance to the canyon. A small stream emptied out of the rocks there, cutting across the trail, before splashing down the hillside. Turning to Kendaric, James said, "Water the horses and keep them from wandering off. We'll be back as soon as we can."

"You're leaving me here alone?" he asked, alarmed.

"Well, if you'd rather go to the goblin camp . . . ?"

"No! It's just, well, alone . . ."

James said, "As much as it pains me to say this, right now you are more important than either Jazhara or my-

self." He thought about it, then added, "Solon, you stay here as well. If we don't come back, go to Miller's Rest and pick up the patrol. Then go to Haldon Head, raise the ship and get the Tear."

Solon seemed to be on the verge of objecting, then saw the wisdom of the plan. "Aye, I'll wait."

James and Jazhara moved up the canyon. After carefully picking their way through the narrow opening, they came to a quarter turn, bending to the left. James peeked around the corner. Then he turned and held up two fingers to Jazhara, and mouthed, "Two guards." She nodded. He glanced up at the rim of the canyon and pointed to a spot slightly behind Jazhara.

Following his gaze, she saw a handhold, and nodded quick agreement. Shouldering her staff across her back, she climbed nimbly up onto the ridge. James followed. At the top he whispered in her ear, "I'm going to move up the draw a bit and see what's there. If there's a way to get past the guards, I'll find it. If not, we'll try the other side."

"What if there is no way on the other side?" she whispered back.

"Then we have to kill the guards and move quickly before we're discovered."

Jazhara's face revealed her reaction to that possibility. "Please find another way," she asked.

James crept along the rim of the canyon, keeping low to reduce the chance of being seen against the still-light sky. He passed the bend and glanced down to make sure he wasn't likely to be spotted by the guard stationed at the opposite side of the canyon, but to his relief the guard was nowhere to be seen.

James continued his slow approach. The rise increased in height as he reached the lip of the box canyon. Below he could see a dozen tents, dominated by a huge one ca-

pable of housing at least a dozen warriors. He sat back on his haunches for a moment and weighed his concerns. The tents were of human origin. Goblins built huts from sticks and branches in their own villages, or stayed in caves or under lean-tos when out foraging or hunting.

Then James saw a human. So: human renegades were behind the goblin raids! He half-expected the man to be wearing the black of the Nighthawks, and was almost disappointed when he approached the fire and revealed himself to be a simple mercenary. James gave that some thought: mercenaries and goblins. It seemed that Bear must be involved in the goblin raids—or whoever was behind Bear . . .

Which left James with a problem to consider at some other time, since right now he needed to focus on rescuing the child.

The mercenary kicked a goblin who grudgingly moved aside so that the human could take out a knife and cut a hunk of meat off a quarter bullock that was roasting on a spit. The man deftly impaled the meat with his dagger, tore off a piece, and turned away from the circle of goblins around the fire. James watched him chew the savory beef.

Then he heard the baby crying. An influx of emotion he hadn't expected accompanied the realization that the child still lived, filling him with relief and a redoubled sense of urgency. James's eyes glanced here and there, his gaze traveling around the camp. The old thief in him spied a course along the canyon rim that would put him above the big tent in which the child lay.

James glanced at the camp below. A couple of goblins sported wounds, obviously from their aborted raid on the Wayfarer the night before. *How to get in and out without being detected?* James wondered.

He looked up at the sky and judged it about three hours before the waning Small Moon rose. Middle Moon was a quarter full, and was now high in the sky. It would set as Small Moon rose. Large Moon was also waning, and would rise an hour after Small Moon.

James calculated. That gave him roughly an hour of relatively deep darkness in which to infiltrate the camp, steal the baby, and return to where Solon and Kendaric waited. As loath as he was to risk passing by the guards three more times, he knew he had to return to Jazhara and discuss his plan with her; he would need her help.

Moving slowly he passed the bend and reached the point above Jazhara. Softly, he whispered her name and from below heard her answer, "Here."

He jumped down.

"What did you find?" Jazhara asked.

"The baby lives and I think I can get to her, but I need to know if you have anything that we can use to keep her quiet. I will almost certainly be discovered if she cries out."

Jazhara said, "I can make something; how much time do we have?"

"I must be back above the tent within the hour."

"Then I have little time. I'll need a small fire and my things are on my horse."

James motioned her to follow. "Quietly," he said. He led her back down the canyon to where Solon and Kendaric waited. At once, Kendaric started to ask questions, but James waved them away. "The child lives and I'll fetch her out, but right now I need a fire."

Solon didn't hesitate. Instantly he started casting around for small branches and twigs. Jazhara took her pack down from her horse, and sat down on the ground, swinging the pack around before her as she did so. She

quickly removed several vials, a small copper vessel, and a pair of thin cloth gloves. While she worked, she said, "Getting the child to drink anything could be difficult and she might cry out in the attempt. I can make a potion that will cause the baby to sleep deeply for a few hours if you can get her to breathe it in. A bit on a cloth, held over her nose and mouth for a few moments, will suffice. Be careful, though, not to breathe the fumes yourself, even at a distance. While it might not put you to sleep, it can disorient you and make it difficult for you to return."

"Get you killed, is what she means," said Kendaric.

Solon said, "Laddie, has anyone ever previously mentioned that at times you possess the charm of a canker on the buttock?"

James chuckled, but Jazhara was all concentration as she poured tiny amounts of liquid and powders from the five vials she had chosen. She added a few drops of water and then with an incantation placed the vessel close to the tiny fire Solon had started.

Pulling an empty vial from her bag, she removed the stopper and deftly picked up the copper vessel, holding it gingerly with two gloved fingers. Quickly she poured the contents into the vial, then replaced the stopper.

She handed the vial to James, saying, "Carefully." Then she rummaged around in her pack. At last she held something out to him. "Here is a clean cloth. Just before you attempt to touch the child, pour a little of the liquid on the cloth, and hold it above the baby's face. A few moments is all it should take. She will not rouse, even if you jostle her or there are loud noises."

"Thank you," James said. "If there's loud noises, it doesn't matter if she wakes or not." He glanced at the sky. "I must hurry. Wait here and have the horses ready for a very fast retreat if I come running." Then he thought a bit

more and said, "Have the horses ready for a very fast retreat no matter what."

"At last a wise suggestion," Kendaric said as he grinned.

James unbuckled his sword-belt, knowing that should
he have need of his blade he and the child would most
likely be facing death, anyway. He checked his dagger
and placed it firmly in its sheath. Tucking the vial and
cloth inside his shirt, he turned and hurried back toward
the entrance of the canyon.

He made his way quickly along the ridge and this time
continued until he was above the tent. Middle Moon had
sunk in the west, and Small Moon and Large Moon were
going to rise soon. The fire had burned low in the center
of the camp and several goblins lay sleeping on the
ground near it. From within several tents, the sound of
snoring told James the entire camp had turned in for the
night, save for whatever guards were on patrol. He prayed
quickly to Ruthia, Goddess of Luck and of thieves, that
the goblins and renegades weren't smart enough to have
set someone to patrolling the rim. He positioned himself
above the largest tent and looked around. Then he began
his careful descent.

When he reached the ground he put his ear next to the
tent and listened, but could hear nothing through the
heavy canvas. The bottom of the tent was tightly staked,
so lifting the canvas and crawling under it was not an option. He pulled out his dagger.

Quietly, he pushed the point into the heavy canvas, and
cut downward in a steady, firm motion, so as not to make
too much noise. He made a slit that was big enough to
peer through and looked inside. The stench that struck
him almost made him vomit. He knew that stink: dead
bodies. He choked down his gag reflex and looked
around.

Three goblins slept on bedrolls on the ground, while another lay upon a raised dais before an altar of some sort. James looked for the baby and saw a small object behind the altar, about the size of a cradle. Slipping through the cut in the canvas, he crept toward the object.

It was indeed a rude cradle and in it the baby lay sleeping. He glanced around and suppressed a shudder. There were body parts lying upon the altar, arranged in a grotesque parody of a human form. An upper torso from a woman lay above the pelvis of a man. A child's arm had been placed to the left, while the arm of an older child or a small woman lay on the right. Equally mismatched legs and feet were positioned below the pelvis. James glanced into the cradle. It seemed likely that this child was to provide the head. He had no idea of what black sorcery was being practiced, and he had no intention of lingering to find out. His recent experience in the Nighthawks' desert stronghold, where he had almost been the guest-of-honor at a demon-summoning, had left him with a strong aversion to such goings-on.

James adroitly removed the vial and cloth from his shirt and, holding his breath, dabbed some liquid on the cloth. When it felt damp, he held out the cloth, and hung it above the child's face. After a moment, he put the cloth down on the edge of the cradle, and returned the stopper to the vial. He put the vial back in his shirt and bent over to pick up the baby.

A startled grunt caused him to look across the altar. The goblin priest who had been sleeping on the other side was standing there, staring at James in wide-eyed amazement. James grabbed the cloth and flipped it, sending it spinning across the altar to cover the goblin's nose and mouth. The priest blinked in surprise then started to reach up, but as his black-clawed fingers touched the cloth, his

eyes rolled back up into his head and he slumped to the floor. Silently, James said, "Thank you, Jazhara," and scooped up the baby.

Taking the child's blanket, he rigged a shoulder sling, and fled the terrible place, carrying the baby as he had often carried treasure after burglarizing houses as a boy. He climbed the rock face and quickly made his way back around the rim, expecting a cry of alarm every step of the way. When he reached a place where it was safe to descend, he jumped down and started running.

It seemed to take forever to get back to the others; but they had the horses ready and were in the saddle by the time he reached them.

"I have her," James said, and Jazhara held out her arms. James handed the child to the magician, then mounted his own horse.

The four of them urged their horses forward and soon were trotting down the trail.

An hour later they found Farmer Toth, sitting beside a small fire waiting anxiously. When they rode into view, he leapt to his feet and hurried toward them.

Seeing the bundle in Jazhara's arms, he cried, "Is that her?"

Jazhara handed the baby down and said, "She will sleep until morning, then she will be a little listless for the next few hours. After that, she will be fine."

"Thank you! Praise the gods! She's still alive and well. Thank you so very much."

James glanced around. "We'll ride with you back toward your farm. The goblins may not realize she's gone until dawn, but it's better to be cautious."

"I'm grateful to you," said the farmer, turning to walk beside them along the trail.

Jazhara said, "We have other—ill—news, I'm sorry to say. Your friend Lane is dead."

Toth said, "I suspected as much when you returned without him."

"He gave the bastards a fight of it," said Solon. He glanced at Kendaric, who was wise enough to stay silent. "He was a hero, of that there is no doubt."

Toth was silent for a moment, then said, "We had yet to name our baby, but I think from now on I shall call her 'Lane' in his memory."

" 'Tis a fine honor," agreed Solon.

As dawn broke, they were miles down the road. They had taken a couple of short breaks and James and Solon had let Toth ride for periods while they carried the baby, Lane.

A little after sunrise the baby stirred and fussed. "She's hungry and her mother's nowhere nearby," said the farmer. "She'll have to wait until we reach my farm and I can milk the goat."

"How far?" asked Kendaric, who was getting a stiff neck from looking back over his shoulder every few minutes.

"Not far," answered Toth. "And with luck, if my missus got any help in Krondor, she might be back at the farm by the time we get there."

James and Jazhara let their horses fall back a little and Jazhara said, "You've been very quiet about what you saw in the camp."

"Yes," agreed James.

"Something disturbed you," she said.

"Yes."

"Something you don't wish to talk about?"

"Yes," James replied, then after a moment, he said, "no, perhaps I should talk about it, to you at any rate.

You're the Prince's advisor on things magical." He described the altar and the body parts.

"Some black necromancy, certainly," said Jazhara. "It's a very bad business, but it fits in with that monster we found in the sewers of Krondor. Someone is creating agents of chaos to unleash upon the Kingdom, but toward what end . . . ?"

"Could it be a coincidence? Maybe the goblins just happened to be interested in the same . . ." The questions petered out under her disapproving look.

"You know better," she replied. "There is an agency behind this, some force that's orchestrating it all."

"The Crawler?" asked James.

Jazhara shrugged. "Perhaps, or perhaps it is someone in league with the Crawler, or someone using the Crawler, or perhaps the coincidence is that there are *two* malevolent forces loose in the West of the Kingdom."

"Wonderful," James muttered. "My old bump of trouble tells me that none of this is unrelated. It's just that we can't see the pattern."

"What if there is no pattern?" mused Jazhara.

"What do you mean?"

"What if everything we see is the product of some set of random choices? What if there is no single plan in place but, rather, a series of events designed to destabilize the region?"

"To whose benefit?" asked James.

Jazhara smiled. "Do you have an hour to run through the entire list, James?"

James nodded, yawning. "I must be getting tired," he confessed. "Kesh, Queg, some of the Eastern Kingdoms even, then a half-dozen minor nobles who would find opportunity in an unstable period to become major nobles, etc."

"Those are just the political realities," said Jazhara. "There are dark forces who have no political aims, but who have social ambitions, or worse."

"What do you mean?"

"I mean forces who are in league with dark powers who would cherish chaos as a kind of smokescreen behind which they may move to preeminence."

Solon turned. "I heard that. She's right, you know. There are forces in the universe whose only aim is to bring misery and darkness upon us all."

James said, "I have always had trouble with that as an idea, but then again I've never been a mad priest of a dark power."

Jazhara laughed, and even Solon was forced to chuckle. "Well, then, at least you're wise enough to admit something you can't imagine exists," said the monk, letting his horse fall back a little so he could ride abreast of James and the magician.

James said, "I can imagine a lot. And what you just said about forces whose only aim is misery and chaos is certainly in character with our current mission."

"Aye," agreed the monk. "There is that."

They continued on in silence until they reached Farmer Toth's farm. A dozen horses were tied to a fence a short distance from the farm. There was a company of militia in the yard and James was surprised to see a familiar face leading them.

"Jonathan!" he called out. "What brings you this far from the city?"

The son of the former Sheriff of Krondor turned and held up his hand in greeting. "Things are still being sorted out, Squire, so His Highness thought it best if I was out of the way for a little while."

James dismounted and handed his reins to a nearby

soldier, while Farmer Toth and his wife had a joyous re-
union. James motioned for Jonathan Means to step away
and said, "What's that mean?"

"It means Captain Garruth is trying to convince His
Highness to do away with the office of sheriff and con-
solidate all enforcement of municipal order in the city
guard's office."

"And thereby elevate his own power and authority,"
said James.

"And importance," said Jonathan. "I don't seek the office for myself, but there's always been a Sheriff of Krondor."

James shook his head. "Sometimes . . ." He let out his
breath slowly. "It's never been wise to turn the city into a
private estate of the Crown. The founding princes of the
city learned that the hard way. A court of magistrates and
a sheriff's office that is outside the court has always been
the wisest way to deal with petty crimes and civil disputes." He looked directly at Jonathan. "I'll speak to
Arutha about it when I get back. I doubt he'll agree to
Garruth's proposal." Almost to himself he added, "So
then what is the reason he got you out of town?"

Means had never struck James as someone with an
abundance of humor, but he did smile as he replied, "Perhaps to return with some word from you regarding things
in the north?"

James said, "Too iffy, unless you had other instructions
after coming to the relief of the farmer and his wife."

Jonathan nodded and they moved farther away from
the others. "Arutha says there are reports of some fairly
horrific things going on in this vicinity. Alan, his factor,
has sent along several such reports in the last two
weeks—livestock sickening, monsters in the woods, children vanishing, and similar tales. You're to concentrate

upon your mission, but you should be cautious. I am to rendezvous with the patrol heading up to Miller's Rest, and be ready to render aid."

James said, "So Arutha thinks a dozen Krondorian regulars might not be enough?"

"Apparently," said Jonathan. "Be wary once you're past the cut-off road to Miller's Rest. From there to Haldon Head you are on your own until we get word to come fetch you out."

"Thank you," said James. With an inclination of his head he indicated that Jonathan should return to his men.

Left alone with his thoughts for a moment, James again wondered at the scope of the attempt to seize the Tear. How did that fit into the seemingly patternless mess made up of Nighthawks, dead thieves, monsters, sorcerers, mad priests, and all the rest they had encountered since the betrayal at Krondor engineered by Makala and the other Tsurani magicians? There had always been a third player in the mix, he knew. Not the Crawler, and certainly not the Brotherhood of the Dark Path, nor even the mad priests who had seized control of the Nighthawks.

He sensed that Jazhara was right; there was an overriding presence behind all that had occurred in the last year, and he was determined before all was said and done to unmask that presence and rid the West of it for good.

Eleven

◆

ḥaldon ḥead

For two days they traveled.

James and his companions found no patrol waiting at Miller's Rest. They had little reason to linger, so they purchased some provisions at a small store near the mill that gave the town its name, and headed north toward the village of Haldon Head.

South of the village a small road branched off to the west, and led down through coastal cliffs to a broad beach. James dismounted and said, "We're only a short walk from the Point." He indicated a promontory of land jutting out into the sea. "If the maps back at the palace are correct, we should find a headland below those cliffs just around the bend."

They watered and tied up the horses, then started walking. "We have a few hours of daylight left," said James as they trudged through the sand. "Kendaric, how long does the spell take?"

"Minutes," said the wrecker. "I can raise the ship and hold it above the waves long enough to gain entrance and retrieve whatever it is you're looking for."

"We'll need a boat, then," observed Solon.

Kendaric laughed. "Not so, monk. For the genius of

my spell is that not only can one man cast it, has he the talent, but it also solidifies the water around the ship. You can walk over to it and retrieve your bauble."

James grinned. "Perhaps we'll get lucky and retrieve this 'bauble' easily."

They rounded the promontory and discovered that the prince's map was indeed accurate. A long finger of rock and soil extended out into the sea. The afternoon weather was moderate, and lazy combers rose and fell off the Point. They could see a few masts poking above the water, remnants of old wrecks not yet completely consumed by the sea. They made their way along the natural breakwater, until they reached the end.

Kendaric surveyed the wrecks revealed by the relatively low tide, the dozens of tilting masts like so many cemetery markers. He frowned. "Which one am I supposed to raise?" he asked.

James replied, "I have no idea."

Solon came over to them. "This is a place of death," he said portentously. "A graveyard of ships and men."

Solon gazed at the wreckage and was about to speak again when Kendaric said, "What's that smell? Like before a storm . . . sharp . . ."

Jazhara was the last to reach the point and she shouted, "It's magic!"

Gusts of wind seemed to arise out of nowhere, buffeting them and tearing at their clothes. Around them the sea began to roil, while a short distance away all was calm.

A sudden blow sent Solon reeling and he fell hard onto the rocks. James had his sword out, yet he could not see anything to strike. Kendaric dropped down, keeping as low as possible, while Jazhara raised her staff above her head and shouted, "Let the truth be revealed!"

A brilliant white light erupted from her staff, blinding

enough to cause James to avert his eyes and blink away tears.

Then James heard Jazhara shout, "Look!"

He cleared his vision and, looking ahead, saw two creatures floating in the air above one of the ships' masts. Both appeared to be roughly reptilian, with long, sinuous necks and tails. Large bat-like wings beat furiously, causing the buffeting winds. The heads were almost devoid of features, save for two ruby-colored eyes and a slit for a mouth that opened and closed, like a fish gulping water.

Jazhara kept her feet and had to shout an incantation in order to be heard. A crimson ball of energy appeared in her hand and she cast the spell at the creatures. The ball of red light struck the creature on the right and it opened its mouth as if shrieking in pain. But all they could hear was a renewed howling of the winds. The monster on the left dove straight at the party, and James leapt to his feet, sword poised, as Solon also rose, flourishing his warhammer.

The creature was heading straight for Jazhara, and James cut at it. As his blade touched it white-hot sparks exploded from it as the creature opened its mouth in apparent shock. The sound of shrieking wind rang in their ears. The monster faltered, and Solon stepped forward, striking downward with his huge warhammer. Stunned by the blow, the creature fell to the rocks.

The tip of one wing struck the ground, and instantly a green flame erupted there and traveled quickly up the wing, engulfing the monster. It writhed for a moment on the rocks, flopping around helplessly, as James and his companions stepped back. Then it was gone, the faint smoke of its passing swept away by the wind, which blew only half as strongly as before.

The second creature had thrown off the effects of

Jazhara's spell and was circling. It hooted, making a noise that sounded like wind gusting through a hollow tree.

Jazhara pointed, "Look!"

Another creature appeared out of the air, circled once, then joined the first. Again the wind that buffeted them redoubled in intensity and they had to struggle to stay upright.

Once more Jazhara cast a spell, this one a single piercing line of crimson energy that struck the first monster in the face. It writhed in agony, losing its orientation, and rolled over, as if trying to lie upon its side in midair, then started a slow tumble into the sea below. As soon as it touched the water, it vanished in a flare of green flames, as the first one had done.

James glanced around and found himself a rock that was large enough to have some heft, but small enough to hold. He reared back and threw it as hard as he could at the remaining creature. It too had started to make the hooting noise, which James took to be a summoning call. The rock smashed the monster in the face, interrupting the summoning.

"Jazhara!" James shouted. "If you've got anything left to deal with that thing, use it now before it calls yet another of its kind."

Jazhara said, "I have one trick left to try!"

She pointed her staff and a ball of flames erupted from the tip. James and Solon both turned aside as it flew between them, for they could feel its blistering heat. The fire went unerringly to the creature and surrounded it. The flames suddenly turned bright green, and the creature vanished from sight.

Instantly the winds ceased.

Slowly, Kendaric stood up. Looking around as if expecting another attack, he said, "What were those things?"

Jazhara said, "Air elementals, I believe, though I've never seen them before. My mentors claimed things like that once attacked Stardock."

James nodded. "I've heard that story from Gardan. If they touch fire, water, or earth they're consumed."

Kendaric nodded vigorously. "I hope to the gods that's the last we see of them!"

Solon said, "Someone doesn't wish us to raise that ship."

"All the more reason to raise it before whoever set those guardians over the ship returns," observed Jazhara.

"But which ship?" asked Kendaric.

Solon said, "You're a slab-headed fool. That one!" He pointed.

"How do you know?" asked Kendaric.

James laughed. "Because that's the one those elementals were guarding!"

Solon closed his eyes for a moment. "And I sense something down there, as well."

"What?" asked the wrecker.

"What we've come here to recover," replied the monk.

"Very well," said Kendaric. "Let me have the scroll."

Jazhara set down her backpack, and opened it. She reached in and withdrew the scroll she had been carrying since finding it in Kendaric's room and handed it to him. He took it, read it, then nodded. "I could do it alone, but with your help, magician, we should be able to do this quickly." He pointed at two places in the spell and said, "Make this incantation with me, then this other passage here. For a spell-caster of your power, this should be easy."

"I've examined your spell," Jazhara said judiciously. "I will do what I can to help."

Turning to face the sea, Kendaric pointed one hand at the mast of the ship in question and began to chant. Jazhara joined in at the passage Kendaric had indicated, and their voices filled the air with mystic words.

A fog appeared where Kendaric had pointed. It coalesced above the water, and the sea began to roil with mystic energies. A keening sound filled the air and James saw the top of the mast start to vibrate.

Abruptly, everything ceased. The fog vanished, the water calmed, and the ship stopped moving.

"I think your spell needs work," said James.

"No," contradicted Jazhara. "It wasn't his spell. As we cast it, I felt something fighting against us. Someone else did this to us."

Kendaric glanced back up at the cliffs as if seeking sight of someone. "She's right. I felt it, too."

Solon's gaze also went to the cliffs behind them. "Then we'll have to locate the source of the interference. For if we do not, the entire Order of Ishap may be in jeopardy and one of its deepest mysteries may fall into the hands of the enemy!"

Kendaric looked at James as if questioning whether this was an exaggeration. James returned a grim expression.

Kendaric nodded, and Jazhara led the way back toward the horses.

Haldon Head was a small village, comprised of only a dozen or so buildings around a crossroads. The north–south route of the King's Road ran from Miller's Rest to Questor's View. The east–west route led from

Widow's Point out to farms scattered between the village and the forested foothills.

At the center of the village sat an inn, the Sailor's Rest. As the travelers rode in, they saw two men standing in front of the inn, arguing loudly.

One of them—a farmer, judging by his rough dress—was shouting. "This has gone on long enough! She must be stopped! You should have had those soldiers execute her when they were here!"

The other man wore a well-made tunic with a sleeveless over-jacket. He was of middle years and rather portly. He shouted back, "You've no proof, Alton. With all the pain we've gone through, you want to cause more?"

"You keep this up, Toddy, and you won't be mayor much longer. Hell, you keep this up and there won't be a village much longer. Lyle told me that—"

As James and his companions reined in, the man named Toddy interrupted, "Lyle is a drunk! If he thinks we are going to . . ." The arrival of strangers finally caught his attention.

The farmer said, "Looks like we've got visitors."

"Welcome to Haldon Head, strangers. Will you be staying long?" the mayor asked.

The farmer interjected, "Not if they know what's good for them."

"Alton! There's other business you'd best be attending."

The man named Alton replied, "We'll talk about this later, Toddy. By the heavens, we will!"

Farmer Alton turned and walked quickly away. The other man said, "I apologize for Farmer Alton's rudeness. He's a bit upset about some recent troubles."

"What was he saying about soldiers?" Jazhara asked.

"A squad of Krondorian guardsmen came through here a few days ago, chasing a fugitive, I think."

Jazhara glanced at James. "William's company?"

James nodded. "Could be."

Solon dismounted. "What were the troubles the farmer was referring to?" he asked.

Toddy glanced down at the ground, then looked up again. "We . . . uh . . . We've had some problems with wolves lately. What with the long winter and all . . . Now, if you'll excuse me, I must be getting back to the inn. You'd do well to join me, as I only keep the doors open for an hour or two after sunset, and I'd hate to see you trapped outside . . ." He hurried inside the inn and closed the door.

"That was odd," observed Kendaric.

James indicated that they should ride to the rear of the inn, and by the time they had reached the stabling yard, a boy was hurrying to take their horses. James instructed the boy on the care they required, then they walked back to the front of the inn and entered through the main door.

The inn was pleasant enough, if small. The lower floor was occupied by a taproom and kitchen, with a single flight of stairs running up the rear wall leading to the second floor. A fireplace off to the left contained a roaring blaze. A savory-smelling broth simmered in a huge copper kettle that hung before the fire. To one side a large spit stood ready for whatever meat was to be that evening's fare.

Toddy appeared a moment later carrying a large, spitted haunch of beef, which he put into the spit cradle. "Maureen!" he bellowed. "Come turn the beef!"

An older woman hurried out of the kitchen and nodded as she passed the innkeeper. Toddy turned to James and his companions. "I'm glad you decided to spend the night here. It may not be as fancy as you're used to, but I'd like

you to consider it a home away from home. I can serve you an ale, if you like."

"That would be a start," said Kendaric.

"Well, then," said the innkeeper. "Seat yourselves and I'll fetch the ale."

He was back in a few minutes with four ceramic mugs full of frothy ale. "My name is Aganathos Toddhunter. Folks around here call me 'Toddy.' I'm both innkeeper and mayor of this small village. Hold the Prince's writ to act as justice in misdemeanor and justice of the peace in civil issues," he noted with some pride.

"Quite a bit of responsibility," said James, dryly.

"Not really," Toddy said, looking a bit deflated. "Truth is, the worst is usually a pig who wanders onto a neighbor's property and having to decide who pays damages or who keeps the pig." The attempt at humor was forced.

Jazhara said, "Why don't you join us for a drink?"

"Ah, you're being kind to spread so much cheer on this cheerless night," Toddy said. He retreated to the bar and poured himself a mug of ale, then returned and remained standing next to the table. "My thanks." He took a long pull on his ale.

Jazhara asked, "Why so cheerless?"

"Well, with the . . . wolves and all . . . we've lost several villagers already."

Solon looked hard at Toddy and said, "Wolves this near the coast are unusual. They tend to stay away from populated areas. Is there no one who will hunt them?"

Toddy took another drink of his ale. Then he said, "Please, I'm sorry I mentioned it. It's not your concern. Simply enjoy yourselves tonight. But I beg you not to go outside tonight."

James studied the innkeeper and saw a man trying his mightiest to hide a deep fear. Changing the subject, James

asked, "You mentioned some guardsmen earlier. Do you know anything else about them?"

"They stayed here a single night, two days ago, and then moved on."

Jazhara asked, "Do you recall who led them?"

"A rather young officer. William, I think his name was. One of his trackers found the trail of their fugitive somewhere east of here." He drained the last of his ale and said, "Now, please excuse me while I take care of my duties. When you're ready to turn in, I'll show you to your rooms."

The only other customer in the inn was a man sitting by himself in the corner, staring deeply into his cup.

James leaned forward, so as not to be overheard by the lone drinker, and said, "Well, does anyone have any bright notions of what we should do next?"

Kendaric said, "I can't understand why my spell failed. It should have worked, but some other force . . . balked me. There is something in this area that is working against us."

Jazhara said, "It is possible that some other enchantment is in place keeping the ship under the waves until such time as Bear or whoever is employing him is ready to raise the ship himself. If that's the case, when *that* spell is removed, *your* spell will work."

James was silent for a moment. Then he said, "So what we have to do is find the source of this blocking magic and remove it?"

Solon nodded. "Easier said than done, laddie. While my knowledge of the mystic arts is far different than Jazhara's, I know such a spell is not fashioned by a dabbler. Whoever put the charm on that ship to keep it below the waves is no mean practitioner of the magician's arts."

Kendaric nodded in agreement. "This must be true. For

no known force should have kept my spell from working."

James sighed. "Just once I'd like a plan to go as originally designed." With only slightly feigned frustration he added, "Wouldn't it be lovely to be back in Krondor tomorrow and say, 'Why, no, Highness, no troubles at all. We just strolled up to Widow's Point, raised the ship, got the Tear, wandered back down the coast, and here we are.' Wouldn't that be fine?" He sighed again. They fell silent.

After a few minutes of quiet drinking, the party was approached by the innkeeper. "Will you be eating?"

Noting the dearth of customers at the tables, James said, "Anywhere else around here to eat?"

"No," said Toddy with a pained smile. "It's just that some travelers are trying to keep expenses down and bring their own, that's all."

"We'll be eating," said James, nodding to where the woman was turning the side of beef.

"Food should be ready in an hour," said the innkeeper.

As he was about to depart, Jazhara asked, "Sir, a moment."

The innkeeper paused. "Milady?"

Jazhara said, "There seems to be some trouble here, or am I mistaken?"

Solon added, "We couldn't help but notice that the town seems almost deserted. What vexes this place?"

Toddy looked concerned, but he forced a smile and said, "Oh . . . well . . . just a little slow this time of year. No harvests in yet, no grain caravans . . . you know how small villages can be."

James looked directly at the mayor. "Frankly, sir, we've heard some strange things about this area. What truth is there to these rumors?"

The mayor glanced around, as if someone might be lis-

tening. "Well . . . some folks say that Widow's Point is haunted by the souls of the drowned, kept from Lims-Kragma's Hall by an ancient and horrible evil . . ." He lowered his voice. "Others claim that witchcraft has cursed our town, but I think it's all superstitious nonsense."

"This 'witchcraft' has been mentioned several times," said Jazhara.

James studied the man's face and said, "Sir, I am on the Prince's business. You are not free to repeat that to anyone, but I am on a mission of some urgency and the situation around here may prove difficult for the completion of my mission. Now, I urge you to be forthright with me or Haldon Head will have a new mayor as soon as I return to Krondor. What is going on around here? Why are the streets deserted during the day?"

The man looked defeated. At last, he nodded. "People are frightened, sir. They hurry from one place to another, and dare spend as little time outdoors as they can, even during the day. At night they bar their doors and cling close to their hearths. There is evil afoot."

"What sort of evil?" asked Solon.

Letting out his breath slowly, Toddy said, "Well, I guess I need to tell someone. This town is beset by some creature—or creatures—that stalk the night, killing good townsfolk, and stealing their souls. Even Father Rowland has been powerless to stop them."

"Who is Father Rowland?" Solon asked.

"The good father is a devotee of Sung. He's been in the area for a number of years, but he's recently decided that the witch is responsible for our troubles." At the mention of the word "witch" Jazhara stiffened her posture, but kept silent. Toddy continued. "Now, I'd expect that kind

of thinking from someone like Farmer Alton, but not a priest of Sung the Merciful and Pure."

Jazhara nodded. " 'Witchcraft' does not exist. Either someone is a natural healer, and uses true magic, or simply knows the medicinal value of certain herbs and roots. 'Witchcraft' is an ignorant belief."

"You're right, of course," agreed Toddy. "The old woman has helped some of the townsfolk with poultices and brews in the past, and has been kind to most people who ask for help, but you know how people are: with the troubles now, they've come to fear what they don't understand. She lives up near the promontory above Widow's Point, if you'd care to speak with her yourself." He scratched his head, and dropped his voice to a conspiratorial whisper. "I know she's not involved with these horrors, but she may know something that will help you decide if our troubles are a danger to your mission for the Prince."

"Have you reported these troubles to the Prince?" asked James.

"Only to that patrol that went through here a few days ago, and they seemed intent upon another mission. Alan, the Prince's factor in the area, was due here last week, but he never showed up. That happens from time to time if he's on special business for the Crown. I was thinking of sending a boy with a message south, but no parent is willing to risk a child on the road . . . given the horrors we've seen."

"How did they begin?" asked James.

"I wish I knew," answered the mayor. "One day things were as they always were, the next . . . It began over a month ago. A woodcutter and his family who live a few miles to the east of the village disappeared.We don't know when exactly, but the woodcutter missed his usual

delivery of wood for the village, so we began to worry. Six men went to his shack the next day, but only two returned."

"What did the two who returned tell you?" asked an alarmed Kendaric.

"Nathan and Malcolm? Malcolm, Lims-Kragma guide him, was killed last night by . . . whatever creature is responsible for this terrible situation. Nathan boarded himself up in his house and hasn't come out since. He has my stable-boy bring him food every day."

"Will he speak with us?" asked James.

"You can try. His house is less than a ten-minute walk from here. I would wait until the morning, though, sir, as he will almost certainly refuse to speak to anyone after dark." Pointing to the solitary drinker in the corner, Toddy said, "Lyle over there was a close friend of Malcolm." Leaning toward them, he added, "But I'd weigh his words carefully; his love of the spirits"—he made a drinking motion—"often clouds his judgment."

James stood up and Jazhara followed. Kendaric started to rise, but Solon reached out with one of his massive hands, firmly gripped the guildsman's arm, and pushed him back into his seat, shaking his head gently. Then the cleric rose and followed James and Jazhara. Kendaric opened his mouth to object, but Solon silenced him merely by pointing at the man's ale, indicating that he should continue to drink.

James, Jazhara, and Solon crossed to where the solitary figure sat staring into an empty mug. "Buy you a drink?" asked James.

The man looked up and said, "Never one to say no to that, stranger."

James motioned for Toddy to bring over a fresh tankard of ale, and when it was placed before the man,

James pulled out a chair and sat down. "Your name is Lyle?"

"That's me," the man agreed.

"I understand you're friends with one of the men who survived some sort of attack here."

"Malcolm, he was my friend," agreed the man. "Died last night." He hoisted the ale flagon and said, "To Malcolm!" Then he drained it.

James waved for another and when it was placed before him, Lyle asked, "What do you want?"

"We want information," James replied.

"Tell us about this 'witch,'" added Jazhara.

Lyle said, "Everyone thinks she's in league with dark powers, but I don't believe it! She's a kind old woman. You can go see for yourself. Take the trail to the point and when it cuts down to the beach, stay on the small path up to the point. You'll find her in her hut most times when she's not out gathering herbs." He sighed deeply. "No, the real source of this evil is something else."

"What?" asked James.

Lowering his voice, Lyle said, "Blood-drinkers."

James's gaze narrowed and he looked at Jazhara before returning his attention to Lyle and repeating, "Blood-drinkers?"

"Night creatures. The dead returned to life."

Jazhara gasped. "Vampires!"

James looked at her. "Vampires?"

"Creatures of legend. Created by the foulest necromancy," she replied.

Remembering the dead bodies being arrayed by the goblins and the creatures in the sewers of Krondor, James said, "We've encountered a lot of that lately."

Jazhara said, "They drink the blood of the living to

slake their unholy thirst, and those whose blood they take rise to join their number."

James closed his eyes for a moment, then said, "And I suppose because they're already dead, they're very difficult to kill again?"

Jazhara nodded. "They can be destroyed by magic or fire, or by cutting them up."

"Which they usually object to, I'll wager," said James dryly.

"They came from the woodcutter's shack!" said Lyle. "The woodcutter and his wife had lived there just a few months before they vanished. Six good men went to look in on that poor family. Whatever was up there killed four of 'em, and scared Nathan and poor Malcolm out of their wits."

"What happened to Malcolm?" asked James.

"Dead. Dead at the hands of those monsters. Malcolm always knew they'd come for him once he and Nathan got away, so he tried to get them first. He thought he could hide and watch for them, the old fool. He knew they came from the woodcutter's shack, but once he told me they'd desecrated our graveyard, too. He got a couple of them, first, though. Poor old sod."

"How'd he get them?" asked James.

"He found one in a grave, asleep during the daylight. He doused it with some oil we use to clear the fields, and set fire to it. Went up like a torch, he said. The other was just waking up at sundown; he cut its head off with his old sword from his duty during the Riftwar. Threw the head in the river and watched it wash away. Went back to the grave the next day and said the body had turned to dust. But there were just too many of them. They caught him out last night, old fool."

Solon, who had remained silent so far, could contain

himself no longer. "Vampires, you say? Man, are you sure? They're the stuff of legend, things to scare small children on dark nights."

Jazhara nodded agreement. "I always thought they were mythical."

"But after what we've seen so far . . . ?" James asked.

Lyle said, "Nay, good sir and lady, they're real. Nathan says they come for him every night! That's why he locks himself in. He's got no fear of dying, but if those creatures get him, he says they'll keep his soul and he'll never take his turn on Lims-Kragma's Wheel of Life again!"

" 'Tis a foul blasphemy, indeed, if true," agreed Solon.

James stood up. "Well, it seems this Nathan is the only one here in Haldon Head who has seen these creatures. I suspect we'd best go talk to him."

"I'd be cautious," Lyle said. "It's almost sundown and once the sun sets, Toddy locks the door and nothing you say will get you back inside."

"How far is it to Nathan's place?" asked Solon.

"Open the door," replied Lyle, "and you're looking straight at the road leading to it. Can't miss it. You'll pass two shops, and the first house on the left is Nathan's shack."

"We have time," James said, "if we hurry."

They collected Kendaric and hurried to the door. As they made to leave, Mayor Toddhunter shouted out, "Be back before the sun sets, or you'll spend the night outside!"

After they left the inn, Kendaric said, "Why are we doing this? I heard every word. Blood-drinkers! Are you mad?"

James said, "Do you think there might be another reason why your spell didn't work?"

"I have no idea why it didn't work," admitted Kendaric. "But vampires? They can't be real!"

"I hope you're right," said Solon. "Holy writ is clear on the living dead. Specifically, they are an abomination to Lims-Kragma, and to Ishap, for they defy the natural order of the world."

"Not to mention they'll almost certainly try to kill us," added James.

Kendaric glanced at the setting sun and said, "We have maybe a half-hour, Squire."

"Then we'd better hurry," said James.

They reached Nathan's house in five minutes, and even if Lyle hadn't told them where to look, it would have been easy to find. The small house, little more than a shack, was boarded up. All the windows had stout planks nailed across them; the door, obviously the only point of entry, was shut tight; nail points protruding from its perimeter indicated that it was similarly covered from within. In the red light of sunset, it looked almost deserted, though James saw a glint of flame escaping through a crack in the boards, no doubt coming from a lantern or fire pot.

"Hello, the house!" Kendaric shouted from the front stoop, a wooden platform in need of some repair. "We'd like to speak with you!"

From inside the house came a reply. "Go away, foul beasts! You'll never get me to quit my house!"

"Hello," said James. "I'm Squire James, from the Prince's court in Krondor."

"Leave me in peace, you bloody demons! I can see through your evil tricks."

James looked at Jazhara and shrugged.

Jazhara said, "Sir, I am the court magician to the Prince. We need some information about these creatures that trouble you. We may be able to help!"

"Ah, very clever, very clever indeed," came the reply. "Go away, you soul-sucking fiends!"

James shook his head in defeat. "What's it going to take to convince you, friend?"

"Go away!"

James turned to Jazhara. "Maybe you can do better?"

Solon said, "Let me try." He stepped up to the boarded door and shouted, "In the name of Mighty Ishap, the One Above All, I bid you let us enter!"

There was a long moment of silence and then Nathan said, "That's good. I didn't know you blood-stealers could invoke the name of the gods! Almost had me for a moment there, with that bad dwarven accent!"

Solon's face flushed with anger. " 'Tis not a bad dwarven accent, ya gibbering loon. I grew up near Dorgin!"

James turned to Jazhara and said, "It does get more pronounced when he gets upset, did you notice?"

Jazhara said, "Let me try again." Speaking up, she said, "Sir, I am a magician and could enter your house at will, but would not violate the sanctity of your home. If you won't let us enter, at least tell us what you know about the evil that besets this town. Perhaps we can help. We have our own reasons for wanting to see it banished."

There was another long silence, then Nathan said through the boards, "Almost got me with that one, you monster!" He laughed madly. "Trying to find out how much I know so you can plot against me! Well, I'm not falling for it."

Kendaric said, "James—"

James waved him to silence. "Look, Nathan, if you don't want to come out, you don't have to, but we need to find the cause of all this trouble in the area. We have, as my friend said, our own reasons for wanting to see it come to an end. If these 'vampires,' as you call them, are

real, they may be causing us our problem and we'll deal with them."

"You'll get your chance soon enough!" shouted Nathan.

"James—" Kendaric repeated.

James again waved his hand and said, "Just a minute!"

As he was about to speak again, James felt his arm gripped by Kendaric, who swung him around to face down the path to the house. "James!" shouted the wrecker. "It looks like we get our chance now."

As the sun was dropping below the horizon, dark shadows seemed to coalesce in the air at the edge of the nearby woods. In the darkness other shapes could be seen moving, and suddenly human forms appeared where there had been empty air a moment before.

James slowly drew his sword and said, "Solon, Jazhara, any advice would be greatly appreciated."

A half-dozen figures advanced from the nearby woods. They appeared human, save for their deathly pale white skin color, and eyes that seemed to glow with a reddish light. Several of them showed gaping wounds on their necks and they shambled with an awkward gait.

The one in the front spoke. "Nathan . . . Come to us . . . We miss you so . . ."

From behind it others called, "You should have stayed with us, Nathan. There's no need to fear us, Nathan."

With rising revulsion, James saw that one of the figures was a child, a little girl of no more than seven years of age.

Solon said, "There's but one piece of advice I can give, laddie. Destroy them all." He raised his warhammer and advanced on the first figure.

Twelve

◆

Dark Magic

James charged after Solon.

Jazhara shouted, "Be wary, you must destroy them by fire or cut their heads from their bodies!"

Kendaric hung behind the magician, holding his short sword, but appearing ready to bolt if the opportunity presented itself. Jazhara began an incantation and lowered her staff, pointing it toward the group of oncoming creatures. A ball of green flame erupted from the tip of her staff and shot across the space between them, engulfing four of the creatures in mystic flame. They howled and writhed, and stumbled forward, staggering for a few paces before falling face-down onto the ground.

Solon reached out with a gauntlet-covered hand and seized the child-creature, hurling the small form backward, into the green flame. The tiny creature shrieked and thrashed, then lay still.

"May Ishap bring you peace, child," shouted the monk. He swung his huge warhammer at an adult-sized creature, smashing the thing's shoulder, but still it lunged at him, its one remaining arm outstretched, the fingers bent like talons trying to rend and tear.

Solon lashed back the other way, and his hammer

caved in the creature's skull. It fell to the ground and lay writhing, but despite having half its head pulped, it still tried to rise. Jazhara ran up to the monk and shouted, "Stand back!" He retreated and she lowered her staff. In a moment, the creature was aflame.

James was having difficulty with a particularly powerful man—*or creature, rather,* he corrected himself. The thing had obviously been the woodcutter Lyle had first told them of. He had been a big, broad-shouldered man, and his arms were long and meaty. He tried to grapple with James, who dodged aside. But the damage inflicted on the creature by James's rapier did little to slow it.

"Kendaric!" James shouted. "I could use some help!"

The wrecker stood with his back to Nathan's doorway, his sword clutched in his hand. "Doing what?" he shouted back.

"My blade isn't exactly a meat cleaver."

Kendaric waved his short sword and said, "And this is?"

James ducked under a huge hand swinging through the air, and shouted, "It's a better blade for hacking than what I've got!"

"I'm not going to loan it to you!" cried Kendaric, watching as other creatures came into sight. "I've got problems of my own."

Suddenly Jazhara was at Kendaric's side and she wrenched the blade from his hand. "Yes, a decided attack of cowardice," she said with contempt. Throwing the sword so that it sailed through the air, she shouted, "James, catch!"

With a speed bordering on the supernatural, James lashed out with his rapier, cutting the shambling creature across the back of the leg. Then he leapt into the air,

catching the short sword with his left hand. He tossed his rapier and the short sword in a juggle, ending up with the rapier in his left hand and the short sword in his right. The thing that had been a woodcutter stumbled onto one knee, and James lashed down with the sword, cleanly severing the creature's neck, so that the head came rolling free.

James threw the short sword back to Kendaric, and shouted, "Better lend a hand here, unless you're anxious to end up like them!"

More creatures were emerging from the woods and Jazhara unleashed several bolts of her mystic flame. She shouted, "James, I can't keep this up! I'm almost exhausted."

"We have to get to someplace defensible!" said Brother Solon, as he slammed his hammer into yet another creature, knocking it backward a half-dozen feet.

James hurried to the door of Nathan's house and pounded on it as he cried, "By the gods, man, let us in!"

"No, it's a trick and I won't be fooled!" came a shout from inside.

"Let us in, or I'll burn this place down around your ears," said James. "Jazhara, do you have one shot of that fire left?"

"I can manage," said the magician.

Loudly, but in measured, calm tones, James said, "Open this door or you're going to get very warm. Which will it be?"

After a moment of silence, they heard the creak of nails being pulled and a series of thumps as heavy boards hit the floor. Finally the door-bolt slid free, and the door cracked open a bit. A pinched-faced man peered out at James and said, "You don't *look* like a vampire."

James nodded. "I'm glad you finally recognize the obvious. Clear the way while I go help my friends. We'll be

right back. We'll hammer the boards back into place once we're all inside."

James didn't wait to see the man's nod, but turned and hurried to intercept a particularly nasty-looking creature heading straight for Kendaric. The wrecker waved his sword ineffectually in the direction of the creature, which paused to consider the potential for injury.

That pause gave James just the opening he needed to circle behind the creature and hamstring it with his rapier. "It won't kill him," shouted the squire, "but it'll slow him down! Try to cut his head off."

Kendaric's expression left no room for doubt as to how he felt about that suggestion. He backed away, putting distance between himself and the creature.

"Kendaric, you useless bag of pig-swill," shouted Solon. He ran over and used his warhammer to break the creature's spine.

Kendaric proffered his sword. "*You* cut its head off!"

"Ya gibbering jackass! Holy orders prevent me from cutting flesh with a blade. If I do, I lose my sanctity and must be cleansed for a year by holy rite, fasting, and meditation! I donna ha' a year to waste on such foolishness! We ha' work to do."

Jazhara said to James, "You're right, the accent does get thicker when he's upset."

James shouted, "Open the door!" More creatures were coming into sight, and James had no doubt they would soon be overwhelmed.

Kendaric was at the door, and pounded on the planks. Nathan swung the door wide with one hand, as he brandished a hunting knife in the other. "Get inside!" shouted the villager. Kendaric entered the cottage as the others began to rush toward the house. Suddenly James wheeled at the sound of a footstep behind him, slashing out with

his blade, and slicing through the throat of what had once been a young woman. She didn't fall, but faltered long enough for him to turn and run. Solon smashed another in the face and also ran.

Jazhara hurried through the door, Solon and James on her heels.

Nathan slammed the door shut behind them and threw the bolt. He then picked up one of planks he had just removed and cried, "Start boarding this up!"

Solon picked up another piece of wood and used his warhammer to drive heavy nails back into the doorframe. "This will not hold if they get determined," said the monk.

"It'll hold," said the townsman. "They're persistent but stupid and don't work well as a group. If they did, I'd have been dead four nights back."

James sheathed his rapier and sat down on a small trunk next to the fireplace. He glanced around. The building was a single room with a small kitchen off to one side. A feather bed, a table, a chest of drawers and the trunk upon which he sat were the sole contents of the room.

Their host was a wiry man of middle years, his dark hair and beard shot through with gray. He had the weather-beaten look of a farmer: once-broken fingers and heavy calluses betrayed the hands of a man who had worked all his life.

Letting out a slow breath, James said, "Just what is going on?"

"So, then we started hearing about others vanishing, from farms outlying the village. There's the odd homestead up in the hills, and some nice meadows that folks use to graze herds or grow summer wheat. Some of those

creatures that attacked earlier tonight were the poor souls who lived up there. Not townspeople, but folks we knew from when they'd come in to buy provisions or sell their wares." He shook his head as if he still had trouble believing what he was describing.

James and the others had been listening to the farmer for over an hour. The narrative had been rambling and disjointed at times, but a pattern had emerged.

"Let me sum up," said James. "Someone or something has come to the area. It has infected your community with a horrible curse that is turning ordinary people into blood-drinkers. Is that right?"

The farmer nodded. "Yes."

James continued. "These creatures are feeding on others, thereby turning them into blood-drinkers, too."

"Vampires," said Jazhara. "The stories about them are full of superstition."

"But these are real enough," said Kendaric.

"Yes," agreed Solon. "But Jazhara is right. There are legends about these creatures that have nothing to do with truth, flights of fancy and tales told to frighten naughty children."

"I must be a naughty child, then," said Kendaric with an angry edge to his voice, "because I for one am very frightened."

James said, "So the woodcutter and his family were the first around here to be turned into these creatures?"

Nathan said, "Yes. Six of us went to investigate. Only two of us survived. We found a dozen or so of those creatures waiting there. A few of them were the folks from the nearby farms I spoke of; a couple were unknown to me."

"Then who was the first?" asked James.

Nathan looked around blankly. "I don't know," he said in a weary voice.

"Is that important?" asked Kendaric.

"Yes," said Jazhara, "because as James said, someone or something had to bring this plague here."

Solon said, "This sort of magic is evil beyond description."

James sat on the floor with his back against the wall. "But to what end? Why plague *this* little village of all places?"

Kendaric said, "Because they can?"

James looked at the wrecker and said, "What do you mean?"

Kendaric shrugged and said, "They have to start somewhere. If they get enough people around here to . . . become like them, they can send some of their number to other locations and . . . well, it's like you said, a plague."

"Which means we'll have to stamp out this infection here," said Solon.

James could hear the shuffle of feet outside.

Nathan shouted, "Keep away, you murderous bloodsuckers!"

From outside, voices called, "Come with us. Join us."

Jazhara shivered. "I know little of these creatures, save for legends. But already I can see the legends are only partially correct."

James looked at Nathan and said, "Got anything to drink?"

"Water," said the farmer, pointing to a large crock near the table.

As James fetched a cup and went to the crock, he said to Jazhara, "What do you mean 'only partially correct?' "

Jazhara said, "The legends of the vampires tell us of great and powerful magic-users, able to alter their shapes and commune with animals, such as rats and wolves. The pitiful creatures we face here, while far from harmless,

could have all been put to rest tonight, had we a trained squad of soldiers with us."

James quietly reflected on this as he remembered a time in Krondor when, as a boy, he and Prince Arutha had faced the undying minions of the false moredhel prophet, Murmandamus. "My experience tells me that things that hard to kill are far more dangerous than they seem."

Nathan added, "Besides, lady, you miss the obvious. These aren't great and powerful magic-users. These were farmers and laborers."

James said, "So that would mean the great and powerful magic-using vampire is out there somewhere. And he—it—is behind all this."

Solon said, "Aye. The Temple teaches what it knows about the forces of darkness. The blood-drinkers are an old and powerful line of evil, said to have descended from a single, cursed magician who lived ages ago in some distant and unknown land. No one knows if the tale is true, but it has been told in the chronicles that from time to time such a cursed one appears, and woe betide those who chance upon him."

"Why?" asked Kendaric.

All eyes turned to him.

Solon asked, "Why does 'woe betide' those who chance across him?"

"No, I mean why do such creatures exist?"

Solon replied, "No one knows. What the Temple teaches is that the forces of darkness often benefit when chaos reigns, so much of what they do is merely to cause problems for order and good."

Kendaric nodded. "All right, I can accept that. But why here?"

James said, "It should be obvious. Someone doesn't want us to reach the Tear."

"The Tear?" Farmer Nathan asked, bewildered.

James waved away the question with a gesture. "You don't really wish to know, trust me. Just suffice it to say that magic around here is not what it should be."

"That is the truth," agreed Jazhara.

"It must be that witch," said Nathan. "She's the only user of magic in these parts."

Jazhara said, "Has she been a problem before?"

"No," admitted the farmer. "But . . . well, who else could it be?"

"That is what we must find out," said James. Listening to the voices from outside, he added, "How long will they keep this up?"

Nathan said, "Until first light. They perish from its touch, it is said."

James said, "Said by whom?"

Nathan blinked. "Sir?"

"Never mind," said James, as he lay down on the floor. "I'm dubious as to the origin of many beliefs. It's a character flaw. Wake me when they go away."

Jazhara nodded and said, "Then what do we do?"

"Find this magic-using vampire and put him out of his misery."

"Aye," said Solon. "If we can do that, the rest will fade away, it is said."

James resisted the urge to ask again "by whom" and merely said, "There can't be many places around here for such a one to hide."

"Oh, I can tell you where one such place is," said Nathan.

James sat upright. "Where?"

"In the graveyard, south of the village. There's a crypt there that has been broken into. There's something in there, I'm certain."

"Why didn't you tell anyone?"

"I did," said Nathan. "But Toddy and the others wanted to hear no part of it. Father Rowland said something about the forces of the gods would protect the properly buried, or something like that, and ignored me."

"That's odd," said Solon. "A priest of Sung the Pure would be among those most interested in investigating such a desecration. Their order is in the forefront of the battle against just these kinds of dark forces."

"Maybe others are," said Nathan. "But he just holds his prayer meetings and rails against the witch. Maybe he's right."

"Again, 'the witch!' " said Jazhara with open contempt. "What has this woman done?"

"Well, Farmer Alton claims she's poisoned his cows, and Farmer Merrick's little girl lies abed with some cursed sickness the witch sent her way."

"But why?" asked Solon. "If this woman has been kind to you before, why'd she turn her hand on you now?"

Nathan shrugged. "You tell me. You're a priest—"

"Monk," corrected Solon.

"—monk, so you must know why these things happen."

Shaking his head, Solon said, "Ah, if only it were so. No, the ways of evil are a mystery."

James said, "Hold the theological debate down, will you? I'm going to get some sleep."

Listening to the low voices from outside and the shuffling of footsteps around the house, Kendaric said, "How can you sleep with that going on?"

James opened one eye and said, "Practice." He closed it and within minutes was asleep.

* * *

Just before sunrise the voices ceased. James woke up to find Solon sound asleep on the floor, while a fatigued Jazhara sat with her arms around her knees, her staff at hand, watching the door. Nathan sat silently nearby. Kendaric had succumbed to sleep and lay on the wooden floor, snoring.

James rolled over, his joints protesting a night spent on such an unyielding surface, and got to his feet. He gently nudged Kendaric with his boot. The wrecker sat up with an alarmed expression on his face, shouting, "What!"

Solon was instantly awake, then realizing it was only Kendaric making the noise, sat back again. "Sunrise?"

James nodded.

Nathan stood as well and asked, "What will you do this day?"

Jazhara said, "Find the source of this evil."

"Then look to the witch up on Widow's Point," said Nathan. "I still think she must be behind all this. Someone has to destroy her!"

Solon said, "Have faith, friend. We will crush her evil just as we destroyed the evil that has plagued you."

"If she is, indeed, the source of this evil," said Jazhara pointedly.

Nathan said, "Are you mad? You did nothing last night. Don't you think I've fought those things before? Except for one or two you burned with magic fire or beheaded, the rest will return. In the darkness they can't be destroyed!"

"Well, we'll see what we can do," said a tired James. "But first we need to get something to eat."

"Toddy will open the door for you once the sun is up," said Nathan. "Tell him to send my food over, would you, please?"

"What will you do?" asked Kendaric.

"Barricade my door again." Then his voice took on a frantic quality. "But you know they'll get me in the end, turn me into one of them. It's just a matter of time."

"Easy," said Solon. "We'll have none of that, laddie. With Ishap's divine guidance, we'll see an end to the troubles that plague this poor village."

James and Solon removed the boards that were nailed across the door and went outside. Before they were off the porch, they could hear Nathan again nailing them into place. Kendaric looked at the sky.

"What is it?" asked James. "Rain?"

"No, something . . . odd," said the wrecker. "For nearly twenty years I've worked the sea and I've never seen a sky like that."

"Like what?" asked Jazhara. "I don't see anything odd."

"Look toward the sunrise."

They did so and after a moment, Solon said, "Ishap's mercy! What has happened to the sun?"

In the distance the sun rose, but despite the air being clear and there being no clouds in sight, the light seemed muted, and although the sun glowed, its brilliance was dimmed.

"Magic," said Jazhara. She paused, as if listening to something. "There is something in the air which drinks the light. We didn't notice it yesterday, because we arrived near sundown, but some dark agency is lessening the sun's radiance here."

"What could do that?" asked James.

Jazhara shrugged. "A relic of great power, or a spell forged by a magician of great arts. It would have to cover a very large area indeed to dull the sun's brilliance."

"I thought it a little overcast when we arrived," said James. "But I didn't note if there were clouds over the cliffs or not."

"There is nothing natural in this," affirmed Kendaric. "But to what purpose has this been done?"

"So that things that walk the night can walk the day?" mused Solon.

James said, "Forget breaking our fast. We must go to confront this witch now."

Without further comment, James turned toward the peak at Widow's Point on the other side of Haldon Head and started walking.

As they walked through the village, they saw Toddy hurrying from his inn. "You!" he said with a broad grin as he spied James and his companions. "You survived the night!"

James smiled. "Surviving is something we do well. You seem to be in a hurry."

The mayor of the village lost his smile. "Farmer Merrick's daughter is ill, and he's gathered some of the village folk at his home. I think they mean some mischief."

James glanced at Jazhara, who returned a slight nod. They fell into step behind the portly innkeeper, who was hurrying along as best as his girth permitted.

When they arrived at Farmer Merrick's house, they found a half-dozen of the village's men, and an equal number of women, gathered before the farmer's door. The farmer and his wife stood in the doorway. A florid-faced, stocky man was saying, "We must do something. This has gone on too long!"

Toddy pushed through the small crowd. "What is this, then?"

The florid-faced man shouted, "We're going to do something about that witch, Toddy!"

"Now, now," said the mayor, holding up his hands. "Let's not do anything rash. This lad here"—he indicated

James—"is a representative of the Crown and will take care of things."

Instantly all speaking stopped and eyes turned to James. James threw a dark look Toddy's way, then said, "Very well. Now, we're here on a matter of interest to the Crown and what has been going on around here is of importance to His Highness. So, who can tell me what has occurred?"

Instantly everyone started speaking at once. James held up his hand and said, "Wait a minute. One at a time." He pointed to the florid-faced man who had been railing when they arrived and said, "You. Speak your piece."

"My cows come down sick!" the man shouted. Then he realized he didn't need to be shouting over others, and he lowered his voice. "My cows come down sick, and it's that witch. She's sent a curse to make them die slowly."

A woman in the crowd spoke up. "And we're losing our daylight, little by little. Sunrise has been coming later every morning; sundown earlier every evening. And what sunlight we do have is, I don't know how to explain it, but look around, it's different. Pretty soon we won't have any daylight at all. And you know what that means!" she sobbed.

Muttering broke out among the small crowd. James held up his hand for silence.

From the doorway, the farmer named Merrick spoke. "It's not only our cows that're sick. Our little girl, she's gravely ill."

James looked at Merrick and said, "What ails the girl?"

"She's cursed," shouted a woman from the edge of the group gathered in the yard.

Jazhara said, "May I see her?"

"Who are you?" asked the frantic-looking woman by Merrick's side, her face pinched and pale.

"I am Prince Arutha's personal advisor on magic," Jazhara answered.

Brother Solon added, "And I am a monk of Ishap's Temple. If there's evil magic afoot, we'll root it out."

The woman nodded and motioned them into the small house.

Inside they found a single room, with a small hearth on the wall opposite the door. A pair of beds stood there, one obviously big enough for the farmer and his wife and the other a child's bed. A small girl, her features wan, occupied this bed. Jazhara knelt by the side of the bed and put her hand upon the girl's forehead. "She has no fever," said the magician. "What can you tell me?"

The farmer said, "Nothing, save she's become too weak to walk or stay awake for more than a few minutes at a time. When she is awake, she seems unable to recognize us."

The farmer's wife added, "Sometimes she'll shake."

Brother Solon knelt beside Jazhara and examined the girl. "What is this?" he asked, fingering a small amulet. "This looks to be the sign of Sung."

"Father Rowland gave it to us," said the woman. Then she blurted, "I went to the old woman on Widow's Point, and she gave me a charm to heal my child. She told me a great darkness was trying to take the children. She was trying to protect them."

"Larissa!" scolded the man. "I told you not to speak of this."

"Go on," said James to the woman.

Defiantly, she looked at her husband. "She was trying to protect our daughter."

"Like she 'protected' Remy's son?"

"Yes, exactly like that!" She turned to James. "She was too late to save Remy's boy, but when I got home and put

the charm under the bed, my girl stopped shaking. She wasn't getting better, but she wasn't getting any worse! Then Father Rowland returned from a journey and came here. He prayed all last night, and my daughter began shaking again. When the sun rose, I swear he seemed irritated she was still alive!" The woman's look was one of desperation.

"Larissa, that's blasphemy!" said Merrick. "The good father was trying to save her soul. It's the witch's fault. He said as much before he left."

"But what if it's not?" asked the woman.

"May I see the charm the 'witch' gave you?" Jazhara asked.

The woman drew it out from under the bed and handed it to Jazhara. She looked at the small wooden box, within which she found several herbs and some crystals. She closed her eyes and held the box for a long minute, then said, "There is nothing malicious in this. This is a simple ward to help the child's natural energy heal herself." Then she looked at the child. "But there is something . . ."

She reached out and took the small amulet from the girl's throat, then suddenly withdrew her hand as if it had been burned. "Brother Solon. You know more of clerical arts than I; will you please examine that ward?"

Solon gently touched the amulet. He closed his eyes and made a short incantation, and then his eyes snapped open. "This is no ward of Sung!" The amulet began to change and he withdrew his fingers from it. The metal seemed to ripple and warp and darken, until suddenly what had appeared to be a simple metal icon of Sung became something resembling a tiny maw, a mouth of black lips and ebony teeth. It opened wide, as if to bite, then the girl coughed. A plume of green gas erupted from her nostrils and mouth, to be sucked into the tiny black orifice.

Solon grabbed the trinket and ripped it from the unconscious child's neck. The girl gasped slightly, and her tiny body convulsed once, then settled down into the bed. With a sigh she took a deep breath, then seemed to breathe more easily.

Jazhara examined the child and declared, "Already she seems a little stronger."

Solon held out the trinket, which was now revealed to be a claw holding a black pearl. "I would venture that this is the cause of the child's illness."

Merrick looked confounded. "But it was given to her by Father Rowland!"

James looked at Jazhara and the others and said, "Before we go rushing off to burn out an old woman, I think we need to have a serious 'talk' with this Father Rowland."

He didn't wait for an answer, but walked out of the tiny farmhouse.

Thirteen

◆

Misdirection

James halted.

Looking skyward for a moment, he then turned to Jazhara and the others hurrying to keep up with him and said, "Is it me, or is it getting darker?"

Kendaric glanced to the west. "There is no weather front approaching, and I see no clouds."

Solon looked at the sky and after a few seconds said, "No, it isn't you. It *is* getting darker."

Jazhara looked to the east, and pointed. "Look at the sun!"

They all turned to face the sunrise, and as they watched with a fascination that turned quickly to dread, the sun dimmed. The brilliant white had now darkened to a dull yellow.

Jazhara said, "I can feel the heat upon my face, but the light is fading!"

Solon said, "Yes, you have the right of it. Something is stealing the light from the very air!"

"What does this mean?" Kendaric asked anxiously.

"I don't know," Jazhara said. "I know of no magic that should be able to do this."

Kendaric repeated doggedly, "But what does it mean?"

James moved to stand before the now-terrified wrecker. "Pull yourself together! What it means should be obvious."

"So what does it mean?" demanded Kendaric.

"It means that soon our friends from last night will be able to walk abroad at any time."

People were hurrying past and James overheard some-one say, "Father Rowland will know what to do!"

The florid-faced man who had been inciting the others in front of Merrick's house approached and said, "If you're a servant of the Prince as you claim, you'll go burn that witch out right now!"

"And who are you?" James asked.

"My name's Alton. After I spoke against the woman at a town meeting, she fixed my cows with the evil eye, and put the wasting curse on them. Ask any of my neighbors. They've seen my animals dying. And she's done worse."

"Such as?" said James, impatiently.

"Well, take the woodcutter and his family. They were nice, normal folks, then suddenly they vanished. Then the blood-drinkers showed up. And Remy's little boy; he took ill after spying her one day up at Widow's Point. Died a fortnight later."

James said, "Your mayor doesn't seem to think she's the cause of these ills."

"Toddy's a wonderful, kind man, but he can be a bit of a fool."

James shook his head as other townspeople hurried by. "Where's Father Rowland?" he asked Alton.

"Just follow everyone else to the church across the square. That's where we're going." Suddenly, he gasped. "Look!" He pointed to the east and they could see how the sun was now darkening to an orange color as if heavy smoke were obscuring the orb.

As the farmer pointed, James noticed a glint of metal around his neck, a chain that moved as his tunic shifted. At the base he caught a glimpse of something black.

James had not been called "Jimmy the Hand" as a boy for nothing. With startling swiftness, he reached out and pulled the chain high enough to reveal a black pearl in a metal hand hanging from the chain. "Who gave this to you?"

The farmer's eyes grew round and he stepped back as James released the chain. "I . . . I found it."

"Where?"

"Ah . . ."

"We found a similar charm—around Merrick's daughter's neck," said Jazhara.

"It's just a simple bauble," said Farmer Alton.

Solon moved suddenly, far quicker than one would expect of a man his size, and came to stand just behind Alton. "Don't be thinking of leaving any time soon, my friend."

James drew his sword slowly for dramatic purpose. He didn't think this blustering farmer was particularly dangerous. But he also felt time was running short and he needed answers. "Again: Who gave you that charm?"

Alton attempted to move away, but Solon grabbed his arm and held him fast. "I think you'd best answer the lad; he doesn't appear to be in a mood for foolishness."

Alton glanced at Jazhara, whose expression was cold, then to Kendaric, who also looked as if he were running out of patience. Suddenly the farmer blurted, "I'll tell you everything! It wasn't my idea. I was just an honest farmer, minding my own business when he came to me. I trusted him; everyone does. He offered me gold, lots of gold, to poison my own cows and blame the witch, so I agreed. She's just one old lady, and she's going to die

soon, anyway. But I didn't know what he really was. I thought he was human when I agreed to work for him. I didn't know—" Suddenly the man's tumbling words were cut off by a strangled, gurgling sound as the chain around his neck abruptly tightened. Alton staggered backward, his eyes bulging and his face turning crimson as he clawed at his neck. Solon found himself holding the man upright as his knees buckled, and he let the farmer slowly sink to the ground. Blood began to flow from the wound in Alton's neck. As the farmer's eyes rolled up into his head, the sounds of muscles snapping and bones breaking could be heard. A moment later, the farmer's head rolled free from his body and dropped to the ground. Solon released the man's arm and the body crumpled to the dust.

James stared at the corpse and then at the darkening sun. He motioned for the others to follow and hurried toward a small building on the edge of the village common. Upon reaching it, they saw it was a simple church with a large, open entrance. No benches or pews were provided, so the congregation stood, listening to a man in white robes, who must surely be Father Rowland.

"Again, I say, if we wait much longer, we will be swept away by a tide of evil. And where, must I ask, is the justice in this? I will tell you where justice lies. It lies in the strength of our arms, the purity of our souls, and the burning that will rid the world of the witch's evil!"

Several of the townspeople shouted agreement.

"He sounds a wee bit harsh for a priest of Sung," Solon observed.

James nodded. "He does seem to be in an awful hurry to get rid of the 'witch.' "

"And to have others do the deed for him," Jazhara added.

The priest's voice rose. "Some say this witch has summoned wolves who walk like men at night, blood-drinkers who devour the souls of the innocent, turning them into monsters like themselves! I say she has summoned darkness incarnate—spirits so foul they drain the life from good people like you and me. Either way, the blame for this lies on her doorstep. This darkness approaching signals the final attack! *We must move now!*"

Some of the men cheered and shouted threats, but James could discern their fear for many of the responses were halfhearted and weak. He pushed through the villagers to stand before the priest.

"Welcome, stranger," said Father Rowland. He was a man of middle height, with dark hair and a small, pointed beard. Around his neck hung a simple ward of the Order of Sung. His white robes showed faint stains and dirt, as if old and oft-washed. "Have you come to help rid us of this blight?"

James regarded him steadily. "I have, but I doubt the blight is what you say."

The priest looked at James, his eyes narrowing. "What do you mean?"

"Alton is dead," James said.

The priest looked shocked. "Farmer Alton is dead? Another victim of that wicked woman!" Looking past James, the priest shouted, "Is this not enough? Isn't it time for us to act?"

More voices were raised in agreement, but James heard Jazhara shout, "James, be wary! There is something not right here!"

James looked and saw that several of those who were shouting had a vacant expression, their staring eyes fixed and lifeless. James turned toward the priest, then with unexpected swiftness, reached out and grabbed at the

amulet around the man's neck. With a single yank, he tore it away and held it up. Before his eyes it shifted and changed, from the benign icon of Sung to a hand holding a black pearl.

"These are servants of the Dark One! They must die!" shouted the priest, his hands reaching for James's throat, fingers bent like talons.

James tried to jump backward, but suddenly was seized by hands, holding him in place. He could hear Jazhara shouting, "The people are innocents! They are possessed! Try not to harm them!"

James felt the priest's fingers at his throat and shouted, "I'll try to keep that in mind!" He let his body go limp and dropped away, the priest's fingers slipping over his head for a moment. From the floor, James could not draw his sword, but he could reach the dagger that was tucked in the top of his right boot. He drew it and slashed upward, striking the priest in the leg.

Father Rowland shouted in pain and fell backward, and James rolled his legs under him in a crouch as strong hands tried to hold him in place. Then he leapt forward with all his strength and, as he had hoped, the hands lost their grip upon him.

Several townspeople stumbled forward, and he barely avoided being pulled down from behind. The priest was retreating. James glanced quickly from one side to the other. Jazhara was wheeling her staff, keeping the villagers at bay. Kendaric was being borne down, pinned to the floor by a pair of strong farmers, while another was attempting to kick him in the head. Brother Solon was using his warhammer to shove people away as much as strike them, in his attempt to reach the wrecker's side and render aid.

James tossed his dagger from his right hand to his left,

and drew his sword in one fluid motion. He shifted his blade and struck the closest man across the head with the flat; even so, the rapier's thin blade still cut the man, but it wasn't a deep wound.

The blow sent the man staggering back a step, blocking those behind him for an instant. An instant was all James needed. He lunged forward, as Father Rowland began to weave a magic spell. Before the priest had finished, James had skewered him through the stomach.

The man looked down in stunned amazement, then his eyes widened in pain as James yanked free his blade. Then the priest's eyes rolled back into his head. But rather than fall, he continued to stand. His head lolled back and his mouth hung open, but from within a deep, alien voice declared, "Though our servant lies dead, our power remains undimmed. Taste the bitter draught of evil . . . and despair."

The priest crumpled to the floor and James wheeled, ready for the next attack, but rather than being assaulted, James was met with the sight of the townspeople standing around, blinking in confusion. Several looked at one another, or at Kendaric and Solon, or Jazhara, and then the babble of voices began.

"What happened?"

"How did we get here?"

"Why are you bleeding?"

James held up his hand and cried, "Silence!"

Voices stilled. James continued, "This man was no priest of Sung. He was an agent of the very darkness he claimed to be fighting. He kept you distracted from the true source of the evil."

One of the women in the group screamed. "The sun!" she shouted, pointing at the morning sun.

James turned. It was even darker. "It'll be night soon," he

said, not trying to explain what he couldn't. "Get to your homes and bar the doors. We'll see to the cause of this."

The villagers fled. Some had to be helped by friends, because of the battering they had taken from Jazhara's staff and Solon's warhammer, but James was relieved to see that the only corpse in the room was Rowland's.

Kendaric looked frightened, but he also seemed to have kept his composure. He brushed himself off as they all gathered around James.

"Did the rest of you hear what he said?" James asked.

"No," answered Kendaric. "I was too busy being attacked."

Jazhara said, "I heard him speak, but not what he said."

"I heard it," said Brother Solon. "He was an agent of darkness, there's no doubt of that. That he could take the guise of a servant of the Pure One is troubling. Even a false icon such as he wore should be difficult to endure by a servant of evil."

"These are very powerful enemies," said James. "I've heard that voice before."

"When?" asked Jazhara.

"Years ago, from the mouth of a Black Slayer. The servants of Murmandamus."

"But Murmandamus was destroyed," said Jazhara. Then she glanced at Solon and Kendaric, unsure of what more she should say. As Arutha's court mage, James had told her some of the truth behind Arutha's slaying of the false moredhel prophet, and the recent troubles in the Dimwood, for there were rumors that he was still alive.

James nodded. "I know he was, but while we may not be dealing with that black heart, we are certainly facing someone who is nearly his equal in power. And that means we're up against something far more dangerous than we thought."

"You knew it was dangerous when we told you about our ship being taken," said Solon. "You're not backing out now, are you?"

"No," said James, glancing at the darkening sun. "Especially not now. I can feel things rushing forward and if we hesitate, I think we are lost." He realized he was still holding his weapons and he put them up. "We don't have time to send for reinforcements, and we don't know how effective William will continue to be at keeping Bear away from here. I think this will end before more than two days pass, one way or the other."

"What now?" asked Kendaric, crossing his arms as if cold.

James let out a long breath. "When darkness finally comes, those blood-drinkers will be back, and I think they are here for no other reason than to keep us busy. So whatever we do, we have to do it quickly." He looked at Jazhara. "One thing strikes me. Rowland and Alton were too anxious to get rid of that witch for it to have only been about finding a scapegoat. There's something about her they feared."

Jazhara said, "Then we should go talk to her." Glancing at the sun, she added, "And quickly. I think we have less than two hours before night falls again."

James nodded. Walking past Jazhara he said, "Let us go visit the witch at Widow's Point."

As they climbed the hillside toward Widow's Point, the woods turned ominously dark. The fading sun created darker shadows on the trail than usual. "It's like traveling at twilight," whispered Solon.

James laughed. "I feel the need to speak softly, too."

Jazhara said, "Stealth may be prudent, but time is fleeting."

As they rounded a bend in the trail, James held up his hand. "Someone's ahead," he whispered.

They moved forward and James soon clearly saw a figure crouched in the gloom. It was a boy of no more than nine years of age. James walked up behind him, making no effort to be silent, yet the child's attention remained fixed upon a small hut near the cliffs. When James put his hand on the child's shoulder, the boy shouted in alarm and nearly fell down in surprise.

"Don't be afraid," said Jazhara. "We mean you no harm."

The boy's eyes were large with terror. "Who are you?" he asked.

"I am Jazhara, and this is Squire James of Krondor. That's Brother Solon, and Kendaric. Who are you?"

The boy's voice lost its quaver, but he still looked frightened. "I'm Alaric. I'm here to watch the witch. Pa says they're going to burn her real soon, so I wanted to see her do some black magic stuff before they get her."

"I think you should hurry home before it gets much darker," said James.

Jazhara asked, "Is she in the hut now?"

"I haven't seen her. Sometimes she wanders the beach below Widow's Point. I'd be careful; she's really dangerous."

James said, "Thank you. Now, get on home. Your family will be worried about you."

The boy didn't need any more urging and turned and ran down the trail.

They walked on toward the dwelling and James shouted, "Hello, in the hut!"

There was no answer.

James approached and climbed the single step to a wooden porch.

The small stoop had an overhang from which hung a variety of gourds. Jazhara inspected the corpses of a couple of small animals hung there to dry and then an assortment of herbs. "This 'witch' is either a practitioner of magic or simply an old woman well-versed in the arts of remedy. I recognize several of these plants. They are used for poultices and herbal teas."

The hut had been constructed on a wooden platform, the porch extended out a few feet from the front wall. Looking down, Solon said, "At least she's dry when it rains."

"And it rains a lot along this part of the coast," Kendaric added. He wrapped his arms around himself as if he were cold and said, "Not only is it getting darker, but it feels like rain is coming."

"Just what we need," said James. He pushed aside a piece of hide strung across the lintel, serving as a door. Inside the hut were a crude table and a single stool. A cauldron simmered before a fire.

Kendaric looked at the brown mixture. "Not a witch? Then what's that?"

James walked over and inspected the bubbling liquid. He took a ladle from a hook over the fireplace and dipped it into the cauldron. Raising it he sniffed, then sipped it. Turning to Kendaric he said, "Soup. And very good, too."

He replaced the ladle when a voice at the door said, "Come to burn me?"

James turned to see a frail-looking old woman standing in the entrance, holding a bundle of sticks.

"Well, don't just stand there, staring. You expect an old woman to gather all the wood for her own burning?"

The old woman looked barely larger than the child they had just sent home. Her skin was almost translucent with age, and her hair was completely white. Her tiny fingers

looked like skin over bones, but she had all her teeth and her eyes were bright and alive.

James smiled. "We're not here to burn you, woman."

"Oh, that's what they all say," she said, pushing past Kendaric and throwing the bundle of sticks down next to the hearth.

Jazhara said, "You practice magic?"

The old woman sat down on her small stool and shrugged. "I know a thing or two. But mostly I mix up remedies for people, or tell fortunes." Her eyes got a faraway look. "Sometimes I see things, but that's . . . difficult. It's rarely pleasant."

Kendaric said, "I'm from the Wreckers' Guild in Krondor and I've tried to raise a ship recently sunk off the Point. Something is blocking my magic. It's powerful and I need to know what it is."

The old woman studied Kendaric for a moment, then turned to face Jazhara. "You practice the craft?"

Jazhara said, "I am the court magician to Prince Arutha."

"Ah," said the old woman, a bemused smile on her face. "A woman magician. Time was you'd have been put to death for even claiming to know the arts in Krondor."

"Times change," said James.

"In some ways, maybe," said the old woman. "Others, not at all."

James said, "Well, perhaps someday we can sit in more comfortable surroundings and discuss it. But right now we have other worries." He gestured outside at the fading sun.

"I saw," said the woman. "That's why I thought you might be from the village, come to burn me."

Jazhara said, "That was 'Father' Rowland. He was rallying the villagers to come here and do just that."

"How did you stop him?" asked the woman.

James said, "With my rapier. He was no priest of Sung."

"I could have told you that," said the old woman. "His pores just oozed evil. I think that's one of the reasons he wanted me gone; he realized I knew him to be a charlatan."

"There had to be another reason," said Solon. "You would hardly have been a compelling witness against him just because you sensed the evil in him."

The woman nodded. "It is because I know the secret of Haldon Head and Widow's Point."

James said, "Will the secret explain what is going on around here, and why we cannot raise that ship?"

"Undoubtedly," said the old woman.

Jazhara asked, "What is your name?"

The old crone paused and then laughed. "It's been so long since anyone has called me anything but 'witch' or 'old woman' I can scarcely remember." She sighed. "Call me Hilda."

"Hilda," asked James. "What is the secret you spoke of?"

The old woman looked around, as if fearful of being overheard. "Below the cliffs, in a deep cavern, lies an ancient place. It is a temple of evil, older than the memory of the oldest living human."

"What sort of temple?" asked Solon, his hand reflexively going to the hilt of his warhammer.

Hilda stood slowly and crossed to an old wooden chest. She threw back the lid and reached inside. From within she removed a small cloth pouch. Handing it to Solon, she said, "Open it."

The monk did so, and when he saw what was inside, he seemed loath to touch it. "This is like those others," he whispered. He shook the thing into his hand and held it

out. Upon his palm was a carved metal hand of either pewter or iron, within which rested a black orb, fashioned from a stone like obsidian. But unlike obsidian, however, it did not reflect the light of the fire.

The old woman said, "I do not know who first built the Black Pearl Temple, but they were not human."

Solon put the artifact back into its pouch. "My order has a catalogue of every cult and faith known to man in the Kingdom, the East, and down through Kesh. As a Defender of the Faithful, I have studied those documents. I have never heard of such an order as the Black Pearl."

The old woman sighed. "And yet it exists." She took the pouch from Solon. "What lies below the cliffs is a festering evil. It is partially to blame for why so many ships are drawn to their demise on the rocks below. It is why few try to farm the good land that lies between the village and my hut. Those who do try grow restless or fearful and leave after a season or two. Even the hunters avoid the woods around here."

"How is it you can abide?" asked Kendaric.

"This," said the old woman, holding up the pouch. "It is a talisman and protects me from their evil, as if I were already one of their own. I'd like you to have it, for you face a grave challenge." She looked into the eyes of each of her guests before handing the pouch to Solon, who accepted the gift with a nod of thanks. She sat down again, and said, "And it is more."

"What?" asked James.

"It's a key. If you go down the pathway to the rocks below, turn into what appears to be a small alcove fashioned by the sea in the rocks. There you will see a small, faint pattern in the rocks, at my eye level. With this key, a door in the rocks will open."

"You've seen this done?" asked Jazhara.

"Yes," said Hilda. "Many times I have spied upon those who come and go below. One of my talents is conceal-ment. I was standing but a few feet from the porch when you passed, yet you had no inkling, right?"

Jazhara smiled and nodded. "True."

"Have you tried to use this to get in?" asked James.

"Yes," admitted Hilda. "I've tried. But I did not get in."

"Why not?" asked Kendaric.

"Because only those who are sworn in the service of those black powers in the temple can use it. I tried, but the door would not open."

James said, "Then how can we use the key?"

"I believe you have one choice," said the woman. "In the village a creature hides. I do not know who he is or what his name is, but that he is there is certain. He is the one who first infected those who became blood-drinkers. He is a servant of those dark powers below. I don't un-derstand his purpose, for it's only a matter of time before the Prince comes to Haldon Head with his army to set things right."

"We know why he's here," said James. "To keep us busy and away from the Point."

"So his master can raise the ship," added Kendaric.

"How do we use this knowledge to get inside the tem-ple?" James probed.

"Find the monster who has killed so many. Kill him and remove his hand at his wrist. Bind the talisman to the hand. Then the door should open."

"Where do we find this monster?" asked James.

The old woman said, "There is an ancient crypt in the graveyard. The oldest family in this area, the Haldons, built it. None live today, but it is kept up out of respect for the town's founder. Inside is where I think you'll find the monster. And if you find him, you'll find the cause of this

darkness. And when you do, please return, so that I may know that I have not sent you to your death."

James said, "We must be going. For by the time we reach the graveyard, those things will be wakening, and I would rather put paid to this before they're upon us."

They hurried from the hut and the old woman crossed to the door and stood there, watching them flee down the path toward the town. Softly she said, "May the gods watch over you, children." Then she slowly hobbled back to her stool, to wait.

Fourteen

◆

Vampire

The sky darkened.

As James and the others approached the south edge of town, where Hilda had indicated they'd find the burial crypt, the light faded.

"It's getting darker," said Kendaric, his voice almost quavering with fear.

"Expect the worst," said Solon. "Assume the bleeders know we're coming for them."

Kendaric asked, "Doesn't your order have some sort of magic prayer-thing that makes these types of creatures just . . . vanish?"

"Ha!" replied the monk. "Wish it were so, laddie. The only order with the power to do so are those who worship Lims-Kragma."

Kendaric glanced around. "I thought they'd be in league with these creatures."

"Nay, boy," said Solon, the tension of the moment thickening his accent again. "They're servants of the right order of things, and despise any creature that thwarts their mistress's will. The creatures we're facing are more of an abomination to her servants than they are to us. That's

why our mission is to send them along to her so she can sort the buggers out."

"Well, here comes your chance," said James as a half-dozen creatures appeared to rise up out of the gloom, from among a field of headstones. He drew his sword and dagger, but kept moving. "Don't let them delay you too long. If Hilda is correct, once we locate their master and deal with him, these will fall."

Kendaric said, "So, you're telling us to fight through these creatures, but be efficient about it?"

"That's wha' the man said, laddie," replied Solon, pulling out his warhammer, and swinging it before him in a lazy circle. "Just crack a head or cut off a leg or some such, and keep goin'."

Kendaric's face was pale, but he attempted to look resolute. "Sure. No problem."

Jazhara said, "I'll deal with this first batch." She lowered her staff and the air crackled with energy. A brilliant flash of actinic light shot out, as if lightning had been released from a bottle. It bounced across the ground like a ball. As it landed before the first of the undead creatures, it split into smaller balls, each lashing out in electric fury to encapsulate the vampires. They stiffened and howled in agony as the crackling energy seared their flesh and rendered them motionless.

James started to run. "We need to move fast!" he shouted. "There's the crypt!"

In the center of the small graveyard, a stone building rose, a small mausoleum with a peaked roof, its doors open. Within, they could see at least a half-dozen marble catafalques, upon which stone coffins rested. "Why couldn't they burn their dead properly," Kendaric muttered, "like the rest of the Kingdom?"

"We're close to Yabon," said Solon. "Burial is still popular up here."

"For once," said Jazhara, lowering her staff and pointing it toward the door, "I agree with Kendaric."

Inside the crypt, an eerie red glow illuminated figures moving behind the stone coffins. "We've got to fight our way in," said James.

Jazhara unleashed another bolt of energy and several of the creatures in the first row stiffened. James raced past them, only to be confronted by a burly-looking man, his skin pale and his eyes seeming to glow with a reddish light. Behind him, James spied another figure, not as bulky, but radiating immense power, and he knew he was looking at the master vampire.

"Kill that one!" James shouted.

The master vampire laughed. "Child of woe, I was dead before you were born!"

The burly vampire lashed out at James, and his fingers were curled like talons. James didn't attempt to parry the blow. Instead, he ducked below the swing, then rose and kicked out with his right leg, planting his boot in the vampire's chest. He shoved and the burly man was thrown backward into the path of the Vampire Lord. Then James lunged and attempted to hamstring the approaching master vampire, but the creature leapt aside with astonishing speed. James suddenly felt afraid. Nothing living should move that quickly. James's previous experience with the supernatural had been entirely unpleasant, and his one advantage in those cases had been his combination of instinct and speed. His plan had been to render the master vampire helpless by cutting his legs from under him, or otherwise injuring him, then leaving it to Jazhara to burn him with her mystical fire.

He now saw that his plan was not going to work.

"Get back!" James shouted. "We have to burn them in here!"

Solon crushed the skull of one vampire, and Kendaric managed to inflict enough damage on another that it was keeping its distance from him.

Jazhara used her staff to good advantage, tripping two of the creatures and causing a third to fall over them. She now busied herself with breaking heads with her staff; but, as they had been warned, the damage merely slowed the creatures down rather than causing permanent damage.

They started to retreat, Jazhara and Solon attempting to clear a path for James. James fought down panic. He had to back away from the pair of advancing vampires, and the burly man was shrewd enough not to let James trip him again.

James risked a glance backward and almost had his head taken from his shoulders for his trouble. Only by lashing out with his rapier did he manage to drive the Vampire Lord back.

Suddenly Solon charged forward, swinging his warhammer with both hands. He smashed it into the burly vampire's chest, sending the creature flying backward thorough the air, into its master.

The Vampire Lord was knocked off his feet, but again he sprang up with supernatural ease and speed, throwing the other vampire aside like a doll. The burly vampire, however, lay upon the stone floor, writhing in agony.

The unexpected counterattack gave James the time he needed to leap away, through the doorway of the small mausoleum.

"Close the doors!" James shouted. "Jazhara, burn them!"

Jazhara lowered her staff and a gout of green flame exploded from its tip. Kendaric struggled with one door, while Solon easily moved the other.

As James watched, his eyes widening in disbelief, the master vampire walked through the flames, unburned.

At last the doors slammed shut. Solon threw his weight against them.

"We need to block them!" shouted James.

Jazhara grabbed Kendaric by the collar of his tunic and pulled him around. "Stones!" she shouted as the wrecker almost fell over, only regaining his balance at the last moment.

They hurried to a small headstone that rose from a grave and together managed to pull it out of the ground. "Thank you, whoever you were," Jazhara directed toward the now-unmarked grave as she and Kendaric dragged the stone over to the mausoleum doors.

James and Solon had thrown their shoulders against the doors that bulged outward as the master vampire threw his unnatural strength against them. First one, then another stone was piled in place, until the door refused to give.

"I don't know how much time we've bought," said James, out of breath. "But I saw that thing walk through your fire, Jazhara. It didn't faze him."

"Then I don't know what to do," she replied.

"Maybe it has to be natural fire," said Kendaric. "We could build a fire, then light a bundle of rags in oil. Toss it in."

"I doubt it would make a difference," said the magician. She pondered. "Perhaps Hilda can tell us what to do."

Solon said, "You two run back to Hilda, while Kendaric and I endeavor to keep these doors shut." As if to punctuate this statement, there came a dull thud from within the crypt and the doors shook and rattled against the headstones. "Hurry!" Solon urged. "He may not be

able to move those stone doors, but he can certainly reduce them to rubble in time."

James nodded, turned to look at Jazhara, who nodded. They set off at a jog back north through the town and toward Widow's Peak.

Nearly breathless, they reached the hut overlooking the cliffs. Hilda heard them approaching and came to stand out on the porch.

"Naught goes well," she observed.

James nodded, attempting to catch his wind. He took a deep breath then said, "The master vampire won't die."

"The Vampire Lord will be difficult to destroy," said Hilda. "But he is no god."

"He will not burn," said Jazhara.

"Ah!" the old woman responded, looking thoughtful. "Then he has placed his essence somewhere else."

James looked at Jazhara who returned a blank expression. "I do not understand," she said to Hilda.

Hilda shrugged. "I am no expert. Necromancy is the foulest of the arts and to be shunned." She paused, then added, "But over time one hears things."

"Such as?" asked James.

"It is said that some of the servants of the dark powers are not truly living; even those poor souls captured by this vampire master have a thread of life within; cut it and they fade," Hilda explained. "But a few of the more powerful servants of evil have conspired to rid their bodies of mortality completely."

"Then how do we destroy those?" asked Jazhara.

"Find the soul vessel. To attain such power, sacrifices are made, and what one gains on one hand"—she held out one hand—"one loses on the other." She extended her other hand. "To make the body immortal, the spirit essence

is placed somewhere close by. It is often protected by wards or hidden in such a way it is unlikely to be found."

"We don't have time for this," said James. "That Vampire Lord is strong. Even now he may be out of the crypt and have overcome Solon and Kendaric."

Jazhara said, "And if we lose Kendaric—"

James nodded grimly. "We had no choice but to leave him with Solon. But we must hurry."

Jazhara said, "Where should we look? Will it be in the crypt with the master vampire?"

Hilda shook her head. "Unlikely. He will have brought it with him, but placed it someplace safe, as soon as he arrived."

"Where was the first place he was seen?" asked James.

"The woodcutter's cabin," Hilda replied.

"Then that's where we'll look," said James. "Which way do we go?"

"Run to Farmer Alton's farm, and follow the road that passes east before his house. A mile beyond the last fence you'll see a path into the woods and another mile beyond that is the woodcutter's home. Tread lightly, for the Vampire Lord will have other allies."

James glanced around. "It's almost as dark as night now. Have you a lantern or torches?"

The old woman nodded. "Torches. I'll get them." She went inside and a moment later reappeared with three torches—one was burning; the remaining two were held in the crook of her arm. "These are all I have."

James took the burning one and Jazhara took the two others. James said, "They will have to do. Thank you, Hilda, for all your help."

"No thanks are needed."

Jazhara said, "When all is done, I shall return and tell you of Stardock."

"I will listen," said the old woman.

James took a last look at the old woman's face. "Good-bye," he called. Then he turned, and hurried back toward the village. Jazhara followed him.

The old woman watched until they were out of sight, then turned and slowly walked back into her hut.

James and Jazhara ran most of the way, stopping only when feeling at risk. Through the town they went and onto the eastern road, until they left the road when they found the indicated trail.

The forest was plunged into darkness, as if noon and midnight had exchanged places. Moreover, no moon illuminated the way, and the murk was both unnatural and ominous. The trail was well-traveled, but narrow, and James had to fight the urge to jump at every single noise.

The daybirds had ceased singing, but the soft hooting of their nocturnal counterparts was also missing. The air was unnaturally still, as if the magic dampening the sun was also silencing the wind.

Suddenly the night air was rent by the sound of a distant howl. It was quickly answered by others.

"Wolves!" said James.

"Hurry," Jazhara cried, and James started to go at such a pace that they risked injury on the narrow trail.

Dodging between the boles of trees and along rocky footing, they at last came to a small hut in a clearing. From within the hut came a red glow, which seeped through the cracks around the door and the tiny window next to it.

"Someone's inside," James cautioned.

"Someone's outside," said Jazhara, pointing.

Four figures emerged from behind the hut, all walking purposefully toward James and Jazhara.

Jazhara lowered her staff and again blinding lightning spilled forth from the tip. The leaves on the ground smoked as the lightning bounced along to strike the four creatures. The vampires struggled to keep moving but their bodies just twitched and shivered uncontrollably.

"Get inside!" Jazhara shouted. "I'll deal with these."

James ran past the quivering figures, two having fallen to the ground where they flopped like landed fish. He hardly slowed, but lifted his right leg and kicked hard against the door, smashing it inward.

A woman sat on a stool, appearing to care for a baby in a bassinet, but as soon as she turned at James's intrusion it was clear that she was a vampire. She rose, snarling, from her stool and launched herself at James, her fingers clawed talons and her fangs bared.

James dodged to one side and cut at the back of her leg, hamstringing her. She fell with a shriek of pain and outrage and James slashed her across the neck. His light blade struck bone and was turned aside, and at that moment he wished for a heavier blade.

He pulled the rapier free of the woman's neck and hacked away at her outstretched arms. She recoiled in pain, scrambled backward, then tried to rise.

As she stood, James leapt forward, put his foot to her stomach and pushed her outside. Her wounded leg betrayed her: as she fell backward, James lashed out with his torch, catching the hem of her skirt with the flame and igniting it.

In moments the woman was rolling on the ground, trying to extinguish the blaze. James turned his attention to the interior of the hut. There was nothing in it except for a small table, the bassinet, and a bucket near the fireplace. There was no obvious hiding place, no chest or likely receptacle for an important item such as the vampire's soul vessel.

James stepped forward and looked into the bassinet. He grimaced at what he saw: the body of a baby lay in it. It had obviously been dead for some time. Its tiny body was shrunken, the skin stretched over the fragile bones. But what was most repulsive was the red light which emanated from its body.

James hesitated, reluctant to touch the little corpse. Then, he put aside his revulsion and touched the child's stomach. Something hard resisted his finger. He pulled out his dagger, swallowed hard and cut into the infant's flesh. Inside the baby's rib-cage a large ruby-colored stone glowed with an evil brilliance.

James was forced to break two ribs to remove the object. By the time he had done so, Jazhara had reached the door. "They're all dead—" She stopped, aghast. "What is that?"

James said, "I'm not sure, but I think the baby is the vessel."

Jazhara stared at the red jewel. "Then that would be the Soul Stone," she mused. She closed her eyes and made an incantation, then opened them and said, "There is a great deal of magic locked within that gem. And it reeks of evil."

"What do we do with it?" asked James.

"Take it outside," said Jazhara.

The howling of wolves could be heard, getting closer by the moment.

"Hurry," she insisted.

James complied with alacrity.

Once they were both outside, Jazhara looked around. "There!" she said, pointing to the woodcutter's work-shed. In the corner was a small bellows and forge, where tools could be repaired and sharpened. She located at once what she was looking for.

"Put the gem on this anvil," she instructed.

James did so. Jazhara reached over and took a small iron hammer and lifted it. "Avert your eyes!" she commanded, and James looked away.

He heard the smash of the hammer on the gem, then felt his skin crawl. A wash of energy made him physically ill and he had to fight to keep from retching. Next came a sense of loss and haplessness, a futility that seeped into his bones; that was followed by a blast of anger and rage that caused his heart to race and his eyes to tear.

He gasped and heard Jazhara also gasping. When he opened his eyes, he saw she had been unsuccessful in controlling her nausea.

Despite feeling light-headed and disoriented, the howl of the approaching wolves made him focus; he forced himself to become alert.

Then the sky shattered. Like a latticework of faint lines, the darkness was shot through with light. As if shards of a broken window fell from above, the black night disappeared. It looked as though pieces of the dark sky were falling down, only to dissolve and fade to insubstantial mist before striking the tops of the nearby trees. From behind each shard the brilliance of the day's light shone.

Then, abruptly, there was daylight again—total daylight.

The howling of the wolf pack ceased, and the daybirds started singing.

"I didn't expect that," said Jazhara.

"Well, expected or not, I'm glad to see the sun again," James replied. He glanced in the direction of the fiery orb and remarked, "It's barely midday."

"A lot has happened," she said. "Come, we must return to the graveyard and see what has transpired there."

They hurried back through the town and down the road to the graveyard. Along the way they saw the townspeople looking out of their doors and windows, astonished and delighted at the return of daylight. A few hardier souls had ventured outside, and were now looking at one another as if seeking reassurance that something approaching normalcy was returning.

They were out of breath and sweating from the returned heat of the sun by the time they reached the vault. Solon and Kendaric were still blocking the crypt door.

"Where have you been?!" cried Kendaric.

"You did something," said the monk. "All manner of madness erupted inside here and then the sky above shattered. I assume the two were related?"

"We found and smashed the soul-gem," said Jazhara.

James said, "I thought he would . . . die or something when we smashed the stone."

"I'm no expert in this sort of thing," Jazhara mused. "Hilda might know more. But I'm wagering now that since the gem has been destroyed, we can find a way to destroy him, too."

Kendaric asked, "Can't we just leave them locked up until they wither away?"

"Not if he's the source of whatever is blocking your spell."

Kendaric stood with a resigned expression on this face. Then he started to haul away the first of the headstones blocking the crypt door. "Care to give me some help?"

"Not really," answered James, but he set to picking up another headstone.

"Do we have a plan?" asked Solon.

"We must cut off one of the Vampire Lord's hands," Jazhara reminded him.

James said, "We let them open the doors. They don't

like the light, so maybe that will weaken them. I encountered a demon not too long ago whose flesh burned in the sunlight. Perhaps it's the same with these."

"With the lesser vampires, perhaps," said Solon, heaving away another stone. "But I suspect the master vampire will find it only somewhat irritating."

"Maybe we can kill them one at a time as they come through," suggested Kendaric as he dropped a stone a few yards away, and returned to pick up another.

The door started to move, as the vampires inside threw their weight against it. "We can't burn them," said Jazhara, "or at least we can't burn the leader; we need his hand."

"Maybe we can get him to stick it out," suggested Kendaric, "then lop it off and run like hell."

Solon chuckled. "We break heads and cut throats. It's simple."

James stepped back from the doors as they began to push outward. "Yes, it's simple." Then the door swung suddenly outward and two figures leapt at him. "But that doesn't mean easy!"

James slashed the closest vampire across the throat as it staggered in the unexpected daylight. As soon as the sun touched the creature, its flesh started to blacken and it began to howl in pain.

The second vampire turned and tried to reenter the crypt, but was pushed back by two more coming after it. Solon laid about him with his warhammer and knocked them first to one side, then the other.

Jazhara struck downward with the iron end of her staff, and soon three corpses lay smoking in the sunlight. James peered into the gloom of the crypt. The bright sun made the interior dark and indistinct. Nothing appeared to move.

"I think we're going to have to go in and get him,"

James said softly. Turning to Kendaric, he nodded toward the wrecker's sword. "You've got the only blade that could cut that thing's head off. If we get him down, try not to chop either Solon or me while you're at it."

Kendaric went pale, but nodded.

James looked then at Jazhara and raised an eyebrow. Then he spoke again to Kendaric. "Should she be forced to set him alight, I want you to be ready to run in and chop off a hand."

Kendaric wiped perspiration from his upper lip with the back of his sleeve. "Which hand?"

"Either should do, I think," said James. He nodded once to Solon and they both charged into the crypt. They raced inside, one on either side of a central catafalque, their eyes darting to left and right.

Three sets of three catafalques dominated the floor of the crypt and both men knew that crouched behind one of them was the Vampire Lord. As James reached the second set, he had a premonition. "Solon, look up!" he shouted.

As the monk obeyed, a figure dropped from the peak of the roof, and only James's warning saved him. Reacting swiftly, he spun and swung his warhammer, smashing the Vampire Lord's ribs.

The master vampire flew across the room, slamming into the stone wall before James, who swung his rapier and lunged, attempting to skewer the creature on the floor, but with supernatural speed the creature was up and on his feet, slipping right past James's sword.

Then a second vampire dropped from above, and suddenly James was borne down to the floor. The stink of carrion assaulted his sense of smell as he struggled against the power and weight of the two vampires. "Solon!" he shouted.

The powerful monk closed upon the three figures on

the floor in two strides. He gripped one by the collar of his tunic and threw him toward the door. The creature slid into the light of day and started to shriek in agony.

Kendaric stepped forward and with as powerful a blow as he could muster he chopped off the creature's head.

Jazhara cried, "Duck!"

At once, Solon crouched. Jazhara pointed her staff upward and unleashed a blast of green fire. The flames danced along the stone ceiling and two more vampires fell, writhing in burning agony.

James found himself struggling against the strongest foe he had ever grappled with. The Vampire Lord was only the size of a tall man, but his hands gripped James's chin and turned his head as easily as James might have turned a child's head. As hard as he tried, James could not resist. His neck muscles felt as if they were being ripped apart, and he tried desperately to keep his head turned toward his foe. Out of the corner of his eye he could see the creature's fangs, and realized with horror that he was about to have his throat ripped out.

Frantically, he tried to convulse his body to buy himself a moment of freedom, but the Vampire Lord had the strength of three men. Then he saw Solon appear behind the vampire. The powerful monk gripped the monster by his long flowing hair and yanked his head back. James heard Jazhara shout, "Close your eyes!"

Jabbing with the end of her staff, Jazhara smashed the Vampire Lord right in the mouth. His eyes opened wide with surprise and he froze for a moment as if appalled by this unexpected attack.

Then Jazhara uttered a quick phrase and energy exploded from the tip of her staff. The creature's head erupted in a gout of white flame, and the room filled with the stench of burning flesh.

The Vampire Lord rose howling and Jazhara pulled her staff free. James scrambled backward the instant he felt the weight lift from his body.

Kendaric hurried over and with careful aim threw his weight behind his blade, and in a single circular motion sheared the creature's head from its body. The Vampire Lord's body fell like a stone.

Kendaric looked as if he was going to be sick.

James said, "Thank you; all of you." Looking at Kendaric, he added, "Cut off the hand."

Kendaric shook his head and reversed the blade, holding it out to James. "If you don't mind, you do it. I don't think I have it in me anymore." Then his eyes rolled up into his skull and he fell to the floor in a faint.

Later that afternoon, they took their ease at the inn. James savored a bitter, refreshing draught of ale, while trying to ignore the pain in his wrenched neck.

"What now?" asked Kendaric, still embarrassed at having fainted.

"We wait until morning," said James. "We are all tired and in need of rest. Then at first light we'll try to raise the ship. If it fails, we'll know Hilda was right and it's not just the Vampire Lord but whatever's down there in that temple."

"What about help?" asked Kendaric.

"I'll send for the garrison down in Miller's Rest in the morning. They'll be here in two days."

"Do we wait?" asked Solon.

"No, we'll explore the old temple. I've done that sort of thing a few times before. It's unlikely there's anyone down there. If there were, someone from the village would have seen something before this recent outbreak of trouble."

Jazhara sipped her ale, then said, "I am still disturbed by two things."

James nodded. "Who's behind all this?"

"Yes," said the magician. "It's clear that someone wants to keep this area isolated and allow his minions to seize the prize." She glanced around to see if any of the locals in the inn could overhear her. "The Tear," she said softly.

"What's the other thing that troubles you, lady?" asked Solon.

"Where are William and the Krondorian Guard?" Jazhara said.

James understood the double reference at once, for while Solon and Kendaric would assume she was concerned only about Bear's whereabouts, he knew she also was worried about William's safety.

James sipped his ale. He thought about those two issues and realized he was just as troubled as Jazhara by them.

Fifteen

◆

Two Fangs

William watched.

Just above the top of distant trees, he could see Two Fangs Pass, silhouetted in black relief by the rising sun. Two large rocks, one to each side of the trail, rose up like a viper's fangs, giving the place its name. On either side of the fangs two clearings could be seen. As he faced north, William could see that a stand of thick forest bordered the right-hand clearing and rose up the hillside. On the left, a clearing topped a cliff overlooking a deep river gorge.

"Are they here already, do you think?" asked Sergeant Hartag.

"I can feel it in my bones," replied William. "Tonight's the new Small Moon and this is the morning the Grey Talons were supposed to lead us to the slaughter."

"We did the best we could getting here, Will," said Hartag. "If we'd pushed any more the horses would be dead and the men couldn't fight."

"Well, at least we know we're in for a fight and they're out there somewhere."

"How do we play it?" asked the sergeant.

"You're an old campaigner, Sergeant. What's your thought?"

The sergeant was quiet as he considered, then he said, "They're certain to be in those trees. But I'll wager Bear's got a dozen or so lying low in that meadow on the left, by the cliff. It rises then falls off behind, and I think he's got some archers crouched down over there, where we can't see them. I think his plan is to bait us to charge the pass, so the lads flee over the summit. Then we come hard right after them, and as we get to the Fangs, he hits us from the right, and as we wheel to charge, his archers take us from behind."

"That's my thinking, too," said William. "So if we see him put riders up there on the crest, watching for the mercenaries' arrival, we know you're right."

Less than an hour later, a pair of riders appeared from out of the line of the woods and took up position at the bottom of the rise. "Well," said William. "Looks like we've found the Bear."

"Shall I send the Pathfinders?"

"Send them up through the trees and have them get up as far as they can, and report back on numbers. I want them back here by midday at the latest."

Time passed slowly while they waited, and William gave orders for the men to ready themselves for a fight. He suspected Bear had a larger body of men hidden in the woods. William was counting on the absence of the Grey Talon mercenaries to tip the balance in his favor.

A little before midday the two Pathfinders, Maric and Jackson, returned. "There's about fifty of them scattered through the woods, sir."

"Horse or foot?"

"Both. Looks like they plan on tempting us by showing us foot, then riding horse over us once we take the bait."

William considered and said, "We can't play his game." He knew he was outnumbered: his thirty-six men against Bear's fifty or more. "Take a half-dozen men into the

trees," he ordered the Pathfinders. "No matter what you hear, wait, then when you hear Bear's men given the order to leave the woods, strike from behind. Don't linger, but draw off as many of the horsemen as you can." He pointed to the left side of the pass. "That's where we hit first."

"How do we proceed?" asked Hartag.

"Thirty of us ride calmly to there"—he pointed to a large boulder near the bottom of the rise—"and then we charge the archers. We take them out as fast as we can, and force Bear to charge us. Either he's on foot or he's forced to retreat and mount. If Jackson, Maric, and the others can draw off some of his riders, he'll be forced to reorganize on the fly. Either he retreats and we keep following, or he charges us piecemeal and gives us the chance we need to finish him."

"If he retreats?"

"We follow and don't press until it's to our advantage. As much as I want that murderous dog, our mission is successful if we keep him from his goal."

"And that is?" asked the sergeant.

"Widow's Peak above Haldon Head."

The sergeant glanced around. "By my reckoning, sir, that's where he's leading us."

William said, "What?"

Sergeant Hartag said, "Over that rise, to the west, you'll find a trail that cuts over those peaks and leads down into a woodland just east of Haldon Head. It's less than two days' hard ride from here. If we left now, we'd be there at sundown tomorrow."

"Damn," said William. "It's not on any maps I've seen."

The sergeant smiled. "Lots of things don't get put on the royal maps, Will. Best to always ask travelers when you can, or the lads who grew up in the area."

"Thanks. I'll remember that."

"So, what then?"

"Then we don't let him get away." Will looked around. "Surprise is all we have going for us. They outnumber us, so if the fight goes badly, make for the river below."

Hartag said, "The river? Are you daft, Will? Even if we could survive the fall, those rapids below will drown a man quicker than—"

"No. If we start taking a beating, rally the men and head south. If he's bound for Haldon Head, he will not follow. We'll retreat to the portage we passed yesterday, and build rafts. We can get to Haldon Head before Bear if we use the river while he's forced to rest his horses."

"Ah," said the sergeant. "So you weren't suggesting we jump from that cliff over there?"

"Well, if it's that or be killed . . ."

"Last resort, it is," said Hartag.

William shaded his eyes as he surveyed their surroundings once again. "How soon?"

"Maric and the others should be in place now."

"Pass orders. We form up and ride at a trot until I give the command, then charge the left."

"Understood."

William waited while the men formed up, and when everyone was in position, he took his place at the head of the column. Glancing at Sergeant Hartag, he half-whispered, "First time in my life I'm wishing Captain Treggar was here."

Hartag laughed. While Treggar was an above-average officer, he had been a thorn in the side of every other bachelor officer at the garrison since before William's arrival, and while he and William had come to a sort of understanding based on mutual respect, he was still a tough man to be around socially. The sergeant said, "Yes, despite his crust, he's a man for a tight spot."

"Well, as he's not here, it's my neck on the chopping block. Ride!"

The column moved forward at a trot. William felt his stomach tighten and forced himself to breathe slowly. As soon as he heard the twang of a bowstring or sharp clatter of metal upon metal, he knew he would lose his edginess and achieve a state of mental clarity that never failed to surprise him despite the many battles in which he had fought. In the course of a fight, chaos was the rule, and whatever plans he had made always evaporated during the first moment of contact with the enemy. Early on, William had discovered that in battle he could somehow sense how things were going and what needed to be done.

Despite his falling-out with his father over his choice to leave the community of magicians at Stardock and join the army, William knew this was his true calling, the craft for which he was particularly gifted. His horse snorted in excitement, and William sent the animal calming, reassuring thoughts. There were times when his singular ability to speak mentally to animals had its uses, he thought.

When William's column reached the lowest portion of the road, the two decoy riders appeared above the crest. They made a show of riding a few yards over the crest, being "surprised," and turning to flee.

William raised his arm and shouted, "Charge!"

But rather than follow the decoy riders up the hillside, the men turned and charged across the meadow. The meadow rose to a small flat area before quickly dropping off. As William had anticipated, about a dozen archers crouched on the grass, ready to rise up and fire at William's men from behind.

Suddenly they had cavalry upon them and while a few got shots off, most were ridden down and killed before

they could rally. William ordered his men to form a line, then reined in his horse.

The orders were simple. Stand until the enemy showed himself. As expected, Bear's reaction didn't deviate much from what William had predicted. A band of footmen raced from the trees and stood as if ready to charge. William did a quick head-count and saw that eighteen had been placed as bait. That meant over thirty men on horses were waiting just inside the woods. "Steady!" he commanded.

Bear's men stood in line and when it was apparent they weren't going to be charged, they started pounding their shields and taunting the Krondorians.

"Steady!" repeated William.

The two sides stood facing one another for long, tense minutes, and Hartag asked, "Should we raise the stakes, Will?"

"Do so," instructed the young officer.

"Archers!" shouted Hartag, and a half-dozen Krondorians switched weapons. "Draw and fire at will; fire!" he commanded and the Krondorian archers let loose their arrows.

Six of Bear's men fell. By the time the bowmen had nocked and drawn their second set of arrows, the remaining twelve mercenaries had turned and were in full flight. They reached the trees and vanished into the gloom. The bowmen let loose, but there were no targets on the other side by the time the arrows struck.

"Shoulder those bows!" commanded Hartag.

The bowmen did as ordered, then drew swords and hefted their shields.

Silence fell. Bear and his men waited for the Krondorians to charge; but William was determined they would fight in the open.

"What now?" asked one soldier nearby as they waited.

Hartag said, "We see who scratches their ass first, my boy."

William sat and wondered how long they'd have to wait.

Kendaric stood on the reef at Widow's Point, looking at the mast of the ship Solon had previously identified. He said, "Keep an eye out for any more of those creatures who tried to stop us last time."

James pulled his sword and said, "Get on with it."

Kendaric tried his spell again, and again it failed. He turned and said in frustration, "Nothing. Something still blocks it."

Jazhara shrugged. "As we suspected it would. Hilda told us that the Vampire Lord was not the ultimate evil."

"Time is short. We need to find that cave," suggested Solon.

They returned to the beach behind the reef and found the cave with surprising ease. It was shallow, only a dozen yards deep, and the morning light from outside cut through the gloom. At the rear of the cave they found a pattern of stones. James pressed on one, experimentally, and it moved. He listened. There was no sound.

"It's not mechanical," said James.

"Which means it's magic," said Jazhara.

"And that means I don't know how to pick this lock."

"What next?" asked Kendaric.

"We have the hand and the artifact," said Solon.

James unshouldered his backpack and took out the talisman and the vampire hand. He wrapped the fingers of the dead hand around the charm and raised it to the portal. He tried a half-dozen combinations of pressure and patterns, and finally put it down.

"Hilda didn't tell us everything," James observed as he replaced the items in his backpack.

"But she did tell us to return," Jazhara reminded him.

"Let's go ask her," said James. He reshouldered his pack and stood up.

The walk up to the top of the point took less than a half-hour. Hilda was waiting for them when they reached the hut. "Got the vampire, did you?" she asked.

"Yes," said James. "How did you know?"

"It didn't take magic, boy. If you hadn't gotten him, he'd have gotten you and you wouldn't be standing here." She turned and said, "Come in and listen."

They followed, and once inside the old woman said, "Give me the hand."

James opened his backpack and gave her the creature's hand. She took a large iron skillet from a hook above the fire and placed the vampire's hand in it. Thrusting it into the flames, she said, "This is the unpleasant part."

The flesh of the creature's hand shriveled and blackened, then a putrid blue flame sprang up around it. In a few moments, only blackened bones remained.

She pulled the pan out and set it on the stone hearth. "Let it cool for a moment."

"Can you tell us something of what we face?" asked Jazhara.

Hilda looked grim. "That is why I didn't tell you about the need to reduce the creature's hand to ash. That is why I didn't give you the pattern of the lock." She looked from face to face. "You are about to face a great evil and I had to know you are worthy. Your defeat of the Vampire Lord shows that you have the necessary determination and bravery. But you face a far worse foe.

"For many years I've known the Black Pearl Temple

was under the cliffs. I have never been able to see inside, except by my arts. And what little of that I can see is evil beyond imagining."

"What 'great evil' do you speak of?" asked Solon.

"Where to start?" asked Hilda rhetorically. "The sailors who've died offshore, and there have been many, have never known true rest. Instead, their souls are enslaved to whatever dark power rules in the temple. I can feel its presence, like a great eye. It was closed for years, but now it is open and it is watching this area."

James thought about the battle at Sethanon, when the false prophet of the moredhel, Murmandamus, captured the dying energy of his servants to fuel his attempt to seize the Lifestone under Sethanon. "So we can assume that this plan—whatever it is," he added quickly, so as not to inadvertently mention the recovery of the Tear to Hilda, "has been underway for a great deal of time."

"Assuredly," said Hilda. She stood and moved over to her chest, opened it and retrieved an artifact. "But the eye didn't know that it was being watched." She held out a long, slender object, a wand or stick seemingly fashioned from frosty crystal. "I dared used this but once, and I have put it away since in anticipation of this moment. I caution you, what you see may be disturbing."

She waved the object in the air and intoned a spell, and suddenly a rift appeared in the air before them, black, but somehow with the suggestion of color within. Then an image sprang to life, and they could see the interior of a cavern. An ornate mirror hung on a stone wall. They could see a figure approaching, reflected in the mirror before them, and Jazhara and Solon both muttered quiet oaths. The figure was one James had seen before, or rather its like, a long-dead priest or magician, animated by the black arts. He had faced such a one as this under

the ancient abandoned Keshian fortress in the south of the Kingdom months before, and knew that there was a link between what had been discovered there and what was occurring now.

The figure waved a bony hand and the image of a man appeared in the mirror. The man was hawk-beaked, with eyes that seemed to possess a burning black fire. His pate was bald, and he let his long gray hair flow down around his shoulders. He wore clothing of nondescript fashion, looking as much like a merchant as anything else. Then they heard the voice of the undead magician.

"They come," he said.

The man in the mirror asked, "Is the guildsman with them?"

"As planned. They will be sacrificed at dawn. Do you have the amulet?"

"No," answered the man. "My pawn still has it."

The undead creature said, "You held it, but it was the voice of our god that filled it with power. It has chosen another, just as it chose you over me."

The man in the mirror evidenced irritation at that comment. "But he is not worthy of the power."

"Nevertheless, without the amulet, we cannot proceed."

"I will find him. And when I do . . ."

Suddenly the image shifted and there upon the rocks of Widow's Point a gathering of creatures from the lowest depths of hell stood arrayed. James could barely resist the urge to speak, for he recognized some of these creatures, but others were even more fearsome and powerful. Finally, he whispered, "Who is that?"

Hilda said, "A mage of most puissant and dark powers, boy. I know not his name, but I know his handiwork, and

he is allied with forces even darker than those you see in the image. Watch and learn."

The man turned to face the assembled creatures, and James's eyes widened as he saw his own body lying on the rocks, his chest torn open as if by a great hand. Nearby lay Solon and Jazhara. Still alive but bound like a calf to the slaughter, Kendaric struggled against his ropes. A massive amulet with a blood-red ruby hung from a chain around the man's neck. And in one hand he held a long blade of black. In the other he held a huge stone of ice blue. Solon whispered, "The Tear!"

With a single motion, the magician knelt and cut into Kendaric's chest, then plunged his hand into the cavity and ripped out Kendaric's heart. Holding the still-beating organ, he dripped blood over the Tear as the magician turned to show it to the demons. The Tear's color changed from ice blue to blood red and the throng shouted in triumph. Suddenly, the picture vanished.

Hilda said, "Don't let these visions overwhelm you."

Kendaric sounded on the edge of hysteria. "But they're going to kill me! Us!"

Hilda said, "They're going to try, boy. But the future is not set in stone. And evil is most adept at seeing what it wants to see. That's its weakness. It doesn't anticipate the possibility of failure. And now you do; and more, you know the price of your failure."

"Then these visions . . . ?" asked Jazhara.

"Serve as a warning. You now know more about your enemy, and what he plans, than he does about you. He knows you seek to recover the Tear of the Gods—"

Solon's hand dropped to his warhammer. "How do you know this, woman?"

Hilda waved her hand dismissively. "You are not the only ones who know how the universe plays, Ishapian. I

was old before your grandmother was born and if the gods are kind, I'll live until your grandchildren die. But if I do not, I will have been a servant of good in my own way, and that contents me. Perhaps it is my fate only to be here to teach you, and after you succeed or fail, I will end my days. I do not know. But I do know that should you fail, I will not be alone in meeting a terrible ending.

"Always remember, visions are potent magic, but even the best of visions is only an illusion, a reflection of possibilities. You still can change your future. And you must!" She rose. "Now go, for time is short and there is much you must do. That creature you saw is called a liche in the old tongue. He is alive by the most powerful and blackest arts. He will lead you to whatever it is that prevents you from raising the ship. You must find him, destroy him, and end the plague that causes sailors to be entombed in their drowned vessels, servants of darkness to walk the night, and old women to have bad dreams. And you must do so before the other appears, for he is even more dangerous, I judge, and for him to have that amulet . . . well, you saw what he plans."

Hilda stood and walked over to the now-cool skillet. "Brother Solon, the talisman, if you please."

Solon took the pouch from inside his tunic. At Hilda's instruction, he held open the sack as the old woman positioned a small silver funnel over the pouch's mouth and poured the ashen remains of the vampire hand into the bag. Taking the pouch from Solon, Hilda retied the strings, murmured a brief incantation, and shook the bag before handing it back to the monk.

"Now," she said, "you have the key to the temple. To use it, you must make the following pattern at the rockface door." She traced a pattern in the air, a simple weaving of four movements. "Then the door should open."

Jazhara said, "Please show us again."

Hilda repeated the pattern and James and Jazhara both nodded.

Jazhara took the old woman's hand. "You are truly amazing. You are a storehouse of wisdom." She glanced around. "When I first entered this place, I was astonished by your knowledge of medicinal and magical herbs and plants. Now I see you have much more to offer. I will return when we are done and tell you of Stardock. It would profit the world for you to join the community there and share your wisdom."

The old woman smiled, but there was a shadow of doubt in her eyes. "First return, girl. Then we'll talk."

Jazhara nodded and then followed the others outside.

The old woman watched them retreat. When they had at last vanished into the trees, she moved back to the fire, for she felt a chill, in spite of the warmth of the sun.

"Now!" William shouted, pointing to the tree-line. As one, his men spurred on their horses and charged the riders who were thundering out of the woods. It had taken nearly an hour for Bear to run out of patience and now William felt he had a chance, since they were fighting on open ground. He might be outnumbered, but he knew his men were better armed and trained. As the Krondorians charged across the road, William prayed silently that his eight raiders at the rear of Bear's men were distracting them enough to divide their forces.

"Keep the line! Watch your flanks!" shouted Sergeant Hartag, and the Krondorians pointed their swords, keeping their bucklers ready to block, their reins lashing the necks of their mounts, as they urged their horses on.

William's world turned to a blur of images. As it always did in combat, he found his attention focused on

one thing and one thing only: the man before him. A rider came in, rising up in his stirrups, his sword high to come down hard at William's head or shoulders.

In a fluid motion, William leaned to the right, raised his left arm above his head, and let his buckler deflect the blow, while his own short-sword slashed at the rider's right leg. The man cried out and then William was past him.

William didn't know if the man had kept his seat or fallen, and he didn't look to see. For in front of him another rider was charging toward him, and in an instant the first rider was forgotten. This man came in from William's left side, giving the young officer an easy block, but making a counter-strike with the short-sword difficult. For an instant, William appreciated the Keshian's use of the scimitar, with its long curved blade, or even the Eastern Kingdoms' saber for fighting on horseback. A longer, lighter blade would serve better now.

William let the thought slip away as he timed his response. At the last instant, he ducked under the blow, instead of blocking it, and wheeled his horse about, then spurred it on after the rider who had just passed. The man was bearing down on a dismounted Krondorian soldier when William overtook him. A single blow from behind and the man was unseated, tumbling hard to the ground and rolling to his death at the hands of the soldier he had been attempting to ride down just seconds before.

Suddenly William's luck took a turn for the worse. His horse screamed and he felt it going out from under him. Without thinking, he kicked loose of his stirrups and let the horse's momentum throw him from the saddle. He let go of his short-sword, but gripped his buckler tightly. He tucked in his chin and tried to roll on his left shoulder,

using the buckler as a point of leverage, unable to use his shoulders because of the long-sword in the sheath across his back.

The roll brought him to his feet behind a mercenary who was fighting one of William's men. William bashed the man with his buckler, letting the other soldier kill him. In a flash he secured his buckler to his belt, then reached over his shoulder and drew his long-sword, ignoring the sting from his protesting, bruised muscles.

William laid about him with two-handed efficiency. As always, the world contracted around him as he concentrated on staying alive. But through it all he still had a sense of the flow of battle and he knew things were not going well.

A squad of Bear's horsemen emerged from the woods, bloodied and looking over their shoulders. The eight raiders at the rear of the struggle had obviously done some damage, but now the battle was about to swing Bear's way.

William cut down a mercenary before him, and then stood still for a second. He sent one image with all his strength at the charging horses: *Lion!*

He attempted to mimic the loud roar of the great lions of the northern forest and suggested the scent of the hunter on the wind.

The horses went crazy, bucking and snorting, several throwing their riders.

William turned and started hacking at another opponent. Moments later, he realized that the mercenaries were fleeing.

William spun full circle and saw his men either chasing those who were running or converging on the single knot of Bear's men who held fast and continued to fight. William felt a rush of exultation. The battle was on the

verge of being won. And he now knew where his enemy stood. He ran forward, eager to engage Talia's murderer, to dispense vengeance.

As he closed on him, something caused his hair to stand on end, and he recognized that magic was in play. He recalled his experience as a boy at Stardock and instantly knew that his anticipation of victory had been premature.

A Krondorian staggered toward William, blood running down his face. "William!" the man cried as he fell to his knees. "He's immune to our weapons!" Then he collapsed.

William saw other men falling away. Bear's companions had no such immunity, and by the time William reached the conflict, Bear stood alone. Like his namesake creature brought to bay, Bear stood defiantly, surrounded by a circle of six Krondorian soldiers. "You call that an attack!" he shouted in defiance.

Chills ran down William's spine when he saw one of his men strike Bear from behind, only to see the blade of the sword glance off his back as if he wore invisible armor. Bear deftly reversed his sword, and stabbed backward, gutting the soldier. His one good eye was wide with madness. He laughed as if it were all a child's game. "Who's the next to die?" he shouted.

While Bear's sword was reversed, one Krondorian took the opportunity to lunge at him, but the blade glanced off his arm without leaving a mark. Bear didn't even bother to pull his sword from the dying man behind him; he simply kicked the man in front of him in the face, sending him sprawling. "You puny excuse for a soldier! You wouldn't last a day in my company!"

William spied the amulet around Bear's neck. He saw the red stone in the center aglow with a bloody light and

knew that was where Bear's power came from. William grabbed the shoulder of one of his men. "Get to his right side and distract him!" he ordered.

William's plan was desperate, but he could see it was his only choice; somehow he had to get that amulet off Bear's neck.

William looked as if he was hesitating, and at that moment the other soldier struck at Bear. Despite being invulnerable, Bear had human reflexes and he turned toward the blow. At once, William thrust with his long-sword rather than cutting, but instead of trying to skewer the man he attempted to get the point of his sword under the heavy chain around Bear's neck. The links of the chain were large enough that William hoped he could flip the amulet like this, and then take great pleasure in killing him.

Instead, Bear reacted with unnatural speed, reaching out and grabbing the heavy blade. Shock ran up William's arms as the blade froze as if stuck in a vise. With an evil smile and a mocking laugh, Bear looked at William. "Smart one, are you?"

Ignoring the frantic attacks by William's men on his back and side, Bear moved toward William, forcing him to retreat or let go of his sword.

William released the hilt of his sword and dove for Bear's legs. He tackled the man at mid-thigh, and lifted. Bear's own momentum added to William's lift and sent the huge pirate flying over William's shoulders. "Pile on him!" William commanded.

Instantly a half-dozen soldiers obeyed, leaping atop Bear and attempting to pin him to the ground.

"Get that amulet off his neck!" William shouted.

Men clawed frantically at the chain as William ran around to try and seize the amulet. The pile of men heaved, but with unbelievable power Bear rose up, shak-

ing the men from his back as a father might his playful children. He slapped William's hand away and shouted, "Enough!"

With evil glee, Bear reached out with his right hand and crushed the throat of one man near him, while smashing the skull of another with a backhanded blow from his left. William stepped back, his eyes wide with shock as Bear systematically killed every man within reach.

The remaining two men backed away from behind Bear, and William shouted, "Run!"

They needed no second command and turned to flee. Now Bear faced William. He took one step toward the young officer. William feigned a move to his left, but then leapt to his right; Bear countered the move, staying between William and the road.

Suddenly William knew he had no other choice. Bear had been playing with his men the entire time. They had routed his mercenaries, but he himself was invulnerable, and he had lured them close enough to kill as many as possible with his bare hands.

William turned and ran straight for the cliffs. Bear hesitated, then gave chase. William didn't look behind him, for he knew even a half-step could be the difference between escape and death. A leap off the cliffs would give him a chance, albeit a very slim one.

Reaching the edge of the cliffs William resisted the urge to slow and look down. Trusting to blind chance, he ran off the cliffs, kicking out as far out as possible, hoping he could hit the deepest part of the river below, a fall of nearly one hundred feet, for otherwise the rocks would surely kill him.

The fall seemed to last forever, with Bear's curses ringing in his ears. Then William struck the water and crashed into darkness.

Sixteen

◆

Temple

ames hesitated.

He closed his eyes for a moment, then nodded to himself. The pattern he had discovered in the rock face matched with what he remembered Hilda telling him. He took the ash-covered artifact and touched each plate in sequence, then waited.

They felt a low rumbling through the soles of their feet, then a section of the wall moved back, and slid to the left. James took out a torch and lit it.

They moved slowly into a dark entrance hall. It appeared to be carved out of the stones of the cliff, a rough tunnel somewhat resembling an abandoned mineshaft.

"Wait," James said as they went through. He watched the door, silently counting. After a little more than one minute, it slid shut. He examined the wall around the door and found the release mechanism. He tripped it and the door slid open. Then he motioned for them to continue to wait and counted again. At approximately the same interval as before, it shut. James knelt and put the artifact back into his pack. "Just in case there's another lock down the passage."

Kendaric said, "Well, it's good to know we can get through there in a hurry without it, if need be."

"Agreed," said Solon.

They started to walk slowly down the corridor, two abreast. James and Jazhara were in the lead, Solon and Kendaric close behind them. After traveling a hundred yards, Solon said, "Hold a moment." He pointed to a spot on the wall and said to James, "Hold your torch there."

James did so and Solon inspected the wall.

"This tunnel is ancient," he said. "Centuries old. It was carved out of the rock long before the Kingdom came to these shores."

"How do you know?" asked Kendaric.

"You spend your boyhood with dwarven lads, you pick up a thing or two about mining."

"But these tracks aren't old," James said as he turned his attention to the ground beneath them.

Kendaric looked down. "What tracks?"

James pointed to odd bits of sand and mud at various intervals. "There's no dust, but these bits are fresh, no doubt from boots that have been past here recently." He peered into the darkness ahead. "Keep alert."

Kendaric said, "As if you need to tell us, Squire."

They proceeded slowly, and moved deeper into the cliffs below Widow's Point.

They walked in tense silence for ten minutes until they reached a portal that opened into a large chamber that they entered with caution. The firelight from James's torch cast eerie shadows on the rough-hewn rock walls. Solon's hand flew reflexively to the hilt of his warhammer when he spied the first skeleton. Nine niches had been carved into the walls at intervals around the chamber. In each stood a skeleton wearing an ornate suit of armor; all had weapons and shields at their sides. A complex set of symbols had been carved into the stone floor,

just deep enough to be seen in the flickering torchlight, without fully revealing their pattern.

As best as James could judge, the chamber was nearly thirty feet in height, a vast half-circle dominated by the far wall. As they approached the wall, its bas-relief design was revealed.

"Gods!" Kendaric whispered.

Creatures of nightmare were depicted in myriad ways, many of them involved with humans, frequently being sacrificed. The depravity of the scenes was abundantly clear.

Solon said, "Hike yer torch up, laddie!" in the thickest brogue they'd heard so far.

James lifted his torch to throw more illumination as they neared the wall.

"Abide!" instructed Solon, as he reached out toward Jazhara. "Lass, another brand! Hurry!" Jazhara unwrapped a torch and handed it to the monk, who lit it from the one James held. He handed it to Kendaric and said, "Stand ye over there!" pointing to the left.

"What?"

"Ah said, stand over there, y' stone-crowned loon."

Solon took another pair of torches from Jazhara and lit them. He gave a torch to Jazhara, and instructed her to stand over to the right. He raised a torch himself and walked forward. As he did so, the entire panorama of the carvings was revealed.

"By the Holy Saints and Heroes of Ishap," he whispered.

"What is it?" asked James.

"Ya see the center, lad?" Solon pointed to a blank area that looked like a round window, around which the most horrible of the creatures knelt in worship.

"Yes," James said, "it's empty."

"Nay, 'tis not empty, m'friend. It's occupied by somethin' ye canna see."

Solon paced back and forth along the wall, stopping occasionally to study closely one detail or another. Finally, he wedged his torch into a pile of rocks, and motioned to the others that they could lower their arms.

"What is this all about?" asked Kendaric.

Solon fixed each of his companions in turn with an unsmiling stare. "You must all remember what I say now. Engrave it upon your memories as you have nothing else in your lives." He turned and pointed to the wall. "This wall tells the history of a very cruel time." He stopped, and took a deep breath. "It is taught in the Temple that after the Chaos Wars, a period of great darkness descended upon parts of the world, as the forces of good and evil fought for a balance. Places like this have been found before, homes to demons and other ill-natured creatures, beings not of this world which must be banished whenever they are encountered.

"This wall tells a story. The details are not important. What *is* important, and what must be conveyed to my temple, is the news of this place, the very fact of its existence. No matter what else occurs, there are two things that we absolutely must do.

"First, we must return to tell my order so that they can cleanse it and seal it for all time. And, whatever else you may forget, you must remember to describe what you call the 'empty window,' and to tell the High Priest that I was certain it was the work of those who follow the Nameless."

"The Nameless?" asked Kendaric. "Who is that?"

"If fate is kind to you, lad," said Solon, "you will never know." He glanced around. "Though I fear that fate is being anything but kind to us now."

"You said there were two things," observed James. "What's the other?"

"That we must not fail in fetching home the Tear of the

Gods. For not only would its loss prove crippling to us, I now know why it is being sought and by whom."

"Why?" asked Jazhara.

Pointing to the blank space on the wall, Solon said, "To open a portal much like that one, and should that portal ever be opened, woe beyond imagining will fall upon us. No human, elf, or dwarf—not even the Dark Brothers, goblins, or trolls—nothing mortal will be able to withstand it. The mightiest of priests and magicians will be swept away like chaff before the wind. Even the lesser gods will tremble." He pointed to the carvings showing inhuman creatures eating or raping humans and added, "And such would be the fate of the survivors. We would be as cattle, raised for their appetites."

Kendaric's face drained of color.

James said, "You faint again and I'll leave you here."

Kendaric took a deep breath and said, "I'll be all right. Let's just get on with this and find whatever is blocking my magic."

They moved to a large pair of closed doors to their left. "They're locked," James said as he inspected them, and pointed to a pattern of jewels set in the door.

"Can you open it?" asked Kendaric.

"I can try," said James. He inspected the device then said, "It's a . . . magical lock, I think." He swore. "Those are always the worst."

"Why?" asked Kendaric.

"Because," said James, "mechanical locks only stick poison needles in your thumb or blow up with a fireball if you make a mistake. I once had to open one that shot a nasty blade out that would cut your hand off if you didn't move it in time, but magic locks can do . . . anything."

Kendaric stepped back. "Are you sure you want to be . . . fiddling with this?"

"I'm open to other suggestions," said James impatiently. He studied the lock closely. "There are six gems. And six holes with a faint color around them. Something that looks like a ruby, and a red hole. A green gem and a green hole." He leaned in toward the doors, almost putting his nose to the lock. "There are tiny mirrors around the edge." He sat back on his heels. He touched a small white gem in the middle. Suddenly light shot out in six spokes. "Oh, damn!" he said. He began frantically to move the tiny mirrors around the edge of the circular lock.

"What is it?" asked Kendaric.

Jazhara said, "I think James has to move each gem and mirror so that the light moves through the gem, changes color, and is reflected into the right hole."

James said nothing, as he desperately tried to do just that.

"What's the problem?"

Jazhara said, "Given James's concentration on the problem, I suspect there may be a limit on how much time one can spend on it."

James was about to move the sixth mirror-gem combination when suddenly the light went out.

Nothing happened.

Then from behind them came a sound.

Solon had his warhammer raised and James his sword out by the time they turned.

Within all nine niches, the skeletal warriors were picking up their weapons and shields and stepping down to the floor.

"This is bad," Kendaric whispered.

William lay in darkness.

His last memory had been of striking the water and being swept along by the raging currents, then hitting his head against a rock.

He stood up and found himself dry. He looked at his hands and down at his body and saw no wound. He tentatively touched his face and head and felt no injury. No soreness or ache, not even a cut or bruise.

For a moment he wondered if he was dead and was somewhere inside Lims-Kragma's Hall.

"William!"

He spun and found that he was standing inside the Rainbow Parrot. Before him, Bear held Talia by the throat, shaking her as a terrier shakes a rat. The huge man tossed her aside and she slammed hard against the wall. Her attacker hurried off through the door leading to the rear of the inn.

William attempted to move toward the girl, but something held his feet in place. *I'm dreaming,* he thought.

A pillar of flame erupted around Talia and she rose up from the floor screaming in agony. Creatures of flame, demons with animal heads, appeared and surrounded Talia's flame-prison. "William!" she screamed.

Suddenly he found he could move. He was wearing armor and carrying a sword of blinding light. He struck the first demon from behind and it shrieked in pain.

All the creatures turned as one and began to move in concert against William, who stood resolute, refusing to concede a foot to them, and laid about with his sword. But for each one he cut, another took its place. Hot talons struck at his shield and armor. He felt pain and heat, yet the armor remained intact. He found that his arm was tiring and his legs were growing shaky, but he continued to stand fast and deal out injury with every thrust.

After a seemingly endless time, his lungs were fit to burst and he had to will each blow as if commanding an unwilling servant; his arms and legs were so reluctant to

obey him. Yet the demons continued to press him, and an increasing number of their blows were getting through.

Still he could see no damage to his armor and no wounds were visible on his body, though he could still feel each talon and fang, feel the searing heat of their touch on his flesh. They bore him back and he felt despair engulf him, but each time he thought it impossible to continue, Talia's pleading voice would reach him: "William! Save me! William, help me!"

He raised his arm again, the pain threatening to overwhelm him, and unleashed another blow.

Slowly the tide turned. A demon fell, and no other appeared. He turned his pain-racked body to attack the next creature about its head and shoulders till it was gone.

As each creature fell, renewed hope rose up within William and he drove himself onward. Depths of strength he did not realize existed within him were plumbed, and he struck, again and again.

Then suddenly the last demon was gone. He stumbled, barely able to put one foot before the other. Somehow, he reached the tower of flame trapping Talia. She stood there calmly, smiling at him.

His parched lips parted and in a voice as dry as sand he said, "Talia?"

When he reached out to touch the flames, they vanished. The girl he loved hung suspended in the air and her smile was radiant.

Softly, William said, "We did it, Talia. It's over."

A rumble arose around them and the Rainbow Parrot's taproom shattered like a mirror, the shards falling away into nothing. They stood facing one another in a featureless black void.

William reached out to touch Talia, but before his hand

could reach her cheek, a voice boomed out: "No, son of conDoin. Though you have freed Talia's soul from being consumed, your part in this has only begun."

Talia looked at William and her lips were motionless, but he could still hear her dying declaration in his mind.

"I swear by Kahooli I will have my vengeance!"

The deep voice came again: "I am Kahooli, God of Vengeance, and your dedication calls to me. Because of your dedication I will answer this woman's dying prayer. You will not be alone in what lies ahead of you."

Talia began to fade before his eyes. William reached for her, but his fingers passed through her image, as if through smoke.

Weeping, he cried, "Talia, please stay!"

Talia's eyes also shed tears as she spoke in a voice like a whispering breeze. "Say good-bye to me, please . . ."

At the last instant before she became insubstantial, William whispered, "Good-bye, my love."

Suddenly, his body was racked with agony and his lungs burned as if on fire. He rolled over, retching as water spilled from his lungs. Coughing, he felt strong hands help him to sit upright.

He blinked and cleared his vision. He was drenched in water, wearing the armor he had worn when facing Bear, not the mystical plate he had worn when facing the demons.

A face swam before him, slowly coming into focus. A hawk-beaked man with intense eyes regarded him.

After a moment, William said, "I know you!"

"Yes, my young friend," said the man, sitting back on his heels upon the riverbank, watching William. "You are that young officer I met some weeks ago, escorting some dignitary from a foreign land on a hunt, if I recall. My name is Sidi.

"I saw you floating in the river, and since it is unusual to see a lad swimming in armor, I deduced you were in some need of aid. It appears that I was correct."

Glancing around, William asked, "Where am I?"

"On the banks of the river, obviously." Pointing downstream, Sidi added, "That ways lies a town called Haldon Head and beyond it, the sea."

William looked around again. They were in a stretch of woodlands, and there was little to be seen nearby save trees. "What were you doing here?"

"I was looking for someone."

"Who?"

"A murderous butcher, one who goes by the name of Bear."

William felt the fuzziness in his head start to clear. "It's good you didn't find him, then. I came upon him with thirty Krondorian regulars and he routed us all by himself."

"The amulet," said Sidi. He nodded to himself. At last, he said, "Come, we'll talk as we walk."

"You know of the amulet?" asked William.

"As I told you when last we met, I am a trader, a trafficker in rare and valuable objects as well as more mundane goods. That amulet is a particularly ancient and valuable artifact. Unfortunately, besides offering the wearer significant power, it also has a tendency to drive him mad. It was intended to be kept in the possession of a magician of great art and intelligence, not a brute like Bear."

"How did he come by it?"

Sidi glanced sidelong at William. "How he got it is immaterial. How we're going to get it back is the question."

"We?"

"As you observed, if thirty-one young soldiers could not best Bear, how could I, a lone old man, hope to do

so?" Then he smiled. "But you and I together . . ." He let the sentence trail off.

" 'You will not be alone in what lies ahead of you,' he said," William muttered.

"What?"

William looked at him. "I think I was told that you would help me." William glanced down at himself, then over at his companion. "Given I'm without weapons—"

"That amulet is just as impervious to weapons as it is to magic, so any attack upon Bear must be by misdirection and stealth. But I have resources, my young friend. Just get me close to Bear and I'll help you retrieve the amulet. You take him away to justice and I'll return the bauble to its rightful owner."

"I don't know if I can promise that, sir," William said. "Everything we recover will have to be sent to Krondor for the Prince's examination. If you have a claim on the item, and the Prince judges it not to be a threat to his domain, then you may petition for its return."

Sidi smiled. "That's a matter for later consideration. Our first objective is to get it from Bear. Once we have removed him from the picture, then we can discuss the final disposition of the amulet. Come, we must hurry. Time grows short and Bear will almost certainly reach Haldon Head before we do."

William shook his head to clear it. There was something he felt he must ask this man, but he couldn't quite put his finger on what it was. But whatever else, he was right about one thing: Bear must be stopped and to do so would require removing the amulet from him.

Jazhara lowered her staff and held up her hand. A ball of crimson light sprang from her palm and played on the

closest skeleton-warrior as if from a lantern. The creature hesitated, then began to tremble.

Solon held up his warhammer high with one hand, and with the other inscribed a pattern in the air while he cast an incantation. Two of the warriors hesitated, then turned as if to put as much distance as possible between them and the monk.

There were still six figures approaching.

Solon charged, lashing out with his warhammer. The first warrior he attacked deftly blocked with his shield. His blow rang out and the cavern echoed with the sound. The battle was joined.

The skeleton Jazhara had cast a spell upon lay on the floor twitching and shivering. She turned her attention to the rest coming closer. Shifting her staff, she lashed out, but with unexpected speed the skeletal warrior blocked the blow with his shield and slashed at her with a long curved sword. She barely had time to dodge backward. Suddenly she realized that the wall was only a few feet behind her. Getting pinned there would be a trap. So she began to slip to her right, attempting to gain herself as much room in which to maneuver as possible.

Kendaric tried to be resolute, but as soon as the skeleton-warrior facing him struck out, he fell to the floor and rolled. His foot caught the warrior's ankle and the creature lost its balance, toppling over. Kendaric lashed out with his boot and it felt as if he had struck iron, but he was rewarded with a cracking sound.

He rolled to his feet as another warrior slashed down and he barely avoided being decapitated. Trying to run, he slammed into another warrior, knocking it backward. He rebounded off it and again fell to the floor. This time he fell across the back of the legs of the creature facing Solon.

The skeleton-warrior fell forward and Solon smashed down with his hammer, shattering its skull. The skeleton twitched and was still; then its bones fell apart.

Kendaric turned and scrambled forward on his knees, over the now-loose bones. Solon looked on in amusement. He said, "You're an ambulatory disaster disguised as a man, but at least this time you're causin' them more annoyance than us." He bashed another skeleton-warrior with his warhammer, sending it backward, then reached down and hauled Kendaric to his feet by the collar. "Now, go see if you can trip up another one without getting yourself killed. That's a good lad." He gave Kendaric a push and smashed at the shield of the nearest warrior.

James dueled with another spectral creature and found it no match for his swordsmanship. But the problem was inflicting damage. His rapier would slide off the bones and occasionally nick them, but there was nothing to hit. He was bound to tire eventually, and then the creature would surely injure him.

James glanced over and saw that Jazhara had successfully gotten herself some distance from the foe she faced, while another creature crept up on her from behind.

"Look out behind you!" he called to her.

She turned and ducked as a sword slashed through the air, and, with a deft blow, got her staff between the warrior's feet. The thing went to the floor literally with a bone-rattling crash.

James had an idea. "Get them on the floor!" he shouted. "Trip them!"

Jazhara reversed her staff one more time and tangled the feet of the creature that had first been stalking her, sending it clattering to the floor. James feigned high, then went low. He dove between the creature's legs, grabbing

them one in each hand, then stood up, toppling the creature behind him. Instantly, he turned and leapt into the air, landing on the creature's skull with all his weight. A shock ran up his legs as if he had jumped upon hard rock, but he heard a satisfying crunch and felt the bones break beneath his boots.

Kendaric scrambled like a crab, ducking under blows and rolling from side to side. Jazhara followed James's example and crushed the skull of one warrior with her staff while the second sought to regain its feet.

James hurried to where Jazhara stood and kicked at the rear of the creature's legs, and she brought her staff down with a savage blow. James looked around the chamber. "Three down."

"Four," she said, as Solon crushed the skull of another warrior.

"Let's work together!" James shouted.

"How?" Kendaric cried as he ducked under another savage sword-blow, blindly waving his own weapon above his head as if it would somehow dissuade the creature's attack. He scrambled away from the warrior that was pressing him, right into the path of another. With a terrified squeak of alarm he jumped to his feet, and fell backward into a third, knocking it down before Solon.

Jazhara tripped another, enabling James to smash its skull, while Solon finished the one that Kendaric had tripped.

Soon it was quiet, and the only skeletal warriors left were the two still trying to escape from Solon's magic. Jazhara dispatched them with her crimson flames, and at last they had a chance to catch their breath.

"My gods!" Kendaric said. "That was too much. What more is there to expect?"

"Worse," said James, turning his attention back to the

lock. "Almost certainly, there will be worse." He studied the arrangement of gems, mirrors, and holes, and said, "A moment of quiet, please."

He pressed the center of the lock and the light erupted. With deft precision, he moved the gems and mirrors swiftly into place. When the last, a topaz-like gem, threw a yellow light into a yellow hole, they heard a click followed by deep rumbling, and the doors swung wide.

The area before them was vast, and they could smell sea salt as the scent of water reached them. Moving forward, they saw two immense pools, providing narrow walkways on either side or between the two.

"We have to go there?" asked Kendaric.

"You see another route, laddie?" asked Solon.

James hesitated, then said, "Wait."

He took off his pack and unbuckled it, removing the artifact that had got them through the outside door.

"I think it might be wise to have this handy."

They set off down the center walkway and when they reached a point halfway between the doors and a distant wall, two pairs of enormous tentacles rose up from the water on either side of them. Kendaric let out a yelp of terror, but James merely held the artifact high above his head.

The tentacles stood poised, as if ready to strike. They quivered in anticipation, but they didn't attack.

Jazhara whispered, "How did you know?"

"I didn't," James replied. "I guessed."

Solon looked over his shoulder as they moved out of striking range of the tentacles, which then slipped back down into the brine. "Good thing, lad. Those would crush us like bugs."

James said nothing, leading them deeper into the darkness.

Seventeen

◆

Black Pearl

Ⓚendaric pointed.

"What is that?"

Solon whispered, "It looks like a temple, albeit more of a pit of black madness, and unless I'm mistaken these are archives."

They were entering another vast chamber, full of floor-to-ceiling shelves stacked with rolled parchments and ancient leather-bound tomes. Above them, a series of suspended walkways vanished into the gloom. Light from an occasional torch broke the darkness of the room, while sconces in the wall and torch-brackets on the shelves themselves remained empty. James observed, "If they used it, it would be better lit. Those torches are placed only to help people navigate through this vault."

They were warned of someone's approach by the sound of boots upon stone, and James led them away from the lights, behind some shelves. Peeking between scrolls piled upon the shelves, they saw a small company of goblins hurry by.

After the goblins had vanished, James said, "Well, now we know those raiders were not just coming down from the mountains."

"What are goblins doing here?" asked Kendaric.

"Establishing a base, I'll wager," said Solon. "This temple is huge and must have barracks. The goblins must be there."

James waited for a moment, and said, "What I don't understand is how all the recent troubles in Krondor fit in with this, now?"

"Maybe they don't," observed Jazhara. "From what you told me, there is a connection between this Crawler and his plans to take over the underground in Krondor, and whoever is behind this attempt to steal the Tear of the Gods, but it may be they are partial allies, nothing more."

James said, "I wonder if I'll ever plumb the depths of this mystery." He looked ahead into the gloom. "Come along," he whispered.

They moved cautiously and at one point paused for James to get his bearings. Two lights showed in opposition to one another, at right angles to the path of their march, and James tried to establish his bearings, knowing that what they sought was almost certain to be in the deepest part of the temple, far below the surface of the earth and sea.

Jazhara read the spine of a text and whispered, "Merciful gods above!"

"What?" asked Solon.

Pointing to a tome, she said, "That text is Keshian, but ancient. If I read it correctly, this is a most powerful, black volume on necromancy."

James said, "That fits with everything else we've seen so far."

Kendaric said, "I'm just a poor wrecker. What is it about necromancy that so disturbs the rest of you priests and magicians?"

It was Solon who answered. "There is a basic order to the universe, and there are limits to power, or at least there should be. Those who deal in the essences of life and who flout death violate the most fundamental tenets of that order. Or are you too thick ta' understand that?"

"I was just asking," said Kendaric, his voice approaching a whine. He touched the binding and said, "Nice cover."

Jazhara said, "It's human skin."

Kendaric pulled his hand away as if he had touched a hot iron.

"Come on," said James. They moved deeper into the temple.

Time passed and they continued to wend their way through the stone halls. Several times they paused while James scouted ahead. They heard others in the vast temple, and at times were forced to hide, but they managed to avoid contact and kept moving.

An hour after entering the temple, they reached a vast, long hall with a gigantic statue at the far end, a heroic figure seated upon a throne. When they reached the base of the statue, they stared up. It rose two stories into the air above them.

The figure was apparently human, with broad shoulders and powerful arms as it sat there in a position of repose. Sandaled feet of carved stone poked out from under the hem of a floor-length robe.

"Look," said Kendaric. "Look at the face." The entire face of the statue had been chipped away.

"Why has it been defaced like that?"

Jazhara spoke softly. "As a ward against the evil that it represents."

"Who is it?" asked Kendaric. "Which god?"

Solon put a hand gently upon Kendaric's shoulder. "You will never know, and for that give thanks."

James motioned for them to continue.

James stopped and smelled the air. He held up his hand.

"What?" whispered Kendaric.

Solon moved forward and whispered, "Can't you smell it?"

"I can smell something," said Kendaric. "What is it?"

"Goblins," said James.

He held up his hand to indicate that they should stay put, then he knelt and duckwalked toward an open door. He moved smoothly onto his stomach for the final four feet and wriggled forward to peer into the room.

Then he turned, crawling backward, and leapt to his feet in a single fluid motion. As he came toward them, he drew his sword. "That patrol we saw had most of them; there are two sleeping on the beds and two eating something out of a pot at the far end," he said softly.

"I can take care of the ones who are eating without a sound," said Jazhara.

"Good," replied James. "I'll silence the other two."

Jazhara closed her eyes and James felt the hair on his arms rising again, in response to her magic. She remained motionless for a good two minutes, then opened her eyes. "I'm ready."

Kendaric said, "What was that?"

"A slow cast. The spell is almost done. I need only to make a final incantation and it goes off. Very useful for accuracy. Not very useful if you're in a hurry."

"Ah," he said as if he understood. But it was clear that he didn't.

James motioned her forward. They reached the door and she stepped through. She spoke her phrase aloud.

One goblin heard the first words and his head came up. He started to rise, but Jazhara's spell discharged and he was paralyzed, trapped like an insect in amber. His companion sat back on his haunches, his bowl in his lap and his hand halfway to his mouth.

They both remained motionless, caught in a sheer energy field of scintillating white, a field like gauze flecked with diamond dust.

James moved purposefully to the bunks where the two sleeping goblins lay, and quickly cut their throats. He then did the same to the two frozen goblins. To his companions he said, "We must hurry. That patrol will almost certainly be back before the end of the day."

They hurried to the far end of the barracks room and James opened a door. Beyond it, a kitchen stood empty, with a bubbling cauldron before a fire.

Kendaric went pale and had to clutch the doorjamb while Jazhara's face also drained of color. On the butcher's block rested the remains of what had once been a human torso. A head lay cast aside in the corner, along with a hand and foot.

"Mother of gods!" whispered Solon.

James was speechless. He merely motioned for them to follow him. Leaving the kitchen, they moved down a short, dark passage, and again James halted.

"Smell that?"

"Goblins?" asked Kendaric.

"Sweat and filth," answered Jazhara.

They turned into a long hallway, carved into the rock. They could see light at the other end. They crept down the passage until they could clearly identify what lay ahead of them, then James held up his hand and moved forward

alone. He reached an open doorway, and glanced around the room beyond it, then motioned the others forward. The room was square, with two passages crossing in the middle between four huge cages. A few dozen humans were packed in each cage. Most appeared to be sailors, though a few looked to be farmers or townspeople.

One of the prisoners looked up and elbowed the man next to him as James's party moved into sight. They both leapt forward and gripped the bars.

One man whispered, "Thank Dala that you've come!"

James looked around the cages. Other prisoners started to spread the word and soon the bars were packed with eager people.

James held up his hands for silence. He knelt and inspected the locks, then asked, "Who has the key?"

"We don't know his name," said the man closest to the cage door. "He's the leader of the goblins. We call him Jailer."

"Probably out leading that patrol we saw earlier," said Solon.

James took off his backpack. He rummaged around and pulled out a small pouch in which he had several picks. He selected one and tested the lock with it.

"Interesting," observed Jazhara.

James didn't take his eyes off the lock as he said, "Old habits."

There was a click and the door opened. "Wait," commanded James, "until I get the others."

After a few more minutes, all four cages were open.

"Do you know the way out?" asked Jazhara.

"Yes, ma'am," said a sailor. "We're laborers here and when they don't slaughter one of us for food, they have us cleaning up this place. It looks like they're getting it ready for the arrival of more goblins."

"Can you find weapons?"

"There's a barracks nearby, with a weapons room, but there are goblins in there," said a thin man.

"Only four," answered James, "and they're dead."

The men muttered excitedly.

James was silent for a minute, then said, "Would you do us a service?"

The thin man said, "They were going to eat us if you didn't come. They killed one of us each day. Of course we will. What would you have us do?"

"Wait here—I'll leave the doors unlocked, but keep them closed—in case someone comes by before we've finished our mission. If you hear any sounds of fighting, run to the barracks room and get weapons, then fight your way out. If you don't hear anything in, say, an hour's time, you're free to go. Is that agreeable?"

The man looked around and saw several others nod. "It is," he said.

"Good," said James. The men returned to their cages. The doors were shut and one man sat down and began a slow rhythmic count, to track the time till the hour was up.

As they left the slave pens, James said, "See you in Haldon Head. There should be a Kingdom garrison there by now. If there is and we're not back, tell them what you've seen here."

"I will." The thin man looked at James and asked, "Where do you go now?"

"To the heart of this black place," answered Solon.

"Then be wary of the leader," replied the prisoner.

"You've seen him?"

"Yes," the thin man whispered.

"What did he look like?"

"I suppose he was a man, once, but now . . . he is an undead . . . thing! He's all rotten and decayed, wearing

tattered robes that stink to heaven, and he's guarded by creatures I can't even name. We didn't see him often; he stays in the lower levels and few of us are taken there, and only infrequently."

"May the gods be with you," said James.

The man nodded.

James led his companions off down another dark hallway.

They went down a stairway they had passed a few minutes earlier that led to a series of tunnels. Several times James had paused and decided that the best course of action was to continue along the main passageway that ran from the base of the stairs, on the assumption that the shortest course would take them to the heart of the temple, and all other passages led off to other areas. At least he hoped that would prove to be true.

Before long they came to an opening in a stone wall and they passed through it. On the other side they discovered what could only be called a gallery—a huge room, all four walls of which contained niches every few feet. Instead of containing skeletal warriors, these niches held statues. Some depicted humans, but many did not, and James didn't recognize all the races memorialized in stone.

Heroic statues—of figures garbed in warrior dress or robes—stood atop pedestals placed at regular intervals around the floor. There was a consistent look of evil to all of them.

At the far side of the hall was a pair of doors. James tested the latch and it clicked open. He pushed slightly and peeked through the crack. "This is it," he whispered.

He pushed aside the door to reveal yet another square room. Three walls were lined with human skulls and the fourth was tiled with a huge mosaic depicting the same

tableaux as the bas-reliefs they had seen at the entrance to the temple. The "empty window" dominated the center of the images as it had before.

Four huge columns supported the ceiling, carved stone showing human skulls entangled by tentacles. The floor was inscribed with arcane runes.

In the middle of the floor rested a giant altar, caked with blood so ancient it was black, and inches thick. Above this sacrificial surface rested a giant clawed hand, apparently made of silver or platinum. Clutched in its fingers was a giant black pearl, twice the size of a man's head. Its surface shimmered with mystical energy. Faint colors radiated across the surface, like the dark rainbow of oil on water.

Jazhara said, "Yes, this is indeed 'it.' "

She hurried to the object. "This is the source of the mystic energy that blocks your spell, Kendaric. I am certain of it."

"Let's destroy it and be on our way," said Solon, unlimbering his warhammer.

"That would be imprudent," said a dry voice emanating from the shadows.

A figure emerged from a dark alcove. It was clothed in tattered robes, and James instantly recognized the figure from the vision. Jazhara reacted instantly, lowering her staff and unleashing a bolt of crimson energy.

The creature waved his hand and the energy deflected away from him, so that it struck the wall, where it crackled and spread before diffusing. It left smoking char where it had hit.

"Foolish woman," he whispered, his voice an ancient wind that sang with evil. "Leave me the guildsman and you may leave with your pitiful lives. I have need of his talents. Resist and you die."

Kendaric stepped behind Solon without a thought. "Me?" James said, "No."

The creature then pointed at them and ordered, "Kill them!"

From doors at each end of the room two giant figures appeared. Each was a skeleton-warrior similar in appearance to the others they had fought earlier, but these were taller again by half. Nearly nine feet tall from foot to helm, each of the giant creatures also possessed four arms and held a long, curved blade. Their heads were covered with wide flaring helms of crimson trimmed with gold.

"This isn't good," said Kendaric. "No, not at all."

Solon reached behind him and grabbed Kendaric by the sleeve, pulling him aside. "Try not to get in the way, that's a good lad."

With an unexpected burst of speed, the monk charged, his warhammer held high above his head and cried, "Ishap give me strength!"

The skeletal warrior closest to Solon hesitated for only an instant before its swords became a blur of motion. With surprising deftness, Solon's hammer took blow after blow as he blocked the warrior's attack. Then he knelt and delivered a crushing blow to the skeleton-warrior's left foot. An audible crack filled the room as the bones of the creature's big toe shattered.

Blades flashed as the silent creature registered no pain or reaction to the damage, and Solon barely escaped with his head. His arms and shoulders bore several cuts and he was forced to retreat and concentrate on defending himself.

James said to Jazhara, "Help him out. I'll see if I can distract the other one."

James hurried to face the creature approaching from

the far door while Jazhara lowered her staff and unleashed a spell against the warrior attacking Solon. The
spell that had proved effective in the first chamber simply
bathed the creature in scintillating pale blue light for a
moment before winking out. Solon used the creature's
momentary pause as an opportunity to dart in, smash at
the same foot as before, then retreat quickly.

The creature teetered slightly when it advanced.

James charged the second creature and tried to gauge
the pattern of its blade strokes. If there was one, it wasn't
apparent, so he was reluctant to get too close. Still, he had
to keep the thing distracted if they were to have any
chance of survival. Together, the creatures would overwhelm them in a matter of minutes.

James started counting silently, and as the first blow
from the creature's sword descended upon his head, he
recognized the pattern. Up went James's blade, deflecting
the first blow, then he blocked to the right, then down to
the right, then across to the left side of his body, turning
slightly. The hall rang with the sound of steel on steel,
and James knew that he could only block this creature's
attacks for a minute or two at the most. He tried not to
think about what would happen if the creature changed
the pattern of its blows.

Jazhara attempted another spell and it also failed. So
she leapt forward with her staff above her head, as if trying to block the multiple sword-blows. At the last second, she let her right hand slide across to her left,
leaving her holding the staff like a long club. She
smashed down with all her strength on the same foot
Solon had damaged, and was rewarded by the sound of
cracking bone.

She barely escaped with her head, and took a long
nasty cut to her left shoulder. Blood flowed as she dodged

to the side and then Solon was back, attacking the same foot.

The creature slashed and Solon took the point of a blade on his breastplate. The armor held, but the force of the blow sent him sprawling. The creature advanced and it was clear the monk would not regain his feet in time to survive.

Kendaric watched in mute horror as the creature advanced on the fallen monk. Jazhara tried to flank the skeleton and was rebuffed with a sidelong thrust of a blade, then the creature bore down on Solon.

Kendaric threw himself away from the wall where he was crouching. He leapt in front of Solon, frantically slashing in all directions with his blade.

"No!" shouted the liche. "Don't kill him!"

The creature hesitated, and Solon rolled over, got to his knees, and rose up, warhammer held with both hands above his head. He smashed down with as much might as he could muster and shattered the creature's left foot.

As Kendaric and Solon backed away, the creature attempted to advance. It teetered and then fell forward, crashing into the floor at Solon's feet. Kendaric hesitated only for a second, then he reached down and grabbed the base of the creature's ornate helm. He ripped the helm away just as Solon's hammer again smashed down with a force driven by desperation.

A dry crack filled the hall, and the creature's skull shattered. The skeleton went limp and rattled against the stone floor.

Jazhara was already approaching the creature with which James was engaged. The former thief declared, "I could use some help over here." He was drenched in perspiration and his arms were heavy with fatigue, but he was successfully blocking the warrior's blows.

Solon turned to the liche. "We don't have time to try to take down the other warrior," he said to Kendaric.

Kendaric nodded, gripping his sword.

They advanced upon the dead magician, who held up his hand. A blast of white energy shot toward Solon, who barely had time to dodge aside. Kendaric ran forward and impaled the creature on his sword point.

The liche looked down contemptuously. "You can't destroy me, boy," it said as its bony hand shot out and grabbed Kendaric's arm. "And now I have you!"

"Solon!" shouted the wrecker despairingly. "He won't die!"

Jazhara was trying to distract the second skeletal warrior in order to give James a reprieve. She turned and shouted, "He must have placed his soul in a vessel!"

Solon hesitated, then shouted, "Where?"

Jazhara looked wildly around the room. "It could be anywhere. It could be in another room or even . . . the pearl!"

Solon moved with purpose toward the pearl on the altar.

"No!" shouted the liche.

Solon raised his hammer and struck down, landing a powerful blow on the pearl. The black surface swam with angry energies, tiny lines of hot white fire spreading out in a latticework pattern across its skin. He struck again, and the pearl emitted a dark fog. A third blow shattered the pearl, and it exploded with enough force to throw the monk of Ishap back across the room.

The liche looked upon the scene with wide-eyed horror. "What have you done?" it asked softly.

Kendaric felt the grip on his arm release, and the liche turned and said, "You still have not succeeded, guildsman."

The second skeleton-warrior began to tremble and his attack slowed. James staggered backward, barely able to lift his arms, and Jazhara offered him a supporting hand. The creature took two drunken steps, then went crashing to the stones.

The liche groped toward Kendaric. "I am not done with you, my friend."

Kendaric's hand reached out and he grabbed the hilt of his sword, which was still protruding from the liche's stomach. He gave the blade a twist and the liche contorted in pain.

"But *I* am done with *you!*" Kendaric declared. "Now, it's time for you to die." He yanked the blade free and the undead magician shuddered in pain and fell to his knees. Kendaric turned with unhesitating precision and cut through the dead man's neck. The skin parted like dry paper and the bones snapped like brittle wood. The liche's head rolled free and bounced across the floor.

James stood with his arm draped across Jazhara's shoulder and said, "Well, that was interesting."

Solon pulled himself to his feet, his face covered in tiny cuts from the shattering pearl. "That's not the word I'd choose, laddie, but your point is taken."

"What now?" asked Kendaric.

"We need to look around," said James. "There may be others down here who will cause us trouble."

Jazhara said, "I think as we go, we should scourge this place with fire."

"Yes," said Solon. "Evil is so entrenched here that this place must be purified. And if we wait for my temple to send others to purge it, much of the evil here may flee to another location."

They went to where the liche's body lay. Behind the alcove where he had appeared stood a door. Passing

through it, they came into a large room, obviously the liche's private quarters. Large and small jars were amassed on tables, and in the far corner a cage had been fastened to the stone walls.

Inside the cage a creature rested, somewhat resembling the thing they had encountered in the sewers of Krondor. It looked at them with pain-filled eyes and beckoned with a clawed hand. They approached slowly and when they were close, the creature's mouth opened. A child's voice said, "Please . . ."

Jazhara's eyes grew bright with tears and she whispered, "Is there no end to this evil?"

"Apparently not," said Solon.

James moved behind the creature as it spoke. "Pain . . . please."

With a quick thrust of his sword, James cut the back of the child-turned-monster's neck and it slumped to the floor without a sound. His face was set in a mask of fury.

Jazhara looked at James and said nothing.

Finally, Solon said, "It was a mercy."

"What now?" asked Kendaric.

Softly, James said, "Burn it. Burn everything." He hurried to a wall where tomes and scrolls were arrayed. He grabbed the shelf and toppled it. A small brazier rested on the worktable nearest the shelf and he grabbed it. Hurling it, he sent flames and coals into the paper on the floor and the fire spread rapidly.

"Look over here!" Kendaric said.

They turned and saw that the wrecker had found another pearl. Unlike the other orb, this one appeared to be translucent, and within it they could see an image of Haldon Head.

Jazhara said, "This is a powerful scrying device."

The image shifted and they could see Widow's Point and the hut of the old woman, Hilda.

"Could this have been what was countering my spell?" asked Kendaric.

"Yes, I think so," said Jazhara. "This creates a wide field of magic in the area under observation. Not all magic is blunted, but this could have been used specifically to prevent your spell from working until they had you in their control."

The flames behind them were spreading. James asked, "What do we do with it?"

Jazhara picked up the large pearl and threw it into the fire. "That should take care of it."

"Good," said James. "We should leave now. Get torches and set fire to anything that burns as we leave."

"What if the goblins object?" asked Kendaric.

Solon, looking resolute despite his wounds, said, "Well, if the escaping prisoners haven't sorted them out, we'll just have to do it ourselves, won't we?"

James nodded. "Come on. Let's go raise a ship."

They started their return to the surface.

Eighteen

◆

Tear of the Gods

The sun was low in the west as they left the cavern.

James asked Kendaric, "Can you raise the ship?"

"Now?" He shook his head. "I can try, but I thought that after all we've been through, we'd wait until morning."

"Actually, after all we've been through, I'm not inclined to wait. Bear is out there somewhere and the faster we can find the Tear and get it back to Krondor, the happier I'll be."

Solon nodded. He was bleeding from several small wounds all over his body. They had encountered a few servants of the dead liche during their escape—a pair of goblins who had put up a struggle, and two more of the skeleton-warriors. They had also come upon the mayhem that had been visited upon other servants of the Black Pearl Temple as they worked their way back to the surface. The escaping prisoners had clearly found weapons in the barracks armory and had been unkind to any who attempted to stop them.

Jazhara nursed a rough compress she had fashioned to staunch the bleeding in her shoulder. She said, "I fear that if we encounter trouble from here on, we may be outmatched."

James motioned to the others to walk out to the end of the rock spire. "We've been outmatched every step of the way," he said. "But we've been lucky."

"Luck is the result of hard work," Solon said, "or at least my father told me so."

"I'll still make a large votive offering to Ruthia when I get back to Krondor," James observed, mentioning the name of the Goddess of Luck, the patron goddess of thieves. He added in a mutter, "Even if she is a fickle bitch at times."

Solon overheard this remark and chuckled.

They reached the end of the rocks, and Kendaric said, "If this works, the ship will rise and a fog will form from here to the hull and it will become solid. It should last long enough for us to get to the ship, offload the Tear and return."

"Should?" asked James. "How long is 'should'?"

Kendaric smiled and shrugged. "Well, I never had a chance to test it. I am still working on duration. Eventually, the spell will hold a ship on the surface until all the cargo can be offloaded. Now, well, maybe an hour."

"*Maybe* an hour?" James shook his head in disgust. "Well, we can't start any sooner."

Kendaric closed his eyes, and held out his hand to Jazhara, who had carried the spell-scroll in her backpack. She handed it to him and he began reading.

First the sea around the ship calmed, the combers and breakers seeming to flow around the ship in an ever-widening ring of calm water. Then a fog appeared on the surface and suddenly the mast of the ship began to twitch. Then it shook, and the ship began to rise. First broken spars and tattered sails could be seen, then dripping ropes that dangled from yardarms and limp banners that hung from the flagstaffs. In minutes it was floating upon the surface, bobbing as water flowed from its decks.

Seaweed clung to the railings and crabs scuttled off the deck to fall back into the sea. The fog around the base of the ship thickened and solidified and after a few moments the ship stopped moving.

Kendaric turned to Jazhara and James, amazement lighting his face. "It worked!"

Solon said, "You had doubts?"

"Well, not really, but you never know . . ."

James regarded Kendaric with barely-concealed rage. "Try not to think what I would have done to you had we discovered the artifact in the temple had nothing to do with you failing last time. If it had just been 'the spell doesn't work' . . ." He forced himself to calmness. "Let's get to the ship."

Kendaric touched the toe of his boot to the solid fog experimentally, then put his whole weight on it. "A little soft," he observed.

Solon stepped past him. "We are wasting time!"

The others followed the monk as he hurried across the mystic fog toward the ship.

They reached the side of the ship and found several dangling ropes to climb. James and Kendaric climbed up easily, but the wounded Jazhara and Solon took some time and needed help. When they all had reached the deck they looked around.

Slime covered the decks and decaying bodies trapped by falling timbers or ropes were already beginning to fill the air with a malodorous reek. The scent of rotting flesh, brackish water, and salt was enough to make Kendaric gag.

"Where do we go?" asked James.

"This way," said Solon, indicating a rear door into the sterncastle, leading down to the lower decks. They held

tight to soaking rope handrails as they climbed down slippery wooden steps in the narrow companionway.

At the bottom of the steps, Jazhara lit a torch, since the interior of the ship was as dark as night. The flickering light threw the scene into stark relief, and shadows danced upon the walls as they walked. The water was slow in draining from the lower decks and the hold, so they found themselves wading through knee-deep brine.

"That way," said Solon, pointing to a rear door.

Halfway across the deck, Kendaric let out a yelp.

"What?" asked James, drawing his sword.

"Something brushed against my leg!"

James let out a long, exasperated breath. "Fish. Fish swim in the ocean."

Kendaric looked unconvinced. "There could be a monster lurking down here."

James shook his head and said nothing.

They reached the door and found it jammed shut. James examined it. "Someone broke this lock, but the flow of water must have closed it again, and now it's totally jammed into place. Better break it off its hinges."

Solon used his hammer on the hinges, knocking them loose, and the door exploded outward with a sheet of water. Dead bodies were swept along as the water in the two compartments equalized. Solon looked down at one corpse that floated at his feet. Flesh was rotting off the bones, and signs of fish having feasted on the face were obvious. The eye sockets were empty.

"Good and faithful servant of Ishap," Solon said with respect. Then he saw something and reached down. He pulled a large warhammer from the corpse's belt and declared, "The Warhammer of Luc d'Orbain! It once belonged to an Ishapian saint from Bas-Tyra. It's a relic treasured by the Temple and awarded as a mark of serv-

ice to my order's leader. It's a magic talisman of great power. Not a bad weapon, either." He looked down at the corpse again. "That was Brother Michael of Salador." He shook his head regretfully. "It would be logical that he would personally lead the group protecting the Tear."

"Well, bring it along," said James, "but let's find the Tear and get off this ship before it goes down again."

"That way," said Solon. He indicated a passageway to a rear cargo hold.

When they reached the next door, Solon said, "Wait." He reached into his tunic and pulled out a tiny chain from which hung a small blue gem. The gem glowed faintly. "The Tear of the Gods is near."

"What is that?" asked James.

"A shard from the old Tear. It was given me by the High Priest to help us locate the Tear if it had been removed from the ship."

James reached for the door-latch and again Solon said, "Wait!"

"What is it now?" asked James.

"There is a ward around the Tear. If Bear or one of his men got too close to the Tear before the ship sank, it may have been triggered."

"And this ward does what?" asked James, obviously irritated at hearing this at the last possible minute.

"The soul of a . . . dragon was captured and confined. It manifests itself and will attack whoever comes close to the Tear if certain rituals are not observed."

"You were going to tell us this sooner or later, right?" asked James, his voice dripping with sarcasm.

"Until we found the Tear there was no reason, Squire. Look, the beast is mindless and will attack any of us if it's been released."

"How can a dragon fit in that cargo hold?" asked Kendaric wonderingly. "They're really big, right?"

"It's not a dragon, but the spirit of one. A ghost, if you will."

"Nothing you're saying is making me any happier, Solon," James observed. "Why don't you tell us something good?"

"I have the ritual to banish the creature and return it to the spirit realm."

"That's good," said James.

"But it'll take time."

"And that's not good," said James. "Let me guess: the dragon will attack us while you're trying to banish it."

"Yes."

"And the ship might sink while we're fighting the dragon while you're trying to banish it."

Kendaric said, "Yes."

James said, "This has not been a good day, and it just keeps getting worse." Grabbing the door-latch, he said, "So, let's get this over with."

He flung open the door to reveal a room bare of any furnishings save a single table.

"This is the captain's cabin," said James. "He must have turned it over to the temple and slept elsewhere."

"And that's the Tear," said Solon.

A single large box, carved with the image of a dragon, sat atop the table. It glowed with a mystic blue light and even James could feel the magic emanating from it.

A flickering of light around the box was the only warning they had. Suddenly a gust of wind swept through the cabin. An invisible blow struck Kendaric, knocking him off his feet into the ankle-deep water.

An image formed in the air, a floating dragon made up

of faint golden mist. Solon shouted, "Keep it away from me, else I won't be able to banish it!"

James waved his sword, attempting to distract the creature, while Jazhara kept her eye on Kendaric to make sure he didn't drown. Then she raised her staff, holding it high above her head with both hands, and started a spell.

The dragon turned its attention to James. Its spectral head darted forward. James felt the air pressure build before the creature's snout, and he rolled his head back with the blow. The punch was still significant. He let out an "oof" of pain while trying to draw the creature away from Solon.

Glancing at the monk, he saw that he brandished the Hammer of Luc d'Orbain before him, his eyes closed and lips moving furiously in ritual incantations.

Jazhara finished her casting and a sheet of crimson energy erupted into the air. It flowed across the ceiling of the cabin and then fell upon the dragon, encasing it in a ruby net. The creature thrashed and attempted to attack Jazhara, but it was bound in the netting.

"How long will that hold?" James asked.

"I don't know," said Jazhara. "I've never done this before."

"How's Kendaric?"

"Unconscious, but he'll live, I think."

The wrecker sat slumped against the bulkhead, chin on chest, as if asleep.

James said, "Glad to hear it. That thing hits like a mule kicks."

They turned toward Solon as his voice rose, obviously nearing the end of his incantation. They watched in amazement as the golden dragon expanded, seeming to stretch the ruby netting to its breaking point. As the final words of Solon's prayer rang through the cabin, the

dragon began to shrink till it was a mere golden pinpoint of light that winked out before their eyes.

Suddenly the netting was empty and floated down to the water where it vanished.

"It's done," Solon pronounced.

"Good," said James. "Now let's rescue that damn box and get off this ship before things get any worse!"

Solon nodded, hung the second warhammer on his belt, and gently picked up the box containing the Tear of the Gods. James and Jazhara grabbed Kendaric by the arms and lifted him. He started to rouse as they moved him. "What?" he mumbled.

"Come on," said James. "Time to go home."

Kendaric said, "Best thing I've heard in days." He took his arms off their shoulders and said, "I can walk."

They scrambled up the slippery companionway, Solon having to hand up the box with the Tear in it to James, then reclaiming it when they were on deck. James, Jazhara, and Kendaric went down ropes into the mystic fog and then Solon tossed the box down to James, and followed.

They hurried along the fog as night fell. Just as they were nearing the rocky point, James said, "Damn."

"What?" asked Kendaric.

"Armed men, on the beach."

"The escaped prisoners?" asked Jazhara.

"I don't think so," James answered. "Look!"

Coming down a path from the hills above they could see a massive figure, a dark silhouette. But from his chest a red glow emanated.

"Bear!" said James.

"This fog is starting to weaken," said Solon, and even as he spoke, James felt his feet sinking a bit.

They hurried the last dozen yards to the rocks and

walked toward the beach. "Do we have any choices?" asked James.

Solon said, "None. We must fight."

From the gloom of the rocks, Bear's voice boomed: "Your choices are few and my patience grows short. You will give me the Tear, or we will slaughter you."

"Why do you seek the Tear?" asked Jazhara. "What use can it be to you?"

They stopped where the rocks met the sand, and Bear's men approached, their weapons drawn.

"Ha!" said the huge man. "Hasn't the monk told you? The Tear allows us to talk to gods, doesn't it, Ishapian? And there are other gods besides Ishap!"

Solon shouted, "You are a fool not to fear the power of Ishap!"

"I've got all I need to take care of you . . . Ishapians!" said Bear, fingering the amulet around his neck. "You can never touch me." He drew a large sword. "But *I* can touch *you*! Now, give me the Tear!"

Suddenly from the rocks above him a figure emerged, crouched and leapt. William hurled himself into Bear, knocking the giant man over.

The surprise of the ambush shocked everyone. The mercenary closest to James turned away toward the commotion, and James took advantage of the opening to pull his sword and plunge it into the man's back. The man died before he could even turn to face James.

Solon set the box containing the Tear on the sand and pulled out the Warhammer of Luc d'Orbain, silently mouthing a prayer to Ishap. Jazhara lowered her staff, pointed the end of it at a cluster of Bear's men and let loose a bolt of energy.

Kendaric drew his sword. "I'll guard the Tear!" he cried.

William grappled for a moment with the huge pirate, trying to pull the amulet from his neck. Then Bear reached back with a thundering blow, and clubbed William aside.

William landed hard on the ground, his armor transmitting the shock through his body, but still he rolled and came to his feet.

Bear leapt up quickly, and with an evil smile said, "Bravely done, boy. For that alone I'll kill you quickly."

William looked up to the ledge above where Sidi stood watching. "Help me!"

Sidi shrugged. "I said get the amulet, lad, and I'd help you. Without it, you're on your own." He looked contrite.

Frustration overwhelmed William and he shouted, "Kahooli! You said I'd not be alone!"

Bear laughed. "Kahooli? You call upon a lesser god!" He held up his amulet, and pointed to where the Tear rested in the sand. "With this amulet I'm invincible. With the Tear in my possession, I'll have the power of the gods. I will *be* a god!"

William again threw back his head. "Kahooli, give me vengeance!"

A loud keening sound commenced, causing James, Jazhara, and several of the pirates to cover their ears in pain. Even Bear was forced to step away from the source. Only William seemed unaffected by the shrill whine. Then a form appeared between Bear and William, translucent and pale, but recognizable.

"Talia!" William breathed.

The girl smiled and said, "You are not alone, William."

She moved toward William and stepped into his body. He glowed with the light of the apparition and his armor seemed to flow and shift over him.

Before everyone's astonished eyes, William was trans-

formed. He grew in stature so that his already-broad shoulders became even more massive. The armor darkened from the silver chain of a Krondorian officer to a blood-red plate so dark it bordered on black. A helm appeared over his head, hiding all his features, and the eye-slits glowed with a crimson light. A voice that was neither William's nor Talia's, spoke: "I am Kahooli. I am the God of Vengeance."

The figure raised its hand and a sword of flames appeared. With a blindingly quick blow, the blade cut across Bear's arm.

Bear flinched and retreated, his good eye wide with astonishment. "I'm bleeding! I can feel pain!"

He pulled out his sword and struck at the figure in red, and shock ran up his arm as the incarnation of the god took the blow. Then Kahooli's avatar slashed out and Bear looked down to see a wide bleeding cut on his chest. Staggering backward, Bear cried, "No, this cannot be!"

Bear swung again, but one more time the spirit of the God of Vengeance, manifested in William's body, took the blow and turned it. Then with a straight thrust, it ran its sword up to the hilt in Bear's stomach.

Bear sank to his knees, clutching the flaming blade. "No," he said in disbelief. "You said this couldn't happen. I can't die. You promised me! You said I'd never die!" He fell over on the sand, his one eye staring at the night sky. "You said . . . I couldn't . . . die . . ."

The figure stood above him for a moment, looking down, then it shimmered and transformed itself back into the shape of William.

The young warrior staggered, as if suddenly weak. He dropped to his knees and looked around. The shade of Talia appeared once more. Softly he said to her, "We did it, Talia. It's over."

The spirit of the young girl smiled at him. "And now I may rest. Thank you, William."

William's cheeks were wet with his tears. "Talia, no! Please stay."

As she faded from sight, Talia's spirit whispered, "No, William. Life is for the living. You have a long life ahead of you and I must take my new place upon the wheel. Say good-bye to me, please."

Just before she vanished, for the briefest instant, she seemed to shine with a bright light. She reached out and her hand touched William's cheek. Then she faded from view.

Tears running down his face, William said softly, "Good-bye, Talia."

James looked around and saw that Bear's remaining men had fled. He put up his sword and saw that Solon had safely gathered up the Tear.

James and Jazhara moved to where the still-kneeling warrior rested. James said, "Well done, Will. She is avenged."

Jazhara placed her hand gently on William's shoulder. "And the Tear is safe."

William said, "So it is true what he said about the Tear?"

"And more," said Solon. "The Tear commands great power, and you've seen to it that its power will not be used for evil." He held tightly to the case containing the Tear. "However, this was only a minor skirmish. The war is not yet won."

Jazhara said, "What of Bear's amulet?"

"It's too powerful an artifact to leave here," said Kendaric.

James used his sword to pick it up. "I wouldn't touch this for any price," he said. "It seems to bring out the vicious side of a man's nature."

He walked back to the point of the rocks overlooking the sea and reached back. Using the sword for leverage, he hurled the amulet as far out into the water as he could. In the gloom they didn't see it strike the waves.

He walked back to where his companions waited. "If the fates are kind, there's a column of soldiers up in Haldon Head and we'll have an escort back to Krondor."

Battered and bruised, they limped up the path toward Haldon Head.

Dawn arrived with rose- and golden-tinged clouds in the eastern sky as Jazhara walked through the woods to Hilda's hut. She reached the clearing and as she caught sight of the building, she felt a stab of concern.

The hut was deserted. She could tell even at that distance, for not only did no sign of a fire or light come from within, but the door hung open. And the plants and herbs hanging from the porch roof were missing.

Slowly she climbed the step to the porch and entered the hut. Inside, the single table and stool were all that remained. The chest and other personal belongings were gone.

On the table rested a single piece of parchment.

Jazhara picked it up.

Girl, it read,

My time is done. I was placed here to keep watch over evil until such time as someone came to rid this place of it. You are brave and resourceful young people. The future is yours. Serve the forces of good.

                                        Hilda

"She's gone," Jazhara said to the person who had quietly mounted the porch after her.

William stepped into the hut. "Who was she?"

"A witch, they say," replied Jazhara.

"You don't believe that," said William. Raised on Stardock, he knew as well as she the prejudices toward women who practiced magic in the Kingdom. "Who was she really?"

"A wise woman," answered Jazhara, folding the note and putting it in her belt. "A servant of good. She's gone now."

"Did she say where?"

"No," said the young magician. She glanced around, then looked at William. "Why did you follow me?"

"I wanted to talk before we were surrounded by others, on the long trip back to Krondor."

Jazhara said, "We can talk while we return."

William stepped aside as she moved through the door, then fell into step beside her on the path back to Haldon Head. After a few steps, Jazhara said, "Talk. I'm listening."

William let out a deep breath. "This is awkward."

"It doesn't have to be."

"I said some things—"

She stopped and touched his arm. "We both said some things. You were young . . . we both were young. But that . . . misunderstanding, that's in the past."

"Then we are all right with each other?"

Jazhara nodded. "We are all right."

William started walking again. "Good. I've lost . . . someone I cared about, and . . . I didn't want to lose another friend."

Jazhara said, "You'll never lose me, William." She was silent for a while. "I'm sorry about your loss. I know Talia was special to you."

William glanced at Jazhara. "She was. As are you."

Jazhara smiled. "And as you are to me."

"We're going to be seeing a lot of each other in the years to come. I just didn't want it to remain difficult."

"Me neither."

They continued on in silence the rest of the way, content to have begun healing the rift between them.

The return journey to Krondor went without incident. The relief column from Miller's Rest was in Haldon Head waiting for them when they reached the summit. It escorted the four of them back to Krondor.

Without ceremony they rode through the city four days later and into the marshaling yard of the palace. Grooms and lackeys took charge of mounts and James, Jazhara, Solon, Kendaric, and William were directed straight to the Prince's private reception quarters.

A horseman had been dispatched as they had approached the city, and the Prince had alerted the High Priest of the Temple of Ishap, who now waited with the Prince for the weary party.

James led the way, with Solon at his side, holding tightly the case containing the Tear. Kendaric, William, and Jazhara entered behind them.

James bowed. "Sire, with great pleasure I report we have achieved our goals. Brother Solon holds the Tear of the Gods."

Solon looked at the High Priest, who stepped forward and opened the box the monk held. Within the box rested a large pale blue crystal, the size of a large man's forearm. It seemed to glow with an inner light and as they beheld it, a faint tone, as if distant music filled the air, could be heard.

"Few not of our order have ever seen the Tear of the

Gods, Highness," said the High Priest. "All here are more than worthy of the honor."

They stood transfixed for a while, then the High Priest closed the box. "We leave at dawn to transport the Tear to our mother temple in Rillanon," said the High Priest. "Brother Solon will personally oversee the transport."

"If you don't mind," said Prince Arutha, "I'll just happen to have a full company of lancers riding along behind."

Bowing slightly, the High Priest indicated that he had no objection.

To Solon, Arutha said, "You serve your god well."

The High Priest added, "He is our good and faithful servant. He shall be elevated to replace Michael of Salador. Solon, we entrust to you the leadership of the Brothers of Ishap's Hammer, and entrust to you the safekeeping of the Hammer of Luc d'Orbain."

"I am honored, Father," said the monk.

To the others in the room, the High Priest said, "Your bravery, and the strength of your spirit, have restored to us that which is the cornerstone of our faith. The Temple of Ishap owes you all its eternal gratitude."

Arutha said, "As does the court of Krondor to you, Brother Solon." Looking at William, he added, "You've acquitted yourself admirably, Lieutenant. You're an honor to the Household Guard."

William bowed.

"Guildsman Kendaric," said Arutha.

The wrecker stepped forward and bowed. "Highness."

"You've done the Crown a great service. We are in your debt. We understand that with the death of your master, the Guild is currently in disarray. As it is a patent guild, dependent upon the Crown's favor, it is our desire that you assume the rank of Guild Master and restore your fellowship."

"Your Highness," said Kendaric. "I am honored, but the Guild is in ruin. Jorath's embezzlement left us without a copper, the other journeymen who've left . . ."

"We shall attend to those details. The Crown is not ungenerous to those who serve us. We shall restore your treasury and ensure you recover."

"Your Highness is most generous," said the new Guild Master.

Then Arutha said, "Lady Jazhara. You have proven my choice of court magician a wise one."

Jazhara inclined her head and said, "Highness."

The Prince of Krondor rarely smiled, but this time his expression was almost expansive. With pride in his eyes, he said, "James, as always you are a good and faithful servant. You have my personal thanks." He stood, and said, "You've all done well."

James spoke on behalf of the others. "Our duty and our pleasure, sire."

"I have asked that a celebration in your honor be readied for tonight," Arutha said. "Retire to your quarters and return this evening as my guests."

He departed the throne room, motioning for James to follow him.

Jazhara turned to Solon and said, "Will you join us?"

"Nay, lass," said the large monk from Dorgin. "As head of my order I must ensure the safety of the Tear until we reach Rillanon. It will not leave my sight until then. Fare you well, all of you." He motioned for two monks who had stood silently in the corner to approach. They turned and bowed respectfully to the High Priest. The two monks fell in behind the High Priest and Brother Solon and left the room with the Tear.

William asked Kendaric, "What now?"

Kendaric said, "I will go to Morraine and bring her

with me tonight. As Guild Master I will earn enough to satisfy even her family. We shall be wed as soon as we can."

Jazhara said, "I am happy to hear that."

Kendaric nodded enthusiastically. "I must hurry off. I'll see you both later."

William said, "May I escort you back to your quarters, lady?"

"No need," said Jazhara. "I have to learn to find my way around this place sooner or later. If I get lost I'll just ask a page for directions."

William knew she knew the way. He smiled. "Until tonight."

As he started to leave, she said, "William?"

"Yes, Jazhara?"

She stepped forward and lightly kissed his cheek. "It is good to be here with you again."

He looked into her dark brown eyes and for a moment he was speechless. Then he returned the kiss and said, "Yes, it is good."

They parted and went their separate ways.

Arutha sat behind his desk. "You can give me a full report tomorrow," he said to James. "You look like you could use some rest before this evening's festivities."

"Well, four days' riding was hardly restful, but most of the bruises and cuts are healing."

"The Tear is safe, which is the main thing. What else did you discover?"

James said, "Of the Crawler, nothing. I think the man was one of several agents of a man called Sidi."

William had told James all he knew of Sidi, both at the time of the attack on the Duke of Olasko, and during this latest encounter. James recounted what William had said

to him, finishing with, "He seems to be a trader of some sort, a renegade, dealing with the goblins and those north of the mountains as well as those in more legitimate commerce. At least that's what he *appears* to be."

"You suspect more?"

"Much more. He just knew too much and . . ." James paused. "I caught but a glimpse of him on the cliffs above the beach while William fought with the pirate, Bear. He makes my skin itch, Highness. I think he's much more than a mere trader."

"A magician or a priest?"

"Possibly. Certainly he was desperate to get back the amulet that Bear wore, and I suspect he gave it to Bear in the first place."

"What dark agency do we face?" asked Arutha.

James said, "That question, Highness, plagues me as well." Arutha was silent as he rose from his desk and crossed to the window overlooking the marshaling yard below. Soldiers were at drill, and he saw young William hurrying to the bachelor officers' barracks. "William did well," said the prince.

"He'll be Knight-Marshal of Krondor some day," said James, "if you ever decide to let Gardan retire."

The prince turned and faced him with what could only be called a grin, an expression James had not seen from Arutha more than a few times in the ten years and more during which he'd served him. "He told me the next time he's just going to walk out, and take ship to Crydee. Then let me send soldiers to fetch him back."

"What are you going to do?"

"Let him serve a bit longer, then recall Locklear and give him the position."

"Locklear, Knight-Marshal?"

"You yourself have told me that as long as I run the

army I should use an administrator. Locklear certainly
has the knack for that job."

"Indeed," agreed James. "Never had much use for accounts, myself."

"I'm going to let him sit for one more winter with
Baron Moyet, then I'll fetch him back and send Gardan
home."

"For real this time?"

Arutha laughed. "Yes, I'll let him return to Crydee and
sit on Martin's dock fishing, if that's what he really desires."

James stood. "I have a few things I need to do before
tonight, Highness. With your leave?"

Arutha waved James from the room. "Until tonight."

James said, "Highness," and showed himself out of the
room.

Arutha, Prince of Krondor and second most powerful
man in the Kingdom of the Isles, stood at his window in
a reflective mood. A young man when he had taken command at the Siege of Crydee during the Riftwar, he was
now middle-aged.

He had many years before him, if the gods were kind,
but he felt a calm reassurance knowing that the fate of his
kingdom rested in the competent hands of younger men
and women, men and women like James, Jazhara, and
William. He allowed himself the luxury of one more
peaceful moment, then returned to his desk and the reports that begged for his attention.

James hurried through the palace. He needed to send
word to Jonathan Means, and two of his other agents, to
let them know that he was back in Krondor. Then he
needed to duck into the streets for a quick visit to one of

his informants who was keeping an eye out for signs of activity by the Crawler and his gang. Now that the matter of the Tear of the Gods was settled, James was determined to turn his attention to this would-be crime lord and find out once and for all who he was. Then he would rid the city of his presence.

James counted down the things he needed to do. If he hurried, he would just have time to return for a bath and change of clothing before the Prince's celebration.

He was tired, but there would be time to sleep tomorrow. At this moment he was doing what he wanted to do more than anything: serving his Prince. And he was where he wanted to be more than anywhere in the world: Krondor.

Epilogue
Challenge

The solitary figure dripped water as it slogged along the dark corridor of the long tunnel. The air reeked of smoke and dead bodies.

Sidi found that the small fire he had started that morning was still burning. He fetched a torch from a wall-sconce. Lighting it, he continued his journey.

Finally, he reached the room in which the dead liche lay, its body quickly turning to dust. "Idiot!" he shouted again at the unhearing form.

He moved behind the throne and found the secret latch. He tripped it and a section of wall moved aside. He entered a room even the liche hadn't known of, one Sidi used exclusively for himself.

As he entered, a voice said, "You've lost."

"No, I haven't, old woman!" he shouted to the voice in the air. He stripped off his dripping tunic.

"You didn't find the amulet." There was mockery in her voice.

"I'll keep looking. It's only been four days."

"Even if you find it, what will you do? You have no servants or allies."

"Talking to the air is tedious. Show yourself."

A faint figure appeared, translucent and without much color, but recognizable as a woman of middle age. Stripping off his trousers, the magician reached for a blanket and wrapped it around himself. "I tire of cold and damp places . . . what are you calling yourself these days?"

"Hilda, most recently."

"Yes, Hilda. I am tired of this place. Servants I can get with gold. That I have in abundance. Allies are almost as easy, once I discover what they desire." He looked at the pale image. "You know, I sensed you've been close by for some years now, but didn't think I needed to ferret you out."

"You can't get rid of me, and we both know it."

The man sighed. "You have no worshipers, no clerics, not one person in ten million on this world who even knows your name, yet you persist in lingering. That's very bad form for a goddess."

The shade who had once been the old woman in the hut said, "It is my nature. As long as you seek to serve your master, I must oppose him."

"My master lives!" said Sidi, pointing his finger at the image. "You don't even have the good grace to admit you're dead and go away!"

The figure vanished.

Instantly Sidi felt regret. As much as he disliked the woman and all her incarnations, she had been a part of his life for several centuries. He had been the first to discover the amulet in over a thousand years. He had succumbed to its power. For years he had felt impulses he couldn't explain and heard voices no one else had. He had grown in his power, and for a long time, in his madness. Then his mind had gained clarity beyond madness. He had learned whom he served: the Nameless One.

He had used the amulet before, to trap others in his

master's service, such as the liche Savan and his brother. That had been a mistake. He sighed. Serving darkness required you to use whatever came your way.

The old woman had appeared soon after he had gained his powers. She was the opponent of the Nameless One, and she had refused to give Sidi any rest. He was forced to admit she was the only person—if one could call the ghost of a dead goddess a person—he had known for longer than a few years. Most of the others had got themselves killed in one grisly fashion or another. In a strange way, he was somewhat fond of the old goddess.

He sighed. The battle had been lost, but the war would continue, and he would seek to do his master's bidding. Eventually his master would return to this world. It might take centuries, but Sidi had time. His master demanded a high price for his service, but he rewarded as well. Sidi might look to be a man of fifty, yet he had lived nearly five times that number of years.

He lay down on the bed. "I must find a better place to live, soon," he sighed.

Coming Soon in Hardcover!
An all-new epic fantasy saga from
***New York Times* Bestselling Author**
RAYMOND E. FEIST

—◦◦◦—

TALON OF THE SILVER HAWK:
BOOK ONE OF CONCLAVE OF SHADOWS

In a distant land, high among snow-capped mountains, a peaceful nation is put to the sword and afforded neither mercy nor quarter . . . leaving but one lone survivor. Little more than a boy, young Talon of the Silver Hawk must somehow carry on alone until, someday, he can avenge his murdered people.

TALON OF THE SILVER HAWK is the first installment in an all-new tale of adventure and danger, magic and intrigue from bestselling author Raymond E. Feist.